# THE DISCORD
OF GODS

# THE
# DISCORD
## OF
# GODS

## JENN LYONS

**A TOM DOHERTY
ASSOCIATES BOOK**
*New York*

THE DISCORD OF GODS

A Tor Book
Published by Tom Doherty Associates
120 Broadway
New York, NY 10271

www.tor-forge.com

Tor® is a registered trademark of Macmillan Publishing Group, LLC.

The Library of Congress Cataloging-in-Publication Data is available upon request.

ISBN 978-1-250-17568-7 (hardcover)
ISBN 978-1-250-17569-4 (ebook)

Our books may be purchased in bulk for promotional, educational, or business use. Please contact your local bookseller or the Macmillan Corporate and Premium Sales Department at 1-800-221-7945, extension 5442, or by email at MacmillanSpecialMarkets@macmillan.com.

First Edition: 2022

Printed in the United States of America

0  9  8  7  6  5  4  3  2  1

*For Kendall.*
*I wish I could*
*bring you back.*

# PRECIS

Our story starts a little over four months previously. Also, four years previously. And four hundred years previously . . . and four thousand years . . . and fourteen thousand years.

Let's work our way forward.

**Fourteen thousand years ago,** human settlers invaded this dimension from another, fleeing the death of their universe. They were ill-prepared to deal with a world where magic existed and where they could neither easily die nor reproduce. They survived and made a home here, but it's most important that you know this: two of the settlers were brothers named S'arric and Rev'arric. S'arric was popular. Rev'arric was smart. Eventually, Rev'arric came to loathe that difference.

**Four thousand years ago,** a second invasion occurred, this time by a race of telepathic, incorporeal monsters who thrived on pain and fear. This invasion damaged the barrier between this world and its twin, a shadowy Afterlife from which all souls came and eventually returned. Afterward, humans could be killed and could have children, but this seemed an ill reward for being slowly destroyed by demons they couldn't fight.

Rev'arric, smart man that he was, figured out a way. He devised a ritual to empower Eight Guardians, giving them godlike powers and the ability to follow demons even into the Afterlife. But he assumed he'd be one of the people picked to receive these powers, and when his brother was chosen instead, Rev'arric was overwhelmed with jealousy and hate.

So, when he discovered that the dimensional breach the demons had created would eventually annihilate the universe, he didn't hesitate at a solution that required his brother's destruction. He tricked his brother into participating in a second ritual, meant to elevate Rev'arric and turn his brother into a thrall under his control. Instead, it turned Rev'arric and the eight other participants into insane dragons and turned S'arric into a horrifying monster under no one's control. This obliterated their country, formed the Blight, killed millions, and created both the Cornerstones and the sword Urthaenriel. Their people, the voras, eventually imprisoned S'arric (now called Vol Karoth) at the cost of their immortality, but not before he killed the rest of the original Eight Guardians. One of the Cornerstones, the Stone of Shackles, was used to bind the demons, effectively ending the war. But it was too late: the voras had been plunged into a dark age from which they never recovered. A cycle in which Vol Karoth's prison would weaken and could only be repaired by the sacrifice of an entire people's immortality would repeat several times.

**Over four hundred years ago**, Vol Karoth's prison weakened once more, but this time he woke. The Eight Guardians (now called the Eight Immortals) had been resurrected, but none of them were prepared to fight their former leader. Worse, upon waking Vol Karoth broke the sun, turning it from yellow to orange-red. After repairing Vol Karoth's prison, the Quuros emperor, Kandor, invaded the Manol and was slain. Kandor's wife, Elana, snuck into the Blight to bargain with the morgage. While there, she remembered that she'd once been S'arric's lover, C'indrol, and so tried to separate S'arric from "Vol Karoth." She succeeded, after a fashion, sending fragments of S'arric's souls into the Afterlife, where he slowly healed. S'arric, Kandor, and Elana would all later volunteer to be reincarnated to stop Vol Karoth, joined by the first emperor of Quur, Simillion.

**Four years ago,** a street thief named Kihrin stumbled upon a demonic summoning, gaining the attention of a particularly evil necromancer named Gadrith, a particularly evil demon named Xaltorath, and a particularly evil Quuros prince named Darzin. The latter snatched the boy up, claiming to be Kihrin's father. In reality, Darzin's master, that necromancer, Gadrith, wanted an artifact that Kihrin unknowingly wore: the Stone of Shackles. Kihrin ran away, and while he technically escaped Darzin, he didn't escape being sold into slavery and auctioned off in a far-away land. There, he was almost purchased by Rev'arric (now cured of his insanity, passing himself off as human, and going by the name Relos Var). Instead, Kihrin was purchased by a cult working for the Goddess of Death, Thaena (one of the Eight Immortals). Kihrin spent the next four years on a tropical island, training. Also falling in love, having his heart broken, running afoul of a different dragon, discovering he was the reincarnation of S'arric, and trying to convince himself that his feelings for Thaena's son, Teraeth (the reincarnation of Kandor), weren't romantic.

**Four months ago,** Kihrin returned to the Capital City with Teraeth and a weather witch named Tyentso, in order to stop Gadrith's plans and free Gadrith's son Thurvishar (who was the reincarnation of Simillion). Instead, Gadrith captured Kihrin, gained the Stone of Shackles, sacrificed Kihrin to Xaltorath, sparked a Hellmarch, and swapped bodies with the Emperor of Quur. But Kihrin didn't stay dead, and he uncovered what Gadrith had been seeking: the god-slaying sword, Urthaenriel, which Kihrin promptly used to kill Darzin and Gadrith, and destroy the Stone of Shackles. This broke all the gaeshe that kept demons under control, unleashing chaos. Also, Tyentso ended up becoming the Empress of Quur.

Kihrin fled the Capital, hoping to find an ally against Relos Var in the form of a mysterious figure called the Black Knight. This turned out to be Janel, the reincarnation of Elana and the last of the four volunteers. She'd fought her own battles against Xaltorath and Relos Var, but now wanted Kihrin's help killing the dragon Morios, whom she believed would soon destroy the Jorat capital, Atrine. Although this threat was real, it was also a trap set by Relos

Var, meant to separate Kihrin from Urthaenriel. It worked. It also woke Vol Karoth and damaged his prison.

**Four fortnights ago**, the Eight Immortals dispatched Kihrin, Teraeth, Janel, and Thurvishar to the Manol in order to make sure the last immortal race did their part to repair Vol Karoth's prison. The vané king said no—by drugging the four and leaving them in the Blight to die. In the aftermath, they realized the situation was more complicated than they'd realized, and that the Eight Immortals weren't pure of intentions. When Thaena proved willing to murder her own son and destroy an entire nation to repair Vol Karoth's prison, Kihrin was forced to ally with Relos Var to stop her. By the time the dust settled, four immortals, including Thaena, were dead. Kihrin decided on a rash course of action: to merge back with Vol Karoth in the hope of ruining Relos Var's plans to replace the Eight Immortals with himself.

**Four days ago,** Relos Var's apprentice Senera switched sides. She kidnapped a dozen people during a dual kraken/dragon attack on the island of Devors and took them to a magical lighthouse outside the normal flow of time. She'd hoped that Kihrin's loved ones would help him fight off Vol Karoth, but the group realized it was the wrong approach: Kihrin and Vol Karoth were no longer separate entities. The only way to "win" was to help Kihrin—and themselves—overcome his trauma.

**And in a few minutes,** Kihrin—once called Vol Karoth, and before that, S'arric—will break free from his prison. Janel and Teraeth will return to the Manol to reclaim a throne. Thurvishar and Senera will try to recover Urthaenriel. Empress Tyentso will struggle to save an empire that's always hated her. Relos Var will begin his final plans to control the dragons, enslave Vol Karoth, heal the dimensional breach, and make himself a god. Lastly, Xaltorath will attempt to steal enough energy to unravel the universe.

And here we go.

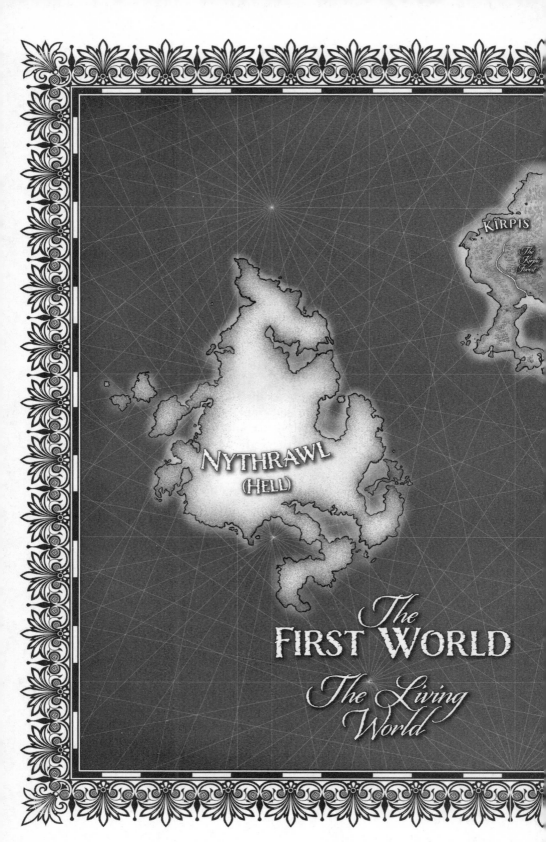

KIRPIS

The
Kirpis
Forest

NYTHRAWL
(HELL)

The
FIRST WORLD

The Living
World

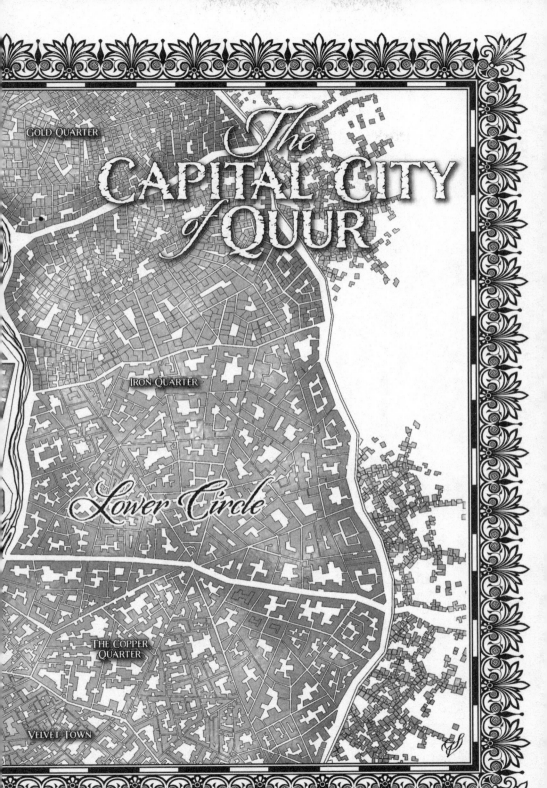

GOLD QUARTER

# The CAPITAL CITY of QUUR

IRON QUARTER

*Lower Circle*

THE COPPER
QUARTER

VELVET TOWN

# PART I

## SETTING UP
## THE PIECES

# 1. Step One: Gather Information

### Kihrin's story
### (in which Kihrin's plan is revealed to be exactly the opposite)
### Wandering in the Blight
### The day of Vol Karoth's escape, just after dawn

I'd started contemplating next steps before I'd freed myself from that ever-so-lovely prison in Kharas Gulgoth. Or what had been my prison. The Korthaen Blight looked much the same as it always had, as it had since everything had gone wrong.

In some ways, remembering its previous existence was far more painful. This had been a garden full of life and beauty, growing wild and lush under a yellow sun. The city of Karolaen had been a wonder—even if it had ultimately been a refugee camp for the voras as we ran from Nythrawl and the demon invasion.

Now, it was a corrupted, ruined landscape. The devastation was so total that it had fractured the earth itself, creating a hot spot that fed toxic thermal springs and sulfur-laced fumes. The damage poisoned the ground so utterly it was a shock that anything had ever been able to grow there at all.

*Korthaen* meant "the Land of Death." Perhaps not the most original of names, but certainly accurate. It still amazed me that the morgage had found a way to survive here, but they'd been extremely, *extremely* dedicated to keeping people away from Vol Karoth's prison.

That had been before Vol Karoth had woken. Afterward, even the morgage had been forced to flee.

It wouldn't have been safe for them to return. Much as I wanted to think that everything would be fine now that I was "whole" again, that just wasn't true. I couldn't hold so much as a stone picked up off the ground without it disintegrating in my grip. I kept trying. It was a problem I'd need to solve.

Before I'd escaped (back when we were all still in that strange liminal space that was both Kharas Gulgoth *and* the Lighthouse at Shadrag Gor),[1] I'd given the others tasks to accomplish: we'd discussed strategies, how to keep Relos Var from discovering our plans, and how to avoid the people who might

---

[1] The two locations were merged thanks to Senera.—Thurvishar

I'm unsure whether it would be better or worse to confess that I didn't do it on purpose.—Senera

cause problems. I'd gone out of my way to make sure everyone knew that I had objectives, a definite scheme, even if I was being cagey about the details. S'arric the general, leader of the Guardians, could naturally be counted on to formulate a battle plan for fighting the enemy, right?

I hadn't been lying exactly . . .

Okay, fine. I'd been lying. There was no plan. Nothing even resembling a plan.

Rather, I had a plan for making a plan. A real and proper strategy would be impossible while there were so many unknown variables beyond my control. I was going to need information and a lot of it before any such plan could be formed.

Senera had used the Name of All Things for every question we imagined before she'd then used the Cornerstone to cure Drehemia's insanity, destroying it as a result.[2] But even such an artifact had limits. It couldn't answer every question. It especially couldn't answer questions about events that hadn't yet occurred, that had occurred before its creation, or that might have occurred in an alternate timeline.

As far as the strategy itself, well . . .

I had no intention of behaving the way S'arric would have. Relos Var knew his brother far too well. No. I planned to take my cues from a more recent mentor: my adoptive mother, Ola. Who had been by her own admission a crook, a schemer, a rogue, and a swindler down to her core. Relos Var thought of his brother as being first and foremost a soldier: I had no intention of behaving like one.

Ola Nathera always used to say that the key to a good con lay in three factors: organization, execution, and finding an utter bastard.[3]

Whether said bastard was the con artist or the mark? Ah, now that was flexible and, depending on the answer, required a different approach. Once you figured out which was which, the rest was a matter of logistics.

Either one made for a successful con, but most of the time, it was safe to assume the "bastard" in question would be the con artist themselves. That's because most of the time, the mark wasn't a bad person.

This whole idea that you couldn't con an honest man? Nonsense. Most cons didn't exploit greed or lust. Most cons exploited *benevolence*. They appealed to the sincere desire that most people genuinely had to help someone in need, then lured them in with the revelation that such assistance also rewarded the mark for their altruism. What could possibly be more appealing than a charitable deed and profit wrapped up in a single act?[4] These people wanted to help, and knowing that there was literally no downside made it an easy de-

---

[2] Technically speaking, the Name of All Things wasn't destroyed, simply merged back with its paired dragon, in exactly the same way Grizzst merged Cynosure and Relos Var in order to cure Relos Var's insanity.—S

[3] Which Kihrin absolutely was, at least in terms of birth, if perhaps not personality.—T

    Oh, I think he might have qualified in personality too.—S

[4] A great many of the scams common to the Lower Circle hinge on some kind of "reward" that the con artist offers to share with the victim in exchange for a small favor or concession, which either is the whole point or which opens up the victim to blackmail later.—T

cision. It made the entire situation *fair* to everyone involved so that ultimately everyone won.

At least, that was the sell. I would argue that it wasn't greed but this desire for equity that took most marks by the hand and led them those final, fatal steps into the trap.

And then there was the other kind of bastard.

That was when the mark was someone who didn't give a shit who needed their help. Helping others wasn't a persuasive motivation, not even if they'd be rewarded for it. They were, in fact, suspicious of such rewards, more likely to leave such a situation alone unless they could verify and double-verify. No, what they needed was a situation where someone *else* was vulnerable. Where they, the mark, believed they were in a position to exploit that vulnerability. These were the bastards who could be convinced to betray confidences, take advantage of the weak, leave their partners out to dry. They didn't fall prey to the con because they were good people but because they thought they were smarter than the con artist. Smarter, wickeder, and more cunning. They assumed that because they were hunters, they would never be prey.[5]

If there was any lesson that I'd learned at Ola's knee, it was that sooner or later, everyone was prey.

I always preferred the second kind of mark, because I'm not a complete bastard,[6] and I always felt bad about exploiting the first kind of mark. Even in a city as notoriously corrupt as the Capital, however, that second variety was harder to find. A con man might approach a regular person out of the cold, beg them for aid. A bastard, on the other hand, needed to think they weren't helping; that they had in fact gotten the drop on you, that you needed them far more than they needed you. They had to think that they had all the power. A bastard was too suspicious of the darker aspects of humanity to accept that anyone was free from ulterior motives. A good con made them think that they were the ones taking advantage of the con artist, rather than the reverse.

All of this was a long-winded way of explaining that Relos Var had always been a strange mixture of both. While it would be easy to say that Var was a bastard and leave it at that, I was fully aware that by Relos Var's standards, he firmly and genuinely believed that he was saving the world (with the side effect of becoming its kindly if tyrannical god) in what might be described as the ultimate expression of "rewarded benevolence."

Plus, a further complication: Relos Var was already involved in his own scheme. Conning certain types of people—other con artists, spies, smugglers, almost any royal—was made more difficult because they were people with agendas, people on missions. The only way to distract one of those groups

---

[5] The citizens of Eamithon even have a phrase for this: *The hawk hunts the mongoose that hunts the snake.*—T

[6] Except by birth, as established.—S

True for Kihrin D'Mon, but the situation is more complicated now. By all accounts I've been able to discover, S'arric and Rev'arric's parents were married, while Kihrin's birth form (we need a better vocabulary for this type of discussion) is no longer being used.—T

That's a good and annoying point. Stop it.—S

was to present them with something better than what they already thought they were getting. Otherwise, there was simply no motivation to trade their old schemes for new ones.

Considering Relos Var was attempting to destroy the other Immortals and rule the world (after he fixed it), I was finding myself hard-pressed to describe what "better than he was already getting" might look like. Especially when I had only the faintest idea how Relos Var planned to accomplish it.

Normally, a con artist either picked a scam and found a mark that fit, or picked a mark and tailored the scam accordingly. In this case, there was really only one option. I couldn't sub in my own game pieces until I understood Relos Var's better. Fortunately, there was someone I could ask.

Although perhaps *ask* was the wrong word.

Still, I had to find it just a little hilarious—downright *ironic*—that in order to mess with Relos Var, I'd first have to mess with Xaltorath.

Honestly, I was even looking forward to it.

So with that in mind, I escaped my prison and set out in search of an old friend.

## 2. Dreams of Sins Past

*Tyentso's story*
*The Soaring Halls, the Upper Circle of the Capital City of Quur*
*The day of Vol Karoth's escape, just after dawn*

The sunlight was a flare of hot red, glinting off the rolling waves with mirror brightness. Tyentso already had a headache from the reflection, and she wasn't even manning a position on deck. The splash of waves created a steady background roar against the ship's hull, counterpoint to the blinding glare. Counterpoint as well to the sound of groaning slaves down in the hold of the ship.

Wait.

She glanced around, blinking as she tried to make some measure of sense out of her view. This was the *Misery*. She hadn't been back on board the *Misery* in years. The *Misery* didn't even exist anymore, long since destroyed in a tug-of-war between a kraken and a dragon. But that had never stopped the nightmares. This was all too familiar.

Except in the important ways that it was not.

Kihrin sat on one of the water barrels, watching men work who either couldn't see him or chose to ignore him. The Stone of Shackles shone a deep blue against his bronze skin. He looked older than the sixteen years he would have been in her memories, with less baby fat in his cheeks and infinitely older eyes.

Normally . . . Normally in her dreams, he'd be tied to the mainmast by this point, back washed crimson from the cat-o'-nine-tails the first mate, Delon, had used on him. That particular nightmare always started off in those moments when Captain Juval had been forced to choose between killing Kihrin and something arguably worse. When he'd demanded Tyentso summon up a demon to section off a piece of Kihrin's soul and gaesh the boy as a compromise.

Captain Juval always picked a death sentence in her nightmares. Always ordered her to be the one to carry it out. Every time, Tyentso would know with absolute certainty that if she didn't carry out the command, she would take Kihrin's place. And every time, Tyentso killed the boy. No matter how much she screamed inside, she always made the same choice.

She'd always done whatever it took to survive.

"Do you always dream about this?" Kihrin turned his head to stare at her. Instantly, she knew this wasn't a normal dream. That this wasn't a dream at all in any typical sense of the word.

"Sometimes I dream about the Academy executing my mother for witch-craft," Tyentso admitted. "Or my father Gadrith murdering me. Or . . . Well. My life is a fertile spring for spawning nightmares. Plenty of fuel for any number of horrific scenarios, replayed nightly for my amusement." She paused, an ugly twisting in her gut. "I dreamed you died, you know. A few weeks back. I dreamed that mimic, Talon, put her hand through your chest."

A part of her whispered that she shouldn't be talking about this. That someone might have found a way to intrude on her dreams and use it to ferret out secrets. But she quieted that voice. She knew this was Kihrin. She could feel it.

Kihrin coughed out an awkward laugh. "You know, I really should've expected that you'd sense that."

Tyentso's heart lurched in her chest, knocked against her ribs. "What? *Scamp.*" Tyentso loved the damn kid in her own way, but this was nothing to joke about—

He shrugged. "What can I say? Talon put her hand through my chest. I kind of died."

Tyentso stared harder. "Was this before or after Thaena's death?"

"After. It's part of why I'm here."

"Tell me you didn't use Grimward. Tell me you're not a damn vampire now, Scamp."

Kihrin's mouth twisted into something a little too sarcastic to be a proper smile. "No, I didn't use Grimward." He gestured toward the hold, toward the source of that faint, painful noise. "How many slaves do you think you helped Juval deliver to the auction block? You did this for something like twenty years, right? So it can't be hundreds. We're talking *thousands,* aren't we?"

Tyentso felt her stomach flip, the knots tangle. "Scamp, I've already done my absolution for that."

"Yeah, but said absolution was with Thaena. And for some reason, I don't trust the judgment of a woman who was willing to wipe out the entire Manol vané population just to keep"—he paused—"Vol Karoth imprisoned for a few more decades. I wouldn't trust her to even understand what the word *redemption* means."

"So what are you saying, Kihrin? I'm not done atoning?" Tyentso wasn't sure if she was angry or frustrated. She wasn't proud of what she'd done, but damn it, she'd been trying to survive . . .

"You already know the answer to that, Ty. Or you wouldn't be still having the nightmares." He raised an eyebrow at her. "Believe me, I know something about committing sins that you'll never make right. It gets easier—it really does—but you'll never be able to proclaim yourself *innocent.*" He glanced at her, for just a moment, but it was enough for her to be certain that he must have heard about what she'd done in the Capital. What she'd done to the high lords.

No. She was definitely not free from sin.

Tyentso felt herself frowning. "When did you stop being younger than me, Scamp? You used to be a child. I could see it in your eyes, in the way you gazed out at the world. But now—" She stood. "You're not Kihrin, are you?"

He chuckled and patted the barrel next to him, inviting her to take a seat. "Relax, Tyentso. I really am Kihrin."

"But why—?"

"I'm also S'arric," he said. "And, uh, much as it pains me to use the damn title, I suppose from a technical point of view I'm also Vol Karoth.[1] Which is why we're meeting in a dream instead of in person. It's kind of difficult for me to be around people at the moment. At least, it's difficult for me to be around anyone I care to keep safe." He made a sweeping motion with his arm. "We're also having this chat in a dream because Relos Var has a couple of ways to eavesdrop on people, but as far as I know, not a single one to spy on a dream."

Tyentso didn't sit on the barrel. Instead, she stood there and contemplated Kihrin with dread itching through her veins as all the color washed out of the world.

Vol Karoth? What the *fuck* had happened to Kihrin while she was busy playing emperor?

Her fingers began moving of their own volition, the desire to do something so intense that she couldn't resist it.

Kihrin smiled at her. "It's still me, Ty. Same soul. Same memories. Just more of both." The corner of his mouth twisted. "The body's new. Or should I say really old? The original, as it were. Can't say I don't miss the newer version, though, because boy, do I ever miss the newer version."

Tyentso took a deep breath. He *sounded* like Kihrin. Sounded like Kihrin in a way she had a difficult time imagining *Vol Karoth* ever would. The ship seemed to tilt, and she realized it was just that she'd sat down on the barrel, after all.

"Fucking hell, Scamp," she muttered. "Does Teraeth know about this?"

"He does," Kihrin admitted, after a beat of hesitation that spoke volumes about how well that conversation must have gone. "Has anyone gotten around to telling you he's King of the Manol these days?"

Tyentso blinked, then shook her head and looked away. "I guess I've missed a few things."

"But not Thaena's death."

She scoffed. "No, not Thaena's death. I felt that one." She'd nursed an ugly, hollowed-out feeling ever since, all the purpose and clarity that had been there for her for the past few years evaporated like seawater on board the *Misery*'s deck. Nothing left behind but stains and salt. "I don't even know what happened to her. It wasn't you, I hope."

"The short version is that Thaena insisted on the vané conducting the Ritual of Night, only it turned out that the vané were never a separate race. They

---

[1] Few people have even heard the name Vol Karoth, and fewer still understand that it's a title, not a name, meaning simply "King of Demons."—T

Something of a misnomer, since he's not a demon.—S

were just humans with a much better educational system. So it didn't work. Apparently, Doc had known and kept it from her, and she was so angry that she murdered him—"

"Fuck," Tyentso muttered.

"—then she used an enchantment to force Teraeth to carry out a ritual that would have killed every citizen of the Manol to gain the power she needed. She intended to use that power to recharge the faulty control crystal keeping Vol Karoth's prison intact. Of course, a bunch of folks went to stop her, and it was big and it was nasty." He sighed. "Taja died. Argas and Galava too. And at one point, Thaena picked up Urthaenriel. A huge mistake: it broke the enchantment she had on Teraeth. So when she tossed the sword to the side in order to better concentrate on killing me, he picked it up and used it on her."

The whole world seemed to just go dark, the breath freezing inside her lungs. She ground her teeth and covered her mouth with a hand. She couldn't imagine it—and yet she also absolutely could. There was never any anger worse, any betrayal worse, than the ones committed by the people who were supposed to love you.

"Oh," she said.

"So a few things. First is that it's apparently possible to be a demon without being evil, although currently there are only two examples of the not-evil kind, and they're both children of Qoran Milligreest, so I'm not sure what that says about the Milligreest bloodline."[2]

Tyentso blinked at him. "What."

"Janel and Jarith are both demons. In Janel's case, you probably wouldn't even notice because she's possessing her original body, but Jarith's a different story. And I'm explaining this to you because it's rather important that you *not kill him*."

She couldn't believe what she was hearing. The idea that Janel had been infected was bad enough—she'd liked that girl—but Jarith? How was she supposed to believe—her brain latched on to a more immediate issue. "That implies I'll have the opportunity."

"Contacting me is tricky at the moment. Jarith can manage it. And it's difficult to stop him from going wherever he feels like, which makes Jarith my official go-between. If you need a message to reach me, all you have to do is tell him."

"You've got to be fucking joking."

A flicker of irritation crossed his face. "Trust me, he's not terribly happy to be a demon either, Ty. But it is what it is. And there's an excellent chance you will need to be able to send messages to me. In the meantime, I've asked him to watch your back."

"I don't—" She closed her eyes. Tyentso didn't even know Jarith Milligreest. He'd been born after she'd been exiled from Quur.

---

[2] Nothing. While Jarith was targeted because of his biological relationship with Janel, it might just as easily have been anyone else. Frankly, I'm surprised Xaltorath didn't turn Janel's adoptive parents into demons.

Poor Qoran, though. He'd be devastated once he figured out what had happened to his son.

Kihrin took her silence as an opportunity to move on to the next topic. "The second thing is that soon you'll be receiving the news that Vol Karoth has escaped his prison—broken free entirely. I'm sure Relos Var felt it as it happened, and if Xaltorath doesn't already know, they will soon. At which point, both will start their endgame scenarios. In the case of Xaltorath—" He shrugged. "I suspect Xaltorath's just looking for power. Tenyé and as much of it as they can manage. Which obviously we have to deny them."

"Obviously," Tyentso agreed, numb.

Kihrin grinned at her. "But the bigger problem is Relos Var. I know what he wants, but I'm less sure about exactly how he intends to get there."

"Okay, I'll play. What does Relos Var want?"

"He wants to puppet-walk my ass into the Nythrawl Wound and use me to seal it from the other side. For the moment, he thinks he needs Urthaenriel to do it, because when last he checked, Urthaenriel could be used to control Vol Karoth."

Tyentso narrowed her eyes. "And that's no longer true?"

Kihrin grinned, wide and bright and achingly mischievous. "That's no longer true. But don't tell him. I wouldn't want to spoil the surprise."

Tyentso snorted. "And I assume this is why you're coming to me. You know you made me promise I wouldn't return that stupid sword to you just because you asked, right?"

"And that hasn't changed," Kihrin said, "but it does mean that Relos Var is going to be coming for you."

She scoffed. "Why? He shouldn't have any idea that I have it. I haven't told anyone."

"I don't think that matters," Kihrin said. "Look, I know that we've all been raised on stories of Godslayer, or Urthaenriel, or whatever you want to call the damn sword. We all know that you can't use magic to find it, but"—he gave her a sharp look—"that's not entirely true. I could *sense* that sword even when I was mortal. I don't think it's just me. I'm willing to bet metal that nine dragons out there, including my dear brother, all share that same connection. The first time Relos Var dropped by the Upper Circle to have a drink at the Culling Fields, he knew exactly where Urthaenriel was hidden."

"No," Tyentso protested. "No, that doesn't make any sense, because if that were true, Kaen wouldn't have been hunting the four corners of the globe for the thing. He just would have asked his court wizard, *Relos Var*."[3]

"Why would Relos Var volunteer that information to Kaen before he was ready? More, why would Relos Var remove the sword from a location where it was secure and he could retrieve it anytime he felt like it? That sword was hidden in the perfect place. But now? *Now* we've put Urthaenriel where he

---

[3] Just a reminder that Relos Var served as court wizard for Duke Azhen Kaen for a number of years, and Duke Kaen did indeed want to locate Urthaenriel, for many reasons.—T

See: *The Ruin of Kings* and *The Name of All Things* for more information.—S

can't reach it anymore. That's going to be a problem for him. A problem he needs to fix. He *will* make a move against you. He has to."

That made a certain ugly sense. And it would certainly put Relos Var in a spot, wouldn't it? Kill Tyentso and the Crown and Scepter reverted back to their "base" positions in the Arena until the next Contest. That meant weeks, at minimum, before a new emperor was crowned. Until that happened, the Vaults were closed off to everyone but the Immortals themselves—who hated Relos Var.

Depending on what Xaltorath was up to, Relos Var might not have weeks.[4]

"Wait. Who has the Stone of Shackles?" Tyentso asked. That was how her father, Gadrith, had gotten around the situation before, after all. He'd just switched bodies with the current emperor, neatly giving himself a throne in the process.

Kihrin said, "Not Relos Var."

"Thank fuck."

"Oh, my sentiments exactly," Kihrin said. "I figure that means he either has to bribe you, enchant you, or extort you. That last one probably by threatening someone you care about. You know how he loves moving at people through their families."

Tyentso let out a bark of laughter. "People I consider family is a fucking short list, Scamp. And something tells me Var can't threaten you any harder than he already is."

Kihrin didn't respond for a moment. He was staring out at nothing—or maybe he was looking at the spot on the mast where they'd whipped him. It was hard to tell. "You mean to tell me you wouldn't care what happens to Qoran Milligreest?"

Tyentso's gut clenched. She wanted to say yes. It had been over between the two of them for a very long time, and the relationship hadn't ended on good terms. Even so. "Shit."

"Told you." At least he didn't sound smug about it. Mostly resigned.

It still made her defensive. "We haven't become lovers again, you know. I'd have sooner chewed out my own tongue. He broke my fucking heart, Scamp. I have no desire to let him stomp on it a second time."

"That doesn't change my question. You would care, right?" He glanced over at her.

"I'd be really sad at Qoran's funeral, Scamp," Tyentso snapped. "But I wouldn't give Relos Var a fucking thing."

Kihrin smiled, although if he was impressed or just hearing what he'd expected was more difficult to gauge. "Fortunately, it won't come to that."

"How do you figure? If you're right, it's either this or try to sway me with an enchantment, and knowing that bastard, it'll probably be both."

"Because it's part of the plan. He's going to come at you for Urthaenriel. And I want you to let him succeed."

---

[4] As it turns out, he didn't even have days.—S

# 3. ROYAL OBLIGATIONS

### Janel's story
### The Mother of Trees, the Manol
### The day of Vol Karoth's escape

The vané soldiers came to attention as the star portal spun into existence, brightened to blinding intensity, and then faded, leaving its passengers behind.

Most of the star portals that linked the different parts of the Manol to each other were inside, kept deep in the center of sky trees or locked away in well-hidden, equally well-guarded rooms where access was strictly controlled. Few outsiders knew of the existence of the portals. Those who did assumed they didn't link to the outside world. And as it happened, that assumption was incorrect.

There'd been one outsider who'd had a permanent invitation to the heart of the Manol capital.

"Well," Teraeth said as he stepped forward. "I suppose that answers the question on whether or not Grizzst kept visiting Khaevatz after he resurrected the Eight Immortals."[1] The amused look on his face faded as more soldiers rushed into the room, clearly caught unaware by the sudden appearance of newcomers. They all had weapons ready.

Teraeth narrowed his eyes at the soldiers. His soldiers. "Seriously?"

Janel thought the problem was less likely to be an issue with Teraeth than his guests. Just as Teraeth was recognizably and distinctly Manol vané, Xivan, "Kihrin," and Janel were all distinctly . . . not. She could hardly blame the vané for being inhospitable to obviously Quuros visitors. Most especially unexpected Quuros visitors arriving through a gate no Quuros should even know exists, let alone be able to access.

"Put those away," Teraeth snapped. "We don't have time for this."

"Teraeth." Kihrin put a hand on Teraeth's arm; Janel hid her flinch.

Because it wasn't Kihrin. It was the mimic, Talon, pretending to be Kihrin. Which she was doing because Kihrin had specifically requested it. Much as Janel hated it, Talon was doing her job. All Janel had to do in return was act like she tolerated the fake Kihrin without wanting to rip the mimic into tiny

---

[1] What she saw in him is a mystery I suspect will never be answered.—S
   He could very charming when he felt like it.—T
   There's no proof of that.—S

little pieces. Pretend that she was looking at one of the men she loved and not his murderer.[2]

Anyway, they had different problems that took precedence. "Forytu, would you be so kind as to escort us to His Majesty? I know he's not expecting us, but we had no way to send word ahead of our arrival."

The guard's eyes slid over to Teraeth, lingered for a moment, and then back again to Janel.

Perhaps the Quuros people weren't the only issue here.

"I know," she told him. "But surely His Majesty gave instructions for this?"

"Janel? A word?" Teraeth grabbed her arm and nudged her to the side. "*His Majesty?* What is going on?"

She snaked an arm around his waist. Janel could hardly blame him for being concerned. He likely expected to return to find either Khaeriel, his niece, or Valathea, his stepmother, running things, and neither one of those would ever use the title "His Majesty." "Do you trust me?"

"Yes, but—"

The soldier, Forytu, interrupted. "My apologies. We *were* given instructions. Please come with us. His Majesty will want to speak with you."

The other soldiers fell around them in a technically "polite" circle that Janel was choosing to interpret as an honor guard rather than an armed escort.

"You know what's going on?" Talon addressed Janel directly.

Janel wished Talon wouldn't try to talk to her, but appearances had to be maintained.

"I do," Janel said primly. She motioned for everyone else to follow her. "Let's go quickly, shall we? The sooner we sort this out, the sooner we can do what we came here for."

Janel appreciated the irony: she *had* told Teraeth what was going on, but he'd just been too out of it at the time to process the information in any meaningful or lasting fashion.

The streets of the Mother of Trees, the capital city of the Manol nation, were silent and solemn. Not deserted, but those few who walked its avenues did so with quiet purpose, grimly putting themselves to work repairing the damage to the country. The vané were better off than the Quuros, but that didn't mean they hadn't taken significant damage. The loss of the Well of Spirals had hit the vané hard. So too had the loss of four of the Eight Guardians. For while the vané may not have worshipped them as gods, that didn't mean they were ignorant of their true role. And that wasn't even counting the psychological toll resulting from the vané discovering the true nature of their own "immortality."

In some ways, the vané were worse off than the Quuros. The citizens of the latter didn't really understand how bad the situation was. They had hope that this would just be temporary, that someone—emperor, high lords, gods— would save them. They understood demons, but the vast majority of Quuros

---

[2] We may need a new definition for this word when the so-called murder victim is still an active living agent.—T

had never heard the names Relos Var or Vol Karoth. The vané, on the other hand, were well educated. Many of them were old enough to remember the specific people and events precipitating this catastrophe.

The vané were *terrified*.

As Janel walked through the vané streets, she felt a keen, piercing homesickness for Jorat. She yearned for wide fields and waving grasses, herds of roaming horses, the crack of thunder from summer storms. She wanted the ground under her feet and Arasgon nudging her shoulder with an impossibly soft velvet nose.[3] She missed Dorna and the scent of roasting tamarane meats pulling her from the training grounds. She longed for the apple orchards of Tolamer and the smell of snow and pine coming down from the mountains.

She wasn't going to get any of that and didn't know when—or worse, *if*—that would change.

This particular portal locale had been so heavily guarded precisely because it existed just inside the palace walls, well inside the boundaries of checkpoints meant to weed out impostors, assassins, and general ne'er-do-wells. Fortunately, they weren't trying to slip anything past anyone, although Teraeth certainly could have managed it if he'd wanted. The group was escorted past extraordinary, intricate illusions layered over interiors that were in and of themselves astonishing works of art.

Finally, they found themselves, still under heavy guard, in a waiting room while one of the vané left to announce them in the throne room.

"That could have gone worse," Teraeth murmured.

Xivan nodded tightly. She looked like she kept expecting Talea to be there and kept being upset when that proved not to be the case.

Janel didn't say anything. Neither did Talon. There were still too many things that could go wrong, and the palace didn't feel like a sanctuary for any of them. This was no time to lower one's guard.

That feeling was only exacerbated when the doors opened. A slew of diplomats, courtiers, and dignitaries were firmly, quickly escorted outside, muttering their protests about the indignity of it all. Someone had just ordered the court emptied.

Emptied of threats—or witnesses.

"You may enter," a herald called to them.

Janel took Teraeth's arm and led him into the audience chamber.

It didn't look *exactly* the same as the last time she'd been there. Some of the decorations had been changed or removed—more obvious, fantastical illusions were visible than the last time too. That was largely because the illusions supporting the Manol vané craftsmanship accentuated it instead of hiding it. Now carved wooden walls were allowed to show their natural beauty, the illusions creating bas-relief bees that flitted from marquetry flower to flower,

---

[3] I can hardly blame her for missing Arasgon. He didn't like me back in the day, but I always thought he was a magnificent example of his species.—S

You mean you wanted to give him carrots and a nice rubdown.—T

"Wanted" implies I don't still feel that way.—S

swaying in imaginary winds. The sprouting trees were real, but the stars and universes sparkling from the depths of their leaves were not.

And sitting on the throne at the end of the hall was a beautiful, black-skinned Manol vané man.

Teraeth.

## 4. THE MOST SECURE VAULT

***Thurvishar's story***
***Arena Park, the Capital City of Quur***
***The day of Vol Karoth's escape, just after dawn***

Senera, Thurvishar, and Talea stood on one of the paths surrounding the Arena. Dawn painted the sky in stripes of violet and pink, casting long shadows through the trees and on paved pathways deserted so early in the day.

"Can we please be quick about this?" Senera said. "If the wrong people see us, I shudder to think how this will go."

"I have no idea what you mean." Thurvishar smiled at her. "I'm not wanted for treason."

Senera glared.

"Oh, it would be awfully unlucky of them to spot us, wouldn't it?" Talea said brightly.

Thurvishar managed not to laugh even as Senera sighed. But Thurvishar's teasing was also a not-too-subtle reminder that Senera was labeled as a terrorist by the Quuros Empire—a status that Senera had earned.

Not that Thurvishar was in any position to compare. He could attribute his own free status entirely to the fact that his house had been considered too important to eliminate, one of history's many examples of money and power pardoning any number of crimes.[1]

Talea reached out a hand to the iridescent wall of force surrounding the Arena. It shimmered at the contact, then spread out into a door shape familiar to anyone who'd ever entered the Arena or stopped by the Culling Fields to watch a duel. A safe point of entry. Senera walked through, followed by Thurvishar, with Talea closing the door behind herself.

"This shouldn't take more than a moment." Talea walked with a determined stride toward the vaults. The freestanding buildings looked much as Thurvishar remembered them—plain, unassuming stone squares with empty, dark doorways and much darker reputations.

His father, Sandus, had died for the contents of those buildings. At least Thurvishar had one consolation: that his murderer, Gadrith, hadn't lived long enough to claim his spoils.

"I'll just dash inside and pick up the other talismans," Talea said.

---

[1] At least you can admit it, I suppose.—S

Talea was the only one of them who could safely enter any of these buildings. They'd been enchanted so that only the Emperor of Quur or one of the Eight Immortals could safely enter.

Talea qualified as one of the latter, which was certainly not true of either wizard.

Talea walked inside. Ten minutes later, she hadn't come out. Senera crossed her arms over her chest and glanced around.

"We're surrounded by woods," Thurvishar said. "Who can see us?"

She pursed her lips. "Fine." The unease rolled off her in waves, like ripples in the air on a hot day.

"But," Thurvishar said, prodding the woman to continue.

"*But* I hate being back in the Upper Circle," Senera admitted. "Even here. I wouldn't mind never returning. Or burning this city to the ground. The whole place vibrates with cruelty and anger. It's even worse than I remember."

"The demons are trying to help with that second one. I know this is difficult—" Thurvishar paused. Senera wasn't wrong. There was something in the air. Something unpleasant and furious hanging heavy over the streets.

Thurvishar shuddered. He'd never wanted to leave the Capital so badly before.

The doorway to the vault's interior space shimmered before disgorging Talea, whose expression was as unhappy as Thurvishar had ever seen. Worse, she wasn't holding anything in her hands.

"What happened?" Senera asked the question first.

Talea shook her head. "It's gone. All of it. Urthaenriel too. Whoever took them wasn't interested in any of the treasure—they only stole Urthaenriel and the Greater Talismans."

"No reason to panic," Thurvishar said, although he was well aware that his caution wouldn't be enough to prevent Senera from doing exactly that. "Maybe one of the other Immortals claimed them. Possibly Tyentso decided it was safest to take Urthaenriel with her or move its location."

Senera threw him a dirty look. "What in the Veils possessed you to give Urthaenriel to *Tyentso*?"

Thurvishar raised an eyebrow at her disapproval. He suspected her bias against Quuros imperialism was showing. Senera *liked* Tyentso. "Because after all the effort Gadrith went through to rob the vaults in the belief that Urthaenriel was here, no one would expect the sword to actually be here. And Tyentso has a close relationship with Kihrin. It was an easy choice." He paused then. "You don't think Tyentso can be trusted with it?"

"Can we just ask the empress what happened to the sword?" Talea suggested.

"Thurvishar can," Senera said. "It would be best if I didn't, even if I'm a huge fan of her recent work."

"You mean the way she slaughtered most of the high lords," Thurvishar said.

"Yes," Senera said with a fond smile at the very idea. "I do mean that."[2]

"I can't do anything else here." Talea tugged on Thurvishar's sleeve. "Mind taking me back down to the Manol? Maybe we can make it in time to help Xivan."

"What I should do is teach you how to transport yourself," Thurvishar said, but he knew they didn't have time for that.

He was more concerned about the way the entire city psychically teetered on the verge of exploding. Everything felt wrong. Unfortunately, they didn't have time to investigate it.

"By all means," Thurvishar said. "Let's return you to Xivan's side."

---

[2] Seriously wish I could have been there. Purely for the historical record, of course.—S

# 5. A Simple Favor

*Sheloran's story*
*The Ivory District, the Upper Circle of the Capital City of Quur*
*The day of Vol Karoth's escape, morning*

"We should have asked Thurvishar to open a gate directly into the Rose Palace," Qown complained.

Galen chuckled as he squeezed the other man's arm. "I don't think he wanted to be attacked by several hundred twitchy House D'Talus guards," the D'Mon prince responded. "And that's not even counting Sheloran's parents."

Sheloran said nothing. She continued watching the riot.

It was, undeniably, a riot, although she was unclear if it was a riot composed of suspiciously early risers or if they'd simply stayed up all night looting and burning. Sheloran could taste the hatred in the air, although she could be forgiven for confusing that with the lingering stench of burning flesh and buildings. The trio perched on top of the Temple of Bertok, one of the more minor gods,[1] trying to stay as unobtrusive as possible as the tide of people heaved through the streets below. Most of the rioters were from the Lower Circle. Under normal circumstances, they never should have made it up into the Upper Circle. Somehow they had, and now the riots seemed determined to lay siege to the Court of Gems.

As a result, Sheloran, Galen, and Qown hadn't made it anywhere near their intended destination.

They were trapped, although at least none of them was dressed like a royal. The Zheriasian clothing they'd worn for the past few weeks while traveling was the only thing keeping them from becoming open targets for rioters.[2]

But even that wouldn't mean a thing if anyone ventured close enough to notice the color of their eyes.

"Maybe the center?" Qown suggested.

The princess blinked at him. "What do you mean?"

"Toward the center," he repeated, pointing for emphasis. "Toward Arena Park, where Thurvishar, Senera, and Talea went? I don't know how well Taunna will react to seeing us again at the Culling Fields, but I'm sure she

---

[1] Technically a god of war, but most specifically associated with hot tempers and killings committed in anger.—T

He sounds charming.—S

[2] That, and may I suggest that being on the roof of a temple also helped?—S

must know that what happened wasn't our fault . . . It has to be safer than here.[3] Surely there'll be a way to get a message to your mother?"

Sheloran frowned. She wasn't comfortable assuming that would be possible or easy. The most obvious method of contacting her mother (besides walking into the Rose Palace) would have been visiting the Temple of Caless in the Ivory Quarter, but it lay on the opposite side of the district from their present location. Given the way the rioting was spilling out of the Court of Gems into the temple district, she thought that would be only nominally safer than braving the crowds to reach the D'Talus palace directly.

Perhaps Qown's idea held merit. She didn't relish the idea of fighting her way through rioters to reach the palace. They could; the three of them were hardly defenseless. In point of fact, they'd left the Lighthouse with a number of specialty glyphs and protections custom designed for their needs, including a variation of Relos Var's "need help" signal.

Of course, they meant to use that against *Relos Var,* not Quuros rioters. It would be a matter of grave embarrassment to come here with so simple a task as "please go talk to your mother" and almost immediately need to have Senera or Thurvishar rescue them.[4]

Riots seldom happened without a reason. For the citizens of the Capital to be so incensed that they were willing to fling themselves against the Royal Houses?

Something had gone very wrong.

Sheloran's eyes met Galen's. He shrugged. "The army's guarding everything near the imperial palace. I imagine it'll be safer if only because fewer people will be allowed in the area."

The three of them all turned toward the center circle of green, and the few buildings that surrounded it. It did seem peaceful compared to the chaos below. Suspiciously so. One could imagine that the magical bubble that surrounded the Arena had expanded outward until it protected the entirety of the city center.

Part of that calm was undoubtedly attributable to the fact the rioters were focused on the Royal House palaces. Those areas formed the outer ring of the Upper Circle. People hadn't yet shifted the blame to the empire itself.

Although that would come.[5]

Sheloran shivered. She felt naked and exposed for more reasons than just returning to the Capital to find it awash in fear and anger. They all had much more personal reasons for thinking themselves at risk.

---

[3] Given that the last time they were at the Culling Fields, someone filled the place with toxic Lysian gas, I'm not convinced Taunna's cooperation should have been assumed.–T

[4] It would hardly be the first time.–S

   Still embarrassing. Remember, they're kids.–T

   And you're not?–S

   Only by certain definitions.–T

[5] As well it should. The "empire" is a myth created by the power-mongers of the so-called Royal Houses. The entire point was nothing so much as an excuse to perpetuate their wealth and power in a wordplay circumvention of the Celestial Concordance.–S

   Yes, but how do you really feel about it?–T

"Let's try it," Galen said. "If trouble finds us, run. We can't afford to be dragged into a fight."

"Trust me, fighting is the last thing I want to do," Qown said. He stared at Galen, and something about what he saw (the intensity of that gaze, the color of Galen's eyes, oh, it could have been anything) made Qown blush and look away.

Sheloran stamped down on a sigh. Her boys. It didn't even matter that Qown had admitted he liked Galen too. The former priest was still as skittish as a feral kitten. She put a hand on her fan, tucked into her belt sash, and only at the last minute reminded herself that she was not under any circumstances to use the damn thing. It was too clearly valuable, too obviously the sort of monstrously expensive item only a royal would be able to afford. At that moment, being identified as a royal wasn't in her best interest.

Galen climbed down off the roof and helped the other two down. Qown was especially flustered when Galen's hands ended up on his waist.

Honestly. The entire empire was falling apart, and Qown was discovering *puberty*. Which Galen was gleefully, purposefully encouraging. She knew her husband far too well to believe that all this touching had been "accidental." It would have been adorable—*at any other time*.

As it was, if she bit her lip any harder to keep from sighing or rolling her eyes, she was going to leave permanent scars.

Sheloran pointed toward an alley. "That way should lead to Arena Park."

The Arena was technically the land inside the magical field of energy where the Imperial Contest was held, so it naturally fell that the area surrounding that was called Arena Park. It was larger than most people realized, housing not only a few businesses and the Citadel but several other important government buildings. Including the Soaring Halls—the imperial palace.

So it was not entirely unexpected to find the entrance to Arena Park blocked by a large contingent of Quuros soldiers, accompanied by Academy wizards and even some witch-hunters. Certainly, more than enough to keep out any rioters who might have mistakenly thought this an easier target.

"How are we going to get past them?" Qown whispered.

"Why don't we tell them the truth?" Galen suggested and darted forward.

"What? Damn it, Galen!" Sheloran missed grabbing the man's misha. She didn't dare use magic, for fear of setting off a nervous retaliation from one of the wizards or witch-hunters at the scene.

Qown sighed in exasperation and ran after him.

*D'Mons,* Sheloran thought.[6]

She followed, her pace quick but nothing like Galen's annoyingly long-legged run. By the time she reached her husband's side, he was already deep in conversation with a guard, gesturing wildly.

It wasn't going well.

---

[6] She speaks for all of us.—S

"I don't care if you're the empress herself."[7] The soldier practically vibrated with anger. "Nobody comes in or out without a pass, which you don't have." The guard examined Galen with a sneering regard. "You're not a royal, are you?"

Galen was about to answer when Sheloran grabbed his hand. "No," she said quickly. "If we were, we'd be sheltering at one of the palaces, wouldn't we?"

The guard narrowed his eyes at her. "You have god-cursed eyes."

"Yes, well, it turns out you don't lose those just because you're an unacknowledged bastard," she answered.[8]

The guard huffed. "Whatever. You can wait with everyone else."

Galen sighed. "All I need is for you to deliver a message to my cousin Eledore Milligreest. I know she's in there."

Recognition flashed across the other man's face. For just a second, Sheloran thought Galen might have dropped the right name. Then the guard's face shuttered away all expression save anger, and he gestured for Galen to step back. "Not my problem. Now walk away. You're not the only person here waiting for the chance to waste my time."

Which was sadly true, even so early in the morning. They weren't the only people attempting to gain entry. Most of the others appeared to be merchants and workers who wanted nothing to do with the chaos and bloodshed but couldn't shelter behind palace walls. Their numbers included a distressingly large number of children. Sheloran could remember a time when these streets had been spotlessly clean and kept largely deserted by regular guard patrols. Now they were a mess, filled with people, many of whom seemed to be actively living on the streets.

Were any demons to show themselves just then, a great many people would die.

She touched Galen's arm. "Let's go."

Qown's mouth twisted. "Go where?"

"I have an idea," was all Sheloran said. Which she certainly had no intention of spelling out in front of this many witnesses. She turned around and began walking across the street, toward a ruined shop that appeared to have once sold flowers. Said flowers lay strewn about the ground, trampled and burned, but there might be some undamaged stems if one searched carefully. The air was an unsettling mixture of orchid, jasmine, and scorched wood that matched the devastated state of the shop itself. It would need to be torn down and rebuilt, assuming its owners were in any condition to do so. More likely, the owners were dead.

Galen and Qown followed her. Galen gave her an especially bemused look. "And why are we picking flowers?"

---

[7] There was some back-and-forth on whether or not the title should be gendered. Evidently, the ultimate answer was *yes.*–T

Because it would be such a shame if anyone were to accidentally forget Tyentso's gender.–S

[8] As opposed to an acknowledged bastard, or Ogenra.–T

She paused. "They're a standard prayer offering, Blue."

"Oh!" Qown blinked at her. "Your mother—"

She nodded, fighting down the fluttery feeling of dread that idea gave her. There would be no denying that she knew the truth after that. Was she ready to confront her mother about her secret—that Sheloran knew her mother was really the god-queen Caless, Goddess of Love?

Galen began looking for flowers as well. He hadn't been doing so for more than a minute or so when he crouched behind an overturned cart.

"Why, hello there," he said. "Aren't you a cute little thing?"

Sheloran glanced over at him. It would be just like Galen to have found a stray dog or an alley cat. He liked to pretend that she was the soft touch for strays, but he had always been the one who really—

Then Galen said, "Where are your parents?"

Sheloran froze.

Whoever was hiding underneath the cart—most certainly *not* a puppy—burst into tears.

"Um." Qown crouched down next to Galen. "Oh dear."

Sheloran looked around. No one was paying any attention. Certainly not the sort of attention one might be expected to pay to one's own offspring in distress. It was impossible to say, though—too many people looked too upset, too numb. Any one of them might be missing a child or might not have noticed that theirs had wandered off.

Meanwhile, Galen and Qown were still trying to coax the child out from its hiding place.

"This isn't—" Sheloran cut herself off before she said something she'd regret. There was absolutely no way that either Galen or Qown was going to leave a child terrified and abandoned on the street, no matter what else they were in the middle of doing. She rubbed her forehead.

"We're not going to hurt you," Galen whispered.

Sheloran pulled one of the shanathá filigree pieces off her fan. She studied it, let its tenyé hover heavy and sweet, a veil of invisible energy weaving around her fingers like delicate lace. She willed the tenyé to change, the metal to shift in response, so that the transition was a minor, delicate thing, easily overlooked. The Upper Circle was always awash in magic. As long as she didn't do any casting right in front of the witch-hunters, she was probably safe enough. She opened her hand and tossed its contents into the air. Food would undoubtedly have been a better lure, but she'd work with what she had.

A metal dragonfly hovered, delicate wings beating fast, then flew under the cart, landing on the broken wheel.

Someone under the cart let out a small gasp.

"Leave them be," Sheloran said. When both the men turned to her, angry retorts on their lips, she laughed. "Have you never tried to lure out a scared cat? The harder you push, the more they hide." She gestured to the steps of the burned-out shop. "Help me clear this so we can set up a shrine."

The two men stepped away from the cart with obvious reluctance. They shoved aside debris while Sheloran knelt. She peeled away another piece of metal filigree from her fan and let this one go molten, pouring it between her fingers until it formed a perfect, mirror-bright circle on the ground. She solidified the metal and then set her gathered flowers on top.

Sheloran ignored the snuffling noise coming from the wagon, the sound of someone rubbing a runny nose.

Sheloran bowed her head. "Caless," she said out loud, "please accept this poor offering, token though it may be from your daughter." That part sounded normal enough, even if it was less of a metaphor in her case than for other worshippers of the Goddess of Love. "If you can hear me, please know I'm trying to enter Arena Park through the South Jade Road."

With that, Sheloran set the flowers on fire.

She heard a small shriek and couldn't tell if it was fear or laughter. She glanced backward. A small child—impossible to say if they were a boy or a girl—had climbed out from under the wreckage and gazed at the three of them with a stare both wary and fascinated.

The child held up the now-inert metal dragonfly. "Make it work, please."

Sheloran's mouth twisted. The child's accent was baby soft, but surprisingly coherent for their age. Surely not older than three years. It was difficult to say if the child had been raised in an Upper Circle household or not. They were filthy and their clothing was in rags, but again—that didn't mean anything, given the current state of the empire. They seemed educated, but that was a lot of guesswork to hang off the word *please*.

Galen knelt next to the child. "You said *please*. That's very good. Now what's your name?"[9]

The small child looked at Galen with a blank expression, like they had found themselves faced off against a tiger and didn't dare move for fear of being eaten. They looked about five seconds from diving right back under the flower cart again.

Sheloran set the dragonfly's wings beating, letting the movement catch the child's attention. The ploy worked brilliantly. The child gasped again, staring at it, any concerns about strange people forgotten.

The ploy worked too well, as the small child ran into Sheloran's arms.

Sheloran rocked back to keep from being pushed off balance and falling. She didn't quite know what to do. At all. She gave Galen a helpless look and motioned for him to take the toddler away.

Galen shook his head, his lips quirked in an obvious attempt to forestall open laughter. "Oh no," he said. "He clearly wants you."

She glared at him, but her husband was too busy enjoying this to feel guilty. She put a hand under the toddler, the other around its waist, and carefully

[9] What impressed me was that the boy had figured out Sheloran was responsible for making the dragonfly work in the first place. I'll bet metal to dirt that child develops a witchgift before puberty.—S

stood. The child was back to crying again, although this seemed more like relief than fear. Apparently, Sheloran was "safe."[10]

The princess sighed. She could *feel* the child wiping snot all over her raisigi.

Galen's expression slipped, turned bemused. "I thought you liked children," he whispered.

"Oh, I adore them," Sheloran agreed. "Most especially when someone *else* is taking care of them." She gave one last wistful glance around—if only she knew how to summon up a nanny just with longing! But no such babysitter appeared.

Qown held out his arms. "I'll take them."

Never mind. That would do.

"Him," Galen said. "It's a boy."

Qown frowned. "How can you be sure?"

"I can't. But it's safer for him if he is, regardless of the truth."

Qown clearly didn't understand but didn't ask for an explanation either. Instead, he unwrapped his agolé from his waist and twisted it around his torso. Then he made gentle soothing sounds—as though he were talking to a particularly skittish horse—while he pried the child away from Sheloran. To her surprise, the child allowed this without protest.

"Sheloran."

She turned at the sound of her mother's voice. And stared, because for a split second, she hadn't recognized her own mother. Lessoral's bright scarlet hair was now a dark Marakori red. Her eyes were as brown as any Quuros woman's rather than furnace hot. Her clothing was clean enough, nice enough—but nice for a merchant's wife, not nice for a high lord's. Definitely not nice enough for a god-queen. She had a permanent frown plastered on her face, where Sheloran was used to smiles. If she wore the Stone of Shackles (and Sheloran had to assume she did), she'd hidden it.

The two women stared at each other, while the men looked awkwardly uncomfortable, and the child continued to try to burrow into Qown's chest.

There could be no hiding. Sheloran knew that her mother was really Caless, the Goddess of Love or Lust or Whores or all of the above depending on whom one asked. And Caless knew that Sheloran knew. She felt her throat close up, her body overwhelmed by so many different emotions she didn't know if she should be feeling anger or relief or bitter resentment.

Then Sheloran was in her mother's arms, powerless to stop the tears. She had no idea which of those emotions was responsible. Perhaps all of them.

Caless pushed her daughter away from her. "Where have you *been*? Do you have any idea how dangerous it is to be wandering the city right now? They're killing—" She swallowed whatever she'd been about to say and looked around herself with frantic zeal, scanning for anyone who might be too close. "When no one could find you, we thought the worst. *How could you?*"

---

[10] Said no man, ever, who's seen her on the battlefield.—S

"I love you too." Sheloran scowled and plucked at her mother's clothing. "What's this? Are you . . . are you *hiding*?"

Caless sniffed. "It's not safe to be a royal at the moment." She gave the two men an unfriendly stare; Sheloran felt the back of her neck prickle. "We'll have to do something about your eye color and clothing."

Galen stepped forward like he was stepping in front of a sword. "When did the rioting start?"

"A few days ago." Caless sneered as though it were a stupid question to which Galen should have known the answer. "Right around the time the food shipments stopped."

The three young people all stared at each other, wide-eyed.

"Um . . ." Sheloran had no idea what to say. *The food shipments had stopped?* The Gatestone system linked every part of the empire. Even in the middle of a Hellmarch, the Capital City still had access to food. Or should have had access to food. If that had changed, then the rioting made a great deal more sense. In point of fact, if that had changed, the rioting became mandatory.

"Follow me, and stick close," Caless ordered. She began walking back toward the entrance to the imperial grounds.

Sheloran started to move when she realized Qown hadn't put down the little boy.

She raised both eyebrows at him, but he was defiantly unapologetic. "Where's his family?" Qown mouthed over the boy's head.

Sheloran examined the street and sighed. These people looked like refugees who'd decided to go inward to safety rather than outward. They were still singed from fires, bloody from injuries. For all she knew, the child's family could be right there.

"Bring him," Galen said. The child's head swiveled, and the toddler frowned. It was rather cute, like he was deciding whether or not this was a good idea.

A better idea than staying on the streets until something horrific happened. Sheloran and Galen sponsored several orphanages in the Lower Circle, although at the moment, she could only hope that those places remained safe. Assuming they were, however, then at least they had a place where they could put the boy and possibly find his family later. Staying with Sheloran, Galen, and Qown long-term wasn't viable. Or healthy.

Her mother noted the exchange, but made no comment on it. She simply walked up to the guards, who had so vehemently resisted letting them have access, and spoke a few words. The man waved the other guards aside so they could pass. Many of those same guards scowled at Galen and Sheloran both, as though contemplating whether or not they should be placed under immediate arrest.

Once past the barricade, their journey became smoother, although no less hectic. Here, instead of riots, it was army encampments. The military had bivouacked in the fields surrounding the Arena in preparation of leaving through gates to other locales. Although in order to accomplish what, Sheloran didn't know. They weren't needed in Devors anymore. *That* situation had been handled.[11]

But no. The food shipments had stopped. That was the emergency now. An empire the size of Quur lived or died through its infrastructure. If that system had failed . . .

Galen leaned over to Sheloran. "I'd never have thought of praying. That was smart."

"I have my moments," Sheloran murmured, but her attention was largely focused on her mother, who seemed remarkably ill-tempered and out of sorts. Probably because she'd been forced to abandon the Rose Palace. "Why are you staying in the Soaring Halls?"

Her mother rolled her eyes. "Why aren't I under siege back in the Red District, you mean?"

"Am I supposed to think that a mob of rioters would be any threat to you or Father?" Sheloran responded to her mother's rhetorical question with one of her own.

Caless snorted. "Just because they can't hurt me doesn't mean I need to suffer through watching them try. And the servants are easy enough to kill." She scowled, her expression that of a person tasting something off. "There's a great deal that's happened. But let's go back first. Your father will want to know that you're still alive. Then we can talk."

---

[11] That situation being an attack by a kraken and a dragon at the same time.–T

## 6. ALL HAIL THE KING

### Janel's story
### The Mother of Trees, the Manol
### The day of Vol Karoth's escape, morning

Janel trapped Teraeth's arm as he reached for his knives. She sympathized with his reaction, but she also knew more than he did about current events.

"Calm, my love," Janel whispered. "Trust me."

"Close the door," King "Teraeth" ordered as he stood from the throne.

"A little warning would have been polite, Janel," Xivan whispered.

"I wasn't precisely sure who would be in charge," Janel responded without looking away from the approaching figure.

The image of the king wavered like a sea-born mirage in the distance, breaking up into hazy strips that rearranged themselves as a very different-looking figure. Not Teraeth at all, but someone far more petite and feminine, a violet flower given life as a woman.

Chainbreaker sparkled green and glittering against Valathea's bosom as she smiled warmly.[1] "My apologies, Teraeth. A small but necessary deception. The first days of power are always so uncertain, and I knew you were in no condition to take the reins for this transition." She floated down from the dais and kissed her stepson on the cheeks. She barely had to lean up to do it, a reminder that for all Valathea's flowerlike delicacy, she was as tall as most vané.

"I admit, I hadn't thought—" Teraeth blinked.

"It's good to see you again, Valathea," Xivan said.

"When you say *uncertain*," "Kihrin" said, "you're referring to my mother, aren't you? You were afraid she'd try to take the throne back if no one was here to defend it."

Talon meant Kihrin's mother, Khaeriel, not Talon's own mother (whoever that had been). Janel forced herself to smile at the mimic, to pretend this was one of the men she loved.

*Fields.* How was she possibly going to maintain this ruse? It was like wearing a coat made of broken glass. She couldn't even look at the damn mimic without flinching now that she knew the truth.

---

[1] You do realize this implies that she was using Chainbreaker for this illusion, yes? When all signs point to a much more prosaic illusion being responsible.—S

True, but Janel assumed she was using Chainbreaker at this point.—T

A mighty bang echoed in the throne room as someone pushed open the double doors at the end of the room and stormed in.

Kihrin's mother, Khaeriel.

Janel glanced over at Talon. "Nice job on *that* summoning."

"Your Majesty," Khaeriel snapped, "why was I only just now told that you—" She paused as she saw who was in the room, her expression softening in response to Kihrin before focusing on the important presence: Teraeth. He was standing in the wrong place, dressed in the wrong clothing. Khaeriel's gaze slipped from him to the woman standing before the throne.

It wasn't difficult to leap to the correct conclusion.

Khaeriel had apparently been enjoying her return to the vané capital, even if she was no doubt disappointed not to be returning as its queen. Still, she dressed to make it clear she *should* have been. Her gold hair was capped with a fret studded with emeralds, and she wore a dress of green silk and gold mail that sparkled in the reflected mage-light. Her skin was dark enough to make her Manol ancestry clear, but her eyes were gold.

Not a stitch of blue. Janel suspected that Khaeriel would never wear the color blue again.

Khaeriel's shock transformed into sly pleasure as she took in Valathea's presence. "I am sure you are aware of just how many laws you have broken, Valathea. Impersonating the sovereign? That will not be easily forgiven."

"You'll have to save the treason charges for another day," Teraeth said dismissively. "She was acting under my orders."

Which Janel knew for a fact wasn't true.

Khaeriel's narrowed eyes suggested she also knew it wasn't true. But short of dragging Teraeth to the Parliament of Flowers for questioning under a truth spell, calling his bluff was problematic. "Was she? And what possible reason could you have had to be absent from the Manol after the catastrophes we've suffered?"[2]

"The best reason," Teraeth answered. "Vol Karoth's escaped."

The derision dropped entirely from Khaeriel's face, leaving behind a flash of stunned horror, quickly concealed. Her ability to cover her emotions was to be commended. It had no doubt served her well when she had been House D'Mon's seneschal.

Janel realized that somewhere along the way, she'd decided she didn't *like* Kihrin's mother. Quite possibly she harbored a bias stemming from the opinions of her friends: Doc and Valathea, for example, or Galen and Sheloran.

"This must have happened recently," Khaeriel said, "as word had not reached us of such a calamity. And yet Your Majesty has been gone for much longer than that, if my guess is correct." She was just this side of civil to Teraeth, but her glare toward Valathea was not.

Khaeriel hadn't made a secret of wanting the throne and, not so long ago, had thought she would get it—or half of it. But Teraeth's father, Terindel, had

[2] So killing your mother who's just tried to murder you after successfully killing your father counts for nothing then? I would've thought that an excellent excuse.—S

betrayed her to grab it all.[3] No matter how noble his reasons or, for that matter, that it had likely saved Khaeriel's life, she seemed to have transferred her resentment to Terindel's wife, Valathea.

"Was there a question in that?" Teraeth stared at Khaeriel with narrowed eyes.

Talon/Kihrin stepped forward before Khaeriel could respond. "Is my father here with you?" he asked Khaeriel.

The vané woman exhaled. "Kihrin . . ." It wasn't clear exactly what she'd intended to say. Possibly she hadn't known herself.

"I need to talk to him," Kihrin said. "It's important." His entire posture was tightly coiled, his fists clenched by his sides. He was playing up the Vol Karoth angle for all it was worth. Given that Kihrin's mother knew he was inextricably linked to the newly escaped dark god, he played to an audience primed to believe him.

There was no overwhelming plan that required Therin's involvement, no pressing business. They weren't there for Therin D'Mon.

Honestly, Janel almost admired Talon's skill. Almost. The mimic had neatly tripped up Khaeriel's momentum and any trouble she might otherwise have stirred up. Not to say Khaeriel wouldn't still be a problem, but she'd have to be a problem after she'd dealt with her own family dramas.

Khaeriel deflated. "Yes, well. I suppose I should take you to him. He will be well pleased to see you returned safe."

Janel didn't flinch in response to the suggestion that Kihrin was "safe." She hoped she hadn't, although the concerned way Valathea stared at her suggested otherwise. Hopefully, that was a general concern and not a more specific "why *wouldn't* you think Kihrin's safe?" concern.

Oh, how Janel loathed the idea that at some point in the future—if they survived all this, if there was anything left worth surviving—someone would have to explain to Khaeriel that her son Kihrin was dead. Had been dead for well over a week.[4]

And if this all went as planned, also not dead by certain definitions. Because the world was strange like that.

Kihrin moved expectantly toward the door and then turned back to Khaeriel. "Thanks." He made it very clear that he meant to leave now and not after Khaeriel was finished with her business.

Khaeriel's departure left a thin, stilted silence in her wake.

After a pause, Teraeth said, "I admit to being surprised."

Valathea smiled. "Oh?"

"We all know I didn't ask you to cover for me, and I wouldn't have thought you'd be so determined to see me stay on the throne. Not knowing what you do."

Valathea seemed genuinely confused for a moment. "Why wouldn't I want

---

[3] He was rightfully entitled to the Kirpis vané half of the throne.—T
[4] Honestly, given that family's relationship with the Stone of Shackles, I should think they'd be used to these sorts of family tree snarls by this point.—S
Plays hell on the genealogists, though.—T

my stepson to—" Her expression cleared. "Oh, you're referring to the delightful irony of who you used to be in your past life?" She grinned then, without
the slightest trace of malice to her expression. "Making the reincarnation of
Atrin Kandor sit on the vané throne strikes me as an appropriate punishment
for past sins. Wouldn't you agree?"

Teraeth didn't look amused—which proved Valathea's point.[5]

The former vané queen examined each member of the group in turn with
mild interest. Then she said to Teraeth, "I also assume your purpose in returning here wasn't to reclaim your throne, so how may I be of assistance?"

"Who can hear us right now?" Teraeth asked.

Valathea stopped, concentrated. "No one," she said.

Janel's focus sharpened. "Are you using Chainbreaker to do that?"

A vaguely embarrassed look flickered across Valathea's face. "Yes, although
I admit that using Chainbreaker on all three of you at once stands right at the
limits of my skill."

"You used Chainbreaker on *Thaena*," Teraeth reminded her.

Valathea waved a hand. "Using Chainbreaker on a single person is easy,
even if that person is a Guardian. Using Chainbreaker on large numbers has
proved . . . more challenging." She lifted her chin. "And don't tell me how
Terindel could sow illusions into the minds of hundreds of people simultaneously. I'm aware. But he had centuries to master this. I've had weeks."

Janel and Teraeth glanced at each other. There was an excellent chance
that they would need just that: someone who could use Chainbreaker on
hundreds simultaneously. Maybe they'd get lucky and just have to deal with
a few people. Maybe they wouldn't. There was no way to know in advance.

Teraeth turned back to his stepmother. "Not a problem," he said. "As it
happens, we wanted to talk to you about resurrecting Doc."[6]

That placid expression, normally so composed, cracked. The longing on
her face was almost startling in its intensity, before she carefully put it away,
hidden under elegant concern.

"Oh," Valathea said. "Why didn't you say—" She paused.

There was a shiver across the universe that was probably Valathea releasing her control using Chainbreaker. With the illusion banished, suddenly an
alarm rang out in the room, a bright, sharp warning klaxon.

"The wards have detected a mimic," Valathea explained, frowning.

Janel, Teraeth, and Xivan all simultaneously shared a panicked look.

Janel fought the temptation to curse. When last they'd checked, the palace
wards couldn't detect Talon. So either another, entirely different mimic was
loose in the palace . . . or *someone had updated the magical security to include Talon.*

In either case, they had a problem.

---

[5] Remind me to send her "let's be friends" flowers at some point.—S
[6] We would have wanted to Return Doc even if we hadn't needed him for Chainbreaker.—T
    Yes, but not quite so urgently.—S

# 7. STEP TWO: HANDLE UNEXPECTED COMPLICATIONS

*Kihrin's story*
*The Korthaen Blight*
*The day of Vol Karoth's escape*

I'd thought the dragons were going to be my biggest problem.

I'd known for years that Vol Karoth maintained a link with the monsters. Indeed, ever since the Old Man[1], I'd been under the impression that Vol Karoth shouldered some of the blame for the general state of "absolutely insane" that swirled around most dragons. Then my relationship with Vol Karoth had become, um, more personal, and I'd confirmed that connection firsthand. I was aware of their voices, whispers at the edge of my hearing, hissing and scratching for attention.

If that had been all there was to the situation, I'd have coped. Hell, I'd probably have wrested control away from the more dangerous dragons and forcibly enlisted their help fighting my enemies. But there was a reason, a good one, why I hadn't done that.

Relos Var. Who was also a dragon.

I *knew* I couldn't control Relos Var. And worse, I couldn't be certain that Relos Var wouldn't be able to feel it if I tried to exercise control over the other eight dragons. Or, I suppose I should clarify, if I attempted to exert rational, coherent control. Vol Karoth had been whispering into the minds of the dragons for years, even while imprisoned. Those whispers and nudges had only grown worse when Vol Karoth had woken—Rol'amar attacking the lake house in the Manol, for instance, had happened precisely because Vol Karoth had ordered it. Yes, I could absolutely rant and scream and throw god-level temper tantrums all I wanted without raising any suspicions.

The first time I gave a lucid order, though?

I had a terrible suspicion that Relos Var would recognize the truth. Which meant that as much as I wanted to force all the dragons to play nice, it was best to leave them alone. In fact, I shut them out, erecting a mental barricade

---

[1] Real name: Sharanakal, child of Thaena and Ompher and associated with Worldhearth. Also the universe's most mobile volcano.—S

to guarantee Relos Var couldn't sense just how deeply "Vol Karoth" had changed.[2]

If that had been my biggest problem, it all would have been milk and honey. Unfortunately, it was far from it.

I hadn't yet even physically left the Blight when the *real* problem presented itself: I became hungry.

This wasn't a normal hunger. Ola had always done right by me, but I'd had plenty of opportunities during my journey as a slave to become familiar with the feeling of missed meals. I knew what it felt like to be hungry and not know when or if the next meal would happen. There was always a tipping point where the body numbed the sharp edges, settled physical need into a dull stupor. Even if I imagined the hungriest that I'd ever been in my entire life—the feeling like a blade twisting inside my stomach, an animal weakness sweeping back and forth through me like the motion of my fellow rowers in the slave galley, it was nothing compared to what I felt now. This hunger grew stronger, fouler, more heated and painful, an agony burning me with a desperate and ravenous need for sustenance.

I needed to eat. *What* I needed to eat was less clear. Food wouldn't solve my problem. In hindsight, it had been naïve to assume that fixing my mental state would do anything to solve the curse that my brother had twisted around my existence. I was Kihrin, yes.

I was also *still* Vol Karoth.

The pain redoubled its assault, expanding into an agony so powerful I couldn't move or think or do anything but float midair and scream.

Into that hunger, voices manifested.

**You should have listened to us. We would have helped you. We would have shown you how to deal with this. We've had to learn ourselves.**

I opened my eyes to gaze across the fetid landscape of the Korthaen Blight. Understanding flashed through me, leaving me in a state of terrifying dread. Nothing existed near me. *Nothing at all.* I had destroyed anything within thirty feet.

I hadn't even realized I was doing it.[3]

**What will you do now?** the voices asked. **You can't return to what you used to be. You're our child, you know. We made you. You were born of our hunger, our hate.**

Shadows lurked at the edges of my vision. Swirling darkness manifested, something other than the remains of my ravenous destruction. The voices were too coherent to be dragons—dragon voices were nearly incomprehensible swirls of chaotic energies. This was a different kind of monster, although still one I recognized.

Demons.

---

[2] I suspect that the only reason this tactic proved successful was because Relos Var himself had already erected strong mental barriers in order to keep Vol Karoth out of his own mind. Thus, this was the telepathic equivalent of two people refusing to look at each other.—T

[3] Not everything. As there was no shock wave, we will assume he didn't destroy all air within thirty feet.—T

Not just any demons either. These were the princes who had corrupted Relos Var's second Guardian ritual, the same ones that had turned S'arric from the well-intentioned sun god to the ravenously angry avatar of annihilation. I had become their greatest triumph and their greatest mistake, and wasted no time devouring their demonic tenyé rather than showing anything like gratitude. I'd devoured their tenyé—but I clearly hadn't devoured *them*. Rather, I'd kept these demons imprisoned in a manner not too dissimilar to the mindscape where I'd imprisoned myself. Or . . . where Vol Karoth had imprisoned himself. Something like that. As that prison had shattered, evidently this one had too.

Which meant everyone was free.

"You have no tenyé," I reminded them. "No power. You're nothing but ghosts."

*Then why haven't you destroyed us?*

That question sparked a realization so painfully obvious that it slammed into me with all the force of blunt fact: they thought I was one of them. A demon. I suppose that made sense given the whole King of Demons title and the way they'd tried to claim me as their own, but they were mistaken. If I had ended up as a demon, I'd probably be in a better position to heal the damage done to me.

Hunger shuddered through my body again. What I'd absorbed from my surroundings hadn't been enough to sate my appetite.

*It hurts, doesn't it? But there are ways to feed. Fear has so much more energy than you'd think. Pain is good too. And souls . . . Oh, the energy of souls . . . We can show you how.*

"Shut up," I snapped.

*We're right here. Don't you want to satisfy your need?*

Why hadn't I destroyed the demon princes? Laughable. The most obvious answer was because I couldn't. Or at least, S'arric hadn't been able to. And even if that hadn't been the case, we'd been in the middle of a war when all of this had happened. Vol Karoth would have kept these demons prisoner so they could be questioned.

I gazed up at the sky. One of the Three Sisters, Jhyr, hadn't set yet, even though the red-orange sun was in the sky. That moon remained visible, shimmering through the colors of Tya's Veil. A lovely sight, but I was more interested in practical applications.

Any of the moons would be a long way from anyone I might hurt by accident.

Traveling there was as easy as a thought. I vanished from one landscape and appeared in another even more desolate. Had I needed to breathe, I'd have suffocated, but fortunately, that hadn't been necessary for my survival for a long time indeed. Above my head, the blue-and-white swirls of the planet on which I—Kihrin, to be specific—had been born glowed vibrantly. The rest of the sky lay black and lush under the shining caress of stars.

This was one of the moons, one of the Three Sisters. It never had and never would support life, which at this moment was exactly what I wanted. Nothing I did here would hurt anyone but myself.

On the other hand, nothing I did here would improve my situation either. I bent over and picked up a rock, concentrating on it.

Bits of it began to flake away, in spite of all my efforts to keep the rock intact and whole. Fuck.

*You'll hide? Surely all those centuries locked away haven't made you so weak.*

"Oh, that's quite enough from you lot. Try me and find out just how easy it would be to destroy you."

*If you were going to, you'd have done it by now. Could it be that you need us?*

I paused to give the question serious consideration. I didn't want to believe that was the case, but I wouldn't dismiss the idea unexamined either. Giant swaths of memory lay buried, still too painful to be resurrected and dragged into daylight. The demons lived in those lands. So it was possible that I might have some lingering attachment, a desire for anyone who might give what I suffered some meaning.

"I still want to know why your people did all this," I murmured. "Why invade? Why attack us? We were no threat to you. We'd done *nothing* to you."

*Done nothing? Done everything! How quickly you forget. You abandoned us. You left us to die in a universe grown sepulchral and cold.*

My response was swallowed as I gritted my teeth in pain. Despite my best efforts, a circle of disintegrating rock slowly ate away at reality in a rapidly expanding sphere around me. I felt the rush of tenyé as the energy released slammed inward.

But it wasn't enough. It would never be enough.

So yeah. No doubt about it.

*This* was a problem.

# 8. The Purpose of an Emperor

*Tyentso's story*
**The Soaring Halls, the Upper Circle of the Capital City of Quur
The day of Vol Karoth's escape, an hour after dawn**

Tyentso woke slowly, blinking open her eyes to gaze up at the enameled ceiling. She wasn't used to living in the imperial palace, to say nothing of the emperor's quarters. It was almost funny how much time—how little time—had passed since she took hold of the crown.

At some point in the distant past, someone must have decided the imperial bedchamber needed a ceiling decorated with enough flowers to fill every garden in Eamithon. Stunning in their realism even if these were picked out in an intricate mosaic of ceramic tile. Undeniably beautiful and completely out of character for the tone of the palace, which was otherwise cold, majestic, and dedicated to showcasing the imperial might of Quur.

Tyentso began laughing.

The young man in bed next to her groaned and rubbed the back of his hand against his forehead. "By all the gods, what time is it?"

"It's morning," Tyentso said. "Which I realize is normally your bedtime, but get up, anyway."

"Whatever you say, Your Majesty."

She frowned at him. For a moment, he'd sounded sincere. Which was extremely out of character for him, too. As was what he said next: "Nightmares?"

Tyentso flicked her gaze to him for a second. He seemed like he gave a damn, which meant that this really was too early for the High Council representative. "I was just thinking that I've fucked the man who made this." She nodded up at the ceiling.

He laughed. "I'm pretty sure the man who made *that* was Atrin Kandor."

Tyentso gazed at him coolly. "I said what I said."[1]

A hint of doubt entered those pretty brown eyes. But then everything about Fayrin was pretty, from those thickly lashed eyes to the well-muscled body of someone who was . . . Well.

Not quite half her age, although she suspected he held the record for the youngest person to ever serve on the High Council. If she kept this up, she was going to have to admit she'd developed a taste for younger men.

---

[1] Tyentso and Teraeth were lovers on Ynisthana. It was apparently a purely physical relationship. See: *The Ruin of Kings.*—T

What Fayrin saw in her was easier to guess: power.

"You're not *that* old," Fayrin murmured.

Tyentso tucked her hands behind her head and continued staring at the ceiling mosaic. Almost certainly made by Atrin for his wife, Elana. She doubted that the people Atrin and Elana had reincarnated as—Teraeth and Janel—either remembered or gave a damn.

She mentally slapped herself. She didn't give a damn either. What she did care about was Kihrin—and that dream.

The bed shifted as Fayrin crawled out of it, probably heading to the wash-room for a little early-morning bladder emptying. She heard his feet slap against the warm marble floor.

She was sure the dream had been real—or rather, a real visitation by some-one. But by Kihrin? That was the hard part. Because it was hardly lost on Tyentso that ordering her to give Urthaenriel to Relos Var was very much in line with Relos Var's plans too. And something that Kihrin wanted to prevent by any means necessary.

She'd never heard of Relos Var being able to visit dreams before. Surely he'd have used the power by now if he'd had it.

And gods, Kihrin had gotten so many details right. Not the things on the *Misery*—if he'd been right, that was her doing. But the details on himself, right down to the gleam of that damn Stone of Shackles around his neck and the particular pattern of bleeding whip wounds on his back.

That was not a certain insurance of authenticity, however.

She levered herself up on an elbow as the scent of freshly ground coffee wafted in her direction. Fayrin was using magic, but she wasn't going to com-plain about him taking a shortcut.

"I'd hardly blame you if it was a nightmare." Fayrin didn't raise his head from where he was concentrating on turning coffee beans into fine powder. "I can only imagine the vast ocean of inspiration you've stockpiled." He flashed a grin at her. "Of course, my definition of nightmare is being stuck somewhere without a proper selection of Quuros wines."

Tyentso rolled her eyes. It wasn't the alcohol selection that gave her night-mares about her years on board the *Misery*. "Oh, I doubt that. You're Ogenra, aren't you?"

His second glance was far warier. "Most everyone on the council is. Was. Even debauched rakes only there to collect easy bribes and seduce everyone's daughters."

Tyentso doubted he limited himself to the daughters, but that was neither here nor there. "Qoran once told me you were the most brilliantly wasted mind he'd ever encountered."

A brief, uncomfortable flicker crossed the man's face as he turned several cups of fresh water into the copper pot and began to stir. "Really? How dis-appointing. I thought I'd done a much better job of convincing that man I'd never been good for anything at all. I'll have to try harder."

"Oh, never fear. He absolutely believes you're a waste of his time." Tyentso threw off the sheets and walked to where the servants had left out clothing the night before. She ignored those, naturally. That set existed to give the assassins something to poison if the mood struck them. "Which family? Given your eye color, there are only four options."[2]

His voice was carefully neutral. "I don't know that it matters."

A feeling came over Tyentso then, a disquiet that whispered that it did, in fact, matter a great deal. Or maybe she was still trying to distract herself from thinking too much about what Kihrin had said.

"I suppose I'm just wondering if I executed your father."

His hand jerked. Fayrin nearly spilled his coffeepot. He set it carefully back down on the metal plate he'd heated. "What?" His laughter stood on the precipice of hysterical. "No. Gods no. My father died over a decade ago. Murdered by some little slave girl who was defending herself from the creep."[3]

"Your father sounds charming."

"Yeah, he sure was." After checking to make sure he'd caused no permanent damage to the warming coffee, Fayrin added, "I mean, you're right to assume he was a high lord." A curious expression crossed his face; he frowned before a scoff escaped his lips. Fayrin twirled his fingers as though presenting a card trick, something frivolous and unimportant. "House D'Jorax."

"A D'Jorax high lord died at the banquet."

"My half brother," Fayrin explained in a voice as empty of emotion as a blank piece of paper. "Also perfectly charming. I won't be filing any petitions with the Church of Thaena, even if that were still an option." He sniffed and refocused his attention on the coffee. "Haven't I said thank you enough? I'll have to try harder for that too."

She finished wrapping one of her silk agolé around herself. "Is that why you're fucking me? As a *thank-you*?"

Fayrin snorted. "No, I'm fucking you because it's incredibly sexy when you boss everyone around."

She snorted. Yeah, she didn't believe *that* was the reason for one white-hot second. "You always say the nicest things."

"That's because my greatest ambition in life is to be a kept man who lounges around all day looking pretty." He twisted out a strand of his hair. "At least the looking-pretty part is easy."

Her response was interrupted by a knock at the bedroom door. She glanced at Fayrin and then tilted her head toward it.

Fayrin looked torn between coffee and following her unspoken order. Reluctantly, he set the coffee aside and answered the door while she finished dressing.

She often wondered at the clothing. Tyentso hadn't ordered any of it made for her. It was just . . . there. Along with an entire staff of servants and officials who had apparently been waiting their entire lives to serve an emperor who

[2] Of the twelve royal families, only eight are god-cursed. The other four are late additions and use magic to change their eye color. Thus a child of Houses D'Kard, D'Moló, D'Jorax, or D'Knofra will be born with perfectly normal eye colors.–T

[3] Is he talking about you, Senera?–T

If he is, I'll never admit it.–S

bothered to live at the imperial palace. Although for all she knew, they might have been giving her the magically preserved castoffs of the last dozen emperor's concubines. She didn't much care. They were beautiful and clean, not to mention delightfully free from curses, poisons, or baleful enchantments.[4]

When Fayrin came back from the door, he was frowning.

"There isn't a problem with the march, is there?" Tyentso had ordered the army to be ready to leave immediately. While the Quuros army traveled with a speed that gave its neighbors nightmares, it was still a lot of people that all needed to be coordinated. They wouldn't leave until the afternoon, if then.

"No," Fayrin murmured. "Just a messenger who wanted me to let you know that the high general's returned to the palace along with his son and daughter-in-law."

Tyentso kept her face expressionless. "And why is that a problem?"

Fayrin straightened. "I never said it was a problem."

"The expression on your remarkably pretty face suggests otherwise."

Fayrin looked her right in the eyes, and for once, there was nothing about him that seemed frivolous or lecherous. "It's just . . . Jarith's dead."

Fuck. She should have answered the door herself. "People do come back from the dead. I've done it myself when the occasion called for it."

"Sure, or you wouldn't be here now. But—"

"But?" She waited for the explanation.

"But you told me *Thaena died.* And I distinctly remember hearing that Jarith was killed by a demon prince, which means either his soul was eaten or he was turned into a demon himself. In either case, he wouldn't be showing up with his wife and father. So the question I'm wondering is: Who's wandering the palace pretending to be Jarith Milligreest?"

"Fuck," Tyentso muttered under her breath.

The last thing she wanted was Fayrin Jhelora running around the palace blabbing out a theory that was lamentably close to reality. Of course, it all depended on whether or not "Kihrin" had been telling the truth, didn't it? And the decision she'd wanted to put off for as long as humanly possible was suddenly a decision she had to make *now.*

"My point exactly," Fayrin said.

"Finish your coffee," Tyentso snapped. "I'll take care of this personally."

She teleported out of the room.

---

[4] Or at least they're delightfully free of such things until the assassins get a hold of them.—S

## 9. Return to the Capital

***Jarith's story***
***The Soaring Halls, the Upper Circle of the Capital City of Quur***
***The day of Vol Karoth's escape, early morning***

It wasn't exactly a homecoming.

They didn't return home, for one thing. Not to the Milligreest estate in the Upper Circle, nor to their home in Khorvesh. Qoran Milligreest ordered the mages with him to open up a portal straight to the Soaring Halls. The Milligreest estate wasn't safe.

Jarith stared at the marble surfaces as if he'd never seen them before, which was true after a fashion. He'd never seen them like this, not as complex shapes but as interactions of matter and energy, less energetic, less vital than the souls around him with their fleshy coverings. Only important in that he was pretending to have a fleshy covering of his own and so had to limit himself to the sort of interactions made with muscle, skin, and nerves.

He remembered when that was all he knew, when that reality seemed normal. It was such a long time ago.[1]

Jarith didn't react when his father placed a hand on his shoulder. His father knew Jarith's presence, his survival, was an impossibility, but he was too eager to accept the miracle, pushing any questions aside with the desperation of a miner trying to shovel their way out of a cave-in.

Qoran Milligreest radiated a dozen emotions, all pulsing against each other: worry and relief and dread and love floating over an oddly persistent background haze of frustration and anger. Weakness and discomfort too, but that was fading with every step inside the palace walls.

"I'm going to find the empress and let her know the situation's been handled," Qoran said. "Do you want to tell your second that you're back?"

"Please, no," Kalindra protested. "Can we wait before we try to set my husband to work again? He needs food and rest. We all do."

Qoran's expression cracked. Guilt added itself to the heady mix already swarming around Jarith's father. "You're right," he said. "Of course you're right. There's a private banquet hall down that corridor, left-hand side, second door from the end. You should all eat something, and then we'll find you quarters."

"Is Eledore all right?" Jarith hoped he'd managed to convey the right

---

[1] For definitions of "long time" that equal just a hair under two months.—S

amount of sincerity and worry. He was certain he loved his sister. She'd been on the List.[2]

Qoran nodded. "She's here too." His mouth twisted. "It's no safer down in Khorvesh. Stonegate Pass was overrun."

Jarith nodded. He was aware, and in ways that would have horrified his father.

"I'd like to see her," Jarith said.

"Of course." Qoran stared at his son, searching. It probably all seemed too good to be true.

Which it was, but not for the reasons his father thought. Jarith wasn't a mimic. He wasn't someone using an illusion. He was the worst of all possible outcomes: a shape-changed demon, just not one pretending to be Qoran's son. Unfortunately, his father was unlikely to make that distinction. Demons were evil. They always had been. It was a reliable, predictable truth.

"I have to take care of talking to the empress first. We'll find your sister when I return." Qoran Milligreest gave his son one more clap on the shoulder before he left.

Leaving Jarith, Kalindra, and their son, Nikali, standing in the middle of a hallway, near a window overlooking a courtyard.

After the high general left, Kalindra took Jarith's hand. "Are you going to remain like this?" Her voice was full of dread and hope in equal measure. Her question didn't refer to his physical position. She was asking if he planned to continue looking human.

He wished he could tell her yes, but that would have been a lie. "It's not—" Jarith paused and made a second attempt. "This body isn't real. It's a shell. I can't maintain it indefinitely. I'm not that strong yet." Jarith gently squeezed her hand back. He knew how much this hurt. More than if he hadn't appeared in a simulation of his old form at all. The aura of grief and pain swirled around her in a heady fume.

She closed her eyes and cradled a wide-eyed Nikali closer to her bosom.

"I won't be gone forever," Jarith promised. "I know how to do it now. I'll come back."

He knew it was even possible to come back in a more permanent form. Janel had said she knew of ways. He didn't think he could become mortal again—nothing could return him to that—but he'd be able to pretend.

Jarith wanted to pretend, if only for the sake of his family, for the sake of Kalindra and Nikali.

His musing was interrupted by Kalindra, who was now staring about them with bemusement. "What *is* going on here, anyway? This can't all be because of the attack on Devors."

Jarith followed her gaze. He'd been distracted when they first arrived, but now that she'd drawn his attention to the matter, he saw what he'd missed on first arrival. An encampment of Quuros soldiers sat in the middle of

---

[2] After Jarith had been stripped of much of his memories by Xaltorath, he'd still managed to maintain a "list" of people whom he was not to hurt or allow to be hurt under any circumstances. —T

the imperial palace, their numbers so large that they'd spilled out into every available courtyard and all the grounds outside. But that . . . that wasn't everything.

Jarith took a step forward. The *emotions*.

Even before he'd become a demon, Jarith had been well acquainted with the emotional flavor of a military camp—the boredom, the anticipation, the excitement, and the fear that he associated with preparing for a battle. This was different. He felt rage. Fury. Bitter, resentful anger. A desire for revenge strong enough to verge into a lust for cruelty.

And this wasn't from one person. This was from *every* person—a seething, shifting, bubbling well of red-hot aggression and hate. Stranger still, the vast majority of it wasn't directed at each other. That turbulence was firmly pointed outward, toward forces outside the camp. Toward the enemy.

Whomever the enemy happened to be.

"Something's happened," Jarith murmured. "Something bad." This couldn't possibly have been natural. The emotions were too uniform, too ubiquitous.

His wife gave him a fond look. "Congratulations. You just summarized the last two months."

"This is different," he said. Try as he might, however, he couldn't discern why it was different, why the soldiers were behaving this way. Not without delving deep through memories, which he couldn't do without being discovered. Something must have happened. Something more than a Hellmarch and political upheaval.

"Food, Papa? I'm hungry," Nikali said with all the hopeful longing of a toddler who'd been relegated to eating Devors Monastery boiled vegetables and rice porridge for weeks.

"Yes, food. Let's find you food," Jarith said. He was every bit as hungry as Nikali, but *his* banquet was all around him. He needed to leave before all these raw, red emotions proved too much temptation and forced him to give himself away.

"Yay!"

He led Kalindra down the hall as his father had instructed. The room beyond was a private dining room, elegant and luxurious, large enough to feed several hundred people in royal-appropriate style. It had been converted into an officer's mess, with nothing about it elegant at all. Currently, it was only populated by a few stragglers—people grabbing a bite on the way out the door. It felt like deployment, like the whole army was about to start marching. The emotions here were no less poisonous than the ones Jarith had left behind, but there were fewer people, which made the situation more tolerable.

No sooner had he stepped through the door than a loud crash echoed as someone dropped their tray—plate, food, and all. Jarith recognized the man responsible, someone he'd worked with before. A good man, as he recalled. Gimor? Something like that.

Evidently, he remembered Jarith too.

"You're alive!" Gimor exclaimed. "By all the gods, Thaena Returned you?

I hadn't heard." The soldier ignored the food he'd just splattered all over the ground to focus on Jarith.

Kalindra held out a hand. "We just came back. Food first, then questions."

The man flushed, flinched backward. "You're right. My apologies. I should know better. It's just there's been so few Returned, and we all assumed—" He didn't finish the sentence, but an angry, determined expression slid in to replace the uncertainty. "Now that you're back, we'll really make those bastards pay." Anger slashed across the man with razor flashes of crimson.

Fortunately, Jarith's son wasn't paying attention. Or at least, he wasn't paying attention to the Quuros officer. "Food!" Nikali leaned out of Kalindra's grip and made gimme motions to the plates being carried out to tables.

A feeling bubbled up out of Jarith, nameless and foreign until it finally escaped his lips as laughter. He paused, uncertain and surprised.

Kalindra pulled him over to a table, where the people who worked the kitchens brought them breakfast.

No one mobbed them, but Jarith felt how they wanted to. They wanted to find out how he was, to tell him everything that had happened. So much had happened.

Kalindra didn't have his ability to sense thoughts and emotions, but he knew that she was listening to conversations swirling around them while she fussed over their son and wiped his face and hands. The officers coming and going spoke in low whispers over their meals, like they would be in trouble if the wrong people overheard. They wondered when they would be sent off to Marakor. They wondered what would happen if they caught up with Havar D'Aramarin. They spent a great deal of time cursing all the Royal Houses in general and House D'Aramarin in particular.

They said it was a shame that Empress Tyentso hadn't managed to kill them all.

That was honestly the oddest thing out of everything. He had to look twice to confirm his suspicions: these weren't *Khorveshan* men. The time since his death had been measured in weeks and lifetimes, but it was too soon for the average Quuros soldier to have abandoned the beliefs they'd grown up nursing. The hatred and venom, the conviction that the only ones worthy to serve by their sides were the ones who looked like they did. He should have heard someone complaining about the insult of taking orders from a woman. Then perhaps one of the Khorveshan men would tell that soldier to shut up. Someone would make a puerile joke about where a woman's *real* place was. A fight would start, of varying success depending on who was present.

Nothing. No one said a word against Tyentso. They only spoke her praises.

Jarith leaned close to his wife. "These men are under an enchantment."

She startled and then stared at him, wide-eyed. She didn't respond except to give him a single, terse nod.

It was the only explanation he could imagine. They had to be under some kind of spell. Something subtle enough to escape immediate notice. Something powerful enough to be able to affect hundreds of soldiers—no, thousands of soldiers—simultaneously and for great lengths of time. Days? Weeks? He had no way to know how long this had been occurring. Presumably not longer than his existence as a demon.

He liked to think he would have noticed. Maybe that was just him being naïve.

His son, Nikali, didn't see any of this. He babbled cheerfully all through dinner, making delighted comments about the food, the soldiers, the mage-lights, the carvings on the walls. He only paused after he'd eaten his breakfast, as his eyes began to droop and he started to tire.

Finally, Kalindra bundled him up into her arms. "Let's see if we can track down those quarters your father promised us."

Jarith was still studying the waves of emotion circulating the room, but he nodded in response. "Yes," he said. "And then I'll need to leave for a while."

Kalindra gave him a heartbroken look.

"I know." He kissed her on the temple. "It's only for a while."

**You know I'm needed elsewhere. Hopefully, I won't be gone long.**

Her lips pressed together in a thin line. "I just wish I could help," she murmured, but Kalindra made no other argument. She didn't try to talk him out of it. They'd all agreed on this before leaving Shadrag Gor.

He pulled her into his arms, her back resting against his chest, while she in turn held an increasingly sleepy Nikali. He let himself sink back against the chair, looking weary, like someone it would be best not to disturb. Jarith glared at anyone who didn't get the hint until they went away again.

Finally, his father returned.

Such an odd idea: family. How much time, energy, attention, love, did one really owe people whose major contribution to one's existence was giving one's souls a temporary container? How much did family matter when their links were the most tenuous, faltering chains in shackles that no longer bound? Jarith had become a stranger to the body of his birth, and he was no more the "son" of Qoran Milligreest's incorporeal souls than that of any man, pulled at random from a crowd. His "mother," Jira, had given birth to a physical body Jarith no longer used. In theory, these people meant nothing to him.

And yet . . .

And yet, as he watched his father—grumpy, exhausted, awash in irritation, anger, and worry—cross the room, all Jarith could think about was how much he loved his father. How much he loved his whole family. How they were not inconsequential at all.

Maybe that was the problem with most demons. They'd convinced themselves that if the physical shells of existence didn't matter, the emotions engendered by those shells mattered even less. They'd told themselves that such attachments were irrelevant weaknesses, useful only to be exploited and devoured.

But they were wrong. They were all so wrong. The opposite was true.

Qoran Milligreest reached their table and smiled—a tiny, wan candle-flicker of a smile—as he looked down on his daughter-in-law and grandson.

He whispered, "You should wake her. I'll take you somewhere you all can rest."

Jarith kissed his wife's hair and then touched her shoulder. "Kalindra, it's time to go."

She rubbed her eyes as she stood, picking up their son as if she hadn't been asleep a second earlier. "Right. Let's go."

"Don't . . . don't worry about anything," Jarith's father said. He showed them down a succession of hallways so richly decorated it was a wonder none of the soldiers had tried to go after the embedded filigree and encrusted jewels with a knife. "Just rest for a few days and you can join back up with the army later. Kalindra and Nikali can stay here. It's the safest place. Everything's just very . . . tense . . . right now."

Jarith didn't think his expression changed, but his father must have noticed something. "What is it?"

Jarith said to his father, "Are you taking us to the empress's private quarters?"

Qoran Milligreest made a face. "I know it's a bit much, but I have no other place to put you. Eledore's already there. It's safe. Tyentso's only here for a few more hours before she takes the army south to Khorvesh. You might not even see her."

Jarith huffed. In theory, this was fine—assuming Kihrin had done what he said he would and, more importantly, that Tyentso had *believed* him.

If Tyentso hadn't believed him, though, such a reunion might prove unpleasant.

Kalindra stopped walking. "Sir," she said to Qoran. "I haven't seen my husband in months. Surely you can find someplace for us that's reasonably quiet and that we don't have to share with your daughter? We'll only too happily drop Nikali off for Eledore to watch, but—"

"Qoran, move away from him."

Jarith turned his head. A woman stood in the hallway ahead. She was dressed richly, in dark colors, but her eyes betrayed her identity. Solid black, because she had been a D'Lorus before she grabbed the Crown with both hands. Tyentso wasn't looking at Qoran.

She was staring at Jarith with an unfriendly expression on her face.

Damn.

To Jarith's senses, she was in the center of a yowling hurricane of tenyé and more. Not just magic but all the emotions he'd been sensing ever since they'd arrived swirled around her, as though she were not just the Empress of Quur but an avatar of war. She wore the Crown of Quur on her head and in her hand held the Scepter—which she pointed in his direction.

He knew in that moment why Thurvishar had insisted he avoid Tyentso until her loyalties were confirmed. Because the woman knew what he truly was. Because if she hadn't believed Kihrin, then she was a threat. With just a single glance, Tyentso had identified him as a demon.

And the emperor of Quur's first job—some would argue their *only* real job—was to kill demons.

**I'm sorry.**

Jarith vanished in a swirl of darkness and smoke a split second before a beam of lethal energy screamed through the space where he had stood.

# 10. THE BREAKING OF THE EMPIRE

**Sheloran's story**
**The Soaring Halls, the Upper Circle of the Capital, Quur**
**The day of Vol Karoth's escape, around breakfast**

The palace was a maze of chaos and noise as soldiers, clerks, and every kind of servant scuttled about in a state of barely ordered panic. None of them acted like Caless's presence was unusual or worthy of notice. The same could not be said of Sheloran, Galen, or Qown; hostile eyes followed them the entire way. Caless was known; she was permitted.

They were not.

Finally, Caless turned down a reasonably sedate corridor and opened a doorway into a courtyard filled with soldiers practicing maneuvers. Sheloran's father stood next to stacks of weapons and armor, switching out equipment for the men.

Caless waved at him. When she caught his attention, she pointed at Sheloran.

Sheloran's father scowled. He didn't seem pleased to see them. Sheloran felt a deep sense of dread as he passed a sword off to one of the other Quuros soldiers before heading in their direction.

"Where the hell have you been?" Varik's stare was unfriendly as he examined his daughter and then moved on to her companions. "And why are you all dressed like foreigners?" If he even noticed the presence of the child, he gave no sign.

Sheloran was taken aback, to say the least. Her father seemed actively angry, which made no sense. The idea that he wouldn't be thrilled to see her had never even occurred to her. She was his precious golden girl. He'd never directed his anger at her, only his disappointment—and not often.

"What, no hello? How are you? So nice to see you survived?" Galen was spitting mad. Sheloran could hardly blame him.

"Why would I waste time on the obvious? You're here. You're alive." The former high lord scanned their clothing again. "Although maybe not for much longer if you keep dressing like that."

He didn't seem to be joking.

There was a moment of silence, and then Galen removed the agolé wrapped around his waist and slung it over his shoulder in the traditional manner. Sheloran followed his example. Qown had already done this when he'd shifted his agolé to carry the boy.

"Is there someplace we might speak in private?" Sheloran asked.

"I have work to do," Varik said, suggesting the conversation was over and the answer negative.

At this, Caless frowned. "The soldiers will still be here when you're done."

"I don't care—"

Caless narrowed her eyes. "They haven't been in the City for a while. They need to know what's happened."

Varik grabbed a rag and wiped off his hands, still furious. "Fine. Our room, then." He waved at one of the others. "Keep going. I'll be back after I've dealt with this nonsense."

Sheloran noted the way the soldiers deferred to her father, the way they instantly followed his orders. Not entirely unexpected: House D'Talus had always maintained a strong relationship with the military because of its monopoly on providing arms and armor. But there was a difference between "favorite weapon supplier" and "included in the chain of command."

Sheloran stared at her mother with wide eyes after her father passed. "What is going on?" she mouthed.

Caless shook her head and motioned for the group to follow Varik.

Sheloran hadn't spent much time in the imperial palace beyond the occasional fête, never hosted by an actual emperor. She remembered majestic, flawless halls and superlative construction. For all that the entire building seemed to be on a war footing, the beauty of the palace remained. Everything was impeccably built and decorated, and even the parts of it that seemed old and ancient were magnificent in their monumentality. The rooms they entered were far from the nicest in the palace, but even the poorest rooms in this place were fit for kings.

As soon as they entered one such room, Varik pinched the bridge of his nose before whirling around to face them again. "What on earth were you thinking? We're at war! It's not safe to be a royal or a foreigner at the moment, and here the lot of you show up managing to somehow look like both." At which point, Sheloran's father paused mid-rant and looked to the side. "Why is there a child here?"

Qown started to open his mouth. Galen dug fingers into the other man's arm.

"I was just about to ask that same question," Caless confessed. She pulled out a chair and turned it to face Qown. "Now who is this?" She held out her arms to the little boy.

Sheloran pulled out her fan, waving it against herself while she thought furiously. It felt like her parents had both been replaced by mimics, although at least her mother didn't seem on the verge of committing manslaughter.

The child gave the goddess an intensely wary look, then changed his mind and all but leaped into Caless's arms. Qown's expression turned terrified when it looked like he might accidentally drop the child, but Caless caught the boy. The crisis was averted.

"I haven't the least idea," Sheloran said. "Galen found him hiding under an overturned cart."

Caless set a hand on the child's brow and studied him carefully, giving him a gentle, sweet smile all the while. The boy, in turn, hid his face behind his hands.

Sheloran wondered for just a moment if that meant that Caless was trying to recognize him, to assign him some kind of identity or tie him to a house—then realized it was probably much simpler than that. Her mother was likely trying to ensure the boy wasn't some sort of trap or decoy, magical overlays hiding a more sinister intent.

"I'm Tave," the little boy offered, his lower lip quivering.

"Of course, dear," Caless said. "I'm Lessoral."

"Except that's not true, is it?" Sheloran said before she could stop herself.

"Sheloran," her father chided, "what are you talking about?"

Caless sighed. "She knows, dear."

Sheloran crossed her arms over her chest. "When were you going to tell me? Or should I just assume the answer is *never*?"

"Darling—" Caless's abnormally dark stare flickered over to Galen and then to Qown.

"They know too," Sheloran answered before turning to her father. "And who are you, exactly? *Don't* say 'Varik.'" She took a deep breath, pushing down the bitterness and anger that threatened to overwhelm her. It wouldn't get her what she needed. She was better than this, anyway. Better than tantrums. Better than letting her emotions interfere with what they needed. Too much depended on this.

But the anger was just so easy.

"I don't have to answer—" Varik started to snap.

"It's Bezar, isn't it?" Sheloran said. That would make the most sense, anyway. Bezar was the god of craftsmen and smiths.

Her father scowled at her. "If you already know, why did you ask?"

Sheloran's stomach twisted. Veils. He was. They were *both* god-kings. And neither one of them had ever said a word.

The little boy, Tave, watched this exchange with wide eyes. He'd grabbed one edge of Caless's agolé and was busy attempting to eat it. Caless saw this, tousled the little boy's hair, and gently lowered him to the ground. Giggling, he promptly ran under the table.

Qown lowered himself off his chair to keep an eye on the boy, but he kept glancing at Sheloran's father as though he were expecting violence to break out at any moment.

And no wonder, really. Varik had stood again and was pacing back and forth, clenching and unclenching his fists.

Galen cleared his throat as if this were just an awkward family gathering where one was discussing someone's scandalous behavior at the last party. "I really do hate to ask, but besides all this god-king business, would someone mind telling me *who* we're at war with?"

Varik stared at Galen like he'd lost his mind.

"They don't know," Caless reminded her husband.

"Very well," Varik said. "We're at war with House D'Aramarin, for a start. After Tyentso failed to execute *Galen's grandfather* Havar, he shut down the gate network. Although not before transporting himself, his favorites, and the various soldiers the villain had apparently been hiding all over Quur. So he now has an enormous army in Marakor. An army that is doing an excellent job of making sure no food leaves its borders."

Sheloran stared in shock. Yes, that would do it. She hadn't considered that the easiest way to keep supplies from reaching the empire was simply to cut them off at the source. Marakor provided most of the empire's food, although some dominions—Kazivar, Eamithon, Kirpis, Jorat—had their own farmlands and would no doubt weather the storm with minimal issues. However, the other dominions, Yor, Raenena, and Khorvesh, were heavily dependent on provisions brought in from Marakor. As was the Capital. Those dominions would starve when food supplies ran out. The Capital, already overwhelmed by the destruction caused by the Hellmarch, had simply emptied out their barrels first.

Thus: riots.

"So why don't you stop him?" Sheloran demanded. "Stop Havar D'Aramarin. You're both god-kings!"

"Please lower your voice."

Sheloran rolled her eyes. "You understand my point. You could teleport in there, just . . . kill the man . . . and no one could stop you."

"Really." Caless's stare was flat. She straightened up. "I am touched by your faith in my abilities, but perhaps I should explain just how our lovely empress went about killing the high lords? It's really quite something. I can't help but think her father would have been proud."[1] When three completely blank looks greeted that statement (four if one counted the little boy hiding under the table), she sighed. "Never mind. Havar D'Aramarin is as much a god-king as we are. We haven't stopped him because we can't."

"And the rest of it?" Sheloran asked.

Caless threw a hand up in the air. "The empress publicly announced the execution of every high lord on charges of treason and sedition. Everyone knows that the Royal Houses are the reason they're starving, so that's where the rioting is focused. And if all this had happened before the Hellmarch, it would have been a minor nuisance at best, but with the gates down . . ."

Galen groaned and put his head in his hands. "Everyone's already evacuated to their summer estates, and they can't get back in."

"Not everyone," Caless said, "but certainly enough when you consider many of the Royal Houses are short members in general. See again: Hellmarch."

"Do you need me here for this?" Varik said. "You can explain current events to Sheloran and Galen just as well without me in the room." He walked over to Sheloran, too quickly, so she fought not to flinch. He kissed her forehead, but quickly, absently, clearly distracted. "I'm glad you're back." With that, he swept out of the room.

---

[1] Just as most people don't realize that Gadrith D'Lorus isn't my biological father, most people don't realize that he *was* Tyentso's father.—T

I imagine the fact that she married the man is at least in part responsible for that assumption.—S

Sheloran, Galen, and Qown all watched him go and then all turned back to Caless.

"What the fuck?" Galen asked.

"Everyone's been on edge," Caless explained.

"I've never seen him on edge like *that*," Sheloran said. "Not when those assassins almost killed me or those other assassins almost killed him or Mazrin D'Erinwa illegally used poison in that duel. And if the Royal Houses have been all but declared illegal, then what are you and Father doing here? Even if you survived the empress's attempt to kill you, that doesn't explain why you're being allowed inside the *palace*."

"Tyentso never tried to kill *us*," Caless said. "Your father and I were the ones who helped her execute the other high lords in the first place."

Sheloran felt momentarily dizzy. Her whole body tensed. Whatever plans of revolution and upheaval paled in comparison to just grabbing up the leaders of all the Royal Houses and chopping heads. Well, evidently not all the leaders. Not her parents. And not Havar D'Aramarin. And clearly, Tyentso had underestimated the danger of letting Havar D'Aramarin escape.

Because he was a god-king. But which one?

Caless reached out and patted her daughter's knee. "It was necessary to keep you safe . . ."

"Suless is dead." Sheloran wondered who'd said that for a second before realizing it was herself. She whispered the words in a dull, flat voice.

Her mother's hand froze. "I'm sorry? What did you say?"

Galen took his wife's hand. "Suless is dead," he repeated. "Truly dead. It might be best if we don't explain how for the moment." Galen laced his fingers between Sheloran's and squeezed. "Breathe, Red. Just breathe."

She met his blue eyes and inhaled, feeling like she was surfacing above water, rescued from drowning. Sheloran exhaled again, slower, taking her time. By the count of three, she was fine again. Later, she would have to pull her reaction to finding out her parents had been party to the empress's massacre into the light and give it a good, hard look. She suspected that on a visceral level, she wasn't nearly as comfortable about the idea of being forever rid of royalty as she thought.

Sheloran straightened, then nodded at Caless. "What Galen says is true."

Caless examined each of them in turn. She looked like she was struggling between believing her daughter and . . . well. Several thousand years of looking over her shoulder for her mother were unlikely to be helping her sense of trust. Finally, she nodded. "I believe you."

"That's not why we're here, though." Qown raised his head from where he'd been drawing on the floor with glowing lines of light. The boy, Tave, was captivated.

Caless raised an eyebrow. "You being here for a reason carries with it the implication that you don't intend to stay."

"We can't," Galen said. "It's too dangerous. We've captured the attention of Relos Var."

Silence.

Not the silence of ignorance or incomprehension but the stunned silence of understanding far too well.

"Then you should go into hiding," Caless finally said.

"He'll find us," Qown said with his head still down.

Sheloran took a deep breath. There was no sense putting off the inevitable just because she knew it would be unpleasant. "That's why we came to see you about the Stone of Shackles." She pointed to her mother's chest.

Caless put a hand to her chest, to the agolé guaranteed to be concealing one of the most powerful artifacts in the world. "Sheloran, dear. No."

Sheloran's hands tightened into fists. "You haven't heard the question yet."

"I know what the question is. I'm not giving you the necklace."

"Yes, fine. We're not asking you to," Sheloran said. "In fact, it's safest if it continues to stay with you."

Caless blinked in confusion. "My apologies. Apparently I don't know what the question is."

Qown popped up from under the table, unable to resist a discussion involving one of the Cornerstones even if he was intimidated by the Goddess of Love. "What we thought . . . well, what we wondered. I mean—so here's the thing. We know the Stone of Shackles can allow people at a distance to create gaeshe. Can it also prevent it?"

Caless visibly startled. "Excuse me?"

Galen took over. "Can you use the Stone of Shackles to protect someone from being gaeshed? Not by gaeshing them first. We know that would work, but there are reasons why we don't want to go that route."[2]

"You think someone's going to gaesh you." Caless immediately amended her statement. "You think *Relos Var* will try to gaesh you."

"He's done it before," Qown said softly.

Caless looked thoughtful. "I must admit, that is an interesting idea." She broke herself out of contemplating unusual uses of artifacts and returned her focus to Sheloran. "I assume, with your concerns being what they are, that you don't wish to be burdened by a small child." She gestured toward the little boy. "Fortunately for you, I hear that the high general's daughter-in-law and grandson have just returned to the palace. I believe the Milligreest child is the same age as your shy new friend. Perhaps we might persuade them to take him in, at least temporarily."

Galen's eyes narrowed. "Just daughter-in-law and grandson? Not his son?"

Caless seemed taken aback. "Yes? I thought the high general's son was dead."

Sheloran and Galen shared a look. If word hadn't spread that Jarith had been Returned, it either meant the high general hadn't believed Jarith was his son or someone had recognized Jarith's true nature as a demon.

"That was fast," Sheloran murmured. They had suspected it would be, but that didn't mean she enjoyed the confirmation.

---

[2] Namely, having to do with the fact that the easiest way to cure a gaesh is to kill the gaeshed victim and fix the spiritual injury in the Afterlife before Returning them. Which is somewhat awkward when the Goddess of Death is still learning how to do her job.–T

"So will you help us?" Galen asked. "Because it is urgent. The longer we go without protection, the greater the odds that Relos Var will find us first."

"And that would be bad," Qown elaborated, quite unnecessarily.

Caless didn't answer for several long beats. Then she moved her hand to the blue stone around her neck and motioned them closer. "Very well. Let's see what we can figure out."

# 11. STEP THREE: SCOUT OUT THE ENEMY

*Kihrin's story*
*The moon Jhyr*
*Later that same morning*

The sky above me on Jhyr was more colorful than I would have expected. The sky itself was dark, but the stars were scintillating holes pricked out of the black velvet. The stars didn't twinkle—I suppose they needed an atmosphere for that. The planet, Ompher, lay against the darkness, a bright blue cotton-wrapped jewel of a world. I couldn't see the red-orange sun, but its light still reflected off the planet above, while Tya's Veil glimmered in the upper atmosphere, doing its job of keeping that same red giant from boiling everyone on the planet alive.

That last bit was my fault. Or Vol Karoth's fault. I shuddered to think how close I'd come to destroying everything I'd ever loved.

And the risk wasn't over yet, was it?

I made small talk with the demons while I tried to ignore the hunger that scraped and gnawed my insides clean. Also while I picked up rocks and tried, again and again, to not destroy them. "What did you mean earlier? When we 'abandoned' you?"

***It means exactly what we said. You abandoned us. You left us behind. You escaped and thought nothing about how we had been left trapped in a cold, dead universe.***

I started to protest that the damn things weren't going to give me a straight answer, when a worse idea occurred to me: *that they were.*

We didn't understand much about demons. We never had. We knew they fed on emotions, heat, tenyé. They were gestalt creatures, comprised not of a single soul but of a hive mind of souls. Sometimes instead of adding a victim to their own hive mind, they would infect and twist the soul, turning it into another demon, like a wasp laying her eggs in a cicada. They came from another universe.

But then, so did we.

"Help me understand," I said. "How could we have abandoned you if you were the ones who invaded *us?*"

The demons waited without answering, somehow feeling both smug and hateful. Like they were waiting for me to work it out.

Had anyone ever asked *why* demons were what they were? If they were a race, how could Xaltorath and Janel have independently turned themselves into demons without any demonic "infection" at all? That implied demons weren't a race but a *process,* like becoming a god-king or one of the Immortals.

And if that were the case, what had they been originally?

Maybe I was overthinking this. Maybe we'd always been overthinking this.

"Were you human?" I finally asked.

***By whose definition are we measuring? What does "human" mean?*** The demonic voices howled around me. If they had any power to do so, they surely would have been attacking. I could feel their fury vibrate against my skin.

That hadn't been a denial.

"Did you start off as human? Originally?"

I could tell they didn't want to answer. Their anger turned sullen and refractory. I suppose that might have been the end of it. Perhaps they'd thought there was nothing more I could do to them, that I couldn't make them answer.

But I could. And I did.

## 12. PARENTAL CONCERNS

### *Talon's story*
### *The Mother of Trees, the Manol*
### *The day of Vol Karoth's escape, morning*

There was no small amount of irony to Talon pretending to be Kihrin, pretending that Khaeriel was her mother. Mostly in that, by many standards, Khaeriel *was* her mother. Or at least, the relationship between Khaeriel and Lyrilyn had always been parental, no matter what Talon had once implied to Kihrin in a quest to make him squirm.[1]

Talon was hardly blind to Khaeriel's faults, but the woman had been there for Talon—or rather, for *Lyrilyn*—when no one else had. When no one else cared at all for a poor little slave girl trying to survive the horrors of a Royal House. When it seemed that even Ola had abandoned her.

So it wasn't difficult to pretend to view Khaeriel with familial warmth—because it wasn't pretend.[2]

Talon put her hand on Khaeriel's, still resting on her arm as they walked.

"I very much hope this is important," Khaeriel said. "I was in the middle of something."

"It's not. I just needed to get you out of there before you started a fight," Talon admitted with a smile.

Khaeriel stopped walking. She tried to pull her arm free from Talon's, but Talon's grip tightened on her hand, trapping it.

"No, no," Talon said. "You're trying to cause trouble for my great-great-grandmother and the man I love, and I'm asking you to stop. Please." She turned her head to stare the woman in the eyes, momentarily unnerved by the fact that she was used to Khaeriel being so much taller. Now she was the taller one. Or rather, Kihrin was. Khaeriel's eye color was different too, but not the intelligence and sharp wit in those eyes. Those had stayed the same.

Khaeriel sighed. "I don't like being betrayed," she admitted and continued walking.

Talon bit her lip rather than make a comment on how Khaeriel's own various

---

[1] While taking the form of Alshena D'Mon, Talon had heavily implied that Lyrilyn (Talon's original life) and Khaeriel had been lovers.—T

[2] Whether Khaeriel would return such sentiment, considering that Talon killed Kihrin, is a different matter.—S

sins might have been perceived by others. Betrayal would certainly be one of the words used in that description.

"Who does?" she said instead, keeping her tone light. "But it's not like Teraeth wants to be king. He really doesn't. And I sure as hell don't want to be . . . I don't even know what to call it. Prince consort?"

Khaeriel whirled to face Talon. "Has he asked you to marry him? When did this happen?"

Talon cleared her throat. "I don't think it officially has, but that's beside the point, which is that you'll probably end up queen soon enough. Except that I know Teraeth: he's not going to give you a fucking thing if he thinks you were plotting behind his back."

Khaeriel scoffed, but didn't dispute the sentiment. Probably because she knew it was true.

"Are you staying?" Khaeriel asked instead. Her voice sounded wistful, even a little plaintive; she'd asked the question while already knowing the answer.

"I can't. I–" Talon shook her head. "You heard what Teraeth said. He wasn't exaggerating."

"So you're afraid that if you stay, it's only a matter of time before Vol Karoth comes for you," Khaeriel said with grim finality. "Or he sends more dragons." She'd been at the lake house when Vol Karoth had first sent Rol'amar to wreak havoc and then had reached through Kihrin himself to touch the world. She knew what was at stake.

Or she thought she did. As it happened, Khaeriel was wrong, but this wasn't the time or place to correct her assumptions.

"That and . . . well. Relos Var. There's still the matter of Relos Var. Everything's one great big, giant mess, basically. And I'm not exactly sure how we're going to fix it, only that we have to find a way because I like this world and I want to keep living in it." Talon's throat closed on her–really closed on her and not pretend–as she contemplated how serious the situation was and how little chance that what they were going to try would actually work.

Talea *really* needed to figure out Taja's power set as soon as possible.

Khaeriel stopped again. "You will find a way. I know you can."

Talon smiled. Khaeriel's confidence was entirely bravado, but that didn't make it any less touching. Talon squeezed one of Khaeriel's hands. "Thanks."

Khaeriel studied her son's face for a long minute, then gently smiled. "Of course. Now let us go greet your father. I'm sure he'll be eager to–"

They started to cross through a doorway into the palace, and right away, two things happened. One, Talon crashed into an invisible wall of energy that kept her from moving forward. Two, an alarm began to ring.

A small voice in the back of Talon's mind–Surdyeh, she thought–whispered, *They must have updated their wards against mimics to include you.*[3]

Damn.

Just her luck. When last she'd been to the vané palace, Talon had been able

---

[3] Surdyeh was Kihrin's adoptive father, a blind musician who was also apparently a member of the secret cabal known as the Gryphon Men.–T

to come and go with almost complete immunity because the wards designed specifically to detect mimics were attuned to the twelve original souls who qualified—which Lyrilyn was not. But during that time, she'd impersonated (and to be fair, also killed) the vané queen Miyane. After Talon had been captured, some conscientious vané must have updated the wards, even though Talon had theoretically been sentenced to be stripped of her mimic abilities.

No doubt that same person had thought themselves exceedingly clever after Talon vanished from her cell.[4]

Khaeriel shifted from confusion to fear to furious anger with commendable swiftness. Her spellcasting was faster. Something bright and sharp ripped through Talon's side—a tapestry pole, with a pointed finial at the end, pulled from the wall. It couldn't really harm her even if it still hurt, but Khaeriel wasn't done. A strong wind picked up down the hallway.

"What have you done with Kihrin?" Khaeriel whispered harshly.

Talon didn't move or even dodge. She had one chance, and if she messed it up, the result would be something much worse than death. "I'm here by his orders," she pleaded. "Please. When the guards arrive, tell them that this was a mistake. Blame someone else, make any excuse, but if you don't, then everything Kihrin's trying to do will fall apart."

"*I don't trust you,*" Khaeriel said through clenched teeth.

"Wise of you," Talon agreed. "But nothing's stopping you from changing your mind later. If you don't like my story, you know what I am, and you can rip me apart yourself. But if those guards on their way find out that I'm not Kihrin, this doesn't just fuck *me* over." Talon heard footsteps approaching fast. "Please. I'll tell you everything, but you have to decide now."

Khaeriel stared at Talon, eyes narrowed. Talon was sure she wasn't going to cooperate. Not after what she perceived as Talon's betrayal previously.[5] Certainly not given the general (and not incorrect) perception of mimics. Khaeriel would turn Talon over to the guards, who would use magic to force her into her true shape. Kihrin would go from someone whose location was known to be in the Manol to someone who was missing.

Relos Var would insist on finding him. And that would be that. The whole fucking scheme upended because of a damn ward.

Khaeriel moved her fingers, like wiping away cobwebs. The glow left Talon, and she could move again. The tapestry pole and the fallen tapestry that went with it vanished.

Talon healed the damage to her side and shifted her agolé to cover the hole just as the soldiers showed themselves.

"Your Highnesses," the guards said to both of them, which made Talon lift an eyebrow. Apparently, Valathea had been leaving behind some very specific

---

[4] With a little help from pre-dead Kihrin.—S
    I helped too.—T
[5] Yes, I suspect that's because it was, in fact, actually a betrayal.—S
    Therin appreciated it, though.—T
    That's true. And one could argue that it worked out better for Khaeriel in the end.—S

instructions regarding the treatment of her niece. "The mimic warning was triggered. Are you both all right? Did you see who triggered it?"

"No," Khaeriel said. Behind her back, where the guards couldn't see, Khaeriel did something. Cast a spell, obviously, but Talon wasn't sure what kind. Khaeriel had always been so good at shielding her thoughts.

"We must test you both," the guard said.

Talon's gut twisted. She contemplated how quickly she could get a spell off and if it would do any good.

"I should say so." Khaeriel lifted her chin. "That *is* the protocol."

The guard held up a chain crafted of bits of quartz crystal linked by gold. Each crystal was a slightly different color, although there was no pattern. Silently, Talon counted thirteen crystals and cursed to herself. They weren't tsalis, but the crystals might well be talismans—each one imprinted with a sympathetic copy of a particular soul.[6]

None of the crystals lit up as the guard brought them over to Khaeriel and then Talon.

But Khaeriel's placid expression masked intensely focused concentration. It was entirely possible, Talon decided, that the necklace *had* lit up—and Khaeriel had crafted an illusion so no one saw it.

Just because Khaeriel was good at air magics didn't mean she couldn't cast an illusion or two if necessary.

Khaeriel waved a hand. "Honestly, I saw the ward trigger. It seemed to go off with no one present, so they must have been invisible. Likely the mimic is still around somewhere."

"We shall start the search immediately," the guard said.

"Good. My son and I will be in our chambers." Khaeriel's fingers tightened to the point of pain (or what would have been the point of pain on a normal human) before dragging Talon through the doors a second time and hauling her violently through a hallway beyond. In a matter of moments, she was pushing Talon into a sitting room, where a chestnut-haired man reading a book looked up.

"What—Kihrin?" Therin D'Mon began to smile.

Khaeriel slammed the door shut. "It's not Kihrin. Talon, why are you wearing real clothing?"

Talon raised an eyebrow. "That's the question you decided to lead with? Not 'Why are you impersonating my son?' or 'Where's Kihrin?' or 'Does Teraeth know you're not really his sweetheart?' but 'Why aren't you forming clothing out of your own flesh?'" She ruefully ran a hand over the truthfully excessive hole in her misha. "Speaking of which, I don't suppose you have a sewing kit, do you?"

Khaeriel inhaled, a mannerism Talon was familiar enough with to know usually proceeded an absolute explosion of murderous outrage.

---

[6] There would have originally been twelve stones, with Lyrilyn creating the need for a thirteenth.—T

"If this room isn't warded against eavesdropping," Talon said, "fix that, or we're not talking about anything except the weather and darning techniques."

Therin stood with an unfriendly expression on his face. "Where's Kihrin?"

"Wards first, then talking," Talon snapped.

Therin made a motion as if brushing away crumbs. "Of course the rooms are warded. We're not amateurs. What's going on? Khaeriel?"

The former vané queen crossed her arms over her chest. "As I said, it's Talon. She arrived with Teraeth, Janel, and—" She thought for a minute. "Xivan. So where is our son?"

Our son. It still caught her—or rather, the bit of her who was Kihrin—off guard to hear that referenced so openly. With nobody in the room acting like that was either a surprise or something to be ashamed of.

Talon exhaled as she walked over to a chair and plopped herself down in it. "It's not complicated. Kihrin's off doing something important. He doesn't want Relos Var to know where he is. And the easiest way to do *that* is to make sure Relos Var doesn't ask. And why would the wizard ask if I'm right here?" Talon grinned at Khaeriel. "And I'm wearing clothing because it's not outside the realm of possibility that I might have to do something ridiculous like hold Urthaenriel. I don't really want to find out what happens if I suddenly can't shape-change anymore, after I've already formed clothing out of my flesh." She plucked the edge of her agolé. "Pretty sure it would hurt like you can't even believe."

"You wouldn't . . . revert?" Therin wrinkled his nose.

"I'm not an amorphous blob," Talon said.

"That is not how it works," Khaeriel corrected Therin gently. "A mimic who is unable to use magic simply persists in the last form they took."

"Right," Talon agreed. "What she said. And truthfully, the whole 'turning your skin into an excellent approximation of cloth' is a thing that has to be constantly maintained—which again: kind of painful. And since I'm embarking on a brand-new 'be nice to myself' campaign, I've decided to skip the gratuitous shape-changing."

Khaeriel frowned at her. She seemed to be trying to work something out. Talon, in turn, tried to not let how she was really feeling show.

Because she was extremely, distinctly nervous about the matter. Talon wasn't just copying Kihrin, after all—she was copying Kihrin *perfectly*. Which was certainly possible if Kihrin had been in close contact with Talon for long enough, but the moment Khaeriel realized that Talon also had all of Kihrin's memories . . .

Unfortunately, Khaeriel was smart enough to put two and two together and come up with the idea her son might be dead. Even worse, that although Talon might not be the murderer (and she was), she'd certainly been complicit enough to have access to the corpse.

Awkward for everyone, really.

"I'm going to need proof," Khaeriel announced.

Fuck.

Talon rubbed an eyebrow and sighed. "And what exactly would that proof look like? It's not like Kihrin left me a letter to give you."

"Do your companions know who you really are?" Therin asked.

"Yes, thank you. See? That was a helpful question. And the answer is yes, they do. This is all part of the plan. I invite you to confirm it with them, but I also invite you to do it discreetly and with Valathea using Chainbreaker to make sure no one can eavesdrop." She shrugged. "Like I said, it's of vital importance that Relos Var have no idea that I'm *not* Kihrin." She pointed a finger at the two of them and then back at herself. "We shouldn't be having this conversation right now. At all."

Khaeriel narrowed her eyes. "And yet, we're going to. Now answer this curiosity. Why is Janel so upset with you? If *she* knows you are not Kihrin, then the disagreement cannot be with Kihrin. It must be *you*."

Double fuck. Talon cursed both the fact that Janel was doing a terrible job of hiding her anger toward Talon and that Khaeriel had noticed. They were really going to have to work on that.

Fortunately, Talon wasn't entirely without ways of distracting the couple in front of her. "Oh no. She *is* mad at Kihrin." Talon grinned. "Well, really she's mad at your brother, Kelanis, but since your brother is dead, she's taking it out on Kihrin instead. A feeling that she's transferred to me, since I'm running around looking like the father of her unborn child."

"What." Khaeriel's hand dug so hard into the arm of the chair where she sat, she was going to leave permanent indentations.

Talon would've been lying if she'd said that the look on Khaeriel's face wasn't absolutely priceless.

"You heard me." Talon paused. "You know, now that I'm thinking about it, this won't even be their first one." She leaned forward and said in a stage whisper, "They had a child together in a past life too. That daughter's even still around, although trust me when I say she should never, ever be invited over to family gatherings."[7]

"How did that happen?" Therin looked like he regretted the words the moment they left his mouth. "I understand the mechanics—"

"After as many kids as you've had, I should damn well think so."[8]

Therin sighed. "I mean, I specifically gave Kihrin protection against that."

Talon shrugged. "Too late, apparently. I gather the lucky deed occurred when they were tossed into a jail cell together by the old king. After being drugged, mind you, so neither one was exactly being rational about the matter."

If Therin looked concerned, Khaeriel looked angry.

"Congratulations on becoming a grandmother," Talon told the woman be-

---

[7] That would be Aeyan'arric, Lady of Storms, the Ice Dragon.—S
  Or as I like to call her, "Auntie Snow Kitten."—T
  You don't call her that.—S
  I might. You can't prove anything.—T
[8] Nine. Seven sons and two daughters.—T
  None of which are still alive.—S

fore waving a hand at Therin. "No congratulations for you. You should be used to it by now."

Therin calmly made a rude gesture at the mimic.

Khaeriel still looked annoyed. In fact, she was wearing what Talon liked to describe as her "plotting bad stuff" face—which looked placid and serene if one didn't know Khaeriel as well as Talon did. "If you're thinking that Janel being pregnant will keep Teraeth from marrying your son, you'll be thrilled to know Teraeth would happily marry both of them. How convenient that happens to be legal here."

"But discouraged in the royal family," Khaeriel pointed out. "It complicates succession to an unreasonable degree."

"Not my problem. And not yours either unless you make it one. Remember, you're hoping that Teraeth gives you the throne." Talon pursed her lips as she regarded the two. "Seriously, I shouldn't have to remind you that Kihrin will absolutely shit goats if anything happens to Janel or their baby." Talon paused and then added, "Teraeth's reaction will be worse."

"Are you implying that I would consider violence against my own grandchild?" The haughtiness and outrage in Khaeriel's voice was razor sharp.

Talon paused to take in the view. Spectacular. There might be friction between Valathea and Khaeriel, but it hadn't stopped Valathea from putting them in the second-nicest suite in the entire palace, and for vané? That was something on a whole different level from a typical Quuros "palace." One entire wall was nothing but windows decorated with sundew lamps and miniature climbing roses. Everything was impossibly lovely, a combination of real, priceless tapestries, furniture, and art and equally unreal, surreal, impossible illusions. Birds flitted from branch to branch on the mural of painted trees, and gilded bees visited every painted flower. No one could argue that the current regime was treating the former queen poorly.

Still, Talon couldn't help but wonder if the pleasant treatment was really meant for Khaeriel or for Valathea's great-grandson Therin.

She suspected the latter.

Talon looked back at Khaeriel. "It does, as you say, complicate succession. And I've lived too long in the Court of Gems not to know what that means. So don't take it personally: I don't mean it as an insult. Just think of it as a friendly reminder of consequences."

"It's an unnecessary warning," Therin said firmly. "We would never do that."

Talon studied the man. Sometimes he still exuded the "my will is law" authority of a high lord. Like just then. But that didn't mean it was true this time.

Therin hadn't asked about the status of the Capital. He hadn't asked how House D'Mon was faring in his absence. Either because he dreaded to know the answer or because he didn't care.[9]

Talon briefly contemplated letting him know that his daughters were dead,

---

[9] It's my personal opinion that he cared a great deal, but sometimes the only way to avoid returning to an addiction is to remove oneself from any exposure to it.—T

lost to greed and the game of empire. That he had, in fact, lost *every* child, including (by biological definitions, anyway) his youngest son, Kihrin.

Probably best not. That seemed counterproductive.

"So," Talon said. "Am I free to go?"

"Obviously not," Khaeriel snapped. "The wards will be reset by now. You would only trigger them again. If the guards arrive to find you there a second time, I believe they might make certain assumptions that would unfortunately prove true."

Talon scowled. Inconveniently, Khaeriel had a point.

Khaeriel kissed Therin on the forehead. "Perhaps I should talk to Valathea—"

Therin stood up. "I'll do it. You know she's more likely to listen to me."

Ah. So Valathea definitely had a bias toward her great-grandson, then.

Khaeriel seemed to contemplate arguing, but sighed and shrugged a shoulder in acquiescence. "Very well. We need her—or Teraeth, I suppose—to shut down the mimic ward, at least temporarily. And please confirm Talon's story."

Therin nodded before turning on his heels and walking out.

Talon bounced a little on the couch as she turned back to Khaeriel. "So! Shall we discuss baby names?"

## 13. The Milligreest Family

### Kalindra's story
### The Soaring Halls, the Upper Circle of the Capital City of Quur
### Just after Empress Tyentso attacked Jarith Milligreest

Shock painted Qoran Milligreest's face an ugly corpse-pale shade. It must have seemed like his son had just died, disintegrated by the Empress of Quur. The howl of the Scepter's blast vibrated through the space Jarith had occupied a moment before, slamming into the far wall, and possibly through walls beyond that. In the distance, a bell began to ring, and through the delicate marble traceries of railings overlooking gorgeous gardens, soldiers ran. What situation they'd be able to handle better than Empress Tyentso, however, was less clear.

Kalindra knew Tyentso hadn't killed Jarith, who'd fled before the beam reached him, but that didn't stop her from being furious. She covered her son's eyes and clutched him to her chest, praying that it had all happened too quickly for him to understand. Too quickly for him to draw the obvious conclusion that his father was once more dead, this time right in front of him.

"Tyentso! What the hell was that?" Qoran screamed and drew his sword.

The empress wasn't impressed or frightened. "That wasn't your son, Qoran."

"Yes, it fucking well was! How dare you!" He looked as angry as Kalindra had ever seen. And unlike his usual brand of temper, this time he seemed willing to back it up with violence.

Unfortunately, this *was* the Empress of Quur.

Tyentso narrowed her eyes and stepped toward him. "It was a demon, Qoran. It only looked like your son. Do you think I can't recognize a demon on sight?"

Kalindra didn't move. It's not that she thought she was in any danger—as she was most definitely not a demon—but the air was so suffocatingly tense, moving felt like a dangerous misstep.

"You need to understand, Qoran—"

Nikali began crying.

She'd been right about not wanting to draw attention. The moment Nikali started screaming, Tyentso whirled to Kalindra. "And you!" she said, pointing. "I know you're not this naïve. You have to be more careful!"

Kalindra cursed the woman and all her ancestors. Tyentso had forgotten—or just didn't care—that Kalindra and she had never "officially" met. *Tyentso wasn't supposed to know her.* Tyentso certainly wasn't supposed to have spent six months with her on Ynisthana after Tyentso joined the Black Brotherhood.

On the other hand, it didn't matter, did it? Thaena was dead, and Kalindra's cover had become her reality.

"I *was*," Kalindra said. "I'm not the one who appeared out of nowhere and attacked—" She choked off what she'd been about to say. Nikali didn't need to hear it.

A flicker of sympathy crossed Tyentso's face. "I *had* to do this."

Kalindra's throat closed on her. Clearly, either Kihrin hadn't spoken to Tyentso, or Tyentso hadn't believed him. And if Kalindra explained, would the other woman believe her? If she told Tyentso to search down deep, to feel out her connection with Thaena, would it still be there? Had Xivan simply picked up the reins of all her predecessor's angels, or was Kalindra the first of the newest Immortal's new servants?

In any event, no one was supposed to know that Xivan was now the Goddess of Death.

Kalindra concentrated on her son, on his crying, which had only grown louder with Tyentso's affirmation about Jarith's status. "Don't talk about this in front of my son."

"Daddy!" Nikali screamed.

Tyentso grimaced. "Oh, for fuck's sake. I'm too busy for this shit."

"Kalindra, take Nikali through the doors at the end of the hall," Qoran ordered. His voice was gentle, for just a moment, then the screaming started up again as he switched his focus to Tyentso. "Damn it, woman! Is that your solution to everything these days? Just kill it first and never use reason? What's wrong with you?"

"We're at war!" Tyentso shouted back. "And I am your empress, and your tone is out of line. Must I forcibly remind you of your place?"

Kalindra looked back over her shoulder, heart pounding. This had just become much more dangerous.

Qoran Milligreest seemed to realize it too. His face, which had been flushed red with anger just a moment before, turned ashen gray. He took a step back as if he'd just been slapped.

"How many times do I have to say it was a demon?" Tyentso snapped. "It was copying your son to get through the wards, and it almost worked."

"Mommy, I don't like it here."

Kalindra wiped her son's tears. "It's okay, little lion."

"I want my daddy!" he pleaded.

"I know," she whispered. "He'll be back soon." Kalindra hoped the woman hadn't heard her. Let her think Kalindra was just telling ugly lies to her son. She wasn't in a position to argue otherwise.

Fortunately, Tyentso wasn't paying attention to her.

"Kneel," Tyentso ordered, her voice whipping out the command.

Kalindra had never seen her father-in-law bow to *anyone*, let alone kneel. She suspected the previous emperor, Sandus, had never once asked. She found herself holding her breath, dreading the violence of his response.

But he barely hesitated. Qoran was down on his knees in an instant.

Kalindra could only stare. What? As far as Qoran Milligreest knew, this woman had either just killed his son or revealed that it had never been his son at all. In neither case did it make any sense that he was prostrating before Tyentso.

"I'll be down the hall if you need me," Kalindra whispered. For a second, she doubted either her father-in-law or the empress heard her, but then Tyentso raised her head and caught Kalindra's eye.

Tyentso mouthed, "Later," to her. She didn't look angry at all, just resigned and sad.

Kalindra stared at her father-in-law, still on his knees. He was mumbling something she couldn't hear. Kalindra had the terrible suspicion he was begging for forgiveness.

Jarith had said something was wrong here. Kalindra didn't know what yet, but she was damned if she wasn't going to find out.

Kalindra hid her shiver as she walked away.

The emperor's (or in this case, empress's) private quarters—a palace in and of themselves in many ways—were honestly not as luxurious as Kalindra expected. They were nice, yes, with marble floors and elegantly inlaid walls, graceful columns, and lovely tapestries. But Kalindra had broken into more than her share of palaces and villas that far outstripped these in terms of material excess. Any of the royal palaces of the Court of Gems would have rooms more extravagant.

These almost looked like rooms a person might live in. Almost.

She set Nikali down and let him cry. She couldn't blame him.

"He'll be back, darling," Kalindra whispered. "You know he'll be back. Daddy just had to leave and take care of some business. He's helping keep people safe."

The little boy rubbed his eyes, sniffling. "That's good. Daddy's good."

"Yes, he is. Now I want you to rest. I'll send for some food and then—"

The door opened a second time as Qoran Milligreest entered. For all that he appeared uninjured, he held himself with the air of someone nursing a wound. He didn't notice Kalindra and Nikali, or at least he didn't look at them. He sat down at a table and stared out at nothing. His face was a curious mix of apathy, anger, and grim determination.

Kalindra rubbed a knuckle into her temple. When she lowered her hand, she said, "Look, we need to talk about Jarith."

Qoran suddenly looked his age. "There's nothing to talk about. We both wanted it to be true so badly we were willing to overlook all the reasons why that was impossible."

"Except Tyentso's wrong."

"Her Majesty," Qoran said.

Kalindra raised both eyebrows while she smoothed Nikali's hair. He was still sniffling and might launch himself into tears again any second. She didn't want to risk it, so she kept her voice low. "What was that?"

"You will address her as Her Majesty," Qoran growled.

". . . fine," Kalindra said after a moment. "Her Majesty is wrong."

The high general glared at her. "I saw what vanished from that hallway, Kalindra. That was a demon. I've seen enough of them to know the difference."

"Yes, but I don't think you're considering that those aren't mutually exclusive concepts," Kalindra said. "He can be a demon *and* be Jarith. It's not like he's the only one of your children Xaltorath has—"

Qoran slammed a hand down on the table.

Kalindra glared as she gathered Nikali back to her chest, who was staring at his grandfather with wide-eyed shock. She was less impressed: Kalindra was far past the age where that sort of trick would be capable of frightening her into submission. "You already have one child who's a demon. Is there some sort of rule that says you can't have two?"

He knew perfectly well who she was talking about, and after they locked stares for a few seconds, he broke first and looked away. "I didn't realize you'd become so close to Janel in such a short time on Devors."

"You'd be amazed how much two people can communicate when it really matters."

Qoran just shook his head. "It's not the same. Janel's been cursed since she was a child. Jarith was *slain*. It's not even close to being the same. I understand. Believe me, I understand. But that's not . . ." His face twisted.

"Perhaps it is different, but that was still my husband who came back with us, and it was still your son."

"It wasn't." A stubborn, angry flush crept over the man's face.

Kalindra knew there'd be no reaching him. Maybe with time, they could talk him around. She wasn't sure they had it.

"The morgage are invading," Qoran whispered. He still wouldn't look at her.

"What." Something deep inside her twisted, and she tasted bile. Even for someone like her, born with one foot in Khorvesh and the other in Zherias, she knew the stories about the morgage. Knew about the terror and destruction they'd spread the last time they'd come pouring out of the Blight into Khorvesh.

"And if that was all there was . . ." He scoffed. Qoran wandered over to a cabinet set against one wall with the assuredness of old familiarity and pulled down a bottle of sassibim brandy and two glasses. He poured one for himself and another for his daughter-in-law.

Never mind that it was still breakfast.

He gulped down a glassful and then held on to the half-empty glass like it was a talisman. "Tyentso tried to clean house," he explained. "It didn't completely work. She missed High Lord Havar D'Aramarin, who took all his people and . . ." Qoran laughed harshly. "He must have been expecting it. He had all his pieces already in place. Small mercenary bands spread out across the empire. Maybe spread out across the whole world. But they're all in Marakor now, obeying his commands. And he's shut down the Gatestones, so the only way goods are getting to their destinations is by land. So that's war number two. I suppose the demons count as war number three." He closed his eyes. "There is no way that Quur can survive this."

"Don't sell us off yet." Kalindra set Nikali down on a couch large enough to do as an impromptu bed until she figured out which door led to a real one. He was worn out from all the crying, but that didn't change the fact that it was still morning. This was too early for nap time, and her son knew it. She gave the boy his toy bag and let him cuddle up against her side.

She glanced back at her father-in-law. "You can make more Gatestones, can't you?"

"As it happens, no. We can't. That was a D'Aramarin secret technique.[1] So we can open up a gate if a wizard does it themselves, but how many wizards are strong enough for that? Maybe a dozen? Two dozen? Tops?" He scoffed and took a healthy swig of brandy. "Tyentso can open up gates herself. Large enough to transport troops. But she's just one person. And in the meantime, D'Aramarin is cementing his position in Marakor and stopping all the food shipments."

Kalindra blinked. "Oh."

"Right. *Oh*."

"But surely Eamithon and Kirpis—"

"Eamithon will do its part. But neither Kirpis nor Kazivar are farming dominions. Eamithon can't harvest enough to feed everyone—Khorvesh, Yor, the Capital. If we don't do something soon, people will starve—"

"Kalindra! Kalindra, where have you been?" A door from one of the other rooms opened, and a young woman rushed through—Eledore Milligreest, Jarith's youngest sister.

She looked a lot like her brother, although she wore her hair tightly braided in a line across her head that was disturbingly similar to Janel's laevos, only without the shaved sides. Eledore was a pretty girl too, with even brown skin and a figure honed to the height of Khorveshan sensibilities—athletic, trained to fight from her youth. Kalindra had always liked her, perhaps because they shared a similar temper.

She had that slightly weakened air of someone who had spent a great many days crying, screaming, or both, and had only recently decided to rejoin the world.

"Hey, Elly, I am indeed back. Quiet, though. Nikali's been through a lot." Kalindra's words were immediately belied by Nikali wiggling out of her arms and running over to his aunt.

"Oh!" Eledore knelt. "Who are you?" she asked Nikali with faux seriousness. "You look like my nephew, but you're much too large! My nephew's this big." She held her thumb and forefinger about two inches apart.

Kalindra's son tugged on Eledore's arm. "No, I'm not! I'm big now!"

Eledore pretended not to hear him. "Such a shame nobody's seen him. I have toys for my nephew too . . ."

---

[1] Not that secret. Clearly, Grizzst knew how to do it.—T
 If only Grizzst had been available to walk them through the method.—S

"It's me, Auntie El! I'm your nephew!" Nikali started to make his wide-eyed puppy face, the one which so easily translated to either laughter or tears depending on circumstances and need.

"Nikali? Why, it *is* you!" Eledore quickly lifted her nephew up into the air and spun around, to his great delight and laughter. "I didn't even recognize you. Who told you that you could keep growing like this? You're like a giant person now!"

He began giggling.

Eledore lifted her head toward Kalindra and motioned to herself, Nikali, and a back room. The message was clear: *Do you want me to watch him for a while?*

"Bless you," Kalindra stage-whispered.

But as Eledore took Nikali into the back, someone else took her place in the doorway. Kalindra paused, because it wasn't anyone that she'd expected to see, and her presence meant that it was every bit as bad in Khorvesh as Qoran had said. The older woman's resemblance to Eledore was obvious, as was the resemblance to Jarith. This woman too was dressed for a fight, which was only prudent, considering.

Qoran's wife, Jira, moved her narrow-eyed gaze from her husband to rest on Kalindra. She smiled, although it was a thin veneer over the anger burning behind her eyes. "Hello, my dears. It's nice to see you both back safe and sound."

# 14. The Edge of a Knife

*Kalindra's story*
*The Soaring Halls, the Upper Circle of the Capital City of Quur*
*One hour after the attack on Jarith Milligreest*

Kalindra admitted to being a little taken aback when she discovered that she couldn't just walk into Tyentso's room, in spite of the fact that she was in theory staying in the woman's own living quarters. That space was divided up in such a way that there was a further subdivision where the empress apparently slept, and that was guarded by a small man in Devoran robes whom Kalindra unfortunately recognized.

Caerowan. A Voice of the Council. And also a man obsessed with the damn prophecies.

Considering that she now knew that some of those prophecies weren't exactly complimentary of Kalindra, she also understood why Caerowan had always treated her so coldly. There were quatrains out there that made Kalindra sound like the Queen of Evil. Devoran priests had literally tried to murder her over them.

Which made her request less than ideal.

"Is Tyentso in? I'll just be a second—" Kalindra hoped that rolling over any objection might be the smart way to play this.

No luck.

Caerowan managed to be in front of her with a speed even she found impressive.

"She's not in the Capital at the moment," Caerowan said, smiling. It was not a sincere smile. That thing his lips were doing didn't even live on the same continent as a sincere smile. It was flat and sharp and used entirely to underline the unspoken "you bitch" at the end of his statement.

"She is," Kalindra said. "I saw her this morning. I know she's back. It's important."

He bowed his head to the side. "Perhaps you'd like to make an appointment?" He was infuriatingly calm.

Kalindra inhaled. "Listen to me, you sanctimonious piece of shit. I need to talk to her right now."

Caerowan raised an eyebrow. "My earliest open appointment is next week."

"Since when are *you* her secretary? You're a Voice of the Council!"

"We're short-staffed everywhere," Caerowan replied placidly. The smile tightened, though, overlaying a barely-concealed glare that vacillated between threat and insult.

"Gods-damn it! I'm not—"

"Caerowan, it's fine," Tyentso said. "I asked her to come around. I have a few minutes before I leave."

A flash of sour irritation moved over Caerowan's face, barely there before it was hidden behind that peaceful expression and calm voice. "Of course, Your Majesty."

Gods. Kalindra fought back the temptation to stick her tongue out at the odious man when she passed him.

As Kalindra stepped inside the woman's private (more private?) rooms, she couldn't help but glance around, if only because the rooms were so different from the rest of the palace. A lot more flowers, for one thing.

"Was this the harem?" Kalindra asked before she could stop herself.

"No, but it was the only room Kandor shared with his wife, Elana, I'm told." Tyentso gave Kalindra a dry look. "Who happen to be Teraeth and Janel in this life, so don't let Teraeth ever try to tell you he's not a romantic fool."

Kalindra ignored the obvious attempt to remind her that they were supposed to be on the same side, knew all the same people, had both been angels of the Goddess of Death. "Can anyone hear us? No servants hiding in secret niches? I know how palaces are."

Tyentso's mouth flattened. "I suppose I owe you an explanation."

The Black Brotherhood assassin scowled as she met the empress's gaze. "I don't know. *Do you?*"

Someone had left out several small cups of coffee, which either had just been made by ghosts or someone had kept magically warm. Tyentso claimed one. Then she frowned. "This isn't about me upsetting your son," she mused. "You fell in love with Jarith? Really?"

Kalindra felt a flush of heat along her neck, rising up over her cheeks. But like hell she was going to let this woman be the one who shamed her. "Fuck off," Kalindra snapped. "I don't need your judgment. But you almost made a serious damn mistake back there, and you need to know—"

Tyentso sighed and poured herself a drink. "Jarith's a demon, but not a *bad* demon. Yes, I've been told."

Kalindra frowned. "*Who* told you?"

"Kihrin," Tyentso said, looking at Kalindra over the rim of her cup as she drank. "He explained it."

Any embarrassment Kalindra felt very quickly transformed into anger. "If you knew, then why did you attack him? Do you have any idea—?"

Tyentso made a cutting motion with her hand. An invisible hand squeezed Kalindra's throat and then released, leaving her coughing.

Kalindra contemplated what her chances would be if she just knifed the woman. Unfortunately, not good.

Tyentso seemed to know it too. She leaned toward Kalindra, scowling. "I'm going to have to do a lot of things I won't enjoy before this whole fucking mess is over." Absolutely nothing about her expression was apologetic. "But this isn't my fault, Kalindra. Why the hell did you bring Jarith with you? You don't think there aren't people here smart enough to put the clues together and come up with the idea that Jarith must not be . . . Jarith? A mimic or a demon or *something*? And when someone comes to me with their suspicions—and someone *did*—I have to act on it or it seems suspicious. And precisely no one who understands what the Crown and Scepter lets me do would just shrug and ignore it if I blindly overlooked a fucking demon roaming the imperial halls!"

Kalindra floundered for how to respond to that. So she didn't. Instead, she said, "You missed on purpose."

"Of course, I fucking missed on purpose!" Tyentso snapped. "I'm a bitch, not a fool."

Kalindra blinked at her and said, "My mistake."

"You don't have to sound so damned shocked about it." The new Empress of Quur flopped herself down on a heavily embroidered and even more heavily bejeweled chair and said, "You need to leave."

"You invited me here—" Kalindra started to say.

"Not leave my parlor," Tyentso said. "Leave the damn palace, the damn city. You and the rest of the Milligreests need to *leave the Capital*. It's not safe for you here. Don't tell me you can't feel it." She sighed and waved a hand. "Whatever the fuck is in the air?"

Kalindra paused. Did she feel something? No. Not as such. But that meant nothing. "Jarith said there was something wrong."

Tyentso nodded emphatically. "Jarith's right. You saw how Qoran behaved back there."

"You didn't have to order him to kneel."

"He didn't have to do it! But whatever is happening started about a week ago, and it's getting worse. Everyone's short-tempered, everyone's violent. Everyone hangs on my every damn word, no matter what I tell them to do. And you have a child now, Kalindra. You can't stay here."

Kalindra was getting tired of people demanding she uproot herself and retreat to some other location for her own "safety." After all, Devors had turned out to be so safe, hadn't it?

"You have no idea why this is happening?" Kalindra asked. "If we can find the cause, maybe we can stop it."

Tyentso nibbled on the edge of a nail. "Not a clue."

Kalindra took the opportunity to really look at the other woman. Her appearance had changed a great deal even in the six months Kalindra had spent with her on Ynisthana. Now she was a strong-featured woman with lavender-gray cloudcurl hair and midnight-black eyes. And even though she looked considerably younger than the "hag" Tyentso had been playing at when they first met, her eyes were so much older. She was tired and jumpy, a person it would be unsafe to surprise.

Tyentso raised her head. "The other day, I lost my temper at one of my generals and suggested he kill himself. Which he promptly did."

Kalindra fought back a violent shudder. "You're joking."

"I wish," the empress agreed with a tired, shaky laugh. "Right in front of me. He didn't fucking hesitate. That asshole hated my guts, Kalindra. He'd have sooner stuck that sword in me than take his own life just because I suggested it. But when I'm not ordering them around? Well. People are fighting each other at the drop of a glass. Lashing out, accusing each other, losing their tempers—often to the point of violence. Those riots? As far as I've been able to tell, those riots are happening because every citizen of the Lower Circle has taken it upon themselves to dispense a little street justice against those 'traitors' in the Royal Houses. I've actually had to send out a list of 'good' houses versus 'bad' to keep them from killing random people in the street."

"That doesn't make sense," Kalindra said.

Tyentso barked out a laugh. "You don't say."

The woman's insistence that Kalindra leave was starting to sound like wisdom. Certainly, Kalindra had no desire to see Qoran Milligreest go from his normal short-tempered self to someone with magically enhanced anger. Or Jira. Or Eledore. Hell, there wasn't a single member of that family that didn't have a terrible temper if given the opportunity. Unfortunately, there was a problem. "And go where, Ty? If the morgage are invading Khorvesh and there's a civil war in Marakor . . ."

Tyentso rolled her eyes, exasperated. "There are more dominions in the empire than Khorvesh and Marakor. Maybe the Academy in Kirpis. If you aren't safe surrounded by a thousand wizards, I don't know where you would be."

Kalindra narrowed her eyes. "Don't you *hate* the Academy?"

Tyentso nodded enthusiastically. "Oh, with all my black, twisted little heart. But I don't . . ." She sighed. "Qoran might be targeted because of me. And through him, you. I'm sure we would both feel a lot better if you knew your family was safe."

"Targeted because of you?" Kalindra blinked as she realized what that had to mean. Oh hell, Tyentso was one of Qoran's trysts? She choked back a laugh. "Tyentso! You never said that you and *Qoran* used to be an item."

"Because we weren't," Tyentso said. "We weren't anything at all."

Kalindra studied the older woman. Nothing the woman had said made a relationship impossible, just bitter and full of bad memories. Kalindra remembered Jarith once telling her that people were always trying to blackmail his parents over their affairs. Enemies were always shocked to discover what they assumed to be dreadful marital secrets were anything but. That Qoran and Jira were never going to leave each other, no matter who they took as lovers on the side.

"Right," Kalindra agreed.

Tyentso took Kalindra's dry answer as skepticism of the entire conversation. "I understand how you feel, Kalindra, but please just take my advice and go. Whatever is causing this takes a little while to ramp up, but I haven't seen anyone who's immune."

"You seem to be immune," Kalindra pointed out. "Although you look like shit."

"Fuck you too. Anyway, I'm the eye of the hurricane, the Empress of Quur.

I *am* the empire." She tossed out the words like ingredients on a shopping list or a nursery rhyme recitation. Not like something believed but something she'd heard so many people around her say that it had become an insincere mantra. "Everyone's sudden bout of patriotism is directed to my benefit."

Which was a problem. Certainly, Kalindra didn't want to keep her family around it. At the same time . . . "You're dealing with an invasion and a civil war. You're seriously complaining because everyone's following your orders without question?"

"The assholes back at the Academy always had a saying: never drink a potion you didn't brew yourself. Now in their case, it was because the seniors had an ongoing contest to see who could trick the most freshmen into accidentally drinking magical laxatives, but the point stands.[1] Yes, it's convenient. But I can't control it, and I don't know why it's happening, so I can't trust it."

"Yeah, fine. Makes sense." It did. Kalindra hated it. Now she had to both find someplace to take the family (yes, perhaps the Academy as Tyentso had suggested) and also convince the rest of the Milligreests to come with her. She didn't expect that to be an easy sell.

Tyentso waved a hand in dismissal. "Now would you kindly fuck off? I have two wars to win."

Kalindra was on her way to the door when a thought struck her. She turned back to Tyentso. "Qoran won't leave with me, you know. He's going to insist on staying by your side."

The other woman sighed. "I know. He was always an asshole when it came to duty. But at least you can get everyone else out. And, Kalindra?"

"Yes?"

Tyentso smiled, a little apologetic, a little wan. It was a real smile, if ill-nourished and sad. "Nice to see you again."

Kalindra nodded. "You too."

[1] I believe that's now something of an established tradition.–T
As if I wasn't already glad I never attended that stupid school.–S

# 15. THE SYMPTOMS OF A GREATER PROBLEM

### Qown's story
### The Soaring Halls, the Upper Circle of the Capital City of Quur
### Same day as their arrival, just before lunch

Everyone stayed at the table after Caless left, uncomfortable and skittish. The worst part of it was that they couldn't be sure that she could help them with the Stone of Shackles. Not that she wanted to help them—she clearly did—but whether or not it was even possible. The only way they could test was, unfortunately, to attempt to gaesh one of them. Even if Qown had been willing (he wasn't), Caless had refused to try.

The three people remaining (four if one was counting the little boy) were quiet in that absence. No one knew what to say.

Then the little boy started tugging at his uisigi and looking around the room in clear distress. Galen knelt next to the child. "Do you need to use the toilet?"

The boy stared at him, wide-eyed, and nodded quickly.

He held out his arms to the child. Tave had apparently decided Galen was acceptable company, because he scrambled into Galen's hold quickly. "I'll be back," Galen told the others.

Qown watched him leave and wondered if he should have gone too, if for no other reason than he had no idea where the washrooms even were. A problem he'd have to tackle himself before too much longer, although hopefully with less impromptu dancing.

Sheloran folded several pieces of sag bread around a thick filling of spiced root vegetables and set the plate in front of Qown. "Eat," she suggested.

Qown huffed. "I'm fine."

"Eat something, anyway. Please?"

He stared at her for a few seconds. How was he supposed to eat? His stomach was twisted in knots. But it would make Sheloran happy, and no doubt Galen would start nagging too when he returned, so he managed to scarf down a few pieces. "If this doesn't work . . . ," he started to say.

"It had better work," Sheloran said. "It *will* work."

"But if it doesn't—"

"Qown!" Sheloran's stare was all flames and searing heat.

"If it doesn't," Qown persisted, "then we need to consider what we can do to minimize the damage. Obviously, Relos Var cannot be allowed to gaesh us." He unfolded two pieces of paper and set them in front of her. On each was written half of a glyph.

Sheloran stared at the paper and then raised her gaze to him. "What is this?"

"I asked Senera to make it," Qown said. "It's . . . um. It's a worst case. I admit that. And it can't activate until both halves are drawn on the same body, obviously. But Senera promised it would be painless. And it'll keep the body from decaying, at least for a while."

She didn't understand right away, and then Sheloran turned gray. "Qown." Her voice was very quiet.

"It's not what you think," Qown said. "I mean, it *is* what you think, but just consider: with what we know . . . who we know . . . and the body being undamaged . . . There are only two certain ways of curing a gaesh. Either destroy the Stone of Shackles, or kill the person, destroy their gaesh control talisman, and unite the pieces of their souls in the Afterlife before Returning them. So."

So something they could accomplish. He wished he could spell it out more bluntly, but Sheloran was smart enough to fill in the lines. She knew what he meant. Under normal circumstances, yes, it would be suicide, but when they had Xivan on their side and the enemy didn't know that she'd already become the new Goddess of Death?

Dying became a tactical retreat, a strategic choice. Nothing more than that.

She peered at him over the lip of her metal fan. "And you waited until Galen was out of the room to explain this because . . . ?"

Qown gave her a bittersweet smile. "You know why."

Because Galen would have absolutely refused under any and all circumstances. Whereas Sheloran was more pragmatic about such things. She understood the need. She wouldn't like it, but she'd understand it.

Sheloran picked up the two pieces of paper and tucked them into her raisigi. "I don't like it."

"Oh, neither do I, so let's hope your mother's method works." He paused. "You realize we still need the Stone of Shackles. We have to convince her to give it to us."

"Yes, but at this point, Mother's going to refuse anyone who asks out of general principle," Sheloran said. "Don't worry. We'll talk her into it eventually."

"I hope so."

The quiet spread out between them once more. Suddenly, the room seemed small and cramped. Qown felt boxed in, which never usually bothered him but suddenly seemed suffocating. He needed something to do. Something that could help. Something. Anything.

A dark thought occurred to him. "No one's looking to arrest Galen, are they?"

Sheloran paused her fanning. "What?"

"I mean, not just because of the high lord business. What about the Lysian gas at the Culling Fields? Even if Gerisea is dead, do you think there might still be a warrant out for Galen's arrest?" He paused. "Or mine?"

Sheloran closed her fan. She looked concerned. "It's possible," she admitted. "We should have asked."[1]

"I'm sure I can find your father by the soldiers." The thought made him wince. He'd been intimidated enough by Sheloran's father the last time they'd met, and that was before knowing that the man was a god-king. His recent behavior was only compounding the issue. Still, finding out might prove important.

Sheloran nodded. "If you'd be so kind."

Qown didn't wander far. The nearby courtyard opened to sky, the weather fair enough to encourage the soldiers using the location to train and spar. The air was scented thick with sweat, leather, and blood as groups of men practiced killing each other—or at least pretended they were trying to kill each other. Teachers wandered between them making corrections. The air thrummed with violence, the energy a rasp against Qown's skin, the hairs at the back of his neck. Several of the practice bouts seemed impossibly close to the real thing.

Qown found Sheloran's father, Varik, at the same place where he'd been before, helping the troops with weapons. The former high lord raised an eyebrow at him as he approached, but didn't shout at him to go away. Qown took that as a good sign.

"A word, if I may?" Qown asked.

Varik gave him a flat look. Qown thought he might have passed judgment too soon on whether or not Varik was going to start shouting. But the former high lord handed over his task to an assistant and gestured for Qown to follow him to the back.

"What is it?" His irritation softened for just a moment as he gave Qown an appraising look. "You know, I might have something that would fit you. Yes, I'm almost sure of it. Any idea how to use a sword?"

"What? Oh no." Qown cleared his throat. "I was just talking with your daughter, and we realized we didn't know if there were still any active warrants out for Galen—or for any of us, really—because of what happened with that Lysian gas at the Culling Fields. So . . . are there?"

Varik checked to see if anyone obvious was listening before turning back to Qown. "No. You were all lucky about the timing. They were still able to check with Gerisea's guards."

"Check with—?" It took a moment for Qown to make the connection: Thaena had still been alive when the assassination attempt at the Culling Fields had occurred. So her priests would have been able to ask the souls of the dead what they knew. Gerisea hadn't just murdered her sister, Tishenya, and her soldiers; Gerisea had left her own guards to die there too. While it was unlikely that most of those guards had known important details, the dead

---

[1] I can hardly blame them for having other priorities.—S

had included the sorcerer responsible for creating the Lysian gas in the first place. *He* had almost certainly known the truth.[2]

"No one's going to come looking for Galen if he doesn't force the issue," Varik said. "Everyone knows Gerisea was head of House D'Mon when she died. And that speech Galen gave at Jarith Milligreest's funeral denouncing the royals might just end up being the smartest thing he ever did. Word's gotten around."

"I can't believe—" Qown shook his head. "I can't believe it's all falling apart so fast."

"That's what happens when you close down the gates and leave everyone to starve. People start to realize you were never on their side."

*But that only happened after Tyentso had ordered the high lords executed,* Qown thought. He wondered what was going to happen to all the members of the Royal Houses who weren't themselves royalty, who had been members because it was the only way to legally work with magic. Those people provided essential, vital services, and now what? Were they being dragged out into the street by rioters? Absorbed into some larger imperial amalgam? What happened to them?

"Yes, they most certainly do," Qown said. "Thank you."

Varik clapped him on the shoulder in a manner that might almost have been considered friendly before he stalked back to his tent.

Which left Qown in front of the training yard. He wrinkled his nose as he watched the men fight. He'd never spent time around Quuros soldiers, so he had no basis for comparison, but these men seemed to be a particularly violent example of the breed. Janel's soldiers had been much more prone to laughter and teasing each other while they sparred. But maybe it wasn't a proper comparison: Janel's troops had been largely outlaws and criminals. And not that interested in killing anyone.

These men were very interested in killing.

As Qown watched, two soldiers who were earnestly driving weapons at each other escalated their bout into a more serious altercation. One of them managed to slice the other with his sword. These weren't practice blades; the quick swipe past the other's defenses opened up a stripe of red along the arm, slicing along veins, an artery. Blood sprayed with lethal ferocity.

Silence, then cheers and jeers. Nobody moved to help the man. Qown started to run forward. As he did, one of the teachers tossed the man a rag and said, "Clean that off and keep to it."

The man rolled his eyes in response and wiped the blood off his arm.

Qown found himself pulling up sharply. *The man had stopped bleeding.* The red liquid seeped thick and sluggish, more like tar than blood. The soldier ignored his own injury.

---

[2] Gerisea must not have thought the sorcerer would die. Otherwise, this was unforgivably sloppy.—S

It still is, in my opinion.—T

Qown felt himself shudder. He looked around. No one noticed. No one seemed to think what had just happened particularly remarkable.

Qown backed away slowly, concerned that he not draw attention to himself. Perhaps . . .

Perhaps the soldier knew magic. But that couldn't have been so normal, so taken for granted, that no one would have even remarked upon it. Or it was possible that the man hadn't been human at all, but a demon possessing a corpse. That seemed unlikely here in the royal palace, though. And even less likely not to draw attention. Again, no one seemed to think it odd. Training continued.

"What in all the world—" Qown blinked. There was a third option. Qown might not have even thought of it except that Cornerstones were such the topic of the day.

"Oh no," Qown whispered. "Warmonger."

Relos Var had wanted Galen to retrieve the Cornerstone Grimward for him, but Relos Var already possessed Warmonger. Qown had never fully understood its abilities, but he knew that it had once been owned by Nemesan, the god-king of Laragraen, who'd used it to keep both the Kirpis vané and Quuros Empire at bay for centuries. According to the stories, Warmonger had made Laragraen's soldiers almost impossible to kill, and equally thirsty for the blood of their enemies.

If Warmonger was being used on Quur's imperial army . . .

Oh, but it was worse than that, Qown realized. Warmonger didn't just affect an army. Qown didn't know what the range was, but if it had been large enough to cover an area the size of Kazivar, then surely it was large enough to affect the entire Capital. Anyone who was an enemy of the nation supported by Warmonger's owner would suffer the consequences. Riots were just one symptom.

Relos Var had either given the stone away or he was close by. And Qown didn't think Relos Var's plans had reached a point where he was willing to give away any more Cornerstones. That meant Relos Var had to be present, *physically present,* inside the Soaring Halls.

Galen and Sheloran needed to know. Hell, everyone needed to know. He turned around to run back.

Relos Var's henchman Anlyr blocked his path.

"Hello, Qown. It's been a spell, hasn't it?" Anlyr smiled cheerfully. "The boss wants to talk to you."

# 16. NEMESAN GAMBITS

*Tyentso's story*
***The Soaring Halls, the Upper Circle of the Capital City of Quur***
***Ten minutes after Kalindra left***

Tyentso had two hours before the army would be ready, or so she'd been told. The army didn't need her until then. The Quuros army hadn't depended on orders from the emperor since Kandor, and even then, he'd been very good at creating a military apparatus capable of organizing itself.[1]

In theory, she had nothing to do.

That theory bore no resemblance to reality.

Just a handful of minutes after speaking with Kalindra, Tyentso appeared in Jorat, checking on the second front.

Technically speaking, it wasn't a front *yet*. Ever since Havar D'Aramarin had retreated to Marakor with his armies and cut off the Gatestone network, the Royal Houses who had gone with him had been solidifying their positions. They'd been building defensive fortifications and setting up a warding system that made it difficult–if not actively impossible–for anyone to teleport into the territory they now controlled. It was disturbingly similar to the barrier the Manol vané used around their nation.[2] Tyentso was reasonably sure that certain individuals–the Immortals, for example–could blow through those wards, but there weren't too many of those left anymore. And those who remained had better things to do with their time.

Everyone knew that they were heading for war. The refugee camp that had sprung up in the shadow of Atrine's ruins was a massive sprawl of distinctive Joratese tents (Ashok? They were called something like that[3]) that took up two to three times the area of the original city. The air smelled of horses and hay, though not nearly as much of human waste as she would have expected. Indeed, there was an odd petrichor scent to the air, which mystified her for a few minutes with its haunting familiarity until she identified it as the smell of Demon Falls itself–millions of tons of water washing over the white granite

---

[1] Can I admit that there's a part of me that genuinely wants to see what Teraeth would do with the Manol vané throne? Because I do.–S
[2] I could have told her how to get past that.–S
[3] Azhock, which are considerably larger and more refined than anything being used elsewhere in Quur.–S

dam works crafted by Ompher, before falling thousands of feet down into the Zaibur River below.

The tent city was organized with military precision. A sour taste filled her mouth. She had hoped the curse—whatever it was—hadn't reached Jorat. This already boded ill for that idea.

Then a group of children ran in front of her, laughing. Tyentso was invisible; they'd have run right smack into her if she hadn't dodged out of the way. The kids were the wide range of odd hues that one might expect of Joratese children, but it was impossible to miss the flashes of Marakori red. They played some kind of game, kicking a leather ball between them. As Tyentso watched, an old man started to shoo them away from the tents, laughing as he promised them treats later as a bribe for a few hours' peace. There was nothing like anger in anyone's voices.

She exhaled slowly. It had been weeks since she'd seen anyone smile like that in the Capital.

Normally, Tyentso didn't teleport in blind to a location. She didn't have to. Her witchgift was clairvoyance; she'd learned how to spy on others from a distance literally before she'd learned how to read.[4] Unfortunately, it was possible to block such scrying. Whoever was in charge of setting up the magical defenses for the Joratese duchy had done so. Reassuring, given the magical nature of their enemies in Marakor, but personally inconvenient in her case. Tyentso had been able to scry where imperial command was located; she hoped that she'd find the Joratese duchess nearby. She hadn't spoken to the woman for long when Ninavis had visited the Capital, but she did remember the woman mentioning that she operated in a tent close to the main military camp.

Tyentso didn't remove the invisibility until she'd found said tent. She would have done the expectedly dramatic "turn visible right in front of the duchess having sauntered past every guard," but she was relieved to discover that the tent was magically warded to the sky. So much so that even she would have a difficult time breaking through without being noticed or stopped outright.

As she contemplated the magical protections, a horse nearby snorted at her and tossed its head.

Only . . . it wasn't a horse. A fireblood. One that seemed familiar—black with red stripes on its legs.[5] The creature was standing over by the side of the ducal tent along with a dozen other similarly-sized firebloods. The grouping didn't resemble a herd of horses being stabled together so much as a group of soldiers standing guard.

Which is exactly what they were.

Tyentso glanced around, but her invisibility charm seemed to be holding up. The soldiers didn't see her. The firebloods *did*.

She walked over in their direction.

"I need to speak to Ninavis," Tyentso said, pushing down any feelings of

---

[4] I am given to understand that it is, in fact, how she learned to read.—T
[5] That would be either Arasgon or his brother Telaras.—S

embarrassment engendered by the idea of speaking to someone who looked like a horse. "Tell her the Emp—" She remembered being told the Joratese didn't gender their titles. Oh right. Ninavis was the Joratese *duke,* wasn't she? "The Emperor of Quur wants to see her."[6]

The fireblood gave her a remarkably unimpressed look, but he raised his head in a gesture that might be generously described as a nod of agreement. Then he trotted past her and over toward one of the larger tents. Halfway there, the fireblood stopped and looked back over his shoulder at her in a motion which seemed to suggest *"What are you waiting for?"*

Tyentso followed him.

The ~~horse~~fireblood made a loud whinny-like noise at the mouth of the tent, at which point the flap of the tent pulled to the side all on its own. The fireblood tapped a hoof against the ground with impatience. The message seemed clear enough: *"get in there."*

"Thank you," Tyentso murmured and walked inside.

The tent was larger than any general's tent in the army. Given the importance that the Joratese placed on these things as part of their cultural legacy as a nomadic people, Tyentso suspected it was sturdier. The walls were decorated in a combination of banners, which included the horse banner of Jorat, a less familiar banner decorated with a jaguar head, and a third banner that might have been an exaggerated flower of some kind—perhaps a lotus.[7] A kettle steamed on a small hearth set to one side. A number of collapsible chairs and cushions were scattered about. Light from hanging lanterns threw geometric patterns around the room.

A large group (including, dear gods, another fireblood) clustered around a map spread out on a table. Most of them looked Joratese and were unfamiliar. A few she knew: a large, plainly dressed man with a white blaze over one eye, a Quuros military general she recognized, and the person she was here to see—Duchess Ninavis Theranon.[8] Duke Theranon, she mentally corrected.

The woman was dressed a bit differently from when they'd met in the Capital. There, she'd presented herself in modest, sober western Quuros fashion—embroidered agolé, ribbon-trimmed raisigi, a long, elegant cotton skirt. The way she'd worn her hair had made it possible to miss—or at least overlook—the splash of maroon skin painted down one side of her face.

Now, Ninavis she wore her hair braided in a stripe down the center of her head, each plait decorated with gold beadwork and jewels. Rubies at her ears, nearly the same color as her darker skin, drew attention to the difference in skin color. She wore a kef like a man, crafted from leather in a way abso-

---

[6] This is incorrect. The Joratese do gender their titles. It's just that they always define their leaders as men—regardless of that person's biological sex.—S

[7] That would be the Joratese, Stavira, and Tolamer banners, respectively, all of which are territories now under the control of Ninavis. Not bad for a woman who started out as an immigrant farm wife turned bandit.—S

[8] I should note that although it is customary for many nobles to refer to themselves by the name of their holding, Quur's dukes do not. Thus Janel Theranon might have once identified herself as Count Tolamer, but Duke Kaen was never addressed as Duke Yor. Similarly, Ninavis Theranon is never Duke Jorat.—T

lutely no one from the Capital would dare unless they were using magic to keep from suffocating in the heat. No agolé at all, but a quilted velvet jacket embroidered with scenes of hunting cats and firebloods. It was as if someone had told her that all the fashionable people wore their most expensive jewelry when going to war.[9]

"We need to talk." Tyentso ignored everyone else in the room.

One of the others—someone Tyentso didn't recognize—scowled. "Who the hell are you—?"

The Quuros general—Lavrin?—glanced over at her, and then his eyes widened. He stood so quickly he nearly toppled the chair he'd been using, and gave her a deep bow. "Your Majesty," he said loudly.

Tyentso valiantly fought to keep from grinning. Sometimes it was nice to be recognized.

Ninavis paused in the middle of whatever they'd been doing. "I need the room, everyone. Go grab something to eat. I'll send messengers when we're ready to pick up again."

The group shuffled out, with the white-and-gold fireblood that had been evidently taking part of the conversation giving Tyentso a surprisingly elegant tilt of their head as they passed.

She waited until they were all gone.

"I was wondering when I'd see you," Ninavis said. "You really fucked things up, didn't you?"

Tyentso blinked. "Excuse me?"

"Oh yeah. Excuse you indeed," the duke snapped. "I couldn't quite believe it when I heard that you'd assassinated most of the Royal House heads, but then I realized it was only that you'd *tried* to kill the bastards off. You hadn't *succeeded*. And now my people have to deal with the consequences."

If there'd been any doubt in Tyentso's mind that Jorat was not experiencing whatever it was that seemed to be holding the Capital in a tight-fisted grip of fanatical devotion, this neatly spat on the idea. Ninavis was in no way inclined to do whatever Tyentso said without question. Quite the opposite.

"It's not my fault that Havar never showed," Tyentso said. "I thought he had. It looked for all the world like Havar had personally attended. But either he's so powerful he was able to shrug off temperatures that would melt steel or it was never him at all. Maybe a stand-in or some sort of illusion. I don't know." She dug a knuckle into the side of her head. "He had this planned. That much is quite obvious. Too much was too ready too quickly. And he's a god-king to boot."

"What," Ninavis said.

"Havar D'Aramarin is a god-king," Tyentso repeated. "Turns out the Royal Houses were just lousy with fucking god-kings, and I had no idea. Boy, is my face red. I don't know which one he is, mind you—"

---

[9] In fact, Ninavis is dressed as a man, or "stallion," of high rank, in the Joratese fashion.—S

"Murad," Ninavis said. It would have seemed like a non sequitur, except . . . well. That was a Quuros god. Not exactly one of Tyentso's favorites either.

Tyentso froze. "What *about* Murad?"

"*He's* Murad," Ninavis said. "Havar D'Aramarin, I mean. He has to be. I have damn few spies left now because the bastard's killing anyone who he even slightly suspects might be one, but those who've survived tell me that altars of Murad are going up all over the damn place in Marakor. Which seemed a bit out of character when I'm told House D'Erinwa is so decimated by just . . . everything . . . that they hardly have a presence in Marakor at all. But if you're right and Havar's one of these bow-down-and-worship-me bastards, then I would assume *his* particular flavor of religion would be the one he's pushing the hardest. And that's Murad."

Tyentso pulled out one of the chairs and sat down. Murad was not a minor god. How could he be when he was the God of Justice and Slavery and the whole damn Quuros economy ran on his back? But Tyentso had thought he was the patron god of House D'Erinwa, since that had been the Royal House who controlled the slavers.

The idea that Murad was the head of a completely *different* house, the first ranked and most powerful house . . .

She was going to need to talk to Lessoral about this.[10]

"Well, isn't that just fucking lovely." She took a deep breath. "It's a gods-damn Nemesan gambit."

Ninavis raised an eyebrow.

Tyentso gestured angrily. "The morgage are invading Khorvesh. Havar—fucking *Murad*—is setting up shop in Marakor and cutting off all the supply chains. I either split my forces and leave both sides weak enough to be easily crushed, or I concentrate on one enemy and let the other one run roughshod over the whole fucking empire. No matter what choice I pick, I *lose*."

Ninavis poured them both a drink. "You're just lucky that Jorat was already in the middle of an undeclared war against Marakor before all this started. We're already prepared. This only upped the timetable. But Janel warned me that the morgage would leave the Blight—"

"Janel." Tyentso squinted. "Where *is* Janel?"

"Busy," Ninavis said. "But she's checking in nightly. And I know the brat well enough to know exactly what she'd say in this case."

"Please enlighten me." Tyentso grabbed her drink, silently checked for poison because the past few months had hardly made her less paranoid, and gulped down a mouthful of fire. "What the fuck—?"

"Ara," Ninavis explained. "Sip it next time. It grows on you. Anyway, her advice would be: there's always a move you can make once you stop playing by *their* fucking rules. Only, to be fair, she probably wouldn't use the word *fucking*. For someone raised by Dorna, she's surprisingly decorous."

---

[10] Lessoral, of course, being the alias used by Caless. I can't imagine Tyentso had realized Lessoral was Caless, or she'd have come up with a very different strategy for being rid of the high lords.–T

Tyentso snorted. "Stop playing by their rules? You think I want to be dealing with two different invasions?"

"What's happening here won't be them invading us," Ninavis said. "Marakor's hunkering down and getting ready for a siege. Only they have all the food."

"Same difference. It's going to come down to a fight, and there's something–" Tyentso clamped down on her impulse to explain what was happening to everyone in the Capital. It sounded crazy. Who'd ever heard of a spell that could affect that many people simultaneously? Even if the Capital's normal population had gone down because people had fled the city or died for any number of horrifying reasons, it was still the largest city in the empire.

And she was missing something. Tyentso knew she was missing something. The entire situation felt . . . disturbingly familiar. Like she had at some point read about something very much like this happening before. But she couldn't remember where, and it was infuriating. She wasn't thinking clearly–and she was pretty sure she knew why.

"Murad, huh?" Tyentso shook her head as she took a sip of the well-named "fire" that Ninavis was serving her. She could see how one might get used to it.

"I could always be wrong," Ninavis allowed, "but I just can't see the bastard putting up shrines to Murad if he's really Jaakar."[11]

"No, that wouldn't make any sense," Tyentso agreed absently. She'd seriously underestimated Havar D'Aramarin. True, one could argue that he'd underestimated her first, but he wouldn't make that mistake again.

She'd damn well better not either.

"So what do you think he'll do next?" she asked Ninavis. "You're closer to the ground on this than I am."

Ninavis snorted. "I think he wants to wait us out. Make it so costly in terms of all the people starving to death that you have no choice but to come to the table and offer him peace terms. And then he cuts a deal. All he has to do is be less immediately threatening than the morgage or the Yorans."

"Wait." Tyentso leaned forward. "What about the Yorans?"

Ninavis raised an eyebrow. "If the food stops coming into Yor, you don't think they're going to politely *stay* up there and starve to death, do you? They'll move south. That means heading into Jorat. And once that happens, we'll be too busy dealing with a Yoran invasion to pay attention to what Havar is doing in Marakor. He's already set that in motion. Again, all he had to do was stop the food shipments. Turns out Quur's biggest strength–that amazing gate system that let us move freight from once side of the empire to the other in a matter of hours instead of weeks–is also its biggest weakness."

"Fuck," Tyentso muttered. "Is there . . . is there any way we can stop that? There has to be something . . ."

"Sure, send food."

Tyentso laughed once, loud and bitter. "Fantastic. I'm so glad I came in person to talk to you." Tyentso set the glass on the table and glanced at the map. There were far too many blank spaces on it and far too many places

[11] Jaakar is the god of sports and physical prowess.–T

where the enemy might easily slip through their defenses without being noticed.

Tyentso tapped the part of the map labeled "the Kulma Swamp." It was a significant chunk of southern Marakor, just north of the Blight. She remembered once hearing that it was where all the trash of the Zaibur basin drained.

"If we *could* fix their food situation, do you think the Yorans might work with us?" Tyentso asked. "Or do you think there's just too much bad blood?"

"Are you proposing giving the Kulma Swamp to *Yor*? I think that if you expect the Yorans are going to be terribly keen on relocating down to one of the hottest, most miserable parts of the entire continent, you maybe have never been to either Yor or the Kulma." She gave a definite nod to the section of map where Tyentso's fingers still lurked. "I grew up in that hellhole. Trust me when I say that no one *but no one* lives in the Kulma Swamp because they want to. It's so damn humid you might as well be trying to breathe underwater."

Tyentso sighed. Ninavis was right, of course. That was a ridiculous offer to make, and it was highly unlikely the Yorans would ever agree.

Tyentso stood up. "We'll have to come up with something. Figure out a way to get in contact with *someone* who can speak for the Yorans. Do it soon, before Havar hires them in exchange for resuming food shipments. Thanks for the drink."

"Sure, don't mention—"

Tyentso teleported out.

# 17. STEP FOUR: ENCOURAGE ALLIES TO COOPERATE

### Kihrin's story
### The moon Jhyr
### The day of Vol Karoth's escape, midday

I'd be lying if I said that I knew delving deep into the mind of an elder demon was a mistake the moment I'd done it.

Because I'd known *before* I'd done it.

It was just that I didn't realize how large a mistake it was. My only salvation turned out to be one of logistics: the souls that comprised the demon's gestalt core were so condensed, compacted, and cellular that they could no longer be treated as individual elements. They had to be treated as a whole, which meant I wasn't washed away in a tidal wave of memories and personalities.

I would've been. Anyone would've been. I'd miscalculated the number of souls involved. Given these were the toughest of the tough—the catastrophe-level demon princes—I'd expected thousands. I'd prepared myself to shut out most of the voices to concentrate on just a few souls and hopefully find out what I needed.

But it wasn't thousands. It was *billions*.

And yes, they'd been human.

Shortly on the heels of discovering how to open portals into parallel universes came the well-intentioned "let's send people there" because we'd known our own universe was dying. Not in a cataclysmic apocalypse, mind you. No, our universe was just old. Everything was winding down, and eventually—in a few billion years—would settle to a slow, dark halt. Humanity intended to survive—just somewhere else.

We hadn't brought everyone with us; we *couldn't* bring everyone with us. But it's not like we'd been leaving the rest of humanity to die—the universe had been old, but not a corpse. Could it really be considered abandonment when they still had something like twenty million lifetimes ahead of them?

I don't think any of us had considered that time might move at different speeds between that universe and this one. That humanity would indeed survive for long enough to watch the beginning of that black wave come tumbling down. The aging stars, the expanding distance, the quickening time. Humanity must have been staring down the slow dissolution of existence or the hope that some spark would set off a rebirth they'd never live to see.

Calling it an apocalypse of ice or cold wasn't even correct. It was stillness and oblivion. No motion anywhere, down to the tiniest levels.

Well.

Humanity did what we always do: we found a way to survive.

Material bodies became a problem, so they shucked those away like rice hulls. Humanity ascended, but it wasn't an ennobling, divine juxtaposition of mind and souls. Humanity ascended, discarded their bodies, and became a thousand times crueler. Where they had once waged wars over land and water, now they did so over stars, galaxies, and the last, tiniest scraps of energy.

Making a bad situation worse.

By the time they'd started cannibalizing each other, I doubt much about them existed that could be called *human* any longer. Those with the strongest wills, the worst resentment, the greatest ferocity, devoured the rest. The sentient life of entire planets numbering in the billions became single individuals, hunting each other. Humanity condensed, transformed from a race spanning galaxies to a few thousand horrifying demons.

Demons who yearned for and hated what they'd lost.

I couldn't tell if they'd followed us deliberately. The demons' memories were scattered and barely organized. Maybe they'd just felt along the cracks of their reality the way one might search for the edge of a door in the dark. Maybe some well-intentioned fool had tried to reach backward from our world to theirs, guided by an excess of nostalgia, and had accidentally opened up an exploitable weakness. Maybe the trail had always been there, demons pouring through the one open window we'd left behind us.

I yanked my mind away as soon as I had my answers. Believe me, if I could have scrubbed my brain clean with vinegar and soap, I would have. I settled for ripping the demon's soul away and tossing it back in with the others. And then it was the usual: ignoring their howls for revenge, the demands for redress, the mocking insults, the angry threats.

"Be quiet," I snapped, "or I'll find out what kind of tsali stone a demon makes."[1]

That shut them up. For the moment.

One thing was certain: I needed to find Thurvishar.

We had a problem.

---

[1] This is a fantastic example of the consequences of a lack of formal education. Demons treat tsali exactly like bodies—yet another container to be slipped into or out of at will.—T

Or here's a thought: while this is Kihrin, this is also a millennia-old S'arric. Possibly he knows something you don't.—S

# 18. Mimic Hunt

***Teraeth's story***
***The Mother of Trees, the Manol***
***The day of Vol Karoth's escape, just after noon***

The palace descended into a mess of not-very-well-controlled chaos. Prior to a few months ago, no mimic had dared trespass the Mother of Trees for centuries. It was assumed that mimics had all departed for other lands, where it was safer, because no one knew how to deal with their powers. Yet recently, a mimic had infiltrated the palace, murdered the king's double, replaced the Queen, murdered said Queen, and who knows what else.[1] The vané guards were understandably paranoid.

Teraeth contemplated ordering them to stand down, but it would've looked odd. Especially so when more than a few guards remembered delivering Teraeth to a throne room that already contained a Teraeth. They knew something was wrong, and after losing a member of royalty to a mimic only recently, they didn't intend to do so again.

Teraeth hoped that Talon could escape whatever trouble she'd accidentally triggered. He'd have to apologize at a later date for not realizing that security had been upgraded to include her. In the meantime, he acted like catching the mimic was something he wanted. Even though it was quite the reverse.

Teraeth ordered extra guards to man the exits (where Talon wouldn't go). Further, he demanded immediate reports on what had been seen and what information they had. He ordered analysis done on the methods used, far too early to be of any use. Normally, he'd let competent people do their job, but in this case, he hamstrung them. He felt like someone had hung weights on his belt as he slowly walked over and sat down on the throne.

Teraeth hated this so much.

The courtiers gave him knowing looks. It didn't take him a second to realize why. Teraeth had arrived with two women and the former vané queen's only son. Teraeth's memories of the aftermath of the Battle of the Well of Spirals were fuzzy, but he suspected every damn vané in the Mother of Trees knew the nature of his relationship with both Kihrin and Janel. It must have seemed like he was bringing a whole stable of lovers with him.

"Perhaps our conversation should wait until after this unpleasantness has been dealt with, Your Majesty?" Valathea smiled warmly at her stepson.

[1] So they're saying that even for a mimic, Talon is unpredictable. —S

"Yes," he agreed. "I think that would be wise. And perhaps all of us might retire to some location less formal?" Because while he hadn't spent a great deal of time in the vané throne room, he still recalled enough. Any conversations here would be stilted, unbearably formal, and eavesdropped on by dozens of people unless Teraeth literally forced all the guards and all the courtiers out of the room. And even then, there would still be listening posts and magical spells designed to keep the room under constant surveillance.

"Why yes, I believe that can be arranged." Valathea paused to turn to Xivan. "Apologies for earlier." She tilted her head. "Is Talea well?"

Xivan scratched at the back of her neck. "Uh, thank you. And Talea's fine. In fact, we are expecting her to join us very soon."

"Oh good. She's always delightful. And I must say, Xivan, you're looking exceptionally well yourself."

Teraeth's mouth twisted to the side. Indeed, Xivan looked extremely hale—so much so that someone staring at her would likely never imagine that she was anything but a living, breathing, perfectly healthy Khorveshan woman. She didn't look dead. Mostly because Teraeth didn't think she was anymore. It seemed that the one sure way to be Returned from the dead even after the Goddess of Death had been slain was to take the job for oneself.

Another reminder, cold and pointed as a sharp knife sliding between ribs: the only reason that position had been vacant was because Teraeth had killed his own mother.

Janel cleared her throat, and when Teraeth glanced at her, she winked at him in return. He gave her a tiny, private smile, grateful that she was there to keep him from drowning in memories. They still had a great deal to do; Kihrin needed them.

After several hours of thankfully fruitless searching (proving Teraeth's trust in Talon's ability to escape capture had not been misplaced), Teraeth pretended at irritability and called off the search. Then he retired to the king's private chambers for lunch. To Teraeth's private chambers, he supposed. At least until they Returned his father.

Those rooms were all that he'd expected. Ridiculously luxurious. Endless silks and rare woods trained to grow into exquisite interlocking shapes. Enough room for several families, all decorated in green and brown forest colors, with no sharp edges anywhere. If the furniture sprouted flowers made from glass and gemstone and the carpets had the inviting lush nap of meadow grass, it did nothing to limit the sense of wilderness. Of wildness. Teraeth could only shake his head in admiration of the artistry of it all.

In this lifetime, he'd grown up in a cave. This felt like someone else's property. Likely because prior to Teraeth's own coronation, it *had* been someone else's property: his nephew, Kelanis.[2] And now here he was, the same soul who had once been the Emperor of Quur, now crowned as the very thing

---

[2] Nephew on his mother's side. Had his father been inhabiting Terindel's original body when Teraeth was conceived, Kelanis would also have been his cousin—but since he wasn't, there's no paternal biological relationship.—T

he'd attempted to invade the Manol in order to destroy. He reached for the arrowhead around his neck and clenched it until the edges bit into his fingers.

Janel took his hand. "Just breathe. This is only temporary."

"It had better be," Teraeth growled.

There'd be a dinner that evening he'd be expected to attend. Probably some sort of dance. Teraeth would be expected to attend that too.

He wouldn't.

Valathea called for wine and food as she gave the tour. The closet alone seemed like it would take weeks to sort through. There were too many clothes.

It wasn't just his ascetic upbringing at work there. The clothing provided was intricate, sumptuous, incredibly detailed, and perfect in craftsmanship. Many of these pieces would have taken months to make. Some might have taken years. Which meant there was no possibility that any of it had been made for *him*.

He looked over at Valathea, a clear question in his eyes.

"It's not our habit to throw anything away," Valathea explained. "Consider this a private history of the vané royal family in sartorial form." She reached over to one of the racks and pulled down a suit of meticulously embroidered gold satin. "I believe this was made for my brother-in-law, Kelindel. And this"—she went all the way back to the end of the row and removed a strange, shifting dress of green and gold—"my mother-in-law, Queen Terrin." She smiled at Teraeth. "First ruler of the vané."

Teraeth could only blink. There had to be some extraordinary preservation spells at work in this room. Some of these clothes were millennia old. All of it was the oddest, strangest reminder of how old Teraeth *wasn't*. Even if he counted his first life as Emperor Atrin Kandor of Quur, he was still an infant compared to the oldest vané. Compared to someone like Valathea, who'd been there from the start.

"Fuck," Xivan muttered. "What happens if you spill your soup?"

Valathea looked amused. "I would imagine you change your outfit."

Janel shook her head. Her expression wasn't contempt. Far from it. She was hardly one to mock anyone for wearing extravagant decorations; Teraeth had never seen her pass up the opportunity to wear as much jewelry as humanly possible. This meant something to her that he didn't understand. He made a mental note to ask her about it later, when they weren't surrounded by servants waiting to cater to his every whim, eavesdrop on him, and in general hover. The fun thing about being Emperor of Quur had always been that he'd been able to come and go as he pleased. Who could follow him if he wanted to escape? All he had to do was teleport away. If he wanted to wander the countryside in disguise, such was his prerogative. If he wanted to take control of the army, that was his right too. He had never been expected to stay in his palace, sit on his throne, smile, and look pretty. Whereas that was very much what would be required of him here.

It bothered him.

Teraeth suspected Valathea knew that and was having a bit of fun with him. She acted completely unconcerned about anything that wasn't ensuring all the pillows in the royal bedroom were properly fluffed and his wineglass was full.

Until some ineffable milestone passed, at which point Valathea dismissed the servants. The moment the doors shut with only Teraeth, Janel, Xivan, and Valathea inside, her attitude changed.

"These rooms are well warded," Valathea said. "They're as private as any place on the Mother of Trees can be, and I have ensured they are even more so." She tapped the emerald stone Chainbreaker around her neck. "Now why don't you tell me exactly what it is that you have in mind. And frankly, how it would even be possible. Because if Returning Terindel was easy, I'd have done it by now."

Xivan cleared her throat, but didn't say anything.

Janel was staring at Teraeth. With a sinking feeling, he realized she was going to let him have this conversation. Since this was his father they were discussing and he was king here. His idorrá, his speech.[3]

Teraeth exhaled slowly. "We have a plan. It's better that you don't know the details. The plan needs Chainbreaker, and it may need someone who can use Chainbreaker on a lot of people at once."

"Thus, you need your father."

"Or you master Chainbreaker in a hurry," Teraeth said. "But even if you did, it would still be better this way."

"Oh, I agree," Valathea said.

Teraeth shook his head. "Probably not for the reasons you're thinking. Chainbreaker has limitations. One of the largest is that it's not a passive illusion. If you don't know someone's there, then you can't affect them. So if everyone knows you have Chainbreaker, and everyone also knows that your husband—my father—is dead . . ."

Valathea studied him carefully. "You want me to be a decoy."

"We want you to cover for Doc," Janel corrected. "Because you can hide him with illusions that are passive while he concentrates on using Chainbreaker."

"And you want me to be a decoy," Valathea added.

"And we want you to be a decoy," Janel agreed.

Thankfully, Valathea didn't look completely opposed to the idea, but then she frowned. "That all makes a great deal of sense. There's just one problem: I don't understand how you'll ever manage it. Bringing my husband back from the dead, I mean." Her gaze flicked over to Janel. "I know you can travel to the Afterlife, but I wasn't under the impression it was in your power to bring souls *back*."

"That's where I step in," Xivan said. She bit her lip, looking as nervous as Teraeth had ever seen her. She let out a slightly hysterical laugh while shaking

---

[3] Idorrá is a Joratese concept of dominance and protection that roughly summarizes Joratese beliefs about the ideal qualities of a ruler, and also of a man.—T

Which the Joratese view as synonyms. Rulers are always men, even if, technically speaking, they aren't male at all.—S

her head. "Oh, I am so very much not used to this. I don't even know where to start."

"Sometimes it's best to just say it," Valathea said kindly.

Xivan made a face, but clearly didn't disagree. "I'm Thaena."

Valathea stared at her. A flicker of confusion flashed across her expression.

"Apparently, the position is transferable," Teraeth said. "She's the new Goddess of Death."

Valathea's face twisted in shock, and for a second, she looked like she might do . . . something. Perhaps turn invisible using Chainbreaker or wrap Xivan in illusions or perhaps just punch her. "That's not possible."

"Oh, it is," Teraeth said. "Tya and Taja figured out a way."

"It's possible to transfer the conceptual link to a new recipient," Janel quickly qualified. "Which has the end result of transferring the position. Thus, Xivan is now Thaena."

That time, the shock lacked any associated threat of violence, but it was as profound and total as anything Teraeth had ever seen. "And you know this? You know this for a fact?"

"We do," Janel said but didn't explain further.

"My mother knew about it," Teraeth said. "It was a point of contention between Tya, Taja, and herself. They'd created these talismans that could only be triggered if one of the Guardians died. If they were picked up and carried by a person with the right synergies, then it would form a link and transform them, transferring the associated concept and all its powers. Xivan can't use all of Thaena's powers yet, but she's figuring it out. We've seen her Return people."

"Honesty compels me to admit that I didn't have to cross over the Veils when I did it," Xivan said, "which will be a lot harder. The only question is: What would I be bringing him back to? Did you preserve the body?"

That snapped Valathea out of her fugue. "What kind of magically immortal race do you think we are? Of course we preserved the body. It's been under spells since the night–" She didn't finish the sentence. Since the night Terindel was murdered. Since the night Teraeth was crowned. Since the Battle of the Well of Spirals.

Since half the Immortals died.

"Excellent," Janel said. "That will make this much easier."

"Which is handy," Teraeth added, "because it won't be easy at all."

Valathea looked bemused. "Won't it? Can't she just . . . bring him back?"

Xivan shrugged to indicate she had no idea.

"That depends on where my mother put him," Teraeth answered, "and how far along Xivan's powers have grown by that point. The Afterlife is a big place. As big as this world. It would be like looking for a single person in the entire world. What are the odds that you'd just stumble across them?"

When he paused, he realized he'd actually been waiting for Talea to answer. He wasn't the only one, to judge from the look on Xivan's face.

Hopefully, she'd be back soon.

"It's not just Thaena," Janel said. "Talea—you remember Talea?—she's become Taja."

Valathea put a hand to her mouth. The emotions on her face were complex and conflicted.

Teraeth understood. Valathea had to have known all the Immortals for a very long time, and she was Kirpis vané. Taja had *also* been Kirpis vané. That meant Valathea had probably known Taja long before she became one of the Guardians. It had to be difficult to see someone else wearing the name.

"I had assumed that—" Valathea swallowed. "I had hoped that however the Immortals had been resurrected the last time would work again." She gave Xivan an apologetic look. "With all respect, of course. I'm sure you'll both do a lovely job. I can't say I especially wanted to have to continue to deal with Khaemezra, but it's a lot to get used to." She looked at Teraeth with large, dewy violet eyes. "Are the others being . . . replaced?" She paused.

"That's the idea," Janel said. "Talea, Senera, and Thurvishar are off seeing to that right now. Not that Tya or Khored can be replaced—they're still alive." She added, "And I'd like them to stay that way."

"I'm sure they'd appreciate that as well," Valathea replied.

The food and drink had gone untouched until this point, but Valathea remembered its existence, probably to buy herself an excuse to think over things in silence. She nibbled at canapés and drank the wine in long, slow gulps. Everyone else did too, although with more food and less wine.

Finally, she set down her glass on the tabletop with solid finality. "So what is the plan?"

Janel started to wait for Teraeth again, and he waved her on. "No, no. You explain it."

"It's not complicated," Janel admitted. "Once Talea arrives, the three of us—Xivan, Talea, and myself—will enter the Afterlife and begin our search for Terindel. We're hoping that Xivan will be able to track him down using her powers. Or if that doesn't work, then because of Talea, we'll just be lucky."

"I'm going with you," Valathea said.

"No, you're not," Teraeth corrected and, when she glared defiantly at him, added, "Not because we don't want you to but because you can't. I'd be going too if it were that easy. It makes no sense to give Xivan *three* people to Return when she's just figuring out how her powers work. Talea and Janel can travel on their own without outside assistance. You and I can't."

"Talea can pass through the Veil?" Valathea shook her head immediately. "She's a Guardian now. You explained this. I apologize."

"It's a great deal of information to absorb," Janel said, "but even if that weren't true, what do you think are the realistic odds that Relos Var isn't tracking you in some manner? You, of all people? You're lucky enough, if such a term can be used, to be one of the few individuals Relos Var takes seriously. So you can't simply vanish from the Living World without him searching for you."

"Nor can you!" Valathea protested.

"I won't," Janel said, smiling. "I'm doing nothing more than sleeping at night, an activity that I assure you is perfectly normal behavior for me. Relos Var knows where I journey at night, and he knows he can't stop it. He won't waste the energy."

Valathea sighed bitterly, then pulled herself together. "Yes. Very well, but I don't like it," Valathea said.

"Noted," Teraeth replied while swallowing the additional "but I don't care" at the end. Ah, diplomacy. "You and I shall stay here with Kihrin—"

"You mean with Talon," Valathea corrected.

Teraeth and Janel both froze.

Right. The downside to his stepmother being smart was that she also wasn't stupid.

Valathea rolled her eyes at Teraeth and his companions. "Do you honestly expect I wouldn't notice when we have a mimic ward activate and Kihrin's the only one not in the throne room? Oh yes, and then there's the little issue of how Kihrin and Thurvishar are the two who broke Talon out of her imprisonment in the first place. Which I had to cover up for you, by the way." She paused. "I assume you're all aware of her identity and she's operating with your full consent?"

"Yes," Janel said. "It's important that we continue to maintain that ruse as well."

"Ah. Well, word of advice, then: generally speaking, people make eye contact with their lovers."

Janel grimaced.

"I told you that you were going to have to get over that," Teraeth told her.

"If I touch her, I want to throw up," Janel said primly.

"Where *is* Kihrin?" Valathea asked.

Everyone hesitated.

"Busy," Janel said and, when Valathea visibly began to protest, added, "Truly, it's better that you don't know. And it's of critical importance that Relos Var not know. When the time's right, Kihrin will explain."

Valathea studied the woman for a long minute, then turned her attention to Teraeth. "And you're not worried?" she asked.

"Of course I'm worried," Teraeth said, "but that doesn't change anything. He's doing what he has to do. Janel, Talea, and Xivan will do their part. You and I will stay here and make preparations for when they return. We want this to be as easy for Xivan as possible, so we'll need—" He cleared his throat. "We'll need my father's body."

"And you'll get it," Valathea said, "but not tonight. The mimic wards were activated, and that means certain facilities are under lockdown. Because a mimic is involved, any place where bodies are stored is under especially tight security right now. You may be king, but it will look odd if you were to override such protocols."

Teraeth sighed. That wasn't the best news in the world, but it wasn't insurmountable. They could wait a day.

"Tomorrow it is, then." He didn't ask what was the worst that could happen. Teraeth liked to think he could learn from his mistakes.

"Thank you," Valathea said. "I admit that I had grown frustrated I might not be able to make good on my promise to Thaena before—" Her eyes flickered over to Teraeth, and then the rest of that sentence shriveled up and died. "I apologize. That was inappropriate."

Teraeth gave her a thin, tight smile. "No need. You didn't finish the sentence." She hadn't, after all, actually said the words. Not *matricide* or *deicide* or even *before you decapitated her.*

"I didn't have to," Valathea responded.

"If I may be so bold," Xivan said, "the old Thaena can rot in hell. She's not going to be helping us. For obvious reasons."

"I don't want you to get your hopes up, Athea,"[4] Janel said. "If Khaemezra threw Terindel into the Font of Souls, there's nothing we can do to recover him, other than wait for him to be born again."

"She didn't do that," Teraeth said immediately, rarely so certain of anything as he was of that. "My mother wouldn't have done that. She wanted him to suffer, not to be reincarnated. I don't think she'd have given him to the demons either. He's probably locked up in a basement somewhere, forever waiting for her to return so the torture can begin."

"I can't believe I used to like her," Janel said.

Teraeth nodded. "My mother was on occasion a horrible woman." Then he frowned. It would've been easy if that's all she'd ever been, but no. Most of the time she hadn't been a horrible woman. Not at all.

Valathea reached over and put a hand on Teraeth's shoulder, her own expression blank. Teraeth felt his breath grow ragged and cursed the fact that Valathea had quickly made it clear that she'd treat him like her own son and not just her husband's. It manifested in moments like this, when he could tell that she'd almost forgotten herself and hugged him.

Janel stood. "We should find Talon—I mean Kihrin. And then"—her next words looked physically painful for her to speak—"we should allow everyone to grow used to the idea that we're sharing quarters and no doubt hosting orgies nightly." She gave Teraeth a sharp look. "And no, we will most certainly *not* be hosting orgies nightly."

"Now that is a shame." Teraeth grinned sharklike at his lover. "But I suppose if I must, for the good of all."

Valathea stood up. "Barring any further misadventures by your missing companions, I expect we'll move forward with plans tomorrow. This night, on the other hand, act as normally as possible. That means attending dinner."

"Is there a dance after?" Teraeth asked, already knowing the answer and

---

[4] Prior to joining the vané, Valathea's voras name was Athea'val or A'val. Evidently, a great many vané took up the practice of shifting around their given and family names to indicate their new allegiance, and thus Athea'val became Valathea.–T

dreading it with every drop of blood in him. "I won't be attending. Make whatever excuse is necessary."

"But, Teraeth, you love danc—" Janel bit off the word.

She was no doubt considering the last time he'd danced in any capacity: the ritual his mother had controlled him into performing in order to wipe out the Manol vané.

"Yes, of course," Janel said. "No dancing."

# 19. The Freer of All Slaves

**_Tyentso's story_**
**_The Soaring Halls, the Upper Circle of the Capital City of Quur_**
**_After returning to the Capital, lunchtime_**

"Fayrin!" Tyentso shouted when she returned to her suite. No sooner did his name leave her mouth, however, than she knew he was probably in his own rooms, rather than lounging around hers.

That's because of the small, screaming child.

Qoran's youngest daughter, Eledore, was bouncing the toddler on her hip as she (unsuccessfully) tried to convince the boy to calm down. He was having none of it. And that kid's screams could cut glass. Indeed, Tyentso was rather surprised to see that any of the mirrors in the salon remained intact. She stuck a finger in one ear and made a face.

"Where's the boy's mother—?"

She wouldn't have thought it possible, but the boy took one look at Tyentso and managed to scream louder.

Eledore gave Tyentso a desperate look. "I thought Kalindra left to go speak with you. I suppose she's probably with Daddy. Then Nikali started crying, and I swear one of the servants was about to slap him, so I yelled for them all to get out. She was lucky I didn't cut her open gullet to groin." She made shushing sounds to her nephew, whose face was screwed up in an ugly scowl while snot ran down his nose. "But he won't stop. I swear he's not normally like this. Maybe he has an ear infection."

"I'm . . . probably not helping," Tyentso admitted. He was a cute kid (when he wasn't doing the screaming thing). If she had even an ounce of maternal instinct, she'd be fussing over the damn toddler and making all kinds of idiotic cooing noises. But she didn't and she wouldn't, so mostly she just found herself wishing he'd shut the fuck up.

The boy had started babbling something into his aunt's raisigi. Tyentso was pretty sure it was something along the lines of "make the bad woman leave."

Valid. The rest of the Milligreests might not have a damn clue, but that baby knew what was up with the D'Lorus clan.[1]

Tyentso sighed. "Have you seen Fayrin?" She paused. "Do you even know who I'm talking about?"

---

[1] I take exception to that.—T
 In every sense of the word, I imagine, as you're not really a D'Lorus.—S

"Shhhh," Eledore whispered to the little boy, who had quieted less because he was growing calmer than because he was too tired to keep up the tears. Just as Tyentso started to wonder if Eledore had heard her—or if she intended to respond—the young woman glanced up. "I know who you mean. Daddy told him that if he came anywhere near me, he'd make him eat his own gonads."

Tyentso raised her eyebrows. "Has Fayrin been bothering you?"

Eledore shook her head. "No!" She rolled her eyes before adding, "I mean . . . he said I was too young." She looked exasperated by the idea, and more than a little insulted.

Tyentso exhaled. Oh. Of course. She would have had a little "talk" with Fayrin if he'd been making passes at Qoran's youngest. Eledore making passes at him, however, was more excusable—just as long as Fayrin kept his dick in his pants. "He's right. You're too young."

"I'm an adult!"

"No, you're of legal age. That's not the same thing, kid. So have you seen Fayrin?"

Both Eledore's hands were taken up holding the small, sniffling child, but she used her chin to gesture toward the door out to the private garden.

"Thank you." Tyentso paused before leaving. "When you see Kalindra, tell her that I meant what I said earlier."

"Sure?" Whether or not Eledore would remember was anyone's guess.

"Thank you."

Tyentso shouldn't have been too surprised. While the palace had always been maintained, someone had taken special pains to care for the small, intricate garden that, theoretically, was meant for the emperor. Fayrin seemed inordinately fond of the place, and she suspected he was the one responsible for its upkeep.

Given that this was one of the few places in the entire palace—including her bedroom—where one might hope to pass a few minutes undisturbed, it was rapidly turning into one of her favorite places too.

She was surprised to see the young man meditating cross-legged under the branches of a cherry tree. Then she noticed several wine bottles next to him.

"Did you start drinking the moment I left?" Tyentso asked.

He opened his eyes and slowly blinked at her. "You weren't here to tell me no. Later on, I plan on inviting some of the girls over too."

Tyentso rolled her eyes. People had been so fond of joking that Fayrin had once turned the Soaring Halls into a brothel that Tyentso had assumed it couldn't possibly be true.

It was.

In theory, because he knew how much it scandalized the other members of the High Council. At least, that was Fayrin's official story. Tyentso had her own theories, mostly involving how she suspected that every single one of Fayrin's "whores" was also a world-class spy.

He wasn't hosting orgies. He was debriefing agents.

"Whatever," Tyentso said. "I don't care."

Fayrin gave her an odd look she couldn't decipher. She wasn't in the mood to try to figure it out.

Tyentso tossed a rolled-up sheet of paper at him. "Sober up, and hold off on calling in your velvets. I need you to deliver a new proclamation to the High Council."

He squinted as he unrolled the piece of paper and began to read. She saw the moment exactly when what he was reading sank in. The moment when a shiver burned through the alcohol in his veins and left him very sober indeed.

Fayrin stared at her, open-mouthed. "You can't be serious."

"Serious as death."

He stood up, wobbled a little as gravity tried to trick him, and shot his best glare her way. "You can't–" He shook his head. "They'll never agree to this. Ever. You can't just wave a hand and make *slavery illegal*."

Tyentso thought about it for a moment. "Why not? Isn't that how most laws happen? Someone declares it so, and enough people go along with it?"

"No, there's a council. We vote. I should know: letting people buy my vote is my main source of income."

"You vote because the emperors stopped enforcing their will after Kandor marched off to an early grave in the Manol. Prior to that, the council only made laws when the emperor was too busy waging wars to be bothered. Well, congratulations: I'm bothering."

Fayrin clenched his fists in exasperation. "Don't enough people want to kill you?"

"All the people who would want to kill me because of *this* already want me dead," she said. "Keep reading, by the way. A little ways down, I declare worshipping Murad illegal too."

Fayrin quickly examined the sheet of paper again as if he expected she might have just been joking. She wasn't. His eyes widened, and he looked back up at her again. "The council will *never* approve this."

She laughed and tapped Fayrin's cheek. "You keep assuming I give a fuck what the council does or doesn't approve. But don't worry: right now, they'll do anything I say and fight each other for the privilege of being the first to do so. Honestly, I'm impressed as hell with your willpower." She smoothed a hand over the back of her cloudcurls. "It has to happen, Fayrin. Never mind that it's the right thing. Turns out it's the tactically smart thing too—remove the threat of slavery, the slaves themselves, and a whole lot of prayers to Murad vanish. Nobody will have any reason to light candles in that bastard's name."

"I don't understand why that matters."

Tyentso sighed. "Murad. The god-king? Well, he's either helping Havar or he *is* Havar, and either way, cutting him off from his power base is for the best. But I'll never be able to stop people from leaving out their little offerings to Murad unless I remove the reason they do it—and a lot more of those reasons have to do with slavery than justice."

"Havar D'Aramarin is . . . Murad?" His stare was glassy-eyed. Maybe he hadn't completely sobered up yet.

"Yes, that's what I said." She wondered if she was going to have to use magic to purge the alcohol from him. This would really go more easily if he didn't look drunk while relaying her orders.

"Fuck."

"Whereas that's *not* what I said, but I agree with the sentiment." Tyentso pointed at the scroll. "Give that to the council. Let them know this is how it's going to be. I've already sent copies to all the dukes and to my generals, so this is happening whether they like it or not. Once you're done, you can party as much as you like."

"Wait. You want me—" He took a deep breath. "I'm not coming with you to Khorvesh?"

"No. I want you to stay here, do damage control, and twist a few arms if you have to. It'll be fine. I'm taking Caerowan with me." When Fayrin barely concealed his grimace in response, Tyentso said, "Would you rather I left him here and took you instead?"

"No, no! By all means, let the toady little monk boy go on an adventure. His status reports are more legible than mine, and he won't complain about the bad food. Just don't . . ." His face twisted. "Whatever you do, don't give him any authority."

Tyentso stared. "He's a *Voice of the Council.*"

"He's a Devoran priest who has lived his entire life crossing off prophecy quatrains like they're a to-do list. He doesn't make decisions based on logic or reason but on bad poetry." Fayrin wrinkled his nose. "I vastly prefer men who are greedy or power-hungry or think with their dicks. Those are motivations I can work with. Caerowan's only real loyalty is to the fickleness of vague fortune-telling."

"Careful, Fayrin, or I might forget you're a louche rake who only cares about the softness of his bedsheets."

He smirked at her and grabbed one of the wine bottles, examining it to see how much was left. "I have no idea what you mean. My life's ambitions have never been anything other than whores and wine. Do you want me to blackmail any council members if it proves necessary?"

"I doubt it will be, but yes." She gave him a twisted smile. "And let me know how everyone behaves while I'm gone."

It would be an interesting test to see if whatever was causing this weird change in everyone's behavior was based on location or based on *her* location. She honestly wasn't sure which one was worse.

"Don't do anything I wouldn't do," Fayrin told her.

*Hilarious.*

# 20. Evacuations

*Kalindra's story*
**The Soaring Halls, the Upper Circle of the Capital City of Quur**
*Around the same time Tyentso was shocking Fayrin*

Qoran Milligreest had agreed that leaving the city was a good idea. He'd been less helpful on how to make that happen when every mage who could open a gate was being sent down to Khorvesh with the empress.

That meant he didn't know about Caless. Unfortunately, Kalindra didn't feel like explaining how she knew without upsetting the god-queen. She'd have to confess that she knew Sheloran and Galen and use that connection to try to convince the woman. Honestly, it sounded like so much work. And all that was assuming that Caless hadn't already been drafted to help Tyentso move the army.

Fortunately, that wasn't her only resource.

"Jarith? Jarith, are you here?" she whispered once she was alone again.

Kalindra wasn't sure if he was there, wasn't sure if he could hear her. But she was very sure that she didn't want to stay in the Capital. Jarith had been right: something was wrong here.

Jarith's mother, Jira, whom he'd always taken after in terms of calm, unflappable temper, had spent a full thirty minutes screaming at her daughter Eledore, who'd been more than happy to return the favor. Eledore had wanted to stay in Khorvesh and fight off the morgage. Jira had wanted to keep her only remaining child safe. Both were convinced the other was being unreasonable. Eledore went so far as to call her mother a traitor.

They were starting to feel like entirely different people. Darker, angrier people.

"Jarith, please answer," Kalindra whispered.

She felt his presence—a darkness draping over her soul—a moment before the shadows thickened and Jarith re-formed. His attempt wasn't perfect—his hair tended to fade into smoke, and dark eddies whirled around his legs—but it was close enough.

He put his hands around her and kissed her cheeks, then her forehead. **I'm here.**

"I need you to pass a message to Thurvishar," Kalindra said. "We can't stay here, but there isn't anyone here who can open a portal to take us elsewhere." She paused. "I tried asking for Tyentso again, but apparently requesting a personal meeting with the empress is rude. I know Lessoral D'Talus can do it, but that would mean admitting I know she's Caless . . ."

**You're right to want to leave. It's not safe.** He paused. **Where will you go?**

"The Academy at Alavel," Kalindra said. "It's a long way away from any front, and it's filled with wizards. Probably as safe as it gets."

He didn't smile, but something in his eyes shifted. It made him look pleased. He probably was.

Kalindra hated the idea that she was a distraction, a source of worry. She wanted to be able to do more to help . . .

Who knew? Maybe she'd find some way to help at the school.

**I'll return with Thurvishar.**

Which he must have, because not a half hour later, there was a knock at the suite door. When Eledore went to answer it, Thurvishar D'Lorus was standing there.

"Hello," Thurvishar said. "May I come in?"

Eledore blinked. "You? What the hell are *you* doing here?"

"Eledore, who is it?" Jira called out.

"It's that jerk who—" *Who Jarith challenged to a duel*, she probably meant to say, but she choked on the words. "What do you *want*?" Eledore finished.

"Thurvishar?" Kalindra called out. "Eledore, let him in. He's here to see me."

Thurvishar gently nudged the door open with his foot.

Eledore's scowl deepened. "What do you want?" Her glance back at the wizard was scathing. "And how are you even still alive? I thought all you high lords died."

Jira scowled at her daughter. "Don't talk to people like that! What's wrong with you? And if he's still alive, there's a good reason." She glanced back over her shoulder at Kalindra. "There had better be a good reason."

"I'm only here for a few minutes," Thurvishar said calmly, looking not even slightly bothered by the insults. "Kalindra, you wanted a gate opened to Alavel. Do you have a place to stay once you're there?"

"I thought we'd find an inn," Kalindra said with a shrug. She moved over to where Nikali was coloring on the marble tile with pieces of chalk.

Jira turned to her with a visibly hurt expression. "You're not staying?"

"*We're* not staying," Kalindra corrected. "None of us are. Get your belongings. That goes for you too, Eledore. We'll all be safer in Kirpis."

"I'm not just leaving—" Jira started to protest.

Kalindra cut her off. "It was the empress's idea. She wants us someplace safe."

That drew Jira short.

Although Kalindra had only been at the palace for six hours or so, she hadn't missed the fact that everyone suddenly seemed to live or die by the empress's word. Which was really fucking odd considering how little most Quuros normally cared about a largely absent position that didn't mean a damn thing in terms of their everyday lives. And that was when the emperors had all been men. A woman in that position? Kalindra would have expected scorn and mockery.

Not this weird devotion.

Jira turned her head. "Eledore, gather your things."

"Mom! If he can take us to Kirpis, he can take us back to Khorvesh!" She all but stomped a foot in frustration.

"Grab your things, you spoiled child, or we'll leave without them," Jira growled.

"I don't want—"

"Eledore." Kalindra gave the girl a flat look. "Obey your mother now."

The girl sullenly crossed her arms over her chest before disappearing into one of the back rooms in a huff.

Thurvishar didn't comment. Kalindra still had the feeling he was counting the seconds until they left.

Kalindra knelt beside Nikali. "Hey, little lion. It's time to go."

He smashed the chalk against the floor. "No! No, I don't want—"

She picked him up and held him as he began screaming. Kalindra shot Thurvishar a desperate, panicked look.

"I see . . . ," he said. He regarded the boy with those somber too-dark D'Lorus eyes. Tyentso's eyes, although Kalindra supposed that made sense since she'd once belonged to House D'Lorus too. "Shhh," Thurvishar said gently to Nikali.

Nikali stopped crying immediately and stared at the wizard with wide-eyed awe.

Kalindra allowed herself the briefest moment to wonder if Thurvishar would ever consider babysitting.[1]

"I think leaving would be an excellent idea," Thurvishar continued. "As I was about to say, if you need a place to stay, House D'Lorus keeps a villa on the campus grounds. It's unoccupied at the moment and should be safe enough." He paused thoughtfully. "As long as you stay out of the attic. Or the basement."

"Is that all?"

He pondered that. "Or the conservatory. Or anything in the library that's in a case or behind a lock."

Kalindra raised her eyebrows. "Shall I assume the demon-summoning chamber is forbidden, then?"

"I already said the basement's off-limits," Thurvishar replied.

"What a delightful childhood you must have had," Kalindra commented dryly.

Thurvishar shrugged. "I try not to think about it."

"Um, Kalindra dear?" Jira stared at her with a visibly worried expression. "How do you know Lord D'Lorus?" She managed to convey volumes of concern in those two questions.

"We met on Devors," Kalindra said, which happened to be the truth. "Nikali

[1] No.–T

and I wouldn't be alive right now if it wasn't for him and some of his friends."
She hefted Nikali to a hip while the little boy attempted to stuff most of his
shirt into his mouth. Thurvishar picked up Kalindra's bags without being
asked, which was nice of him. A few minutes later, Eledore came out with a
bag of her own, still sulking.

Kalindra noticed that Jira hadn't packed. "You don't need your things?"

The older woman walked over to a cabinet and pulled out a satchel before
slinging it over her shoulder. "I always keep a bag packed," she replied, ad-
justing the sword hanging from her belt.

"Right," Kalindra said, blinking. "Good practice."

"Shall we, then?" Thurvishar waited politely for them all to agree before
he magically opened a portal.

# 21. A TOUCH OF DARKNESS

*Tyentso's story*
**The Soaring Halls, the Upper Circle of the Capital City of Quur**
**One hour later**

Of all the wizards who might once have been reliably expected to open a magical gate and keep it open while an army poured through, less than a half-dozen people remained. Two of those people were Varik and Lessoral D'Talus, worth dozens of wizards all on their own.

Tyentso was the last one on the staging grounds. Everyone else waited on her.

She looked out over the assembled troops and felt a profound sense of disbelief. What the hell was she even doing there? Defending the empire? Saving it? If Kihrin had told her four months previously that she'd end up as Emperor of Quur, she'd have laughed and then told him to go fuck himself. It was a ridiculous notion.

Since when had she ever given a damn about Quur?

More worrying still was the fanatical gleam she saw in every eye. She wasn't half so naïve as to think it had anything to do with her own personal charm. She had no personal charm. She never had. This was something else.

She didn't waste time on speeches. Tyentso suspected they wouldn't have mattered, in any event. These people were already operating on a level of fervent devotion that she neither understood nor deserved.

But as Tyentso looked over the assembled soldiers and began to give the order to start opening gates, a flash of movement from a palace window caught her attention. A corner-of-the-eye glimpse, quick enough that exactly what she'd seen sank in only after her gaze had already slid past.

*Gadrith* had been watching her from the window.

She blinked and snapped her attention back to that position. The window was empty.

"I'll be right back," she told Qoran and teleported.

She appeared again in the hallway that led to that same window. Nothing. There was no one there. No footsteps echoed as someone retreated. The corridor was deserted.

Tyentso felt a chill.

Gadrith was dead. She *knew* Gadrith was dead. So she was seeing things. Certainly possible. No one could argue that she hadn't been under more than a little stress.

Tyentso glanced back down the hallway. Under normal circumstances, she might not have been certain of her location. The Crown and Scepter gave her a perfect knowledge of the entire palace layout; not only did Tyentso know exactly where she was, but she knew that only three doors and two flights of stairs separated the hallways she stood from her private chambers.

She bent down and picked up a single black hair.

It meant nothing. Lots of people had black hair. *Most* people had black hair.

She held the hair up to the light and cast a minor spell—one known in the inner circles of the Royal Houses. One that she knew because she had, after all, been a lord heir's wife.

The hair caught fire and flared black before fading.

She stared. Whoever had owned this hair was a blood relative of the D'Lorus line As far as she knew, there was only one living person who qualified: herself. She didn't have black hair.

Tyentso lowered a shaking hand. So it hadn't been her imagination: she'd seen something. But had she seen *her father*?

Unlikely. But perhaps there was an Ogenra out there who'd escaped Gadrith's attention, who'd avoided being claimed. Someone that High Lord Cedric had sequestered away, perhaps.

It couldn't be Gadrith D'Lorus.

It just couldn't.

She teleported back to the staging ground and began the process of transferring troops down to Khorvesh.

# 22. A PALE IMITATION

### *Janel's story*
### *The Mother of Trees, the Manol*
### *The same day as their arrival, afternoon*

"Why would I have thought they'd added Talon to the security wards?" Talon complained. "The vané were going to strip her of her body in a couple of weeks, put her in some other, non-shape-changing form. They shouldn't have needed to add her to the wards—it was about to be redundant!"

Janel could only assume Talon referred to herself in the third person because she still looked like Kihrin. Janel hated it, but there wasn't anything to be done about it. Talon had come back to them a few hours after Teraeth had ordered the wards lowered, explaining how she'd had to tell Khaeriel and Therin at least part of what was going on in order to convince them not to kill her.

Janel was loath to admit Talon had done as well as could be managed under the circumstances. None of them had considered that Talon might trigger the wards. It just hadn't factored into their plans. It had been risky, but not irreparably so—all of Relos Var's favorite ways of scrying on his enemies were currently working for their side.[1]

An upset Talea had returned from the Capital, at which point she and Xivan had retired to their own rooms. That left Teraeth, "Kihrin," and Janel to likewise return to the king's chambers to sleep. An idea that didn't seem to bother Teraeth or Talon in the slightest.

It bothered Janel a great deal.

So she paced, and the other two readied for bed.

"I just wish you hadn't told Khaeriel that Janel is pregnant," Teraeth said.

Janel's mouth twisted. She had a feeling she knew why Teraeth was so concerned, and it was a thought as paranoid as it was dark. That Khaeriel might try to get rid of any competing children in her quest to make sure that Kihrin married Teraeth and eventually had an heir between them.[2] At some point Khaeriel had gotten it into her head that this was the perfect solution to all the issues of succession haunting the united Kirpis and Manol vané people, and nothing Teraeth had said since had seemed to dissuade her.

---

[1] Unfortunately, this was an incorrect assumption.—T
[2] This would only be possible if Teraeth decided to follow in the footsteps of his voramer maternal line, who are born male and become female as they age. He's shown no inclination toward this. By which I mean he's flatly refused to even consider it. Maybe Khaeriel shouldn't have assumed.—S

Janel could only hope that Khaeriel remembered that this was Khaeriel's grandchild as well. Unfortunately, Janel couldn't exactly explain that it was also the *only* child Khaeriel's biological son would ever have.

And anyway, the pregnancy was far too early for such assumptions. Any number of things could go wrong. Janel lived a dangerous life and had no intention of taking it easy when the fate of the whole world was at stake. It would be a miracle if she somehow managed to make it through all this without miscarrying.

Janel realized she was tapping her fingers against her stomach and forced herself to stop.

"I had to," Talon said. "Sorry. She was coming uncomfortably close to guessing too much, and if that had happened, all the 'this is what Kihrin wants' in the whole world wouldn't have been enough to stop her from tearing Talon into tiny little itty-bitty pieces. And Therin would have helped." Talon grinned. "A real bonding moment for them, I'm sure."

"We should stop talking about this," Janel said. "We can't assume there's no one listening." She turned toward the shape-changed mimic.

"Kihrin" paused with his misha pulled halfway over his head. The dark bronze skin of his back was broken up by a horrifying crisscrossed network of shiny raised lines—old and healed, but still an obvious reminder of the terrible things human beings were willing to do to each other.

Janel froze. How many times had she seen Kihrin without clothes? How many times had she seen his back? In all their travels together? Possibly at the Quarry, but if so she'd been in too much of a drugged daze to understand or remember. She'd have accused Talon of having made up this detail, but she knew that was nonsense. If Talon wore whip scars while pretending to be Kihrin, it could only be because Kihrin had worn them first.

Teraeth must have noticed her reaction, must have known what caused it. "He was trapped in the rowing galley of a slave ship for three months, Janel," Teraeth explained in a voice that managed to be both soft and furious. "When he was sixteen." He turned to Talon. "Go on, tell her *why* you ended up on a slave ship."[3]

Talon's lips pressed into a thin line of annoyance. "Does it matter?"

Teraeth's bitter sarcasm gave Janel some idea of what the answer had to be. Janel inhaled deeply, tried to find a sense of internal equilibrium, and then moved quickly toward Kihrin, grabbing him by the shoulders and shoving him up against one of the pillars in the room. "Let me guess," Janel whispered. "Talon had something to do with it."[4]

"That slave ship was better than what would have happened if I'd stayed," Talon said, because damn if she wasn't a professional. She wasn't breaking character for *anything*. "Darzin hadn't planned on letting me live, you know."

Janel hated this. She hated everything about this. She logically knew it was

---

[3] Wait. Janel never read your book?—S

    When would she have had time?—T

[4] Talon had everything to do with it.—T

Talon, but all her senses told her that this was Kihrin. Shirtless, close enough to smell the scent of his soap and his skin, close enough to see the Manol humidity bead up like tiny jewels sliding down the side of his neck.

Talon strained forward against her hold and whispered, "I know this is difficult. This sucks and I'm sorry. I would do this differently if I could."

Talon sounded just like Kihrin. It was even something Kihrin would say, said the way he would have said it. Staring into those blue eyes, it was impossible not to feel that it *was* Kihrin. Even though she knew the truth. Even though she was aware of the full extent of the deception.

Janel pulled Talon's head down to hers and kissed her false Kihrin. She held nothing back, let all of her frustration, anger, and passion show in the clash of tongues and teeth. She felt Kihrin's lips against hers, soft and warm, the taste of him in her mouth, the beat of his heart hammering away next to hers. His body was slick and hot against her skin; it would have been so easy to just pretend.

But no. That wasn't true. In point of fact, it was utterly impossible to pretend.

Janel heard movement behind her as Teraeth approached, although to what purpose was less clear.

It was a fantastic kiss.

But it wasn't Kihrin. No amount of identical body, perfect acting, and all the memories a mimic could steal made up for the fact that it wasn't Kihrin. She felt it; she tasted it; the knowledge of it singed her like sparks from a forge. Kihrin's souls weren't there, and the rest of this was nothing but a pretty shell, housing someone she didn't love at all.

Janel released Talon and backed away. She felt strangely better, as though she had just plunged a burned hand into a bucket of ice water. Janel raised shaking fingers up to the beaded braids of her laevos. Janel felt wrung out, scraped over rocks. Clean, but worn thinner too.

"Thank you," she murmured. "That helped."

Talon didn't seem particularly upset. She grinned impishly at Janel and spread her hands. "You know I'm here for whatever you need."

Janel scoffed. "I need for this all to be over, but I have my doubts you can pull that off any faster than you're already trying."

Teraeth touched her arm. "Are you going to be all right?" He started to slide his arm around her waist and gave her a hurt look when she slipped away from him.

Janel smiled fondly at him. What a loaded question that was. Was she going to be all right? But Janel knew he meant on a much more immediate level. Was she going to be okay right now. Was she going to be okay as long as they had to continue this horrible charade.

Janel took Teraeth's hand and kissed each finger in turn. "I'll be fine. And it's not you. I just need a little time to myself. I'm going to go for a walk." When Teraeth started to protest, she added, "We're in the palace. I'm not naïve enough to say nothing could happen here, but it's likely the safest we can manage. I'll be back in time for Talea and Xivan, don't worry."

Teraeth pulled her to him and kissed her forehead. She didn't fight it this time; it was clearly meant as a way of saying goodbye and not an attempt to keep her by his side.

Janel kissed him back on the mouth and then left.

## 23. STEP FIVE: WHEN NECESSARY, CONSULT EXPERTS

*Kihrin's story*
*Grizzst's Tower*
*Afternoon*

Finding Thurvishar was easier said than done. Not because Thurvishar was difficult to find but because, well, Vol Karoth.

I was still running around as a man-size hole cut into the fabric of reality, picking up random stones and trying with all my might not to disintegrate them. Hardly ideal for a clandestine meeting with one's coconspirators.

Fun fact: I was also a naked man-size hole cut into the fabric of reality, although I doubt anyone who met me would notice what with all the screaming and running away. I had zero desire to roam around letting it all fly free, but I didn't have a choice; see once again the part where I kept disintegrating anything I touched, which included clothing. If hunger got the better of me or I became distracted, everything within a few dozen feet paid the cost.

Which meant I ideally needed to find Thurvishar without being closer than a few dozen feet to the man. Even better, without being closer than a few dozen miles.

This is where that whole mental projection business really came into its own. The trick of it was making sure that the mental projection on the other side didn't also start destroying everything around it (which I already knew I was perfectly capable of doing) and also that said projection looked like something other than a big, naked silhouette.

That last part took the most practice. Teraeth would have been so much better at this. Or his father, Doc. Alas, neither of them had been cursed millennia ago to exist as perpetually hungry incarnations of the void, so I was forced to deal with what I had.

I practiced. Made sure I could hold up my end of a conversation without accidental mass murders. Then I projected an image to Grizzst's Tower on Rainbow Lake. It was midday in Eamithon, a gentle lullaby of a day where nothing terrible could ever happen and nothing ever hurt. The titular lake sparkled in the sun, flashes of feldspar shimmering underneath crystal waters. The wind rustled through a bamboo forest on the shore, although an ugly wound of trampled greenery spoke of recent violence.[1]

I could see and hear, but not smell or touch. The lack of sense created a disconnected feeling, like I was dreaming.

Senera was pinning pieces of paper to a large map on one of the first floor walls.

I cleared my throat from just inside the doorway I would have entered had I'd been physically present.

She jumped, which I'd expected. What I hadn't expected was the look of absolute horror that scuttled across her face before a blank expression slammed down over it. "Who are you?"

I cocked my head. "What do you think–?" I glanced down at myself.

All that practice. I'd still shown up looking like S'arric.

"Ah," I said. "Let me fix this." I shifted the illusion to look like myself again. That had been a sloppy mistake. There was always a chance that Relos Var or one of his people might notice me in two places at once. Awkward, and it would raise questions.

But not nearly the questions that would be raised if someone saw me who recognized *S'arric*.

Senera deflated as my appearance changed, a heavy sigh of relief escaping her. "Veils. Don't do that. You scared the hell out of me."

I grimaced. "Sorry about that."

Senera rubbed the back of her neck. "I didn't realize you two looked so much alike."

That made me pause.

She was right. Rev'arric and S'arric looked *a lot* alike–if one ignored the way we wore our hair and dressed and spoke and virtually everything about our personalities. When we'd been kids, we were often mistaken for twins by someone who'd only seen us from afar. (No one who knew us made that mistake. Attitude was everything.) But it had been a long, long time since Relos Var had run around looking like Rev'arric. If my brother had one weakness above all others, it was his need to make sure everyone knew he was the smartest man around–and being exceedingly pretty didn't help that goal.

I squinted. "How do you know what Relos Var really looks like?"

A faint blush rose on her skin. "One time, I used the Name of All Things and drew a portrait of him. I never told him that I'd done it. I didn't think he'd have approved."[2]

"I think you're right." I purposefully ignored the implications about Senera's feelings for Relos Var. My time at the Lighthouse at Shadrag Gor had

---

[1] I believe that would be from when Gorokai decided to leave Rainbow Lake and attack the Temple of Light in order to steal Skyfire.–S

[2] If the Name of All Things can't "see" before its own creation, how was it able to show you what Relos Var really looked like?–T

Because when Grizzst merged Relos Var and Cynosure, the human shape he assumed was his birth form. And that took place after the Cornerstones were created.–S confirmed that their relationship had been more emotionally convoluted than "mentor figure" in spite of Senera's insistence that she had no interest in romantic relationships.

I was going to go with "tangled mess" as the most appropriate descriptor.[3]

I avoided touching anything. Between Thurvishar and Senera, they'd done a commendable job of organizing the place. Given another five years or so, I imagined it might even be possible to find something one needed in a timely manner.

"Is Thurvishar here?" I asked her.

"Yes," Senera said. "You're not, though, are you? Really here, I mean."

I grinned. "Be honest: Was your first clue the fact that you're still alive to ask me that question?"

"That's a rather big clue, yes." She dug a knuckle into her temple. "How's godhood treating you?"

"Unlimited power turns out to be a lot more limiting than I'd expected. Someone should really revise the god-king tales to reflect that."

"I'll take your word for it." Senera stretched her fingers out in front of her and wriggled them as if imagining casting a spell. "Let me tell Thurvishar you're here—"

"No need." Thurvishar opened the doorway from the stairs leading to one of the lower levels of the tower. "Kihrin? Why aren't you down in the Manol?" He asked the question like an accusation. Thurvishar didn't look happy to see me.

I understood. If I was really Talon, then I'd departed precipitously from the plan. And if I was really me, then I'd torn the plan to shreds and lit it on fire.[4] I could hardly blame the man for being upset. As much as I knew that our plans needed to stay flexible (on account of how much of it I was making up as I went along), I also knew Thurvishar was less comfortable with that idea.

I bet Thurvishar couldn't sense me telepathically either, which had to be tripping every warning bell the wizard had.

"Something came up," I said and purposefully didn't grin as his expression darkened. "And yes, it's really me. But I figured out what demons are."

Thurvishar shared a look with Senera. "Really you? Really you, jeopardizing the whole plan, you mean?"

"Oh, if Relos Var's eavesdropping on us, we're already fucked," I said. "Anyway, this is more important."

"And this is why I haven't been sleeping well," Senera said. "What do you mean, 'what demons are'? We already know that."

"Do we." Thurvishar's expression turned contemplative, pensive. Also, still very annoyed. Thurvishar was a man who believed in order, and I was messing

---

[3] That is sadly accurate. At least I have the consolation that Relos Var never once attempted to exploit our relationship in that particular regard.—S

Oh no. He exploited your relationship as much as possible, in unhealthy, unethical ways. He just didn't try to have sex with you.—T

[4] No, surely not. Kihrin would never do that.—S

Unless he had a good reason. For example, because reality exists.—T

with it. "Perhaps you should first let us know why this is so important you had to drop everything else and jeopardize all our plans to come tell us?"

"They're humans." I raised a hand as Senera opened her mouth to object. "They're the humans we left behind when we migrated from our old universe to this one. Except they evolved. They shed their bodies and devoured . . . everything. And then they followed us here."

The two wizards stared at me.

"That . . ." Senera blinked. "That is interesting. And horrible. But could you please get to why we care right now?"

"How do you know this?" Thurvishar pressed.

"I found out from the demons," I answered. "And no, they didn't willingly give up the information. But here's where I need your opinion, because of all of us, I think we are the three who know Relos Var best. Do you think he's figured this out?"

Senera squinted at me. "Why?"

"Because do you really think that Var's plans don't include getting rid of the demons? He can't just seal off the Wound as long as the demons are still here. They might be capable of ripping open another hole, which will put us right back where we started. He has to eliminate them."

They both stared at me. They weren't telling me that I was wrong, they clearly just didn't have a clue why it was important. Or rather, why we shouldn't be cheering the bastard on, at least about this one thing.

"Okay, let me try this a different way," I said. "Demons are amalgams of all the souls that they've eaten. But we assumed, everyone assumed, that the first demons who came here were singular entities. Each demon a single soul, at least until they declared it dinnertime on the human race and started adding on to themselves like snowballs rolling down a hill. With me so far?"

"Don't be condescending," Senera snapped.

"I'll take that as a yes," I said. "Well, we were wrong. That assumption was . . . okay . . . maybe *incorrect* is the wrong term, but incomplete. The demons who invaded were never individuals. It would be like looking at a mosaic on a wall and saying, 'Yes, that is a single piece of art.' Which yes, sure. That picture is a single thing. But it's also made up of thousands of individual bits of tile, and each of those tiles is also an individual piece. This idea of unity was an illusion; each of those invading demons was never a single soul at all. And why this is important is because of the Font of Souls."

I knew they didn't yet understand, but they seemed willing to listen, so I continued. "From the start, we had a problem with what to do with a demon once we defeated one. Tossing them into the Nythrawl Wound meant nothing—they'd just come back through. But eventually, we realized that we could get rid of a demon by throwing them into the Font of Souls. It was the perfect solution. Demons would be trapped in the Font forever, because they are spiritual beings with no physical counterparts in the Living World to reincarnate into. As far as we've ever been able to tell, the Font exists to channel souls from the Afterlife to reincarnate in the Living World. And it works along racial lines! Daughters of Laaka are reincarnated as Daughters of Laaka. Elephants only reincarnate as elephants. Humans *only* reincarnate as humans . . ."

"But you just said demons used to be . . ." Senera's eyes widened.

Thurvishar looked like he'd just eaten a bug.

"Human. Exactly right. Which means demons haven't been staying inside the Font after all. They've been reincarnating as humans, because they *do* have physical counterparts. Us. But—" I raised a finger. "It gets worse."

"*How?*" Senera growled.

"Because people aren't being born *demons*," I explained. "If a demonic soul—an entirely spiritual entity that doesn't require a physical body in any way—was shoved into a newborn baby's body, it would stay there for about two seconds and then would likely kill everyone in the room, starting with the mother. That doesn't happen. And the only reasonable explanation that I can come up with for why that doesn't happen is that the Font of Souls is breaking every demon down to component parts. Smashing the mosaics so each individual tile can . . . well . . . I admit I lose the metaphor here, but my point is that not only is it likely that some humans are in fact reincarnated demons, but . . . it's probably a large number." I shook my head. "I'm not even sure that the Font has ever created human souls at all. I want to talk to Galava about this, and I'm annoyed that I can't."

Thurvishar started to nod. I saw the moment the realization hit him, when his eyes widened in horror. "You think Relos Var is going to use a sympathetic magic ritual to target the demons." It wasn't a question.

"What can I say? My brother loves his rituals. Except I'm wondering what the odds are that sympathetically targeting 'demon' souls won't also get all the souls that have been reborn as normal human beings since."

"How many—?" Senera's voice cracked. She started over. "Let's assume for the moment that you're right. This universe isn't responsible for creating any human souls. That everything we have, we either brought with us or have unwittingly recycled from demons. That would make every single soul—" She covered her mouth with a hand, and I honestly wondered if she might be sick. "Founders' souls make star tears when they're tsali'd. Do you have any idea how few souls form a star tear? The vast majority don't by a large percentage." Senera turned to Thurvishar. "Gadrith was constantly doing that to people. How often did you see a star tear?"

"Almost never," Thurvishar said numbly. He shook his head as if to wake himself. "Maybe once or twice? It was rare."

Senera swallowed as she returned her attention to me. "You're right, of course. Relos Var is planning to do this. Which I didn't think was a problem. Why would I? Do you realize how many people would die?"

"Oh yes," I said. "Almost everyone. *Now* do you understand why this is important?"

## 24. BORDER TOWN

*Jarith's story*
**The imperial camp near Stonegate Pass**
*After Tyentso left the Capital City*

When Jarith found the Empress of Quur, she was in the middle of leaving the Capital, yelling orders at soldiers, secretaries, and councillors. The woman was so sharp in tone it seemed impossible that people wouldn't leave her presence bleeding. Jarith felt the tension vibrating off everyone who came into her presence. She looked the same as when Jarith had seen her last—the center of a swirling tornado of magical energy and furious negative emotions.

But at least her ability to sense his demonic nature seemed to be limited to her ability to physically see him. As long as he remained invisible, she didn't know he was there. Still, he had the impression that if she really concentrated on an area, she'd sense him. Thus his existence became an extended game of ducking behind people, columns, and furniture, trying to stay out of the woman's direct line of sight. In theory, she knew about him. In theory, Kihrin had filled her in. In reality?

Caution would be prudent.

Jarith's father, Qoran, traveled with her. The man was uneasy, but the high general stoically kept a straight face and followed her every order. Everyone did. Jarith wondered if any of them stopped and wondered at how the empress was suddenly commanding such complete and total loyalty.

Seeing the troops gathered was a truly awe-inspiring sight; Jarith would have been moved had this happened only a few months earlier. It was all the more extraordinary because it was illegal. The imperial army had its command quarters stationed in the Upper Circle, but armies were not allowed to gather there. Clearly, no one had explained that to Empress Tyentso, or if they had, she'd ignored them. Now there were thousands of men gathered in neat rows, equipment slung and ready to travel by gate to their next destination—Khorvesh.

The soldiers all had a uniformity to them that was odd even for Quuros soldiers, normally renowned for the consistency of their training. It wasn't their appearance but rather their expressions—identical sneers lined every face for as far as Jarith could see. All of them radiated that same anger and rage, the same focus and dedication to their goals.

These were thousands of men who'd throw their lives away if Tyentso so much as snapped her fingers, and given all the challenges since she'd gained the Crown, Jarith didn't think she'd refuse such an opportunity.

He followed the column of men through a portal, noting as he did that clearly not all the wizards capable of opening portals had gone with Havar D'Aramarin when he'd left to splinter off his own segment of the empire. Which was handy, because nobody wanted the long march through hot desert that would have otherwise been required to reach Stonegate Pass.

When they arrived, the troops made camp outside the town, and Tyentso called a meeting.

"Do we have intelligence on the nearest troop movements?" she asked the team of generals gathered in her tent.

Blank stares met her question.

"Troop movements?" Qoran Milligreest asked. "You mean the morgage?"

Tyentso rolled her eyes. "Of course I mean the morgage. Do you think Vol Karoth suddenly has troops?"

"I'm not sure I'd claim the morgage do either," one of the other men muttered. He was new, someone who'd been stationed here at Stonegate rather than someone who'd come in through the gate with the others.

Tyentso turned to him. "What was that?" Her voice had a warning edge to it.

The man cleared his throat and stood taller. "Your Majesty, the morgage are here, it's true, but they're hardly invading."

Tyentso seemed distinctly unimpressed with that explanation. "Are they inside the Quuros borders?"

"Well, yes, but—"

"Then they're invading," Tyentso snapped. "Or they will be just as soon as they realize that the only way they're going to find food is by stealing what little the Khorveshans have. We need to crush them before that happens."

Most of the men fell into immediate and vocal agreement, but that newcomer grimaced. "Your Majesty, they're refugees. They brought their women and children."

Tyentso stared at him flatly. "What's your name?"

He looked nervous. Not so difficult to understand why, considering the angry looks the other men at the table were throwing in his direction. "Fosrin, Your Majesty," he said.

"Well, Fosrin, try to remember that this isn't the real threat. The real threat is what's going on in Marakor right now. But we can only be expected to fight on so many fronts. There's a chance that if we smash the morgage immediately—smash them hard—that we'll scatter them so completely that we'll have the breathing room we need to concentrate on that real problem. Also, morgage women *are* warriors—and wizards too. Don't underestimate them just because of their sex. Are we understood?"

The man was at least smart enough to understand the possibility that his survival might depend on how he answered, so he nodded and without a trace of reluctance said, "Your will be done, Your Majesty."

Tyentso studied the man as if deciding whether it was worth it to enact some more lasting punitive action, and if so for what reason. Finally, she waved him back.

"As I was saying. I want the morgage gone from Quuros lands. Then we can concentrate on Marakor."

Jarith slipped out before she finished her meeting. He'd heard enough.

# 25. THE ERODING LINE

*Tyentso's story*
*The imperial war camp*
*Afternoon*

Tyentso returned to her tent and fought the temptation to collapse onto the bed. There was too much work to be done. Honestly, what was the point of being in charge of everything if she had to do all this damn paperwork? Caerowan hadn't yet made any serious mistakes, but he had to know she was double-checking all his work. Tyentso knew that if she didn't at least keep an eye on that paperwork, on making sure that everyone was pulling their weight fairly, any amount of funny business might sneak through.

She stopped herself. That wasn't true. She knew that wasn't true. Everyone was too tightly wound up in duty and devotion and giving their lives for the empire to do something like that. Yet her immediate, visceral reaction was still to assume the worst of intentions. In Caerowan's case, though . . .

Fayrin wasn't wrong. Caerowan's problem was that he might cause trouble with the best of intentions, convinced he was acting for the good of the empire. She did need to keep an eye on him.

She stared down at the desk in her tent and then, gradually, focused on the paperweight on top of one of the stacks of papers. It was new.

It was a tsali stone.

She slipped her sight past the Veil to confirm that it wasn't some sort of trap before touching the stone. Yes, it was a tsali stone. A recently made one. Red, fading to a subtle orange along its length. It rested on top of a piece of torn cloth, folded into quarters.

Tyentso unfolded the piece of cloth, recognizing the embroidery: the crossed swords over the Crown and Scepter of Quur. A general's insignia. The edge of the cloth was bloodstained. She examined the way the light caught at the darker stain.

Still wet.

Whoever had placed this in her tent had done so only minutes before. And since her wards were intact, they'd done so with enough skill to avoid magical detection.

She felt a chill.

Tyentso stripped the wards in seconds and built a new set, this one based on a much more obscure set of techniques. Then she crafted another spell that would dampen all the heat signatures in the room. Lastly, she overlaid an illusion so that if someone managed to get through all that, they'd see Tyentso doing paperwork.

That was about as much as she could do to ensure privacy. She'd just have to hope no one was really committed to seeing what she was up to when she was alone.

Or at least, when she seemed to be alone.

"Jarith, are you responsible for this?" Tyentso asked. "I know you're here. I can sense you. I knew you were following me before we left the Capital."

Nothing happened for several long seconds. Then the shadows deepened and coalesced into a man-shaped cloud of darkness, topped with an eyeless white porcelain mask.

"Veils," Tyentso murmured. She'd assumed he'd at least *look* human. But this was . . .

The darkness shuddered and changed again. This time, it morphed in front of her eyes into a human man.

Tyentso had only seen Jarith once, after he was already dead, but it was enough to recognize him. But even if the creature in front of her looked like Jarith, there was something decidedly wrong about his eyes, his blank expression. If this was Jarith, it was a Jarith who had seen things, done things, that had twisted him forever.

**No. I didn't do this. I stayed with you after we left the meeting.** Jarith's voice echoed in her mind.

"Great." She held out the tsali stone. "Then whose soul is this? Can you tell?"

Tyentso hadn't been certain that he'd be able to pick up the stone, but he reached out and plucked the rock from her fingers. He stared at the rock with peculiar intentness.

**Fosrin.** He gave the stone back to her.

Tyentso stared. "Fosrin? General Fosrin? Jarith, we were *just* talking to him! Just a few minutes ago—"

She thought back. She hadn't gone straight to her tent from that meeting. She'd stopped by the mess for a cup of coffee and then spoke to one of the cartographers about the accuracy of the local maps. Twenty, maybe thirty minutes, not counting the time to walk the distance. She had walked too—teleporting everyplace played hell on assassin planning schedules, but it also denied her the opportunity to mingle with her soldiers.

That was enough time, perhaps, to commit a murder and leave the proof sitting on her desk. She swallowed and closed her hand into a fist. A tsali. Fuck.

Someone was trying quite hard to make Tyentso feel like Gadrith was alive again.

She let out a long, shuddering breath and sat down. Clearly, not everyone in the camp loved her. This was a mind game, another gentle nudge to leave her off-balance.

**You need to stop this.**

Tyentso's head snapped up as she felt a rush of heat come over her in response to Jarith's chastising. "Be more specific."

**The morgage aren't your enemy.**

Tyentso felt black laughter bubble up in her. "Aren't my enemy? Oh, I beg to differ. Look, I understand that they're just trying to survive. So am I. And the only way that I'll do that is if I deal with them so quickly and so decisively that they cannot possibly be a threat to Khorvesh." She waved her hand holding the stone. "And deal with whoever thinks *this* is cute. Havar, I assume."

**Is that you speaking, or the anger? The fear?**

A shudder rippled through her. "How do you know—?"

**I'm a *demon*, Your Majesty. I feel it, taste it. This whole camp is soaked in unnatural anger and hate.**

"I realize that, but I'm fine."

**You're not fine. None of you are. And none of you are *thinking clearly*.** Jarith narrowed his eyes at the tsali stone. **Someone's trying to feed that anger, make it grow. Someone wants to make it worse.**

Tyentso collapsed back into a chair. He was right. None of them were thinking. Fosrin, perhaps, but he was already dead. He'd already been in Khorvesh when the rest of the army arrived. Meaning he hadn't been exposed to whatever was causing this. She wondered if that was why he'd been targeted—because he might otherwise have been a voice of reason.

She rubbed her face and tried to slow the pounding of her heartbeat, which even now was drumming out a tempo that screamed she should be attacking, that she was in danger. Everything made her angry. Everything made her lash out.

Made much worse by the fact that someone in the camp *was* her enemy.

But what was Tyentso supposed to do? Wait for some second-string House D'Lorus Ogenra to finish toying with her? Just withdraw and let the morgage rampage across Khorvesh? Give them an entire dominion and just shrug? Sit down and bargain with them?

Wait.

*Fuck.* Everyone expected her to fight the morgage.

Why *not* bargain with them?

There was only one enemy she planned on fighting, and that was Havar. The morgage? The Yorans? Those weren't her enemies. They were distractions, meant to siphon away her energy, pick off her people, make her ill-prepared to face the real threat.

Murad, or Havar, or whatever the hell his real name was, had invested quite a bit of energy into putting her in an impossible situation. He was likely responsible for whatever curse was causing everyone to behave so recklessly. He had *planned* this.

No, no, no. She wasn't a fool. *Relos Var* had planned this. Whether Havar D'Aramarin realized it or not was inconsequential. She knew who the real puppet master was. He would try to use the people she cared about against her, strike at her through what he perceived as her weaknesses. Even this, leaving a fucking tsali behind for her, smacked of someone who knew her too well. Havar may not have known about her relationship with her father, Gadrith D'Lorus, who did so dearly love creating tsali stones from his victims . . . but Relos Var did.

Jarith was right. Whoever was responsible for killing one of her people had done so simply to keep her off-kilter and upset. Not thinking clearly.

Tyentso still felt angry. She still felt like she was two steps from committing a murder with every breath.

"You're right. I'll try to control this better—"

But the demon was already gone.

## 26. Warning Signals

***Thurvishar's story***
***Grizzst's Tower, Rainbow Lake, Eamithon***
***Later that afternoon***

One of the gems on the wall of Grizzst's Tower began blinking.

It was, in fact, precisely the same wall that used to monitor the status of Vol Karoth's prison, but that particular use was no longer necessary, since the status of Vol Karoth's prison was known: broken. Instead, the stonework had been covered with new glyphs and new gems, all of which glowed like faint candles in the dim light.

One of the lights began to blink, and a chiming sound filled the tower.

Senera reached the room first, with Thurvishar just a few steps behind her.

"Who is it?" Thurvishar asked before he'd closed the distance between them.

"Qown," Senera said. "Why did we think blocking tracking was a good idea?" She immediately checked the other gems, but that was the only one blinking, the only one in distress. Sheloran and Galen seemed to be fine.

A spot of darkness in the corner became animate, re-forming in a column next to Thurvishar, topped with a ceramic white face mask.

"Nice timing, Jarith," Thurvishar said. "Would you please do me a favor? Check in on Qown. There's a problem."

The demon nodded once and then vanished.

Senera watched the blinking gem against the wall and bit the side of her thumb. "You think it's started?"

Thurvishar sighed. "It started when we couldn't find Urthaenriel. And I'm afraid of what it means."

"He needs the sword," Senera said.

Thurvishar knew she wasn't talking about Kihrin. She meant Relos Var. *He* needed the sword, for whatever it was he was going to do next. Something a little more final than killing a few gods.

"I never thought we'd be able to keep it from him," Thurvishar admitted. "Not permanently. I'll send out the danger warning."

"We should ask everyone to check their baskets," Senera added. She began writing out multiple notes on small cards.

Not long thereafter, Sheloran's and Galen's gems began to blink too.

# 27. Expectations

*Janel's story*
*The Mother of Trees, the Manol*
*Twilight*

The vané palace was a queer place.

Magical, of course. So magical that it seeped into the very wood, into every tapestry and piece of furniture. The parts of the palace shaped from the sky tree hosting them were so overflowing with life that Janel couldn't imagine the vané were unaware. It almost felt like a soul. Almost.

She suspected her inability to perceive the sky tree's soul was a flaw in herself, not a lack of soul in the sky tree. A flea, trying to see the whole of the wolf.

She walked down beautiful, impossible hallways until she found a balcony that either really overlooked the jungle surrounding them or had been so heavily covered with illusions that it was impossible to tell the difference. The darkness was heavy with the smell of flowers and a hot, humid odor of greenery and decay. The air itself was thick enough to cut, the sort of humidity that slicked up skin and forced its way into lungs. Janel was used to much colder environments; even the Capital City of Quur seemed temperate in comparison. But it's not like the heat would bother her, and the clothing the vané preferred was designed to wick away sweat and keep the skin dry. She could put up with it for a few minutes if it meant taking in that view.

The irony was that there was theoretically no view to take in. Under the heavy sky tree canopy, the jungle should have been a dark place, eternal night on a grand scale. Yet such wasn't the case. The channeled sundew of a thousand sky trees spiraled down trunks in lazy glowing rivers before spilling out in bright fans of light. Phosphorescent birds and butterflies flitted around to pick off prey or take advantage of glowing flowers. The longer she stared, the more was revealed, until the Manol seemed like a dark jeweled landscape, lush with glittering facets.

Janel heard movement behind her and glanced back. She sighed internally.

"Hello, Janel," Khaeriel said. "I thought we might talk."

Janel didn't hide her frown, but motioned for the older woman to join her. She just had to hope that Teraeth was wrong and Khaeriel was in fact too smart to do something as stupid as attack her. If that proved not to be the case, then Janel would make Khaeriel pay for the mistake and send her apologies to Kihrin later.

"Let me guess: you wish to discuss intentions and whether or not I'll do the honorable thing and marry your son."

Khaeriel tilted her head as she walked out onto the balcony. "I'm sure a woman such as yourself–"

"I'm not a woman," Janel corrected.

Khaeriel paused. A flicker of confusion appeared and vanished as quickly.

"In my land," Janel said, "whether you are a man or a woman depends on your role, your nature. These are not the same thing as one's birth sex."

Khaeriel's eyes widened with understanding. "Oh, I see. That's not an issue here." She waved a hand. "Although with the vané, it is customary to change one's body to match in such cases." She shrugged one shoulder. "But even then, not everyone does. I didn't think that was a custom in Quur."

"That tells me you never visited Jorat," Janel said.

"No," Khaeriel acknowledged.

Silence wrapped around them both.

"Are you keeping the baby?" Khaeriel asked.

"Yes," Janel said, "although it won't be the first child I've had with your son."

Khaeriel visibly startled. "Someone had mentioned . . . but I didn't think . . ."

Janel smiled to herself. She was being a bit of an ass at the moment, but she found no shame in it whatsoever. "I know you've been told that Kihrin is the reincarnation of one of the Guardians. And I am the reincarnation of his lover. We had a child together."

Khaeriel exhaled slowly. "I had assumed that source of information was unreliable."[1]

"No, they were telling the truth. The dragon, Aeyan'arric." Janel shrugged. "If only she were sane. If only she were capable of recognizing us."

"You're not–" Khaeriel paused, collected herself, and then tried again. "You're not as young as you seem, are you?"

"In some ways, I am," Janel said. "But for the most part–" She shook her head ruefully at Khaeriel. "No. Not in the least."

Khaeriel gave her a tiny smile. "I'm beginning to think trying to keep you away from my son is a lost cause."

"Such a lost cause. And we're a package deal: Kihrin, Teraeth, and myself. If Teraeth is the youngest of us, that doesn't mean we have any intention of leaving him behind." Janel turned around, leaning her back against the railing. "But I have a question for you."

Khaeriel drew herself up. "Yes?"

"What was it like to switch bodies using the Stone of Shackles?"

Khaeriel was visibly taken aback by the shift in topic. Not a surprise, considering the unexpected nature of the question. "You mean when Miyathreall murdered me?"

"Did you use the Stone of Shackles some other time I don't know about?"

---

[1] It's true. Mimics do lie a lot. –S

Khaeriel sniffed. And then stared at Janel with obvious curiosity when it became evident that she waited on the answer.

Kihrin's mother's gaze drifted over the bright light limning the edges of darkness. Her expression was contemplative, even wistful. "I had no idea what wearing the Stone of Shackles would do. Nothing had prepared me. It happened so slowly and so very fast. The moment she killed me, it was . . . It took a shockingly long time to kick in. I was dead, but being kept alive for long enough to make the transfer, long enough to ensure my soul didn't inconveniently leave. I remember she yelled at me: 'What have you done?' As if I had any idea. And it hurt. It was without question the most agonizing experience I have ever suffered, and yes, that includes childbirth. As if my core were being ripped apart, ripped away, and then shoved into another body while hot lead was dripped over my souls to make sure they didn't stray. That wasn't the worst part, though."

Janel brushed her fingertips over the living wood of the balcony railing and waited.

"The worst part were the memories," Khaeriel explained. "Because although my souls were now trapped inside Miyathreall's body, they were strangers there. It is the reason one cannot cast magic at first after the transfer—because magic is a product of the mind, and you are living in a mind that has been shaped for someone else. Until my souls could reshape that mind to fit me, it was like living in the shadow of an eclipse. Everything doubled and blurred. My memories came with my souls, but also the echoes of memories left behind by Miya. For several months, I knew everything she knew." Her mouth twisted. "Had I been slightly smarter about the whole matter—" Khaeriel paused. "Well, no. I suppose I might have outwitted my brother, but I most certainly would not have outwitted my grandmother Khaemezra. She knew exactly what the Stone did, after all. She'd planned all of it."

"It sounds awful," Janel mused. "Dreadful."

"I do not recommend trying it for yourself," Khaeriel said. "Especially not now, but that goes without saying. How far along are you?"

Janel studied Khaeriel carefully before answering. "Not far at all. Six weeks."

"How humorous it would be if our children were born near the same time," Khaeriel said. Then she brightened. "If morning sickness has been an issue, I know a very effective potion for helping with such difficulties."

Janel was sure she'd rather let a venomous snake nibble on her breasts before she'd willingly drink any herbal concoction given to her by Khaeriel, but that wasn't a diplomatic response. So, she truthfully said, "I thank you for the offer, but I haven't experienced any morning sickness."

Khaeriel stared at her.

Janel shrugged. "I realize that's not normal. I've been pregnant before in previous lives. Elana had terrible morning sickness from the start. Whereas this time, other than an aversion to coffee and a preference for certain foods, I've barely noticed any change whatsoever."

"I believe I am obligated to hate you now," Khaeriel told her flatly.

Janel thought she was joking. She hoped the woman was joking. It was difficult to tell.

"My mother is the Goddess of Magic," Janel said. "So let's not discount the possibility that my lack of discomfort has had assistance from the child's *other* grandmother."

A complicated set of emotions made their way across Khaeriel's face. "You said your mother was a dancing girl."

"She was," Janel said. "But that's hardly *all* she was." She pushed herself away from the railing and toward the hallway. "I should probably try to sleep. We both should, if such a thing is possible." Janel stopped at the doorway, however, and looked back at the former vané queen. "I love your son a great deal, Your Highness. Love him so much dying hasn't been able to keep us apart. It would please me if I had your permission to marry him. If such ends up being possible by the time this is all done."

Khaeriel pursed her lips but then finally nodded. "I will not object, but the final decision must ultimately be his."

Janel smiled. Well, in that one regard, Khaeriel was definitely wiser than her grandmother Khaemezra. Actually, in more than one regard: Khaeriel had never shown the slightest inclination toward filicide.

"I wouldn't have it any other way," Janel said. "Sleep well."

# 28. A HINT OF BETRAYAL

### Galen's story
### The Soaring Halls, the Upper Circle of the Capital City of Quur
### After finding a washroom

Galen's return to his in-laws' suite of rooms was delayed inasmuch as Tave insisted that he was a big boy and could walk all by himself. Galen noted that the "boy" part of that had turned out to be correct, not that it particularly mattered at that age.

On the walk over, Galen hadn't been able to help but wonder at details no one had yet taken the time to explain. Had Caless and Varik evacuated everyone at the Rose Palace? Had the D'Talus servants been bundled up for safety, or were they still there, keeping the doors barred and the windows barred against a siege they could only pray never made its way inside? Or was it much worse than that, and they'd already been dragged out into the streets?

Caless and Varik could come and go as they liked. They were powerful enough to be able to teleport directly. All the people who worked for them were a different story.

Halfway back, Tave decided he was tired after all and had begun crying until Galen picked him up. By the time Galen finally managed to make it back to the rooms, Tave was fast asleep and Sheloran was in the D'Talus rooms alone. She had a cup of tea in her hand and a faraway expression on her face Galen couldn't quite interpret. He saw no sign of Qown.

He set the boy on one of the beds and tucked a blanket around him. Tave promptly curled up like a cat wrapping itself in its own tail. If the gods were kind, perhaps the child might manage to stay asleep for a few hours. Galen thought the kid was adorable, but that suggestion Caless had made about finding the Milligreests was sounding better and better.

He pulled a chair over to his wife and sat down. "Are you all right?"

Sheloran sipped her tea without answering, staring at the bed where Tave was already asleep. She didn't answer, which made Galen frown, but he decided against pressing her. Instead, he made his own cup of tea and sat down with some of the leftovers from the earlier meal.

"No," she said, so long after he'd asked the question that it took him a moment to connect the answer to his query. "I had hoped—" Sheloran shook her head. "It's all falling apart, Blue. The empire's falling apart right in front of our eyes. The irony is that after all that talk about wanting my parents—my mother, in particular—to do something, to change something, she *is*. And

I don't know how I feel about it. I feel weirdly betrayed. And angry." She frowned. "I feel *so* angry."

Galen scooted closer and wrapped his arm around her. "I think that's perfectly reasonable. Something weird's going on here, don't deny it. I've never seen your father act like that. Not ever."

"No. Never. And as far as I can tell, the two of them are alive because they helped set up the other high lords. That's . . . a lot." Sheloran grimaced and drank a healthy gulp of her tea.

"Yes, well." Galen sighed. "I suppose one can argue that both of your parents were doing what they had to in order to survive."

"I sense a 'but,'" Sheloran said.

Galen nodded. "*But* I heard some gossip while I was out. Did you know they're calling the dinner where the empress assassinated all the high lords 'the Glittering Feast'? Sounds romantic, doesn't it?"

Sheloran's face went blank. "Do I want to know why they're calling it that?"

"No," Galen said.

She hesitated.

Galen simply waited.

"Fine!" She waved her fan frantically. "Tell me anyway."

"On the surface, it sounds like the Glittering Feast is just what everyone's said. Tyentso held a party, invited all the high lords, made it sound like a nice 'let's put our differences aside and pretend to be friends until the crisis is over' sort of diplomatic gesture. And then the glitter started to fall."

Sheloran squinted. "I thought that was just poetic license. Glitter? Actual glitter?" Her voice hitched in a mild expression of horror, probably thinking about finding pieces of the damn stuff in her clothing for the next five years.

Galen smiled. "You act like that's unusual. Remember the year House D'Jorax rained down rose petals in all the royal colors?"

"Oh, that was so tacky."

"Or the year House D'Kaje had colored mage-lights spelling out blessings?"

"Well, yes, but–"

"House D'Mon. Those oversize Manol Jungle plants."

Sheloran cleared her throat and glared at Galen. "Yes, I understand your point. Everyone assumed this was more of the same. An overwrought royal conceit."

"But it wasn't. Because it seems there's a metal out there that burns when heated? Not just melts the way most metal does but burns extremely hot."

Sheloran's eyes widened. "Ataras? You're referring to ataras?"

"I don't know what it's called. I imagine you would, though. So picture it: tiny flakes of this special metal floating down in graceful little spirals all over the entire feast hall. Then Tyentso erects a magical field of energy surrounding the place and just"–he made a motion with his fingers–"lights it on fire."

"It's not that easy to set alight," Sheloran said, but then immediately rebutted her own protest. "I suppose if you gave it more surface area. Reduced it to a powder . . . or flakes . . . it would be easier. Powdered platinum melts at a lower temperature than ingots. But in that state? Burning ataras would have caused a massive explosion. The ataras flakes would have burned up all the air in a fire so bright and hot it would blind anyone watching with the naked eye." She made a strangled sound. "I begin to understand why my father was involved, and how."

"Yes. He made the empress a whole mess of tiny little glittery metal flakes, and by doing so won House D'Talus an exemption from whatever punishments Tyentso decided to hand down."

"At least their deaths were quick."

"Not everyone's," Galen said. "My grandfather survived it." He couldn't begin to imagine how Havar D'Aramarin had done so, but he'd found a way.

Which meant Havar had to be a god-king too. But which one? Galen wasn't sure he wanted to know.

Sheloran examined the small boy as if he might wake with nightmares from what they were whispering to each other. When she'd collected herself, she returned her attention to Galen. "Ataras can melt through shanathá in seconds, Blue. It can melt through *drussian*. It would have charred those people to ashes before they even realized they were dead."

He shrugged. "And yet. The whole 'invading Marakor and cutting off the food supply to the Capital' suggests he survived. And that he's been planning something like this for a long time."

Sheloran had nothing to say to that. Galen could hardly blame her. He didn't want to think about it himself, except he suddenly had more sympathy toward Sheloran's shock at discovering her mother was a god-queen.

Several hours later, they were still there, brooding. Galen was starting to fidget, wondering what had happened to Qown. He would have expected him back already.

The little boy made an unhappy, distressed sound in his sleep. "What are we going to do about that one? Find his family?" Sheloran made a moue.

"How? His real name can't be Tave," Galen said.[1]

"One would hope not," Sheloran said, "but he's three at best, and I assume that such was his caretaker's nickname for him. There's no way to know whether or not he's a royal—"

"His eyes," Galen started to protest.

"D'Jorax, D'Moló, D'Kard, and D'Knofra are all born with normal eye colors because they were not among the original eight. He could easily come from one of those houses. I'm not sure what to do with him. We haven't checked in with any of the orphanages."

---

[1] Under the assumption that any later translations of this text that may occur will presumably not translate common names into their prosaic meanings, I shall point out that *tave* is the Guarem word for "baby."–T

"I'll be surprised if any of those are still in the city. We told our people to get out if there was trouble. There's been a lot of trouble."

They both watched the sleeping child. This was also "not their problem" right now. At least, Galen was all too aware that such is how his father would have framed the situation. His grandfather. Sheloran's parents too, probably. Not their problem. Everyone needed help. Everyone's situation was dire. They weren't in any position to provide charity.

Sheloran wouldn't care. Galen knew her well enough to know she'd help, anyway. Kihrin probably would have done the same. Which way Qown would lean was obvious.

Galen's father would have mocked them all.

"Your mother had a good idea about seeing if the Milligreests would let him be a playmate for their youngest," Galen said. "I'd suggest he stay with us, but that's not safe, is it?"

Sheloran squeezed his hand. "No, it's not."

"We'll just have to see—"

Qown threw open the door and all but ran into the room. He looked spooked, so much so that he barely glanced at Galen.

"Is something the matter?" Sheloran asked him.

"No, I—" Qown looked back toward the door, then visibly shook himself. "No, I mean, yes. Would you . . . would you mind coming with me? There's something I need to show you."

Galen stood up. Qown was skittish—and in this place, that might mean any number of things. It wasn't directed at Galen personally; that would have involved more blushing.

"Did something happen?" Galen asked.

"I just—please. We have to hurry." Qown's eyes scanned the room as though he expected someone—Caless, perhaps—to pop up behind one of the chairs and shout, "Surprise!" His stare stopped cold on Tave, still asleep. He grimaced, although Galen couldn't tell if it was annoyance, concern, or some other emotion.

Galen grabbed his sword. "All right, then. Let's go."

"Both of you," Qown said, when Sheloran seemed more inclined to stay with the baby. "I want you to see this too."

"Oh, but we can't leave him." Sheloran gestured toward the sleeping child.

"Then don't," Qown said. "Please, we have to hurry."

Galen stared helplessly at Sheloran, who shrugged her confusion in turn. Tave stirred when Sheloran bundled him up then immediately settled into a more comfortable position and fell right back to sleep again.

"Quickly!"

Galen scowled at the healer's back. He'd barely even looked at Galen since entering the room. And even without that personal failing, it just seemed off that he wouldn't give them more information before taking them . . . wherever it was that he was taking them.

The sense of wrongness spiraled as Galen noticed Qown acting too familiar with the corridors and turns of the Soaring Halls; Qown had never been to the imperial palace before. Galen found the place almost impossible to navigate after having been there several times.

Then Galen heard the chimes.

Sheloran hesitated for a fraction of a second. "Is this something to do with the Lash?" Sheloran asked as they hurried. She cradled the back of the boy's head as she looked at Galen out of the corner of her eye.

She'd heard it too.

The noise hadn't been random. It was one of the precautions that they'd set up before leaving the Lighthouse at Shadrag Gor. Senera's last actions with the Name of All Things had been a furious bout of researching sigils that might prove useful. Several of the sigils did little more than send a noise to specific people, but they'd assigned meaning to those sounds. Two such had just played.

First, report back. Second, one of us is in danger.

The first wasn't possible at the moment. The second Galen had figured out all on his own.

Qown stopped at a door and began to fiddle with the latch. "Just let me–"

"Please allow me," Sheloran said. The metal turned into a swarm of metallic ants, which all scurried away from where the locking mechanism had once been. "Now about the Lash?"

"Oh!" Qown took a deep breath and rushed to enter the room. "Yes," he said as he turned back toward them. "I was looking for more information on him since he escaped with Grimward and–"

Galen unsheathed his sword and aimed its point at the other man's throat.

"Hmm." Qown looked down at the drawn weapon. The corner of his mouth twitched. He slowly raised his hands. "What gave me away?" he inquired.

"The Lash isn't a man," Sheloran said. "She isn't even human."

The person (presumably cloaked in an excellent illusion) laughed. "You mean that little shit lied to me? I didn't think he had it in him."

Galen felt a flash of dread shiver through him. He nudged the sword under the man's chin. "What have you done with Qown?"

Before the man could answer, he looked over Galen's shoulder and smiled.

Galen rolled his eyes. "Do you honestly think that's going to work?"

"Um, Blue–" The nervous twinge in Sheloran's voice was far more effective than any amount of smirking *"look behind you"* pantomime.

Then a voice Galen loathed spoke.

"I believe in this case," Relos Var said, "it will work because it's not a bluff. Now would you mind stepping inside? This isn't a coversation for the hallway."

Tave woke and started to make fidgety noises. Sheloran shushed him, unsuccessfully.

Relos Var made a shooing motion with his hands toward the doorway. "And please don't try anything rash, Lady D'Mon. You may not be expendable in my plans, but your husband is a different story. And you so thought-fully brought me a spare."

Anger flashed through Galen. He meant the child. Relos Var was talking about hurting the child. Galen knew—knew down to his sinews and marrow—that Var wasn't bluffing either. He'd no more hesitate to kill a baby than Ga-drith the Twisted would have.[2]

"Come on, Red." He sheathed his sword.

Sheloran seemed to be weighing the odds, but Galen didn't have to try hard to know which way she'd decided. She bounced the increasingly unhappy little boy on her hip while she gave Relos Var a glare that promised centuries of pain, and walked inside. Var clearly thought her implied threat adorable.

Relos Var followed them into the room and closed the door behind them.

The room was some sort of parlor, not so much packed away as covered with tarps and cloths and then forgotten. The fake-Qown walked over to a bundle of linens, which was shifting around suspiciously for something sup-posedly inanimate. He removed the top sheet.

Qown lay underneath, gagged and struggling.

Galen immediately darted forward. Qown had been *beaten*. He had a nasty purple bruise around one eye and a cheekbone, blood still trickling from the corner of his mouth. His hands . . . Galen clenched his jaw so hard he thought he might crack a tooth.

They'd broken Qown's fingers.

He supposed that answered the question of whether or not Qown had will-ingly betrayed them. Torture wouldn't have been required if Qown had been loyal and cooperative.

Relos Var gazed at his former student without expression. Then he turned to the other man. "Anlyr, was that necessary?"

Galen whipped around to glare at the fake-Qown, because he recognized the name of the man who'd once pretended to be a House D'Mon guard.

Anlyr made a gesture with his fingers and dropped the illusion. "Appar-ently, no. I guess it really is true what they say about torture not working, but I figured it was worth a shot."

Tave began openly crying. Galen had no idea why. It could have been anything.

"Well, somebody's hungry," Anlyr commented, apparently more willing to make assumptions.

Relos Var stared at the child, like it was something inexplicable, something beyond his comprehension. The question in his eyes was clear, but he didn't ask it. Instead, the wizard did something elegant and complicated with one hand, which opened up a small portal not much larger than a dinner plate. He reached through the opening, pulled back a skewer of sugar-dipped fruit, and handed it to the boy.

---

[2] Oh, I don't think that's true at all. Gadrith would kill a child the way one might swat at a mos-quito. It wouldn't even occur to him not to. Relos Var wouldn't hurt a child without a reason.—T

He'd still kill the child if he had a reason, though.—S

Oh, without question.—T

Galen found himself wondering how Relos Var had managed that. Did he have a secret stash of candy somewhere, or was there a very confused shop-keeper who'd just seen a hand appear out of thin air and grab his wares?

Tave, no fool, didn't care how the wizard had managed it. The small boy reached for it without hesitation. He promptly stopped crying in favor of chewing on the candy.

"Is that supposed to impress me?" Sheloran sounded rather bored. She cast a level eye around the room and sniffed as if smelling something off. That gaze landed on Qown and then slid right off him again, as if his welfare didn't matter at all.

Which just proved Sheloran was the smart one. Relos Var didn't seem to think Qown was a bargaining chip. He'd threatened Galen and Tave, but he hadn't tried to use Qown against her. He hadn't specifically threatened Qown, the better to make it perfectly clear that violence was very much an option. So it seemed that Relos Var was assuming that although Qown had been ordered to gain Galen's confidence, he had *only* succeeded with Galen, if at all.

Galen just didn't know if that was a good thing. Qown being useful as a hostage also meant Relos Var had a motive for keeping Qown alive. If Relos Var had decided that Qown couldn't be trusted—which seemed to be the case—then Qown was in incredible danger.

Galen wished he knew what had given Qown away.

"It's a rare day when candy won't shut up a child," Relos Var said. "And why *is* there a child here?"

No one answered.

Galen kept his expression neutral. He supposed he was lucky—if such was the right word—that he had practice dealing with powerful men who'd re-spond violently to the slightest hint of disrespect.

"What is it that you want, Var? We can't give you Grimward. We never pried it out of the Lash's hands." He gestured toward Qown. "He must have told you all this."

"We can't trust anything he says for some reason," Anlyr confessed as he ran a finger over one of Qown's bruises, making him whimper.

Galen was going to *kill* Anlyr. He didn't care if it was slow or fast, just as long as it was final.

"Although I know you won't believe me, I'm not a fan of torture," Anlyr said. "But funny thing: as you may have noticed, I'm a bit of a wizard too. And one of the, uh—let's call it a spell—that I know lets me read minds. Now a month ago? Torture wouldn't have been necessary because I could read Qown's mind. And your mind. Little Shelly-doll's mind too. Now? Why, I think the last time I was in a room with this many people immune to that ability I was crashing a witch-hunter chapter house meeting." He met Relos Var's eyes. "So Qown lied to us. I can't even be mad; our little boy's growing up."

Ah, so that was it. The irony was laughable.

Their new defenses, courtesy of Senera, were what had given them away.[3]

Relos Var scoffed. "You're easy to lie to, Anlyr. You're so used to reading minds that you've forgotten how to read people." Ignoring the man's indignation, Var turned back to Galen and Sheloran. "Very well. As I don't have time for subtlety, we're going to take a trip. You'll cooperate with everything I ask. If you do, then there's a better-than-average chance that no one will be hurt." He gave Sheloran a stern, parental look. "If you don't cooperate, I'll start with Galen. Or rather, Anlyr will. He can be inventive when the occasion calls for it. And if a threat to Galen can't persuade you . . ." He gave a pointed look to the toddler.

"Don't you fucking dare," Sheloran said.

The corner of Relos Var's mouth quirked. "That's your choice, Your Highness."

"I'll ask again: What do you want?" Galen dug his nails into his palms to keep from doing something immensely stupid, like going for his sword. But oh, how he wanted to.

"The Stone of Shackles," Relos Var replied.

Galen glanced at Sheloran, in spite of himself. "You have to know she doesn't have—" But then his breath stuttered to a halt, as he felt like a fool. Sheloran was the one Relos Var needed because *she* was the hostage. Everyone else was just collateral damage.

"I'm starting to not like you, old man," Galen said softly.

At that, Relos Var actually smiled. "Yes, your father felt the same. I imagine pursuing that grudge won't go any better for you than it did for him. I do find it ironic that I'm in a shockingly similar position to the one Gadrith was in when he was trying to pry that damn rock from my brother's hands. And as I too don't feel like taking the time to grab it off its current wearer's corpse, I'm going to resort to similar tactics. By hurting the people Caless loves until she does the sensible thing."

Xivan tried that too, Galen thought, but it wouldn't have been wise to bring that up. The difference between a threat from Relos Var and a threat from Xivan was immeasurable. Relos Var could make it work.

He felt awash in warring emotions: horror, but also relief. He didn't so much as glance at Qown. He didn't dare. Because when it came to people the Goddess of Love held close to her heart, Qown wasn't even in the same room as the piece of paper the list was written on. Assuming neither he nor Sheloran gave it away, Var was unlikely to think threatening Qown was a means of persuading them either.

Veils. He suddenly understood how Kihrin must have felt when Gadrith started killing his way through the D'Mon family.

Except that wasn't right either. He wasn't Kihrin in this scenario. He was still Galen—still the hostage and game piece on someone else's board.

While Galen contemplated his lack of options, Relos Var walked over to

---

[3] It was really a "damned if we do, damned if we don't" situation.—S

one of the tables and opened a small jewelry box. He removed its contents—a single piece of jewelry.

It wasn't really jewelry, though. Galen recognized the stone well enough. It was the final, irrevocable sign that Relos Var had decided he was done wasting time on his former apprentice, Qown.

He'd reclaimed Worldhearth.

## 29. To Hunt in Dreams

*Janel's story*
*The Mother of Trees, the Manol*
*The day of their arrival, evening*

When Janel returned to the royal suite, she found Talea and Xivan waiting in addition to Teraeth and "Kihrin."

Janel lay down on the bed. "Shall we do this?"

Talea seemed more interested in the room, likely because she hadn't been there for Valathea's grand tour earlier in the day. "Did no one make a fuss about the three of you all staying here?"

Janel smiled. "Why would they? The vané saw how Kihrin and I were acting around Teraeth when we brought him back from the Well of Spirals. The odd part would've been if we'd done all that and weren't sharing a room."

Teraeth was openly pacing. Janel was surprised he wasn't tossing a knife from hand to hand. As it was, he reminded her of a caged black jaguar, which was hardly the first time she'd likened the man to a hunting cat. He'd always worn the predator close to the surface.

"You two know how to get past the Veil into the Afterlife?" Teraeth asked Xivan and Talea.

The two women shared a look.

"I've done it before," Xivan said. "I'm pretty sure I can do it again."

Teraeth looked expectantly at Talea.

Who shrugged. "How hard could it be?"

Teraeth began cursing under his breath.

"If she doesn't figure it out, you can keep her company until Xivan and I return," Janel said. She wasn't worried, though. Talea had been the first one to gain a Greater Talisman and seemed to have transitioned quickly. The small mental duplicate of the former goddess who appeared to Talea and Talea alone—Eshi—was more than capable of talking the fledgling luck goddess through the right skills.

"Teraeth, stop wearing a track in the carpet, please," Janel said. "We'll be careful, and we'll bring your father back."

Teraeth walked over to where she lay and kissed her. Xivan cleared her throat when said kiss turned overexuberant.

Reluctantly, he released her. "Go raise hell," he told her.

"Hopefully not," Janel said. "I'd rather just Return your father."

She closed her eyes in that world and opened them a moment later in a different one.

## 30. THE DRY MOTHERS

*Tyentso's story*
*The imperial war camp*
*Evening*

The advantage of having the fanatical devotion of most of the men around herself, Tyentso discovered, was that no one questioned it when her orders changed from "kill on sight" to "capture all the morgage you can, unharmed, especially any old women."

Not that old morgage women proved easy to capture.

But by early evening, a messenger relayed that such an old woman had been located and was even expected to live now that they'd gotten her to the healers.

Lovely.

Even before Tyentso's arrival, the local garrison had set up a prison camp for captured morgage on those rare occasions when they didn't fight to the last person. As they passed through the bedraggled and sorry-looking prisoners, the empress turned to one of the wardens who had shown up to escort her. "I know that the morgage aren't the most well-behaved prisoners, but if I find out that any soldiers have been assaulting any of them, abusing any of them, I will personally see that soldier executed. Do you understand?"

The warden turned gray. "Uh, yes, Your Majesty."

"Good," Tyentso said. "Now take me to this old woman."

The morgage woman in question sat on the only piece of scrap that might generously be considered a chair. She was decrepit, her side bandaged and bruises visible on her face. Her coloring along her back side was dark gray, with a lighter color, almost white, along her face and neck.

"Do you understand Guarem?" Tyentso asked.

Another morgage woman—younger but by no means *young*—looked up. "She does not. I do." This woman was an indigo blue, almost black, color, with a swath of delicate silver scales striping across her head and down her side.

"What's your name?" Tyentso asked her.

Neither woman answered.

Tyentso sighed. Both women had sullen, uncooperative expressions on their faces.

"Fucking bitches," the warden said as he raised a whip. "The empress asked you a question!"

Tyentso used magic to rip the whip from the man's hand. "Touch either of them and I'll use this on you."

His eyes widened in surprise, and then he bowed. "Uh . . . yes. Yes, Your Majesty."

"Leave us," Tyentso ordered. She really should have learned the man's name. Threats were so much more effective when made on a first-name basis. "Now."

He backed away, still bowing.

Tyentso grabbed both women by the arm and teleported them to a different location.

No sooner had she done so than the younger woman twisted her hand and set red-hot, burning fingers against Tyentso's skin. At the same time, the old woman attempted to boil the blood in Tyentso's veins.

Of course they both knew magic. They'd just been waiting for the right opportunity.

And it would have been the right opportunity—with someone else.

Tyentso broke the younger woman's arm before pushing her away so hard it sent her flying. As soon as she landed, the rocks turned liquid and mud-like around her before hardening again, trapping her. Tyentso turned to the older woman and glared as she pulled the moisture from the morgage priestess's lungs. The morgage collapsed in the middle of an asthma attack.

Tyentso snapped her fingers and let the old woman breathe properly again. She knelt next to her while she gasped for air.

"Let's try this again," Tyentso said. "I am the Empress of Quur, Tyentso, holy daughter of Thaena. And you are?"

Despite the younger woman's claim that the older woman couldn't understand Guarem, the old morgage woman began to chuckle, a thick, wheezing noise. She put a hand to her chest as her lungs heaved. "I am Durgala . . ." More laughter. "*Also* a holy daughter of Thaena."

A chuckle forced itself free before Tyentso could stop it. Ah. Yes, there was some humor in that.

"Mother—" The daughter called out. She was in a particularly uncomfortable position, trapped on her back, unable to move any limbs. Which had to hurt considering the angle of her broken arm.

"Would you free my child?" Durgala asked. "I vow we will cause you no more trouble. As one angel of Death to another."

Tyentso waved a hand and lowered the spell. "If you're lying to me—" She smiled. "It will be no great effort to recapture you. But I thought we might talk woman-to-woman."

The younger morgage woman muttered something in a language Tyentso didn't understand.

"What was that?" Tyentso asked.

Durgala said, "She said, 'We've been waiting five hundred years to talk woman-to-woman. What kept you?'" She tilted her head and gazed around them. "Where . . . are we?"

A fair question. They were nowhere near Khorvesh, that was certain. They rested on an island of lush, green grass, but all around them, dark water shimmered in the moonlight while frogs croaked out mating calls from lotus pads. A forestlike maze of trees grew from the water in the distance, limbs hanging heavy with moss. The air was sticky and humid, the shadows full of secrets. It probably looked worse in the daytime, but at night, this was an enchanted sort of place, both dangerous and beautiful.

By human standards, this place was a pit. Tyentso could understand now why Ninavis had openly mocked the idea of offering it to the Yorans. But compared to the Korthaen Blight? Where any liquid was either a poison or an acid and the air itself hurt to breathe?

Paradise.[1]

"This is the Kulma Swamp," Tyentso said. "Do you like it?"

The daughter reached down to the water and pulled up a handful of swamp water. She smelled it, then let the water trickle through her fingers. Her eyes were very bright. "So much clean water," she murmured.

"All this life, just . . . here. Out in the open." Durgala shook her head. "Is it poisonous?"

"Not to my knowledge," Tyentso said. "Do you want it?"

Durgala scowled and started to stand, anger clearly overwhelming any good-natured camaraderie their earlier fight had engendered. "How dare you mock–!"

"No mocking," Tyentso said. "I'm offering your people the Kulma Swamp."

Both women paused with stunned expressions.

"We don't use the place," Tyentso explained. "It's too wet, too hot, too wild. Gods, I'm not sure you can take a breath without swallowing a mosquito out here. I've been told that there's one Marakori tribe that lives here, but they can be moved." She made a gesture toward the trees. "The Kulma Swamp is massive. Large enough for every morgage. And if you and your people are willing to help me, it's *yours*."

Durgala's expression was disbelieving. "You're going to just . . . give . . . us the Green Lands?" She scoffed.[2]

Understandable. Tyentso too would be a bit skeptical of an offer that seemed too good to be true.

"No," Tyentso corrected. "Oh, not at all. You'll earn it. The 'helping me' part is fucking dangerous, and I guarantee that a great many of your people will die. But the way I see it, a lot of your people are going to die no matter what happens, and at least this way, there's something worth fighting for at the end–a new home in the Green Lands. Which is fucking dangerous and full of disease, and if you don't really watch yourselves, a lot of your people will die just trying to survive. But you'll be here and Warchild won't.[3] Help

---

[1] Technically, waters inside the Blight are usually alkaline, not acidic, but still undrinkable.–T
[2] I find it curious that the "Green Lands"–which seems to be an important promised land in morgage culture–translates in Guarem as "Marakor."–T
[3] I'm honestly impressed that Tyentso remembered that this is what the morgage call Vol Karoth.–S

me, give me your finest warriors and witches, and in return, I'll give you the Kulma Swamp."

"For how long?" the other woman asked suspiciously.

"Really, what *is* your name?"

"Sighoris," she answered.

"All right, Sighoris," Tyentso said. "Until you don't want it anymore. I'm granting it to you for you to rule as you see fit. Now personally? I would strongly suggest that you stay with the empire just so no future emperors decide to win themselves fame and glory by reclaiming it, but that's your call. The point is, our peoples don't have to keep fighting. If you can convince the rest of the Dry Mothers to stand down, I'll give all this to you." She waved a finger. "But no more attacking us. No more of your men proving their worth by assaulting our women. In return, you'll have water again." She pointed to the east. "The Kulma Swamp goes right down to the ocean. So you'll have access to that too if you want it. I'm sure you have some cousins living out there who would love to see you again."

Sighoris murmured something to her mother.

"It doesn't matter anymore," Durgala snapped. "None of that matters anymore. Our vows are fulfilled. We have done what we promised."

Tyentso hoped that they hadn't vowed to keep Vol Karoth imprisoned, because if that were the case, then they'd also failed at it. Probably best to just keep that to herself.

Durgala turned to her. "I will have to ask the other Dry Mothers, but I already know what they're going to say."

"And?" Tyentso raised an eyebrow.

"They're going to say yes."

# 31. Xivan's Teacher

*Xivan's story*
*The Afterlife*
*That evening*

Xivan could only hope that Talea had figured out how to move past the Veil on her own because for the life of her (ha), Xivan couldn't explain it.

It felt like all of reality was on the other side of a massive curtain, or—no—that was the wrong metaphor. People spoke of the First Veil and the Second Veil, but it wasn't like that at all.

The separation of the two worlds wasn't a pair of veils, it was a single thing. And it was more like a waterfall. Or no: a river rushing perpendicular to the world.

One could dip one's fingers into this river, play in a little eddy formed by one's own awareness; this is what people called "seeing past the First Veil." It was safe and easy and required little effort. No one would ever drown in those shallows.

But crossing the river was a different story. Removed from the shelter of a physical body, the soul was both drawn to and buffeted by the force of that barrier. The strain to the lower soul, the cost in tenyé, was great enough that few could cross over completely. Most were swept away by the river, spinning down to its end, which was also, paradoxically, its source, where they would be washed back into the First World.

Reborn.

A cycle; an endless, elegant loop of life and death.

That's how it was for most people. Xivan wasn't most people. She hadn't been for decades, a dead person trapped in the Living World. But ever since Talea had slid a sword in its scabbard to her in the rain, she'd become something else. The sword had just been the excuse for the scabbard, and the scabbard had changed her life. Or rather, her death.

To her, the barrier was neither a curtain nor a river; it was a road. One she walked across at will in either direction.

She did this now.

The view around her changed as she stepped across, and she was struck once again by the terrible beauty of the place.

Before she became the new Thaena, she hadn't expected the Afterlife to be beautiful. It seemed inappropriate for the literal place of death to be attractive. Or perhaps it was a matter of perspective; others might find the woods dark and foreboding, the ravens and vultures sinister, the tangled vines and poisonous toadstools harbingers of doom.

But they were beautiful in her eyes. She loved the way the fog hugged close to the ground and glowed a cool bluish-green in the perpetual evening light. The lichen made mazes of decorative patterns on the trunks of trees, and the chill touch of moist air hinted at approaching rain.

She reached out a hand to a tangle of twisted, thorny vines and watched as they bloomed in response to her touch. Roses the color of arterial blood, black in the faint light and heavy with the weight of petals. The fragrance was heady.

No wonder Thaena had loved roses.

She broke off a flower, the thorns smoothing out at her touch, and turned just in time to tuck the rose behind a surprised Talea's ear.

"Beautiful," Xivan whispered.

Talea stood, momentarily speechless, then slid into Xivan's arms like coming home.

It would be the work of but a second, Xivan knew, to find a pleasant bower—or make one. There, she could spend hours in Talea's arms if she wanted.

And she wanted.

Janel cleared her throat, bringing Xivan back to reality.

The pair broke apart, both blushing. Janel's expression of fond amusement showed no hint of irritation, but there was a steel in her expression to remind them that they were there on business and under a time limit.

Janel was dressed in black armor rather than the vané garments she'd worn in the Living World. Her laevos was brighter red here, the ends brushing her shoulders with fire.

"So," Janel said as if she hadn't just interrupted them in the middle of a passionate embrace, "the trick will be to discover where Thaena—the old Thaena—trapped Doc's souls. I would think someplace where she wouldn't have to worry about him wandering off, but also where the demons can't find him and spoil her fun."

"The Land of Peace," Talea suggested.

Xivan pursed her lips. "I don't know. That seems a little too nice—"

"Not the Land of Peace," an old woman said from the tree line. "How would you stop him from wandering into his next life? Do try to use that brain I imagine is somewhere in that skull."

Xivan turned, her eyes narrowing.

"What is it?" Talea asked, glancing around.

Janel drew her sword, and slowly scanned the edges of the clearing.

Xivan frowned at Talea, making a vague gesture toward the old woman.

"Pardon the expression, but you look like you've seen a ghost," Talea said, then paused. "Wait: Are you seeing a ghost? Is that a thing you can do here?" She searched the area, but her gaze passed right over the newcomer without a reaction.

Xivan stared at the old woman. No, not old: ancient. Hoary and withered and, given the mirror finish of her eyes, some variety of voramer. Her skin was pale to the point of translucency, splashed with liver spots, and her hair a white, spindly tangle. Xivan couldn't imagine a more perfect image of a witch for such a setting. She wore robes that had once been funeral white, but age and the swampy nature of the locale had turned them a dingy gray. She leaned heavily on a gnarled and twisted walking stick. The woman seemed familiar to Xivan, although she couldn't place where she'd seen this particular old crone before.

Neither of Xivan's companions could see the old woman.

"Who are you?" Xivan asked.

The old woman chuckled, although it wasn't a friendly sound. Her expression turned even more sinister as she said, "The one you've been waiting for, I should imagine." She flashed a grin full of too-sharp, impossibly-bright teeth. "Why don't you call me Khae." It seemed less a suggestion than an order.

Xivan exhaled loudly as she realized why the woman looked so familiar. Not someone Xivan had ever met but she'd remembered reading her description.

"You're Khaemezra," Xivan stated.

"What?" Janel dropped into a defensive stance. "*Thaena's* here?"

Talea looked around wildly, but saw nothing out of the ordinary (if such a term applied in this place).

"No," the old woman snapped, "I'm most certainly *not* Khaemezra. Didn't anyone explain how this works to you? Or do I have to do all the damn work myself? As usual." She rapped her walking stick against the ground. "Fine. Let's get this over with. We have a lot of ground to go over if you're going to be anything but a complete waste of death."

"What was that?" Janel asked.

Xivan whipped her head to look at her. "Did you hear—"

Janel cut her off with a slash of one hand. "Listen!"

"Oh bother," the old woman said. "Here we go again."

Xivan tried to ignore Khae. She did hear it: hooting and ululating and screaming and shouting; the sounds of battle. Distant, but growing closer, and quickly.

"What is it?" Talea asked.

Janel's brows drew together, but her lips curled in a feral grin. "Demons," she said, sounding entirely too pleased about the idea.

"I do hate those things," the old woman muttered to herself. Xivan glanced over and blinked. Khae now sat on a tree branch some fifteen or so feet off the ground, dangling her legs and kicking. "Well? Don't just sit there like a princess visiting a farm for the first time. You have a job to do, don't you? *Kill them.*"

## 32. The Ruins of a Lighthouse

*Qown's story*
*Shadrag Gor*
*After being taken prisoner by Relos Var*

Relos Var wasted no time removing the group from the Soaring Halls. Qown knew right away where the wizard was taking them. There was only one location where it was necessary to open a magical gate underneath the feet of the entire group because it was of vital importance that they all arrived at their destination at the exact same time: the Lighthouse at Shadrag Gor. Which meant that Relos Var planned on doing something that would take *time*.

Gaeshing them, for instance.[1]

Qown shivered as Relos Var gestured in the air and wove together the spell. The portal irised out into position under their feet, dropping them all through.

Onto nothing.

The air was bitterly cold and smelled of ocean salt, petrichor, and years of accumulated bird droppings. The sky was darkening into evening, the sun already fallen behind the mountains to the east. There was nothing below them but a long drop down onto sharp rocks and tempest-torn seas. They'd come out of the magical gate in midair. At least a hundred feet of empty space stretched down underneath them, with no supports at all.

So they fell.

Before Qown could even begin properly screaming, a second portal opened under their feet. They landed somewhere else—mud and marble blocks and the smell of bamboo forests this time. But even a wizard like Relos Var could only cast complicated gate spells so fast when he'd been taken by surprise. They'd dropped twenty feet—maybe closer to thirty feet—before hitting solid ground with all the finality of throwing eggs at a stone wall. Qown landed poorly; something in his leg snapped.

The screaming was for a different reason than surprise that time.

Qown choked on the pain. He didn't want to look down at his leg, so clearly bent the wrong way. A femur break, almost certainly. The bone had pierced skin.

"Fuck," Galen groaned. He rolled, his body wrapped around the tod-

---

[1] Gaeshing can be done anywhere, of course, but the ritual is complicated and takes hours. As Relos Var seemed to be on something of a schedule, it's understandable that he would have wanted to perform said ritual at a location where that time wouldn't hinder his plans.—S

dler. While neither of them seemed seriously injured, neither was happy either. No amount of candied fruit was going to stop Tave from bawling this time.

"Qown, can you—" Galen seemed to flinch, then cursed again. "Damn. Heal yourself first, I guess."

"I'd love to, but I can't." Even if the broken fingers weren't an issue—and they were—Anlyr had weighed him down with enough talismans to keep him from doing anything that might harm others or help himself.

Sheloran seemed fine, but she still had access to her full magical abilities. She wouldn't have had a difficult time slowing her descent. Galen was fussing over the child and hadn't so much as glanced at Qown after giving him that impossible order. Which Galen knew perfectly well was impossible. Qown suspected he was trying his damnedest to act like Qown's fate concerned him not at all.

Relos Var stood off to the side, cursing.

Anlyr bent down over Qown. "I've got you," he said gently and started breaking the wires holding the talisman coins with a dagger's edge. "Can hardly heal yourself wearing these fun little gems, now can you?"

"You should know. You put them on me," Qown said through gritted teeth.

"And now I'm removing them. Straightening the leg's going to hurt, but then you already knew that."

"You were never in any danger," Qown murmured. "When we first met, when those assassins attacked Galen's carriage back in the Capital. Relos Var was the one who healed you. Were you even injured at all?"

Anlyr smiled wryly. "Not really, no, but I'm fantastic at faking it. And who do you think sent the assassins?" He stage-whispered, "Here's a hint: it wasn't Gerisea."

Galen scoffed, having apparently overheard. The child was crying again, and who could blame him? Qown was crying too. He'd genuinely thought he was about to die. Of all the dangers he'd faced in the past four years, it struck him as horribly unfair to think what finally killed him would be something as simple as a miscast gate spell.

Except Relos Var didn't miscast spells. So what had happened?

"What was *that*?" Sheloran's voice cracked with hysterical laughter. "I would think that if you wanted to break one of our healer's legs, there were easier ways to accomplish the task."

Relos Var made a sound that could only charitably be called laughter. "Indeed there are." He took stock of his former apprentice's situation with an apathetic eye before he focused on Sheloran. "Still bored?"

Sheloran flushed and didn't answer. Galen looked between Qown and Sheloran, clearly trying to decide if it was worth breaking character to see if Qown was all right.

Qown shook his head minutely and hoped Anlyr didn't notice.

Galen narrowed his eyes. Then he moved over to Sheloran with the boy still in his arms.

"I don't want to hold him," Sheloran snapped. "He was your idea."

Anlyr laughed, looking delighted. "Oh, it's a little late to pretend you don't care about the tyke. Terribly sorry, but that baby boy is officially on the 'useful hostage' list, so you might as well try to see if you can dry his tears and make sure he knows his mommy loves him." He waved the hand that he wasn't using to remove Qown's talismans. "Or keep up the acting. I always appreciate a good performance. You're good."

"You're a monster," Sheloran spat.

"You have *no idea,*" Anlyr agreed amiably. He continued removing talismans from Qown with quick flicks of that blade. "Now, Lord Var, I am curious about something. Weren't we supposed to be going to the Lighthouse at Shadrag Gor? Because I couldn't help but notice a distinct lack of Lighthouse in our immediate vicinity."

"Yes," Relos Var answered dryly. "I noticed that too."

"I've always admired your skills at observation," Anlyr continued. "Only *why* was there no Lighthouse?"

Var leveled a look at Anlyr sharp enough to cut through steel, a look that clearly said the man could push his luck too far. Anlyr grinned a mischievous smile, then ducked his head and returned to concentrating on Qown. The priest felt a warmth fill his thigh as magical energy flowed into him, then numbness. That was galling, on multiple levels. Anlyr had just used a Vishai healing technique. Qown knew it well. And so did Anlyr. And why wouldn't he? Qown had learned the method from Relos Var, even if he hadn't known his mentor's true identity at the time. Had Anlyr studied at the Temple of Light, some nameless acolyte Qown had never met? Or had they met, and Qown hadn't remembered him?

"You might want to clench your teeth for this next part," Anlyr advised.

"Yes, thank you." Qown did. He knew what was coming and wasn't disappointed when the most horrible, sharp pain gripped him, shooting up his leg directly into his spine. The world went white, then black.

When he blinked his universe into some semblance of coherence, he still lay down on the ground, but Anlyr had walked away. The little boy, Tave, had stopped crying and had been set down. He'd walked over to Qown, where he was wiping Qown's hair away from his eyes. The gesture might have been better appreciated if Tave's fingers weren't still sticky with sugar candy, but that was truly the least of Qown's worries at that moment.

Qown smiled at him, then his gaze shifted back to Galen, worried and tense. They met each other's eyes, and Qown nearly flinched at the despair that slouched in Galen's stare.

"You good now?" the little boy asked, before solemnly clarifying why exactly Qown might be feeling a little out of sorts: "You fell wrong."

"Yes, I did," Qown answered. "Thank you." He dragged himself up into a sitting position and finally saw where they'd landed.

The Temple of Light, in Eamithon. What remained of it. The former temple was mostly open field and burial mounds at that moment, rows of neatly stacked white marble that might one day be reused to build . . . something.

The area had been cleansed of the more macabre and obscene twisted details that Qown had witnessed when they were last there, in the aftermath of Goro-kai the dragon's attack. He didn't know what Relos Var had done with the bodies, with the warped bits of stone. And Relos Var himself . . .

Relos Var watched Qown with eyes devoid of all expression. Qown felt a chill. Whatever tenderness or affection had ever been there was truly gone now. Relos Var was done pretending to be a creature capable of love. Or maybe whatever affection he might have once felt toward Qown just didn't matter. No amount of friendship, love, or loyalty would impede Relos Var's goals. But Qown suspected this was more personal—their relationship had been more personal. More paternal. The worst possibility was that Relos Var had viewed Qown as much a son as Qown had viewed the wizard a father. And if Var was allowed to betray, use, and manipulate Qown, the reverse wasn't true.

Qown's throat closed. He'd thought he might bluff his way through when Anlyr had come for him. He'd tried, he really had. Qown had failed in his mission to reclaim Grimward, yes, but there'd been no reason to think Relos Var would punish him for it. Relos Var had never been one to punish fail-ure with any sting more lingering than parental disappointment. It had been Qown's first mission; he'd messed up. Relos Var must have known there was a chance he would.

Because Qown had been trying to bluff, trying to pretend that he was still a loyal lapdog, he'd even handed Worldhearth over without hesitation when Relos Var had asked for it. It's what Qown would have done, back in the days when he thought Relos Var was someone to be trusted.

It was only once Relos Var had Worldhearth again in his possession that Qown realized that he hadn't fooled the man at all. When Qown had tried to explain himself with the cover story they'd created, Relos Var's stare had turned flinty, then ice cold. Var had known Qown was lying.[2]

This had become a more personal enmity.

No, Qown had been wrong. Relos Var's stare wasn't expressionless at all. It was full of hate. Qown didn't think his odds of surviving this were looking good.

"What happens now?" Sheloran asked the wizard.

"What I'd wanted was to take you all back to Shadrag Gor so we could do this with some modicum of decorum. Take our time. But it seems that's no longer possible."

Anlyr looked up. "Isn't the Lighthouse at Shadrag Gor supposed to be indestructible?"

"Yes," Relos Var growled, "it *is*."

Qown saw Galen's eyes widen. It wasn't hard to guess why. If the Light-house at Shadrag Gor was gone now, if it was destroyed, what were the odds that the group of people Senera had taken there hadn't had something to

---

[2] Well, he is something like fourteen thousand years old. Unfortunately, we may not have paid enough attention to the fact that he's just very, very good at reading people.—S

do with that destruction? That *Kihrin* hadn't had something to do with that destruction? Qown gave the other man a minute shake of his head. This was not a subject to be discussed under any circumstances. Hell, the whole reason Senera had marked those glyphs on them to keep their minds from being read was because it had been so incredibly, vitally important that no one knew the truth about what had really happened back at the Lighthouse.

And this? They'd fallen right into the worst-case scenario. It was infuriating how little time it had taken Relos Var to come this close to the secrets he was never supposed to know. Now they'd find out if Caless's attempt to use the Stone of Shackles to ward them against gaeshe worked.

Or else Qown would have to resort to more desperate measures.

A shadow off in the bushes caught Qown's attention. It was behind Relos Var, behind Anlyr as well. For a split second, it coalesced into something recognizable, if only as a shadowy form too cohesive to be merely a trick of the light through trees. The blank ceramic mask, though—that was the giveaway.

Jarith Milligreest.

The shadow demon vanished again as if he had never been.

Qown just had to pray, if that would ever again be the right choice of words, that Jarith was still listening. "Was it you who gave Warmonger to Tyentso?" he asked Relos Var. "It must have been you, yes? Although I suppose Tyentso doesn't have to be the one carrying it, as long as it's someone close by, right?"

Relos Var paused. "You noticed that."

"It's difficult not to, if you know what to look for," Qown said. "The heightened aggression, the extreme resistance to pain that all the soldiers seem to have, the tribal loyalties. All that sounds just the thing for Warmonger, and I know you're the last one who was in possession of it."

"What are you talking about?" Sheloran asked.

Qown struggled to make his speech seem casual, chatty. "Warmonger is one of the Cornerstones. Relos Var used it a few months ago to lure Kihrin D'Mon into a trap, and Relos Var didn't give it away afterward. But now it seems like Empress Tyentso's become the beneficiary of its powers. Which has some unfortunate implications about her loyalties. Someone close to the empress—and I hope it's not the empress herself—must be working for Relos Var here."

He hoped that was enough. That Jarith had heard all that and would bring word back to the others in time to do something.

"Enough," Relos Var said. "I'm not interested in gossiping about Warmonger. I want to know what happened to the Lighthouse. Tell me." Var's voice was velvet soft.

Qown shifted his gaze back to Relos Var. "The Lighthouse? You know what I know. I didn't think the Lighthouse could be destroyed."

"What are you talking about?" Galen asked.

Var stared at both men very carefully. "It seems I won't have enough time to gaesh you, after all."

A whole-body shudder ran down Qown's spine and along his limbs.

"Gaesh?" Sheloran's eyes showed white around the edges. He admired what a good actress she was; they'd known from the start this was a risk.

"Do control yourself, Lady D'Mon," Relos Var cautioned, "and try to remember just how out of patience I am."

Sheloran stepped back. Galen picked up Tave.

"Here's what we're going to do," Var said. "We shall travel to a location more suitable for keeping the three of you under control. After that, I'll craft a few talismans to make sure none of you cause trouble and Anlyr will keep watch on you, while I visit your mother, Lady D'Mon."

Sheloran's face went blank. "She won't give you the stone."

"You're mistaken. I happen to have something in my possession she desperately hopes not to lose."

"He means you, Red," Galen whispered.

"I know that," she snapped. "Have I mentioned how much I really hate being seen as nothing more than a bargaining chip?"

"Be glad of it," Var said. "As it's the only incentive I have to keep you alive." He turned to Anlyr. "Can he be moved?"

Qown bit back on the urge to remind Var that Qown could answer for himself. It didn't seem wise to draw the man's anger.

"Yes," Anlyr said. To underscore that statement, he picked up Qown with an arm under his shoulder and another under his knees, ignoring the healer's squawk. "Where to?"

"Senera's," Relos Var answered. "She's not answering her summons. After recent events, I'm starting to take the silences personally." He began weaving the spell for the gate, this one a more standard open portal they would have to walk through—which prevented any mistakes like what had happened at the Lighthouse.

Qown had a good idea he knew what had happened at the Lighthouse. Senera had linked Vol Karoth's prison at Kharas Gulgoth to the Lighthouse at Shadrag Gor. Depending on the strength of that link, it was possible that when Kihrin broke free of his prison, he created a reciprocal, sympathetic act of destruction at the Lighthouse too.

They had, without meaning to, annihilated one of the most magical—and magically exploited—locations in the entire world.[3]

Qown found himself feeling very, very grateful that Kihrin had waited until they'd all left before he'd performed his jailbreak.

Relos Var gestured toward the open portal. "After you," he told Galen and Sheloran.

The princess looked ready to flay the man with a stare, but Relos Var give that threat all the attention he thought it deserved—which is to say none at all. Galen seemed quieter and less openly rebellious, but he was carrying a small child at this point, which made it difficult to hold a sword. Qown assumed Galen had done the math well enough to know that his survival was only of

---

[3] I would argue the Lighthouse claims first place here. Everyone used that location for their schemes at one point or another, including us.—T

secondary importance to his mother-in-law. She'd want Galen back, yes, but she'd still make the deal if it was only for her daughter.

Galen was, as Relos Var had mentioned several times already, expendable. The child, Tave? Very expendable.

And Qown himself? Qown wasn't on the list. Relos Var wasn't interested in ransoming him—or letting him live.

When they stepped through the portal, the cold air slapped across the sinuses. It was evening, and although Qown had been to Senera's sanctuary only once previously in the flesh (and another time as a scrying spirit), he still had no idea where the cottage was located. Someplace considerably farther north than he was used to.[4]

Then the smell of ash and smoke wiped any other odors from Qown's mind. There were more pressing concerns than the geographic location of Senera's cottage.

The entire house had burned to the ground.

Var stared at the faintly glowing embers of the house with a look of pure fury on his face. "Oh. *I see.*"

"Shit," Anlyr cursed. "She . . . Someone must have found her." He lowered Qown to the ground.

"Watch the others. You know what to do if someone makes trouble."

"Of course," the man murmured.

Relos Var slowly walked through the still-red-hot ashes of the ruin. He wasn't bothered by the heat, but then, it made sense that he wouldn't have been. Var searched the cottage, although what he searched for was unclear. Possibly Senera's body. When he returned, however, his expression had only grown colder.

"She's not in there?" Anlyr asked, sounding like he genuinely dreaded the answer.

"Nothing's in there," Var said. "Not a piece of paper, not a book. Someone emptied the cottage out and then burned it to the ground. Unfortunately, I suspected something like this. There are times when I do hate being right."

Anlyr cursed.

"Who are we talking about?" Sheloran asked.

Qown thought it was a mistake to draw attention to herself like that, even if it was as an attempt to reassure Var that she was ignorant of details such as Senera's identity. Thurvishar and Senera must have moved her possessions before setting the house on fire, but it would hardly be wise to voice such a theory out loud.[5]

Var started to give what probably would've been a sarcastic response, but then he stopped and stared at Sheloran. His gaze slowly flickered to Galen, then to Qown.

---

[4] It's in northern Kirpis.—S

[5] In hindsight, we really should have made copies of all the books and research notes to give him something to find.—S

Yes, but there was no time. Even Shadrag Gor has its limits.—T

"I thought she'd been kidnapped," Relos Var said. "But I was wrong. I lost both of you, didn't I?"

Qown's stomach twisted. *No, no, no.*

"Boss?" Anlyr raised an eyebrow. "What are you thinking?" He shook his head to refute the wizard's declaration. "No, come on. Not Senera. She'd never. Something must have happened to her. Someone must have found her and ambushed her."

Relos Var didn't seem to be listening. He'd already made up his mind. "Keep an eye on them," Var said. "I'll return shortly."

Relos Var vanished from the clearing.

# 33. A Demon's Appetites

### *Xivan's story*
### *The Afterlife*
### *After meeting "Khae" for the first time*

"Oh, this brings back memories," Janel muttered as the first wave of demons broke from the tree line. Demon hounds—mostly bestial but with the faintest uncomfortable traces of human features still discernible. As the hounds raced toward them, Janel said, "Careful with these ones. They're not dangerous by themselves, but they'll overwhelm you in large numbers—"

She broke off as the hounds shot past her, past Xivan and Talea, and raced toward the other side of the clearing.

"—at least that's what they normally try to do," Janel finished. She sounded as confused as Xivan felt.

Before they had time to discuss the odd behavior, more demons entered the clearing. These were proper demons in horrific chimerical forms. Many of them resembled monstrous knights astride equally awful steeds. One spotted the three women and couched its lance. The demon's trajectory was off, but it didn't bother making a course correction; instead, the demon and its mount galloped past, a few yards to Talea's right.

A second wave followed the first.

"I'm starting to feel offended," Janel said as she watched the retreating demons. "I swear this is not how they normally behave—"

"Heads up!" Talea called out.

A third wave of demons entered the clearing. Unlike the first two, this wave came in walking, stumbling, tripping. A fighting retreat. These demons were battling something—something large enough and strong enough that they could neither easily defeat it nor easily run. Crashing sounds echoed through the woods as their opponent smashed trees to splinters while in pursuit.

That destruction became more personal when the last trees into the clearing exploded, showering the three women in daggerlike shards. The shrapnel flew in all directions, bounced off Janel's arm, and never even came close to touching Talea. Xivan expected to be impaled herself, but the wood ricocheted off her upraised arm, either because she was harder to hurt in the Afterlife or because the woods themselves refused to harm her.

"Oh. It's *that* demon. I hate *that* demon," the old woman in the tree said.

"Joy," Janel said at the same time. "Really, I should have known."

Xivan lowered her arms to see. A writhing mass of animal demons seethed around a central figure, snapping and clawing as they tried to prevent it from advancing. The target of their wrath was huge; a humanoid male with obscene muscles, arms dipped in blood to his elbows, huge sharp teeth in a too-large mouth, and a crocodile's tail that lashed to and fro.

A lionlike demon with razor-sharp quills launched itself at the huge figure, only to be caught mid-flight. The blood-drenched central demon grabbed his attacker and bit down, a ghastly, oversize bite that would have cut the other demon in half if it hadn't dispersed. Xivan *felt* the tenyé of the weaker demon flow into its killer.

"Is that—?" Talea started to ask.

"Xaltorath!" Janel screamed.

***HELLO, DAUGHTER!*** Xaltorath "said," his words battering at their minds like a siege ram.[1] ***WHAT A PLEASANT SURPRISE. LET ME FINISH YOUR LESSER COUSINS, AND THEN WE CAN HAVE A REUNION. OH, AND YOU BROUGHT ME SOME IMMORTALS. HOW LOVELY. I HAVEN'T TASTED THEIR KIND IN DAYS.***

"Run," suggested Talea.

***YES, PLEASE DO,*** Xaltorath said, scooping up and consuming a few more demons. ***YOU KNOW HOW I LOVE THE CHASE.***

Janel scowled and took up a battle stance. She wasn't going anywhere. On the other hand, the look on her face suggested unpleasant consequences for everyone who stayed, herself included. "Go!" she shouted at Xivan and Talea.

The demons too stupid to run were ignoring the three of them for the moment, but that was only because Xaltorath had their attention. Given the rate at which he was eating his way through the enemy forces, it wouldn't be long before Xaltorath was free to focus on them.

"I think the little girl's right," Khae said from the tree. "Retreat. You're not ready for this fight."

"And how exactly are we supposed to escape him?" Xivan snapped.

The old woman blinked, baffled. Then she scoffed and leaped down from the tree. "Not on foot! Oh, you really are the first fish in the net, aren't you? Like this!" The old woman disappeared from her original position and reappeared directly in front of Xivan. With her walking stick, she hit Xivan in the shoulder, the hip, the belly.

Xivan blinked. She felt that. How the hell had she *felt* that . . . ?

Khae moved to attack her again, and this time, Xivan parried the blows. Across the way, Xaltorath ripped a demon in half with his teeth, tossed both parts aside, and advanced on Janel, grinning.

***YOUR TURN.***

---

[1] Gender pronouns are a bit tricky for a demon like Xaltorath, who sometimes appears male and sometimes female. Janel typically refers to the demon as "she," but it's clear that there are times when Xaltorath refers to themselves as a "he"—so we've chosen to use the pronouns matching the form Xaltorath is holding at the time, and "they" for those instances when gender preference is unclear.–T & S

Janel readied her sword and shield. Talea took up a position next to her.

The old woman gave Xivan an evil, pleased smile. "Good! Now again, but this time use your tenyé as you block. Here! Here! Here!"

The old woman attacked a third time; Xivan didn't make her do it a fourth. As Xivan parried the last blow, she pushed out with her tenyé. The world around her changed. Just like that, Xivan and her companions were somewhere else.

She thought she could feel Xaltorath's scream of rage echo through the very rocks.

## 34. SKYFIRE

**_Tyentso's story_**
**_The imperial military camp, Khorvesh_**
**_Later that evening_**

*[Tyentso, are you alone?]*

Tyentso raised her head as she heard Kihrin's voice. She double-checked each ward and then exhaled.

"I am," she said. She had, in fact, been about to go to bed. Sleep wasn't an opportunity she could afford to let escape her.

*[I need a favor.]*

It sounded like Kihrin . . . sort of. It also sounded viscerally wrong, like hearing his thoughts magnified and strained through a dozen pieces of silk. Like he was speaking with hurricane ferocity, but from miles away.

She blinked in surprise. "*You?* You need a favor?" It's not that she wasn't willing to help, but she was having a difficult time wrapping her mind around the idea of why he'd need one. "What can I do that you can't?"

*[Hold something without destroying it.]*

"Oh."

*[Are you familiar with a dragon named Gorokai?]*

"Distantly. I don't remember exactly—he hasn't been very active, I don't think."

Kihrin sounded amused. *[He's very active, but seldom in a form anyone would recognize. Gorokai is a shape-changer. He's in possession of a Cornerstone that he stole from Relos Var recently—Skyfire. I need you to retrieve the stone.]*

"Scamp, I'm a little busy right now. It's not like I can drop dealing with two different armies just to go dragon hunting . . ."

*[I'm not asking you to fight Gorokai. He'll give you the Cornerstone when you ask, but you're going to have to collect it now. The timing's tricky on this. If I want to make sure Var doesn't sense me nudging Gorokai, I'm going to have to make it quick. That's why I can't send the dragon to you. You have to go to him.]*

"Are you . . . are you all right?"

Silence. Then: *[As well as I can be, Ty. But you're the one I'm worried about right now.]*

"I'm fine." She started to wave away the concern, and then stopped herself. "Okay, no. No, I'm not fine." Tyentso exhaled. "Someone's fucking with my people. Cursed them or something. I'm not sure. But it's making everyone angry and violent all the time. And then . . ." She dry swallowed. "Someone's also going the extra step to make it seem like Gadrith's still alive. They're trying to scare me."

*[You should talk to Thurvishar and Senera,]* Kihrin suggested. *[They might recognize what's going on. As for Gadrith . . . ]* He hesitated.

"Spit it out, Scamp."

*[Ty . . . I'm not saying that this is what's happening, because I don't know, but I think you should remember just how much Relos Var likes to strike at people through their family.]*

"Yes, I know that. We've had this conversation—"

*[Gadrith's still your family. And just because you don't like your father doesn't mean he isn't a sore spot, a weakness. Relos Var knows that.]*

She scowled. He wasn't telling her anything new. "Well, whoever's responsible either is a member of House D'Lorus or has access to one. They left some hair behind, and I tested it."

Kihrin paused again. *[So what if it really is Gadrith?]*

"That's *impossible*. You killed him, Scamp. And Thaena would never let Gadrith—" She stumbled over her words and made a choking noise. "Fuck."

She was being an idiot.

Thaena was dead. Which meant no one was keeping Gadrith's soul locked away *anywhere*. And given what a talented necromancer Gadrith had been, there were any number of ways that he might have engineered his return now that the gates were unguarded, including (but hardly limited to) ghostly possession. She damn well knew *that* was possible. Gadrith dead and gone?

It would be foolish in the extreme to assume it *couldn't* be Gadrith.

"Thanks, Scamp," she said faintly. "You've given me . . . a lot to think about. I'm going to have to take some steps."

*[But you'll still go get Skyfire, right?]*

"Only because you're the one who's asking."

*[Thank you. Head to the D'Moló emerald mines in the Dragonspires. Go to a tavern called the Four Riches.]*

Tyentso paused, surprised. "A tavern? You want me to find a dragon in a tavern?"

*[He likes to gamble,]* Kihrin said as if that context somehow made sense. *[Be careful. Of all the dragons besides my brother, he's the most dangerous.]*

### The Dragonspires
### Immediately after talking to Kihrin

The D'Moló emerald mines were more of a mining town, a small community of several thousand people nestled in the foot of the Dragonspires. The population was entirely male save for the velvet girls that worked their trade there. On the whole the community seemed ramshackle and temporary. If House D'Moló had spent any of their money on the town, it was on the mines themselves and not on the areas where workers lived. Those were shanties, barely holding up under their own weight.

The Four Riches looked like it was the seediest tavern in the entire mining town, and that was saying something. She watched three men with broken arms spill out the front door as she approached, cursing to themselves and moaning. Tyentso didn't see a bouncer specifically throwing them out, but she thought that could be assumed. Enough noise filtered through the thin walls to make her wonder if someone was staging fights inside.

Tyentso thought about staying invisible, but there were so many people crowding the streets near the entrance—all the boisterous drunks looking for a fun night out—that it was impossible she wouldn't bump into someone. So instead, she plastered her best *"don't mess with me"* glare on her face and strong-armed her way inside. She pushed aside anyone who tried to stop her. Or magically shocked them. Or both.

The tavern lived up to all her expectations, dim and smoky and smelling of stale beer, piss, and blood. It was a raucous place trying whenever possible to separate miners from their metal. A large crowd gathered on one side of the bar to watch some sort of arm-wrestling contest. Still more people gathered around the bar, working diligently on improving their drinking skills. People shouted at each other, traded insults and drinks.

Tyentso was supposed to find a *dragon* here?

"Hey, you want anything?" A bar wench approached her, looked her up and down, and quickly decided that she was a customer and not anyone related to the velvet industry. Possibly those D'Lorus black eyes gave it away, although in this lighting, it was hard to say. The brightest corner of the whole tavern shone from somewhere beyond the crowd gathered around the wrestling contest, blocked by the wall of bodies. Probably a firepit.

"Give me a rice wine." Tyentso placed enough thrones on the woman's tray to pay for a whole night of drinks. "Keep the change. Have you seen anything odd—"

A sharp, snapping sound filled the air, followed immediately by a man's scream and a child's mocking laughter.

Tyentso stared in the direction of the crowd.

"Well, yeah." The woman picked up the coins, gave them an appreciative once-over, and then leaned in to stage-whisper, "Gorokai's back, and that's plenty odd. But I wouldn't mess with that, ma'am, not unless you want to end up hurt. He's bad news."

Tyentso blinked at the woman.

*Gorokai's back.* Sure. Said like any old piece of gossip. Said the way one might explain that the local bully had come back—unwelcome, but too tough to run out of town. *Keep away from the dragon, ma'am, if you know what's good for you.*

Tyentso pushed her way to the front of the crowd.

A giant bruiser of a man cradled his savagely broken arm with tears running down his face. Sitting across from him, laughing, was a small, pale-skinned boy with silver hair.[1]

The boy banged the table in front of him. "Next!" When no one immediately stepped up, the child pointed to the mound of coins, notes, and raw gems piled up in front of him. "Oh, come on, doesn't anyone want to be rich?"

The crowd grumbled, unhappy. Clearly, they all wanted to be rich, and equally clearly, no one would end up that way by accepting the boy's wager. Tyentso wondered why no one had tried to steal the gems, but then she noticed the blood under the table. She corrected her opinion: several someones had already tried. And failed.

The crowd could only watch, salivating over the treasure like a pack of dogs scenting raw steak. She didn't blame them. The gems in that pile were . . .

Tyentso cursed.

A shockingly large yellow diamond perched at the apex of that pile, reflecting the light from the nearby fireplace so intensely that it seemed to glow.

Tyentso's breath left her in a sharp huff. Skyfire. That was the fucking Cornerstone, right there, being used to sweeten a betting pool. Which meant . . .

Which meant the little boy was the dragon Gorokai.

At that moment, said dragon-disguised-as-child turned and stared straight at her before a remarkably sinister grin spread over his face.

"You." Gorokai pointed at Tyentso. "Oh, you're strong. What an aura you have." He put his elbow on the table and wriggled his fingers. "Fight me."

"I don't arm wrestle," Tyentso said.

"Fight me," Gorokai repeated, "or I'll get upset." He narrowed his eyes. "When I'm upset, I might do *anything*."

She glanced at the crowd, who were muttering to themselves. No one was exactly cheering the boy on, although they had been quite vocal earlier—probably egging on the man they had hoped would win. More important was the fact that the building wasn't large enough to hold this gathering *and* a full-size dragon.

The threat was clear enough: play the dragon's game, or watch as the dragon threw a temper tantrum that would level the entire camp.

Tyentso gestured toward the Cornerstone. "You're supposed to give that to me."

Gorokai beamed at her. The context of knowing what he really was made an otherwise adorable smile creepy as hell. "Win against me in a game and it's yours."

"I thought you preferred riddles," she said as she sat down in the chair the wounded man had vacated.

The boy rolled his eyes. "You're thinking of Baelosh."

---

[1] I'm sure it's no coincidence that such a description greatly resembles the original Taja, who was Gorokai's daughter.—T

*Kihrin,* Tyentso thought, *I thought you said he was going to give the damn Cornerstone to me.*

She could all but feel Kihrin sighing. *[He was supposed to. Unfortunately, he's very good at not doing what he's supposed to do. You know what that means.]*

*I'm going to have to play.*

*[You're going to have to play, yes.]*

"Don't do it, lady," one of the men said lowly. "That one isn't just breaking arms. He's ripping them off too."

Gorokai's violet gaze flicked over to the miner who'd said that. A low growl rumbled from him that was far larger than his small size and shook the floorboards.

The miner turned gray and backed away.

Tyentso put her elbow on the table and presented her hand. "Promise me you'll leave these people alone no matter who wins," she said.

"I thought you wanted Skyfire," the little boy said. "Make up your mind." The glee in his voice was wire tight and promised all manner of ugliness.

She shuddered. Tyentso hoped that the fact the barmaid had recognized him—had identified him—meant that he wouldn't destroy the town. This was his playground. He'd been here before, enough to be a known, if feared, factor.

But no. That was wishful thinking. Gorokai didn't give a fuck. He'd wipe out this town for a laugh. Or any town.

"If you expect to win," Tyentso said, "then what's the harm in promising both?"

"I haven't seen what you're offering," Gorokai said. "It would need to be twice as good." He pointed to the circlet on her head. "I'll have that." Then he pointed to the wand at her belt. "And that."

"They're yours," Tyentso said, "if I lose—and if you can take them."

If Tyentso lost, she'd be dead—and in those circumstances, the Crown and Scepter would teleport back to the Arena in the Capital.

Good luck getting those artifacts then.

The little boy sniffed. "Acceptable." He reached up and put his hand in hers, so that she had to shift the angle a little to let the boy's elbow reach the table. It felt like a child's hand, soft and warm and showing no signs that he'd been mutilating arms all evening for giggles. She felt sorry for the miners, who had no way to know that this was just a trap, that trying to win against this "child" would be like betting someone they could lift a rock off the ground only to discover said rock was one of the Dragonspires. He only looked like a child.

He was still a dragon.

Gorokai grinned at her and started to lower his arm, fast and hard with the full force of all his immortal draconic strength. He stopped smiling as her arm didn't budge.

Tyentso may not have been a Guardian or an Immortal, but by the Veil, she was the Empress of Quur, and that *meant* something. In many ways, it was like being a god-king. The patriotic fervor and power of a nation channeled tenyé into her every second of the day. It was a heady, intoxicating bounty. If she wanted to channel that power into keeping a damn dragon from ripping off her arm, she could.

But she saw the problem immediately: she wasn't *winning* either. Neither was Gorokai. They just sat there, staring at each other while their tenyé built up like the air pressure before a tornado. Coins began to bounce and slide across the table. The air shimmered with magical energy.

The miners witnessing this confrontation began to back away, while those in the rear of the crowd ran. Even people otherwise fully insensitive to magic felt the tremendous potential for destruction vibrating in the air.

Gorokai's smile returned, but this time, it was far more feral, with very little of the cute child in it. The whites showed all around his irises; he didn't look sane. The skin along his arm rippled, as though something under his skin had decided it was time to crawl out.

Probably true.

*Okay, Scamp. Do your thing.*

Tyentso couldn't hear or feel what Kihrin did, but Gorokai flinched as though someone had just screamed in his ear.[2]

That second of distraction was all she needed. Tyentso burned through a stunning amount of magical energy as she slammed the dragon's arm down through the table, shattering it and sending the pile of treasure bouncing to the ground. She caught the yellow diamond before it rolled away.

"Run! Keep running!" Tyentso screamed at any bar patrons or staff stupid enough to try to collect any of that treasure. In theory, she'd won, and that meant Gorokai would leave without killing anyone. In theory.

She didn't trust that theory. She was confident that if she left the dragon there, he'd go back on his word and level the damn place just for spite. But that was the trick, wasn't it? Gorokai might not do what he was told, but he was also easily distracted. Dealing with him was just a matter of giving the damn baby a different toy to rip apart.

Whatever Kihrin was doing, he was still doing it. Gorokai bent over, clutching his head. He paid no attention to his surroundings.

"You lose," she told the dragon.

Tyentso opened up a gate under his feet.

---

[2] I believe that's exactly what happened.—T

# 35. Step Six: Don't Avoid Working in the Field

***Kihrin's story***
***Teraeth's dreams***
***Just after midnight***

"What am I doing here?" Teraeth glanced around the black-sand beach of Ynisthana with obvious distrust, which was understandable considering the whole "destroyed in a violent cataclysm" fate the island had suffered only a few months earlier. In the real world, what was left of Ynisthana hadn't even finished cooling down. Perhaps it was possible to walk across the island without burning one's feet, but I wouldn't bet on it.

"Oh, that's my fault," I said. "You fell asleep, and I took advantage. I have to say this dream stuff is pretty fun."

I leaned back on an elbow as I lay against the sand, one leg crossed over the other, dressed in Ynisthana cultist white. Overhead, seagulls chased each other against the teal sky. Waves caressed the shore with foamy white fingers, scattering sea spray and salt. Everything was brilliantly highlighted by the red-orange sun in the sky, glaring to the point of being washed out.

Teraeth turned and examined me for a long minute.

"What's the password?" Teraeth asked.

"Cold clam broth," I replied, grinning. A joke between the two of us started while we'd been trapped in the Korthaen Blight, but one we'd continued.

"Oh, thank fuck," Teraeth said as he threw himself into my arms. "I'd have been so pissed if I'd just invented this to torture myself."

I decided it would probably be best not to point out that since Teraeth knew the password, he could still have created a dream involving me knowing the password. That might have interrupted the kissing.

I was rather enjoying the kissing.

When we finally came up for air, Teraeth began nibbling down the side of my neck. Laughing, I had to put my hands on the other man's shoulders to stop him. "Much as I love this, I'm here to talk to you, not to make out."

"That's the brilliant part. We can talk after we make out," Teraeth suggested. His clever hands slipped under my shirt and slid across my skin in a delightful tease.

So possibly the decision to have this dream happen in a fairly sexy location had been a mistake.

"It's about your mother."

Teraeth sat up. "You could have just said no."

I pulled my legs up under me, leaned over to kiss Teraeth's cheek. "That would imply I didn't want to, which would be a lie. But I do need to talk to you about your mother."

Teraeth scowled and looked away. He was still turned away when he said, "So talk."

"I think Relos Var may be trying to do something that will kill a whole lot of people. A great deal more than we'd assumed his plans would endanger. I'd like to confirm that before I change course in response, and the two people most likely to know are Galava and Thaena—the "your mother" version of Thaena. Galava's souls have been eaten by Xaltorath, so I can't talk to her until I've dealt with them, but Thaena is a different song."

"Khaemezra." Teraeth spat his mother's name like an expletive. "I thought she *couldn't* be resurrected. I thought that was the whole fucking point."

"While she was a Guardian, yes," I said. "Although even that's not completely true."

Teraeth turned back to me. "What?"

I took a deep breath. Part of what I hated about this conversation was the way it made me dig into memories I'd have rather left in their graves. "You killed Khaemezra last time, but she's died before, and that time, I was responsible. I didn't just kill her, Teraeth. I *destroyed* her. I destroyed all of them. Their souls were spread out, yes, but as far as I can tell, Grizzst figured out the solution to that problem right away. The problem was finding a body that could safely contain that energy. Now that she's *not* a Guardian, though—because someone else has come along and snaked the job away from her—that's no longer a problem. She could theoretically be Returned. She wouldn't be a Guardian, but she'd be alive. If only she hadn't died trying to wipe out the one group of people with the skill to both repair her body and preserve it until that could happen, right?"

Teraeth winced.

I scooted closer to him, wrapped an arm around him so I could rub the small of his back. He wasn't technically shirtless, but he might as well have been. "Likewise, since she's not Thaena anymore, there's no reason to think her souls didn't go to the Afterlife, the way souls are supposed to. Just another person wandering the forests of the dead without their memories."

Teraeth snorted.

"Yeah, I'm not betting any metal on the idea your mother can't remember either. Which is what I'm hoping, because I need her memory intact."

As Teraeth stared out at the ocean, his eyes wet and brilliantly green. He pulled his knees up to his chest and wrapped his arms around them. "And so . . . what? You want me to tell you how to find her? I'm not sure I could do that."

"No, I want you to come along."

Teraeth's head whipped around, and he stared. "Are you joking?" His voice was thick and ground-glass rough. "You must be joking."

"No," I said. "I'm not. Now, I can't make you go. I would never dream of demanding that you go. You are under absolutely no obligation. But I would never forgive myself if I didn't at least give you the option. If you want to see her one last time, this is your chance."

"Sure, maybe I can murder her again."

"You didn't murder her last time."

"I wouldn't say that in front of her if you want her to cooperate with any of your plans," Teraeth snapped. He tipped his head back and stared up at the sky. A thin, horrible laugh trailed from his throat, riding the border between hysteria and tears. "And I wouldn't bring *me* along either."

"You're still her son."

"I've gotten the feeling that doesn't mean as much as I once assumed."

I nodded. None of this was a surprise. I'd given it slim odds that Teraeth would want to see her again, even if it was just to curse her out—which she deserved. I'd also had a pretty good idea that Teraeth would refuse any such suggestion. Still, I had to give Teraeth the option.

Also, it had only been a day, but I missed him.

"I understand." I kissed his shoulder, smoothed a hand over the skin there. "When this is all done—" But I didn't finish the sentence. I couldn't. I kept flashing back to a body I couldn't control well enough to keep from disintegrating everything I touched. I still destroyed every rock I picked up. Being with Teraeth in his dreams was lovely, but the knowledge that it might be the only way I could ever touch Teraeth again? Less so.

Best not to think about it. Best to plan for a future where *that* wouldn't be my destiny. Best to find another way, like I'd promised Teraeth and Janel I would.

"I didn't say I wasn't going." Teraeth picked up a seashell from the beach and threw it petulantly. "I said you shouldn't bring me."

"Oh, I see. You're right, that's completely different."

Teraeth threw me a lopsided grin, then hopped up to his feet. "Good of you to agree with me. I'm excited about this plan. When do we go?" He hesitated. "Only . . . you have a way to bring me back, right? Pretty sure my mother's not capable of helping this time. Call it a hunch."

"Me?" I chuckled, mostly at the look of dismay on Teraeth's face. "I think you're forgetting an important detail."

Teraeth raised an eyebrow. "What?"

"Elana *liked* Kandor, remember? She did the same thing to him that she did to herself. So there's no reason you can't move between the Living World and the Afterlife the same way Janel can. That means that you can come back all by yourself."

# 36. AN UNGRATEFUL STUDENT

*Xivan's story*
***The Land of Peace, the Afterlife***
***Just after fleeing Xaltorath***

For an awful, tense moment, Xivan wasn't sure if she'd brought Janel and Talea with her. She didn't know if she'd accidentally left them behind to fight Xaltorath alone. There was so much she didn't understand about what had just happened, why it had worked, or what she had done (under Khae's instruction). She didn't know if Khae was petty enough to have left Xivan's companions behind.

No. The problem was that she *did* know Khae was petty enough.

Then she heard Janel curse. Xivan glanced over to see both Janel and Talea were standing there, still ready for battle in a fight that had been rendered obsolete.

She exhaled.

"Where are we?" Talea asked.

"A place I haven't been to in a lifetime," Janel answered.

"Is it a place that can be described with a proper noun, though?" Talea grinned. "And why were the demons fighting Xaltorath. I thought he . . . or she? I suppose *she*. I thought she was their queen?"

"Self-proclaimed," Janel said, "but it's a fair question. Although from what I saw, I don't think they were fighting her by choice. She was hunting them." Janel glanced at Xivan. "How did you manage this? I'm not complaining, but I wasn't aware that you'd stepped so much as a foot inside this place."

It was a palace; that much was obvious. A beautiful palace crafted of white marble. Delicate columns supported domed ceilings. Soft rugs lined the floors. Silk tapestries and bas-reliefs on the walls depicted hunting scenes involving massive elephants trampling demons. Jeweled lanterns threw ruby diamonds across the walls, and the air smelled of funereal incense and roses.

"I haven't," Xivan retorted, "and I have no idea where we are."

"We're exactly where you wanted to be," Khae snapped, her posture tight with offense.

Xivan stared at the old woman. "Since I don't know where we are, I'd say that's damn unlikely."

"What?" Janel asked.

Talea put a hand on Janel's arm. She grinned happily. "She's not talking to us. Xivan's finally found her Eshi."[1]

The old woman spat to the side. "What a revolting comparison. Tell her to never do it again," she ordered Xivan. "And yes, you did want to come here. You wanted someplace safe, and this is the safest place in the Afterlife. This is the Land of Peace."

"Right," Janel said in response to Talea's reminder. "So this is the Land of Peace."

Oh, that was going to be a problem. Xivan held up a hand. "Stop. You're both talking at once."

Khae shrugged. "Tell her to stop talking, then. This is *your* sanctum. You give the orders here."

"Janel can't hear you," Xivan said. "Whereas you know damn well that you're talking over other people. Give me a minute, would you?" Xivan turned to Janel. "I didn't imagine that, did I? Xaltorath was *eating* those demons?"

"She's consolidating power." Janel's worried expression was doing nothing for Xivan's sense of calm.

"Consolidating power is when you make all the chieftains swear an oath and sign trade agreements. It's not *eating* the rest of the nation."

Talea smiled and rocked a hand from side to side. "Maybe it is for demons?"

"I still can't believe they chose you," Khae mumbled.

Xivan whirled back to the "phantom" memory of Khaemezra. "Excuse me! Do you have a problem?"

"Obviously." The old woman looked visibly affronted.

"Get over it." Xivan paused. "Do you have a problem with Khorveshans?"

"I don't even know what a Khorveshan *is*," Khae hissed, stabbing her cane down into the ground for emphasis. What it emphasized was that Khae wasn't really there, that she was a helpful figment of Xivan's imagination; the cane made no impact whatsoever on the slick marble floor. "Who chose you? They should have at least picked another voramer."

"No, they shouldn't have," Xivan snapped. "The voramer don't exist anymore."

Khae inhaled sharply at the news about her people. Xivan supposed she wouldn't have known, would she? Talea had been under the impression that while the seven remaining members of the Eight Immortals had all sat down and let themselves be subject to a curious sort of duplication, Thaena had been the least willing, the most uncooperative. While the others repeated the process over the years, keeping their magical "doubles" current with their own memories, Thaena hadn't. She'd allowed it exactly once and then just tossed her talisman in the darkest, deepest hole she could find while she tried to forget that it ever existed. Khae's idea of current events was millennia out of date.

"There aren't any voramer left, just like there aren't any voras left," Xivan elaborated. "Or vordredd, for that matter. All the races are mortal now, splin-

[1] The "shadow" of Taja who mentored Talea through using her powers called herself Eshi, a nickname derived from the original Taja's full name, Eshimavari.—T

tered and fragmented. Everyone gets to die. And really, you couldn't have shown up earlier? I needed your help back in Devors. Or hell, back at the Lighthouse at Shadrag Gor."

"Yes, because the place for me to begin your lessons is in the Land of the *Living*," Khae sneered. "If I was going to begin your lessons, and honestly, I have no idea why I should." At which point, the old woman promptly turned around and began to walk off.

"She just walked away. Just like that," Xivan said, stunned. She turned to Talea. "She's leaving? Can she do that?"

"No, but I don't think she has to talk to you either. And she sounds like such a sweetheart." Talea clasped Janel's arm. "Let's step back and give these two a moment."

"Hm. If you think it's best." Janel directed that comment toward Xivan.

"Probably a good idea," Xivan said. "I need to talk with my 'Eshi.' We'll sort this out."

Khae's voice echoed from down the hallway. "Ah, so you *don't* want my help . . ."

"Eight Immortals, and I get the one who's the biggest fucking bitch in the universe," Xivan muttered.[2] She held up a finger to the other two women. "Just . . . give me one minute."

Xivan trotted down the hallway to catch up with her "teacher"—aware the whole time that this was a ridiculous exercise in subservience. In theory, Khae couldn't "leave" Xivan at all. She was just being dramatic.

When Xivan had Khae in sight again, she shouted, "You're seriously going to turn your back on everyone who needs you because you don't feel properly consulted about your replacement? What if I told you that you *did* pick me? That you, Thaena, personally picked me, put the cup in my hands, and told me to use it if and when anything happened to you."

Khae paused.

Xivan was sorely tempted to let the woman keep walking. And why—*why*—did Khae look like an old woman, anyway? She didn't have to. Xivan knew Khaemezra's true form in life had looked young and beautiful, because all of the Guardians *were immortal*, weren't they?

Khae turned her head. "Did she?"

"Of course not. You were far too scared of death to ever plan for it. Which is, I think, my new favorite definition of irony."

The old woman turned around, furious. She caught Xivan's stare and held it.

After a few seconds, Xivan raised an eyebrow. "Is that supposed to *do* something?"[3]

Khae huffed.

---

[2] Yes, the one Xivan has a "synergy" with.—S

I wasn't going to say anything.—T

[3] The original Thaena was famous for being able to see into one's soul—quite possibly literally—in a manner that most people found overwhelming. Even Relos Var wasn't immune.—T

"This would be a lot easier if you *helped* me," Xivan said.

The old woman wrinkled her nose like she was smelling something rotten. "And why should I help you? I told them that this was a stupid idea. You don't have enough time to grow into the powers you need! And don't say you'll just go to the Lighthouse at Shadrag Gor, because you can't learn some things in that damn place. You have to be *here,* in the Afterlife. This is your world now, not–" She made a vague gesture that Xivan assumed probably meant the Living World.

"So the circumstances aren't ideal. That doesn't change anything."

"They should have brought Khaemezra back to life." Her stubborn insistence on this point was far past the stage of grating on Xivan's nerves.

Xivan leaned against a wall and kicked back her leg. "They couldn't."

"Why not?" Khae demanded. "They know how."

"Grizzst's dead," Xivan explained, "and so's Galava. There's no one alive who knows how to bring Thaena back. I'm not even sure what happens to her souls. Will I find her somewhere here?"

Khae shuddered. "No. No, you won't. That was the problem before. It would have been different if we reacted like a normal person, but our souls behaved . . . oddly. Like oil poured on top of water. We couldn't re-form." Her brow knitted together. "Although I don't know what happens now that you're taking over the job. Perhaps with the connection broken, she'll end up here just like anyone else would and can be reborn like anyone else. Or perhaps she ceased to exist."

What a lovely, cheerful thought. Because it was Xivan's own fate Khae was describing as well. Talea's fate too. "That's a worry for another day. For now, it's enough to know that Vol Karoth is free—really free and not just awake and grouchy."

She thought that the news might make Khae a little more amenable to providing useful information and a badly needed shortcut to finding Terindel. Khae's knowledge was out of date, but she knew Thaena's mind better than anyone else and might know where Thaena would hide her former lover.

Khae reacted to the news like a slap, but only for a moment. Then she martialed herself and refortified her position. "That only makes my statement about you not having enough time all the more relevant. Honestly, why are you bothering? You have a year or two at most before Vol Karoth finishes annihilating everything. My advice is to enjoy the time you have. Your girlfriend's a cute one. Keep her company. Take pleasure in each other. At least make your last moments nice ones."

Xivan rolled her eyes. "Yes, great. Fantastic advice. Don't be surprised when I pay zero attention to it. Anyway, stopping Vol Karoth isn't the problem. Stopping *Relos Var* is the problem."

The old woman looked confused. "Who?"

Xivan exhaled and then fought back laughter. She didn't think the breathing was strictly necessary, but she did it, anyway. Probably because some deep-set animal part of her insisted that she should keep doing it. She told herself to focus.

"Rev'arric," Xivan clarified. "He calls himself Relos Var now, and *he*'s the problem. He's always been the problem. And yes, that means that I need to have this position even if we don't have enough time, even if I'm not who you would have chosen. Because as long as this position is already filled, Rev'arric can't assign it to someone of his own choosing—which he *will* do otherwise. He knows Thaena's dead, and I have it on good authority that he's made plans to usurp the Guardians. So I'm sorry that Khaemezra can't be Returned, but it's a war, and these things happen."

The old woman's eyes narrowed. "Did you have a grudge against Thaena? You did, didn't you?"

"A grudge?" Xivan felt laughter, dark and black, rise from her before she could stop it. And why lie, when the bitter old hag had already made it clear that she didn't feel like cooperating for no good reason other than because she was awful. "Yes, you might say I have a grudge. I hate your fucking guts. Excuse me—*Thaena's* fucking guts. I've hated Thaena since she refused to Return me because my husband had been targeted by Rev'arric. Which played into Rev'arric's hands beautifully, since it meant he could bring me back as an undead creature and thus win my husband's cooperation. I spent the last two decades as one of the soul-bound dead because of Thaena's refusal, and why? Because she was a petty bitch. I hated her even more when I found out everything she'd done, how she treated people, how she treated her own son. Maybe Khaemezra was once a good person, but that was a long time ago."

Xivan rolled her eyes. "Never mind. I don't need your help. I'll figure this out for myself." She stalked back to where the others waited.

Before she'd gone more than fifty feet, she heard Khae speak.

"Wait."

Xivan paused. She didn't turn around.

"How did Thaena die?" Khae asked.

"Do you really want to know?" Xivan didn't mock, though. In Khae's place, Xivan would want to know too.

"Yes. Tell me."

Xivan turned back. "She was in the middle of trying to wipe out the entire vané nation, as well as kill her own son, after she'd murdered his father. And that same son broke free of her control and killed her with Urthaenriel before Thaena could murder his lover too. The same battle where Galava died, by the way, as well as Argas, Taja, and Grizzst. All of which, by the way, ultimately happened because *Thaena was a damn coward.*"

"You have no right to judge her. You have no conception of how terrible Vol Karoth—"

"The fact that her fear was logical doesn't excuse what she was willing to do to avoid it. That's where the cowardice comes in. Somewhere along the way, she decided killing people—even killing millions of people—was all to-tally fine as long as it kept *her* alive."

The old woman cast her gaze at one of the tapestries, but Xivan didn't think she saw it. She was looking at something much further away. "*Killing's* such a useless word," she murmured.

"What was that?"

Khae's glare was scathing. "It's useless! It doesn't mean anything. So a bunch of souls go from the Living World to this one, and you call it *death*. So what? They won't stay here. They'll go back. They always do. It's not like death is nonexistence. It's nothing but going on an extended vacation. And anyway, I'm sure Thaena had a reason."

"Were you not listening to a word I said?" She couldn't help herself. Xivan marched back to Khae. If the phantom of a dead goddess had been anyone else, the look in Xivan's eyes would have been a terrifying thing. "Thaena had a reason, all right. But it was a stupid, petty, craven reason. Ul-timately, she did it because she was willing to justify any sacrifice that kept her alive. Now I don't know how sentient you really are. Talea's version of Taja seems to think she's not alive at all. I'm less certain given the tantrum you're throwing right now. But the closest you will *ever* get to truly living again requires helping me. It doesn't require that you like or approve of me, so stop being such a fucking bitch and teach me what I need to know to do my damn job!"

The old woman seemed to grow several inches taller, her face suffused with rage. Then she started laughing, so abruptly that Xivan wondered if the anger had been staged. "Well done," Khae said, tucking her walking stick under one arm to applaud. "See, I knew you had a brain in there somewhere. But seriously, you have a great deal to learn, and you're already too far be-hind. You should have come here days ago."

"Yeah, well, we were busy," Xivan said. "Still are, in fact. So that motion earlier, combined with tenyé and desire, will take me wherever I want to go?"

"Within reason." Khae nodded.

"What does *that* mean?"

"It means, it can't take you across to the Living World; you have to use a different spell for that. But since you're here, you figured it out already. And it can't take you beyond the Wound . . . or even all that close to it. But other than that, anywhere you want to go in the Afterlife, just imagine it and poof! You're there."

"Great," Xivan said. She made the gesture, dumped some tenyé into it, and stood there looking a little foolish as nothing happened. "Uh . . ." She looked at Khae for an explanation.

"I have no idea," the old woman snapped. "Where did you imagine going?"

"To wherever Terindel's souls are," Xivan said.

The old woman rubbed her hand across her face. "Starting to reconsider that brains thing."

"Listen, you annoying old—"

"Shut up," Khae said, stabbing her phantom walking stick through Xivan's middle. "Think. *Where* is that? Oh, you don't know, do you? You're the one doing the magic; it goes where you tell it to go. But you have to give the order."

"I didn't tell it to go to a place when I brought us *here*."

"No, you didn't," Khae growled. "*I* did. Which worked because I know where the Land of Peace is."

"Then how do we find him?" Xivan asked in exasperation.

"Think of places he might be, and go there instead of expecting the magic to make value judgments based on nonexistent information," Khae replied.

"Fine," Xivan said. "Tell me where his souls are."

"Sorry," Khae said with a shrug. "After my time."

"What does that mean?"

"It means that Khaemezra did whatever she did to Terindel long after I was 'splintered off.' I wasn't present for the big event; it's not like I can ask her, since she's gone and you're taking her place so I. Don't. Know!"

". . . Fuck," Xivan said.

"Would now be a good time to interrupt and ask how everything's going?" Talea said. She and Janel had been slowly walking in their direction until they finally caught up. Janel looked like she was contemplating jumping out a window.

Xivan rolled her eyes. "Khae doesn't know where Terindel is, and I can't just poof us there, because I have to poof us to specific places, not theoretical locations. So unless you know something . . . ?"

"That said, I might have some ideas," Khae said mildly.

Xivan's spine stiffened, her head jerked up. She turned—very, very slowly—to face the old woman. "Are. You. Fucking. Kidding. Me?" The light around her seemed to dim momentarily. Her arm shot out, and her fingers closed around the space that would have been Khae's throat if she had really existed as a complete entity. Xivan pulled, felt tenyé start to flow in her direction.

Talea and Janel both stepped away from her.

"Better," Khae said from several feet away. "*Now* you're getting the hang of being Thaena."

Xivan's hand was empty. She scowled at it before returning her attention to Khae.

"I wasn't around for Terindel's death, so I don't know where Thaena put him . . . but I know where I *would have* put him if it were me . . . so unless a whole lot has changed, there's decent odds that's where he is." The old woman smirked at Xivan.

Talea put her hand on Xivan's arm. "Are you okay?"

Xivan barked a laugh. "No . . . but apparently, I'm getting better." She faced Khae again. "Fine. Where would you have put him?"

Khae's smirk grew wider. "With Xaloma."

"Xaloma?" Xivan's eyebrows shot up toward her hairline. "Who the fuck is Xaloma, and why would she be here in the Afterlife?"

"Oh, I know this one," Janel said wearily. "Xaloma is one of Khaemezra's children.[4] She lives here. In a lake, when last I saw her. Xaloma is a *dragon*."

"Of course she is," Xivan growled.

---

[4] She's the daughter of Thaena and Galava.–T

## 37. FUNERAL ARRANGEMENTS

### *Tyentso's story*
### *The imperial bivouac, Khorvesh*
### *Midnight*

"Where . . . where did you send the dragon?" Qoran Milligreest asked as Tyentso finished filling him in on what had happened. He was half-dressed with a robe wrapped around himself, sitting on the edge of the bed in his tent. Tyentso sat in one of his chairs, feet up on its matching twin.

She'd woken him up in the middle of the night, but she didn't think he'd want to wait until morning to hear the news.

Twenty years on, and Qoran still *hated* to be out of the loop.

That said, she didn't fill him in on everything that had happened. Certainly not the part where Kihrin, in the guise of Vol Karoth, had shouted who-knows-what into the dragon's mind to buy her a distraction. Qoran didn't need to know.

Let the high general think she was just that amazing.

The corner of Tyentso's mouth twitched as she sipped her brandy. Part of her wanted coffee, but it was the middle of the night and she really did hope she might be able to get some sleep at *some* point. "Where else would I send him? The domain capital of Marakor, of course. Dropped him right in Havar D'Aramarin's lap."

His mouth fell open.

She snickered. "Honestly. Why even have this job if you can't be a massively petty bitch about it?"

"Wait. How would that work?" the high general asked. "Havar has wards up all over Marakor. You *can't* just open a gate there."

"At ground level, yes, but Havar didn't ward half a mile up," Tyentso said. "Who knows? Perhaps Gorokai flew right over the city and is heading back here, or went south to the Kulma, or any number of places. But I suspect he couldn't resist playing with all the soldiers, who immediately started shooting things at him." She turned the yellow diamond over in her hand. It was warm and . . . sunny. It felt like spending the day outside lying in a field of flowers, napping in the sun. A pleasant catnap sort of a gemstone. Happy.[1]

---

[1] I suppose that explains why the Vishai were so willing to claim it as theirs. Sounds perfect for them.–S

But it was a Cornerstone, so she assumed that impression was a massive pile of dragon shit.

"What are you going to do with it?" Milligreest frowned at the Cornerstone as though it had somehow managed to personally insult all the man's ancestors.

"Not sure," Tyentso admitted. Ironically, Kihrin hadn't needed the stone—given what he'd told her, he couldn't even safely touch the damn thing. He'd just wanted to make sure that Skyfire had stayed out of the hands of Xaltorath, whom Kihrin assured her would use the incredible energy manipulation abilities of the artifact to do very, very bad things.

As long as Tyentso kept it out of Xaltorath's hands, or Relos Var's, Kihrin didn't care what she did with it.

"I'll figure something out," she murmured. "But that's not why I came to see you. I want to ask you about Gadrith."

Qoran blinked at the unexpected statement. "What about him?"

"What did you do with his body?"

"What?" Qoran frowned. "You mean when Kihrin D'Mon killed—"

She waved a hand. "That wasn't his body. That was Sandus's body. No. What did you do with *Gadrith's* body? The one that was left behind when Gadrith tricked Sandus into killing him while Gadrith was wearing the Stone of Shackles? *That* corpse was Gadrith's original form. What did you do with it?"

"Oh," Qoran said. He paused for a few seconds, then made a face. "He was still a lord heir."

Tyentso frowned. "So?"

"So we returned the body to his father for burial."

Her heart skipped a beat even as she felt a shudder race through her. "You . . . you gave the body back to *Cedric*?" The alcohol suddenly tasted like acid. She set down the cup.

"Of course we did. You think we can just dump a lord heir's body in a shallow grave? We'd never hear the end of it."

Tyentso leaned back in her chair and fought down the strong desire to break out into hysterical laughter. "No," she said. "No, I would expect that you would take the body of a man famous for self-resurrecting as one of the walking dead and cut it into sixteen different pieces. And then I would expect you to throw each of those fucking pieces into a different Red Man forge until they were nothing but ashes, and then take those ashes and spread them over the mouths of sixteen different rivers! Except for his head—that I expected you to toss into an active volcano. Most of all, I would expect you to use your damn brain! *Are you fucking kidding me?*"

The high general shifted on the bed, a scowl on his face. "Now hold on. I did use my damn brain. And I talked to the priests of the Black Gate about it. They said it wouldn't be a problem; Thaena would make sure Gadrith couldn't come back to life."

The laughter did bubble out of her that time. "Thaena would. Right."

Qoran leaned forward. "You don't think . . . you don't think he's somehow Returned, do you?"

"Who would stop him?" Tyentso said bitterly.

Qoran looked like he was having difficulty swallowing. "How . . . how did he come back last time?"

"Grimward," Tyentso said. "Grimward and precautions he'd taken to make sure his souls didn't cross the Veil. So he never entered Thaena's realm at all. But now? I don't think it matters. Someone else would have to bring him back, but I can think of someone with the motive and skill to do exactly that. Our dear friend, Relos Var." She stood up, sighing as she put down her cup. She wasn't getting any sleep, was she? She should have bowed to fate and had the coffee. "Keep the armies from doing anything stupid while I'm gone, would you?"

"Where are you going?"

"I need to talk to some people. If Gadrith's back, he won't just be coming after me."

# 38. Last Goodbyes

***Galen's story***
***Next to the ruins of Senera's cottage, Kirpis***
***After Relos Var left to deal with Caless***

The clearing was quiet with the wizard's absence. Nighttime birds advertised their availability from the tree line nearby, and the sound of waves betrayed the cottage's location near the coast. However, those were peaceful sounds. So at odds with their situation.

Galen walked over to Qown, who stared at him wide-eyed. Galen didn't need to be a telepath to know that Qown was desperately wishing that Galen would stay away from him. Galen wasn't sure which of them he was trying to protect.

"Now you're not going to try anything stupid, are you?" Anlyr asked. "Because I won't enjoy hurting you, but I'll do it. Blah, blah, blah. Fill in obligatory threat about how I'll make you wish you were dead." He managed to make that sound not even the tiniest bit funny.

Sheloran narrowed her eyes at Anlyr, somehow more threatening than anything she'd said or done previously.

Anlyr must have thought so too, because he gestured; a glowing barrier of bright blue energy encircled Sheloran. "Don't let the 'extremely handsome and charming guard' routine throw you. I'm almost as old as Relos Var, and I know magic spells that no one's heard of in a thousand years."

Galen glared at Anlyr as he knelt next to Qown. "And here I thought you were just a pretty face."

"I get that a lot."

Galen resisted the urge to roll his eyes, mostly because Anlyr probably *did*. There was no denying the man was pretty. That Galen fervently wanted to kill him was beside the point. "Relax, I'm not looking to make trouble. I just want to make sure my healer's all right. He's been useful, you know."

Sheloran beat a hand against the magical barrier. It rebounded. "Do you mind?" she growled.

"Just keeping you out of trouble," Anlyr said amiably. "We're all going to have a nice little fête out in this refreshing night air and enjoy the smell of roasting chestnut wood."

It was a beautiful evening. That was honestly the worst part of it. A little cold, yes, but the sort where the air was crisp and pure, as conifers battled with the nearby ocean for which scent would be dominant. If not for the overwhelming scent of woodsmoke, Galen had little doubt he would be over-whelmed in the beauty of it all. Small dots of light blinked off and on above his head—fireflies.

"Are you all right?" Galen asked him.

"I'm fine," Qown said, which seemed an obvious lie. He wasn't fine and hadn't fine for a while now. At least it seemed Anlyr had healed Qown's hands well enough to prevent permanent injury, but he still looked traumatized.

Galen had seen people with that look in their eyes before, but rarely outside the slave quarters. Oh, but he would make Anlyr pay for that.

"So did you two get around to fucking, or have you just been throwing longing glances at each other the whole time?" Anlyr asked Qown. He didn't ask quietly.

Qown flushed red.

"Upset you weren't invited?" Galen glared at the man.

Anlyr laughed. "I'll take that as a no. I'd say now's your last chance to fix that, but, uh, you know it is. Maybe not in front of the baby, right?" He glanced at the small child, and for a moment, his expression turned pensive. "So which one are you picking?"

A chill raced over Galen's skin.

"What do you mean?" Galen asked.

Anlyr laughed. "Oh, come now. You must realize Relos Var's not going to let you take everyone home even if Sheloran's mother cuts a deal. Sheloran, obviously. You'll probably make the cut with the ransom. But Qown? The baby? They're optional. I figure Lord Var will let you have one of them. Which I would have thought would be an easy choice but"—he winked at Tave—"he seems to be growing on you like a vine."

"He's a child," Galen protested.

"You'd be surprised how few people consider that a sufficient argument." He paused. "Well. You *are* Darzin's son. Maybe you wouldn't be surprised."

Qown scoffed under his breath. When Galen glanced in his direction, Qown shook his head. "Don't let him bother you. We both know Relos Var isn't letting me go, no matter what happens."

"Mother knows you're with us," Sheloran said. "She'll make you part of the ransom."

Qown nodded as he stared down at his hands. He'd been drawing the tip of one nail against the palm of his other hand, a nervous tick Galen had never seen before. It almost looked like Qown was practicing drawing a glyph, re-peating the same shape again and again.

Qown looked up and met Galen's eyes. He gave him a sad, apologetic sort of smile. Galen felt a piercing sense of dread.

Galen realized in that moment that Qown didn't think he was going to survive this.

Worse, Galen couldn't guarantee he was wrong.

## 39. STEP SEVEN: SPEND TIME WITH LOVED ONES

### Kihrin's story
### The Afterlife
### After reuniting with Teraeth (in dreams)

"I don't know what it says about me that I've missed this place," Teraeth mused as we made our way through dark woods of the lands of the dead.

The ravens screamed at us as we passed by, but then that fit my last memories of this place too. Plenty of broken flashes of terrified running, stumbling, scrambling madly through blood-tossed mud. The trees were still twisted, the wildlife warped, the weather weirdly damp. If there'd ever been a sun here, I'd never seen it. There had to be a sky, though, right? And what was up there? Were there stars? Moons? Janel had always implied the Afterlife mirrored the Living World in weird, dark ways, but just how far did the duplication go? I hadn't the slightest idea.

No, I didn't miss the Afterlife at all.

I kept my voice light, anyway, trying not to let my worries show. "I think it says you spent most of this lifetime as a member of a death cult of assassins, but that's just a guess."

The last time I'd been here, I'd just been murdered by my brother.[1] Come to think of it, the time before that had also been the result of being murdered by my brother, hadn't it?[2] It had just been a different brother. And a different life.

"You should know that Janel, Xivan, and Talea are here too. Somewhere."

I stopped walking. "Tell me it's because they're going after Doc and not because something happened."

Teraeth grabbed at my arm—and passed his hand right through it. He blinked and then, as comprehension set in, looked personally insulted.

I sighed. "I can't really be here, Teraeth. This is just a projection."

"Even in the Afterlife?" Teraeth swung an arm out to encompass disgusting mud and damp trees as if he were drawing attention to all the benefits of paradise.

"Yes. Even in the Afterlife. Why would this world be any more immune

---

[1] Darzin.—T
[2] Relos Var.—S

to being broken down into tiny pieces than the Living One? It won't be the same kind of damage, but it would still weaken you at a point where you can't afford to be weakened. I couldn't stand it if something happened to you and it was my fault."

"Hm." Teraeth wrinkled his nose and looked like he'd either been drinking some of the local water or was contemplating arguing the point.

I stared at him.

Teraeth stared back.

I said, "You really wanted to have sex with me while we were here, didn't you?"

"Yes, damn it, I really did! Stop laughing!" Teraeth's indignation was quite possibly one of the cutest things I had seen in *years*.

I pressed my lips together and did my best. Or sort of my best. Kind of.

"I'll have you know sex in the Afterlife—morbid and weird as that sounds—has serious advantages. Trust me. If I could just touch you . . ." Teraeth made a face, still grumbling his displeasure over the whole matter.

I believed him. Janel had made similar comments. In a world largely shaped by will and imagination, many of the more unpleasant, sticky, uncomfortable details of sex likely vanished completely.

I gave Teraeth—my beautiful, deadly, extremely enthusiastic Teraeth—a serious look.

"What is it?" Teraeth said, expression sliding into uncertainty.

"I just think it's funny," I said after a moment.

"What is?" His eyes narrowed.

I stepped in close. "That you think I have to touch you. Pretty sure I don't."

"Well, I—" Teraeth's pupils dilated as he processed exactly what I meant. "Excuse me?"

"Oh, you know what I mean." I was close enough by that point that if I'd been physically present, Teraeth would have been able to feel the heat of my breath. "And if we had time—which unfortunately, we don't—I'd make you strip, slowly. And if you were *very* good and asked *very* nicely, I'd let you touch yourself. I would tell you exactly how you were allowed to touch yourself. I would watch you while you did that—maybe in that clearing over there in full view of anyone who might happen along. And then, after a time, because you are good and beautiful and perfect, I'd give you permission to finish." I paused, smiling at the way Teraeth looked breathless after my speech.

Then I grinned evilly. "It's a shame we don't have time for that."

I turned around and continued walking.

Stunned silence filled the air behind me and then a strangled "Kihrin!" filled that void.

I managed to keep from laughing that time, but barely.

When Teraeth caught back up to me, he decided to handle the situation in classic style—by pretending it had never happened. "So, Janel, Talea, and Xivan are fine. Yes, they're going after Doc." He tugged down the hem of his wrap. "I see real potential for a family reunion brewing here. Janel's looking for my father, and here we are about to visit dear old Mom."

I didn't have to look hard to unearth a positive treasure trove of bitterness buried under that sarcasm. If family trauma set upon a table with a mage-light aimed directly at it could be considered "buried." "I don't know how to break this to you, but we have to *find* your mother first. She could be anywhere, and it'll just be worse if she doesn't have her memories."

Teraeth scoffed again, a single deep heave of his chest. "Oh, she'll remember," Teraeth said. "I bet you anything that we'll find my mother in her palace in the Land of Peace, no doubt cursing your name, mine, and everyone we've ever known."

"She'd know where Doc is," I mused, but I also knew she'd never tell us.

"Yes, and she'll never tell us," Teraeth said. "What are you trying to find out from her, anyway?"

I hesitated. Just for a second. It was impossible that Teraeth didn't notice. "I have this theory that Relos Var is going to try to use a ritual to get rid of the demons."

"Yes, because that's gone so well previously." Teraeth waved a hand dismissively. "Not getting rid of the demons. I'm fine with that in general concept. I mean using a ritual to commit genocide in one easy step. Somehow it never works as planned."

"Yes, funny you should mention that . . ."

"But hold on," Teraeth said, scowling. "Because if it were that easy, surely Relos Var would have done it before, yes? Why wait until now?"

I shook my head, my mouth twisted into something only charitably similar to a smile. "Because it wasn't in his best interests. The demons were keeping the Immortals busy, and that meant they weren't spending all their time getting into Relos Var's business. And then there was the small matter where it wouldn't affect *all* the demons. If I'm right, then it won't do anything to Xaltorath. It's possible Var was concerned that he'd be creating a power vacuum that Xaltorath would happily step in to fill. Then he'd be right back where he started, but with demons he couldn't ritual away." I paused. "No, I don't think Var plans to make the attempt until he's dealt with Xaltorath."

Teraeth chewed on that piece of information and his lower lip at the same time. "Why won't it affect Xaltorath?"

"Because there's a difference between the demons that came from the old universe following us, and ones like Suless or Xaltorath who figured it out here." I mentally told myself to stop dancing around the issue and get to the point. "The reason I need to speak to Khaemezra is because I have a theory that all the souls that didn't come with us as part of the original settlement arrived as demons. And every time you or your mother tossed a demon soul into the Font of Souls to destroy it, you were instead releasing more human souls."

"Yes, that was the whole point—"

"Not the demons that were created from humans here. The demons who invaded. Those started out as human souls too."

Teraeth blinked and turned to face me head-on. "What?"

"I realize it sounds a bit far-fetched—"

"For you. It even sounds far-fetched *for you*. Do you realize what a high bar that is?"

I glared. "I'm mighty tempted to say, 'Fuck you,' but I know how you'll respond."

"Hey, I was willing, but apparently, *you're just a projection*."

I rolled my eyes. "That's the one. *Anyway,* trust me when I say that demons used to be human and, because of us, are often becoming human again. My fear is that Relos Var has created a ritual to target the unique idiosyncrasies of those demons, but by doing so, he's targeting every soul that isn't a Founder's."

Teraeth didn't say anything for several long seconds.

"I'm not a reincarnation of a Founder," Teraeth said.

"Yes," I replied. "*I know.*"

Teraeth let out a tense bark of a laugh. "So once again, my life is in jeopardy because of a magical ritual. No wonder everything's feeling so familiar; I've danced to this melody before."

"Don't get too excited about the tune. I'm making a lot of assumptions that might easily be completely and totally wrong. That's why I want to talk to Thaena, or rather, the Thaena who's been doing the job for long enough to know something." I shrugged. "Truthfully, I'd prefer Galava, but since Xaltorath ate her, I'm going with the easier option."

"Could've been worse." Teraeth gestured and continued walking.

I nearly muttered a prayer as if that would have done any good. "I can't believe you just said that. I expected you to know better by now."

"I'm just saying Xaltorath could have eaten *both* of them." Teraeth didn't especially look like the idea upset him.

I supposed I'd have held a bit of a grudge too, in Teraeth's shoes.[3]

As Teraeth started to speak again, I held up a hand. "Do you hear that?"

"Ah, I see you'll be playing the part of Janel tonight. Good to know." Then he frowned. "Okay, yes, I hear it too. Fighting. We must be close to the Chasm. It's hard to see with all these trees blocking things."

"Yes. I'll be right back." I was only there as a mental projection after all—there was no particular reason I had to pay attention to such fiddly little details as gravity if I didn't feel like it.

So I floated up above the tree line. Not dramatically—not in a "look at me!" kind of way—but enough to have a better idea what was happening. I groaned at what I saw and then immediately dropped back down again.

"That good?"

I scowled. "Xaltorath's attacking the Chasm."[4]

[3] I don't know, Kihrin. How have you felt about family members trying to kill you? It's not like you don't have a track record here.—S

[4] We are assuming that Xaltorath started doing this after they lost track of Janel, Xivan, and Talea.—T

The terrible irony of it all was that this was exactly what I wanted—in fact, finding Xaltorath saved me an extraordinary amount of trouble later on. I needed Xaltorath for my plans.

Except . . .

If I was right about Relos Var's plans to be rid of the demons, then Xaltorath's continued existence might well be one of the only things keeping Relos Var from enacting that final ritual. Currently, I was in no position to try to convince Relos Var why he shouldn't do it, let alone stop the wizard. *And* there was the problem of location. The last place I wanted to fight Xaltorath was on top of the Chasm. It would mean fighting Xaltorath with a foot already in position to trip and fall into that other universe. While I'd never firmly established whether or not Relos Var could travel to the Afterlife, it seemed like giving the man too much opportunity to tick off all the boxes on his list of goals.

The collateral damage might overwhelm the harried defenders and destroy the barrier erected so long ago to keep out the worst effects of that other universe. My plans hinged on fighting Xaltorath in the Living World.

Fighting Xaltorath *here* was a terrible idea.

Which was a problem, since we needed to get past him.

Teraeth sighed and started checking his knives. I had to assume that was just reflex since any weapons he had here were inventions of his mind.

"Fine," Teraeth said when he finished. "Let's go scout out the situation and see what can be done."

"I might be able to draw him off," I said. "Distract him. But if I have to stay and keep Xaltorath occupied, you'll have to enter the palace alone."

Teraeth cursed enthusiastically. It wasn't too difficult to imagine that the last thing Teraeth wanted was to go back into the Land of Peace to have a "pleasant" conversation with his dead mother—assuming she was there at all.

"Let's hope it doesn't come to that," I said as a peace offering.[5]

---

[5] It came to that.—T

# 40. THE BARGAIN

***Caless's story***
***The Soaring Halls, the Upper Circle of the Capital City of Quur***
***Early evening***

Caless couldn't find her daughter.

She'd left Sheloran—also Galen; his healer, Qown; and that small child—in her suite of rooms, but when she returned, everyone was gone. She suspected they'd dropped the child off with the highest-ranked babysitters in the empire, but she'd also expected at least Sheloran to still be there. Caless might have thought they'd gotten a jump on that whole leaving business, but there was a problem: not *everything* was missing. The healer's satchel still hung off the back of a chair. Worse—and the thing that made Caless's stomach knot—was the small leather-bound volume left discarded on a bed.

Her son-in-law always kept such a book with him for whenever he felt the need to write his poetry. He never went anywhere without it. They'd left in a rush, too quickly to take the time to leave notes or remove their most important belongings.

So something was wrong.

She felt a flash of anger, quickly suppressed. It had been too easy of late to lose her temper. Easier still to jump to paranoid conclusions. There was likely a perfectly normal explanation for this.

Her gut told her otherwise. Her instincts screamed that something was wrong, that she should start grabbing people and shaking them until they spilled out answers from their mouths like blood.

Perhaps that's part of the reason why she reacted so quickly to the spike of tenyé as someone opened a gate into the room. It wasn't her husband—she'd have recognized his aura. And there was no one else who had any good reason to come calling in such a manner.

Which was why she attacked before whoever it was finished appearing.

The surge of tenyé-spiked energy should have shredded the person immediately. Instead, they *caught it.*

"Caless, I—" The intruder managed to say before the blast of pure energy from Caless smashed into him. The portal he'd stepped through had already closed behind him, or she might have knocked him back whence he came. Instead, she slammed him into the wall and knocked

askew a painting of Simillion and Dana hunting in the woods of Eamithon.[1]

It was far too much to hope that such a paltry attack would seriously injure
the wizard, much less kill him, so she was already weaving her second strike
before the sound of his back hitting the wall had even finished ringing in her
ears.

"Damn it, woman, I–" he said.

She hit him with the bed.

Her favorite bed too. She'd brought it with her from the palace. It was a
magnificent affair. Metal, of course, with room for a custom-made stuffed cotton mattress. It easily weighed a ton; she crashed it into him hard enough to
twist the frame. Potentially break a few ribs, if she was lucky. The bedsheets
covered his face and, more importantly, his eyes. Retaliatory spellcasting became much more difficult if he couldn't see her.

"Enough!" he bellowed. The bed exploded away from him in a hail of metallic shrapnel, every piece flying toward her. She interposed a barrier, which
stopped most of it, but felt a sting where a finger-size splinter of metal pierced
the back of her right hand.

She plucked it free and flicked it back at him, weaving tenyé into it so the
splinter melted into a small orb of shimmering metal that then exploded into
a roiling sphere of flame.

He batted the fiery bolt aside with a gust of frigid wind and launched a trio
of blasts at her; high, low, high again. He alternated between kinetic force,
electricity, and a spell for the breaking of bones.

None of them hit her. She wasn't a novice. While she might not have had
the same weight of centuries behind her as some others, she *was* a god-queen.
She dodged the first, deflected the second so that it went out the window,
setting a curtain on fire in the process, and let the third fail against her own
protective aura.

"Oh please," she said. She reached into a pocket and cast a handful of small
metal flakes at him, agitating them so that they would burst into flames as
they drew near. If it worked on the emperor's enemies, she saw no reason it
wouldn't work on the sorcerer before her.

Except it didn't. The ataras flakes fell to the floor unlit. He shook his head.
"I heard about your little trick," he said. He looked smug, but Caless saw his
eyes dart toward the burning drape fluttering outside the window.

Someone would see that. They would report it. Soon, people would arrive at
the door to her suite: soldiers, witch-hunters, Voices of the Council, perhaps
even the empress herself. It didn't matter where Tyentso was when she could
teleport across the empire in seconds.

Evidently, the stranger didn't feel like dealing with that idea, because her
visitor lost his temper.

---

[1] That never happened, but I suppose it's to be expected that much of that relationship has been
mythologized.–T

He touched his throat, his face twisted in a grimace of pain. With his other hand, he made a complicated gesture.

But nothing happened as far as she could see. Caless drew breath for her next attack and then realized what he'd done.

The intruder had pulled all the good air from the room. Caless began suffocating in a room with open windows.

Windows.

Yes, that was it. She twisted her hands.

"Stop wasting my time," the man said, his voice sounding strange in the fetid air. "I have your daughter and your son-in-law. If you'd like to see them again in this life, cease these pointless attacks and let us parlay." He opened a fan with his free hand.

Caless froze; it was Sheloran's fan. He smirked at her over the edge of it.

Her spell finished. A breeze blew in from outside, pushing the burning curtain into the foul air to smother the flames. But then the fresh air arrived, and she felt the coolness of it like a sharp knife in her lungs. She coughed.

"Wha–" Her voice was a harsh croak. She cleared her throat, tried again. "What is it that you want?"

A closer inspection brought no enlightenment. Caless didn't recognize the man. He wasn't notable—a normal-looking Quuros man, taller than average, but not enough to stand out. His clothes were sturdy, plain and ordinary.

He had the aura of a god-king, which she knew from long experience was a group of people who hated "plain" and "ordinary." She considered herself something of an expert on the subject, having been directly or indirectly responsible for nearly every god-king or god-queen in existence.[2] So not a normal god-king and not a normal wizard and not someone she could afford to underestimate.

She stalled for time and hoped that Varik wouldn't return from his improvised workshop early. With the mood her husband was in, it seemed unlikely—or impossible—that he wouldn't leap at any excuse to start a fight. And her husband didn't have a quarter of her experience at magical dueling.

"Who *are* you?" Caless finally asked.

The corner of the man's mouth quirked. "I don't believe we've had the pleasure. My name is Relos Var."

"Prove it," she snapped back. She did her absolute best to act like the name elicited only mild curiosity and not panic.

He blinked, surprised. "Excuse me?"

Caless crossed her arms over her chest. "You heard me. You're powerful and you know the name of someone powerful, but that doesn't mean you're the same person. Prove that you're Relos Var."

An annoyed expression crossed his face. "I hardly think–"

---

[2] Which is true. With the exception of her parents, Cherthog and Suless, almost all of the first god-kings were either lovers or friends of Caless's. Once the secret was out, those first god-kings rarely shared their knowledge with others, but it still happened often enough to create hundreds of them.–T

"My mother used to talk about you all the time. Ranted, even. So I do have some idea what you *really* look like. Not the dragon form. I'm uninterested in that. Show me your birth form, and then we'll talk."

She didn't doubt the man's identity for a moment, but that wasn't the point. He'd shown up here with her daughter's fan and that knowing look in his eyes, the one that said that he knew exactly how this meeting was going to proceed and intended to control every aspect of it. She knew that look of old. They always thought they'd enter her house and take charge, give the orders.

She went out of her way to prove them wrong.

He might have responded in any number of ways, from attacking her again to ordering her to shut up and listen. Perhaps she'd given him an excuse to do something he'd been wanting to do for ages. His form shimmered, the edges blurring and sliding against each other until they settled into a new shape. His expression twisted from the pain, but not more than one might expect from stubbing a toe.

"Ah." Caless studied him for a moment. The mistake most people would have made was giving themselves voras red eyes. The man in front of her had not. His eyes were blue—not the too-bright cerulean of a D'Mon but a deeper sapphire shade. He was taller than most Quuros but still short for a vané. Dark skinned, but that wasn't unusual. His hair was tightly braided in a style that suggested he wore it that way to control its otherwise rebellious curl.

Caless imagined a great deal about the man hinged on that idea of "control." Keeping it, gaining it. It was a pity that he seemed far too proud to ever acknowledge he always would've been happiest on his knees.[3]

She scoffed under her breath. "Yes, I see it."

Relos Var raised an eyebrow. "This is all quite charming, but I'm here to talk about—"

"Did you know that my mother was deeply infatuated with you?"

Relos Var choked off whatever he'd been about to say. "I'm sorry. *What was that?*"

"Oh, you didn't realize?" She laughed at the delightful joke. Delay, delay, delay. She tried not to consider the irony of having to wait and hope she'd be *rescued.* And how she already knew it wouldn't happen. "She wanted you so badly."

Var's expression turned to one of genuine bafflement. "A moment. Just to confirm. We are talking about *Suless,* aren't we?"[4]

"Who else? She was the only mother I had."

The wizard visibly shuddered. "Suless hated me."

---

[3] Ah, wonderful. That's a mental image I'm never going to be able to scrub free from my mind.—S
  On the other hand, this is her area of expertise. It's possible she's even right.—T
  You're not helping.—S
[4] Su'less, in the original voras style, but I have sadly been unable to discover what her personal name was.—T
  It's probable that there's no longer anyone alive who knows, including her daughter.—S

"Yes, I understand why you would think that. It was impossible to tell the difference between love and hate with her. But she hated *you* in a special way, one that made it obvious her affection was an emotion turned rotten by years wrapped in jealousy. How badly she wanted you. How bitter she was that she couldn't have you. She was hardly alone. Why, I imagine half your fellow professors at that school of yours were madly in love with you, simultaneously desperate for your approval and terrified of your criticism."

He just stared at her. Caless was willing to bet metal that if he hadn't been a millennia old immortal, he'd have been stammering and blushing. She'd shocked the hell out of him.

"You're mistaken," he finally said. "I was never loved."

She studied him carefully, then laughed. "I rather think you're the one who's mistaken. You mean to tell me you never realized? You, walking around, looking like *that*. A perfect mind carried around in that perfect body, that perfect face. You, a marble statue of a man, gorgeous and cold. Untouchable, unassailable, out of everyone's reach. I can just picture the students writing each other love poems about you. Quite a few of the teachers too, I imagine. Surely my mother wasn't the only one." Caless gazed up at him through her eyelashes. "And you were oblivious. How delicious."

"My brother was the one everyone loved." The words seemed to slip past Relos Var's lips in a moment of inattention. The scowl that chased its way onto his face didn't move quickly enough to stop their escape.

"Perhaps it may have seemed that way," Caless said. "But I would wager your admirers were no less ardent. Just more circumspect. People like S'arric are always safe to worship openly. They shine so brightly, it's difficult to look at anyone else. But not everyone wants to blind themselves. I've always preferred moonlight myself."

He was smart enough to see the offer in her words and far too smart to accept. Still, it didn't hurt to try. Sometimes people surprised you.

"I have your daughter," Relos Var spat out, returning at last to the main subject. He seemed genuinely angry now, although Caless suspected that anger was almost entirely aimed at himself.

So she'd gotten to him, just a little. Maybe he'd even been tempted. It was good to know, even as she knew it wouldn't do a thing to change the outcome. She'd take her consolation prizes where she could.

She'd forced him to pull the conversation back under control.

Caless ignored the heaviness in her gut, the feeling of cold weight that would twist and leave her insides spilled out on the floor. "Yes," she said. "Obviously. I assume you want something in exchange."

"The Stone of Shackles." He gestured at the blue gemstone resting on top of her cleavage.

Caless tasted bile, even though she'd known that was what he wanted from the moment he named himself. She'd tried so hard for all these years to stay out of certain paths of destruction. Var had been at the very top of that list. Still, it wasn't unexpected. She was only shocked at how quickly the man had come calling. She couldn't help but think of her son-in-law's confession that he and Sheloran had caught Relos Var's attention.

"Just out of curiosity, was Qown here for the Cornerstone too or for some other reason?" It was a guess, but she thought it likely a good one.

The corner of the man's mouth twitched, even as he didn't answer. But the look in his eyes—half amusement, half admiration—was answer enough. Not necessarily to the boy's orders but at least to the identity of his master.

She had previously wondered who had taken the time to so exquisitely twist that poor boy's mind into knots. Caless couldn't help but wonder if Relos Var had done it deliberately or if he was just too caught up in his own ambitions to notice the damage he had done to a child in his care. She suspected a combination of the two. In her experience, most people thought far more highly of their skill as parents than they deserved, probably because it was too easy to see children as tools or extensions or as second chances for redemption. Goals rather than people.

"Do we have a deal?" Relos Var asked. "Or shall I point out that I left a *mimic* watching your daughter and son-in-law? Perhaps we should hurry this up before it grows hungry."

Caless raised her chin and tried her best to look like every inch the queen she was. "I want all three of them returned." If Qown still worked for Relos Var, she'd find out quickly and take appropriate action. And if he didn't, she certainly wasn't going to leave him in the wizard's care.

"That can be arranged," Var told her, "in exchange for the Cornerstone. Do we have a deal?"

She sighed. As if any other outcome were possible. "We do."

# 41. Hunting the Ghost Dragon

*Janel's story*
*The Afterlife*
*After leaving the Land of Peace*

"It's not exactly, uh . . . scenic, is it?" Talea gazed around them with the somewhat taken-aback air of someone who enjoyed sunlight and open marketplaces and cheerful, laughing children. All descriptions for which exactly none of her current surroundings would ever qualify.

"It grows on you," Janel allowed.

"Not literally, I hope," Talea said.

They both paused as the dense copse of trees and brambles opened up, drawing to the side like curtains as Xivan rejoined them from where she'd gone off to have a little heart-to-heart chat with her "Eshi."

"Any luck?" Talea asked.

Xivan kissed the side of Talea's cheek. "Probably, but I wouldn't call it 'good.' Also, I hate her." She glanced to the side and made a rude gesture. "Yes, and fuck you too."

Janel didn't ask who "her" was. Xivan hadn't had quite the super-friendly first contact with her predecessor's shadow teacher that Talea had. But then, given the two goddesses in question, that made sense.

Xivan rested her head against Talea's for a moment, then sighed and straightened. "You know how much I love dragons."

Talea's smile faltered. "Oh sure. Great fun. Who doesn't love dragons?"

"Anyone who's met one?" Janel said. "But I think this is where I need to point out that I know about Xaloma because I've met Xaloma. Specifically, I helped Kihrin *kill* Xaloma." She flicked out her fingers in annoyance. "Obviously, it didn't last."

Talea's eyes widened. "Wait. That dragon? The dragon in the lake? The one whose heart Kihrin cut out and split between you?"

Xivan winced. "Khae just said, and I quote, 'What the fuck.'"

Talea's laugh had a distinct edge. "What a funny coincidence; Eshi just said that too. Is that a bad thing?" She leaned away from something Janel couldn't see and wrinkled her nose almost exactly the way one might while being shouted at.

Janel scowled. She was almost positive that what Kihrin had done back when they'd first been injured here in the Afterlife—what seemed like lifetimes ago even though it had only been months—wasn't anything . . . permanent.[1] A transfer of tenyé, symbolically represented by the heart of a dragon. Xaloma had presumably healed the damage and gone on about her life—if such a word was appropriate.

It was the *almost* that gave her pause.

"I don't know," Janel admitted. "I don't think so? I think it was just tenyé, really. But there is a reasonable chance that she'll remember me with something other than fond feeling. I'm hoping she doesn't. I wasn't the one who killed her. Kihrin was. But I can't be sure." She gave Xivan a hard look. "You know for a fact that Xaloma has him? I would really hate to go through all that effort only to discover that we were wrong and he's not even there."

Xivan's scowl suggested she too would be extremely unhappy if that proved to be the case. The sort of unhappiness that usually resulted in violence, although to whom was less clear.

"No," the fledgling Goddess of Death said, "but Khae did tell me the different locations where Xaloma typically lairs." She paused. "Understand . . . I've met Doc in person, but as I wasn't yet . . . this . . . I don't know what his soul looks like. But if we go to the different lair locations, any additional souls should stand out like a bonfire against the night sky, simply because Xaloma normally doesn't allow anyone near her. So . . . that narrows down the possibilities."

"The odds are low that Xaloma would be guarding souls for any other reason," Talea murmured.

"Exactly. And it's a better lead than any of our others."

Janel pondered the new information. Unfortunately, it relied on a potentially false premise—that Xaloma wouldn't have any other souls. And considering how many dragons had been in the habit of collecting people as much as treasure (typically to horrifying effect), Janel was unsure that was a wise assumption. But they didn't have any other clues. And while it sounded like the "false" Khaemezra wasn't exactly pleasant, Janel would be surprised to discover this memory of a goddess was interested in betraying them. They may not have been friends, but they weren't enemies.

Talea put a hand on her lover's shoulder, grinning broadly at Xivan. "That doesn't sound too bad."

Xivan's lips curled, just a little, in response, but it didn't dampen the worry in the woman's eyes. "Don't get too excited. Most of Xaloma's lairs—the ones Khae knows about, anyway—are underwater."

Janel squeezed her eyes closed and tilted her head to the sky. It had always been easier when she hadn't known the gods she prayed to on a first-name basis.

When Kihrin and she had run into Xaloma, the dragon had been hiding

[1] The key phrase being "almost positive." In theory, it is possible that some sort of link with Grimward may have been formed, which doesn't seem to be the case. Although I am unsure how one might recognize such a link or what effect it might have had.–T

in a lake. And as Khaemezra's child (and Teraeth's sister, Janel reminded herself) she would be either half or full voramer.[2] She'd like the water. It would remind her of home. Searching for Xaloma in the water made sense.

Janel hated it.

"Do dead Ithlané souls live in the water too, I wonder?" Talea asked.

Xivan answered, "Yes, of course. The Afterlife has oceans too."

Janel nodded. She'd seen such an ocean once—a great wine-purple slick of water stretching as far as the eye could see, luminescent waves crashing down against black-sand beaches where her footprints lingered in glowing red long after she'd gone by. Beautiful. Horrible.

Like most of the Afterlife, really.

Janel gestured toward the world around them. "It's your call, Xivan. Take us where we need to go."

Xivan went through the motions. It was much easier that second time.

---

[2] Xaloma is full voramer, or was before she became a dragon.—T

## 42. Leaving Someone Behind

***Galen's story***
***Outside the ruins of Senera's cottage***
***Sometime after Relos Var left***

The air crackled as a mirror-smooth gate of magical energy irised into being and discharged . . . someone. It wasn't Relos Var. It wasn't, in fact, anyone that Galen had ever seen before.

The man was far closer to his age than that of the wizard's. He was darker in complexion, but his tightly braided hair was lighter in color. Any resemblance ended there: this newcomer was far better-looking than Relos Var.

Since Anlyr didn't react by reaching for a weapon, Galen assumed that this was yet another previously unknown minion of Relos Var's. And Galen mentally added a footnote to his mental picture of Relos Var that included the knowledge he apparently picked his henchmen for aesthetic value as well as talent.

At least, Galen thought that until Anlyr said, "Lord Var? Veils, I almost didn't recognize you. How many centuries has it been since you looked like yourself?"

The man chuckled. "Too many." But he didn't change back to looking like the wizard Galen recognized, nor did he seem inclined to change shape to look like anything else.

He did seem pleased with himself.

As Galen stared hatefully at him, Relos Var turned to Sheloran and said, "Good news, Your Highness."

It was all Galen could do not to lunge at the bastard, because there was no way in hell that any information delivered with that tone could possibly qualify as "good."

"Your mother has agreed to my terms. So you and your husband will both be returned, as promised."

Galen pressed forward as much as he dared. "What about the boy? What about Qown?"

Any pretend friendliness vanished from Relos Var's eyes. "Just the two of you."

Sheloran scoffed. "The hell you say. My mother knows we had a child with us, and she knows we were traveling with Qown. She wouldn't have forgotten them."

"She didn't," Relos Var agreed, "but compromises were made."

"You son of a bitch!" Sheloran slammed into the field of magical energy as she rushed forward.

Relos Var turned away from Sheloran then, the first time since they'd arrived where the focus of his attention shifted to Galen. "You want them as well? Perhaps we too can arrive at a compromise."

Galen found himself snarling. "I thought we didn't have anything you wanted."

"Not true. You have the truth."

Everyone paused. Var and Anlyr might've been the only two people in the clearing who were remembering to breathe.

Then Tave picked up a clod of mud and threw it at Relos Var. The toddler wasn't strong enough to reach Var, but that wasn't stopping him from giving it his full effort. "You're a bad man!" Tave pronounced.

Var didn't seem much offended. "Yes," he agreed. "So I've been told." The wizard turned his attention back to Galen. "As I was saying. You have the truth. There's something going on. First Devors, then the Lighthouse, now Senera's cottage. One unexpected event is an accident. Two is an unfortunate coincidence. Three is a plot. And all of this besides Vol Karoth escaping his prison." He paused and then said in a very soft voice, "Which you already knew."

Galen and Qown might have given it all away right then, but Sheloran saved them. "Of course we did!" she snapped. "Do you think the empress couldn't tell the instant that thing escaped? Or did you really buy that story about her marching her army down to Khorvesh to deal with the *morgage*?"

Relos Var studied her, lips pursed. Then he turned back to Galen. "Tell me what's going on." Relos Var threw Tave an unkind look. "I'll let one of them go."

"The boy doesn't know anything!" Galen protested.

"Oh, Lord Var understands that. He's including the child to be mean," Anlyr provided.

Var glanced at him sideways, but didn't dispute the man's statement.

The wizard's expression changed in an instant, turned amused and friendly. "I admit when I put Qown in your path, I harbored some faint, wistful idea that the two of you would be a good match. I have my moments of sentimentality. But I didn't think you would be the one seducing him."[1]

To which Anlyr said, "Pretty sure he hasn't, yet."

Relos Var threw the mimic an irritated glance. "I didn't mean sex." He turned back to Galen. "You like him. Yes, I know you tried to pretend that he doesn't mean anything to you and it's adorable you thought that would fool me, but let me assure you, it didn't. So let's acknowledge that you do, in fact, care what happens to Qown. Perhaps there's enough there for a longer-term relationship. Something real. It wouldn't surprise me. And the only coin you have to spend to gain him back is telling me what really happened on Devors."

---

[1] No, I imagine not. I do love it when Relos Var messes up. —S

Galen blinked at him.

Under other circumstances, in a different situation, Galen might have believed him. A younger Galen—one who hadn't been murdered by someone he trusted, one who hadn't been betrayed and used by practically *everyone*—might have thought that Relos Var was many things, but typically a man who kept his promises. In his desperation, he might have forgotten Jarith's warning.

But this Galen knew better. This Galen knew that Relos Var was capable of betrayal. These were the last few moves of the whole game, the crescendo to a musical score that Relos Var had been building for over a thousand years. This was when he was most dangerous.

Now, Relos Var *would* lie.

Now, Relos Var *would* kill.

Now, Relos Var was capable of *anything*.

Darzin had once laughingly told him that there were no honest men, just fools or people smart enough to save up their lies for the moments when it mattered most. This was that moment.

Galen was taking too long to answer. Relos Var's expression darkened. "I tire of this." He started to make some movement, cast some spell.

"Fine!" Galen said. "I'll tell you."

"Galen, no!" Sheloran slammed a fist against the magical wall.

"Why not, Red? I don't have any idea what was going on, anyway. What do I care?" Galen swallowed with a desert-dry throat. "We were chasing the Lash, and we did, all the way to the pirate haven, Da'utunse. Except when we arrived, we discovered the Lash wasn't human. The Lash was a Daughter of Laaka who'd been using Grimward to puppet a crew of dead pirates, because hey, turns out people are a lot more comfortable with pirates attacking ships than a kraken doing it. One puts the merchant ships a little more on guard. The other brings out the Quuros armada and all its wizards."

"Are you fucking joking?" Anlyr spat.

Relos Var blinked rapidly, a distant look on his face as though he was reexamining everything he knew about the Lash and how he knew it. "I see. Yes, we did make certain assumptions, didn't we? Continue."

"We found out she was planning to attack Devors, because—" Galen shrugged. "Fuck if I know. Apparently, her girlfriend—a dragon?—was acting weird, and the Lash wanted to cure whatever it was that was wrong with her. We managed to get there ahead of the Lash, barely, but somehow she got through the wards, and . . . and it was a mess. She was . . . she was gigantic. I don't have anything to compare it to, but the legends didn't make it sound like kraken were *that* big."

"Only their oldest matriarchs." Relos Var's gaze turned contemplative. "How old must she be? I would never have thought one of the Laaka would study our people closely enough to counterfeit such a role. How extraordinary."

"If you say so," Galen snapped. "But in the middle of all that, her girlfriend, that dragon, decided to show up, which is when everything really went to shit."

"Really." Var's mouth twisted. "And what did this dragon look like?"

"Black. A bunch of colors, really, but black in basic theme. Starry eyes."

Var's look of distaste slid over into disappointment. "You were doing so well too. But now I know you're lying. If Drehemia had really been there, there's no way you would have seen her at all."

"Galen can see in the dark," Qown said.

Var turned to his former apprentice. "What was that?"

"Galen can see in the dark," Qown said again, louder. "It's his mage-gift. *He* could see her just fine."

Var pondered something in the middle distance for a few angry beats. Probably whether or not he could trust either of them to tell the truth. He must have decided yes, because he then turned back to Galen. "And then what?"

"And then there was a gigantic fight, and we're lucky we survived it," Galen said. "End of story. Getting your rock back was out of the question."

"I would certainly say so." Relos Var gave a short laugh, almost one of relief. He turned to Anlyr. "What do you think?"

"I think the idea of a Daughter of Laaka impersonating a pirate is one of the most ridiculous things I have ever heard, and I've heard a lot of ridiculous shit in my day." Anlyr shrugged.

"Maybe so," Sheloran added, "but several thousand Quuros soldiers, including High General Qoran Milligreest, witnessed it, so you might confirm it with them before you call us liars."

"There's no need," Relos Var said. "I believe you're telling the truth. And besides, your story is, as they say, too ludicrous to be a lie. You're both smart enough to make your lies believable." Var smiled at Galen. "Now that wasn't so hard, was it?"

Galen cursed under his breath. Arrogant bastard.

Relos Var started to cast a spell. Galen even recognized that it was a gate spell because Var had been casting them so often. Then he paused. He closed his fist, ending the spell prematurely, and turned back to Galen.

"There's just one problem with it."

Galen clenched his jaw and said nothing.

"None of that," Relos Var continued, "required you to find a way to protect your mind from telepathy."

Galen's breath hitched. He'd hoped Relos Var would be too intrigued by the story to remember that part.

Unfortunately, he had.

Galen never thought he'd be grateful for the years of practice he had dealing with his terrible father, but if Darzin had taught him anything, it was this. How to lie to a man who wouldn't settle for merely being right but who had to *win*.

The trick was to give them the truth for free and make them fight for the lie.

Galen turned away, not hiding the sullen look on his face.

"I have no time for this," Relos Var reminded him.

"She controls minds!" Sheloran shouted, which was such a perfect interruption that Galen could have kissed her, and their own preferences in bed partners be damned. "He said it would protect us!"

Var narrowed his eyes. "Please clarify the owners of all those pronouns."

"The dragon," Galen said. "Whatever she did when she breathed on people, it made them lose their minds. Start fighting each other. That's the *she*."

"And the *he*?"

And here was the part Galen had been waiting for, which had the bonus of not even being an actual lie, just a giant, steaming pile of omissions. "D'Lorus," Galen growled. "We didn't want to trust him, but what choice did we have?"

"Galen, no!" Qown's voice was choked.

"D'Lorus," Relos Var repeated. "Thurvishar D'Lorus?" He turned that question to Qown, who looked so haunted and guilty it was an answer in and of itself. Galen wasn't even sure that Qown's reaction was faked. If one didn't know better, it would be easy to assume that Galen had broken, that he was telling the whole story rather than this carefully edited version. It was possible Qown thought the worst of him, hypocrisy draped all over betrayal like a new bedspread.

"Gadrith's son? Surely you've heard of him." Galen knew damn well that Thurvishar wasn't related to Gadrith—that he was in fact related to Relos Var standing right there—but it was a piece of information Relos Var had no reason to think Galen knew.

"Thurvishar did this so you wouldn't fall to Drehemia." Var didn't ask it as a question, so Galen didn't respond except with a shrug meant to be interpreted as a yes. His voice went soft and dark. "And who else was he protecting?"

"Janel." Qown was the one who answered that question. "And . . ." He winced. "And Senera. They said they had a way to cure Drehemia's insanity. Which seemed like the best way to get Drehemia to stop attacking us."

The expression on Relos Var's face didn't change.

Galen's stomach flipped. *Relos Var already knew.*[2]

"There's a way to cure a dragon's insanity?" Anlyr sounded utterly mystified. "Is that true?"

"Yes. It's true," Relos Var said, although he looked like it caused him physical pain to admit that fact.[3]

Anlyr's confusion cleared. "Oh! So that girl—"

Relos Var made an angry slashing motion. Anlyr stopped talking.

"I didn't want to tell you," Qown whispered. "I knew you'd be so angry."

The fear in Qown's voice made Galen's gut clench. It was a tone he knew well: the tone of a child who had been horribly treated, who'd learned not to be too loud or too bright or too visible when his caretakers were angry.

---

[2] Looking back, it seems likely that he would have known from the moment Drehemia was cured. This was just him filling in a few details.—S

[3] I wonder why that would be? Could it have anything to do with the fact that he's known how to fix his fellow dragons for millennia and has decided he'd rather have them insane?—S

Insane left him with a controllable dragon and a usable Cornerstone.—T

Galen still didn't know who was responsible for that. If it had been Relos Var
or someone else—someone earlier from Qown's supposedly peaceful, perfect
family in Eamithon. The family Qown never talked about, never visited, and
whom he'd been so grateful to leave even as a child that he'd jumped into the
Vishai's open arms without ever once looking back.

But that . . . was a conversation for another day. If they made it past this
one.

"And did Senera cure Drehemia?" Relos Var asked. "Was she the one who
used the Name of All Things?"

Qown nodded mutely.

Relos Var stood perfectly still for several interminably slow heartbeats. No
one—not even Anlyr—made a sound.

"Very well," Relos Var finally said. "So I'll have to deal with her in due
time." He gestured then, cast some sort of spell.

Galen found himself dragged to his feet by invisible forces.

Var bent over to pick up Tave, who started to kick.

"No! Don't touch! Bad man!" Tave screamed.

The wizard handed the child to Sheloran, saying, "Keep the boy quiet or I
will change my mind about letting you save him."

He cast the gate spell again, this time to completion, before motioning for
Sheloran and Galen to step through. "Quickly now. I have places to be."

Galen didn't step through, though. "What about Qown?"

Relos Var raised an eyebrow. "You honestly expected that I was going to
let Qown go? I didn't think a D'Mon would be that naïve."

Galen threw himself forward toward the wizard. He heard shouting:
Qown's, Sheloran's.

Then a darkness his eyesight couldn't penetrate descended, and he heard
nothing at all.

# 43. THE ENEMY OF OUR ENEMY

*Janel's story*
*The Afterlife*
*Several hours after they began searching for Xaloma*

Fourth time was the charm, as they say.

One of the three other locations they searched was, to Janel's vast amusement, the very lake where she had first met Kihrin. But it didn't look like Xaloma had been there in months—probably not since a certain golden-haired reincarnation of a sun god had literally burned the dragon from the inside out.

No, the place they found her was one of her lairs underneath the ocean.

Swimming through the ocean was . . . uncomfortable.

Janel adjusted easily enough. After a few false starts, both Xivan and Talea were able to come up with spells or something close enough to spells to allow them to "breathe" underwater and communicate with each other, a process that begged several ontological questions they didn't have time to address at the moment. But the water itself tasted of death, and many of the creatures who swam in the dark waters were little more than skeletons. Not all, though. Occasionally, Janel would spot what looked like living fish, sharks, and once, off in the distance, a whale.

She found herself intensely curious about how exactly reincarnation with animals worked. Had these beasts originally been born in the Living World, only to pass into this one when they died? Were they born here? Could one be born here?

So many questions, but this was neither the time nor place to ask.

It didn't take long before they had to summon up mage-lights, because the waters became too dark to see otherwise. Janel also introduced them to the idea that if they traveled too far down, the weight of the water above could begin to suffocate them. It wouldn't kill them—not here—but it would hurt.

Every once in a while, one of the ocean creatures—a shark or an eel, once a massive jellyfish—would approach Xivan. It was an extraordinary thing to see a shark butt up against Xivan's leg like a cat asking to have its back scratched.

As dark and twisted a place as Janel found this to be, she knew that Xivan didn't share her sentiments. Janel had rarely seen her look so content.

"Eshi says Xaloma's the weakest of the dragons," Talea had volunteered before they'd gone for their swim. "Which doesn't make her weak, exactly, just smaller than some of the others."

Thinking of Aeyan'arric, Janel nodded. "It is indeed wise not to confuse those concepts."

Janel's plan was for initial reconnaissance—establishing that Doc was in Xaloma's custody. Once they'd ascertained that, then they would regroup and come up with a solid plan for freeing the man.

Like most things, the plan didn't survive contact with the enemy.

Janel didn't hear so much as feel the vibrations of the dragon's scream. She'd thought that they were too far away for the dragon to detect them, but clearly, she'd underestimated Xaloma's ability to sense people in her native element. Out of the darkness of the seabed, a smooth indigo shape came rushing at Janel with burning eyes.

Xaloma remembered her.

Janel ran. Or swam, rather.

She could only hope that neither of the other two tried to stay and fight. This was the worst possible place to fight a creature like Xaloma. A shadow slowly swept over her, and Janel knew that she was unlikely to escape. Xaloma was catching up.

Janel crafted a spear in her hand. If she could get close enough to Xaloma without dying—if she could touch the dragon—she'd inflict more damage. Unfortunately, there was an excellent chance Xaloma would kill her before she ever had the chance.

"Like this?" Xivan asked empty water. She was talking to Khae, but it was still unnerving to know that even a sliver of the old Thaena was with them. Xivan stretched out an arm; a blast of bright energy shot from that hand and struck the dragon in her rear left flank.

Xaloma screamed again, causing the water around Janel to hammer against her like an overly enthusiastic musician playing a kettledrum. Whatever Xivan had done hurt the dragon, who curled around her own center to turn and face this new threat.

Janel swam harder, back down, trying to catch up before the dragon killed Death.

Jaws gaped, teeth snapped, and Xivan . . .

Wasn't there. Janel felt the buffet of displaced water as the former Yoran duchess appeared next to Janel with Talea in tow.

Xaloma whipped her head back and forth for a second before realizing she had nothing in her teeth. She undulated, flowing in a semicircle to face up toward the three women once more.

Janel imagined that spotting them would be simple as they floated there, between the dragon and the more brightly lit surface of the water above.

Xaloma opened her mouth again, but this time, instead of screaming, she issued forth some other sound that vibrated Janel to her bones. She felt incredible, searing pain as small pieces of her flesh tore away. Talea and Xivan writhed as the same thing happened to them.

The assault ended after an eternity of heartbeats, leaving Janel bleeding from dozens of coin-size wounds. The bits of her that ripped free dissolved into the water. Xaloma was the Dragon of Spirit, of souls . . . and in the Second World most inhabitants were comprised of nothing but souls.[1]

Before she could share this revelation, a new threat materialized; all those sea creatures that had previously amused or disgusted Janel began swimming toward her and the others. It's hard to judge the facial features of a fish, but Janel didn't think they were approaching to be friendly.

Her spear lashed out once, twice, impaling an angler and a pike, a situation she would find ironically humorous later if she survived. A school of herring swarmed around her then, blinding and biting. She thrashed, lashing out this way and that, but it was impossible to target a single fish in the flashing, constantly moving school.

**ENOUGH!** she thought, and unleashed a burst of tenyé, shaped into heat. The water bubbled around her, and hundreds of fish died in a second, their bodies floating away. Janel also found herself several yards above her companions when she could see again, which surprised her.

They had their own problems: Talea was surrounded by jellyfish, their stinging tendrils lashing her arms and face, while Xivan's shark friend had returned, with buddies. They weren't on Xivan's side anymore.

And during all of this, Xaloma drew closer.

**BELOW YOU!** Janel screamed. She pointed her spear at Xaloma and channeled tenyé through it as a lance of heat. It wasn't as strong as what Kihrin did during their first meeting, but it seemed close enough to distract the dragon. Instead of swallowing Xivan whole, Xaloma raked her with a claw as she swam past, heading up for Janel.

Janel swam for the surface, glancing down now and again to judge the distance. At just the right moment, she flipped herself over and dove back down, narrowly missing Xaloma's mouth. She kicked with both legs, so close she could have reached out to touch the spirit dragon. As she reached the bottom of Xaloma's torso, the dragon was just starting to flip around to give chase. Janel lashed out with her spear and again unleashed an inferno.

Xaloma screamed; the shock wave of water sent Janel spinning end over end. She couldn't see how much damage she'd inflicted. By the time she had righted herself, the dragon was on top of her, mouth agape.

Darkness covered the surface above as the dragon's mouth loomed ever closer, and Janel fought off the distraction of a flashback. She'd been through this before. She'd once killed a dragon by tricking him into swallowing her whole, after all. So had Kihrin, if with less intention. She wondered if she had enough energy to pull off such a trick again.

She didn't feel like she did, if she was being honest with herself.

Just as Xaloma stretched forward to take that all-important bite, a tentacle reached out of the darkness above, wrapped itself around the dragon's neck, and yanked.

---

[1] If Kihrin's correct, Xaloma wouldn't be able to permanently destroy a soul, but that doesn't mean it would be pleasant.–T

That hadn't been an octopus's tentacle. It had been too large—and barbed. But the answer was obvious.

If fish could swim in these seas, the Daughters of Laaka could too.

She felt cold. Because this wasn't a case where the enemy of her enemy was a *friend*.

Janel didn't know why she hadn't thought that Daughters of Laaka would end up in the Afterlife too. This one clearly had. It was the largest Daughter of Laaka that she'd ever seen. Except she quickly revised her opinion: it was exactly the same size as the largest she'd ever seen.

Talea tugged on her arm, intent on a retreat. She was bleeding from numerous locations. Some of the jellyfish stings were swollen and red. Xivan swam up also, cradling the stump of her left arm against her body. A shark under Xaloma's control must have gotten in a lucky bite.

Janel pointed down. They still needed to find Doc.

But Xivan shook her head firmly and pointed up. Together, they dragged Janel toward the surface at an angle. At first, Janel wasn't sure why, then she realized that the "ground" was sloping up in that direction; an island.

Which would do exactly nothing to stop Xaloma from chasing them, but at least they'd die on dry land.

Exhausted, they dragged themselves onto the shore and collapsed a few feet above the waterline. If this were the Living World, the island would be lovely: palm trees and white sandy beaches. Just the sort of place Kihrin would love, Janel thought with a weak grin. Here, however, the trees clustered menacingly and giant spiderwebs filled the spaces between. The beach was more sharp stones than sand. At least it wasn't the ocean.

"We have to find Doc," Janel said the moment she'd caught her breath. "Otherwise, this is all for nothing."

"Agreed," Xivan said. "But we need a moment." She turned her head and looked to the side. "Show me," she said, evidently to Khae. After a moment, she nodded. Lifting the base of her severed arm, Xivan concentrated, and the arm began to regrow. All her wounds "healed" at the same time.

Janel frowned at that. She had thought that only demons knew that trick, but why wouldn't Immortals know something similar? Especially Thaena, in her own realm.

Xivan then went to Talea and did the same, then to Janel, who started to wave her away before realizing that no, she really was weakened. In fact, she hadn't felt this weak since Yor. She allowed Xivan to heal her.

"Here," the new Death Goddess said, putting a hand on Janel's shoulder even after the healing was done. "You need energy too." Janel felt tenyé pouring into her. Unlike when it came from her mother, however, she actually *felt* it this time. Probably a lack of practice; Tya had had lifetimes to perfect the trick while this was Xivan's first try. Still, it felt amazing as Janel's strength returned. Yet, at the same time, the demonic side of her hungered for more, always more.

She clamped down on it.

"Was it just my imagination, or was what attacked Xaloma . . . ?" she asked.

"No," Xivan said, looking off into the distance. "That was what you thought it was: a kraken."

**"I prefer the term who,"** a familiar voice said. **"What makes me feel like an object."**

The ocean splashed and rippled as the Lash drew herself tiredly to shore, like a mountain that had decided to heave itself on land. **"Hello again, Xivan,"** she said and then collapsed onto the sand. **"We really have to stop meeting like this."**

## 44. THE LAND OF PEACE

*Teraeth's story*
*The Chasm in the Afterlife*
*Early morning*

Teraeth stared down the people with weapons drawn on him. He didn't recognize them, but that meant little. People came and went from the Chasm defenses, retreating back to the Land of Peace when they were too injured, being replaced as new people volunteered. He'd never been expected to know their names, and he'd never tried. It had always been enough to know that his mother knew their names.

And that was the problem, wasn't it?

"Who told you that I killed her?" He'd have preferred to ask the question quietly, to have this conversation under more private circumstances, but such was not to be. He was left shouting his response while standing next to a howling morass of magical moving rock, the shield Ompher had created to keep anyone approaching too close to the Wound while also keeping the demons in the Afterlife from entering the Land of Peace.

"You killed her!" one of the soldiers shouted. "How could you!"

Seriously, how did they know what had happened? But he answered himself immediately: thousands had died on that battlefield. It was hardly outside the realm of the permissible that one of those souls had arrived here with the knowledge of those events.

Except . . . they shouldn't have remembered. Whoever had told them had remembered everything. And that would have been a far smaller number.

"She's here, isn't she?" Teraeth asked. "My mother's *here*."

"She doesn't want to talk to you!" A Quuros man with the bright green eyes of a D'Aramarin Ogenra shook a spear at him as he shouted.

"Did she tell you that she was forcing me to kill myself?" Teraeth continued. "Forcing me to dance until I completed a ritual that would have taken a million lives? If I betrayed my mother, it is only because she betrayed herself first." He growled as he step forward, pulling his daggers from his belt. "I don't care if she doesn't want to see me. She owes me this. Now give me a path or I will make one."

There was a moment of stillness where Teraeth honestly didn't know how the conversation would go. If they would make him fight people who were in no way his enemy.

They stepped aside.

Teraeth ran across the narrow bridge, which he logically knew was safe. It still always felt like it was seconds from dropping him into the Chasm. This time, it felt even more fragile than normal.

Maybe that was his imagination. Maybe it wasn't.

Teraeth hoped Kihrin was right about him being able to return on his own. He wasn't certain Kihrin could enter the place, and Xivan had no idea he was here. If Teraeth couldn't get out by himself, he had no reason to think he was ever getting out at all.

He threw open the doors to the Death Goddess's palace and walked inside.

Compared to the last time Teraeth was there, the Land of Peace was practically deserted. The reason why was as obvious as it was horrifying: because every soul willing to fight was out at the Chasm, and every soul killed by a demon never made it any further.

So in theory, finding his mother should have been easy.

He'd already finished searching a dozen rooms before it occurred to him that she might well be out at the Chasm fighting too. She'd clearly spoken to the people out there.

But no, he told himself. If she'd been there, she'd have said something. She wouldn't have just let him run off.

The palace was unlike earlier structures built in the first days of the wars with the demons. It wasn't a place of war but as a promise and a goal for souls that might otherwise have wandered through the Afterlife until demons succeeded in hunting them down. A thing that happened far too often at the start.

At least, that's what his mother had always told him.

Had Thaena built the palace herself, or had Ompher helped? Probably the latter. His mother had always grumbled, if quietly, about the Font of Souls being located on land. She'd cordoned it off, fenced it in within a wide garden that meant one couldn't stumble upon it purely by chance. People went to the Font of Souls when they meant to—when they wanted to be reborn.[1] He started to second-guess himself. Teraeth had assumed his mother would look like her voramer self, not the old woman he'd grown up knowing, but maybe he was wrong. Maybe she'd chosen to look like the disguise. Or maybe she hadn't come here at all.

He searched through the garden. He looked through the pools.

Then he realized there was one room he hadn't searched. He'd just assumed it would be empty—in hindsight, that had been naïve. Teraeth looked down at himself, concentrated, and changed into something more appropriate for formal occasions.

Then he went to the ballroom.

---

[1] Given that all the voramer-descended races are amphibious and can breathe air, this wouldn't prevent any of those groups from reincarnating. That said, one does wonder about the fish.—T

That is possibly the single best argument I've heard yet for the idea that animals don't reincarnate.—S

Yes, but what about the Daughters of Laaka? Or the sky trees? I have questions.—T

He had no business mocking the people who were here and not at the Chasm, considering how much time he'd spent here himself in between his first life and this one. Sure, he could claim it was for a good cause—S'arric had needed someone to help him out until Elana had gotten around to dying of old age—but he wouldn't have been fooling anyone, least of all himself. If he'd avoided the place since, it was because it no longer contained the only two souls that had ever made it worth visiting.

Khaemezra had never called it a throne room, but surely the name applied. It was a lavish space of cold marble and glittering beauty. A single bright light source toward the ceiling refracted downward through a chandelier of crystals and created what, Teraeth realized in hindsight, was a pattern of light along the floor very much like being underwater.

And there were indeed people here. Far more than he would have expected under the circumstances. Before the demons were freed, this place would have been packed, a constant dance in motion to rival anything the vané might have hosted. But now? This seemed like hiding. Like cowardice.

Then Teraeth spotted someone he recognized and had to revise all his theories of what was going on.

His father was in the center of the room, dancing.

## 45. The Mimic

**Caless's story**
**The Soaring Halls, the Upper Circle of the Capital City of Quur**
**A few minutes after making a deal with Relos Var**

Logically, it took very little time for Relos Var to return, but emotionally, it felt like aeons. Eventually, another gate opened and spat out four people: Relos Var, Sheloran, Galen, and the small child, Tave.

Caless saw the child and immediately knew that she'd miscalculated.

No, it was worse than that: she'd been *played*.

"Mother, you have to–!" Sheloran said that much before her voice fled her, leaving her with a hand at her throat, staring venom and fury at Relos Var.

"All three, as promised," Relos Var said.

The two powers in the room stared at each other.

Caless knew she could protest. Relos Var knew perfectly well that the spirit of the bargain hadn't been for the return of a child she had naïvely assumed wasn't in jeopardy. (Surely her daughter and son-in-law had already left the boy with the Milligreests, yes?) She'd been expecting Sheloran, Galen, *and* Qown.

But Caless was no fool. She'd agreed to three, Var had delivered three, and if she protested, he'd gleefully take the child back. That was assuming he cooperated at all. If Qown had been one of his people, as Relos Var had suggested, then it was likely that Var had never intended to return him, and any suggestion otherwise had always been fool's gold and shadow plays.

Galen hadn't made the smallest protest, but the way he watched Var, as if he would gleefully charge forward with a sword drawn at the smallest provocation, told Caless all she needed.

Caless pulled the necklace around her throat until the chain released with a soft snap and held it out to Var. "Here," she said. "Take it and go."

Sheloran was pleading at her with her eyes. Caless ignored her.

Var held out his hand under hers so that the stone fell into his outstretched palm. He stared at the stone for a moment, looking inordinately pleased with himself, before tucking it under his belt.

"A pleasure doing business with you," he said. The next second, he was gone.

"Mother!" Sheloran screamed the moment Relos Var vanished. "He still has Qown."

"I know," Caless said. "Do you know where you were? Where he took you?"

"Somewhere in the Kirpis, I suspect. Near a beach," Galen said. "Which would be far more helpful if thousands of miles of coastline didn't qualify." He breathed deep and took Sheloran's hand. "Let's not panic. Even if Relos Var suspects something's wrong, he has no way short of torture to get the information out of Qown. He won't just kill him."

Caless felt a chill. "Torture? Does Relos Var think your Qown knows valuable information?"

Her daughter stared at her. Sheloran had always been good at tracking her moods, so she must have realized that something wasn't quite right. "Yes. We all do. But it's fine: they can't read his mind."

Caless grimaced. "Damn. I assumed—"

Ah, but she'd assumed far too much.

"You assumed what?" Galen asked.

"I assumed Var wanted Qown for punitive reasons, not for information," Caless said angrily. "Relos Var claimed he had a mimic guarding you. Is there any chance he was telling the truth?"

"A mimic? But he didn't have a mimic, just . . . Anlyr?" Galen looked at Sheloran, wide-eyed. "Anlyr can't be a mimic. He was using illusions to impersonate Qown, wasn't he?"

"That's what I thought . . ." Sheloran looked horrified. "Remember when Var said Anlyr was so used to reading minds he'd forgotten how to read people? What if . . . ?"

"You should assume the worst," Caless said. "It was an oddly specific threat to make and a strange one if Relos Var was lying."

Galen closed his eyes and visibly shuddered.

"What you're saying . . ." Sheloran couldn't finish the sentence.

"Can you—" Galen swallowed. "Can you use magic to find Qown? He's not wearing Worldhearth anymore."

"No," Sheloran answered before Caless could. "Because we warded against that, Blue. We can't be tracked." She began laughing, hysterical, while the small boy with her sniffled and looked on the verge of tears.

"You . . . you don't happen to know where Grizzst's Tower is?" Galen asked.

Caless blinked. It suddenly occurred to her that she should have paid a little more attention to exactly what her daughter and son-in-law had been doing in the past month. Because most people, assuming they'd even heard of the place, would have classified Grizzst's Tower firmly in the category of a god-king tale—something mythical.

"It's been a few years," she admitted. "But yes, I know where it is."

For the first time since Caless explained about the mimic, Galen's expression held something other than despair. The faintest hint of hope.

"Then if we might beg a kindness of you," Galen said. "We need a gate opened to that location immediately."

Sheloran handed the small boy to her. "And we'll need you to watch Tave until we return."

# 46. A History of Dragons

*Xivan's story*
*The Afterlife*
*Just after fleeing Xaloma*

The Lash rose high out of the water, which flowed off her sides to crash back into the ocean in sprays of black and silver.

Xivan felt like laughing. Of course. Of fucking course.

The funny thing was, the Lash looked much better than the last time Xivan had seen her. Gone were the cataract eyes, the rotting and discolored flesh, the pale hide that spoke to a body long since past the point where it should continue to function. And yet, there was only one reason that could be true here, in this place.

Someone had slain the Lash.

As Xivan contemplated exactly what she might be able to do—this was her world now, right? She should be able to do *something*.

"Xivan." The Lash's voice was a familiar earthquake rumble. **"That is you, isn't it? It's so hard to tell sometimes. You're all such tiny things."**

Talea flashed Xivan a concerned look, but Xivan waved her back.

"Yes, it's me," Xivan answered. "What are you doing here?"

**"You never struck me as that dumb before,"** the Lash said. **"I would think it's obvious what I'm doing here."** The kraken's voice rose then. **"I was *betrayed*."**

"Betrayed," Xivan said. The number of suspects was low, simply because there were few "people" that the kraken allowed anywhere near her. "Not Boji?"

Xivan had assumed the slimy little toad had run after the battle on Devors, but if he'd been foolish enough to return to the Lash . . .

**"Drehemia,"** the Lash said lowly. **"Drehemia betrayed me."**

"Oh," Talea said. "I'm so sorry."

Janel began quietly cursing. Xivan suspected she knew why. Because depending on just why such a betrayal had occurred, Drehemia might well have absconded with two separate Cornerstones—Grimward, the stone that the Lash had carried, and the Name of All Things, which had been used to stabilize Drehemia's mental state.

So depending on the story, this was either bad or *unbelievably* bad.

The kraken's tentacles made whirls and eddies in the water, constantly in motion. But she wasn't attacking, and she didn't seem to be in any rush to leave either.

"What is it you want?" Xivan asked.

The Daughter of Laaka turned her head so she could stare at Xivan with one obscenely large eye, glittering golden in the faint light. **"You're the new caretaker of this realm, are you not?"**

Xivan blinked. She wouldn't have thought it that obvious, but . . .

"Yes," she admitted. "I am."

**"I thought as much. You have the scent about you."** The Lash somehow managed to convey a sniffing motion. **"I never liked your predecessor. I got along much better with the original before they left."**

Everyone froze.

"I'm sorry?" Talea said. "Did you just—" She swallowed. "Did you just say that there was a Death *before* Khaemezra?"

The Lash paused. A stretching, creaking sound filled the air as the kraken shifted her position so an eye could stare directly at Talea. The salt sea smell of dead fish and storm-tossed kelp hung heavy and thick.

Then the kraken matriarch began to laugh. Great, massive vibrato-rich peals of laughter that sent out ripples along the surface of the water. She even went so far as to slap her tentacles against the ocean waves the way one might slap a thigh.

**"You—"** She laughed some more. **"Did you really think yours were the** *first?*"

Janel stared at Xivan and Talea, wide-eyed.

"Um," she said. "Uh—yes? Yes, we did. Mostly because we were the ones that invented the way to do it. Or Relos Var did, anyway."

**"And who told you that? Relos Var?"**

Xivan felt like the earth under her feet had just shifted. What? "Are you saying . . ." She mentally shook herself. Was it possible that the Lash was just fucking with them? But if so, what did she have to gain by suggesting that Relos Var was a liar? And how the hell did a damn Daughter of Laaka know who Relos Var was, anyway? "Okay. So what happened to them, then? This first caretaker?"

Janel mouthed, "Thank you," at Xivan.

**"Oh, that explains so much. Allow me to further extrapolate,"** the Lash said in a silky-smooth voice. **"You thought that some of your people took on the shape of dragons out of . . . coincidence? Pure happenstance?** *Luck?*"

She lost herself in laughter again.

Xivan shook her head. She had no idea what to think.

Janel didn't seem to either, but she pressed forward. "We thought they took the shape of dragons because the ritual went astray. Because it was flawed."

**"Not flawed. Just not meant for** *your* **people,"** the Lash corrected. **"The first Death was a dragon, naturally. But then all the dragons left."**

"Left?" Talea looked every bit as lost and confused as Xivan felt. "Where . . . where did they go?"

**"As if I know?"** The Lash slapped another tentacle against the water, this time less in humor than frustration. **"I miss them still. Who do you think**

created the glyphs, sang the magics into being, wove the strands of creation into melodies of light and matter? My people didn't leave glyphs carved on land for you to find. Why would we leave such a record in a place where we never go?"

"Glyphs?" Xivan tugged on Janel's arm. "Is she talking about the Name of All Things?"

"Yes and no," Janel said, still looking dumbfounded. "Same idea, older origin. This is . . . You're saying that we . . . Just to make sure there's no misunderstanding. You're saying that Rev'arric *didn't* create the Guardians?"

**"I'm saying that you, like a hermit crab, moved into a seashell already built by another and then complimented yourselves for your skills at architecture. No, you were not the first."** The Lash lowered herself until her eyes were much nearer to the three women. **"The dragons came here and built and shaped things and then later realized we were in the world too. But unlike your lot, they were honorable and left so we might live in peace. We never considered how much damage might be caused by what they'd left behind, if it fell into hands such as yours."**

Xivan's stomach tightened; she felt overwhelmed. She reminded herself that all of this—while interesting and probably important—did nothing to accomplish their reason for being here. She thought back to the conversation before the Lash had accidentally shaken their entire view of the world and their place in it.

"I'm glad you like me better," Xivan said, "and I assume that this means you want something from me?" She paused. "I don't know if I can Return you. I can try."

**"You cannot,"** the Lash said. **"My corporeal body is cinder and ash. I'll go to the wellspring and start anew, as is my right. But I wouldn't mind . . . I wouldn't mind you doing what I cannot."**

"And what would that be?" Xivan asked.

The Lash was silent for several slow, heavy seconds. **"Why were you confronting Xaloma?"** she finally asked.

Xivan glanced over at Talea, but most especially Janel. Just to make sure that it wasn't a poor idea to share this information. Janel gave a single nod.

"She has someone of ours. We wish to rescue him," Xivan said.

The Lash pondered that piece of information. **"If I help you, will you kill Relos Var?"**

"Um." Janel cleared her throat. "To be honest, we were planning on doing that anyway."

**"Then I will help you in this ocean for lack of being able to help you in the other."**

Xivan exhaled. Part of her wanted so much to just laugh and laugh. She never thought she'd be *allying* with the Lash. Doing so with her full consent.

"You'll distract Xaloma while we steal our friend from her lair?" Xivan asked.

**"No,"** the Lash said.

Xivan scowled. "Then how exactly—"

**"Your friend isn't in her lair."** She raised a tentacle the way someone else might raise a finger to stifle any objection. **"I can smell a human swimming in my waters for miles, and I tell you that you three were the only ones anywhere near Xaloma's sleeping lair. I will keep my word and help, but part of that is not letting you throw yourselves against the current. Your friend isn't there."**

Janel threw up her hands.

Xivan plopped herself down on the beach. "Perfect," she said. "I have no idea where to look next." She glared at the old woman who sat farther up the strand. "Very helpful."

The old woman waved a hand dismissively at her. "I can't be right about everything. Clearly, Thaena had some other plans in mind for the man."

She made an effort not to grind her teeth. "We need to find him!"

Khae didn't seem especially sympathetic. "Then I guess you'd better see if Khaemezra's souls ended up here and ask her."

Janel sighed. She looked about ten seconds from lighting the entire beach on fire, and Xivan felt much the same.

"Lash?" Talea asked in a tentative, hesitant voice. "How did you end up here, anyway? I mean, I know you said you were betrayed, but . . . what happened?"

**"Oh,"** the Lash said.

Both Xivan and Janel turned to look at the kraken when she didn't answer.

But it turned out she was just formulating her thoughts. In a deep, rumbling voice, she said, **"Perhaps it won't be too unexpected if I say that what 'happened' was Relos Var."**

# 47. Conversations with Death

*Teraeth's story*
*The Land of Peace, the Afterlife*
*Shortly after crossing the Chasm*

Teraeth made his way past men and women draped in the finest of clothing, velvets and silk brocades. He swore that there were a few he recognized—people who'd died and come to the Land of Peace and had simply never left. Souls who had preferred to instead spend the rest of eternity attending Death's never-ending ball. People tried to dance with him, and he had to politely but firmly refuse them as he headed toward his target.

He'd changed his mind about the identity of the black-skinned vané man dancing in the center of the ballroom almost immediately. Precisely because the man did look like Doc—*after* he'd switched bodies with his murderer, thanks to the Stone of Shackles. Thus, the person dancing there had to be Mithrail, whose body his father had ended up wearing as a permanent reminder to always ask more questions when making deals with wizards.[1] The man's dance partner threw her head back and laughed; Teraeth had his second shock of the evening.

Taja.

Eshimavari, he supposed, since "Taja" was now a former Khorveshan slave girl turned mercenary lieutenant. Still, she was distinctive enough with that silver hair and pale skin that Teraeth felt certain of her identity. "Mithrail's" expression turned sly as he whispered something to the woman.

A shiver raced through Teraeth. The body posture, that smile were hauntingly familiar. And it's not like he hadn't looked for Mithrail in the Afterlife before. He'd been certain the man had gone to the Font already.

Teraeth might have been second-guessing, or third-guessing, himself, but he was changing his mind about the man's identity again.

Maybe it *was* Doc.

"He won't remember you," Khaemezra said. "He doesn't even remember himself at the moment. Although clearly, there is no power in the universe that will make him forget how to flirt." She sighed. "In case it wasn't completely obvious which parent you take after in *that* regard."

---

[1] King Terindel obtained the Stone of Shackles because of the wizard Grizzst, who gave him the Cornerstone in exchange for Valathea's help resurrecting Galava. Grizzst had truthfully told him that the artifact would save his life.—T
Terindel should have asked how.—S

Teraeth turned around and stared at his mother.

She sat in a chair made of fabric stretched across a gold frame—one of many such spaced around the perimeter of the ballroom, nothing special. But the way she rested her head on her hand while pensively watching the dancers transformed it. It was hard for Teraeth to shake the impression of a bored, unhappy queen at court.

"Is Argas around here somewhere?" Teraeth asked, not sure himself if he meant it as a joke or a serious question.

"No, not yet," Khaemezra said. "So we can assume my so-called friends haven't gotten around to replacing *him* yet." She went back to watching Doc and Eshimavari dance, her expression both venomous and strangely wistful. None of that emotion was directed at Teraeth, though. Honestly, he didn't know whether or not he should feel insulted.

She looked like the crone this time, not the pretty young maiden. No one you would want to dance with—no one you would expect to be even capable of dancing. Teraeth had never once seen her in these halls in all the years he'd been there. Then he realized why she'd chosen it: so no one would recognize her as the woman who had once been Death.

His mother had her pride.

Teraeth glanced back at his father. "I would've thought he'd look like a Kirpis vané. Like he did in his first life."

His mother scoffed. "You mean his second life. Yes, I expected that too."

He blinked. Teraeth's father hadn't been a Founder, but Teraeth recalled that he had been older than the demonic invasion, one of the extremely rare children born when the Veil had still been a solid barrier between the twin worlds. Had she known him in that first life? Had there been some sort of connection between them? She'd either tell him or not. He wouldn't ask.

It wasn't why he was there, anyway.

"I didn't come here for him. I'm here to talk to you."

She didn't respond. Khaemezra continued to stare into the crowd, to where Doc danced. It was a clear dismissal, one he chose to ignore.

"Mother—"

She slammed her hand down against the chair's arm and glared at him.

"Really," Khaemezra said. "How can you call me that after what happened?"

"You'll need to be more specific. Do you mean after you murdered my father? After you tried to kill Kihrin? After you tried to murder the entire Manol vané nation, for that matter? Or do you just mean, how can I call you Mother when I'm the one who cut off your head?" People started giving them a wide berth, probably because family arguments had nothing in the "awkward" department compared to family arguments where one member had literally killed the other.

His mother glared at him. Then the corner of her mouth quirked up, and she chuckled. "A bit of all of that. I really should be much more angry at you than I am."

"Yes, I've heard a guilty conscience can blunt self-righteous rage."

Khaemezra gazed at him sideways. "If we'd done things my way, the danger would be over."

"If we'd done things your way, Relos Var and Xaltorath would still be loose in the world. Care to try again?"

"You've been spending too much time with Kihrin."

"Whose idea was that?"

"Evidently yours. I should have known you volunteered too quickly."

"You knew perfectly well that I'd fallen in love with S'arric before I was ever born as your son. You thought it was cute."

She didn't deny that. She just scoffed again and said, "I never should have let the three of you leave the Afterlife."

"Indeed. You should have forced us to stay here, for *him* to stay here against his will while he slowly remembered just who and *what* he really was. That would have worked out so well once it occurred to him just how far you'd deviated from anything remotely resembling your actual job."

"I hadn't–!"

He continued as though she hadn't said anything. "And if it wasn't for us, Gadrith would be emperor, either he or Var would have Urthaenriel, and some other poor hapless bastard would be standing in our shoes, except without our skill sets. Whoever ended up as 'Janel' would have been consumed by Suless, and you'd have bought the world an extra two hundred years during which you'd fuck around and *not get the job done,* just like you've consistently done for the last four thousand." Teraeth paused to catch his breath and then started laughing. "Also, three? I'll have to tell Thurvishar that all his efforts to make you think he's the well-behaved one worked perfectly."[2]

She didn't respond; he hadn't expected her to. What was there to say?

They both watched the dancers. His father looked like he was having a good time.

His mother let out a weighty sigh. "How did you die, anyway?"

Teraeth was taken aback, shocked in spite of himself. He turned to face her. "I didn't."

Khaemezra straightened. "How–?" She seemed to answer her own question before she'd finished asking it. "Are you my replacement, then?"

Teraeth was so astonished by that idea that he could only stare. He shook his head. In lieu of answering, he pulled over a chair, slumping down into it.

"Well?" she pressed.

"No, I'm not." No sooner had he sat than he was immediately back up again, this time to liberate a set of drinks from one of the nearby tables. He handed one of them to his mother and kept the other one for himself. "I've met your replacement. You don't know her."

"Don't assume," Khaemezra snapped.

"Her name's Xivan."

Khaemezra pondered that statement for a long beat.

[2] I'm honestly not sure whether to be proud or insulted that I was apparently the one volunteer for all this whose participation was taken for granted.–T

"I don't know her," she admitted.

Teraeth raised his hands in an *"I told you"* gesture.

Khaemezra downed her wine and set it on the table next to her. "You realize she won't have enough time to learn everything needs to know, don't you? She's never going to be able to take on Vol Karoth. Not in time to make a difference."

"Agreed," Teraeth said. He decided to skip right over why "taking on Vol Karoth" wasn't their focus. "But that sounds like a problem for the people trying to fix this mess, not people hiding out in the Afterlife stalking old lovers."

"If Vol Karoth destroys the Immortals and lets the demons overrun the Land of Peace, it's everyone's problem," Khaemezra snapped. "*That's* why I'm still here, boy. I may not be Thaena anymore, but I'm still a millennia-old wizard who knows more about this side of the Veil than anyone else in existence. Forget that at your peril."

Teraeth wrestled down his anger, his resentment. He didn't know why he would have expected her to admit that she might have made a mistake. That would take lifetimes they didn't have. He scooted his chair around and set his feet up on the table next to her, knocking an empty glass to the ground. He ignored the sound of breaking glass, nearly lost among the clamor of the party.

"I'll worry about that if it becomes an issue," Teraeth said, "which, for right now, it isn't. But I do need information from you. Kihrin has this idea—"

"I hope he didn't hurt himself."

He raised an eyebrow. "The pettiness doesn't become you."

"Can you blame me?"

He didn't even have to think about that one. "You know what? *Yes, I can.* You're sitting here wallowing in self-pity and acting like Kihrin's nothing more than a twenty-year-old street-rat musician turned spoiled Quuros prince, when you know perfectly well who he really is."

"Yes, a magnet for Vol Karoth," she snapped, "which is no blessing!"

Teraeth allowed himself a smirk, although damned if he was going to let her know how much better and worse the truth was. "It's almost comical how terrified you are of Vol Karoth when the reason you ended up here was entirely a situation of your own making. And when it comes to a contest between Kihrin and Vol Karoth, or Kihrin and Relos Var, or Kihrin and the rest of the whole fucking universe, I will bet on Kihrin every time, and *I will win*. You forget *that* at *your* peril."

She glared. "And you expect my help?"

"Didn't you just explain how the Land of Peace being overrun is everyone's problem? How you're still a power in your own right and know more about this place, blah, blah, blah?" Teraeth laughed. "You're dead. At least for now. At least until you decide to be reborn. Or a close family member petitions for your Return. I do understand that could be arranged." He leaned on one arm. "Do you think Sharanakal might put in a request? Or Xaloma perhaps?"

Khaemezra huffed. "You are such an ass."

"I prefer *son of a bitch*," Teraeth corrected and gave his mother a significant look on the off chance she missed the insult. "Anyway, as I was saying, Kihrin has this idea that when we've been tossing demons into the Font, we haven't truly been destroying them."

He watched her carefully, which was the reason he saw the draw of her brows, the briefest twitch at the corners of her eyes.

"A ridiculous notion," Khaemezra snapped. "Do you think I haven't checked? A demon tossed into the Font ceases to be. That's why we do it."

"Okay," Teraeth said, narrowing his eyes. "But now I'm confused. Because if the Font of Souls destroys demons, why have we been working so hard all these years to keep demons away from it? Which is it? Does the Font of Souls destroy demons, or can demons destroy the Font?"

His mother's lip rose in a sneer. "What a simplistic way of looking at things. There's a difference between throwing someone into a furnace and letting them have free access to the fuel. Both outcomes can be true."

"Very well," Teraeth said, ignoring the insult. "But Kihrin doesn't think you're destroying their souls at all."

"*Kihrin* is hardly the expert—"

"He thinks that all the demons who came from that other universe were each composed of thousands—millions—of smaller souls. That the Font breaks those souls apart, but it never destroys them. It merely sends all those component pieces back to the Living World to be reborn as individual humans."

Silence. Then Khaemezra leaned over and stole the glass of wine from Teraeth's hand. She'd already drunk her own.

"Mother."

She drank said wine as petulantly as possible. "And how exactly is that *not* destroying a demon?"

He stared. His mother was grumbling and cranky and clearly upset, but she wasn't even the tiniest bit *surprised*.

"That is what's happening, isn't it?" Teraeth said. "He's right."

She didn't answer for a long beat of hesitation. Then she said, "Why does it matter?"

"Because it does."

"Oh really?" She scowled. "That's your answer? 'Because'? I was being serious. What good is it knowing that before you were Atrin Kandor, you were one infinitesimally small part of a *demon*? Please enlighten me on how that would have made any of your lives even the tiniest bit better."

Teraeth had already figured out that he probably was one of those recycled "demon" souls. He'd figured it out as soon as Kihrin had explained that everyone who didn't have the soul of a Founder likely qualified. The confirmation was still a queasy, ugly feeling.

But she also didn't understand. "It matters, *Mother,* because depending on how someone set up the ritual, trying to affect demons might also affect everyone who ever *was* a demon. Which is apparently a lot of people. Which is a problem if Relos Var decides that's the way we should have been handling our demon problem all along!"

Khaemezra straightened in her seat. She blinked several times, staring out into the distance. Teraeth could almost see the quickening of her pulse, the way her whole body tensed. She understood the ramifications, even though she pretended at nonchalance. "No," she said. "He's not that stupid. Relos Var knows we'd stop him—" She choked off the words as she realized what she was saying.

Who, exactly, was going to stop him? Tya and Khored? A bunch of baby Guardians who had no idea what they were doing?

Teraeth said, "Tell me again why it doesn't matter."

What followed wasn't silence exactly—not with the soaring music and murmurs of the crowds and the jangling laughter and the clinking of glasses. But it felt oddly the same as if there had been no sound of any kind at all. Just a mother and son, all the history behind them, and the terrible realization of what might yet be to come.

But only for a moment.

"And you thought I was bad," Khaemezra finally murmured.

"Oh no. You're not excused just because he's worse," Teraeth spat. "You're both far too good at gilding your crimes with the cracking veneer of necessity. You should have said something. You should have explained this."

"We didn't know back then." Khaemezra suddenly sounded very tired and every bit her age. "Not until after Grizzst brought us back. You should have seen the giant pile of demon souls he handed over, and he'd just finished with that gaeshing project of his. We had a chance to catch our breaths. That was when Galava and I noticed the pattern." She saluted him with her empty glass. "It was a reassuring pattern, child."

"How can you possibly—"

She sighed. "It meant 'demon' wasn't a permanent curse, that the infection could be countered. Yes, you'd have to be reborn, but wasn't that better than the alternative?"

Yes, of course. But the consequences of that knowledge were less enviable.

Teraeth saw it all laid in front of him like dishes at a banquet. Yes, it would have been a reassuring pattern—and it would have made the situation so much worse. Because what must have originally seemed like an emergency that had to be solved, immediately, without delay, or risk the survival of humanity would have suddenly seemed . . . less urgent. A problem, to be sure, but not an insurmountable problem. With the demons gaeshed and their reclamation an understood phenomena, demons would have been instantly relegated to being the lesser evil. Terrible, yes, but gradually more and more *normal*. The greater evil, of course, being not the Daughters of Laaka, the dragons, or even Relos Var, but Vol Karoth. The Guardians had then let themselves become trapped in a stasis of their own making: preoccupied with an enemy they couldn't engage with as long as he was still imprisoned, yet unwilling to focus their attention elsewhere while he remained. And how tempting must it have been when someone came along with all those lovely "prophecies" that suggested that someone else might one day solve all their issues with Vol Karoth. All they had to do was make sure certain events happened, certain people were born, certain game pieces were placed just so.

No wonder Xaltorath had been able to ambush them in so many timelines.

Teraeth didn't answer his mother. He forcibly unclenched his jaw.

"How many souls?" he finally asked. "How many souls do you think this affects?"

She considered the question. "Half."

Teraeth felt sick. "Half. Really?"

"It's a guess," Khaemezra said, waving a hand. "I don't know. But half seems reasonable. With each race that used the Ritual of Night and aligned themselves, more and more souls would have been created by the Font itself. And fewer and fewer of the old demons still exist. So it's a numbers game. The more time passes, the lower that number will drop."[3]

Teraeth sucked his lower lip against his teeth as he remembered Kihrin saying he wasn't even sure the Font produced human souls at all. If that was true . . .

He had to hope that Kihrin wasn't right about that.

His mother's voice dropped until it was barely louder than a whisper. "We never found any evidence that it matters, Teraeth. No suggestion that you're some sort of hidden carrier of demonic taint. If that was ever true, the Font of Souls would have washed it all away. It truly isn't something to lose sleep over." She paused. "You really think Relos Var will target the demons this way?"

"Yes." He didn't even have to think about it.

Khaemezra's face twisted. "You have to stop him."

"I wasn't planning on stepping aside and letting him do what he likes," Teraeth admitted. "Stopping him is the plan. I just regret that I probably won't be able to personally twist the knife. I would have liked that."

"You always did hate him so much." She sounded fond.

He glanced over at his mother. "Not without cause. Remember the part where I fell in love with his brother?"

"Just be careful—" Midsentence, she seemed to realize what she was saying, and to whom. She closed her mouth and looked away.

And maybe if it had been under different circumstances, he'd have let that go unremarked, but he just couldn't. Nor could he keep the venom from his voice. "Don't pretend to care. We both know better."

The more familiar scowl was almost a relief. "Oh yes, my mistake." She made a face as though she was tasting bile. "How silly of me to give a damn about my own child."

He tilted his head. Apparently, it was time to leave. "Are you confusing me with a child that you haven't tried to murder?" Teraeth paused. "*Do* you have a child that you haven't tried to murder? Khaevatz, maybe? Although you did have her daughter assassinated . . ."

---

[3] This is embarrassingly bad logic. If one assumes that the Font of Souls will only "create" a new soul when strictly necessary, then it would only do so if the living population exceeds the number of souls readily available. If Kihrin was correct, and just one of those demon princes was an amalgam of billions of souls, then it seems unlikely that the Font would have ever needed to create new souls, even if it was capable of doing so.–T

"Oh, stop it," Khaemezra snapped. "It wasn't personal."

Teraeth looked back at Doc, then looked at his mother. "No," he said, his voice breaking. "Don't kid yourself. That was very personal. And I haven't forgiven you. I don't think I ever will. I did *everything* for you. Committed every crime that you ever asked of me, swore every vow, bound myself with every leash. I gave you my absolute devotion—"

"Teraeth—"

"And I only *ever* asked for one thing in return: that you be worthy of it."

He didn't say the next part, although it echoed loud enough to break glass: *you weren't.*

Khaemezra just stared for a moment, her face blank. Then that expression became by stages angry, horrified, regretful, and guilt-stricken. She made a sound suspiciously similar to a sob, put a hand to her face, and turned away.

Maybe a better man would have forgiven her then. Kihrin would have forgiven her, he was certain. He was good like that.

Teraeth was his mother's son, and she'd raised him to show mercy to no one.

It wasn't that she didn't matter to him anymore—she did. But there were some hurts that couldn't be healed with an epiphany and tears.

"I'm glad we talked," Teraeth said, his voice as flat as the still sea of numbness he floated on. "Now, I'm going to fetch my father, and we're going to leave. And you won't stop either of us." He pulled his feet off the table and stood.

She closed her eyes and didn't respond, although there was no possibility that she hadn't heard him.

"I am curious about one thing," Teraeth added. "You mentioned he doesn't remember."

Khaemezra opened her silver eyes.

Teraeth continued, "So he doesn't remember the history between the two of you. If you'd shown up here looking the way you really do, you could have been the one he was dancing with, flirting with. Maybe he'd have ignored Taja and spent all his time with you."

She made a small scoffing noise as she wiped a thumb under one of her eyes. "Yes," she said. "That's exactly why I didn't."

Teraeth nodded. Truthfully, he understood. He thought about how miserable he'd been prepared to be, watching Kihrin and Janel together. How angry he'd been and also how determined he'd been to cheerfully cut the throats of anyone who would have dared give them a moment's discomfort. He'd almost lost everything because he'd been too proud to confess his vulnerability. His mother's son indeed.

In any similar situation, he would have been damned (perhaps a poor choice of words) if he'd have been forced to resort to tricks to gain the attention of someone he loved. Not even if it was Kihrin. Not even if it was Janel.

Khaemezra waved him away. "Go. Take him. I don't care."

Teraeth knew that was a lie, but he let it be. It was his way of saying goodbye.

He left to speak to his father.

Eshimavari spotted Teraeth first. From the moment their eyes met, Teraeth knew the former Goddess of Luck's memory was intact. She recognized him.

She winked.

Teraeth felt inexplicably nervous. He'd never spoken to Taja. He'd only ever heard about her or read about her. He felt like he should have some kind of update for her: *Here's how everything's going. Yes, there's a new Taja, and she's coming along fine. Oh yeah, um, Vol Karoth and Kihrin merged, but no worries, everything is under control.*

Teraeth hoped everything was under control.

Before he had a chance to contemplate what he was going to say, though, Doc noticed his dance partner had been distracted. The former Kirpis vané king turned and examined Teraeth, frowning. Something about Teraeth's appearance seemed to bother Doc, although it wasn't clear exactly what.

"I'm your son," Teraeth told him, suspecting it was likely best to get certain facts out of the way immediately.

"Are you?" Doc cocked his head. "I hope I was a good father."

"You were," Teraeth said. Or at least, maybe he would have been, if he'd been given the chance. Taunna seemed like she'd turned out well enough.[4] "I need you to come with me."

"I'm feeling parched; I'm going to get a drink," Eshimavari said before tugging on Doc's shirt. "Listen to him, would you? He's not just pretty; he's smart too. He gets that from you." With that, the former goddess walked off the dance floor, although Teraeth strongly suspected she'd be back at it as soon as she found a new dance partner.

Doc watched her leave—which Teraeth noticed because he'd been watching too—and then gave his son an apologetic, rueful smile. "And where is it you would have us go? I am told on good authority that I cannot leave. That I am . . . dead." He frowned as though the thought left an unpleasant taste in his mouth.

Teraeth frowned at the man's accent, his manner of speech. Far, far more formal than anything he'd ever encountered from Doc. Doubt wormed its way into his heart.

"That's . . . true," Teraeth acknowledged slowly. "But we've been looking for you. Uh, friends have been looking for you too. Including the new Goddess of Death. She's giving you permission to Return."

Doc stared at his son as though Teraeth were speaking a foreign language. "And where is this new Death Goddess, then? I'd hear the words from her." He studied Teraeth, a probing look that felt as though it penetrated all the

---

[4] That's Taunna Milligreest, a distant cousin of Jarith, Janel, and Eledore, who is Doc's adopted daughter.—T

way to the soul. Which, in this world, was distinctly possible. "No, I'm definitely not going to leave. And besides, why should I go back? I'm told that I'm known as a monster in the Living World: a tyrant and villain. Lastly, I'm rather enjoying myself here. I'd ask you to dance, but if you truly are my son, that would probably be scandalous to some present. Perhaps I should find a new partner."

Teraeth grabbed the man's arm as he was about to walk away.

"Remove your hand from my arm before I remove it from yours," Doc said.

Ah. That look in Doc's eyes was far more identifiable.

"Valathea's waiting for you," Teraeth told him. "I'm bringing you back to her."

It was like watching someone surface from underwater. That splash of awareness in the eyes, the focus that came with them, the sudden recognition when his father looked at him. His posture changed, his expression lightened, his eyes began to twinkle.

"Oh," Doc said. "You should've led with that."

They left. Teraeth never looked back at his mother, but he could feel her eyes following him the whole way. The important thing, however, was that she didn't try to stop him and she didn't interfere.

Perhaps that was her way of saying goodbye as well.

## 48. THE PROBLEM WITH ANLYR

**Qown's story**
**Outside the ruins of Senera's cottage**
**After Relos Var left**

Qown stopped shouting quickly, if only because he didn't want to help escalate matters to a point where Galen would be hurt.

More hurt.

As it stood, the wizard had taken one narrow-eyed look at Galen's advancement before casting a familiar healing spell, one easily twisted into pain. Galen fell to the ground screaming. Relos Var left through the gate with Galen's unconscious body, a spitting-angry Sheloran, and a crying child.

He returned a few minutes later with the Stone of Shackles.

Qown exhaled as he slumped down. None of this was going the way it was supposed to, the way it *needed* to go. He couldn't blame Caless for making the trade, but the result tied his stomach into knots.

Qown hated that he'd been right about Var's plans for him.

"We shouldn't stay here," Anlyr said.

Relos Var nodded. "We won't. I have a great many things to take care of. The list is never-ending." He tossed the Stone of Shackles at Anlyr, who caught it with a confused blink. "Hide that. Do not wear it under any circumstances."

"But—" Anlyr glanced down at the stone with something like longing in his expression.

"I need to be able to contact you," Relos Var explained, "which won't be possible if you're wearing that. So please take care of Qown, hide that damn rock in a hole in the ground, and then meet me at the Northern House when you're done."

Anlyr made a face. "Isn't there some other way?"

"We have to know how much of what they just told us is the truth and what they're trying to hide," Relos Var said. "And since we don't have time for gaeshing, I see no other alternative."

All the hairs along Qown's arms rose up. "Take care of Qown" sounded like nothing he'd like. Since they'd just previously established the unreliability of torture, by inference whatever they were planning had to be worse. "What are you talking about?"

Relos Var gave him a brief, cold glance, but otherwise ignored him.

Anlyr shook his head. "Yeah, yeah. I guess. I just hate eating people."

Qown felt a spike of pure fear shoot through him. Because Anlyr hardly seemed like the kind of person to be a cannibal. Or even a weirdly reluctant cannibal. Qown didn't think what he was saying was just a figure of speech. So he was serious. But why would eating Qown allow Anlyr to find out what he knew? The only way that made sense was—

"No," Qown said.

Anlyr glanced at him.

"You're . . . you're a mimic?"

Anlyr winked at him in response.

"But—" Qown shook his head. "No. No, you used illusions to copy me when you lured Galen and Sheloran out. You didn't *shape-change*."

"You're right," Anlyr agreed. "Because shape-changing hurts. Why should I do it if I don't have to? It's not fun."

"Then why . . . why do mimics do it at all?"

"Just between you and me," Anlyr said, "most of my siblings are completely out of their gourds."[1]

"And comments like that"—Relos Var tilted his head in Qown's direction—"are what make this necessary. Because Qown shouldn't have had *any* contact with a mimic. He shouldn't know what sort of behavior is or isn't typical." He sighed. "Needless to say, I'm not staying to watch."

Qown's whole body was shaking, which logically was a bit ridiculous. He'd always known he was going to die here.

But he hadn't known that his death would ruin everything. They hadn't made allowances for protecting themselves from mimics precisely because they had all gotten in the habit of behaving as if Talon were the only one. Who was on their side as much as Talon could be claimed to ever be on any-one's side.

But she wasn't the only mimic, was she? There were at least eleven others in existence. And why *wouldn't* Relos Var have one working for him? They were so useful, after all.

Even the damn sigil that Senera gave him wouldn't work. He'd still leave behind a perfectly whole body, and that meant Anlyr—or whatever his real name was—would still be able to find out every shred of information that Qown knew, including all their plans.

No, the only way this wouldn't work would be if Qown could somehow kill himself in such a way as to leave no body at all, and quite frankly, if he had a way to do that, why wouldn't he instead just kill Anlyr?

While he sat there, trembling, contemplating the enormity of his failure, he nearly didn't notice when Var opened another gate and left.

The field fell silent save the sound of crickets in the distance and the occa-sional crackle of hot embers from the remains of Senera's cottage.

Anlyr scowled at the blue rock in his hand, cursed softly, and tucked the Cornerstone into a pouch at his belt. He cast a spell that summoned up a

---

[1] I wonder if this describes a literal or figurative relationship. Are all mimics related to each oth-er?—T

circle of mage-light, almost the same color and position as a campfire, if very different in all other ways.

"I'm really sorry it had to work out like this," Anlyr said.

When Qown shot him an incredulous look, the mimic shrugged. "I'm as stable as I am precisely because I *don't* eat every single person who comes my way," Anlyr explained. "In fact, I am very particular about the personalities and memories I absorb. It was never really all that much fun, to be honest, and like I said, shape-changing hurts. I'm a fourteen-thousand-year-old wizard. Most of the time, that's enough for any obstacles the world feels like throwing in my path."

"You don't . . . you don't have to kill me," Qown said.

"I kind of do. What Relos Var wants, Relos Var gets." Anlyr sighed. "Why couldn't you have just done your job and stayed loyal, kid? He liked you. He wasn't going to hurt you. You know, he doesn't usually send bodyguards along with the disposable minions. Certainly not *me*. Be extremely flattered."

Qown was desperately trying to buy time, contemplate his options. He did know a few spells that . . . Well. No. None of them were sufficiently destructive in the way he needed.

"I'm not feeling flattered," Qown said. "And I don't think that's true." He was trying to look calm and unconcerned rather than a panicky mess, but even without the telepathy, he didn't think he was fooling Anlyr. "Not the part about bodyguards. The part where he wouldn't have hurt me. I don't think he had a reason to hurt me, but that's not the same thing. He didn't hesitate to order you to kill me at the first sign that I might have had second thoughts, did he?"

The mimic shrugged. "Maybe you shouldn't have betrayed him?"

"Who says I have?!" Qown shouted. "Would I have just handed over World-hearth like that if I was betraying you? I've had a good reason for everything I've done. You all agreed it was a good reason! But you're going to kill me, anyway, *just in case*."[2]

Anlyr chewed on the inside of his mouth for a few seconds, then stood and wiped off his pants. "You have a point."

Qown eyed the man. He didn't think the concession meant that Anlyr was going to let him go. Just the opposite. "You're still going to kill me."

"Yeah, I'm still going to kill you. But I'm going to feel just terrible about it if it turns out to have all been a big misunderstanding." He paused. "Tell me you did at least get a chance to sleep with the cute D'Mon boy?"

Qown shook his head.

Anlyr sighed. "What a waste. Ah well. Maybe in your next life." He started to walk in Qown's direction, and Qown for his part found himself scrabbling backward away from the mimic.

"Please don't," Qown said.

Anlyr just smiled. "Don't worry, Qown. I've always liked you, so I'll make it quick."

---

[2] I think we may not have been giving Qown full credit for his acting skills. This would have made me doubt his guilt, and I knew for a fact that Qown had changed sides. —S

## 49. A Pause for Planning

**Senera's story**
**Grizzst's Tower, Eamithon, Quur**
**A short time after Jarith located Qown,**
**just after sunset**

"Warmonger," Thurvishar cursed as Jarith finished talking. The wizard turned to Senera. "Why would Relos Var give a Cornerstone to the Quuros Empire? Especially *that* Cornerstone? He has to know what it can do!"

Senera started to answer, then she stopped and blinked at Thurvishar, at the waves of anxiety she could feel pouring off him. "Wait. You're far too upset about–" She narrowed her eyes. She'd been trying to block out other people's thoughts, but sometimes it was hard.

Right now, Thurvishar was mentally shouting.

The wizard was upset enough that Rebel ran to him, rubbing her head up against his calf and making little whining noises for attention. He absently reached down and scratched between the dhole's ears, but his focus was elsewhere.

And Senera could tell, just based on what she was feeling from the man, that the anxiety was entirely focused on this particular Cornerstone: Warmonger.

This was . . . personal.

Senera rubbed her forehead. Yes, it probably was personal, but not from this lifetime. She sometimes forgot that for all that Kihrin, Janel, and Teraeth danced around as examples of the "all the lives we've lived before" club, Thurvishar had too–as the first Emperor of Quur. And Emperor Simillion had indeed had history with that particular Cornerstone.

"I never won against Nemesan," Thurvishar said softly. "But he was a nightmare as long as he had that damn stone. I was murdered before I had the chance to figure out a way to counter its effects. It is easy to think Warmonger isn't a dangerous Cornerstone because it can't let you throw lightning or switch souls or raise the dead, but Warmonger is the worst of the lot. Just the scale of the damn thing–"

Senera sat down in one of the chairs. They'd cleared out most of the workshop, but there were still a few projects too odd, too delicate, or too inexplicable to touch. Who knew exactly what Grizzst had been doing?

**What about Galen and the others?** Jarith asked.

Senera inhaled sharply, chiding herself for once again managing to lose track of the demon. "We have to rescue them." She stood again, grabbed her sallí cloak, and threw a matching one to Thurvishar.

Thurvishar caught the cloak, and it seemed to snap him out of whatever fugue had entrapped him. "You can't come with us, Senera," he told her.

"Excuse you," she snapped. "I believe I'm perfectly capable of going where I like."

"If Relos Var finds out–" Thurvishar started to say.

"Relos Var knew the moment he arrived at a cottage already burned to the ground." Senera hadn't even the slightest doubt that was true. "He's had his eye on me for signs of betrayal ever since the Battle of the Well of Spirals when he saw the two of us together. Too much is at stake for him to blindly assume my loyalty."

**Relos Var will leave when he dictates terms to Caless,** Jarith said. **If we wait until then, we'll only have to deal with Anlyr.**

A cold wave of shock picked Senera's skin. "What? Anlyr? *Anlyr's* with them?"

**Yes. He's the guard.**

Senera inhaled deeply. "I see. Damn. I thought he was somewhere else. That . . . that changes things."

"How so?" Thurvishar narrowed his eyes.

Senera spoke to Jarith: "Go back. Keep watch on them. Let us know the second Var leaves, but don't try to take on Anlyr alone. He's much more dangerous than he seems."

Jarith vanished.

Senera concentrated on her breathing. She needed to focus.

"Senera, tell me what's wrong," Thurvishar said.

"You know, you really have a beautiful voice," Senera said absently. Rebel decided to switch targets and pushed up against Senera's leg.

Thurvishar froze in shock. "I'm sorry. What did you just say?"

Senera began petting Rebel and ignored the question. "Let's assume that even if Caless agrees to Relos Var's demands and hands over the Stone of Shackles, Var will keep one of them for himself. My metal is on Qown."

Thurvishar studied Senera's face. "Why would he care? He's already taken Worldhearth. Qown has no value."

Senera decided it would be best not to waste time on long and complicated explanations, so she just went with short, ugly facts. "I made a mistake," she confessed. "When Qown told us about Anlyr, something about him bothered me. He reminded me of one of Relos Var's other people. Different name, same attitude. So I confirmed it, while I still could." She shuddered and then spat out in a rush: "Anlyr's a mimic," she said.

Thurvishar didn't seem to hear her at first, but he was just processing the news. Senera knew he'd truly comprehended when his skin turned gray. He'd understood the ramifications: all the protective glyphs in the world wouldn't protect Qown from having his brain *eaten* by a mimic. At which point, all their secrets would be laid bare.

Senera's mistake was not mentioning it to the others. They had too much on their minds and she had no way to defend against him. Relos Var had him spying on Havar D'Aramarin. Senera had assumed that meant he'd be too busy to cause trouble for them.

"We have to go right now," Thurvishar said. He looked ready to cast a gate spell right that instant. In fact, his hands started to begin the motions.

"No," Senera corrected. "We need to *think*."

Thurvishar paused.

"We need to take a moment and consider our enemy's position on this game board," Senera said. Rebel nudged her head under Senera's hand when the wizard stopped petting for a few seconds. "When—please note that I'm saying *when* not *if—when* we recover Qown, Relos Var will know several things. He will know for certain that I have switched sides, he will know that Sheloran, Galen, and Qown are actively helping us, and he will know that *we* know about Warmonger. Because he's smart enough to realize Qown will tell us. Additionally, he will know that the Name of All Things has been lost. Now what does that mean?"

Thurvishar didn't just throw the question back at her, which Senera appreciated. He steepled his fingers under his chin and contemplated the question. "He's not stupid enough to check on Warmonger's position to make sure it's safe. He might check on the Name of All Things, though."

"Eventually," Senera agreed. "But not first. And I agree that he won't give away Warmonger's location. But he knows that we're going to be looking for it. More specifically, he knows *I'm* going to be looking for it. And he knows I have a contact who is close to the empress. That's the fastest, most logical place for me to start if I'm trying to find out who's carrying Warmonger."

"You have a contact close to the empress?" Thurvishar frowned. "Who?"

"Fayrin Jhelora," Senera said. "The councilman assigned to liaise with the emperor. Also," she added, "the man who controls one of the largest spy networks in the empire. If anyone is going to be able to easily identify who around the empress might be using Warmonger, he will."

"How on earth—"

Senera waved a hand. "We grew up together. That's not important. What is important is that he's the only family I have, and Var *knows* it. All of which makes Fayrin a target. In Var's place, I would send someone to kill, kidnap, or replace Fayrin with a mimic as proved most convenient and then wait for me to show up. And thus once I do show up—" She shrugged. "It could go any number of ways. Best-case scenario, you too have something that Relos Var wants." She pointed to the yellow-green crystal around Thurvishar's neck— the Cornerstone Wildheart.

"He'd have to know how I feel about you," Thurvishar countered.

"Don't assume he doesn't. He's very good at judging people, and you weren't subtle when we parted from each other at the Well of Spirals. Anyway, ransom demands have been working very well for him tonight. Why not one more?"

Thurvishar rubbed his forehead. "Fayrin Jhelora? He's a spymaster? Isn't he the one that got caught renting out part of the imperial palace as a velvet house? He regularly falls asleep during council meetings. He's considered the easiest vote to buy on the entire council—unless someone outbids you, of course."

"It's an act," Senera explained. "It's always been an act."

"Any chance he's secretly working for Relos Var? Knowingly working for Relos Var? Because I have to admit the description you're giving of the man does make him sound like just the type of person Relos Var would recruit."

"No," Senera said. "I tried to recruit him, but he'd been warned off. He never agreed. We had a relationship of cordial ambivalence; for old times' sake, we agreed to stay out of each other's way."

"Warned off? Warned off by who?"

"Sandus," Senera said. "Fayrin worked for your father. And Emperor Sandus was never friends with Relos Var."

Thurvishar's gaze grew distant as he seemed to process that information. Then he nodded. "Then it's an opportunity. We know where they're going to be. And they can't say the same about us."

"Right," Senera said. "And *now* we can leave."

But even as she said the words, a portal spun open in front of them.

They prepared for the worst.

# 50. A Very Good Girl

*Qown's story*
*Outside Senera's cottage, northern Kirpis*
*Just after discovering Anlyr is a mimic*

Anlyr didn't immediately kill Qown, for which Qown was grateful even if he didn't understand the reason for the delay. Given what Qown had learned about mimics from Talon, he thought it reasonable to assume that a mimic's mind fractured a little more with every victim consumed. Talon certainly had (and he didn't doubt continued to have) difficulty sorting the myriad voices taking up space inside her head. If Anlyr had so far largely avoided that, Qown could understand why he would be reluctant to do anything to jeopardize that arrangement.

No, Qown wasn't complaining.

Which was why they were both still sitting sullenly on rocks near the edge of the woods, one of them notably not killing the other, when a strange chirping call sounded from beyond the tree line.

Anlyr heard it too. The mimic frowned, and started looking around. The orange glow of the burned-out cottage highlighted the edges of a fox. It had jumped up on top of a nearby rock, using the height to stare straight at Anlyr with its head down and teeth bared. Then it made an odd yet charming vocalization, a series of short whistles.

Qown's eyes widened. He was wrong. That wasn't a fox.

It was a dhole.

As far as Qown knew, dholes weren't native to this area, weren't even found anywhere west of the Dragonspires, so there was really only one animal it could possibly be.

Senera's pet, Rebel.

He almost couldn't believe it. He'd never been so happy to see an animal before in his life. It *was* Rebel, wasn't it? It had to be. The wild dog was wearing a collar, something that he wouldn't expect to see on a wild dhole or a fox.

"Fuck," Anlyr said, which suggested that the mimic agreed. Without a second's hesitation, the mimic conjured a blast of fire and sent it to explode on the dhole's position. But Rebel moved too fast. She leaped to the side even as Anlyr released the spell, easily clearing the area of effect with an impossibly long, graceful jump.

Rebel was possibly the most heavily warded animal in existence. Senera had layered so many magical protections on her pet that Anlyr could have hit the animal straight on without so much as singeing her red fur.

Rebel slowly stalked forward, never taking her eyes off Anlyr, occasionally letting out another one of those whistles. Normally—*normally*—a dhole was far too skittish a creature to behave this way. They didn't view humans as prey animals but as predators, something to be avoided at all costs.

Rebel continued to advance.

Despite Anlyr's protest that he never shape-changed, he'd formed his right hand into a set of devastatingly fatal-looking claws. He watched Rebel advance warily, clearly contemplating whether or not it was worth fighting the dhole.

There was no way Senera had left Rebel behind at the cottage. Either Relos Var and Anlyr had been wrong about what had happened to Senera—which Qown knew wasn't the case—or she'd have taken Rebel with her.

"You know that whistle's how they call to their pack mates," Qown said, his voice startlingly loud against the quiet of the standoff. "Rebel doesn't think she's out here alone."

Anlyr scowled, but didn't tell Qown he was wrong.

Qown slowly, carefully stood. Anlyr had removed Qown's talismans and even healed his leg. Qown's fingers were still broken, but Anlyr had to be wondering just how effective that would really be in stopping a Vishai healer from fixing himself. At which point, Anlyr would be facing Qown too, in addition to whoever Senera had brought with her. Qown hoped Thurvishar. And Sheloran. And Caless too. *Everyone would be nice.*

"Senera," Anlyr called out. "I know you're out there."

Laughter met his statement—a woman's laugh.

And then, in case there had been any doubt, Senera called from somewhere out in the darkness. "It's been a while, Anlyr. Did Relos Var really leave you here all by yourself? Tsk, tsk, tsk. Whereas I brought all *my* friends."

There was rustling from the edge of the clearing and just enough light to see several shapes moving at the tree line. One of them was recognizably Senera. Another, to the side, was probably Thurvishar, to judge by the silhouette of a large man with a bald head, wearing robes. There were other noises, other sounds.

Anlyr laughed, although not happily. "Satisfy a curiosity for me, if you would. Just how long did you spend figuring out exactly how you'd take me down if we ever fought?"

Qown began concentrating on his fingers. If they were going to have a friendly little chat before the fighting started, he wouldn't waste the opportunity.

Senera said, "Just an afternoon. But I had the Name of All Things. An afternoon was enough."

The mimic stood very still, watching the moving shadows and the more visible dhole. Tension vibrated in the air. Soon, someone would make a move, do something, and everything would explode in a flurry of violence.

Anlyr laughed. "Well, aren't you a lucky bastard, Qown. Looks like you're going to have your chance to not die a virgin, after all."

Several shiny objects streaked across the clearing, metal reflected red in the light. They moved so fast that even Anlyr couldn't dodge them, though he tried. What might have otherwise been a strike to the head and the throat became a graze across a temple and spray of blood at his shoulder. Sadly, neither appeared to be a lethal—or even debilitating—wound. Especially not for a mimic.

A bell rang out. Everyone began moving. But even as Rebel leaped at Anlyr, the mimic vanished.

Senera immediately cast something, fingers spread wide, and then shook her head. "He's really gone."

The clearing fell into quiet again.

Qown held out a hand to the dhole. "Who's a good girl? Who's a very good girl?"

"*I* am," Sheloran said as she walked forward, waving a fan in front of her face.

Qown looked up to see Sheloran, along with Galen and Senera. He was so relieved he started laughing. He stopped, though, when Thurvishar's silhouette vanished only to reappear a second later as a cloud of darkness and smoke, which re-formed in a vaguely man-size shape, topped with an eyeless ceramic mask.

"Thurvishar's *not* here?" Qown asked. He had absolutely zero doubt that Senera by herself wouldn't have been able to drive Anlyr off. And it was even possible that Senera, Rebel, and Sheloran might not have been, although that was a riskier fight. But Jarith fooling Anlyr into thinking Thurvishar had been present too had likely made the decision to run obvious.

Where was the real Thurvishar, though?

"Thurvishar's dealing with a different problem," Senera said. "We're going there next."

Galen started to cross over to Qown when Jarith blocked his way.

"What . . . ?" Qown didn't understand.

The cloud of darkness floated in Qown's direction before hovering right in front of him, the face mask at eye level.

\*\*It is Qown and not an impersonator. The souls match.\*\*

Galen blinked. So did Qown, for that matter. The idea that he might have already been replaced by the mimic hadn't occurred to him. But he supposed that Anlyr could have already eaten him and then used illusions to make it seem like Anlyr was a different person, one who had then "teleported" away . . . He shuddered.

Galen started to pull Qown into his arms, but then stopped, looking down at his fingers. "Your hands—?"

"I'm healing them," Qown said. "But that's not important." He leaned around Galen so he could talk to Senera. "Senera, Relos Var doesn't have the Stone of Shackles anymore. He gave it to Anlyr."

She began cursing.

"But Anlyr isn't wearing it!" Qown interrupted, because Senera *needed* to know this. "Relos Var ordered him not to, because he wanted to make sure that he could locate Anlyr later, and the Stone of Shackles would block that."

Senera stared at him. "You're saying Anlyr can still be scryed."

"Yes," Qown said. "That's exactly what I'm saying."

Senera whirled around to Sheloran. "When you attacked him just now . . . ?"

Sheloran was still fanning herself. "Yes, obviously I planted a marker we can use to track him. As small as I could make it, but I don't think it will last for long. He's bound to notice it soon."

"Maybe we can salvage this after all," Senera murmured. Louder, she said to Qown, "I'll finish healing your fingers in a few minutes. But now we should leave before someone we *don't* want to fight returns. The odds that Anlyr's going to come back with Relos Var are not in our favor."

**Do you want me to tell Kihrin about the Stone of–?**

"Veils, yes! Please!" Senera said. A second later, Jarith vanished, presumably off to do just that.

Senera spelled open a portal. "Let's hurry," she said. "We have places to be."

# 51. How Relos Var Helped Drehemia

### *The Lash's story*
### *Various locations*
### *After fleeing Devors in the previous book*

It had all gone wrong from the very start. The Lash had been so happy, so very profoundly happy, when the small ones had given Drehemia back to her, cured of the curse that had left her beyond the Lash's reach. Drehemia had experienced such periods of . . . irritability . . . before, but never so serious and never for so long. This had been different.

So when Drehemia woke and the Lash saw comprehension and reason and awareness behind her eyes, she had rejoiced.

The rejoicing quickly turned into horror.

Drehemia had taken one look at the area around her, one look at the Lash, and had rushed away, flying and screaming both in a sound of anguish and confusion.

What could the Lash do but follow? Or try to follow, limited as she was to the sea while Drehemia had no such obstacles and could fly with equal felicity. Tracking Drehemia wasn't easy, and the Lash was forced to take refuge in magical skills she seldom needed to keep track of her lover's location.[1] For some time, it seemed Drehemia's movements were random—rage- and chaos-induced blind turns with no goal—but eventually, the dragon began making her way back to her own lair, deep in the waters near Da'utunse.

When the Lash arrived at the lair and tried to say soothing words to her lover, Drehemia attacked her.

"What monstrous outrage is this? What trick? What curse! What have you done to me?!" Drehemia's claws dug deep furrows into the ground as she spat out the words, while all around her the shadows twisted like kelp in a storm.

**"Drehemia, what are you saying?"** the Lash whispered, soothed. **"It's me. You know me. You've known me for ages. I would never hurt you!"**

The reverse didn't seem to be true.

Still, Drehemia's powers were most effective against crowds of small ones, not against a daughter such as the Lash. She tried to claw and bite at the Lash, but quickly found herself constrained by a creature with more than enough arms to trap every limb, and her tail and neck besides.

---

[1] From which we can deduce that Drehemia's ability to pass undetected and invisible requires intention.—S

And then *he* arrived.

The Lash didn't notice him at first. She'd always had a difficult time noticing the small ones unless they were doing something to directly capture her attention. This one seemed normal enough, a collection of browns and drab colors in a body with too few limbs and too small a head. She hadn't thought he was a threat.

That had been her fatal mistake.

"It's normal," the small one said. When the Lash twisted in his direction, he repeated his words. "It's normal. The shock of having her Cornerstone returned to her is great. To her mind, she shouldn't be a dragon, so this seems like a curse. But fortunately, this can be healed."

**"Who are you?"** the Lash demanded. **"How did you get here?"**

"Magic," the man explained, which . . . fine. Yes, likely magic. The small ones were annoyingly good at magic, much to all her kind's remorse. "My name is Relos Var. With your permission, I'd like to help Drehemia better cope with her situation. I know what it's like. I know how difficult it is to adjust to such a change."

She should have said no. She should have told Relos Var to go away or, better yet, struck him where he stood with everything she had, so fast that he wouldn't be able to defend himself.

But alas, she didn't. She'd been in love, and she'd only cared about making Drehemia happy.

"Kindly bring her head down closer," Relos Var said. "This will be easier if she can more readily see me."

Drehemia calmed down right away.

"It's me," Relos Var said. "Rev'arric. I know everything seems horrible right now. You must have so many memories that are nothing but chaos and violence." He reached a hand out and touched the dragon on the nose. "I've been through the same. It's not an easy thing to experience. Will you let me help you? Will you let me show you how to turn back into what you were before?"

Drehemia didn't say anything. Not anything the Lash heard. Perhaps he saw something in her eyes. Perhaps he hadn't actually cared how she answered.

Regardless, he did something. The Lash always wore her shields, her protections against magic, but still she could feel the power of what he'd done.

Drehemia vanished.

The Lash staggered as she found herself holding nothing at all. She nearly fell over.

Now, standing next to this "Relos Var" was another small one, pale white all over and with none of the filaments the small ones so often seemed to have on their heads. She immediately began to sob.

**"Drehemia!"** the Lash pleaded. **"Drehemia, is that you?"**

The woman took a step back, behind the man. "Keep it away from me! Keep it away!"

**"Drehemia!"** The Lash reared back as though she had touched lava. **"What have you done to her? You haven't fixed her. You've made her worse. You've changed her!"**

"People change," Relos Var answered. "And you have it backward, I think. She was cursed when she knew you. Her mind was broken. If it had been otherwise, she never would have been with you at all."

**"No! I don't believe you!"** The Lash roared, meaning to destroy this horrible, spiteful small one who had ruined everything. Everything!

Things happened very quickly after that.

The ground underneath Drehemia opened in a perfect circle, and Drehemia, now small enough to fit easily, fell through. A half second later, there was a surge of motion and pressure.

The walls of the cave exploded as a second dragon appeared in front of the Lash, lunging at her head.

The Lash wasn't so easily killed, however, or more to the point, couldn't be easily killed. She carried Grimward, after all. Killing her was beyond the ability of almost all small ones, even the ones they called "gods."

Then the white dragon pulled her out of the ocean, grabbing one of her tentacles. She found herself stretched between the rocks she had rooted against. His claws grabbed at her. His wings beat with gale-force strength against the water, sending it splashing into the air. She knew she would have to do something quickly to survive this. If Drehemia was the night incarnate, the beauty of secrets and shadows, this was a far less subtle force of nature.

Then the dragon opened his mouth and breathed blue fire at her.

She screamed as she boiled away under a flame hotter than anything she had ever experienced before. She who had played in magma vents in her youth and was doubly protected by both her own wards and the Cornerstone embedded in her flesh. The fire burned, and it seared, and it charred.

And it didn't stop.

From a dim, faraway place, the Lash knew that she'd dropped back down to the water with a thunderous booming noise that would travel halfway around the globe for anyone with the skill to listen. She damned the fake dragon a hundred times, or she would have.

But she didn't live that long. That was the moment she learned that immortal or not, she could still be destroyed.

In the seconds before her soul was pulled into the Current Between Oceans, she saw the white dragon turn back into a small one. He retrieved Grimward from her corpse and then proceeded to vaporize the rest of her corpse until there was nothing left but ash and cinder.

He opened a portal and left.

### Xivan's story
### The Afterlife
### One day after Vol Karoth's escape, early morning

Xivan listened to the story with a growing sense of dread. She'd known roughly how it would go, of course—after all, the Lash was dead—but that didn't mean she didn't still wince at the idea that Relos Var had been the one to slay the Lash.

He had said at some point or another that he'd take the stone back himself if he had to. Relos Var had made good on that promise.

Drehemia, though . . .

Xivan shivered. "What do we know about Drehemia?"

"Before or after she became a dragon?" Janel asked.

"Before."

Janel nodded. "She was Argas's daughter, one of Relos Var's protégés. Very smart. Very clever. Very good at holding secrets close to her chest. And she hung on Relos Var's every word. If there were any of the dragons that I could imagine Var wouldn't mind seeing restored to their full sanity—barring his son, perhaps—it would be Drehemia."

"Fucking fantastic," Xivan muttered. "What about her powers? Is she a walking embodiment of the Name of All Things now?"

"I don't—" Janel made a face. "I don't think so. Relos Var's Cornerstone Cynosure made its wearer immune to the other Cornerstones, but after Grizzst used it to restore Relos Var, *he* didn't have that same immunity."

"But it could be," Xivan pressed.

"Yes. It could be." Janel didn't explain the ramifications, but she didn't need to. Xivan was perfectly aware.

Relos Var having access to the Name of All Things—or someone with the same abilities as the Name of All Things—put the entire plan in jeopardy.

Talea sighed and stood up. "Well, at least we know ahead of time, right? Because I really wouldn't want to let her sneak up on me while something important was going on."

Xivan looked out over the ocean toward the kraken, who had lapsed into uncomfortable silence with the completion of her tale. "Thank you. I'm sorry it worked out like this."

"I curse the day your awful race came to my world," the Lash mourned. "Now keep your promise. Kill Relos Var."

The Daughter of Laaka slipped back into the dark waters, leaving only the ripples behind.

## 52. THE HEIR

**Tyentso's story**
**Lady Lessoral's quarters, the Soaring Halls**
**Late evening**

"Does no one sleep anymore?" Tyentso asked as she appeared in the room. "I honestly expected that you'd scream at me for waking you, but instead I find that not only are you still up but . . ." She frowned. "You're taking care of a small child. Why?"

Lady Lessoral D'Talus looked up from where she was tucking a blanket around an adorable little moppet of a child. Then the most delicate of frowns crossed her face. "Perhaps instead I should yell at you for teleporting into my quarters without asking. It seems that people have been coming and going all night. But I won't, because as you said, there's a baby. How may I help you, Your Majesty?"

Tyentso's mouth quirked. Lessoral really did a good job of playing up the "high lady" bit when she felt like it, although Tyentso had her suspicions there was a lot more going on with the royal than the obvious. "There are a few things," she said. "First, I've been trying to locate the Milligreests, only no one seems to know where they've gone. Second, I just found out that the High Lord of House D'Aramarin, Havar, is apparently the god-king Murad. And I thought to myself, *That's interesting. I wonder how many other high lords and ladies are secretly god-kings.* Obviously, anyone who's still alive is a suspect. I know High Lord Cedric D'Lorus wasn't, and Therin D'Mon would have had a very different life if he was hiding that kind of secret. But then I thought of you."

Lady Lessoral's eyes narrowed. "What exactly are you accusing me of?"

"I just want to know which goddess you are. And what you can tell me about Murad."

Lessoral sighed. She stood up from the couch where the small boy was resting and wandered over to a different chair so she could collapse into it with practiced weariness. Although no. Perhaps Tyentso wasn't giving her enough credit. The woman did seem exhausted. Like she'd just been through a magical duel.

"Where's your husband?" Tyentso asked.

"Resting," Lessoral murmured. "He's not feeling well."

"So he's not a god-king?"

She pursed her lips. "Oh, he is. This is somewhat irregular." She said it with an understated gravity, the same way one might look at a scene of mass slaughter and say there'd been a mild disagreement.

"You don't look like you're feeling fantastic yourself."

"I'm tired. For so many reasons tonight. But there is a curious malaise that seems to have befallen the palace. Perhaps everyone is taking a collective breath now that the army has vacated?" She didn't look like she believed it.

Tyentso sure as hell didn't. Whatever had been causing the emotional changes in everyone must have left when the army did. And in its wake left people drained and tired. The changes had happened quickly too. Half a day, at most.

She was not at all pleased about the ramifications. But she was also aware of just how much of this was a distraction.

"So you were explaining which god-queen you are?" Tyentso continued.

"I wasn't," Lessoral said.

Tyentso smiled tightly. "We're not enemies." *But that could change* went unspoken.

Lessoral sighed.

The two women stared at each other. Tyentso sure as fuck wasn't going to back down.

Finally, Lessoral growled. "It's less and less a secret these days, anyway, I suppose. Caless."

Tyentso blinked. "I wouldn't have expected . . ." She swallowed back any commentary. "All right. Caless it is. And your husband?"

"Bezar. And as for Murad," Caless continued, "I can't provide a great deal of clarity for you except that he's not who he says he is."

"I know that," Tyentso said irritably. "I just told you—"

Caless dismissed her protest. "I don't mean Havar. I mean that Havar—or Murad—is voras. You can tell by the aura if you know what to look for. One of the originals. Do you understand what that means?"

What Tyentso understood was that Caless was being condescending as hell. But on the other hand, Tyentso had just appeared in her rooms unannounced in the middle of the night confessing she hadn't known that there were god-kings in the royal families. The empress swallowed her sneer for the purpose of keeping the woman talking. "No, I must have missed that class in school."

"We first became god-kings out of necessity. The creation of Vol Karoth had blanketed the whole planet in a cloud of ash that lasted *years*. The demons were still free. The Guardians were dead. And the voras were now mortal. In the aftermath of all that, my father used the Stone of Shackles to enslave my mother and force her to teach him the secret of becoming a god-king. And he would have kept that secret to himself and damn anyone unwilling to propitiate him for protection. He wanted to rule humanity. Mother was ordered to say nothing to anyone who wasn't family."

Tyentso was about to order her to get to the damn point, but then that point stabbed her in the gut. If Cherthog had meant to keep it secret, why *were* there any other god-kings at all? If Suless could only tell family, how had the secret gotten out?

Tyentso gave the Goddess of Love a pointed look. Oh. Presumably, Daddy hadn't thought to order his *daughter* not to share.

Caless smiled. "Now you get it. There wasn't a single one of the early god-kings—save my parents, of course—who didn't first share my favor and my bed." She shrugged. "Which creates a narrow window, you understand. All those voras were suddenly mortal, their life spans measured in decades. Murad only had those same decades to learn the secret, either from me or from someone I had taught. I made it a point to be familiar with every single god-king back at the beginning." She stage-whispered, "But I don't know him."

Tyentso rubbed her jaw. "So what are you saying? He faked his identity? That he used to be a *different* god-king?"

"It can be done," Caless said. "You of all people should know that appearances are malleable."

Tyentso scowled and looked away. The fact that Tyentso was an Ogenra was perfectly obvious, but this was the first time that Lessoral—Caless—had ever indicated that she knew *Tyentso* wasn't her real name. Perhaps a lucky guess. Perhaps not.

When Tyentso didn't respond to that bait, Caless continued, "But why would most god-kings bother? It takes years to develop a portfolio, a church, the worshippers to sustain immortality. It's a great deal of work. Why would anyone start from scratch if they didn't have to?"

"Do you know which one he is? Or, I guess, which one he used to be?" Tyentso narrowed her eyes at Caless. She really did wish the woman would just spell out what she knew. "If you've fu—" She winced.

"Just say *fucked*."

"Yeah, well. Who's missing?"

Caless poured herself a glass of water, then one for Tyentso as well. "Quite a few. Mostly because Godslayer exists. Still, we can eliminate some candidates. Our Havar likes green, but he's not particularly keen on snakes. I don't think Ynis would be able to hide that obsession. I don't consider Khorsal a viable candidate for similar reasons."[1]

And even before Urthaenriel had come onto the scene, a lot of god-kings had probably died fighting each other. Even assuming one limited oneself to the men . . .

Well. Caless had been a busy girl.

Then Tyentso realized Caless was watching her. Was waiting to be asked. "Who do *you* think he is?"

A corner of Caless's mouth quirked up. "I really don't know, except . . . I remember a god-king who was good at making portals. Portal barriers too. He

---

[1] Ynis being the self-proclaimed God-King of Death, who also created the thriss (the snake men who live down near the Manol), and Khorsal being the God-King of Horses, whom the Joratese ultimately rebelled against and helped Atrin Kandor slay.—T

had his entire kingdom hidden under one so strong not even the vané could break it. They were extremely frustrated by the experience." She paused for the tiniest of seconds and then said: "Nemesan. The timing would be right too. When he died, versus when Murad first appeared."

"Nemesan? But Nemesan's . . ." Dead. Everyone knew Nemesan was dead. Killed by Simillion—no, wait. *Not* killed by Simillion. The first emperor was assassinated before he could finish the job, leaving it ultimately to one of his successors.

The Crown and Scepter helpfully provided all the details, frustrating in their inadequacy. A corpse was found, yes, but already cold by the time the emperor had arrived—presumed a suicide when Nemesan was too proud to surrender after the defeat of his army. Not nearly enough investigation had been done. They'd been far too eager to announce their victory and annex Laragraen—now Kazivar.

"It's a guess," Caless emphasized. "It may be someone else entirely."

The boy whimpered and turned over violently, flinching in his sleep. Both women turned and looked at the child, now tossing from a nightmare.

Tyentso sighed. She supposed everyone was having nightmares these days.

"Might I ask a favor of you?" Caless moved over to the boy and gently touched his forehead, but she was still talking to Tyentso.

"You can ask."

"My daughter and her husband—" Caless stopped and sighed. "Hmm. It just occurred to me I'll probably have to be the one to tell Galen the truth about his grandfather. Anyway, they're fond of this child, but I really don't think any of us are in a position to look after children at the moment. My daughter asked me to care for him; I intended to entrust the child to the Milligreests. They already have a boy this age, so why not two? I was wondering if you might drop him off with them?"

"This is where I remind you that I don't know where they are."

Caless seemed unconcerned. "I'm sure you'll find them. You're very resourceful."

Tyentso stared. Was this woman seriously expecting her to be a baby-delivering service? She had more important things to do than—

Wait.

She looked down at the boy again. "Who is he?" Tyentso asked softly.

"No one important. A foundling," Caless answered, "of unknown provenance. Likely an orphan."

Tyentso nodded. "All right," she said. "It's not a problem. But I'll need your help with one more thing first."

Caless raised an eyebrow. "Yes?"

"How good are you at faking god-touched eyes?"

## 53. REST AND RECOVERY

### *Thurvishar's story*
### *The Soaring Halls, the Upper Circle, the Capital City of Quur*
### *Simultaneous with Senera rescuing Qown*

The Soaring Halls were always a vanity project gone wrong.

There'd been a palace located on the same site since the founding of Quur. It had been built by the god-king Ghauras, who had used it as the center of his worship and rule. Simillion had taken over the palace without appreciably changing it, and later emperors were typically too busy—and too rarely inside the Capital—to particularly care about the status of the imperial palace. If that had become what was now called the Soaring Halls, Thurvishar would have known the floor plan like he knew his own witchgift.

But no. It wasn't. All because of Atrin Kandor, who had razed the palace to the ground and built it up again from scratch. The man who would go on to create the city of Atrine had started with his own palace first, and he hadn't skimped. Perhaps he had indeed built to his ego, but Thurvishar preferred to think that he had built to intimidate. That the Soaring Halls had been meant as a reminder to the High Council that if they ever stopped playing nice, Daddy would come home and hand out the appropriate punishments. In the meantime, he was content to continually expand the borders of the empire, at least until a Manol vané arrow had put a permanent halt to his ambitions.

The other reason Thurvishar thought the Soaring Halls had been built to intimidate was the other feature the palace shared with Atrine, besides a common architect: both locations were mazes.

A maze that Thurvishar was in no way prepared to navigate. He cursed himself the entire time. Much of their plan depended on him finding Fayrin at the same time Senera was rescuing Qown—leaving Relos Var unaware of what was occurring and giving Anlyr no time to warn him.

That was all for nothing if Thurvishar spent the next thirty minutes trying to locate his target—which was looking increasingly likely. Scant comfort that Senera wouldn't have been any more familiar with the damn place: if he couldn't set down a homing sigil in the right location once he arrived, no reinforcements would be incoming.

Thurvishar finally tracked down the councillor in the apartments set up next to the imperial quarters. He could have broken in, but that risked triggering whatever traps the man had set up—and he assumed there would be traps.

So he politely knocked.

He heard a mumbling sound from inside, so he knocked again.

"Fuck off!"

At least that was intelligible.

"Open the door please. It's important."

He was about to start knocking again when the door swung open, revealing a pretty, slender Quuros man, wearing an open robe and nothing else. "If you've delayed the velvet girls, I–" He paused, blinking in surprise. "High Lord D'Lorus?"[1]

Fayrin Jhelora seemed to be the real deal. Anlyr hadn't gotten to him yet. "May I come in?" Thurvishar asked.

Fayrin raised his eyebrows. "Uh, sure. Let me just, uh–" He seemed to realize his robes were open at that point and wrapped them more tightly around himself. "I didn't expect to see you. And not just because of the Glittering Feast. I don't think you were on the invite list for that one." He backed up into the room, leaving enough room for Thurvishar to follow.

"I wasn't," Thurvishar agreed. "Probably because Her Majesty has no reason to consider me a threat. Now please listen carefully: we don't have much time. Someone is coming to kill you. We need to leave."

Clothing was scattered about the room, as were a number of empty brandy bottles. No one seemed to be in the room except for Fayrin, but the clothes suggested either that hadn't been true recently or Fayrin was a rather extraordinary slob.

Probably the latter. Fayrin picked up a brandy bottle, checked its contents, then threw it down on the ground and tried again. Around the third bottle, he seemed to find one not completely empty and took a healthy swig. "Kill me? Who would want to kill me? Oh, well, besides any number of husbands, I suppose. Not to mention–"

Fayrin's mind was hard to read. Not such a surprise, if Senera was right about who he'd worked for. He almost certainly knew some magic himself. His inebriated state further blurred the lines. He was magnificently drunk.[2]

"Senera sent me," Thurvishar said.

"I'm sorry. Who sent you?" Fayrin squinted. "Oh, someone should light a candle in here or something. You could trip."

Thurvishar looked around. He was running out of time. "She said to tell you he cried like a teething baby. And frankly, I'm not sure I want you to explain what that means."

"Fuck." Fayrin threw the bottle to the floor, where it shattered in a spray of green glass. "Senera did send you."

"How do you know Senera?" Thurvishar asked.

Fayrin straightened. "You don't need to know that." He rubbed his temples. "I feel terrible. Like I'm hungover even though I'm not really . . ." The man

---

[1] Given Fayrin's earlier conversation with Tyentso, it seems likely that this was less about an assignation with courtesans than checking in with his spies.–T

Oh, it's adorable how you're assuming it can't be both.–S

[2] Or at least, pretending to be.–S

paused, his expression openly confused. "Wait. I haven't really been drinking that much, so why do I feel hungover?"

"That is interesting," Thurvishar admitted, "but it doesn't take care of the more immediate problem of saving your life. Which I would like to do. So if you know any good sobering spells, now would be the time."

Fayrin squinted at him. "You were serious about the assassins?"

"Deadly serious," Thurvishar said. He cast a spell; it was as though a giant hand simply pushed the clothing, empty bottles, and other detritus to the side. He cast a second spell, and the markings on one of the carpets began to rearrange themselves to form a glyph. "We have to get you out of here. Come over here and stand—"

The door opened. Senera walked inside. "Fayrin, we need to talk. Where—" Her expression froze as she saw Thurvishar. "Well, that was fast."

Thurvishar was inclined to compliment the mimic on their skill: Senera's appearance and voice were perfect. He'd even managed to copy her clothing, which meant that he must have encountered her when she'd made her attempt to rescue Qown.[3]

However, even if the physical appearance and voice were perfect, Anlyr hadn't copied Senera's mind, not in the way he would have needed to in order to fool Thurvishar. And Thurvishar would know Senera's mind *any-where*.

Thurvishar suspected he was probably supposed to say something clever and witty at this point, just before the fighting started.

Thurvishar skipped the banter and simply attacked.

He cast the spell he developed to deal with Talon. Thurvishar expected it to work—for a mimic to work effectively as, well, a mimic, they couldn't wear talismans. He didn't expect that Anlyr would simply dodge it.

The man moved *incredibly* fast.

In the spot Anlyr had occupied less than a heartbeat ago, a mass of gray ribbons exploded, formed a man-shaped cocoon, and contracted. Had someone been there, they'd have been entirely encased, head to toe, in incredibly strong magic bonds of pure energy.

Instead, the web of energy contracted on nothing and vanished. A pair of sharpened darts flew his way; Thurvishar threw himself backward rather than trying to guess their metal content and erect a suitable barrier. One almost grazed his skin, catching the hem of his misha.

Before he'd recovered his footing, Anlyr was upon him. The fact that he still looked like Senera while doing so was disconcerting. The mimic leaped, landed with both knees on Thurvishar's chest, and knocked him backward. He stumbled, tripped over an embroidered settee, and fell on his back.

He had enough time to whip his head to the side before a heavy mace crashed into the ground where his skull had been a moment ago.

---

[3] I hadn't thought that he'd caught that good of a look at me, but in hindsight there was no reason to suspect he didn't have spectacularly good night vision. I suppose we should be glad that Jarith did such a good impression of Thurvishar and that Galen and Sheloran were present.—S

Thurvishar lifted his hands and cast twisted tenyé into a warping of marble flooring that caught Anlyr's whole body and threw him across the room. The mimic landed on his feet and grinned using Senera's mouth. He looked a little bruised, but no more than that.

*Gods. And I thought Talon was annoying.*

He cast a more familiar spell—one he knew well enough to throw while drunk, drugged, or asleep.[4] A bolt of lightning streaked across the room and hit the mimic in the left shoulder—which shattered in a spray of charred flesh and gore.

"Damn it," Anlyr said, looking down at the stump where his left arm used to be. "I liked that arm."

"It wasn't even yours," Thurvishar said, rising to his feet. "Nothing's stopping you from growing a new one." Even as he said those words, Anlyr was doing exactly that. It was both fascinating and repulsive.

More importantly, Thurvishar couldn't allow it to continue. He threw another lightning bolt at Anlyr and scowled as the mimic deflected the electricity into a nearby bed, destroying it. Fayrin uttered a stricken noise.

"You're right," Anlyr said with Senera's voice. "It's not the arm I like so much as the *idea* of having arms."

The door opened again. Six men armed with short swords and crossbows pushed into the room. The first one's gaze crossed to the mimic, then to Thurvishar, then to Fayrin. He gestured with his left hand before raising his crossbow to aim at Thurvishar.

In that moment, Thurvishar was glad for years of training with Gadrith, duels in the Arena, and the general need to expect attacks from any quarter at any time. He'd had to develop certain instinctive responses. One of them saved his life now. He twitched a finger; the marble floor beside him flowed upward, forming a shield between him and the new arrivals. Three crossbow bolts smashed into the stone, shattering upon impact.

He tracked movement out of both corners of his eyes. Two of the new men headed for Fayrin, now unconscious and slumped over a table, while "Senera" circled the other direction to get behind Thurvishar.

Thurvishar scrambled to his feet and made another shoving motion. The marble shield he'd raised dissolved into dozens of needle-sharp stone fléchettes, which flew at the four soldiers still standing near the door. They were in the process of reloading their crossbows when each was skewered with a dozen six-inch marble shafts. One managed a surprised look before he died.

But the distraction cost Thurvishar dearly. As he swung back to face Anlyr, the mimic was already leaping at him. The mace caught him high on the shoulder; Thurvishar felt pain blossom as his arm broke. At the same time, the mimic thrust at him low and to the outside with a poniard, aiming for his kidneys.

---

[4] This wasn't bragging, was it? You really could do this while drunk.—S

It wouldn't be the first time.—T

Thurvishar couldn't dodge, didn't have time to do anything fancy. He threw the luck-warping spell he only used if he was sure the other person didn't have a lot of auratic protections. He couldn't be certain it would work, but he was growing desperate.

It worked. Anlyr half tripped while closing the distance. Not enough to put him at an exploitable disadvantage, but enough to make his blade skip to the side and slash harmlessly through fabric.

Anlyr made a face and did something, likely an attempt to mitigate the curse. The mimic flipped the blade in his hand and came in again.

Thurvishar allowed himself a brief indulgent moment to wish Sheloran were present. Because Thurvishar would have been very surprised if the blade in Anlyr's hand was common iron or steel. Thurvishar couldn't tell at a glance. That likely wasn't true for the House D'Talus princess. There was nothing to be done about it, though.

He thrust his hands down and then back up, hard. The ground under him cracked and then rose quickly into the air, carrying both Thurvishar and Anlyr toward the ceiling at breakneck speeds.

Just before they smashed into the ceiling, Thurvishar warped a hole in the marble ceiling the same size as his body. The pillars of rising stone slammed into the rock with enough force to shake lose part of the mosaic there, but Thurvishar was perfectly safe in a small bubble of stone.

Thurvishar lowered the stone pillar from the ceiling. He glanced over to where Anlyr's body should have been.

The marble was clean of blood.

Anlyr grinned up at him from ground level. At least the man looked like himself now; Thurvishar had forced him back to that shape, if nothing else. It didn't feel like a victory. To buy himself time while he scrambled to his feet, Thurvishar tossed another lightning bolt at the mimic. This one blew a hole the size of a pineapple in the man's abdomen.

"Stop *doing* that!" Anlyr snarled. Something blurred through the air between them. As the thrown mace smashed into Thurvishar's jaw and broke it, he realized that the mimic had to be using magic to augment his own velocity. He'd underestimated both the mimic's speed and his willingness to lose his weapons.

The only reason the damn thing hadn't smashed his skull like a melon was because Thurvishar still had the luck curse going.

Thurvishar toppled off the pillar and hit the ground hard enough to drive the air from his lungs.

His vision was already blurry from the pain in his shoulder and jaw; this didn't help. About the only good part of the whole thing was that the pillar was now between him and the mimic, so he had all of a second or so more to live. He intended to savor it.

His view, hazy as it was, let him see Fayrin. He'd either been faking unconsciousness earlier or he'd recovered quickly, because he'd managed to slit one of the two soldier's throats with a knife Thurvishar hadn't realized the man had had on him. The councillor was now in the process of slamming the other soldier's head into the corner of the table. So that was nice.

"Ray-Ray?" Fayrin said. "That really you?"

*Ray-Ray? Who the hell is—?*

Thurvishar answered himself immediately. *Senera. He's talking about Senera.*

*No,* he wanted to say. *It's a mimic, here to capture or kill you.* But he couldn't speak; his jaw refused to work properly. He wondered why for a moment. Also, why was all this red staining these nice silk carpets? Someone should do something about that.

A man's voice from somewhere to Thurvishar's left let loose an impressive string of invectives. He hoped he remembered that one about the dreth and the pit full of vipers.

"Fayrin, where's Thurvishar?" Senera's voice.

*Oh, that's right,* Thurvishar thought. *Anlyr's pretending to be Senera. And he's coming to kill me. I should do something about that.*

He gathered up as much tenyé as he felt like he could hold and waited for the mimic to come into view. Perhaps if he hit the damn mimic in the head this time, it would take.

Senera came into view. She wore the same silver-gray misha embroidered with osmanthus she'd been wearing when they'd left Grizzst's Tower. The one Anlyr had so perfectly copied.

But *this* mind was Senera's. What had happened to Anlyr?

She knelt beside him, worry and anger warring in her eyes.

"Ahh hiir," he said.

"What?" she asked, then looked to the side. "Qown, we're over here!"

"Ahn . . . lhiir," Thurvishar repeated, although doing so hurt worse than he'd have thought possible. It was just a jaw. Plenty of people went their entire lives with broken jaws, and he never heard them complaining.

It occurred to Thurvishar that he might be going into shock.

"What's he saying?" Qown came into view, with Galen and Sheloran close behind.

Senera reached out and touched Thurvishar's head. *[I need you to concentrate. What happened?]*

He was so proud of her. Just a week ago, she'd have rather slowly flayed herself than contact someone telepathically.

*[Anlyr was here.]*

"He's saying Anlyr was here," Senera said out loud for the benefit of the non-telepaths in the room. "That must have been the one who teleported out as we arrived."

Thurvishar tried to focus. The fleeing adrenaline was leaving him shaky and weak, very much going into shock. They needed to do something about that. *[He got away? Damn. Did he take his arm with him?]* Thurvishar sent the words into Senera's head rather than trying to speak. That, apparently, wasn't in the cards at the moment.

"His arm? I mean . . . yes?" Senera frowned in confusion.

Someone loomed over him. Thurvishar made an effort to focus and realized that the man above him was Qown, who said, "Now you be quiet, and let's take a look at you. My, you've certainly made a mess of yourself, haven't you?"

"Uh-huh," Thurvishar agreed before deciding that this was, in fact, the ideal time and place to pass out. And so he did.

## 54. RETREAT

**Senera's story**
**Grizzst's Tower**
**After leaving the Soaring Halls**

Senera ushered everyone through the magical gate. Thurvishar was last, carried by Galen and Qown while Rebel supervised both by running around their legs, tail down and anxious. Senera had opened a portal straight to the ground level, glad once again that they'd thought to clear a safe space to make that easier.

Senera fought back a round of hysterical laughter as she thought, *At least we won't get blood on the research notes.*

Fayrin looked bemused as he took in the lowest room of the tower, which Senera thought was a valid reaction. It wasn't clear where they were if one had never been to the tower before, and the architecture was . . . odd . . . if one was used to the Capital. Grizzst's Tower was so old that it was probably one of the only existing examples of voras construction outside of Kharas Gulgoth. Especially now that the Lighthouse at Shadrag Gor had been destroyed.

But she'd misunderstood the reason for his shock.

"Wait," Fayrin said. "You *cleaned*? He let you touch his notes?"

She felt an odd sort of pain stab through her as the air caught in her lungs. Oh. If she'd had any doubts that Fayrin really had been part of the Gryphon Men, they were certainly gone now. He'd given himself away.

"Grizzst's dead," she said.

Fayrin blinked at her, uncomprehending. Not, she thought, the stare of someone who didn't know who she was talking about. More that she told him something that couldn't possibly be true.

"What are we doing here?" Galen asked as he led Thurvishar over to a chair, mostly so he wouldn't have to hold him up while Qown saw to his injuries.

"There's a magic gate downstairs we're going to use," Senera said. "It leads to the capital of the Manol."

Sheloran's head jerked up, and she stared at Senera in disbelief.

Senera shrugged. "The man who built this place was having an affair. He found it convenient to be able to reach his lover quickly. And right now, it is our only way into the Manol that doesn't involve standing around at the border until someone notices us. We can't remain here."

"Um." Fayrin frowned. "Are you sure that's a good idea? I mean, we are Quuros . . ."

"It's fine," Senera said. "Their king's a friend."

Fayrin *stared*.

"We're expected," Senera explained. "Or at least, we planned for the possibility we might need refuge there if things went wrong—which they have." She raised an eyebrow at Sheloran and Galen. "Really. How did you think we were going to go there? If wizards could just open portals into the Manol at will, Quur would have invaded a long time ago."

"I'm almost done," Qown said as he finished ripping the sleeve off Thurvishar's arm. "Then we can move him. He's mostly lost a lot of blood and broke some bones, but nothing more serious than that."

"All right, finish up and—"

A roar sounded from somewhere in the distance.

They all froze.

A shiver crawled over Senera's skin. That sounded large. That sounded *draconic*. Kihrin was supposed to be keeping the dragons away.

But there was one dragon he couldn't control.

Fear quickened through her veins. How stupid of her. With the Lighthouse gone and Senera's cottage destroyed, how many places could Senera and Thurvishar take as refuge, really? Relos Var knew Grizzst kept a gate here to the Manol. It wasn't so great a leap to conclude that either their group would take shelter in the now empty tower of Thurvishar's mentor or they would use it to travel to their only other reliable sanctuary.

Either way, destroying the tower was the smart play.

"Everyone downstairs!" Senera shouted, pointing to the door they needed. "Right now!"

Sheloran used magic to yank the door open by its metal handle even as she was running for the stairs. Galen picked up Thurvishar and tossed him over a shoulder. Qown, Fayrin, and Rebel just ran.

Senera was the last to go. She threw up the strongest magical ward she could just as the room filled with blue fire. The force of the blast threw her backward, down the stairs. Everything was bright light and heat and the most indescribably pure pain.

And then nothing at all.

## 55. Royal Address

### Galen's story
### Grizzt's Tower
### During Relos Var's attack

Galen liked to think he knew something about heat. Not as much as his wife, of course, who had grown up around magical forges and Red Men and all the ways one could possibly melt and shape objects normally quite immune to such treatment. But as familiar with heat as one could be growing up in a household run by men notorious for enjoying temperatures that would send most people straight into heatstroke.

This fire wasn't *right*.

It was blue, for one thing—a bright, searing white-hot blue—and when Senera was blown back through the doorway and came tumbling down the stairs, she was already burning, her skin black and charred. He shuddered to think how it would have gone if his wife hadn't been there. As it was, she'd shut the door the moment Senera was through and raised a magical barrier against the fire.

"It won't hold long!" Sheloran shouted back over her shoulder. "Does *any-one* besides these two know how to get through that gate?"

She gestured to a large, wide circle of stone set into the wall. Maybe it wasn't the portal, but if Galen had to wager on anything in the room being what they were looking for, this was where he'd have bet his metal too.

They only had moments. Even if the fire didn't melt right through the rock—eminently possible—the air was growing scorching hot. Galen didn't know how long it would take to reach oven temperatures, but if they didn't do something soon, they were going to find out.

Sheloran had pulled off her agolé and wrapped it around Senera. And she was crying. Galen couldn't look at either of them. He couldn't . . . he couldn't look at Senera. The dog that Senera had brought with her was making soft whining noises, all the more horrible because of how quiet they were.

Qown set a hand against Thurvishar's head. "Please wake up," he pleaded. "We need you to open up the gate or we're all going to die."

Thurvishar either wasn't as unconscious as they'd feared, or Qown was just that good a healer.

Or Taja liked them.

Thurvishar blinked his dark eyes open. To his credit, the man didn't delay in order to confirm what was going on, ask questions, check on Senera, or try to wriggle himself off Galen's shoulder. He muttered something that sounded suspiciously like a bawdy drinking song[1] and reached out a hand to touch the edge of the portal. The portal activated, different from what Galen was used to. More delicate and beautiful. Like a million points of starlight dancing around a central axis.

But he'd leave contemplating the nature of non–House D'Aramarin portals for another day. He looked back for just long enough to confirm that his wife had Senera and then ran through the gate. He grabbed Qown's hand as he passed to make sure the healer didn't try to do something stupid, like fight off an entire damn dragon all by himself so the rest of them could escape.

Galen set Thurvishar down on the ground the moment he was through, and turned back. Unnecessary, as it turned out. Whatever magic Thurvishar had used to activate the gate closed after the last person–Fayrin–passed through.

The councillor looked down at Senera with a face almost as pale as her normal color. "Is she–?"

"Let me see her!" Qown ripped his arm away from Galen as he scrambled over to where Sheloran had laid the woman.

That was the moment Galen realized they weren't alone.

He couldn't say where they were. It felt like being at the bottom of a gigantic well, with mage-lights forming a spiral pattern upward. More comprehensible, however, were the Manol soldiers with bows aimed at them.

Slowly, Galen raised his hands. Fayrin caught on quickly and did as well. Thankfully, the wild dog was too busy fussing over Senera to feel threatened, and thus too busy to get herself shot.[2]

"We're here to see Teraeth," Thurvishar murmured. Qown must have fixed the man's jaw first, since that sentence was comprehensible. He opened his eyes wider and repeated the same sentence, only louder.[3]

The vané gave zero indication that they'd understood a single word of that. One motioned to his belt, then pointed at Galen.

Probably ordering him to drop his sword.

"Do, uh . . . any of us speak vané?" Galen murmured.

Sheloran raised her head and said something in a language Galen absolutely didn't understand.

She shrugged helplessly at his shocked expression. "Mother taught me. It's never come up before."

"Pretty sure you just offered to cook them breakfast," Thurvishar murmured, still fighting with consciousness himself. He was staring at Senera, his face a wasteland of devastation.

"She'll be fine," Galen said. "Qown's good at this." Galen didn't point out the very worried expression on Qown's face, the one that suggested that being good at this might not be enough.

---

[1] Of course it was a bawdy drinking song. This is Grizzst we're talking about. However, I will not be listing which drinking song here for security reasons.–T

[2] I'd be surprised if arrows–even vané arrows–had any effect on Rebel.–S

[3] Yes, I should have said it in vorem. I wasn't thinking clearly.–T

One of the guards said something to the others and ran off.

He glanced over at Thurvishar. "What did the guard who left say?"

"'I'd better go fetch His Highness,'" Thurvishar translated.

"Okay," Galen said. "Yeah, that's . . . that's good, right?" He couldn't tell if the look on Thurvishar's face was pain because of his injuries or their situation. "Right?"

Thurvishar lifted his chin. "Probably." He added, "except Teraeth should be 'His Majesty' not 'His Highness,' so there's a possibility that something unexpected has happened."

Galen swallowed. They'd discussed this, briefly. Teraeth had been absent from the throne from the moment he'd been crowned. They'd talked about the possibility that someone would try to strip the position from him because of that. "Someone" in this case being Kihrin's mother, Khaeriel, better known to Galen as Miya—the woman who'd murdered him.

He was having a difficult time thinking of the Manol as any kind of shelter.

"Well . . . they're not shooting," Fayrin said. "So far, so good?" He pulled a dagger out of a sleeve and gingerly set it on the floor.

"Yeah," Galen agreed. "So far, doing great." The soldiers didn't seem to be inclined to loose those arrows in their direction so long as any moves they made were slow and involved tossing down weapons, so he was going with that. He slowly unbuckled his scabbard and set the sword on the ground before adding a dagger he kept in a boot.

That seemed to mollify them, but one of the guards made an angry gesture at Fayrin.

"She said, 'All of them,'" Sheloran explained.

Fayrin sighed and pulled another set of daggers from his sleeves. And then two more from inside his robe. A hairpiece that evidently hid a sharpened edge. And an entire brace of daggers that must have been . . . strapped to his thigh?

"Where were you hiding all of those?" Galen asked.

The councilman rolled his eyes. "As if you don't go around armed."

"Not when I'm wearing my bedclothes!"

Fayrin shrugged. "That sounds like your mistake."

The same guard—Galen could only assume she was using magic—made one last angry comment. Sheloran didn't translate. She just raised an eyebrow at Fayrin.

The man sighed and removed a ring, setting it on top of the rest of the weapons.

Galen couldn't be certain, but he thought the vané was grudgingly impressed.

Movement from the stairs alerted Galen to a change. He glanced up to see a group of vané heading their way. The leader wasn't Teraeth—that was obvious enough from skin color, even at a distance. Compared to most of the vané here, this new arrival was drab. His clothing was colorful enough, but his hair was a tame chestnut, his skin nearly the same shade of brown as Galen's own. At least his eyes were—

Wait.

Galen felt his hands close into fists, unable to stop himself. He did manage, barely, to fight off the impulse to stand as straight as possible. To adjust his clothes.

Apparently, when they'd said "His Highness," they hadn't been referring to *vané* royalty, but the Quuros kind.

"Hello, Grandfather," Galen said.

## 56. BAITING THE TRAP

### *Tyentso's story*
### *The Soaring Halls, the Upper Circle of the Capital City of Quur*
### *Just after Thurvishar's fight with Anlyr*

The alarms were already sounding when she teleported near her suite. Normally, she would've gone directly to her rooms, but since she didn't know what she'd find there, and she had a small child in her arms, she decided against taking the chance. She approached on foot, even as the remaining staff at the palace ran to and fro in panic.

Fayrin's rooms were, quite literally, *demolished.*

Just as troubling, the Milligreests who should've returned to her suite by now were still absent. At first, she thought the worst—that Gadrith or Havar or whoever it was who was responsible for all this had already come for them, that he had already made his move.

Then she saw the small black paper sitting on the table, tucked under a bouquet of flowers in a jade vase.

She recognized it and still feared the worst. It was a D'Lorus trick, one she knew well. She flicked a finger against the edge of it, sending a tiny stream of tenyé through the paper.

Silver writing appeared, briefly, before vanishing again.

> *Have taken the general's family to the schoolhouse.—Thurvishar*

Tyentso exhaled.

This would have been a strange form of deception. If one of her enemies had taken them, there was no reason to leave *a fucking note,* at a place where she logically shouldn't be expected to be.[1] There was no reason to claim the note came from Thurvishar. Such a note wouldn't put her on edge—it would calm her. Her enemies didn't seem to want that.

Which meant that there was an excellent chance that Thurvishar had done exactly what the note claimed. That he'd taken the family to the D'Lorus apartments in Alavel, likely because he, not knowing that Gadrith might be alive, had assumed the location safe.

---

[1] Only because she was supposed to be in Khorvesh at the front. Otherwise this is exactly where I'd expect her to be.—T

And even then, the emperor is rather famous for that whole 'teleport anywhere in the empire' power.—S

Unfortunately, if Gadrith was alive again, few places were *less* safe.

The boy was still fast asleep in her arms. She set him down on a couch, because three-year-olds were still heavy if you carried them for long enough. He was a pretty boy, honestly a mark against him for her plans. On the other hand, she could easily lay that blame on the child's father, who could go blissfully unnamed for the time being. She'd been gone for a long time, after all. Anything might have happened, with anyone. Those keeping track of her movements[2] would assume the boy's father had been a Black Brotherhood assassin. They were often exceedingly pretty, which had always made Tyentso roll her eyes. (Assassins shouldn't be pretty. Assassins should be unremarkable.)

She reached down and petted the boy's hair. What once had been brown and straight was now an impossibly soft black cloudcurl, with just the faintest violet sheen to it. If one looked at his eyes, one would see they were deep wells of night—the endless void of D'Lorus black. Who knew where the boy had come from originally, but now? Anyone could tell, with a single glance, that his origins rested solidly with House D'Lorus.

Truly, Caless did amazing work.

Tyentso let herself feel a moment's guilt for what she was about to do. The poor boy had committed no crime except having the bad luck to come to the attention of exactly the wrong people—namely, herself. He certainly didn't deserve what was about to happen to him. She couldn't fool herself: this was risky. She was putting this child in harm's way, fully knowing that he might not survive the experience. Only the most craven of souls would stoop to take a baby and turn them into *bait*.

But Tyentso knew her father, and she knew his weaknesses. And anyway, she'd never made the mistake of thinking of herself as a good person. She knew better.

Tyentso promised herself that she'd make it up to the boy, when this was all done.

Assuming either of them survived.

---

[2] I assume she means Relos Var.—T
She wouldn't be wrong. We *were* checking on her.—S

## 57. Murderers and Healers

*Galen's story*
*The Manol Jungle*
*Just after arrival*

Therin had shaved his beard.

Galen had a difficult time imagining a more inane or unimportant first impression in the grand scheme of things. He'd shaved his beard. Sure. Why not? It's not like there was some damn law that said that Therin D'Mon had to have a beard. Most royals shaved or paid for the magic that made it unnecessary. Yet it was the first thought that came into his head. That his grandfather had shaved the stupid beard, and without it, he looked twenty years younger. He was dressed like a vané too, in layered silks that were nothing like what a Quuros royal would wear. Therin fit in perfectly; he looked like a native, so much so that Galen almost hadn't recognized him.

The resemblance to Kihrin was especially obvious, now that Galen was looking for it, although most people could have been forgiven for assuming Therin was an older brother.

His grandfather's expression tightened at Galen's greeting. He looked every bit as pleased to see Galen as Galen felt about the situation. "What are *you* doing here?"

Gods. Galen's hands felt clammy. The desire to stare at the floor while he stammered out some explanation, an apology, an excuse, nearly overwhelmed him.

Galen forced himself to meet his grandfather's accusing gaze. "That's not important—"

"I asked you a question—"

"And I'm telling you it doesn't matter!" Galen growled. "*Senera's dying.* Are you going to help or not?"

Galen had expected his grandfather to demand to know who the hell Senera was, but apparently the man wasn't oblivious to who Kihrin's allies were. The former high lord stared past Galen to where Qown and Thurvishar hovered over Senera's body. Fayrin and Sheloran stood there with the rigid anxiety of people who wanted to help and couldn't. Therin motioned forward the vané he'd brought with him. They carried a stretcher and had evidently come prepared to deal with injuries.

"Oh Veils," Therin said. "Was it demons?" He rushed past Galen to bend down next to Thurvishar, then barked another order. Two more vané ran off, in a great deal more of a hurry than the original guard.

"No. Relos Var," Thurvishar said. He didn't look great himself, what with the blood and all, but he could talk, and he was conscious. "In dragon form. He breathed fire and . . ." Thurvishar closed his eyes for a second.

"I'm keeping her from dying of shock," Qown said, "but these burns are bad. I don't know–" He didn't finish the sentence. He didn't need to.

Galen caught a glimpse of Senera and had to turn away, fighting back bile. He couldn't recognize her. Even her hair had burned away. Her clothing had *melted*. It was hard to imagine how she could possibly be alive.

"We need to move her," Therin said.

"Where's Mi–?" Galen stopped himself. Not Miya. Not anymore. "Where's Khaeriel?" He loathed how his voice broke on the name.

"This isn't the time for that," Therin snapped.

Galen wanted to grind his teeth. He wanted to scream. Instead, he stayed calm and reasonable and said, "Last I checked, she was still the best physicker in House D'Mon. We could use that skill right now."

His grandfather turned back to him in surprise. It wasn't difficult to guess that Therin had expected a different sort of conversation about the woman. Therin's throat moved as if he were swallowing something, and then he nodded. "She'll meet us upstairs." Then he was concentrating on Senera, on helping Qown with whatever magics he was doing. Therin was, after all, a talented healer himself.

"*Blue,*" Sheloran whispered. "What are you doing?"

"Whatever it takes," he whispered back. He didn't have time to say anything more before the vané were rushing Senera upstairs, leaving the rest to follow as best they could.

"Thank you," Thurvishar said. The dog was sitting at his feet, looking up the stairs with obvious longing, but for whatever reason not leaving Thurvishar's side.

Galen didn't know what the man was thanking him for. He hadn't done anything. It's not like he was a healer, a fact he was regretting more and more of late. Galen gave the wizard a once-over. Still covered in blood, still favoring one arm. He didn't think Qown had fully healed it–it just hadn't been as important as dealing with Senera's injuries. None of that, though, was as bad as the numb look on Thurvishar's face. The one that clearly suggested just how broken he was going to be if Senera didn't pull through.

Galen had no idea what they would do if she didn't make it. The plan didn't hinge on her by any means, but he feared her death would be the blow that made all the others impossible to dodge.

"Let's catch up with the others," Fayrin suggested. "I don't think we want to fall so far behind we end up in the hands of vané who didn't hear the news that we're guests."

"Are we guests?" Galen asked. Just because they were helping didn't mean they were welcome.

"Yes," Thurvishar said with gratifying certainty. "But Fayrin's right. Let's not fall behind."

Galen didn't get a good look at wherever they'd ended up. It was the middle of the night, and they'd been in a rush. He'd seen glowing objects and light sources off in the distance, but he hadn't been paying attention. He was sure that they were wondrous and magical and so beautiful he'd remember it until the end of his days—if only he'd been looking.

Galen didn't care. He was busy.

The vané were surprisingly gracious. Much more so than any Quuros Royal House would have been to a group of foreigners showing up in the middle of the night, unannounced and making demands. They'd been taken someplace that Galen didn't think was the vané equivalent of a Blue House, if only because it was too pretty, too richly appointed, too luxurious. People wearing clothing embroidered with elaborate designs of stars and trees brought food—edible, if nothing Galen recognized. They also brought something that wasn't tea or coffee but was clearly meant to take on the same role. As much as Galen didn't want to eat, the smell reminded him that he hadn't done so in a long time and he should fix that situation while he could.

Thurvishar had vanished. Galen suspected he was helping with the healing in some manner, if perhaps only in providing tenyé for the others. The dog had gone with him.

Those who remained—Galen, Fayrin, Sheloran—ate in silence. Sheloran managed to swallow a few bites before she stood again, looking nauseated. She spent the next few minutes examining the meticulously forged candelabras in the room, twisted to look like trees, with mage-lights instead of candles. Knowing his wife, she was identifying the metal, if for no other reason than to keep her mind off the situation. And also in case they needed weapons.

"I don't—" Fayrin inhaled. "Why did Relos Var attack us?"

"I'm not sure he did," Galen said. "I think he was just destroying a place we might have used for shelter, and he didn't much care if we happened to be there or not at the time." Galen felt a horrible, dark bubble of laughter escape him. "We took some of his toys away, so he did the same to us."

"How equitable of him."

"Sure," Galen said, "and if I ever—"

The door opened. His grandfather walked through, looking a little tired but, much more importantly, looking *pleased.*

Galen all but ran over to him. "Is Senera going to be all right?"

Therin nodded. "Yes, she is. Fortunately, you had a healer with her at the scene immediately, and your friend did all the right things. She's going to be fine—"

Galen punched him.

He hadn't planned it. Not really. It just occurred to Galen that he'd been waiting for years to show his grandfather exactly how he felt about him. It was entirely possible that he'd never have a chance to do so again. Galen couldn't think of a better, more *efficient* way to express his opinion than the punch to the jaw his grandfather so richly deserved—although in hindsight, he really should have blackened one of those blue eyes.

It felt *so* good too. The look of surprise on the damn bastard's face, the way his head flung backward. And then while Therin was distracted reacting to the blow, Galen held his hand out to the side, palm up. He hoped Sheloran was paying attention so he wouldn't look like a fool.

Thankfully, his wife had been, and she followed his lead perfectly. He felt cool metal touch his fingers as Sheloran melted one of the candelabras and re-formed it as a sword in his hand. How many times had they practiced that move in case their enemies took his weapons? He had to say, it worked like a charm.

Worth it for the look in Therin's eyes when he righted himself from the punch only to realize Galen now held a blade to his throat.

"Um . . . ," Fayrin said from somewhere behind him.

"Councilman Jhelora," Galen said lightly, "I need the room, if you don't mind. My grandfather and I are having a conversation."

"Right," Fayrin said. "Well. Far be it from me to get in the way of a proper family reunion. I'll just, uh . . . see how Senera's doing, why don't I?"

"Galen—" Therin started to say.

Galen's fingers tightened on the hilt. In eighteen years, that was the first time he'd ever heard his grandfather say his name with anything that even approached *respect*.

"Perhaps I should go too," Sheloran said. She stopped by Galen's side for long enough to kiss his shoulder. "Don't do anything I wouldn't do, Blue."

His breath stuttered, and he almost cursed her. Because there was a lot that Sheloran wouldn't do that Galen easily might have and because he'd long since come to understand that her opinion mattered to him. Along with Qown and Kihrin and not too many others.

And none of them would want him to hurt his grandfather, no matter how much the son of a bitch deserved it.

The air was thick and hot and still as the two other people left, leaving Galen and Therin alone.

The moment the door closed, Galen took a step back, tossed the improvised sword to the side, and stalked away.

"Galen, that was hardly necessary," Therin said. "Let me explain—"

Galen turned back. "Explain? Explain to me how you can possibly justify running away to the Manol with the woman who *murdered your entire family*?" He paused just long enough to scoff. "She was *your* slave. Yet how is it that you're the only one she didn't kill? We thought you'd been kidnapped, but I have to say, you don't look very kidnapped to me. You look like you're having a great time. But go on. Explain it to me. I fucking dare you."

Therin walked over to the table, sat down, and put his head in his hands.

Galen found that he was so angry he was shaking. And somehow even angrier that Therin hadn't started shouting back. Galen wanted him to. He wanted the bastard to care enough to start yelling about it. But Therin never yelled, did he? He just retreated and let people—Darzin, Miya—do whatever they wanted.

"How is . . . how is everyone . . . ?"

"Dead," Galen snapped.

Therin looked up, startled.

"Dead," Galen repeated with feeling. "There might be a few cousins who survived the last couple of months, I don't know. I was only Returned because my wife has family who give a shit about her, which meant Shel was alive to file the petition for me. Aunt Tishenya was starting to Return some of the family, the ones that wouldn't be a threat—for example, my sisters are fine. Aunt Tishenya sent them to the estate in Kirpis. But there were a lot of family still waiting in that line when Thaena died. And then *that was that*."

His grandfather inhaled, a shuddering, sharp breath.

Galen knew he was sneering. He knew his expression was something dark and ugly. He wrapped it around himself like a thin silk robe—cold and slithering and hiding absolutely nothing. "*Then,*" Galen said, "Aunt Tishenya was murdered by your other daughter Gerisea while she was trying to assassinate me, which means it's probably just as well that you don't give a fuck about your family, because guess what? You don't have one anymore. All your children are *dead*—"

He couldn't stop himself. Galen couldn't shove that sentence back down his throat no matter how much he wanted to, no matter how hard he choked on it.

Galen knew he'd made a mistake the moment he saw his grandfather's brow draw together, his blue eyes turn hard and calculating.

"Except Kihrin, you mean," Therin corrected.

A beat of silence hung in the air.

". . . Except Kihrin," Galen agreed. And because he had to do something, cover for his slip somehow, he added, "Sometimes, I forget that he's your son and not my brother."

Therin scoffed as he looked down at his hands. Galen didn't let himself relax, although he thought his grandfather was buying that explanation. For the moment.

"I can't make excuses—" Therin started to say.

"You're right about that."

"Would you shut up and let me finish?" His grandfather glared at him before his expression settled into something more introspective. "I can't make excuses. And I realize that *sorry* is insufficient in the extreme. But I am sorry. I just . . . I didn't realize how miserable I was in Quur until I left."

"And so you ran away from all your responsibilities, from everyone who was depending on you."

"Don't give me that!" Therin snapped. "As if you wouldn't have been perfectly happy to run away with Kihrin the very first chance you had! You did, in fact, try to do exactly that!"

"I was a fourteen-year-old boy who was being beaten by my father whenever the mood took him, which was pretty fucking often. So yes, I tried to run away with the first person to show me some basic decency. Whereas you didn't have a gods-damn thing wrong with your life that wasn't of your own making!" Probably anyone standing outside the room or in the same hallway, possibly in the same building, could hear him shouting.

And again, he didn't care.

Therin rubbed his jaw where a satisfying purple bruise was forming. He wouldn't look at Galen.

"You left me to pick up the pieces," Galen said, "even though you never made any secret of how I wasn't good enough to do the job."

"No." Therin turned back to face him then. His gaze was a broken, wounded thing. "No, that's not what I said. I never said you weren't good enough."

"Liar!" Galen screamed.

"I said you were too *nice* to do the job." Therin's voice lowered to a whisper. "Too kind. Which I thought meant weak, because I was a fool. I was wrong."

Galen could only stare at him. He couldn't breathe. He couldn't . . .

His eyes were stinging. Galen raised a hand to his face and realized he was crying. He thought Therin would say something. Chide him. Make some kind of comment about how crying was unmanly.

Instead, he did something that Galen wouldn't have predicted if he'd waited until the stars blinked out in the sky. Therin stepped forward and *hugged him*.

It was too much. It was everything. Galen had wanted this his entire life, knowing he could never ask and it would never be offered. Just one of the many reasons his father had pronounced him weak. Why his grandfather had never once defended him.

Galen's instinct was to push his grandfather away. For a split second, he started to. Then he realized what he was about to do and how Darzin would have approved of the rejection. So instead, he threw his arms around his grandfather and let himself cry.

He wasn't precisely sure how long they stayed like that.

Finally, Galen stepped back, rubbing his eyes sheepishly.

Therin just handed him a cloth to wipe his eyes. "I've done so many things I regret, Galen. It's a long, long list. And there came a point where I just . . . couldn't do it anymore. Couldn't live that life. And I would be such a hypocrite for insisting Khaeriel face justice for her crimes when I never did. I had a choice, and I chose selfishly. It's the one thing I don't regret."

Galen's one consolation was that his grandfather's eyes were wet too. Galen hadn't been the only one crying.

Galen wiped his eyes. He felt empty. Flayed. "So you're fine with this? Just moving down to the Manol and becoming Queen Khaeriel's . . ." He searched for a word that wouldn't be horrible, failed, and settled on what he hoped was the least offensive. ". . . Concubine?"

Therin laughed. "Sort of the reverse. She's not queen anymore. Whereas I'm next in line for the throne."

Galen stared at him. "I'm sorry . . . *What did you just say?*"

Therin cleared his throat. "Um, well, Doc died . . ." His face twisted, and Galen thought his grandfather might be the one to break down crying that time. As it was, Therin took a deep breath and visibly clenched his jaw before continuing. "I mean, King Terindel died, which made his only living child, Teraeth, the new king. But Teraeth doesn't have any children of his own, so if anything were to happen to him, the crown would default to the oldest of the descendants of Terindel's deceased daughter. My grandmother."

Galen rubbed the side of his head. "You're serious?"

"To my chagrin, yes," Therin said. "Khaeriel's furious about it, but I'm trying to bring her around to the idea that maybe she's earned a break from politics."

"What does . . . what does that make me?" Galen asked in a small, numb voice.

Therin almost smiled. "Last I checked? Fourth in line for the vané throne. Right after Kihrin. You might want to learn the language."

"But I'm not vané . . . ?" That no one seemed to be paying attention to that fact was deeply disturbing.

"There's not as much difference as we've been led to believe." Therin gestured toward the door. "Come on. Let's go check on your friends and let your wife know that you didn't murder me, after all."

Galen was still sniffling, but it didn't stop him from narrowing his eyes at Therin. "Don't think this means I've forgiven you. Either of you."

Therin nodded as though he'd expected that. The bastard didn't look deterred. He also didn't look like he was taking Galen's threat even slightly seriously. Probably because of all the crying. Bastard. "That's fair. We've more than earned it."

## 58. THE BABYSITTING SERVICE

### *Kalindra's story*
### *The D'Lorus town house, the Academy at Alavel*
### *The morning after Vol Karoth's escape*

"I must admit, I find myself a bit taken aback by the idea that the empress has a child," Jira Milligreest said as she handed Kalindra a cup of morning tea. "But with those eyes, I suppose he'd have to be hers, wouldn't he?"

The child in question was currently siting in the middle of a fortress made out of ink sticks, along with Kalindra's son, Nikali. She wasn't certain where the ink sticks had come from, but it made a certain amount of sense that a house owned by the D'Lorus family would have a truly excessive, decadent supply.

They'd wanted to use books, but Kalindra had put her foot down. If a column of ink sticks fell over, no one would be hurt. The same couldn't be said of many of the tomes kept at the D'Lorus house.

As if to prove her point, her son grabbed several cloth belts he'd pulled from her bag earlier and began spinning them at the impromptu fort. When that failed to give the desired destructive result, he pouted and then shoved to knock the blocks over.

Kalindra felt a chill as she realized her son was reenacting the Lash's attack on Devors.

"Dear?"

Kalindra turned owl eyes on her mother-in-law. "What was that?"

Jira sighed and rubbed the side of her head. "Oh, I don't know, dear. Just commenting on how odd it was that the empress would suddenly reveal out of nowhere that she has a son." The woman squinted at the contents of her teacup before apparently finding the idea of tea wholly inadequate and setting the cup aside.

"Are you all right?" Kalindra took the opportunity to ignore the question and Tyentso and her so-called son.

Because it was bullshit. Kalindra *knew* it was bullshit. Yes, technically, her tenure on Ynisthana in the service of the Black Brotherhood had only overlapped with Tyentso's by around six months or so, but that was enough time that if Tyentso had come to the island already pregnant, Kalindra would have known. Since there wasn't a single soul on the island who hadn't been meticulous about preventing unplanned pregnancies, it was extraordinarily unlikely that Tyentso could have become accidentally pregnant while there. Finally, since Tyentso had returned to Quur along with Teraeth and Kihrin, just a few months previously, the only possible way she could have pulled off a surprise child was if she'd taken a quick vacation over at the Lighthouse at Shadrag Gor so she could birth and raise a toddler. Which seemed logistically impossible for many reasons, not least of which was that she'd have run out of food long before the boy's first birthday.

So yes, it was bullshit. And yet the woman in charge of the entire damn empire had shown up at the D'Lorus estate at some gods-awful hour of the morning with a still-sleeping baby in her arms. Whom she then proclaimed to be her son, Tyrin, and all but begged Jira to take care of the boy while Tyentso was away on march because she didn't trust any of the servants.

Kalindra hadn't said a word in protest, even though the lie was so obvious it was all but lit up in mage-light with a big shiny ribbon tied around it.

She didn't think anyone would blame her for wanting to know what game Tyentso was playing, though. Besides wanting to know the answers to such other questions as: *Where did you find the child? What happened to his parents?* And her personal favorite: *What the fuck is wrong with you?*

In Kalindra's opinion, when the professional assassins started giving someone judgmental stares, that person really needed to take a long, hard look to whatever the hell they were doing, because it had crossed a damn line. She knew from experience.

She was zoning out again. Kalindra snapped herself back in time to realize her mother-in-law was still in the middle of answering her question.

"—and I feel completely dried out, and I didn't even have anything to drink last night. I must be coming down with something." Jira inhaled deeply. "Although I must say, I'd forgotten how calming Alavel is. So at least that's nice."

Eledore was apparently feeling the same way, to the point where she'd decided to skip breakfast and just stay in bed.

A burst of sun-bright laughter echoed through the room as the two boys fell to the ground giggling uncontrollably, presumably because of the way Nikali had sprayed spit everywhere when he was pretending to be the rainstorm over Devors.

At least the children were having a good time.

"It is pretty here," Kalindra agreed. "But I can't help feeling some sympathy with Eledore. I wish we were down in Khorvesh fighting."

"If it weren't for the children, we would be," Jira said after a thoughtful pause. "I haven't missed repelling a morgage incursion in over twenty years, and then only because I was in labor with . . ." Her face started to twist, started to turn haunted. Jira closed her eyes and sat very still, as though she were a cracked cup that would finish shattering if she moved so much as an inch.

"With Jarith," she finished in a much softer voice.

Kalindra reached over and covered her mother-in-law's hand with hers. She wished she could explain about Jarith. She could only imagine—but she could imagine very easily—how painful it would be to lose one's child. And Jarith had been . . . Jarith had been everything, hadn't he? It had never been difficult to tell how loved he'd been by his family and how much he'd loved them in return. They'd loved him so much that they'd only made the most token of protests when he'd announced he was marrying a nobody commoner from Khorvesh. Even those protests had been promptly revoked once Kalindra demonstrated how well she could fight.

"He's not . . . he's not really gone." Kalindra's throat was so dry, speaking those words felt like the rasp of sandpaper. She hated that Jira would take those words as metaphor, that she was telling the truth but not in a way that was *honest.*

*Your son's still here. He still loves you. He still loves us. He's just . . . different now. Please don't hate him because he's not your perfect boy anymore.*

"Sometimes . . ." Jira's voice cracked. "Sometimes I feel like he's still in the room." Her lower lip quivered.

Kalindra knew those moments hadn't been Jira's imagination.

But she couldn't say anything. She only hoped there would be time to explain and that the Milligreests could forgive her for letting them all suffer like this.

"It's not fair," Jira whispered.

Kalindra felt the words like a stiletto to the lungs, leaving her gasping and unable to draw in a breath. It didn't matter that she knew Jarith wasn't dead—or at least, wasn't *gone*—because no matter what else, Jira had spoken true. *It wasn't fair.*

Jarith hadn't deserved what had happened to him, what Xaltorath had done to him. He'd been so young and so beautiful and so breathtakingly *good.* The wrongness of it coated her mouth, poisonous and sticky, acid at the back of her tongue. The guilt she felt at the emotion—grieving for a man not dead—wasn't as strong as the bitter knowledge that things could never be as they were. Jarith still loved her, for which she was eternally grateful, but he couldn't return to being a normal husband, a normal son, a normal *human.* He might learn to cope, to compensate, but . . .

Kalindra didn't want to think of him as broken. That was the wrong metaphor. Broken swords could be reforged, broken pottery repaired. He'd been attacked, infected, *defiled,* and there could be no return to innocence. No fixing this.

And *it wasn't fair.*

She squeezed her mother-in-law's hand. Neither woman moved as one of the estate servants entered the room with a new pot of tea, carrying off the old one.

The old man didn't say a word to either of the women. He didn't even ask if they wanted a new pot of tea. He just set the new pot down with fingers so withered they were shaking and took the emptied pot as its replacement. He bowed, shakily, at the door, eyes flicking down to the children once before backing out of the room.

Still, Kalindra was grateful. The servants were weird and standoffish, forgotten holdovers from days when the D'Lorus family hadn't been all but extinct. She wasn't sure she'd heard more than a dozen words out of any of them since they'd arrived.

But they were attentive. And the tea was a good distraction.

"Here. Yours has grown cold." Kalindra poured new cups for both of them.

"Thank you," Jira murmured, her thoughts so obviously miles away. Or more likely, years away. Imagining better times.

Across the room, the two boys started chasing each other, Nikali flapping his arms while Tyrin giggled. Jira wiped her eyes even as she chuckled, smiling softly.

Kalindra thought it would have been impossible not to smile. Certainly, she hadn't managed it.

Jira shook her head. "Honesty compels me to admit that what I really want to do right now is take my sword and kill . . . someone. Morgage, demons? Just someone. *Anyone.*" She drank her cup of tea. "I was being far too hard on Eledore."

"She wasn't making it easy," Kalindra murmured. Something about the situation had started to bother her. It was subtle. What was it? The servants? The old man was just . . . old. And, honestly, had probably seen some shit. The fact that he'd even survived in the D'Lorus household meant he had to be an absolute expert in the art of not becoming a convenient human sacrifice. But still, something felt off.

The moment she tasted the tea, she knew what it was.

"Jira, don't drink that!" Kalindra snapped, but it was too late.

The older woman looked down at her cup. "What's—" She glanced back up at Kalindra with fear in her eyes. She didn't finish asking what was the matter. Jira wasn't stupid.

Kalindra grabbed a bowl that had been filled with fruit and almonds, dumped the contents onto the table, and then poured the contents of the teapot into the bowl. She looked over the dregs. Nothing obvious. No riscoria weed or dalmarik, no foxglove or other easy "throw some herbs in the pot and stand back" sort of poisons. But the aftertaste—that she recognized as potentially one of several different poisons. None of which were inhalants or acids likely to cause even worse damage if inhaled or regurgitated a second time.

Fine. So vomiting was unlikely to make the situation *worse.*

There was a small, covered bowl of salt on a sideboard, which she grabbed and added to a glass of water.

"I don't feel—" Jira leaned back on the couch. "I do feel a little tired. Whatever this is, it's acting quickly."

Kalindra handed her the glass of salted water. "I need you to drink this and then purge yourself all over the fucking D'Lorus rugs, okay? And then I'm going to start carving my way through the staff until someone talks."

"I would prefer you didn't. These particular servants weren't easy to train."

Kalindra raised her head.

A man stood in the doorway; she hadn't heard him enter. That alone was enough to make her concerned, but the man's appearance raised all the hairs on her arms.

Black hair, blacker eyes, pallid skin. Dressed in D'Lorus robes. He didn't look dead exactly, but Xivan didn't look dead when she'd recently fed either.

Probably for the same reason.

Kalindra may never have had the unique pleasure of meeting the man, but she still knew what Gadrith D'Lorus was supposed to look like. Kalindra also knew he was supposed to be dead, but honestly, when had that ever stopped him? In hindsight, she should also have realized that Jira was of the right generation to have actually met the man.

"Gadrith!" Jira snarled as she drew her sword. She tried to close with the wizard, but halfway there, she teetered. She fell to her knees and then to the ground.

Unconscious, Kalindra thought. Not dead.

"Don't be alarmed," Gadrith said. "The tea wasn't laced with anything fatal, although I am impressed you were able to identify the threat. Unexpected." He didn't look impressed. He also didn't look unimpressed. His face was blank of any identifiable emotion. "But not insurmountable. Throw your weapons over there." His black glare intensified when Kalindra hesitated. "Think of the children. Don't make me prove my sincerity."

Kalindra couldn't help herself; she glanced over at Nikali. The boys had both stopped laughing and stopped playing, and both had gone perfectly still. Rather like baby gazelle hoping the lion wouldn't see them. She repressed a shudder.

It couldn't be a fucking coincidence that Tyentso had dropped off a child who was, at least in theory, the D'Lorus lord heir, just a few hours before Gadrith *the fucking Twisted* decided to show up. Especially not with Gadrith's reputation for killing everyone around him, but most *especially* family members.

Tyentso had all but put a bull's-eye on the poor boy's chest.

Kalindra wordlessly pulled her scabbard off, gracefully stepping a tiny bit to the side as she did. Enough to block line of sight to the boy. There was no point trying to conceal Nikali. Gadrith obviously knew who he was.

"What do you want?" Kalindra asked carefully.

"Nothing more from you than your cooperation," Gadrith told her. "Do so and there's no reason any of you need to come to an unpleasant end." He did something complicated with his hand, and several pieces of paper along with a quill appeared on a nearby table. "I want you to write your father-in-law a letter. I'll tell you what to say."

## 59. Successful Missions

*Janel's story*
*The Mother of Trees, the Manol*
*The morning after Vol Karoth's escape*

Janel woke from sleep that was not sleep. Teraeth lay next to her—eyes open, waiting, resting on an elbow. He'd been watching over her. She saw no sign of Talon, which was a relief.

"Did you sleep at all?" she asked him.

"I'd say something about sleeping when I'm dead, but I think that would be a little too uncomfortably close to certain people I know." He kissed her forehead.

Janel groaned and stretched. "I don't sleep when I'm dead; I'm dead when I sleep. It's not the same at all." She had technically slept, but she wanted to sleep *more*. She felt bone tired. "Unfortunately, I have to return. We weren't successful." She gave Teraeth an apologetic look. She hated that they weren't successful. She'd very much wanted to come back triumphant, to be able to do this one favor for both Valathea and Teraeth.

But Teraeth just grinned and cupped her face to deliver a sweet, lingering kiss. "Kihrin says hello," he whispered.

Janel was confused for a moment. Then she realized what he had to mean. She pulled him back down to her, kissing him again. "What happened?" she whispered.

He held up a star tear and winked at her. "Let's go find Valathea and talk about it, shall we?"[1]

Janel scrambled out of bed. She searched the overly large room, but there was no sign of Talea or Xivan. Since they'd traveled to the Second World physically rather than the way Janel had, she didn't know for sure where they'd reappear or even when.

But it turned out she didn't have to worry.

Just like the other times one of the Immortals had shown themselves, there was no fanfare unless the Immortal wished it. One moment, Teraeth and Janel were alone in the room, and the next minute, they were not.

"You know you're going to have to learn how to dress like goddesses," Teraeth said. "Summon up impractical clothing and the like. It's tradition."

---

[1] I was about to protest that Terindel's soul gem shouldn't have been a star tear since he wasn't a Founder, but then I remembered that he was born before the demons arrived. That means his soul had to have been reincarnated from one of the original settlers.—S

"I'll settle for just knowing how to use my powers in a fight." Xivan noticed the notably pleased expression on Janel's face. "Did something happen?" She immediately qualified. "Something new?"

"Yes," Teraeth said. "Uh, I don't know what happened with your group, but I'm pleased to say that plan B worked."

Talea cocked her head. "We didn't have a plan B."

"No, we didn't," Teraeth agreed. "But that didn't stop it from working."

"Before explanations," Janel said, "we should find Valathea."

"And food," Teraeth said. "I left strict instructions that I was not to be disturbed for anything less than an actual invasion, so if we want breakfast, we're going to need to hunt it down ourselves."

Talea grinned and reached over, taking Xivan's hand. "Sure. Let's do that."

## 60. THE GLITTER OF BLUE

**Kihrin's story**
**The Free States of Doltar**
**Just after dawn, several hours after the attack on**
**Grizzst's Tower**

When Jarith had first brought me the news that Relos Var had the Stone of Shackles—sort of—well, I might have been a touch worried. I really didn't want Relos Var to have that damn rock, for all kinds of reasons.

Then Jarith had also let me know that Anlyr had it, wasn't using it, and indeed had been ordered to hide it. Strangely, it had engendered in me a feeling suspiciously analogous to panic. Because this was what I'd been waiting for.

Relos Var had finally made a mistake.

I say that like he hadn't made mistakes before. He had. But they'd always been recoverable mistakes, errors that sooner or later he twisted to his advantage. Not this time.

I hoped.

Anlyr had stayed on the move after leaving the Soaring Halls. That was the smart play. Even if anyone was tracking him (and we were), by the time another wizard could open up a gate to his current location, he'd already be on to the next one.

Except I didn't care about his current location, because I wasn't interested in finding Anlyr. I cared about the fact that at some point during this jumping game, he'd hidden the Stone of Shackles. I didn't need to know where he was, only where he'd been. So I visited each and every stop he'd made along the way, until I found the right one.

That turned out to be an abandoned sandstone temple half buried by a dune desert in the rain shadow of the Doltari mountains. The desert itself would be miserable by midday, but this was just after dawn, so the air was still cool. The red sun had turned all the yellows and browns to a beautiful pink-orange hue and limned the ruin walls in scarlet light. Tall columns and stepped pyramids spoke of an elaborate structure that would remain visible even after the worst sandstorms.

It was the perfect location, really. Desolate, unlikely to be visited casually, known to very few. If you didn't already know it existed, you'd never find it.

Inside, the ruins had been long since cleaned out by robbers and looters, assuming that there'd ever been anything valuable left in the first place. Anlyr had been at this location for less than fifteen seconds—if he'd hidden the Stone of Shackles here, he would have had to do so quickly.

As it turned out, Anlyr had left the Stone of Shackles lying at the bottom of a clay pot, probably where he'd simply thrown it. And it *was* the Stone of Shackles. I could tell, just looking at it, in a way that had nothing to do with the fact that I'd once worn the damn thing for almost twenty years.

I didn't even try to touch the stone. I still wasn't able to hold any object for a great length of time with 100 percent certainty. The risk was too great.

I teleported both stone and vase back to the moon.

Then I destroyed the entire temple and summoned up a windstorm to fill in the hole left behind. By the time it finished, there was no sign that a building had ever been there at all.

## 61. Father Issues

**Tyentso's story**
**The imperial army bivouac, Khorvesh**
**The day after Vol Karoth's escape, after breakfast**

It was, perhaps, the shortest war to ever occur in Quuros history, if it could even be called a war at all. Still, Tyentso wasn't naïve enough to think that a sudden declaration of peace would halt fighting that had been going on for well over a thousand years. So she'd spent most of the morning barking orders, teleporting across various parts of the empire cementing deals, and in general preparing to move the entire army yet again–this time to Jorat.

Havar was going to get his siege a lot earlier than he'd been expecting.

Her fiercely loyal, if not fanatical, logistics officers might have been willing to follow her every whim, but that didn't mean they were happy about having to pack up and leave literally before they'd even finished settling in from their first move.

She was also trying to limit her time at the camp. Tyentso suspected she was feeling the curse less intensely than her troops precisely because she spent so much of her time teleporting around the empire instead of in camp. The effect didn't seem to be following her, so she assumed that whatever was causing it moved with her troops rather than herself. She would start to worry when she found herself making excuses to stay.

At some point during all of that, she lost track of Qoran Milligreest.

"Where's the high general?" she asked Caerowan.

"I'm not sure?" The Devoran priest looked around with concern, but not panic. It was a massive army camp, after all. The simplest explanation to his absence was just that he was busy elsewhere.

"Your Majesty, um . . ." A runner sprinted into the tent, holding a flat wood case. She was wild-eyed and clearly upset. "Someone . . . someone left this for you. You told us to watch out for anyone placing anything on your desk, but this just appeared. Out of nowhere. And–" The girl swallowed nervously.

"You already opened it," Tyentso said.

"In case it was cursed," the girl confessed. She threw herself on her knees. "I submit to any punishment Your Majesty feels is appropriate."

Veils. "Oh, for fuck's sake, stand up," Tyentso ordered. She inhaled. Given the girl's reaction, whatever this was, it was going to be bad.

She flipped open the box and stared.

Yes, it was bad. Extremely bad.

A severed human hand lay nestled in velvet as though it were a piece of jewelry. And if she'd had any doubts at all as to the original owner of said hand, the ring of office on his finger gave it away.

So no, the high general wasn't just "busy elsewhere."

*Fuck, I'm sorry, Qoran,* Tyentso said. A small note was tucked into the lid, and damn it all, but after so many years, she still recognized Gadrith's handwriting.

It said: *We'll wait for you in the D'Lorus house library.*

There was a great deal Gadrith could have spelled out but hadn't: that if there was any sign of reinforcements, he'd kill Qoran. That if she ignored the message, he'd start sending pieces of the high general back until she stopped.

This was all understood.

She handed the box back to the messenger. "Take that to the physicker's tent and tell them to cast every preservation spell they have on it. I'll want it reunited with its owner as soon as I return with him." She gestured to Caerowan, who had been staring at the severed hand with a look of fierce concentration. The little bastard was probably trying to recall which prophecy quatrain applied to *this*. "Get out."

The small man startled. "Your Majesty?"

"I want to be alone," she said firmly. "Go tell General Pelran he's in charge until I return. He knows what needs to be done."

"Yes, Your Majesty," he said, bowing quickly as he backed out of the tent.

Tyentso didn't teleport directly to Alavel. Not right away. She had some preparations to make. The trick with reinforcements wasn't to ignore them, it was to make sure Gadrith never detected them.

She tossed up spells, because she didn't trust some enterprising aide—and that category most certainly included Caerowan—to eavesdrop.

"Jarith?" Tyentso said to the empty air when she finished. "Are you here?"

He was. He must have been waiting, because she'd barely uttered the words when he swirled into visibility.

**He has my *family*,** Jarith snarled. He sounded . . .

Tya help her. He sounded like he had his own personal demonic chorus backing him up, which she suspected was demonic telepathic shorthand for "seriously fucking angry." If she'd ever doubted that he was a demon . . .

"Has he hurt anyone?" Tyentso immediately winced and raised a finger. "Besides your father. Which we *will* fix."

**No. But I will destroy him for daring to touch them. For daring to share the same air as them. THEY ARE ALL ON MY LIST.**

Tyentso really wasn't sure what the fuck that meant. List? This didn't seem like the right time to ask for an extensive explanation. There was a damn good chance she wouldn't have understood the answer, anyway. Jarith might be one of the "good" demons, but that didn't mean the transformation hadn't left him deeply weird. And creepy.

Also useful. She wasn't complaining.

"I know," Tyentso said. "But we talked about this. We had a plan. It's still a good plan. It's going to work."

That seemed to calm him down, at least for the moment.

**What if it doesn't work?**

"Well, then, go get Thurvishar and avenge my ass, obviously," Tyentso snapped. "But I promise I won't let your family be hurt." Even as she said the words, she could only hope that she wouldn't make herself a liar.

The angry shadows didn't exactly stop lashing, but they moved a little slower.

**Then let's go.**

### Tyentso's story
### The D'Lorus estate at Alavel
### Just after talking to Jarith

This particular D'Lorus property had always unimaginatively been called *the schoolhouse,* mostly because it stood on the school grounds rather than because classes had ever been taught there. The townhouse stood all but deserted. Just Tyentso and the shadows, and if one of those shadows was a little too dark and a little too animated? Well, nobody was around to notice.

Tyentso never had good memories of the place, not exactly, but some of them had been less terrible than others. Years on board a ship had made clean sheets and a large bed her definition of decadence, a yardstick that had given a burnished shine to recollections of luxurious baths and fruit with every meal. She'd also missed the pure bliss of having access to a library that large. Some of the books were technically hers too, part of her wedding dowry. She'd always assumed Gadrith was far more interested in the books she'd inherited from her adoptive father than he'd ever been in her.

In hindsight, she'd assumed too much.

She wondered if Gadrith had ever bothered to investigate her adoptive father's death. If he realized that the dean's error while summoning a demon hadn't been a mistake at all. If he understood the lengths Tyentso had always, always, been willing to pursue while chasing revenge.

She would like to think Gadrith understood. She had, after all, willingly married the fucker, even knowing full well he was her own father, in the hopes of getting close enough to murder the man. And yes, yes, it had been a completely celibate marriage, with no incest ever occurring, but if she was being honest . . .

Well. If she was being honest, incest wouldn't have stopped her from marrying him if it had meant she could hold that bastard's heart in her hand and feel its last, feeble beats.

Yet as she walked through the house, shoes echoing against the fine parquet flooring, she had to wonder if he'd understood at all. But then she didn't really understand what the fuck Gadrith hoped to accomplish here either. She'd expected *Relos Var* to make a move against her.

She hadn't expected Gadrith—at least not until he'd given himself away.

Everyone was, as promised, in the library. Gadrith had warped the furniture, letting chair legs and wooden frames become manacles and bars. Jira looked furious (relatable), Kalindra very calm (terrifying), and Eledore was sleeping (and hopefully just that). Qoran . . . Qoran was trapped in an undignified position, arm still forcibly stretched out, but now missing the hand that should have been at the end. She made a point of giving the two children the tiniest, briefest glance before carefully avoiding looking anywhere in their direction. They were also tied up and looked as scared and pathetic as one could imagine. If she hadn't already promised herself that she was absolutely going to kill Gadrith and make it stick this time, that would have been enough justification to make a go of it.

Every prisoner was covered in magical traps. Gadrith had thoughtfully made the wards especially phosphorescent and obvious, impossible to miss. The threat was clear: no sudden moves or spellcasting, or everyone died. There were more wards on the walls. The usual protections against fire in the library, more defenses designed to stop lightning (that felt directed at her specifically), but nothing to keep a magical portal from being opened.

So at least she could assume Havar D'Aramarin (or Murad or Nemesan or *whoever*) wasn't directly in league with her father.

Gadrith himself sat at a table facing toward the door, reading a book. He had set up a defensive aura so strong it was visible a full two feet out from his body. If she was reading the marks right, it would melt any sword that crossed its threshold and set the holder on fire besides. (That felt directed at all the Khorveshans in the room.)

Gadrith barely glanced up as Tyentso walked into the room. "You're late."

Tyentso ignored him and instead focused her attention on the high general. "Seriously, Qoran? How do you fall into a trap this obvious?" Only when he glared at her in lieu of an answer did Tyentso notice the way his lips seemed glued together. Some sort of spell to keep him from talking.

Gadrith scoffed. "The same way you did, I imagine, because someone you care about is in danger. It's very predictable."

"So congratulations. You got me here. Now what do you want?"

A small portal with an unclear destination opened up a few feet away from her. "First," Gadrith said, "I want you to remove the Crown and Scepter and toss them into that. Nothing in my research indicates that they'll teleport instantly to your side, just instantly to the Arena if you die. Then . . ." He shrugged. "I want what I've always wanted. Urthaenriel. You have it. Give it to me. Then I'll leave."

Tyentso stared at him. Gadrith was far from expressionless, particularly to those who knew him. And what she was sensing from him at that moment wasn't apathy but frustration. Even, dare she say, a certain amount of helpless rage.

"Oh," she said. "This is still being done for Relos Var, isn't it? He brought you back from the dead just to play fetch for him." She raised a finger. "Smart. A good leader knows how to delegate."

He *snarled*. "I would have been a fool not to take the opportunity, regardless of its source. But we're not here to catch up on gossip, daughter. Crown, Scepter, sword. *Now*."

She almost laughed. Oh, that must have chafed. To be pulled back from the Afterlife, stuffed back into his old, thoroughly inferior dead body, only to find that he owed his third chance at grotesque villainy to his most hated enemy.

"Raverí," Jira growled,[1] "just get me out of this and I'll gladly help you gut this bastard." She struggled against the wooden arms wrapped around her limbs.

Tyentso barely glanced at her. "I appreciate your enthusiasm, but do shut up before you get people killed."

Jira scowled, but she also fell silent.

Good enough. Once Gadrith lost his patience—which would happen any second now—he'd start killing people. He'd probably start with Qoran, gods help the poor man, because there was a certain way in which Gadrith was and always had been perpetually chained to the past. A past where Tyentso had been desperately in love with Qoran and had naïvely assumed that he'd run away with her just because he loved her back. Gadrith was already dead (for the first time) when Tyentso had learned the hard way that she'd been mistaken about that. Her father had also missed out on her spending the next twenty years on the run because of it.

That sort of thing would rub the gloss off any affair.

"Don't pay any attention to her. She's still upset about losing her son," Tyentso said. She very pointedly didn't look at the children, not even when one of them decided he'd rested enough to begin crying anew.

And finally . . . finally . . . it drew Gadrith's attention.

"Who's the second child?" he asked, frowning.

"No one important," Kalindra spat out. "Just a playmate we brought to keep Nikali company." She threw a look at Tyentso so venomous that she wanted to check herself for wounds.

Perfect. Kalindra might have played the part better if Tyentso had coached her, but she wouldn't have bet metal on it.

"He's a D'Lorus," Gadrith murmured, looking puzzled. "I didn't think Thurvishar was interested in . . ." His gaze snapped back to Tyentso. "Never mind. So you've finally given me a grandson after all this time? I admit to being surprised."

Tyentso didn't react except with a glare.

The second boy began crying too. She wasn't entirely certain if the new voice was Nikali's or Tyrin's. "Someone wants his mother," Gadrith commented.

"I don't know what you're talking about," Tyentso said from behind clenched teeth. It wasn't hard to give her father a hateful stare. That didn't even require acting.

---

[1] Tyentso's birth name was Raverí. Presumably, Qoran had told his wife about the real identity of Quur's newest emperor.—T

Gadrith presented her with a rare smile. "Yes, you do. Now let's stop play-ing games. I've changed my mind about who I'll punish for your willfulness."

She closed her eyes for a moment, as if in pain. Then she swept the circlet off her brow and tossed both Crown and Scepter into the portal mouth, which snapped shut.

A shadow against a bookcase, one out of Gadrith's line of sight, slid away and vanished.

"Better," her father said. "Now the sword."

"I'll have to cast a portal spell of my own," Tyentso warned. "I don't carry the fucking thing on me."

"Let me remind you that I know what a portal spell looks like," Gadrith said in response. "Do not deviate."

She didn't. This part would be played straight now that she'd confirmed Gadrith was Relos Var's unwilling pawn.

She opened a portal midair; a small, dark sword fell through. She'd known she'd have to transport the damn thing. Fuck if she was going to keep it in such a way that she'd ever have to *touch* it. Urthaenriel landed on the ground with a rather anticlimactic thunk. Tyentso waved a hand and appeared to close the portal.

She didn't. She just made it invisible. Keeping it open was hell on her tenyé reserves, of course. She'd never have managed it before, even if she'd been able to cast that spell. The rules had changed now that she was emperor. She was reasonably sure that the god-kings or the Immortals themselves had access to larger reserves of tenyé, but damn if she wasn't right up there in those ranks. And if that Havar D'Aramarin bastard was good with gates, she'd bet metal that Grizzst, the man who'd created the Crown and Scepter, had been better.

Gadrith picked up Urthaenriel, the artifact he'd spent two lifetimes chasing in vain.

Third time's the charm, Tyentso supposed. What she was really curious about was why on both worlds Relos Var thought that Gadrith would just hand Godslayer over now that he had it. She saw the moment when Gadrith had the same thought.

She also saw the moment he flinched.

Fuck if she didn't know *exactly* what that was. Gaeshe had been her damn business for sixteen years, not even counting the four she'd spent trapped on a tropical island with Kihrin D'Mon. She knew the signs.

Relos Var hadn't just used Grimward to bring Gadrith back as a free agent. *Relos Var had gaeshed him.*

Tyentso's mouth twisted as she contemplated if it might be possible to get her father caught up in a gaesh loop. Possible, but probably not wise to plan on it. Relos Var was unlikely to give easily twistable orders, and Gadrith knew too much about how gaeshe worked.

Gadrith dropped the sword as if it had become molten. Then he pulled a robin's egg out from his robes and crushed it in his hand.

Nothing happened.

Gadrith sat down again.

The two boys quieted, still tired from the first round, but honestly, Tyentso would rather have had them crying or asleep. Cruel, she realized, but far less likely for the little boy she'd basically kidnapped to reveal that not only was Tyentso *not* his mother but he'd never even seen her before.

It was admittedly one of the larger flaws in her plan.

Fortunately, Relos Var's reaction to the signal was fast, even if it wasn't instant. Only a few minutes passed before a shining portal shimmered up out of nothingness and spat out . . .

Someone who wasn't Relos Var. Two someones, in fact, neither of whom was the wizard. Both were young men who varied in attractiveness from exceptionally pretty to "no one would blame you for breaking up with your lover to run off with him" pretty.

Gadrith seemed equally nonplussed. "He couldn't even be bothered to come himself?"

The younger of the two men smiled. Said younger man was in his midtwenties, perhaps? His manner made him seem older, but Tyentso always looked at the hands. He had a young man's hands. His dress was Quuros, but not particularly identifiable as belonging to any Royal House. The clothing wasn't fancy, except for the boots, which probably cost as much as everything else he wore combined. The second man scratched at an itch of recognition—someone she'd probably only met once or twice, and not recently—but she was positive she'd never met the *really* pretty one.

Then said really pretty one started to speak. Tyentso's eyes widened. That was still Relos Var's *voice*. She had to look across the Veil to confirm it, but damn if that wasn't the wizard himself.

"Don't be offended, Gadrith," Relos Var said. "I did come myself. Some things are just that important." He held up a hand, from which dangled a silver chain and small silver skull. "And in case you have any doubts as to my identity, allow me to assure you that I'm still the one who holds your gaesh." His smile was ice cold.

Gadrith took in the man's appearance and gave a disdainful sniff.

Relos Var sighed at his companion. "No one takes me seriously looking like this, Anlyr. Honestly, I should have transitioned to my normal appearance the last time I switched back from being a dragon."

The man shrugged. "No judgment from me. That shit hurts."

Var gestured toward the sword. "Would you be so kind as to do the honors, Anlyr?"

Anlyr grinned. "It's why I'm here." He picked up the sword and made a face. "Ah, this bitch again. But hey, it's the right one. I'm surprised. I expected at least a little trickery. Although I guess he can't, can he? Whoops."

While Anlyr picked up Godslayer, Relos Var's gaze wandered over the other people in the room. He raised an eyebrow at the high general's missing hand but made no other comment. Then he frowned as he stared at the children.[2] His gaze shifted from the boys, over to Tyentso, and then back again.

---

[2] He was probably wondering why one of them looked so familiar.—T

He took note of the missing Crown and Scepter. Then he made a tiny, amused noise from somewhere deep in his chest and turned back to Gadrith.

"You've done well," he told the undead wizard, in exactly the same tone of voice that a teacher might use to praise a student who had finally managed to pass a very basic exam.

"I don't care about your approval." Gadrith held out his hand. "You promised to return my gaesh."

"I did, didn't I?" Relos Var said amiably. "But as I trust you as much as I trust the sun to spin backward, I think I'll hold on to this for a while longer. I have no more time for your games. You will *not* interfere with my plans again."

Gadrith scowled as he visibly flinched in response to what had clearly been a command given to the gaesh. "You're going back on your word?"

"After all that I have done, this is what surprises you?" Relos Var shook his head. "I had such high hopes for you once. Really, I did."

"So is that why you brought me back? Revenge?" Gadrith looked more curious than upset, now that he'd recovered from his earlier flash of embarrassing naïveté.

"Not at all," Relos Var explained. "You're a proficient wizard; I didn't have to bring you up to speed. You already know all the players, and you know both why Urthaenriel is important and how to deal with the sword. Why recreate the horse when I already own a saddle?"[3]

"I hate you," Gadrith said, with more emotion than Tyentso had witnessed from the man in all the time she'd known him.[4]

"Yes. The feeling's mutual. But you did your part and even did it reasonably well. So I won't kill you today as a professional courtesy." And then the bastard gave Tyentso an amused look, as if to say, *"Can you believe this fool?"*

Tyentso had to admit it was pretty naïve to think that Relos Var was going to give up a perfectly good gaeshed wizard like that. Even more naïve to think Relos Var would do it when the wizard in question was the man who'd murdered Relos Var's son.

Tyentso suspected revenge had at least a little to do with this fuckery, no matter how hard Relos Var denied it. Family seemed important to him too. If Relos Var always targeted family, it was only because that was his own weakness.[5]

It also occurred to her that if Relos Var decided to take his new pet wizard with him when he left, then Gadrith might just survive to see another day.

---

[3] A common Joratese expression.—S

[4] That's only because Tyentso was already dead (if only temporarily) when Gadrith had his breakdown after Kihrin claimed Urthaenriel. That was the most emotional I'd ever seen him.—T

*The Ruin of Kings,* chapter 87. Cite your sources, dear.—S

[5] I think Relos Var liked to believe it was his weakness. It's a very romantic idea, that one will rain a fiery death on anyone who messes with family. But if their safety interfered with his goals? He never hesitated.—T

He never saw us as people. That was the problem. We were, all of us, nothing more than tools. And while you obviously kill anyone who tries to steal your tools, that doesn't mean you won't break them yourself to finish the job.—S

Because even if she had felt like fighting Relos Var—which she didn't—doing so wasn't what Kihrin wanted.

Then Gadrith gestured toward the prisoners. "And are any of them necessary to your plans?"

Tyentso narrowed her eyes. *Gadrith, you petty motherfucker.*

"Not in the least." Relos Var opened up another portal. His spellwork was annoyingly graceful. Before he and Anlyr left by it, he said, "Catch up with us in Marakor when you're finished."

Which sounded a lot like permission.

The gate closed behind Relos Var, and Gadrith turned back to them. His black eyes were cold with all the anger he hadn't been able to take out on his "master."

"So. Where shall we start?" Gadrith asked.

## 62. CHILDHOOD FRIENDS

*Senera's story*
*The Mother of Trees, the Manol Jungle*
*The morning after Relos Var's attack on Grizzst's Tower*

When Senera woke, she recognized where she had to be: the Mother of Trees.

She'd never been in the royal palace before, although she knew from her previous visit that a great many of the dwellings in the vané city could only be described with words like *palatial* and *breathtaking*. They were different from the Quuros palaces, though. It was difficult to put her finger on exactly what the differences were; then she realized that for one, they were not color-coded (as almost all the Quuros palaces were), to show with a glance which Royal House controlled them. And there was an elegance to these chambers that spoke of time. Huge swaths of time in a millennia-old city that had only once known war, whose citizens prided themselves on their skill in magic, art, and craftsmanship. People willing to spend centuries decorating a single room.

She didn't know for certain she was even in the royal palace, but she guessed so, largely based on the people in the room with her. Also, the fact that she had initially thought she was outside, lying on a bed incongruously situated under a wide-limbed oak tree, leaves rustling under a golden sun.

Which seemed a ludicrous place for a recovery bed, so it must have been an illusion.

Her hand felt warm. She looked down and saw Thurvishar was holding it. Cradling it really, like it might break if he dared let it drop. He looked terrible. He must not have slept, although someone had finished healing him and must have made him change into something other than black. Gold looked good on him.

"Why does my skin hurt?" Senera said, then winced, because the act of asking the question had brought both the obvious answer and more questions besides. She remembered the fire breaching the walls of the tower, rushing at her . . .

Before she could stop herself, she'd lifted her free hand to touch her face. But she didn't feel burns or bandages. She wasn't wearing her old clothing but rather a thin silk gown. No wounds of any kind. Just normal skin, although unusually soft.

"Your skin was damaged," Khaeriel told her sternly. "So we were forced to replace it. Along with several other organs." The former vané queen was doing something with herbs on a table set up to the side of the surreal meadow. She was dressed very plainly compared to the vané styles Senera remembered–nothing more than several simple layers of dark red robes that would do a fantastic job of hiding the bloodstains.

"My eyes hurt too."

"And your mouth, throat, and lungs, I should imagine. Perhaps you were not directly in the path of the flames, but you must have been close."

"Just how much did you replace–"

"You don't want to know," Thurvishar said.

"You're going to be fine," Qown added. "Like you were never injured at all."

Senera looked around the room. Or what she assumed was a room. She just refused to assume that the vané equivalent of a hospital was an open meadow that couldn't possibly exist anywhere within the borders of the Manol Jungle. The illusion was so damn obvious Senera had to assume it wasn't meant to fool anyone. This was just someone's idea of a peaceful recovery room.

Khaeriel carefully set a ceramic cup into her hand. "Drink this. It will taste awful. There's no help for it."

"She's been dousing all of us with the stuff," Thurvishar explained. "Apparently, we were all poisoned to some degree. I'm sorry about your agolé. I know it was one of your favorites, but they had to destroy all our clothes."

Senera paused with the cup at her lip. Yes, of course. She had known, on some distant intellectual level, that Relos Var's dragon fire was poisonous. He'd warned her often enough to stay away from locations where he'd used it. Something similar to razarras poisoning–an invisible rot that might still kill days or months after exposure. Senera found herself extraordinarily glad that someone had thought to check for it.

"Thank you," Senera murmured and finished the cup in one long gulp. Khaeriel had been right: it was awful.

"What a novel change of pace to have a patient who does the sensible thing without arguing," Khaeriel said. "Now if you will all excuse me, I plan to be elsewhere when the rest of your friends arrive. Lovely seeing you again, Senera." She managed to convey the impression of all but running from the room without ever walking faster than an elegant saunter. The illusion was confirmed. She didn't cross the meadow so much as move a few dozen steps and simply vanish. Presumably having closed the door behind her.

Qown stared after the woman, confused. "Why was she in such a hurry to leave?"

Thurvishar cleared his throat. "Qown, that was Kihrin's mother."

Qown's bewildered expression didn't change.

"The woman who murdered Galen and Sheloran," Senera elaborated.

"Oh light!" Qown turned in the direction the woman had gone, now thoroughly appalled. "But she was so helpful . . . Senera, you're *friends* with her?"

Senera raised an eyebrow at the former Vishai priest until he finally realized how incredibly stupid that question was. He flushed red and became even more flustered. Sweet, in its way. Apparently, someone had forgotten that when it came to mass murder, Khaeriel was an amateur.

Whereas Senera was a professional.

As if to underline that first time she and Qown had encountered each other, she heard Rebel whistle at her. A moment later, the dhole, Fayrin, Galen, Sheloran, and surprisingly, Therin and Valathea entered the room.

"Ray-Ray!" Fayrin called out. "How are you feeling? I have no idea what's going on, but I suspect I'll just have to cope." He paused, looking thoughtful. "Last night's a bit of a blur, but I'm pretty sure I've missed a few things."

Senera levered herself up on the bed with Thurvishar's help and scooted over to the side to make room for Rebel. The dhole leaned against her body and gave her sad eyes while whipping her tail against Senera's legs.

"All right," Senera said. "We should gather everyone together. We need to talk."

### Teraeth's story
### The Mother of Trees
### Breakfast

"So how much do you think Relos Var's figured out?" Teraeth asked everyone.

The group that gathered was large, so much so that the impressively enormous royal rooms felt normal-size by comparison. It was only after Teraeth, Janel, Xivan, and Talea had left the royal suite in search of breakfast they could bring back to Talon (who couldn't leave the royal suite for fear of triggering the mimic wards again) that they discovered their friends had arrived in the middle of the night. With Senera so badly injured that it hadn't been certain she'd live.[1]

But she had, and since the subjects of vane healing typically fell into one of two categories ("perfectly fine" or "dead"), she was also capable of walking on her own and joining them. The fact that Thurvishar insisted on carrying her anyway was, frankly, *hilarious*. The dog was there too, because apparently at some point earlier, a well-meaning vané had tried to shut the dog out, at which point Rebel had simply eaten her way through a magical, solid-wood door and joined them, anyway. Teraeth suspected any attempts to keep Thurvishar away from Senera would meet with a similar fate—although one with more explosions.[2]

Teraeth wasn't certain about the wisdom of including everyone in the room, especially since Valathea couldn't cover them all using Chainbreaker. He would have preferred leaving Therin out, but given that the main point of discussion was resurrecting Doc, he had to allow that was unrealistic.

Fortunately, Qown insisted that he knew how to counter Worldhearth's scrying ability. Between Senera, Thurvishar, and Valathea, there were so many illusions slathered over their location that he suspected even Argas

---

[1] I will simply comment that given our location and Xivan's presence, there was really no chance that I was irrecoverable.—S

Logically, we knew that. Emotionally? A different story.—T

[2] That's basically accurate.—T

himself would've had trouble finding them. It was as good as they were probably going to get without holding the meeting in the Afterlife.

Which was tempting.

Senera had vouched for Fayrin, but Teraeth saw no reason why they should trust the man. Unfortunately, Thurvishar and Senera both wanted to debrief Fayrin, so he was there too, if mostly doing a good job of sitting quietly in a corner and impersonating someone with a painful hangover.

At least Teraeth had been able to keep Khaeriel out of the room. He suspected that had more to do with Galen and Sheloran being present than his own commanding authority.

"Relos Var knows about Drehemia and the Name of All Things," Galen said. "He also knows Senera's switched sides, and he knows the Lighthouse at Shadrag Gor's been destroyed."

Xivan straightened in her seat. "Destroyed? When did that happen?"

Senera sighed as she dug her thumbs into her temples. "I imagine when Vol Karoth escaped his prison. The two locations were linked."

A whole lot of people who had previously been very quiet all started asking questions, all at once.

"Stop." Janel held up a hand. "I can see that we're going to need to lay some ground rules. First, we're not going to explain *everything*. We don't have time. There is a lot going on right now. The fewer people who know certain things, the better. It's not an insult, it's not that I don't trust you—"

"Although in some cases, it actually *is* that we don't trust you," Teraeth corrected, then ducked to the side when "Kihrin" slapped his arm.

"Not helping," Janel singsonged back. "Anyway, we know why the Lighthouse is gone. I'm assuming Relos Var does not?" She glanced at Galen, Sheloran, and Qown for confirmation.

"No, he doesn't know," Qown said.

Teraeth exhaled. That was good. It wasn't a long leap from figuring out exactly what had happened to the Lighthouse to realizing that they must have done something to Vol Karoth himself.

"He already knew about Drehemia," Galen said. "He wasn't as surprised as he should have been."

"Oh, he absolutely already knew," Janel said. "He must have felt it the moment Drehemia gained her sanity back. Or he's just that good at tracking. We came across the Lash in the Afterlife. She's dead—for real this time. He killed her and reclaimed Grimward *and* Drehemia. I don't know that he would have had time to do that after he left you, but he certainly would have had time before."

"Anlyr made a comment about a girl," Galen said to Qown. "And Relos Var shushed him, remember?"

Qown nodded, then his eyes went wide, and he stood. "Oh! Oh, I almost forgot. I'd figured something out just before Anlyr kidnapped me, but I never had a chance to tell anyone—namely, someone's been using Warmonger on the Capital or at least the Quuros army. I don't know if people noticed how short-tempered everyone was? That's one of the symptoms."

"Warmonger?" It was almost funny how at least three different people said that simultaneously. Valathea, Thurvishar, and Senera all looked at each other.

Thurvishar gestured to Valathea. "After you."

Valathea inclined her head. "Thank you. Warmonger is a problem. Of all the Cornerstones, it has the broadest area of effect. Perhaps not an entire nation when we're talking about an empire the size of Quur but certainly an entire dominion. It does indeed make everyone short-tempered. Also fanatically loyal, paranoid, and cruel. While under its effects, people report feeling invincible and are prone to high-risk behavior. It's not entirely unwarranted. You'll heal faster, to the point of actual regeneration, as well as experience increased strength, endurance, and general combat ability. An army under the effects of Warmonger is nearly unstoppable."

"Why . . ." Sheloran wrinkled her nose. "Why would Relos Var want the Quuros army to be nearly unstoppable? Tyentso doesn't even like him."

"Because, as I said, it makes you prone to high-risk behavior," Senera said. "You stop thinking strategically. But mostly–" She sighed. "Mostly because of what happens when you take the stone *away*. Because Warmonger is addictive. Once they remove Warmonger, we'll all be able to experience the unique pleasure of watching an entire country simultaneously go into withdrawal." She tilted her head in Fayrin Jhelora's direction. "How are you feeling?"

"Honestly, Ray-Ray? I feel like shit," Fayrin said.

"Ray-Ray?" Thurvishar asked. "That's really his nickname for you?"

Senera sighed. "We have so many more important things to talk about."

"Oh no," Kihrin said, holding up a hand. "I think we need to discuss this."

"She's Ray-Ray, and I'm Fay-Fay," Fayrin offered with the excessive false cheer of someone pretending they weren't nursing a terrible headache. "Because we're twins."

Everyone paused. Fayrin was visibly a full-blood Quuros man. Senera was . . . Senera. Descended from white-skinned Doltari stock. Rarely had there ever existed two people who seemed less related to each other.

Senera pinched the bridge of her nose. "We're not twins. We did grow up together. And it's not what we need to be concentrating on right now." She held up a hand. "How many of the Cornerstones does Relos Var have? Warmonger, Grimward, and Worldhearth. We don't know if he reclaimed Skyfire, and the Name of All Things is no longer usable. So at least four–"

"What about the Stone of Shackles?" Sheloran asked.

"Someone on our side's recovering that," Thurvishar said, glancing at Kihrin. "Assuming he hasn't already."

"Let's not go into details," Senera said. "It's best if Relos Var thinks Anlyr hid it somewhere, exactly as ordered." She paused, biting her lip. "Relos Var and I have discussed a great many plans over the years. I'm sure he held back, but he had plans for what he'd do if he could recover all the Cornerstones and plans if he couldn't." She waved a hand toward Valathea and Thurvishar, the two people in the room who still held Cornerstones. "If he could recover all of them, he would use them as sympathetic links to strip the Immortals of their powers, channeling that energy into the gems. In effect, the Cornerstones would become full gods, ones that could be controlled by . . . anyone."

"I'm sure he left out the part where he'd then bind those gems, channeling all that power into a single source: himself," Janel commented.

Senera scowled. "Yes. I'm sure he did. However, that plan relies on two prerequisites: all of the gods dead, so they can't protest when he starts the ritual, and that he possess all the Cornerstones. Neither prerequisite has been met."

"So what was the fall-back plan?" Galen asked.

"Oh, there was a plan B and a plan C. Plan D. Plan E . . . You get the idea." Senera exhaled. "I'm personally of the opinion that he is most likely moving forward with his plans to deal with Xaltorath. It's Xaltorath that he considers the real threat. Not Vol Karoth and certainly not Kihrin. That plan looks a lot like the first one. Same ritual. It just doesn't matter whether or not he has all the Cornerstones, because it's all make believe. The point of it is to lure Xaltorath to his location using the idea of all that tenyé as bait. And then Xaltorath triggers the ritual—the real ritual—and effectively kills themselves."

"If that's the case, then the moment Relos Var goes to reclaim the Stone of Shackles from Anlyr's hiding spot, he's going to know it's been stolen," Thurvishar pointed out.

"Yes, we're going to have to make sure Relos Var doesn't think there's any point in bothering," Janel said. She shrugged. "We can't let him do that ritual, anyway. We need Xaltorath for our own reasons." She gave the vané queen an intense look. "No, I won't explain."

"I think the more pressing question is: What do we do now?" Fayrin Jhelora asked. "Someone has to make sure Empress Tyentso knows what's going on."

There was a pause.

"Are we certain she doesn't already know?" Therin asked carefully.

"Yes!" Fayrin protested. "She could never . . . She would never agree to this. She knew something was affecting the temperaments of everyone around her. She wasn't happy about it."

Teraeth took careful note of the quiet outrage in the man's expression and wondered if that loyalty was a side effect of the Cornerstone or if he'd just really hit it off with the woman. Teraeth had some sympathy. Tyentso was proud and hot-tempered and absolutely unafraid to speak her mind. She was also utterly convinced that no man would ever be interested in her without an ulterior motive. It had helped that Teraeth had never wanted a romantic relationship, but he felt sorry for anyone determined to make that work. They'd be trying to scale a very tall cliff without a rope.

"Very well," Valathea said. "Then I believe we have three main goals at the moment. The first, bring word to Tyentso about what is affecting her people. Second, finish what you all started last night and Return my husband. Once that's done—"

"I have him right here." Xivan interrupted as she held up a star tear. Then she paused, looked at the gem, and put it back into a pouch at her belt. She removed a different star tear and held it up. "I mean, *now* I have him right here."

Janel made a strangled sound. "Xivan, *don't* get those confused."

"Don't worry. I can tell them apart."

"Contacting Tyentso will be the easy part," Thurvishar said as he raised his hand. The ruby ring on his finger—the magically enchanted one that connected Tyentso with all the Gryphon Men agents—glinted in the light.

Fayrin shook his head. "You don't think I tried that? It was the first thing I did. She's not responding."

Thurvishar lowered his hand. "That's not good."

"Amazing. That would've never occurred to me. But she can teleport anywhere in the empire instantly. How exactly are we supposed to find her?"

"I don't know," Teraeth said. "But perhaps we should figure something out."

"All right," Janel said. "Here's what we'll do. Teraeth, Xivan, Kihrin, and myself will stay here with Therin and Valathea and see to Returning Doc. Everyone else puts their heads together and sees what they can figure out how to contact Tyentso and warn her about Warmonger."

"And after that, we'll deal with Xaltorath," Senera said.

Janel nodded. "Let's go."

"One last question," Therin said, stepping forward. "Where's my son?"

Everyone halted. Fayrin, because how the hell would he know differently, went as far as to look over at Talon and blink in confusion.

"We can't talk about this right now—" Janel started to say.

"No," Therin said. "We can. And we will. I already know that's Talon." He pointed at the mimic. "And you've explained that Kihrin's off doing something that you can't talk about." Therin paused to give Galen a dirty look. "But I don't think you're being honest with me. Now, I've spoken to Khaeriel and Valathea both, so I know what happened to Kihrin after I died at the Lakehouse . . ."

"You *died*?" Galen asked.

"Why should you be the only one to have all the fun?" Therin said dryly. "Killed by a dragon. I don't recommend it." He turned back to the rest of them. "I know that my son is . . . linked . . . to Vol Karoth. I know what Kihrin used to be in his past life. And now you're all dancing around something that happened to link Vol Karoth's prison to that fucking Lighthouse, and no one will tell me where my son is."

A look of slow horror stole over Valathea's expression.

"Does Vol Karoth have my son?" Therin asked.

"No," Teraeth said. Which was and wasn't a lie, but damn if this wasn't the right time to have this conversation. "And yes, Kihrin is still alive. Believe me, Janel and I would both be acting very differently if he were dead."

Therin stared at him. Teraeth was around 70 percent certain the man didn't believe him, at least not entirely, but that last bit about how Janel and he would act had been fairly convincing.

Slowly, the man nodded.

On the other hand, Teraeth didn't dare meet Valathea's eyes. She'd see right through them both. Valathea knew Janel and Teraeth a lot better than Therin did.

"Now that we have that settled," Janel said. "We have a lot of work to do. Let's begin."

## 63. THE KING RETURNS

**Janel's story**
**The Mother of Trees, the Manol**
**Noon**

Janel felt like she was being pulled in multiple directions at the same time. On the one hand, she wanted to be there for Doc's resurrection. On the other hand, something bad was happening with Tyentso. Janel had only met the woman once, but she'd made a good impression.

And if Janel harbored not so-secret desires to see the Quuros Empire fall, she didn't want it to happen in literal flames. Tyentso had, if only briefly, given Janel the faint hope that such a transition—from oligarchy to something kinder—might happen peacefully.

That was seeming more and more like a dream. The problem with duchies, countries, empires—governments—was that they were all ultimately cute little labels for the purpose of describing giant collections of living, breathing people. It was too easy to forget that. *Revolution* was such a pretty word until one realized that in the turning over societal order, a great many people always fell to their deaths. Even the Joratese version of rebellion, the most bloodless that Janel had ever encountered, that she had ever even heard of in *any* of her lives, generally only happened after someone had made such monumental mistakes that it resulted in mass casualties.

Janel felt sure that losing the empire would be more advantageous to their enemies than to them.

If there was any advantage to the seeming invasion of the vané palace by as many Quuros as it had probably ever hosted in the entirety of its existence, it was that matters were in such a state of chaos that no one noticed what they were doing. Doc's body had to be transferred from the preservation room where it was being kept to Valathea's private quarters, all without anyone noticing. Likewise, the group themselves needed to quietly congregate in Valathea's rooms. This was where the chaotic comings and goings were especially useful.

When Janel arrived, Talon was already there, since the mimic didn't need to leave the royal wing of the palace in order to go from Teraeth's rooms to Valathea's.

Doc's body waited for them, resting on the couch, covered with a cloth. Had the cloth been tucked under his chin, it might've been possible to pretend he was just sleeping.

"You can do this, yes?" Valathea didn't snap at the other woman, but her concern and worry were palpable, prickly points to her normally smooth mannerisms.

Xivan started to answer, then visibly startled and gave a hard glare to an empty area of the room. Janel immediately knew that Khae must have said something—probably something nasty. Xivan returned her attention to Valathea and said, "It might take me a little while. I'm learning as I go. But don't worry, I can do this."

Which proved to be true, just not fast. It was afternoon before she finished.

Xivan slumped back into one of the chairs, the relief and exhaustion on her face both evident. Talea reached over and squeezed the woman's hand.

Doc sat up, gasping, his hand searching around him as if for a weapon.

"Darling." Valathea sat down next to him, drew her hand across his cheek. There was a moment of profound silence as Doc stared back at his wife and then looked around the room. His mouth opened, but no words came as he saw his son, Teraeth, and his best friend, Therin, Kihrin and Janel, Talea and Xivan.

"I'm—" Doc winced as his voice came out in a rasp.

Kihrin poured a goblet of water and handed it to him. Lunch was still spread out on a nearby table, and thankfully, nobody had complained that Janel had been picking at the food the entire time.

"Thank you," Doc murmured. His gaze once more sought out his wife and son. "You're here, so I'm guessing things went well. On the other hand, this is a very small, private group, so I'm guessing things didn't go *that* well."

Therin leaned over and punched Doc's shoulder. "Goatbrains, who told you it was fine to trade your life for mine?"

"Khaeriel," Doc answered and then grimaced. "All right, fine. She didn't explicitly say that, but I feel pretty strongly that she would have, if she'd known what I was planning. You didn't . . . you didn't see how she reacted after you died, Therin. No way was I letting her be the one Thaena took out her frustrations on. Speaking of, where *is* Khaeriel?"

"She's fine," Janel said, holding a bowl of fruit in one hand while she ate with the other. "Just keeping to her rooms right now. Thaena, Galava, Argas, and Taja? Not so fine. So a bit of a mixed bag in terms of how things have gone." She didn't ask him if he remembered what had happened to him in the Afterlife. She didn't think it likely that he would.

Doc wrapped the blanket that had been draped over him more tightly around himself. He was dressed—since the whole point of this exercise had been to bring him back from the dead, leaving him naked had seemed rude. "How—" He licked his lips, frowning. "If Thaena and Galava are both dead, how am I here?"

"We didn't need Galava," Valathea explained, "because Khaemezra killed you without damaging your physical body, which your"—she smiled—"*subjects* were quick to preserve. And as for Thaena, we found a substitute."

Janel fought back laughter as Xivan waved hello to Doc. Without context, that must have seemed inexplicable. Especially since Doc knew Xivan—and knew she wasn't even a wizard, let alone someone of god-level powers.

"I don't understand," Doc said.

"That's fine," Teraeth said. "The most important thing is that you overturned the Law of Daynos."

Doc blinked at his son.

"Because that means," Teraeth continued, "that I'm not king anymore. *You* are."[1] He pointed a forefinger at his father. "And from the bottom of my heart, a most sincere thank-you, because I have places to be and people to kill—namely, Relos Var."

"Don't forget Xaltorath," Janel reminded him.

"Sure, of course," Teraeth said, "but I assumed you had first rights to that?"

"That's so sweet, but I'm willing to share," Janel said. "Everyone can help."

"How did—" Doc shook his head. "I'm sorry, I'm still processing that Thaena's dead. That . . . really? Taja?"

"Yes and no," Talea said. "Do you want something to eat? I don't think Janel's eaten *everything* from lunch yet, or we could send out for something. If you want us to tell you what happened, it'll take a while. It's a bit of a story."

"It's not that much of one," Kihrin/Talon said. "Thaena decided that if she couldn't perform the Ritual of Night, next best was to tweak the ritual to affect a country instead of a race. So she tried to wipe out the vané, and in the battle to stop her, Argas, Taja, Galava, and Thaena herself were killed. With them out of the way, Relos Var's happily skipping along toward whatever nastiness he's been planning from the start while Khored and Tya desperately run around trying to put out demon fires."

Talea wrinkled her nose at the mimic. "You left out the part where the Guardians had figured out how to pass along their positions, so while Khaemezra and Eshimavari are both dead, Thaena and Taja are not."

Doc blinked. "What was that?"

"I'm the new Thaena," Xivan said, then raised Talea's hand, still held in hers. "And this is the new Taja. Not that we've got the full powers of either goddess yet, but it was enough for me to put your souls back in your body."

Doc's expression reflected profound shock. "I . . . I see."

"There's more," Teraeth said.

Janel fought not to wince. She really wasn't looking forward to explaining this part. It's why she'd argued so hard against having Therin in the room, but it was just impossible to keep him out without explaining why he might end up breaking furniture.

So this was going to be uncomfortable. She regarded Teraeth with miles of fondness for stepping up to take the hit.

---

[1] Had the Law of Daynos still been in effect, Terindel would have given up his crown when Thaena slew him and wouldn't have regained it just because he was resurrected.–T

Pretty sure that would have been the shortest reign in vané history. Quite possibly the shortest reign in anyone's history.–S

No, there was a Zheriasian king, Sargo, who was assassinated as he was being crowned. He still holds the record.–T

Teraeth took a deep breath. And then didn't say anything.

"Anytime, handsome," Kihrin said. "We've got all day, and I'm sure Doc's in zero hurry to go somewhere private and play happy reunion with his pretty wife."

"Fuck off," Teraeth muttered absently. "I'm trying to decide how I want to explain this." He inhaled. "All right. So Kihrin is reasonably sure that part of Relos Var's plan includes getting rid of the demons. Now, the way in which he thinks Var is likely to do this wouldn't affect Xaltorath, which means Var probably won't move forward with those plans until he's first taken care of the demon."

"None of that sounds like a problem . . ." Even as Doc said that, he was giving Teraeth and Kihrin an odd look.

Easy enough to understand why. Teraeth had acted like Kihrin was absent when it was obvious that he was right there. Valathea gave Kihrin a considered look; Janel suspected she was debating how much it would disrupt the current conversation to reveal Talon wasn't really Kihrin. The answer must have been "a lot" since she didn't do it.

"Agreed," Xivan said, who was also frowning.

"Let me finish explaining," Teraeth said. "So none of that would be a problem, except for one small detail—the demons we've been fighting, the demons who invaded—all those demons were originally humans from the same universe the first settlers were from."

"Bullshit," Doc said.

"Ridiculous," Valathea agreed.

Janel felt a spike of pure adrenaline. Because it wasn't ridiculous or bullshit *at all*. In fact, it would explain a great deal. And hadn't Xaltorath hinted . . .

"Oh Veils," she said. "'What's the difference between a human and a demon? *Time*.' Xaltorath *bragged* about it."[2]

"I don't, um—" Talea's eyes were wide.

"Janel," Xivan said gently. "Slow down and explain it to the rest of us. You know how you get when you jump ahead a dozen steps."

"We always knew," Janel said, "that demons who were originally infected humans would return to being normal noninfected humans once they entered the Font of Souls and the cycle of reincarnation. The Font realigns them with this universe. That was how Thaena cured them. But if *all* demons were originally human, then . . ." She looked back at Teraeth. "How many souls are we talking about?"

"A lot," Teraeth said. "All the souls of everyone the settlers left behind in that other universe, apparently."

Valathea turned white.

"That would be a large number," the vané queen whispered. "A very large number."

---

[2] She's quoting what Xaltorath said to Elana Milligreest before the demon unlocked her memories in the Korthaen Blight.—T

Note that Elana Kandor was Janel's most immediate previous incarnation.—S

Janel rubbed her temple. "More people than have ever existed on this world, yes."

"I spoke to my mother in the Afterlife," Teraeth said, raising a hand as that won him incredulous looks. "Yes, she's there now. Anyway, she said that she thinks that at least half the population may be comprised of these 'cleansed' demon souls. She and Galava had figured out that it was happening, but since it seemed to be in everyone's best interests, they didn't make a fuss about it."

"Let's hope she's right," Thurvishar said, "because Kihrin theorized that the Font may well have never created human souls, simply because the numbers are so large that it never would have needed to. If so, then if Relos Var does target these demons using a ritual, he might well wipe out everyone who isn't either an original settler or the reincarnation of one."

Janel felt a little dizzy. She looked around the room: the vast majority of people present wouldn't meet the qualification of "original settler."

Doc pointed a finger at Kihrin. "Can we pause for just a moment and talk about why you keep referring to Kihrin like he's not in the room when he's right there." He squinted at his wife. "Are you using illusions? Or is someone else?"

"Yes, and yes," Valathea said, "but it's not what you think."

"Let's deal with that later," Talon suggested. "Fun as I know that conversation is going to be, I'm still trying to wrap my head around 'demons can be reincarnated as *humans*.'"

"Another universe?" Talea said. Her eyes flicked to the side. "Oh. Really? I didn't know that." Talea's conversation with an invisible person might have looked like the behavior of someone less than sane if Janel didn't know about her phantom tutor in godhood.

Therin started to say something. Instead, he walked over to the table and poured himself a cup of tea.

Janel cleared her throat. "So yes. Another universe. We came to this universe from a different one, but not all of our race made the trip. We left a lot of people behind. Far more than we brought with us. Something must have happened to them. Something—" She bit her lip while she chased down the thought. *Time,* Xaltorath had said. Time must have moved more quickly in that other universe, must have given some calamity the opportunity to unfurl. They must have decided that diabolism was the most appropriate solution to whatever problem plagued them. "I need to talk to Kihrin," she murmured.

"The good news is that's more possible than I'd originally thought," Teraeth confessed. "But the main point: the timetable has escalated. Now we don't just need to stop Relos Var, we need to stop him from wiping out at least half of humanity."

Silence.

"Well, that's not ideal," Talea said. "Do you think Relos Var realizes?"

"It wouldn't matter," Janel said. "It wouldn't even slow him down. As long as enough people remain to safely continue the species, he's willing to kill all the rest."

Valathea shuddered. Her violet eyes were haunted as they caught Janel's.

"This is my fault. You tried to tell me how dangerous the man was. I should have listened to you."

An almost physical pain lanced through Janel. "You *did* listen to me. If you hadn't, maybe Relos Var wouldn't have felt like he needed to sacrifice his own brother to gain what the Assembly denied him."

"Can we not point fingers for an event that happened over four thousand years ago?" Teraeth suggested. "I think that ship has sailed." He waved a hand. "Anyway, you all needed to know about that, but truthfully, I don't know that it changes anything other than just making it that much more important that Relos Var not finish *any* fun rituals. The moment Relos Var felt Vol Karoth escape, he would have started hunting Xaltorath. And we have to assume that Xaltorath knows too by this point—"

"Wait, Vol Karoth's free?" Doc straightened. "I thought that wasn't supposed to happen for years yet!"

"We're ahead of schedule," Janel murmured.

"It's fine," Teraeth said.

"*How is that fine?*" Doc started to stand. He looked like he was about to go running off, although Janel had no idea what he thought he'd accomplish.

Teraeth put his hand on his father's shoulder and pushed him back down. "Finish. Listening." His gaze shifted from his father to his stepmother then, and turned contemplative.

Janel had a feeling she knew what he was thinking. Teraeth was wondering just how secure this conversation was, even with all the precautions they'd taken. It was so easy to be paranoid about this when so much was at stake.

Talea caught Janel's eye and winked.

Doc sat back down on the couch. "Explain, then."

Teraeth cleared his throat. "As I was saying. Relos Var and Xaltorath are preparing for what they think is the endgame. Part of that means moving to take control of Vol Karoth, whom they both think is a puppet they can control." Teraeth inhaled.

*Here it comes,* Janel thought.

"What they don't know," Teraeth continued, "is that Kihrin has beaten them to it."

Valathea whirled in her stepson's direction. "What? What do you mean?"

Teraeth started to answer, then gave Janel a pleading look.

She nodded to him, stepping forward to stand by his side. Janel put a hand behind her back so neither Doc nor his wife would see her clench it. "Xaltorath tricked me—or rather, tricked Elana Kandor—into cutting away part of Vol Karoth's souls, which is how Kihrin ended up in a position to be born in the first place. The result was a Vol Karoth who was badly damaged on a spiritual and mental level—little more than an angry child and not quite as intelligent. Xaltorath thus assumed that Vol Karoth would be in no position to stand against his plans. And since Relos Var needs to be able to control Vol Karoth, this fit nicely with his plans as well. So Kihrin fixed the damage. He—"

"*What?*" Valathea repeated.

"What does that mean?" Therin asked. "Fixed the damage how?"

Doc put a hand on his wife's shoulder. His expression grim, he looked back at Janel. "What exactly did that idiot do?"

"He fixed the damage," Teraeth said. "I suppose, if you want to look at it this way, he killed Vol Karoth. In the process, he Returned S'arric."

"He would have had to use *his own souls*," Valathea said with an utterly horrified expression. "It would have either left him as damaged as you say Vol Karoth had been previously, or it would have . . . it would have . . ."

Therin glared at Janel, sharp enough to tear flesh. "You told me my son was still alive." He didn't bother making it sound like anything other than an accusation.

"He is," Janel repeated.

"He's just in a different body now," Talon interjected. "And hey, I know at least two people in this room who know what *that's* like. Three if someone wants to go fetch Khaeriel."

Doc slowly turned and stared at "Kihrin," who waved a hand back again.

"Talon," Doc said.

"In the flesh," Talon agreed. "But pretend I'm Kihrin, please. We really want that to be our little secret until it's time to let Relos Var in on the joke." She glanced down at her fingers. "But honestly, I hope we're done with this soon, because all this 'being good' and 'nice' is seriously ruining my fun. I had no idea Kihrin was such a killjoy."

"Lyrilyn," Talea chided. "Behave."

Talon glanced over at the woman and huffed.

"So is my son . . . ?" Therin paused whatever he'd been about to say. "Where is he now?"

"Roaming around the world pretending to be a damaged and broken Vol Karoth," Teraeth said, "so neither Relos Var nor Xaltorath realize that anything's changed."

"Pretending to be Vol Karoth?" Valathea's voice had gone cold. "Or is he just . . . actually Vol Karoth?"

Janel winced. She knew Valathea well enough to be able to tell that the woman was *furious*.

The silence, as they all tried to think of something to say, was probably answer enough.

"He's fulfilling the prophecies." Therin's voice sounded choked. "You're telling me that he's fulfilling those fucking prophecies."

"The prophecies are a fiction," Janel said. "They've *always* been a fiction. They're not real. I'm not—" She paused. She really didn't want to take the time to explain how those stupid things were both Xaltorath's notes to herself and a way of manipulating the events that she'd wanted to occur. "Just trust me. They're nonsense."

"I have to say they're feeling pretty real right now," Therin snapped. "Tell me the Stone of Shackles was involved, that at least it's my son's souls in Vol Karoth's body. Otherwise, I'm supposed to believe that a twenty-year-old boy just *took over* the mind of the God of Annihilation? Because that's a hard sell."

Janel and Teraeth looked at each other. The argument could have gone worse, but that wasn't to say it was going at all *well*.

"Yes," Teraeth answered. "That's exactly what we're saying. And yes, he did. And frankly, if that wasn't true, he wouldn't have helped recover my father from the Afterlife. Because Kihrin's the one who made that possible. Without him, we wouldn't be having this reunion right now."

Valathea frowned. "I thought you three brought my husband's souls back." She pointed to Janel, Xivan, and Talea.

"We were supposed to, yes," Talea agreed. "It just didn't work. He wasn't where we thought he'd be." She shrugged. "Fortunately, Kihrin and Teraeth stumbled across him while they were doing something else. And take our word for it, it's still Kihrin."

"Yeah," Talon agreed. "If he was really Vol Karoth, he'd be an entirely different flavor of massive killjoy."

Valathea gave the mimic such a flat, hateful look that Janel knew instantly she'd just pieced together *why* Janel had been having trouble pretending the mimic was her lover. That Talon wasn't doing such a fantastic job of impersonating Kihrin because she'd known him for years but because she'd eaten his corpse.[3] Janel just had to hope that Valathea wouldn't say anything—that bit of kindling was the last thing they needed added to the fire.

Doc stood up from the couch and moved over to the table, pulling a chair out and sitting down as though his legs had been cut out from under him. He poured himself a cup of coffee and loaded up a plate with a selection of mixed vegetables and unidentifiable meats. He didn't eat or drink any of it, though, instead staring at the items for an awkwardly long period of time.

"Thank you for taking the time to explain," he finally said. Doc looked up at his son. "I assume you didn't just Return me out of politeness, though."

"My love." Valathea didn't walk to his side so much as glide. She touched his face with a delicate hand, "I would have Returned you no matter what—"

"Everyone knows you're dead," Teraeth said. "And everyone knows you can't be brought back to life because Thaena's dead too."

Janel smiled. "Which means no one's looking for you. And since there's no one alive who has more experience with Chainbreaker than you, we can use that."

---

[3] Just the brain, really. Talon didn't have time to eat more than that.—S

# 64. THE LAST MISTAKE

***Tyentso's story***
***The D'Lorus estate, the Academy at Alavel***
***Right after Relos Var left with Urthaenriel***

"Why are you asking?" Tyentso told her father. "We both know perfectly well where you're going to start." She didn't look at the boy. It was its own kind of tell, if you knew what to look for. Now, Gadrith did.

"True," Gadrith allowed. Then: "What's his name?"

"Leave him alone!" Kalindra screamed. "He's a child, and he's not her son!"

"*Shut up,* Kalindra," Tyentso said, hoping with all her might that the woman would get the fucking hint. "Trust me when I say my father does not care, and he won't believe you." Her gaze sharpened on her father. "But she has a point: he *is* a child, and that's barely an appetizer as far as tenyé goes. Are you really so petty that you'd make a tsali out of Tave's souls for no other reason than because he's my child?"

"Tave?" Gadrith asked.

Tyentso sighed. "It's his nickname."

"Charming," Gadrith said. "But no, I won't kill him. I could use a new apprentice to replace the one I lost."

Tyentso didn't hide the shiver that washed over her that time. That had always been an option too—that Gadrith would decide to gaesh the child and take him away to experience whatever horrors the monster had perpetrated on Thurvishar. Since her plans had hinged on Gadrith trying to kill the boy, this complicated matters.

But not irreparably so.

She'd just have to fall back to plan B.

"So, what happens next?" She squinted at her father. "Fight me for the Crown and Scepter? Try to put a third 'hey, I killed an emperor' notch on your belt? Because I'm not Gendal, and you don't have the Stone of Shackles this time."

"You forget I too wore those artifacts," Gadrith said. "And I've sent them someplace where you cannot use their powers. I don't think you've grown so proficient in just a few months that you can beat me." He pursed his lips. "Especially not when you're blinded by rage and grief."

Tyentso rolled her eyes. "Oh sure. Because that's going to work. You should

have left with Relos Var, Gadrith. You could have walked out of this alive."
Her gaze flickered over him. "Alive by certain definitions, anyway."

Gadrith looked decidedly unimpressed. "You doubt my will?"

Tyentso laughed her very best evil witch laugh—the one she'd spent some
damn energy on back in the day because it had always amused her to no end
to give the sailors nightmares. "Oh no. I know you'll do it. I don't doubt your
determination, just your intelligence. I can't believe you thought you could
extort me into doing what you wanted by threatening other people. I'm not
*Kihrin*, Gadrith. Whose fucking daughter do you think I am?"

The faintest whisper of confusion showed on his face, as he tried to decide
if she was lying. He gestured over his shoulder at the boy. "But he's your—"

"He's *not* my son," Tyentso said with a scoff. "He's some stray I picked up
and had Caless patch up to look like a D'Lorus. Go check if you don't believe
me. You think a kid that adorable could possibly come from *our* bloodline?
Please. In fact, the first time I ever saw this moppet in my life was yesterday
evening. But you know how it is. I wasn't sure that you'd really believe I'd cave
if you were only threatening the Milligreests. It all depended on how much
attention you'd been paying, and I couldn't be certain."

Tyentso pointed to each in turn. "I mean, Qoran dumped me knowing full
well that the witch-hunters were on their way. Jira's the bitch he wouldn't leave
for me. And as for the others—" She shrugged and ignored the increasingly
dark look on Qoran's face. Sure, they'd been getting along since she took the
throne, but he knew what he'd done.

Jira, on the other hand, was giving her an inscrutable look that Tyentso
couldn't quite interpret. It was either a grudging respect or she was contemplating exactly how many times she could stab Tyentso's liver in the next five
seconds. She'd almost freed one of her hands too, although it looked like she'd
dislocated a thumb in the process.

"Why would I care about the others? But it had to seem authentic, or you'd
never have fallen for it. So I thought, what if you found out I was hiding a 'love
child' with the Milligreests? And that worked like a peach. You didn't even
question why I handed over Godslayer without so much as a single lightning
bolt tossed at your ass."

"Wait," Gadrith said. "What do you mean?" He tilted his head. "That
wasn't Urthaenriel?" He started to look genuinely horrified.

He was no doubt starting to consider the possibility that he might have
unintentionally lied to Relos Var. It was tempting to confirm it, just to see if
it triggered the gaesh loop. But no, finding out it wasn't the real Godslayer
(although it had been) would have just compelled him to keep looking until
he located the real one.

Behind him, one of the children let out a tiny, soft gasp. Tyentso made a
point not to respond or look back, but she was reasonably sure that she'd seen
a wisp of shadow curling like fine mist near the couch.

Perfect.

"Not your problem," Tyentso told her father with her most annoying smirk plastered on her face. "That's going to be Relos Var's problem. I mean, come on. You can't tell me that you'd be unhappy to see someone fucking with *him*, would you?"

Gadrith looked supremely torn.

But finally, he shook his head. "I'm afraid I can't allow you to distract me anymore."

"I wasn't *trying* to distract you." Tyentso scoffed. "I fucking well succeeded."

She magically grabbed the enchanted portal she'd kept open through the entire talk with Relos Var and the second conversation with her father after. An instant later, she'd flipped it, pushed it to the floor, and enlarged the circumference. Oh, and stripped the invisibility spell, because she wanted that bastard to understand what she'd done.

Even if Gadrith had known how to block portals (she assumed he did), he couldn't do it with the number of portals he'd needed various people, himself included, to open to make this whole transfer happen. To prevent that from being a problem, he'd spread out the hostages, so none of them were close enough to each other (save the toddlers) to grab with a single well-placed portal spell.

Or that was the theory, anyway. Tyentso assumed no one had bothered to tell Gadrith about the time Relos Var had opened a single portal that covered the entire damn bridge spanning Demon Falls to Atrine. Or that the secret to opening a larger-than-normal portal was just to dump more tenyé into it.

So she made the portal the size of the room. Fuck Gadrith. Some of those books were hers, anyway.

The portal didn't catch her father. She hadn't wanted it to; that had been the whole point of giving him enough warning to protect himself. Which he had. As soon as she opened it, he'd warped part of the wall to create a platform for himself, ensuring that he didn't fall through. She'd done something similar, although less wall and more magical barrier. But that wasn't important.

What was important was that none of the Milligreests were in danger anymore. She'd taken precautions. The room she'd cleared out for them back at the palace was lined with a solid two feet of cotton-stuffed pillows, just to make sure the babies didn't hurt themselves when they fell. Hopefully, no bookcases fell on anyone, but that's why Jarith was tagging along.

Tyentso may have been a monster, but even she had limits.

Their absence left her alone in a very large, very empty room with her father.

Tyentso grinned as lightning played over her hand. "Now that we've put the kids to bed, where did we leave off?"

# 65. THE DUEL, AGAIN

*Tyentso's story*
*The D'Lorus estate, the Academy at Alavel,*
*What used to be the library*
*Just after taking the Milligreests to safety*

Even without the Crown and Scepter to invigorate him, Gadrith was no push-over. This was, after all, a man who had killed two emperors previously, one of whom was ready for the attempt. Since his second reanimation, he'd taken time to craft talismans for himself, and he wore them now. He was prepared: difficult to hurt magically, and nearly impossible to hurt physically.

Of course, Tyentso was also prepared. And even without the Crown and Scepter on her, she could still draw upon the tenyé of Quur. It was nice to have the upper hand against Gadrith for a change.

Also, she had a few other tricks he didn't know about. To that end, she tossed out a bolt of lightning to cover a second portal she opened again in the back of the room. It was easier to have one waiting.

"Clever," Gadrith said, attempting to condense a ball of acid around her head. "How did you open the portal that quickly?"

He wanted to engage in shop talk. How nice.

"Oh see, what I did was—" Tyentso sidestepped the acid ball. "Fuck off. Do you really think I'm going to tell you?" She tossed a ball of roaring fire his way. Her best bet was to cause the bastard enough structural damage that even Grimward couldn't keep him functional.[1]

The flame ball sputtered and died a good two feet in front of Gadrith. That was, without a doubt, the largest aura she'd ever seen. Naturally, he was warded against fire; it was one of the first defenses the Academy taught. But sometimes people forgot the small things. She'd made the mistake of not checking the last time they'd fought. She wasn't going to make that mistake again.

In some ways, a magical duel was like a game of Zaibur. Both wizards planned their strategies while attempting to predict their foe's. In the end, it often came down to who did a better job of it: what sort of protections they'd planned. Would they ward against fire or swords? Would they go all offense, hoping for a quick victory, or would they lean toward defenses, hoping to tire out their opponent? Each spell cast, each protection raised, cost the wizard in terms of available tenyé. This was why knowledge of your enemy was

---

[1] Which we know is possible. See: Relos Var vs. the Lash.—S

important: there was no sense using energy to stop swords if your opponent never used them.

Unless you had simply a ridiculous amount of tenyé at your disposal and could afford to splurge.

Gadrith was playing a defensive game. This told Tyentso that he expected the loss of the Crown and Scepter to drain the elephant's share of her available reserves. It was a good theory, a logical theory.

It was wrong.

For all his arrogant boasting, he hadn't held those artifacts for more than a half hour. Tyentso, on the other hand, had made it a point to ferret out the inner workings of her office tools almost from the moment they came into her hands. Research, research, research.

Gadrith launched a blistering shower of molten metal her way, forcing her to throw up a hurried barrier while skipping backward to avoid the barrage. Clearly, he expected her to be distracted long enough for a follow-up, but she didn't give him time. She turned invisible and then teleported.

He launched a devastating one-two blast of lightning and metal fléchettes through the space where she'd been standing.

He couldn't see it, but she grinned at the momentary confusion on his punchable face. He hadn't expected her to vanish. Maybe he thought she couldn't teleport without the Crown and Scepter. It wasn't even an illogical conclusion; she hadn't been able to teleport prior to becoming emperor, after all.

But his hilarious look of stupefaction wasn't as important as the valuable seconds her stunt had bought her. By the time he pinpointed her new location (she was invisible, not inaudible), it was too late for him; she'd opened another small but extremely important portal just above her right hand.

She caught the large yellow gem that tumbled through.

The rush of tenyé from holding Skyfire made the constant stream from the Crown and Scepter pale by comparison. She almost felt bloated from all the extra energy rushing into her.

"Block this, asshole," Tyentso said, still grinning. She sent a beam of yellow-white superheated flame in his direction. Gadrith raised a hand to block it, but the plasma burned right through, taking out three of his fingers, the wall behind him, the wall behind that . . .

Oops. Apparently, she was going to need to be careful, lest she accidentally start incinerating holes through random students walking around the school campus outside.

Gadrith screamed, which was interesting. Tyentso hadn't entirely been sure how much his undead nerves truly carried pain sensations and how much he just pretended. But that scream sounded pretty real.

Of course, it would be temporary. Grimward held him together, and purple-black energy was already forming finger shapes to fill in the missing pieces. Gadrith turned to face her; Skyfire's brilliance made concepts like invisibility laughably quaint. It was at that moment that a large cloud of black smoke erupted in the center of the room.

Jarith had returned.

He tossed something in Tyentso's direction, but given how fucking bright Skyfire was, she couldn't make out more than one or two vague shapes clattering to the ground near her.

With the finely honed instincts of one who trafficked in demons suddenly seeing a demon that he himself hadn't summoned, Gadrith made a twirling and pulling gesture toward Jarith. Bands of blue-green energy encircled the demon. Whatever it was must have hurt, because Jarith started screaming.

Most wizards knew basic strategies on how to fight demons. Gadrith, with his predilection for soul-based magic, knew better than most. Jarith would have been in a lot of trouble right then if he hadn't been ready for exactly this and brought reinforcements.

It was the reason Tyentso had left the other portal open.

Because everything happened so quickly, Tyentso had to reconstruct it later. But what she figured out was this: Jarith had appeared as a cloud of smoke right in front of Gadrith as a distraction, while Kalindra and Jira used the portal that Tyentso had left them to return to the fight.

Gadrith was warded against swords; any long blades that tried to penetrate that two-foot aura would be turned, harming the wielder as a result. But assassins liked daggers precisely because they were small enough to be shielded from that nonsense by the auras of their wielders, allowing them to slip right past magical defenses that would stop a sword cold.

Kalindra slit Gadrith's throat in both directions, cutting down to cartilage, turning his gloating laugh into a raspy wheeze. She then plunged her blades into his eyes and left them there.

Meanwhile, Jira wasn't idle. It turned out that for all that she preferred to use swords, she knew her way around smaller blades just fine. As Gadrith reached for the daggers stuck in his eyes, Jira darted forward and slit the tendons under his armpits. If he'd been alive, it would have permanently removed his ability to move his arms. As it was, it slowed him down while Grimward's magic compensated.

None of this killed him. Grimward saw to that. But it did neutralize his ability to cast most spells for a handful of seconds.

In a wizard's duel, ten seconds during which your opponent cannot react with magic might as well be an hour. It's all the time in the world.

"All of you, get clear!" Tyentso ordered.

Jarith, freed of the energy bonds, had the fastest reaction time in the room. He grabbed Kalindra, and they both vanished.

Tyentso telekinetically shoved Jira back through the open portal and closed it. It wasn't very dignified, and Tyentso was woman enough to admit she took a small amount of pleasure in that, but it also kept the woman safe. Tyentso had promised Jarith, after all.

Even an undead monster like Gadrith needed eyes to see with, at least in the mortal realms. Gadrith must have slipped his vision past the Veil based on his reaction as Tyentso stepped forward with Skyfire in her hand. She'd never attempted to look at the artifact with wizard's sight herself, but she imagined it must have been like . . . well, like looking at the fucking sun.

Because metaphorically and symbolically, Skyfire *was* the fucking sun.

Clenching the artifact tightly in her fist. Tyentso stepped inside Gadrith's aura. She grabbed the back of his hair with her left hand and pulled his head back, exposing the double slit Kalindra had left across his throat. She then shoved her entire hand, including Skyfire, into that gaping wound and let it do what it did best: *burn.*

The flame flowed like liquid and gas at the same time. It rolled down Gadrith's throat, filling his stomach and intestines. It roiled up, into his head, burning away his brain. Light shone through the holes where his eyes used to be, the holes in his arms and ribs. The daggers still embedded in him softened, melted, and then evaporated. It would be poetic to say that his flesh turned to ash and blew away in a wind, but the truth was that Skyfire's flame was so hot, not even ash remained. A pit in the floor a good five feet across turned to molten rock. If the artifact hadn't been protecting Tyentso, she would have disintegrated right along with her father.

"Come back from *that,* you piece of shit," Tyentso muttered, staggering backward.

She sat down on the floor and just let herself breathe. It felt nice. It would have been nice to just sit there and pretend that all her problems had now been solved.

Sadly not. There was still plenty of work to do.

It wasn't over.

Tyentso pushed herself back up to her feet and cast a spell. She'd learned a bit of necromancy over the years. Of course she had. Everyone who'd ever had the distinct misfortune to have to survive around Gadrith D'Lorus probably learned at least a little, as a survival mechanism, if nothing else. But in her case, her interest had been more personal, had never involved animating corpses, and had predated her ever meeting her father.

Tyentso's interest had been ghosts.

It was an interest that she found grimly helpful at that moment. She even found no small amount of satisfaction in the idea that the only reason she knew how to do this was because of a ghost that Gadrith himself had created.[2] She removed a small crystal sphere from inside her agolé, the stone not much bigger than an eye. It wasn't a tsali stone, and it wouldn't keep Gadrith's soul trapped for more than a few days.

But it would do it for long enough. She'd never personally learned how to make a tsali, but if Caless didn't know the trick of it, Tyentso would eat the Crown and Scepter of Quur.

The crystal began to glow, and she double-checked to make sure he was trapped. Gadrith had killed too many damn people in this house for her to take it as assumed that any lingering ghosts here would automatically be his.

But it was his. She smiled to herself as she tucked the crystal away. That was when she noticed that the Crown and Scepter of Quur were just lying

---

[2] Presumably, she's referring to the ghost of Phaellin D'Erinwa, whom Gadrith murdered when they were both students.—T

there on the floor. She had a feeling that those were the items that Jarith had tossed at her while she'd been fighting her father. She scooped those up, setting the Crown at a jaunty angle over her cloudcurl hair and tucking the wand into her raisigi. Wouldn't have done to forget those, now would it?

Then she opened a portal back to the Capital. She just needed to check in on the Milligreests, and then she could . . .

She ducked to the side as a Khorveshan sword bounced off the magical shield of talismans she wore. It would have been a nice hit too.

"*Do you mind?*" she spat at Jira Milligreest.

The woman didn't look like she minded at all. Nor did she look even the slightest bit guilty about taking a swipe at the first person to step through the gate. She did, however, lower her sword and take an awkward step to the side.

Awkward because of all the pillows.

"Since it's *you*," Jira didn't make that sound like a compliment, "I'll assume that means we won."

Tyentso didn't think she needed to dignify that with an answer. The room was a mess. Someone—probably Jarith, but who knew really?—had broken the furniture to free the whole family. Eledore was awake and fussing over her father, which made sense, what with the severed hand and all. Kalindra was checking on the children, whom Tyentso was pretty sure were about to start building pillow forts.

Everyone was very quiet, and it didn't take Tyentso more than a second to realize why.

Jarith also stood there.

He looked like Jarith too. Well, he mostly looked like Jarith. He still hadn't completely gotten the hang of not leaking shadows around the edges, but nobody would look at him and not think it was Jarith. Or a demonic variation of Jarith.

Tyentso couldn't blame his family for staring in shock. Qoran would probably have been shouting, but he was still under the effect of that silence spell, and he might have been going into real shock besides.

Jira just pointed at him, while still staring at Tyentso. "Explain. I'm going to assume this is your work, and it's not funny."

"It's not her work, Mother," Jarith said.

Jira wouldn't look at him, but tears started welling up at the corners of her eyes. She visibly swallowed. Her finger shook.

"Daddy!" A shout of pure glee came from under a gold-embroidered red velvet cushion.

"No, don't go near—" Jira started to say, panic in her voice.

"Please, it's fine." Kalindra raised her hands. "Don't upset him—"

"What the hell?" Oh good. Eledore must have looked up.

"Get away from my grandson, you monster!"

"Oh, would you all just shut up!" Tyentso yelled. She threw up a magical wall separating the adults in the room. "Everyone be quiet. I seriously do not have time for this shit."

Jarith picked up his son, who was wide-eyed and hid his face against his father's chest. Tave started crying. Kalindra, who was still near the boy, picked him up. Evidently, he was only upset that Nikali was getting picked up while he wasn't, because he quieted immediately.

Thankfully, everyone else stayed silent.

Tyentso pinched the bridge of her nose. "First, yes, Gadrith's dead. Thanks for your help on that. It's appreciated. Nice team effort there. Second, yes, that is Jarith. Believe me, I have spent enough time with him in the last twenty-four hours to guarantee you that there is no demon in the history of the empire who has ever been this well behaved. Thanks for your help on that as well." She lowered her hand. "I swear by all the gods, Qoran. Maybe he is 'technically' a demon, but he's still managing to be the fresh flower of any room he's in." She glared at Jira. "I can't imagine where he gets it from."

Jira made a rude gesture at Tyentso.

"Anyway, let's get Qoran to my physickers so we can reattach his hand. And then I want you all . . . I don't know . . . somewhere else. We'll figure out a safe place. Just not with the army, because I still don't know what's causing everyone to act so strange—"

**It's Warmonger,** Jarith said. **We should return to the Manol and talk to the others.**

"Warmonger?" Tyentso frowned. "You mean the Cornerstone Warmonger? But why—"

Her brain finally caught up. Finally. That nagging piece of information that had been itching at her for well over a day slotted into place, and it all made sense. The Cornerstone that Nemesan had used to keep an entire damn country of raving fanatics under his thrall. The Cornerstone that had made them so hard to hurt, so vicious, so fearless, that the nation of Laragraen had held off both Quur and the Kirpis vané for almost a hundred years. Yes, of course. That fucking *Warmonger*.

"Right," Tyentso said. "Thanks for clearing that up."

"What about *your son*?" Kalindra said flatly, still bouncing Tave on her hip. The boy was looking at Tyentso with big, black eyes.

Her mother always used to say that D'Lorus eyes were terrifying as an adult and adorable as a child. Now Tyentso understood. That kid's puppy dog stare was ridiculous.

Then what Kalindra had actually asked sank in.

"Yeah, no," Tyentso said, waving her fingers at the boy. "You know damn well he's not really my kid. He was a trap. I figured Gadrith would try to tsali him, and when he did, well. It was going to blow up in his face." She paused. "Not literally. Magically." She paused again. "The boy would've been fine."

Kalindra just stared. "You are such an asshole," she said.

Tyentso laughed. Gods, she was tired. "Yeah," she agreed. "Guilty. I am an asshole. I blame my father. My mother was a much nicer person."

Jarith shook his head.

Tyentso raised a finger to the demon. "You're judging me. I can feel you judging me."

"Everyone's judging you but the children," Jira snapped, "and they'd be judging you too if they understood. Kalindra, darling, I agree that she's horrible, but you can't reward that behavior by putting a child in her custody."

Kalindra was obdurate. "She doesn't have to raise him. Royals don't raise their own children, anyway. They pay other people to do it for them. But she claimed this boy was a D'Lorus, so guess what?" She glared at Tyentso. "Congratulations on your adoption. There are now two living members of House D'Lorus. I'm sure Thurvishar will be thrilled to find out that he's an uncle. Or a brother. Or however that works."[3]

"I don't have time to argue this," Tyentso growled.

"Is she going to be my new mommy?" Tave whispered to Kalindra. He had a very strange expression on his face. Like he wasn't quite sure how he wanted to react to that.

Kalindra glanced down at the boy with obvious surprise. Tyentso didn't think he'd talked a lot, not even when he was playing with Nikali. She'd kind of assumed the kid just wasn't very good at it yet. Or more likely, too damn traumatized.

"What happened to your old mommy?" Kalindra asked him.

Tyentso rolled her eyes. She would have thought Kalindra knew better than that by now. That was not a question you asked a little kid who'd clearly been through some shit if you wanted him to stay anywhere in the neighborhood of calm. And sure enough, the boy's face scrunched up, and he started crying all over Kalindra's agolé.

Kalindra had brought that one on herself.

**She burned,** Jarith said. **He remembers, even if he can't say the words.**

No.

Tyentso's breath froze in her lungs. She felt her heart lurch in her chest. For a moment, the whole world stuttered. She couldn't have formed a single coherent thought if her life had depended on it.

Tyentso's head was full of fire and screams and the sound of her mother's voice. It was as if no time had passed at all. As if she were still there. Still watching while those bastards killed her . . . [4]

She snapped herself out of it, breath still straining in her lungs as she stared at the crying child. Jira was right: it was a terrible idea.

She wanted to make it work anyway. Even though she shouldn't be allowed anywhere near children, even though House D'Lorus was not a child-friendly place to grow up. She owed the kid, right? And it's not like she'd outlawed the

---

[3] Technically, Tyentso herself stopped being a member of House D'Lorus when she became empress.—T

[4] Tyentso's mother, Rava, was executed in Alavel for being a witch, which was carried out by burning. I've looked over the evidence, and it's my opinion that Rava didn't know any magic but confessed to pull suspicion away from her daughter, who did. What is less open for speculation is that the man who sentenced her to death, Lamrin Shan, later adopted Tyentso to the bewilderment of all his peers, thus leaving her his entire fortune when he and his wife died horrifically in a demon-summoning accident.—T

Oh, I do appreciate a well-orchestrated revenge.—S

Royal Houses, just certain traitors within them. Maybe making him a prince would be apology enough.

Maybe it could work.

Then Tyentso laughed. She had to hand it to Kalindra. She didn't know if the woman had done it on purpose or not, but damn if she hadn't managed to pull everyone's attention away from the literal demon in the room.

Neat trick, that. If only she could figure out how to pull something similar during council meetings.

"We'll talk about this later," Tyentso finally said. "Let's get Qoran to a healer and go visit some vané, and then you all can scream at me about what a terrible mother I'm going to make to your heart's content. But let's save the world first, okay?"

# PART II

## GAMBITS

# 66. The Tower

*Senera's story*
*Grizzst's Tower*
*After returning from the Manol*

Grizzst's Tower was still burning when Thurvishar and Senera returned to assess just how bad the damage had been.

Bad.

"Move and countermove, I suppose," Senera said. She felt her gut twist as she glared at the inferno.

Everything they'd transferred from her cottage had been—temporarily, anyway—housed at the tower before it could be moved elsewhere. Precisely where hadn't quite been decided yet. Years of artwork, all the books she'd accumulated. All the sigil notes that she'd taken, carefully organized to make sure none of them activated accidentally.

All of that was burning.

Senera felt like such a fool.

Valathea had told them the location of a second star well they could use to return to the Manol, which honestly made Senera wonder just how many secret entrances into the supposedly impregnable Manol existed within the Quuros Empire.[1] Valathea hadn't wanted them to return to the tower at all. That would have been the smart choice, without question.

But Senera had to know. She loaded up Thurvishar and herself with all the protections she knew against razarras poisoning and had insisted they check on the damage personally, even though it broke her heart. Especially because it broke her heart.

Thurvishar had discovered how to use Wildheart to take clear away any lingering poison, so that was one good thing at least.

Thurvishar rubbed a thumb into his temple. "There has to be something . . ." He looked around. Senera imagined he was probably trying to decide the best way to dump the entire contents of Rainbow Lake on the tower. Which was not a spell Senera had ever researched and was reasonably sure Thurvishar didn't know either.

Senera shook her head. "I don't know what we could do. I just—" She took a deep breath, fought the tightening of her throat and the heavy feeling in her

---

[1] Just the two.–T
As far as we know.–S

chest. She couldn't even re-create what had just been lost. She'd destroyed the Name of All Things. All her research. All Grizzst's research. C'indrol's research. Very likely the only extant recording of the original ritual Relos Var had used to create the Eight Immortals in the first place. All of that gone.

Senera wondered if this was the smallest insight to what it must have been like for their ancestors to abandon Nythrawl, knowing as they did so that ten thousand years of magical research and knowledge had been irrevocably lost.

Honestly, she never would have thought Relos Var would be capable of it. Killing people, often in mass amounts? Yes. Of course. Deliberately destroy this much knowledge? It seemed impossible to imagine.

She felt a touch on her hand. Senera met Thurvishar's gaze. She saw the question there and knew that if she said no, he'd respect it. He wouldn't insist that some kind of physical contact was for her own good, that she needed this, that she was just too stubborn, too proud.

Senera grabbed his hand and squeezed. He let her without comment or complaint. He didn't try to pull her into his arms.

Gods, she loved him.[2]

"Do you want to return to the Manol?" he suggested. "We can go find some of the Founders and see if they're willing to talk about magical theory?" He shrugged. "Alternately, we can rob the main Academy library. Your choice."

Senera started laughing. It wasn't that funny, but once she started, she found she couldn't stop. She was left gasping, aware that she was perching on the precipice of devolving into tears. And she'd be damned if she was going to let Relos Var make her cry.

"Let's save our budding career as book thieves for another day," Senera said. "For now, let's just go back . . ." The words trailed away as she continued staring at the burning tower.

There was a curtain over the window on the highest story of the tower. She hated that curtain, had hated it from the moment she'd first set eyes on it, largely because she was reasonably certain it would've been rejected by any self-respecting velvet house. She was equally sure it had never been washed once in the entirety of its existence, because at his heart, Grizzst had been the most horrible slob.

*That* curtain wasn't burning.

Senera blinked. "Are we sure *everything* in the tower is on fire?"

Thurvishar gave her an understandably odd look and then returned his attention to the fire. "I . . ." He paused. "Hold on a minute." He put a hand to his neck; no doubt doing something using Wildheart.

He let out a single, startled laugh. "Grizzst, you absolute madman."

Senera allowed herself to feel the tiniest amount of hope. But yes, thinking back, it did seem odd that a man who'd managed to keep his notes and books

[2] Wait. What was that?—T
   What?—S
   You just . . . is that really what you were thinking?—T
   I couldn't possibly know what you're talking about.—S

intact over several millennia hadn't thought to do anything about accidental fires. Or not-so-accidental ones, in this case.

Or in particular the fires caused by a certain dragon he'd been secretly working with and not-so-secretly didn't trust.

"What was the sigil you looked up that makes things resistant to fire?" Thurvishar asked her.

She took a deep breath and reached for her brush.

The main floor of the tower was a loss. The room was black from soot and ash, literally oven hot even after they'd finally figured out a way to put out the fire. All the furniture down on that level, the tapestries and rugs, were destroyed. The smell of woodsmoke and hot stone overwhelmed the scent of evaporated spilled wine, evidence of the smashed bottles from Grizzst's extensive collection of alcohol. White smoke billowed out the windows, filled the room with fog.

The smell vanished as Senera set up the air glyph on both herself and Thurvishar. Logically, she knew it was probably a much more sensible idea to wait until the fire was completely out before assessing the level of devastation. The fire wasn't likely to cause any permanent damage to the feldspar of the tower, but depending on how hot the temperature had become or how much wood had been used in the tower's construction, it was possible that the building might weaken enough to collapse.

If Grizzst had done something to protect the other floors, she wanted to remove the contents before anything worse happened.

Or before Relos Var returned. They had a few hours leeway; Senera planned to make the most of them.

"Words cannot even begin to express how glad I am that we finished cleaning this room," Thurvishar said.

Senera laughed. Because it was true; they'd taken all the books, the stacks of notes, the centuries' worth of random papers—and, of course, their own notes on recent events—and moved them to the library level where they belonged. The ground floor had been turned into a receiving area for guests, under the general theory that perhaps their most sensitive notes shouldn't be in the first room entered by everyone who visited.

"I reserve my judgment until we see how the other floors are faring," Senera said. She moved her vision past the First Veil as she reached the stairs.

The magical aura surrounding the door to the second floor was blinding bright, impossible to ignore. Said door was made of wood and yet completely unburned, so at the very least, it seemed to be some sort of protection against fire. Quite possibly something more dangerous than that as well.

"You wouldn't happen to be familiar with Grizzst's wards, would you?" Senera asked. "From the weeks you've spent here before? Or your past life."

Thurvishar's mouth twitched. "No, not so much." He took up a position next to her and concentrated on the door as well. "I don't think it's anything actively dangerous, though. Just defensive."

"That's what I'm seeing too," Senera said, "it's only that I don't think 'just defensive' is Grizzst's style."

"An excellent point," Thurvishar said. "Let's look deeper." He squinted as he concentrated on the door.

The problem with someone who was largely self-trained was that one never knew exactly what they'd figured out how to do. Grizzst hadn't shared most of his magical knowledge with, well, anyone. He was credited with writing a book on demonology, but Senera had to assume it had either been a joke or a dare considering it was effectively a treatise on exactly the sort of healthy living Grizzst himself had never once practiced.[3]

One couldn't assume his magic would behave in a predictable way.

"Ah, there it is," Thurvishar said. "If you strip away the first layer of ward, you activate a different layer of ward. Much deadlier." He paused. "Electrified."

"Ah, right up your alley," Senera said.

"Yes," Thurvishar agreed. "Cover me? Just in case something unexpected comes up."

"There goes my plan to abandon you when you need me most," Senera said.

"There's always next time," Thurvishar replied, smiling.

She snorted and forced herself to concentrate on the magic and not the banter.

"Shall we try opening a gate?" Senera suggested.

"Be my guest," Thurvishar said. "I would think the wards are blocking that, but perhaps Grizzst lost some of his paranoia over the centuries."

"When you put it like that, it does seem rather a moot point." She quickly cast the gate spell to come out in the library—a trip she'd made several times.

The gate refused to open on the other side.

It made sense. Grizzst had designed the barrier roses for the Manol vané. Of course he could block gate access to his own tower.

At a guess, the wards had been activated by the fire, a defensive measure that neither Thurvishar, Kihrin, or any of the other visitors had ever activated precisely because none of them had been inclined to set the tower on fire. Senera suspected the wards would persist until someone took them down with a keyed command or the first floor had cooled down. It was possible that there was some sort of lever or device that would trigger the all clear as well, but that would likely be inside the very areas they were trying to access.

Likewise, they could travel from the Manol through the gate in the basement workshop (assuming that access hadn't been shut down) but ironically couldn't access the Manol without first breaking through the wards.

"We could use the other gate, I suppose," Thurvishar said. "Just need to hop over to the Kirpis and hope that those eidolons are still deactivated."

"Oh, I really wish we had Urthaenriel," Senera said. "We could take care of this just like—" She snapped her fingers.

Thurvishar gave her a small, amused smile. "It's a rare thing for a wizard to wish they had Godslayer close by, you know."

She scoffed, shaking her head. "Yes, well. Whoever said I was smart?"

---

[3] It seems to largely operate under the premise that successful demon summoning requires one to be pure of mind and body. Which is nonsense. Personally, I lean toward the "joke" possibility.–T

"I did," Thurvishar replied. "And I do, often. Because you are."

Senera stared at him and felt very odd. She felt warm, which was ludicrous because she was warded every single protection against heat she could . . . Oh.

She was blushing.

There was no way Thurvishar hadn't noticed, but he didn't comment on it. "He wasn't really trying to destroy the tower, you know," he told her. "This was just a flyby."

"I know," Senera said. "Believe me, I know."

Thurvishar returned to contemplating the door. "We'll have to take down both wards at once."

"And if there's a third layer of warding?" Senera asked.

He just raised an eyebrow at her. They both knew well enough what would happen if there was a third layer: they were screwed.

"You're better with lightning spells," Senera said. "I'll take the first layer. You take the second. The timing is going to have to be absolutely perfect, you realize."

"Hmm." Thurvishar offered her his hand.

Senera stared at it for several long heartbeats. Just because she knew that she should have been a telepath, that her real witchgift was something other than copying spell maps, didn't mean that she was automatically good at it. It didn't mean she knew how to use those abilities effectively.

But Thurvishar did.

She clasped his hand and squeezed.

No words were exchanged, not even mental ones. Rather, she felt the anticipation, knew the moment that changed into action, felt the stirrings of mental energy as Thurvishar readied his spell. She found it a challenge to block him out enough to concentrate on her own business instead of on his. There was a moment of hesitation on his part when he was ready but knew she hadn't quite reached the same point. Then she had.

They struck as one.

She felt something like having her ears pop, as a pressure she hadn't even been consciously aware of feeling vanished, leaving her staggered. But nothing else happened.

There hadn't been a third ward.

"Upstairs or downstairs first?" Thurvishar asked.

"Downstairs," she said, although she desperately wanted to check the second floor, where the library was with its books and papers. "That's where the barrier rose gate is, and that's where any sensible person would have left the ward controls."

"Mark your words," Thurvishar said.

She laughed. Indeed, *any sensible person* hardly sounded like a category that had ever included Grizzst the Mad.

They both headed down the stairs to the basement door, which, like the door to the second floor, showed no sign of being burned. Senera reached out to touch it.

Thurvishar grabbed her wrist.

"Please, allow me," he said. He didn't reach for the door himself. Instead, he put a hand to his neck, to where he wore Wildheart. The wooden door seemed to physically withdraw as if it were pulling away from a hot surface. The locking mechanism fell to the ground with a heavy clanging sound.

At exactly that moment, Senera heard movement from the other side of the door, a sharp metal noise of something far heavier than the lock hitting the floor.

"Thurvishar!" Senera grabbed Thurvishar by the collar, pulling him against her, so they were both flush against her side of the stairs.

A second later, a large section of the door disintegrated. A beam of energy Senera normally associated with the Emperors of Quur cut through the space where Thurvishar had stood a moment before.

"Thurvishar?" A querulous, unfamiliar voice called out from the other side. "Fuck! I didn't hurt you, did I?" That was followed by more noises, sharp, hard thuds.

Footsteps.

Thurvishar looked momentarily nonplussed, then his eyes widened, and he gently moved Senera's hands away from his collar. "Grizzst?" he called through the mostly missing doorway.

Something metallic glinted through the doorway. Senera summoned up a ball of mage-light. Then her mouth dropped open.

An articulated metal statue was standing not ten feet from the door, lowering a wand held in its hand. She recognized the statue. It had been lying unused on a table in the basement workshop, one of several of Grizzst's projects they had decided not to move until they'd found the wizard's notes. Really, it was less a statue than a suit of armor, but so complex and enclosed that she'd seen no way for anyone to wear it. She'd suspected that it was an unfinished eidolon or, based on what she'd previously read, a holdover from earlier attempts to resurrect various Guardians. Notably, an empty star tear diamond had been embedded in the forehead of the armor's faceplate, right above the eyes.

The statue tilted his head. "Tell me you're not the one who lit my fucking tower on fire. Because when I find the mother—"

"It was Relos Var," Senera volunteered. "Are you . . . You *are* Grizzst, aren't you?"

"Grizzst! You ridiculous old goat," Thurvishar said. "Why didn't you tell us you were down here? Why didn't you say something?" He gestured toward the suit of armor. "And what is this?"

"Well, shit, that's a lot of questions at once," the armor snapped. It didn't have a mouth and certainly wasn't moving its faceplate, but somehow it was making sound.

Magic.

Grizzst counted off on his gauntlet. "Yes, I'm Grizzst. I didn't say anything because I wasn't awake. Must have miscalculated the power requirements somewhere. And this is a contingency plan. You don't get to be as old as I am without having a few of those around. Now excuse me." He shoved his way past Senera and Thurvishar and stomped his way upstairs to the first floor.

And immediately began cursing.

Senera and Thurvishar had barely made eye contact when the suit of armor was back at the top of the stairs. "You say Var did this?" That question was clearly directed at Senera. "You're not still working for that bastard, are you?"

"No," Thurvishar said. "She's not."

The statue turned his head, giving the impression of listening to Thurvishar, then swiveled back in the direction of Senera.

"It's true," she confirmed. "Relos Var just found out yesterday. I suppose we can assume he's not happy about the situation, although I imagine he's more upset about losing the Name of All Things."

"How did you manage that?"

"We cured Drehemia," Senera said.

"Huh" was Grizzst's only response. "I wondered if anyone was ever going to figure out how Relos Var ended up sane."

"Of course, we found out. We read your notes." Thurvishar still seemed fairly appalled by the whole "animated suit of armor" situation. "Really? A suit of armor? That's your solution to an unexpected death?"

"Yeah?" The statue shook his head, and he picked up the faintly glowing remains of the dining room table. "Look, it's not like I could count on making a really nice tsali and having the vané bring me back, is it? Maybe once, but Khaevatz's kids don't like me nearly as much as their mother did. And I hate to break it to you, but the Eight Immortals may not always be around."

Senera coughed.

The statue froze. "What happened? I'm assuming you stopped that bitch from wiping out the vané . . ."

Senera might have smiled under different circumstances. She'd gone most of her life being forced to put up with the Eight Immortals being treated with such reverence. Omnipotent, omniscient beings who could do no wrong despite the bluntly empirical evidence that they did plenty wrong all the time. It was nice to hear someone else treat Thaena's memory with the gravitas it deserved.

None at all.

"Yes," Thurvishar answered. "We stopped her. She was killed. So was Galava . . . and Argas . . . and Taja."

It was impossible to know what expression the man would have worn since he had nothing that resembled an actual face, but he froze.

"Fuck," Grizzst said succinctly. Then he turned around and marched to the other side of the workshop, where several crystals were embedded in the wall. Or rather, used to be embedded in the wall.

"Fuck!" Grizzst screamed.

"I'm sensing a trend," Senera chuntered.

Grizzst the animated suit of armor swung around to face them again. "Do *not* fucking tell me that Vol Karoth has escaped!"

Senera crossed her arms over her chest and looked away. Thurvishar stared flatly at his old mentor. Neither one said a word.

There was a beat of silence.

"Well? Did he fucking escape?"

"You told us not to tell you," Thurvishar reminded him. "But yes, as it happens, that's exactly what he did."

The two living wizards could only watch for several eternally long minutes while the magically animated statue of the great, mad wizard Grizzst proceeded to throw a temper tantrum. A violent temper tantrum.

"That suit's remarkably strong," Senera commented. "Metal tables don't generally bend that easily."

"True. It is impressive." Thurvishar didn't sound impressed. In point of fact, Thurvishar sounded bored.

Senera smiled fondly at the man.

"Vol Karoth's not the worst of our problems, old man," Thurvishar said.

At first, Senera didn't think Grizzst had heard him. Thurvishar hadn't shouted. He'd said the words in a perfectly normal tone of voice, and Grizzst was being noisy.

Grizzst straightened. "Are we talking long term or short? Because I know Nythrawl's an issue, but we'll have to survive Vol Karoth before the Wound can take us down."

"No," Senera said. "He's not talking about the Wound. He's talking about Relos Var." Senera said to Thurvishar, "Maybe you should explain it."

"Yes," Thurvishar agreed, "but first, a question, Grizzst. I'd like you to confirm something for me, if it's possible. How was Relos Var planning to get rid of the demons?"

Grizzst hesitated. Then the voice answered with clear suspicion, ". . . Why?"

Senera nudged Thurvishar. "Tell him what demons really are."

## 67. THE MAD WIZARD

***Thurvishar's story***
***Grizzst's Tower***
***Three hundred and seventeen bottles of rare alcohol later***

Thurvishar thought Grizzst took the news rather well, all things considered.

"Is he going to stop smashing up his own tower anytime soon?" Senera asked.

Thurvishar grimaced. He supposed "taking it well for Grizzst" and "taking it well" might be considered two different things. "We may want to revisit this conversation in a few hours," he suggested.

"Not happening," Senera said. "The rest of the group did what they were supposed to while we were trying to contact Tyentso. A few interesting twists, but everything worked out. That means we need to head back."

That meant Terindel had been recovered and hopefully, with Xivan's help, was being Returned.

"We'll talk about that with Grizzst as soon as he's calm enough," Thurvishar said. He sat down on a rock across from Senera. They were outside. Rainbow Lake was spectacularly beautiful. It wasn't exactly a hardship, even if the smell of smoke in the air was a constant reminder of what they'd lost. "We should figure out where we might take shelter next. I don't believe the vané are terribly enthusiastic to let us permanently move in to the Mother of Trees, even if we are friends with their king. We're going to need a place . . ." He shook his head. "I suppose Grizzst will want to rebuild."

"Will we have time?" Senera asked. "Apologies, I made that sound like a question, didn't I? You and I both know we don't have time. Hopefully, if Talea thinks of me fondly, Relos Var will be too busy doing whatever terrible things Relos Var is planning to do to think that he needs to come back to Rainbow Lake and finish the job. And if he does have time to do that, then we've clearly failed to keep him sufficiently distracted." She stared down at her hands. "Don't think I'm not still going to take you up on that offer of stealing the Academy library when this is all over, though. I think that's a fine idea. Should have done it years ago."

"Oh, I just assumed we were still doing that," Thurvishar said gently. He reached over and pulled a single errant lock of Senera's hair away from her face. She caught his hand, closed her fingers over his. They locked stares.

He had always thought she was beautiful. From the moment he first saw her, paper white and dressed in silver, trying to embrace winter, ice, and unfeeling cold with all her might so she could deny all the colors that ran through her soul. Like trying to splash white paint over a complicated, brilliant portrait so she could draw something simpler and neater. Easier to recognize, but far less true.

"I don't deserve this." Senera wasn't talking about a burning tower.

"By coincidence, neither do I," Thurvishar said, smiling. Certainly, he had no claim on sainthood. He'd have nightmares for the rest of his life from some of the things Gadrith D'Lorus had made him do. Perhaps surviving was no crime, but that didn't make it a heroic act.

She laughed unhappily. "You know what I've done. You shouldn't care about me."

He nodded. Sadly, he knew every bit as well as she did, possibly even better given how many of her memories she'd repressed. "I do know, yes. And I know you will regret what you've done for the rest of your life."

Senera's eyes turned sharp and wet. "But I don't. That's the thing you need to understand. Don't try to turn me into something I'm not. I don't regret—" She choked on the words.

Thurvishar knew it would be easier if he could speak directly to her mind, but he also knew that wasn't going to happen. It was one thing to learn that you had the power to read minds; quite another to allow someone inside of your own. Especially when you cared how they might judge what they saw.

"You've told yourself that for years, Senera," Thurvishar said. "And you *almost* believe it. But I think you know better. Relos Var got hold of you when you were a *child,* Senera. If he groomed Qown, it was no more than what he did to you."

Her face looked haunted. "Qown hasn't killed anyone. I can't say the same."

Thurvishar nodded. "I'm not saying that you're pardoned for all crimes, but let's acknowledge that you were exploited. You and Teraeth have a lot in common, you know. Both taken in by parental figures and turned into weapons, both told that your sins were justifiable because the cause was righteous. Both lied to about so many things."

She gave him a narrow look out of the corner of her eyes. "And you were different?"

Thurvishar shrugged. "Gadrith never pretended to be righteous. And he didn't need me to believe I was doing the right thing; I was gaeshed." He paused. "He took no small amount of pleasure in the knowledge that I found what he made me do morally repugnant."

"Never thought I'd envy a gaeshed man," she admitted, "but I find myself envying the ability to say, 'I had no choice but to follow his orders.'"

"Kihrin's fond of reminding me that we always have a choice."

Senera snorted. "Kihrin's problem is that he's far too willing to throw himself on the fire. But even knowing what I do, there's a part of me that doesn't think I was wrong, just following the wrong person." She paused. "Which is a problem, because I don't know who the right person would be. Sometimes when I look at you, I wonder—"

"No. Veils no. Don't try to swap Relos Var for me. I'm not the right person.

The right person doesn't exist." When Senera gave him an annoyed look, he elaborated, "It's true. The Guardians weren't bad people. But at some point, the reasons for their duty became the justifications for their authority. The excuse for why they had to stay in power. Honestly, the worst mistake Grizzst ever made in his whole existence was convincing the Guardians to call themselves gods. He thought it was hilarious." He laced his fingers through hers. "But I think you know that trying to tear them down using the bodies of the people they were already stepping on isn't any better. And you can't tell yourself that it's justified just because you're ridding the world of tyrants."

"Ridding the world of tyrants is a good thing, though. You know that's a good thing." Senera sounded so young in that moment. So lost.

"Power is a mountain, Senera. A mountain that humanity climbs to feel safe or give our lives meaning or, I don't know, just bolster our self-esteem. People will never stop climbing, never stop trying to be the one who reaches the top. Never stop trying to make sure that no one else can climb up there and throw them rolling back down. And yet, someone always does. I'm not saying it's wrong to fight them, but keep doing it the way you are, and the inevitable result is that you're going to look down one day and realize the person at the top of the mountain is you. And then you'll have to ask yourself if all the bodies you climbed over to get there were justified. If all the deaths were worth it. If the answer is yes, then you'll have simply replaced what you were fighting. And if the answer is no, then what the hell were you even doing?"

She closed her eyes and put her hand to her mouth. He watched as tears fell in glistening trails down her cheeks. Finally he couldn't stand it anymore, and he smoothed the tears from her face with his fingers.

"You know this is the part where you should kiss her, right?" Grizzst said.

Senera's eyes flashed fire as she whirled to face the wizard. "You know this is the part where you should find out if you can go fuck yourself, right?"

"Oh, I would if I could, beautiful, believe me . . ." The armor shook his head. "Never thought I'd miss being able to shit."

Senera glanced at Thurvishar. "Are we sure we need him?"

Thurvishar sighed. "We might? Best to play it safe."

"Hey, fuck you too, kid," Grizzst snapped.

Thurvishar ignored the insult. That was just a friendly greeting based on Grizzst's normal behavior. "I'd ask you if it's really necessary for you to be so disgusting, but I already know the answer. Grizzst, I haven't needed advice on romance from you for an entire lifetime. If and when Senera decides that she would like to kiss me, that will be entirely up to her. And if she never does, *that's fine too.*"

Grizzst didn't reply for a few dozen seconds, although Thurvishar found it almost hilarious how expressive he was starting to find a faceless suit of armor. Somehow, the way Grizzst was tilting his head managed to perfectly convey *"what the fuck"* as a sentiment.

"Can we skip all this?" Senera snapped. "Because what we should be doing is returning to the Manol so we can talk with the others, not least of which because it seems someone near Empress Tyentso has Warmonger, we haven't managed to track her down yet, and we were really hoping you might have some idea how to help with both problems."[1]

"What? Warmonger?" Grizzst straightened. "Why didn't you say something!"

"Oh, someone was too busy smashing all his favorite alcohol, presumably under the idea that if he can't enjoy impossibly old, priceless liquor, no one else can either."

Grizzst scoffed. "You're quite a bitch, you know that?"

Senera stared at the man flatly. "And you are a horrible, disgusting, egocentric cad who has no doubt been improved by your transition into a walking piece of metal, because at least now no one will care that you never bathe. We didn't center our plans around you, and frankly, had we known you'd found a way to survive, we still wouldn't have, because of the many adjectives that have ever been used to describe you over the years, not once have any of those words included *stable, reliable,* or *trustworthy.* So if you would like to return with us to the Manol where the vané might possibly be persuaded to return you to a body capable of fulfilling your fervent desire for bowel movements, I suggest you make yourself useful and try to fucking keep up!"

With that, she stalked angrily away from them, although where she could possibly go without teleporting was somewhat limited.

For a moment, neither of the two men said a word.

Then Grizzst laughed. "Oh, I really like her."

"Yes," Thurvishar said. "Me too."

---

[1] Jarith had yet to report back both that he'd found Tyentso and that all the events at the D'Lorus estate had happened.—S

# 68. THE DEAL WITH WARMONGER

### *Tyentso's story*
### *Grizzst's Tower*
### *After kicking Gadrith's ass*

"What the fuck happened here?" Tyentso asked as she took in the sight of Grizzst's Tower burning.

Kalindra and Jarith had shown up a few seconds before she did, which had the entirely welcome side effect of making sure that she wasn't met with a rain of spells when she arrived. Not because she was the enemy but because she couldn't blame anyone for being jumpy under the circumstances.

Honestly, they were all just lucky that she hadn't shown up with the whole damn Milligreest family. And she'd *tried*. Tyentso really had, because she was running out of places where she could stash the lot of them without worrying that they were still in the arrow's path. So sure, why not the vané? But Qoran and Jira had both refused, which was when Tyentso learned that the only person in the universe stubborner than the high general was his damn wife. So they'd compromised.

Meaning the Milligreests had insisted on staying at the Capital to try to help deal with the rioting and restore order. Tyentso grew tired of arguing about it.

So anyway, it was just the three of them, facing off against Thurvishar and that white-skinned woman who'd betrayed them all at Atrine. The two wizards both stared at her with blank wariness, like deer that had just spotted a wolf.

Although most deer couldn't toss out the kind of massively destructive spells that these two could, so maybe that was the wrong analogy. Tyentso was too fucking busy to run around trying to arrest terrorists, anyway.

"Not to agree with the bitch or anything," Kalindra said, "but seriously, what the fuck happened here?"

"Rude," Tyentso told her.

"Stop being such a bitch, then," Kalindra said.

Tyentso didn't take it personally. She knew exactly why Kalindra was so upset. "You're not going to forgive me for putting the kids in danger, are you?"

"*No*," the assassin growled. Then she jerked as if struck and gave Jarith a sullen look.[1]

---

[1] I believe Jarith reminded Kalindra here that she herself had put her son, Nikali, in danger on Devors.–T

Nobody likes having their hypocrisy pointed out to them.–S

"Relos Var's what happened," Thurvishar finally answered when it became obvious that Tyentso wasn't about to launch directly into a mage duel. "He turned into a dragon and attacked the tower last night. Just saying hello, really."

He continued to stack books and odd bits that had been recovered from the fire. The tower looked like a loss. It seemed like a damn miracle that any of it was still standing. They were rescuing what they could, although there was some sort of armored construct performing most of the work. Sensible and far less prone to blistering.

"Lovely," Tyentso agreed. "Look, we should get this out of the way–"

The eidolon started moving toward Jarith, lightning-fast.

"Grizzst, no! That's a friend," Thurvishar called out.

The construct froze even as he was raising an arm that had started to glow, presumably a prelude to some sort of attack of extra-special usefulness against demons. "That's a demon," a voice corrected.

It both was and wasn't a familiar voice. Tyentso was quite certain that she'd never heard it before. And yet . . .

The identity of that voice was one of those pieces of information the Crown and Scepter often provided unasked, like the floor plan of the palace or how to teleport anywhere in the empire in an instant. The Crown and Scepter knew his voice because it was the voice of their creator, Grizzst the Mad.

"Grizzst?" Tyentso said. "Named after or . . ." She narrowed her eyes. She'd never been entirely certain whether or not Grizzst was a myth until she'd become emperor, when the Crown and Scepter had confirmed his identity. Still, there were any number of explanations for the creature in front of her. Only one of those was "that is the actual wizard Grizzst."

"No, that is the actual wizard Grizzst," Thurvishar said.

Tyentso took a moment to process that. She suspected that she just didn't have time to be fully briefed on all the shit going down with Kihrin and his friends in time for it to make a difference. She'd probably regret that later, but there was nothing for it. So Grizzst the wizard was also Grizzst the enchanted construct. Weird, but good to know.

"Hey, Grizzst," Tyentso called out. "Leave my friend the fuck alone. I'm vouching for him. He's one of the good demons." She was pretty sure "good demons" was a category that currently contained only Jarith, but someone had to be the trendsetter.[2]

The suit of armor turned in her direction, toward Thurvishar and Senera, then finally stopped in front of Kalindra. "You. Whatever your name is. You seem sensible. Let me try this with you, since none of these assholes are listening. That's a *demon*."

"That's my husband," Kalindra said with stone-hard finality.

"Being a demon doesn't mean what you think it means, Grizzst," Senera said. "Damn it, we *explained* this to you. Please tell me you were listening."

Personally, Tyentso would have used "that's a demon" as a perfect setup to making a ribald joke about Jarith's sexual prowess, but maybe that wasn't

[2] There's no reason she would have known about Janel.—S

a joke-worthy subject these days. Tyentso had no idea how that would work, anyway. Oh yes, also she hadn't slept in a day, had she, because the sex lives of Qoran's children wasn't a subject that she wanted to speculate about or imagine, *ever,* which meant she must be exhausted.

Tyentso surreptitiously cast a rejuvenation spell on herself. She'd pay hell for it later, but she'd burn that bridge when she got to it.[3]

"Great, now that we have that settled . . ." Tyentso could only hope that saying it made it true. "Thurvishar, Gadrith's dead. Again. Hopefully for good."

Thurvishar froze, and his expression went through a dozen emotions before settling on "stoically concerned." "He was Returned?"

"No more than he ever was," Tyentso said. "But Grimward, you know? Anyway, as near as I can tell, after Thaena died, Relos Var must have just immediately tapped in to Grimward to summon up Gadrith from the Afterlife and pin his ass into a body. A body he no longer has, fortunately. I have his soul right here, though." She pulled the small crystal sphere out of her top. "Maybe I can bribe one of you to tsali the fucker later, because I'd like to make a brooch."

Thurvishar blinked, just once, at the small, glowing point of light. He looked exactly like a man who'd just found a great life-affecting event had both happened and been solved before he'd ever found out about it. Clearly, it was emotionally important to him, which Tyentso understood down to her bones, but also, he couldn't do anything. It had already happened.

And hey, maybe it would have done Thurvishar good to have that final face-off with the bastard who'd raised him. But Tyentso didn't think so. To her immense shock, her "son" had apparently managed to get through life with a sense of basic decency in spite of being raised by that monster.[4] Thurvishar had somehow ended up as a genuinely good person. He didn't need to get caught in all the anger and revenge of removing his kidnapper from the world. Maybe it was just enough to know the bastard was finally gone.

And anyway, Tyentso hadn't known where to find Thurvishar.[5]

He nodded slowly. "I see. Yes, we should . . . we should do something about that." He sounded a bit dazed.

"Thurvishar?" Senera put her hand on his arm.

"I'm fine." He shook himself awake and looked down at the woman. They were standing a lot closer to each other than Tyentso would have thought appropriate for two people who had absolutely been enemies only a few weeks earlier. "Let's get back to Teraeth and Janel. We can talk about the rest of this there."

Tyentso whistled as she came out of the twirling circle of stars forming the edge of the vané gate system, the rising lights, the swirl of tree bark and

---

[3] Shouldn't that be "cross that bridge when she comes to it"?—S

    No, she said what she meant to say.—T

[4] Legally, Raverí D'Lorus, a.k.a. Tyentso, is still listed as my mother. I really need to get that fixed.—T

[5] If she had taken two seconds to contact me with the ring, she would have.—T

    This is where that lack of sleep comes in.—S

plants, the smell of sap and fresh, sharp trees. "It's nice to see the craftsman-ship, you know?"

"Thank you," Grizzst said primly.

Tyentso raised an eyebrow. She'd been trying to say something nice about the vané in the interest of diplomacy, so that was interesting.

There was a large contingent of vané soldiers with bows waiting for them on the other side, and wasn't that just a kick? She couldn't help but notice what a fantastic assassination method this would be. If she'd been any other Emperor of Quur, trying a stunt like this at any other time in the empire's history . . .

Well. She'd have fucking deserved the early death, wouldn't she?

Tyentso wasn't sure what was more surreal, retreating to the capital of the Manol like she was stopping by for a cup of tea, or knowing that she was do-ing so as the Empress of Quur. Certainly not a situation she'd ever imagined in her wildest dreams back when she was the *Misery*'s weather witch.

The guards looked . . . exasperated. Tyentso had seen exactly that look on Kalindra's face when she was teaching a class full of novices back on Ynisthana. Every disappointed parent in the universe knew how to make that expression.

"You want to see king?" one of the guards asked. His Guarem was . . . not great. Still, Tyentso understood the question, so clearly it was good enough.

Thurvishar smiled slightly and said in the vané tongue, "Yes, and it's an emergency. He'll wish to speak with these people right away."

The guard clearly wanted nothing so much as to tell everyone there to fuck off. But this was evidently not the first time human visitors had shown up like this recently, because instead of making them wait or turning them away, he just motioned for everyone to follow him. "Yes, king left instructions. Please walk me."

Tyentso gave a surreptitious glance at the others just in case any of them (Kalindra, possibly Senera) couldn't follow what Thurvishar had said. Or laughed. No one looked confused.[6]

So what followed was an interesting walk through the palace (interesting in terms of breathtaking and magical, not interesting as in dangerous or event-ful) before finally being shown into a palatial room that seemed half illusion, half priceless treasures.

And there Teraeth was, wearing a *fucking* crown.[7] He wasn't alone either; Tyentso saw Janel and someone who looked like Kihrin but couldn't possibly be Kihrin. There were four other vané present, two women and two men, several of whom were giving her odd looks. That was normal enough, she supposed, what with this being the vané homeland and all. Less normal was Galen and Sheloran D'Mon, along with another Quuros man she didn't rec-ognize. Also.

---

[6] Unlike the earlier group, everyone in this party spoke Vorem. Except for the demon, who's a telepath.—S

[7] Just a reminder that we were keeping Doc's return a secret at this point, which is why it was still Teraeth wearing the crown.—T

Tyentso blinked. "Fayrin? What the fuck are you doing here?"

He wrinkled his nose. "That's a funny story . . ."

"We rescued him before Relos Var could kill him and replace him with a mimic," Thurvishar explained. "Then we brought him here because we didn't know what else to do with him. You can have him back now."

"Thanks?" Fayrin said.

"Anytime," Thurvishar responded.

Tyentso felt a curious kind of lurch, a wave of electric current washing over her body. Relos Var had targeted Fayrin? Why would Relos Var do that? Sure, they were lovers, but with Fayrin's reputation, why would anyone ever think that their relationship meant anything at all? It was strictly physical, practically transactional. Why would anyone think that Tyentso cared?

Fuck. *Did she care?*

Tyentso tucked that question down deep and promised herself that she'd look at it again never. Anyway, Fayrin likely would've been targeted because of his proximity to her, regardless of the emotions involved. No reason to go looking for a deeper explanation than that.

Janel cocked her head and narrowed her eyes at Grizzst. "Who's that?"

"Grizzst," Senera said.

"I'm right here," Grizzst said. "I can introduce myself."

Senera waved him away like he was a small, annoying insect and not an oversize magical suit of armor who had all but founded the Empire of Quur.[8]

More than a few people in the room looked like they weren't quite sure what to do with that information. Tyentso couldn't blame them.

Janel apparently decided that the best course of action was just to ignore it. "Your Majesty, we need to talk about Warmonger."

"You took the words out of my mouth," Tyentso said. "But we need to find it first."

Teraeth calmly walked over to stand in front of her. Kalindra was still at her back. Tyentso felt the tiniest chill as she realized she was standing between two Black Brotherhood members on foreign soil in a palace built by magic. If they decided Tyentso wasn't their friend . . .

She was still the Empress of Quur. But she'd seen how fast Kalindra could move when she felt like it. Teraeth would be even worse.

He looked good, though. Unless one noticed how tired his eyes were.

"Tyentso," Teraeth said gently. "Please don't be offended. But do *you* have Warmonger?"

Tyentso scowled at him. "What the fuck? Of course I don't have the stupid thing. What the hell kind of question is that?"

"The kind that isn't assuming. You have to admit Warmonger has helped you stay in power," Janel said. "I bet the assassination attempts have all but stopped, haven't they? And no one questions your authority anymore."

---

[8] Excuse me. He very much did not. He just created the artifacts.–T
  Do you really want to claim credit for the founding of Quur?–S
  When you put it that way, no. No, I do not.–T

"That's not a good thing," Tyentso snapped. "And yes, the timing has been . . . advantageous. But I don't know what the cost will be for all this 'help.'"

"It's addictive," Senera explained matter-of-factly.

"What do you mean by 'addictive'?" Tyentso asked, worried for reasons that seemed perfectly obvious.

"I mean that within a few hours of Warmonger being removed from Lara-graen, all of its people and soldiers came down with a horrible, debilitating weakness that left them all but helpless when the Quuros army showed up," Thurvishar said. "They couldn't fight. They could barely walk."

"Oh, I can vouch for this part," Fayrin said. "It sucks."

"Jira and Eledore started complaining about not feeling well not long after we left the Capital," Kalindra said. "Frankly, I'm amazed Jira was able to stand when we were fighting Gadrith, but then again, she was really angry."

"Did you say 'Gadrith'?" one of the vané demanded.

Wait. Tyentso knew that voice. She blinked and gave the man a harder look. "*Therin?* Is that you?" She hesitated. "You shaved."

Galen D'Mon coughed into his fist.

"Really? That's what you're focusing on?" Therin snapped, before narrowing his eyes. "Raverí? That is you, isn't it?"

She wrinkled her nose. Tyentso supposed she had looked different the last time she'd seen him. "Yes, and yes, I'm the emperor, and yes, it's weird for me too." She waved a hand. "We'll catch up later, okay? Right now, we have more important things to worry about."

"And Gadrith?" Therin crossed his arms over his chest.

"Not even on the list, hilariously enough," Tyentso said. "Now can we please get back to talking about Warmonger and it being addictive?"

"Thank you," Thurvishar said. "So as I was saying, if the person who has Warmonger wants to cripple the Quuros army, all they have to do is *leave*. Within a few hours, everyone previously under the Cornerstone's effects will be too sick to fight." He gave Tyentso a pointed look. "I agree with the others that it's not completely out of character for you to use something like War-monger if you had access."

"You used to like me better, Thurvishar. What happened between us?" Tyentso said.

"You killed my adoptive father?" Thurvishar raised an eyebrow.

She stared at him. "*How* is that a mark against me?"

"You didn't invite me to help," he elaborated.

Tyentso sighed. Apparently, he was going to hold a grudge about that.

"But I also know that you'd never make a deal with Relos Var. And if you had Warmonger, you'd be carrying it on you," he continued, ignoring her interruption.

"And you're not," said the person who looked like but wasn't Kihrin.

Tyentso squinted at him. That had to be an illusion, right? There's no way that Teraeth would ever be working with a mimic . . .

"I can confirm," Kalindra said. "She's not working with Relos Var. He wouldn't have raised Gadrith D'Lorus from the dead to try to pry Godslayer out of her hands if he could just order her to hand the sword over. Although she did do that, just under duress."

A couple of people in the room reacted with scowls and curses to that news, but not Teraeth. And not Janel. Or Thurvishar and Senera.

It was interesting to note the people who were in on the plan versus those who were not.

"Well, as I'm in the middle of a war," Tyentso said, "I need to find out where Warmonger is and either get rid of it before it does more damage or make sure they can't remove it from the area until after we've finished this business with Marakor." She thought over that idea. "Ideally, the latter one. The whole thing makes my skin crawl, but I'd rather fight a war using paranoid fanatics than medical patients too weak to get out of bed."

"Speaking of," Fayrin said, "when was the last time you slept?"

Tyentso waved a hand at him. Honestly. He needed to stop trying to be her nanny. "I'll sleep when I'm dead."

Next to Thurvishar, Senera gave Fayrin a hard look.

**I can find Warmonger,** Jarith offered.

It was almost as funny this time, watching who lost their minds about the demon in the room and who didn't seem to care. Almost.

Mostly, it was getting old.

"Enough," Teraeth said, and his voice echoed in a way that seemed to override all others. Tyentso pursed her lips. It had to be that chair. "Jarith's on our side. Yes, he's a demon. Yes, we know. Yes, we trust him. You can save yelling at us for later, or better yet, just shut up and trust that if he was a threat to us, we'd have destroyed him already." He tilted his head toward Jarith. "You were saying?"

**I can find Warmonger.**

Janel frowned like a disapproving older sister. "You can't track a Cornerstone."

**No. But the emotions it engenders are strong. They have a motion, a current. I can follow that current to its source.**

"And now you're my new favorite Milligreest," Tyentso said. "I'll happily help the rest of you with whatever horse business you're all doing, but please help me wrest back control of my army first."

She removed Skyfire from her raisigi and set it, balanced on an edge, on one of the tables. "Now. I think this should serve as collateral on my good intentions, don't you agree?"

## 69. THE ANGEL OF MAGIC

**Kihrin's story**
**The ruins of Atrine, Jorat**
**That afternoon**

From the start, my greatest worry had always been that I'd run into one of the remaining Guardians, who still thought I needed to be destroyed.

This was made worse by the fact that I *needed* to run into one of the remaining Guardians at some point—now that I'd passed up on my opportunity to fight Xaltorath in one of the least appropriate places ever, I was unlikely to be able to bait the demon with anything less than the power of a Guardian. Unfortunately, since I couldn't stop and explain what I was doing, there was a genuine risk that I'd end up fighting said Guardian for real.

I didn't want that.

Unfortunately, as far as Tya, Khored, or Ompher knew, I was Vol Karoth, big, bad God of Annihilation. Of course they'd fight me. They had to. Unfortunately, that meant that I'd have to return the favor. I couldn't guarantee that I wouldn't hurt one of them in the process. I couldn't even guarantee that I wouldn't kill one of them.

Now, since Tya and Khored happened to be closely related to the people I'm madly in love with, I'd decided Ompher was the choice least likely to result in awkward family dinners until the end of time. Of the three remaining, I also thought he was the least powerful and the least likely to get a jump on me. Plus (and this was important) Ompher was going to forget all about going after me the moment Xaltorath showed up. Sure, Vol Karoth was a threat, but Vol Karoth hadn't recently murdered and devoured Ompher's wife, Galava.

Ompher needed to do something about me. He *wanted* to do something about Xaltorath.

As I moved, I picked up a piece of broken marble to see how long I could hold it without destroying it.

*You'll have to kill them all, you know. They'll never listen to you.*

Oh good, the demons were awake again.

"Shut up," I muttered as I watched the marble chunk crumble and flake away. Not bad. A good fifteen minutes that time. Not long enough by half, but I was starting to get the hang of it. It was still a question of balance. Every time I grew hungry, my instinct was to make up for the lack by destroying whatever was around me.

I was still very hungry.

*You know we're right. They'll never trust you. Trusting you is far too risky. You have to be destroyed.*

I wanted to find a way to get word to the Guardians first. I was contemplating this very problem as I toured the remains of the city that Ompher had helped Atrin Kandor create. There'd hardly been enough time to rebuild since Morios the dragon had come crashing through the city for laughs, leaving behind ruins, rubble, and the dead.

I wondered if the Joratese had any intention of rebuilding Atrine. It wouldn't surprise me if they never bothered. The survivors of Morios's attack on the city had simply relocated to the shoreline of Lake Jorat, set up azhock tents, and self-organized into districts, all without the slightest indication that they ever planned to return.

Given that Atrine had never been a city that had been lived in full-time by anyone except for Marakori squatters, the Joratese people didn't seem particularly put out to be operating from "temporary" shelter. They might have even been happier now that they had more immediate access to their horse herds and fireblood allies.

At least, they probably would have been happier if it wasn't for the war.

That there would be a war was undeniable. I was keeping my distance, but it was impossible to miss the Quuros armies moving into the Joratese camp, the preparations, the soldiers. When the Quuros moved to take back Marakor—which they had to do, or watch the whole empire come crumbling down around them—Jorat was the most logical platform from which to launch their attacks. The tent city overflowed with tense excitement, the combined sense of purpose and anxiety that came with preparations for battle.

I didn't roam the city as myself for obvious reasons. So a projection it was, and an invisible one at that. The idea that I'd have been able to travel through the crowded, tent-lined streets without bumping into anyone seemed ludicrous and improbable, but as long as no one could see that they were passing right through me, no one cared.

Truthfully, I drew no small amount of satisfaction from the idea that I was this powerful—knew all this magic, dark god, blah, blah, prophecy, destroy the world, blah—and yet, I was still using the same witchgift I'd figured out when I was a street thief from the Lower Circle to make myself invisible.

Eventually, I located the tent I was looking for, mostly because I wised up and started searching for firebloods instead of people. Once I found Arasgon, the rest was easy.

Seeing the fireblood brought on an immediate wave of longing. It was impossible to think of Arasgon without thinking of Janel. I missed her.

But that would have to wait.

The tent I slipped into was decorated in classic Joratese style: bright colors, flags, and pennants of favorite teams on display. The tent was large enough for a rope bed, a chair, and a chest that was doing double duty as a desk.

Dorna sat at the desk. She looked a lot more pensive than the last time I'd seen her, either through my own eyes or through someone else's memories. I'm not sure what she was supposed to be doing, but it probably wasn't staring out at nothing while she rolled a gold metal ball along the table with the palm of her hand. A nervous gesture.

"Dorna?"

The old woman flinched and stood at the sound of my voice. The gold ball made a break for it and fell off the edge of the desk.

I didn't try to catch it.

"Kihrin? What are you doing–?" She paused. "Is Janel with you? Because I want to have some words with–"

"No," I said. "Janel doesn't even know I'm here. You're the one I need to talk to." I hesitated. "In the interest of honesty, I'm compelled to admit that I need to talk to Tya, but you're the only angel of Tya I know. Which means I need to talk to you so you can pass a message along to her."

Dorna blinked at me. Then she bent over to pick up the ball. Which was when I realized it wasn't a ball; it was a walnut seed, dipped in gold.

It took me a second to make the connection, but then the identity of that particular object struck me with almost physical force.

"Is that Galava's Seed?" Galava's Greater Talisman, the one that would (now that the previous Galava was dead) transform its new owner into the next Goddess of Life.

And *Dorna* had it.

Dorna clenched the seed in her fist as she adjusted her skirts. "So you're familiar with it, are you? I, uh . . ." She inhaled, blinking as if to clear her eyes. "Mithros gave it to me yesterday."

Mithros. Better known to the world at large as Khored, God of Destruction.

I remembered too late that Dorna had been friends with the man in her youth, although she hadn't realized that the mercenary captain who spent so much time on the Joratese tournament circuit was also Jorat's most popular divinity by day.[1]

"Wow. Okay, so . . ." I blinked. I hadn't expected this at all, although in hindsight, I damn well should have. Tya had handpicked Dorna to raise her child.[2] Khored clearly thought the world of Dorna too. Picking her to be the next Galava made perfect sense.

Also, it meant that Tya and Khored were the ones who'd taken the rest of the Greater Talismans, which was a relief. That meant Relos Var likely still didn't know that the Guardians weren't one and done.

"Are you keeping it?" I asked her.

Dorna glanced down at the seed in her hand. "I kind of have to, don't I?"

"Why, no. I don't think you do," I said. "There's no law that says you have to do this."

But the old woman only shook her head, almost violent with the strength of her denial. "Oh, but that's where you're wrong," she said. "I never did

---

[1] It's worth mentioning that Khored isn't associated with destruction in Jorat but rather competition. And given that the Joratese use competition to decide idorrá/thudajé relationships, that arguably makes him the more important deity in their society.–T

It also makes the fact that he participates in these contests himself downright hilarious.–S

[2] That would be Janel.–S

realize how important Galava was to me until she weren't around no more. Someone's gotta do the job, don't they? Tya and Khored want it to be me, and well . . . I don't honestly know how good a job I'd do. Don't seem right that it should be me. I ain't a very nice person, you know."

"Dorna, last I checked, 'nice' wasn't a condition for the job." I paused. "And you *are* nice. You know as well as I do how mad Janel would be if she heard you talking like this. And she'd be very upset at me if I let someone get away with talking about her nurse that way, so stop."

Dorna chuckled. "Ah well. She's always been a bit biased."

"That doesn't mean she's wrong." I grinned. "Seriously, I think you're a great choice. And believe me, I could tell you some stories about Novalan. That's the real name of the woman you call Galava. She could drink any of the rest of us under the table and still go home with everyone's girlfriend. I remember one time she went on a bar crawl that lasted for five days—"

The ground started to shake.

As far as I knew, Jorat wasn't normally prone to earthquakes. Incredibly violent storms and tornadoes, yes. Earthquakes, no. Unfortunately, there were any number of potential explanations: a problem with the Demon Falls dam, unstable ground brought on by Morios waking up from his nap at the bottom of Lake Jorat, an attack by Marakor's armies. Hell, a really big stampede wasn't out of the question.

But it was worse than any of that. I knew it from the moment that the ground inside the tent started to well up, rock building on top of rock until it formed a shape at the apex.

Ompher stepped down.

## 70. THE NAME OF THE GAME

**Jarith's story**
***The imperial army bivouac, just outside Atrine, Jorat***
***Also that afternoon***

The swirl of emotions in Atrine was different from the Capital.

He should have anticipated this problem. The Quuros army was still relocating; they hadn't spent more than a few hours at this new site. That meant that instead of an entire emotional massacre dumping blood for days into the psychic waters, it was the faintest trickle, easily missed. After all, these people were already facing down the stresses of invasion, of war. They were already dealing with aftershocks of demons and dragons. Of course they were anxious and full of tension. But it wasn't the right kind of tension.

He followed Tyentso, Fayrin, and Kalindra invisibly through the camp, paying attention to each group of people they passed. Fear and stress and low-boiling anger, excitement and anticipation and grimly defiant determination. Not even close to the same singular rage and loyalty he felt while they were in the Capital, but Jarith didn't doubt that it would reach that point if they were there for more than a few days.

"You could have warned me that it's cold here," Kalindra muttered, rubbing her hands over her arms.

"Ah damn. I forgot, sorry," Tyentso said. She wasn't sorry. She was deeply amused and fond, and laughing at herself too. The reasons probably made sense to Tyentso but were less than clear to someone like Jarith.

Kalindra threw her a scathing glare, at which point Fayrin shook his head and ordered one of the nearby soldiers to give Kalindra a sallí cloak. Kalindra took it, mollified.

On at least three separate occasions, Fayrin suggested that Tyentso should take a nap first. Each time, she waved him off. Both of them were starting to lose their tempers about it.

They had almost made the full circuit around the camp when Jarith scented a trace of the emotional storm he'd experienced at the Capital. He tugged on Kalindra's misha in the direction he wanted them to go.

He paused.

Kihrin was here. He could feel him, a gathering void, hovering at the borders of his awareness. He was hiding himself, and doing a good job at it, but Kihrin's efforts to restore Jarith's mind had left the demon sensitive to Kihrin's presence.

Jarith thought it best not to mention it.

"How about this way?" Kalindra gestured idly.

Tyentso didn't argue. She headed in that direction.

He tracked the emotions in clusters. A flash of fear here, an appeal to loyalty there. Splashes of blood spreading out drop by drop. Thicker now. Easier to see.

The taint was a slowly widening spiral. At first glance, he had thought it gathered around Tyentso, but the more he examined the situation, the more he realized that she was just the focus of all those emotions. She wasn't the source.

He led them in a circle, tracing where the emotional signatures were stronger or weaker, until he had isolated it down to a single tent.

**I believe it's in there,** Jarith told the woman.

"Oh, fuck me," Tyentso said. "I know whose tent that is."

"That little bastard," Fayrin said.

"Let's see—wait!" Kalindra was too late.

Tyentso had already ducked into the opening and entered.

### Tyentso's story

"Caerowan!" Tyentso shouted.

The Devoran priest looked up from his writing table, set up carefully under no fewer than four mage-lights. He had a stack of letters in front of him—most of which was Tyentso's own correspondence.

He should have bowed and asked her what she needed. Caerowan had always been excruciatingly polite and correct, even in the face of her volatile temper, which was why he made the perfect secretary. He should have responded to Tyentso coming in off the street shouting for him as though it were a perfectly normal thing that happened all the time.[1] And then Tyentso would tell him what she needed, and he'd make it happen, typically with the most immaculately perfect handwriting that she'd ever seen. That *should* have been his normal response.

He didn't do that. Caerowan tilted his head and gave her a single, flat-lidded glance, taking in both her appearance and that of Fayrin behind her. She couldn't have said what tipped him off. Something in one of their expressions, perhaps.

Then he knocked over a small, decorative vase on his desk. It hadn't even hit the ground before gray smoke began billowing out in a thick, smothering blanket.

At least four knives flew into that smoke. Tyentso couldn't have said which ones were Kalindra's and which ones were Fayrin's. In the back of her mind, she noted that the most infamously louche member of the imperial High Council had decided to stop pretending at incompetence.

At just that moment, an explosion boomed, and the ground under their feet

---

[1] Yes, because it apparently was?—S

shook. Tyentso had a sudden, wild thought where she wondered if this was Caerowan's doing, but neither sound nor rolling ground centered on their location. This had happened somewhere else. If Havar had started his invasion early, Tyentso was going to murder the bastard.

Murder him more.

"What the fuck was—" Kalindra started to curse, and Tyentso could hardly blame her.

That second of hesitation cost them dearly. It was all the time Caerowan needed. Magnified by the smoke, a flash of light that Tyentso recognized all too well illuminated all the corners of the tent. She magically swept aside the haze even as Kalindra and Fayrin rushed over to her, but it was too late.

Caerowan had run, opening up and closing a gate so quickly . . .

Tyentso started tearing up the floor using magic. It took no more than a second of looking to find it: a House D'Aramarin Gatestone, hidden under the rugs.

"We could follow him," Fayrin said, but he didn't sound committed to the idea.

And no wonder, really.

Tyentso frowned. "Yeah, that's not happening. Who the fuck knows what Havar will have waiting on the other side."

"So you think Caerowan had the Cornerstone?" Kalindra directed that question to her demon husband.

**Yes,** Jarith said. **The taint is fading.**

Tyentso sighed. That wasn't good news, under the circumstances. It meant that in a short while, however many hours it took, her people would start feeling the effects of being separated from Warmonger.

And her enemy would start exploiting its benefits.

"Fuck me," Tyentso muttered. Then she raised her voice. "Now would someone find out what the hell that explosion was?"

The answer came from the least welcome source.

Jarith whispered, **It was Kihrin. Something's gone wrong.**

## 71. FALLEN STAR

**Kihrin's story
Dorna's tent, Jorat
Immediately after Ompher's arrival**

Ompher was in full Immortal mode. Even for a dreth, he looked like nothing so much as an obsidian statue made animate. His eyes were completely white.[1] Although he was dressed in clothing, there was no appreciable difference between the rock forming his clothing and the rock forming his skin.

He wasn't there for me. Ompher barely even glanced in my direction as he stepped toward Dorna.

"What's your name?" Ompher sneered at Dorna. "I want to know the name of the woman they think can replace *my wife*." He gestured; stone from the ground grew up like it was a fast-growing vine and wrapped around Dorna's legs, trapping her in place.

Shit. I hadn't once considered *this*. That Ompher might take huge exception to one other person besides myself and Xaltorath—namely, whoever was tapped to replace Galava. A person who was, at least for the moment, mortal—and vulnerable.

"What? Who the—" Dorna's piebald face flashed an odd combination of gray and paper white as she realized who Ompher was. Who he had to be. "Ah, goat fucks. Look, I ain't—" She pressed her lips together and shook her head violently. "I never felt anything but love for Galava. She saved my life. I owe her everything. I only ever loved Tya more."

Ompher grabbed Dorna by the throat. "Then why are you holding that seed? Did they tell you that you'd be replacing her? Did they tell you that you'd be *damning her*?"

"*Hanik*, stop it," I snapped.[2]

The God of Earth—more accurately, the Guardian of Matter—stopped and turned, frowning as he seemed to notice me for the very first time.

Yeah, this was . . . bad. Really bad. Maybe not quite "let's fight Xaltorath on top of the Chasm" bad, but damn if it wasn't racing neck and neck for the privilege of being top place on my list of ways I could screw this up.

---

[1] To my knowledge, this is not a normal feature of dreth physiology. I've been unable to find any mention in historical records of dreth with white eyes where the full dreth wasn't also a pale color.–T

[2] Ompher's real name is Hanik Mir.–S

I sighed. I wasn't going to let him hurt Dorna, and all I had to stop him with were words. I had to make them count.

"She's not your enemy," I said. "And this isn't damning Novalan. Think this through. Thaena's dead. So's Grizzst. That means that even once we kill Xaltorath, Novalan will be free from her imprisonment yet still be out of your reach. Spread out across the universe just like last time. But now? Now she's *not* the Guardian of the First World anymore. That means she'll go to the Afterlife. That means you can ask for her to be Returned. This isn't insulting your wife's memory. This is *saving* her."

Ompher let go of Dorna, who clutched her throat and bent over, gasping for air.

"How do you know our real names?" Ompher's eyes widened. "*S'arric?* Is that you? How is that even possible?"

I put on my best fake smile, my best "we're not that close" polite stare. It was bullshit. I didn't think he'd fall for it, but I had to try. "Come on, you remember me. I'm Kihrin. We met right here in Atrine when you asked us to go take that message to King Kelanis. I get it, I do. After all, I know you all say I was S'arric in a past life . . ."

Ompher made a throwing gesture with his left hand, and something streaked toward me, too fast for me to dodge. I didn't need to dodge: a boulder roughly the size and weight of five or six men flew through the space that I technically occupied. It sailed right through as though nothing was there. Because nothing *was* there. Then it crashed into the ground fifty feet away and exploded with a force that made me wince. There was no way that people hadn't been injured from that. Odds were excellent that people had died.

Which meant Ompher wasn't buying my story, and he didn't care who he hurt if it meant taking me out. The boulder had passed right through me because I was just a projection. And the last thing in the universe that would fool the Guardian of Matter was an illusion that didn't have any substance.

"Great talk, Dorna. I'll tell Janel you said hi." I blinked out, canceling the spell. A second later, I returned to my temporary base of operations on one of the moons.

Fuck. I wanted to scream. I could only hope that I'd so distracted Ompher that he'd ignore Dorna and spend all his energy trying to find me. But I couldn't be sure. I couldn't be certain what Ompher would do to Dorna now that I'd left. I feared that leaving might have been a terrible mistake. All I knew was that staying would have been much worse.

Less than a heartbeat later, I realized I'd made a different sort of mistake: I'd underestimated Ompher.

He appeared in the space right beside me on the moon.

I gaped. *That bastard had somehow found a way to track me.* That shouldn't have been possible. Ompher had somehow figured out how to follow my projection back to my actual body, to track that body even after I'd teleported away.

"Don't—" was as far as I managed before Ompher was on me. Although strangely, it wasn't anything like a normal attack. No blasts of energy, no slashes of magically sharpened artifacts, no killing spells. Instead, Ompher just reached out a hand and touched my arm.

That should have disintegrated his hand.

It didn't.

Ompher had come prepared. He wore a strange set of gloves that Argas had probably crafted. Something no doubt designed to protect Ompher from proximity to Vol Karoth, at least for a few seconds. But those few seconds were enough.

Ompher teleported us both.

The next moment, I was back in a location I both recognized and loathed: the Korthaen Blight hadn't grown any less horrendous or Blight-y in the short time since I'd left it. We appeared near the center, within sight of Kharas Gulgoth. A faint scent carried on the wind, dry and sulfurous, as though the Blight were trying to force its way past the barriers surrounding the city.

I had no idea why Ompher would bring me back there, except perhaps that with the morgage gone, it was one of the few places in the world where our fight risked few casualties from collateral damage. So maybe he *did* care about that.

Whether that was Ompher's motivation or not, he wasted no time attacking again. This time, he used physical magic, swinging his arms as though punching me but delivering hits of pure magical energy. The blows were a thousand times harder than anything a normal man—even a normal god-king, if such a term could be used—could accomplish with muscle and bone alone.

It felt like being hit by scorpion war machine casks launched at frightening speed. I staggered back as I was struck two, three, four times. And while I absorbed a great deal of that energy, I didn't absorb enough.

I felt bones crack.

"Good," Ompher said. His grin held no humor, only a rictus mask of grief. "You can be hurt."

He made a pushing motion, then; I flew backward. I should clarify that I *fell* backward; it was as if I'd lost my ability to hover at the same time that up, down, and sideways shuffled around. I slammed against one of the magical walls of force outlining the crumbling structures of the dead city.

I tried to push myself free and discovered that I couldn't. The stone at my back disintegrated as a great weight pressed me into the rock sideways.

Gravity. Because Ompher *wasn't* the God of Earth, never mind that he'd been given its name. Ompher was tied to "matter" in exactly the same way I was tied to "energy."

Perhaps thinking of Ompher as the "weakest" of the surviving Guardians had been a mistake.

I concentrated on resisting Ompher's abilities, exerting my own in response. I slid a foot forward, possibly one of the most difficult feats I'd ever accomplished, and leaned against it. Slowly, I managed to shuffle forward another half step. I then began to feed off the tenyé that Ompher needed to manipulate the gravity crushing me.

It was the first time I'd ever been grateful for my horrifying need to consume energy.

But Ompher and I weren't done. Ompher smiled. The Guardian glanced up toward the sky with an expression I could only describe as supreme satisfaction. A second later, Ompher flew backward away from me, so quickly it would have been easy to believe that Ompher had teleported a second time.

I didn't have time to give chase.

Because a mountain fell on my head.

To be fair, it wasn't a real mountain. Those were difficult to rip out of the ground without drawing a lot more attention to the whole process than Ompher had generated. Never mind that Ompher would have had to keep the mountain from crumbling into a million pieces, which might have been a difficult feat even for him. No, this wasn't even composed of rock.

This was ice and dust and probably non-terrestrial. If I had to guess, Ompher, master of gravity and mass, had just smashed a comet directly into the Korthaen Blight. Or more specifically, had just smashed a comet into me.

So what did I do in response to being hit by a massive object moving that fast?

What anyone would have done.

I died.

## 72. A BRIGHT AND BEAUTIFUL LIGHT

*Teraeth's story*
*The Mother of Trees, the Manol*
*Not long after Tyentso's departure*

The throne room shook.

*Shook* was the wrong word for it. This didn't feel like something had slammed into the section of tree where they currently resided. Rather, the entire tree had bowed as though greeting a passing monarch, and to hell with the city of people living on her branches. Everything—furniture, people, decorations—slid ten feet to one side and then immediately swung back the opposite way when the tree righted itself again.

It was loud too. One of the loudest noises that Teraeth could ever remember hearing. Not a single sound but the accumulation of groans, creaks, screams, and crashes as an entire city full of people began to tip over.

"What was *that*?" Janel called out.

The question on everyone's mind, Teraeth suspected.

"Your Majesty!" A vané courtier—Teraeth hadn't learned her name yet—came running into the throne room, so quickly that she had to have teleported. "There was an explosion in the Korthaen Blight. And a bright light. It was—" Words seemed to fail her.

"How big an explosion?" Valathea asked.

Next to Teraeth, Janel shook her head. "If it was big enough for a shock wave to move the queen sky tree . . ." Teraeth didn't think anyone else heard her murmur.

"The whole . . . the whole Blight. The fireball is gigantic . . ." The woman looked like she was about to go into shock.

"There's a viewing platform upstairs," Khaeriel suggested, but with enough doubt in her voice to suggest she didn't recommend using it.

Teraeth felt something warm on his hand and looked down to see that Janel had laced her fingers through his.

"It's starting," she said.

He picked up her hand and kissed it, then stood. "Find out what's going on," he ordered the room. Teraeth didn't single anyone out. Let them figure out how to best follow the command.

Janel was probably right. It was starting. Kihrin had warned them that a fight with the other Guardians would be devastating.

The worst part was knowing that there was absolutely nothing any of them could do.

# 73. EXTINCTION EVENTS

### *Kihrin's story*
### *The Korthaen Blight*
### *Just after the comet strike*

I didn't stay dead.

This was not the blessing it might have seemed.

The massive flaming chunk of ice, dust, and debris, easily a mile across, smashed into the Blight at an incredible speed. It instantly vaporized itself, a section of the world's mantle, and the ruins of Kharas Gulgoth, finally completing the destruction that had begun thousands of years before.

And it vaporized me. At least, I had no reason to assume otherwise.

Molten stone, superheated gas, plasma, and dust exploded with enough force to be felt all the way in Yor.[1]

The Korthaen Blight had already been a weak point in the planet's crust, again thanks to me. The caldera formed by Vol Karoth's birth had left far too many weak spots, mostly expressed as toxic vents and alkaline hot springs. It was the last place on the planet that should have been hit by such forces *twice*.

The world cracked open. The entire Blight turned into a roiling ocean of plasma and stone so hot that it didn't just liquefy but turned to gas.

I took no pleasure in knowing that Ompher had fucked up. I wasn't sure if Ompher had genuinely made a mistake or had simply reached the point where he no longer gave a damn what happened to anyone else with Galava gone, but he'd put too much force into the strike. The comet had hit too fast and too hard.[2]

And so, high above the boiling inferno of the Blight, Ompher tried with all his power to keep the escaping catastrophe contained. He used his powers to drag all the debris back to earth, collapsing rocks, plasma, and dust back in on itself. The old Ompher—the one S'arric remembered—would have fought with all his might to keep this from being the act that destroyed the whole world. Perhaps that Ompher still existed.

But I didn't think his good intentions would have been enough. Left to his

---

[1] In point of fact, it exploded with enough force to be felt in the Free States of Doltar on the southern continent.–T

[2] Depending on exactly how Ompher accomplished that attack, he may not have had any choice in the matter.–T

own devices, the man would have unleashed a world-breaking catastrophe on the very people he'd tried to save.

As it turned out, however, Ompher wasn't on his own.

Tya and Khored appeared nearby shortly after the initial impact. Tya screamed something, demanded an explanation, but there was neither time nor the ability to hear above the howling winds and screaming tumults of the blast. So instead, Tya spread her hands wide and created another Veil.

Why not? She'd created the first one too. If that one had been crafted to protect the planet from a sun that had become catastrophically large, this one was more localized. Once again, she was cleaning up the messes made by her fellow Guardians.

Tya's smaller Veil was a dome-shaped barrier of pure tenyé surrounding the Blight. Maintaining the Veil had always been a taxing endeavor, even for a Guardian. I'm personally of the opinion that a great deal of Quur's bullshit had only gone unchecked through the empire's existence because Tya had been left too weak to kick the right asses. Maintaining a second barrier—one actively being pummeled by a violent conflagration—took all the energy Tya had remaining. Sweat broke out all over her as she struggled to keep the spreading devastation within from spilling out and destroying—well, certainly, all life within a large radius. Khorvesh. Marakor. The northern Manol. But eventually, the majority of life on the entire planet.

Khored helped too, destroying any rocks or bits of lava that escaped, but his abilities weren't an ideal match to the problem.

Inside the dome, the trapped energies of the massive explosion rebounded off Tya's shield before being pulled back down by Ompher's gravity. More stone melted. What had been an explosion became a forge. Hundreds of spontaneous eruptions gushed lava and poisonous gases into the air, while any rock that might have solidified immediately turned molten once more.

Slowly, though, equilibrium returned; as the plasma melted rock, it cooled enough to become liquid.

The land outside the Blight for several miles in every direction heated, sagged, became lava. Had Stonegate still been inhabited, the entire city would have perished in an instant. It was a small blessing that limited the death toll, but even so, well over a thousand people—Khorveshan and morgage, vané and thriss—died in seconds. A section of the Kulma Swamp boiled, so it was just as well that the morgage hadn't moved in yet. The last few mountains in the Dragonspires chain began erupting.

It wasn't nearly as bad as what it could have been. The stone absorbed a great deal of the energy, Tya's newly created barrier halted the spread of death.

Inside the dome, it was every bit as horrifying as one might expect. The temperatures were so hot that it vaporized everything inside, person or god, in a heartbeat.

I knew this because my body kept attempting to re-form only to be destroyed by superheated gases again several seconds later. It was too much energy even for me, which was my second clue (the first being that initial attack by Ompher) that my body had limits to how much energy it could devour at once. I hadn't thought I *had* limits. I was wrong.

*Interesting–*

*–I don't seem–*

*–to be able to–*

*–die,* I thought in the brief moments of existence before the pain became too intense, before the screaming began. Although I wasn't being given much time to think through the ramifications, on some level, I knew that this was an anomaly, different from the other Guardians, different from the dragons. Or perhaps not so dissimilar to the dragons, but where it might take them hours or days to regenerate after a fatal injury, it seemed to take me seconds. Around eight seconds. I counted.

I could die, technically. I just wouldn't stay that way for long.

Eight seconds was enough; I could work with that.

After four iterations of this treatment, I'd recovered enough to defend myself, able to concentrate on absorbing and consuming all the energy around myself instead of letting it overwhelm me. But I couldn't absorb the entire explosion. I was more powerful than any single Guardian, but now I was choking down that ugly fact about limits. My physical body could only hold so much power. Trying to devour the entire explosion might easily jump my entire system into the sort of explosive overload that would surely finish what Ompher had started.

Gradually, I pushed out a sphere of influence around myself, a buffer against the firestorm's onslaught. Past the storm clouds of rock vapor, dust, and flying magma, Tya's magical field was a glittering dome over the Blight. A beautiful shroud to keep the rest of the world from burning.

By that point, I was aware enough to make smart choices (or choices, in any event),[3] so I teleported myself outside Tya's barrier, to fresh, cool air. The absence of pain was so abrupt it felt like knives.

Below me, Khored put a hand on Tya's shoulder, sharing tenyé with the woman. On the ground, Ompher visibly strained to contain the planet-killing forces that he'd created.

I had to give credit where it was due; it looked like they'd largely succeeded in stopping the explosion from leaving the Blight. Or from dumping enough dust and ash into the atmosphere to create a winter lasting years.

That's not to say I wasn't tempted to hit Ompher at that moment. It wasn't a nice thought. Let's call it a Vol Karoth sort of thought, the sort of idea worthy of my older, angrier, cursed self. The one who wanted to survive more than anything. The one who didn't believe these people had ever really been his friends. That anyone had ever been his friend.

That Vol Karoth still lived in me, much to my regret, and he screamed at me to strike while I could. Ompher's entire attention focused on the seething

[3] At least he qualified that.—S

chaos inside the Blight. The Guardian hadn't noticed that I'd worked my way free. I could've killed him right then.

**You should. You know you should. Look at all that tenyé. You know that would keep you fed for days.**

Okay, so maybe it was also the demons talking. I really needed to rid myself of those bastards.

Ompher wasn't my enemy. I knew that. Of course, he'd attacked me. Of course, he'd spent centuries figuring out what he would do if Vol Karoth ever freed himself and, in that final calculus, had decided that the deaths of all these people was an acceptable loss for taking me down. It was a far smaller number than Thaena had been comfortable sacrificing. As far as Ompher knew, the alternative was the death of everything.

It's not like I was in a position to sit him down and spell out how this was all a big misunderstanding.

I should've left. That would've been the sensible option. No one knew I was there—the last anyone had seen of me, I'd been vacillating between solid and gas inside the Blight. And much as I hadn't wanted to be forced to fight a single Guardian, I really didn't want to fight *all three* surviving ones.

But my timing was off. Even as I started to give thought to where I might go, the universe provided me with ample evidence that my earlier theory was correct. That a fight between myself and the other Guardians would be guaranteed to draw the attention of Xaltorath.

***DO YOU KNOW, IN ALL THE TIMES I'VE DONE THIS BEFORE, *THIS* HAS NEVER HAPPENED?***

Damn.

Xaltorath appeared, this time in female form. She had six arms, all of which ended in stingers or bone swords. Three of those arms pointed back toward Tya's wall, clearly the "this" in her statement, which pulsed in rippling waves across its surface as the fireball inside its area churned.

Yes, fine, this had been part of my plan. I admit it. But I can't say I was happy to see how it was playing out. I'd harbored a faint hope that I could warn the other Guardians first, maybe even enlist their help. That was the whole reason I'd dropped by to have a chat with Dorna.

Xaltorath sounded so pleased with herself. Almost giddy. She gave the scintillating magical wall one last fond look before she turned her attention to the Guardians. She paid no attention to me. None whatsoever. I might as well have not even been there. Her red eyes passed right over me. Lest I felt slighted, however, she did the same to Khored and Tya.

Because Xaltorath could never pass by the chance to stick her thumb into an open wound.

***COME JOIN US, OMPHER. YOUR WIFE MISSES YOU,*** the demon taunted, arms held wide as though inviting Ompher to join her in the world's most ill-advised hug. She was so obviously provoking an attack that anyone could see closing in on her was playing to her strengths.

Ompher didn't care. I'd been right about that too, to my deepest regret. Because Ompher forgot about the mess he'd made in the Blight, he forgot about me, he forgot about saving anyone. He forgot about everything except revenge. That part he remembered just fine.

Ompher screamed as he lunged at Xaltorath, while the earth around them shattered into razor-sharp spears.

Meanwhile, Khored locked eyes with me.

# 74. Very Bad Timing

### Kihrin's story
### Just outside the Blight
### Just after Xaltorath crashed the party

"Vol Karoth!" Khored bellowed. If anyone besides myself heard him, they were too distracted with their own issues to pay attention. The God of Destruction pointed his red glass sword at me and launched a blast of seething red tenyé in my direction.

He was at his strongest. Just as his draconic brother, Morios, was made stronger by violence, Khored was empowered by destruction.

The Korthaen Blight had just seen a lot of destruction.

Which is also why I don't think Khored was really trying. He hadn't thrown that attack my way in order to hurt me; he'd done it to send a bright red bolt of magic across the sky to catch Tya's and Ompher's attention and remind them I was still around. I easily absorbed the strike; it didn't do much more than make my skin tingle.

*"Help Ompher!"* I screamed at him.

I didn't expect Khored to listen, and he didn't disappoint. Why would he? I was the bad guy. I couldn't even blame him for believing the rumors, paying attention to hearsay and myth; *I'd killed him once.* Pretty difficult to let go of the "villain" label under such circumstances.

He had every reason to want to kick my ass. Not so long ago, the Korthaen Blight would have been the perfect place to have this confrontation.

Ompher's little trick changed things, though. Now, the Korthaen Blight wasn't a safe place. If Tya took a stray shot, the chaos below would boil out and cause untold damage to neighboring lands: Khorvesh, the Manol, the Kulma Swamp. I needed to take this fight somewhere else.

I didn't wait for Khored to close with me. Instead, I flew down and to the side. I used the same tenyé Khored had so graciously gifted me to unleash a torrent of kinetic energy at Ompher and Xaltorath both.

Solid hits. I truly think that if my targets had been anyone else, I'd have killed at least one of them, caused serious, crippling injuries.

Instead, I just knocked them both away from the Blight.

I followed them. I didn't turn back to look, but I knew Khored was chasing after me. I hoped that Tya wasn't. With as much tenyé as she was throwing into maintaining two different magical barriers, she was already too vulnerable.

Ompher lifted himself from the ground, looking slightly singed but about as unharmed as I would expect for a Guardian. He spotted me first, his eyes wide with outrage and shock.

"Impossible!" Ompher said. "There's no way you survived that. *I broke the planet to kill you!*"

*"If it makes you feel better, you succeeded."* But I really couldn't stop to chat. Instead, I flew right past the Guardian and slammed into Xaltorath.

I grabbed the demon queen; bits of claw, scales, and tentacle-stingers began to flake away to ash under my grip. Now here was someone I was only too glad to kill.

Pretty sure when Xaltorath had attacked me on the streets of the Capital all those years ago, *this* hadn't been the outcome she'd expected.

I did some damage. Unfortunately, Xaltorath's physical form had always been more suggestion than fact. Xaltorath vanished out of my hands and reappeared several yards away. The ground at her feet iced over as she drew every bit of available heat up into her body to heal the damage.

***WHY ARE YOU OPPOSING ME, IDIOT-GOD OF ANNIHILATION?*** Xaltorath sounded genuinely perplexed. ***WE SEEK THE SAME THING. WE SHOULD WORK TOGETHER. HERE: YOU KILL ENTROPY, AND I WILL FINISH DEVOURING THIS ONE.***

The unintended reminder that Khored was also in this battle was well timed. A second red blast of energy passed through the space I'd occupied a second earlier. This one had meant business. It dissolved giant chunks of the ground behind me.

Xaltorath hadn't waited for my reply. The demon queen instead leaped on Ompher, rending and devouring.

Ompher retaliated by attempting to turn Xaltorath's personal gravity inward, to make the demon implode. Clever. I liked it; I was glad he hadn't tried it on me. The trick might have worked against another demon too, but this one had eaten gods, had eaten Galava. The amount of energy necessary to overload Xaltorath's defenses would have taken everything Ompher had to give and then some. I'm sure Ompher didn't think it was worth it, since I was still in the fight.

My survival must have shaken the hell out of him. It had taken millennia for Ompher and the other Guardians to resurrect after I'd destroyed their bodies. Even then, they hadn't been able to manage it on their own. Ompher must have expected me to obey the same rules. And yet here I was, back after only *seconds*.

Which meant he'd killed a lot of people for nothing.

I turned back to face Khored. *"Damn it, Mithros, stop! I'm not your enemy! Would you stop being such a damn flamingo?"* I kept waiting for one of the Guardians to comment on the fact that I was talking, reacting, responding to them like a rational, intelligent being. But then I remembered that I'd been perfectly capable of speech that first time too. That time when I'd murdered them all. They'd never encountered the mentally amputated version of me.

All the same, though, I was a *lot* chattier this time around.

Eventually, Khored noticed, although he wasn't ready to pronounce me his friend again. "Not my enemy?" Khored pointed up. "Then explain that."

That was exactly one step removed from shouting, *"Look, air!"* at someone so they'd glance away at a crucial moment. Which was cute and funny under different circumstances, but I wasn't in the mood. I teleported three hundred feet to the side and in a random direction so I could see whatever Khored meant before I had to return my attention to him.

It wasn't air. Instead, it was this: a flowing cloud, headed in our direction, dark and wispy as it rode the inferno-hot winds gushing out of the Blight. Bits of the cloud at the edges seemed to ignite, burn, and flake away.

I sharpened my vision.

It wasn't a cloud either, which made sense considering its extremely uncloud-like behavior. Rather, it was a flock of birds, thousands strong.

No. I revised my estimate immediately. Millions strong. So many birds I could only guess at the numbers. All different species and sizes, many of them so physically damaged that they shouldn't have been capable of flight.

Coincidentally, they were also all dead.

The shadow of a much larger winged creature—gigantic, skeletal—flew in the center of that giant, decomposing flock.

Rol'amar the dragon had re-formed—and was flying our way.[1]

I supposed it was possible that the dragon had been drawn to the area by the giant, glowing magic wall that could be seen by half the planet. But that wouldn't explain why he was heading toward us. Toward me.

It occurred to me that the dragons—all the dragons—might have noticed that uncomfortable cycle of deaths and resurrections that I'd "enjoyed" inside the Blight. Irony: Rol'amar might have been flying over to help me.

I thought about telepathically contacting the dragon and forcing it away, but if Relos Var had noticed the deaths too, he might be paying more attention than normal. I didn't know how strong Relos Var's links to the other dragons were. Certainly, when I—when Vol Karoth—had been imprisoned, Relos Var's control had been much stronger, even as Vol Karoth whispered hate and revenge from the shadows. Now I had more control, but that didn't mean Relos Var wouldn't be able to hear me if I started shouting orders. Too much had already gone wrong.

I couldn't risk it.

"Shit," I cursed as the cloud dove at us.

I held up my hand and summoned up a barrier of energy around myself. Although *energy* was the wrong word for it. It was the opposite of that. Anything that hit the field disintegrated, with the energy released flowing back into myself even as black flakes floated in the air.

It was unnecessary; the birds came nowhere near me. They instead flew

[1] Rol'amar is the only son of Tya (Ir'amar, also known as Irisia) and Relos Var (Rev'arric). Which makes him S'arric's nephew and my uncle.–T

I think you might be missing the more important fact: that Kihrin destroyed Rol'amar while channeling Vol Karoth's power. We had thought it possible Rol'amar wouldn't be able to come back from that, and we were wrong.–S

directly at Khored, attempting to claw and pick at his flesh in a hundred places as they flew past in a never-ending flow of feather, bone, and exposed muscle. Khored, though, was more like Vol Karoth than the man would ever admit; the shield that Khored erected was remarkably similar to my own. Birds who ventured too close were annihilated, turned to nothing but clouds of ash tossed by the winds.

If only Rol'amar himself were so easily cast aside. The undead dragon slapped Khored as he flew past. Part of the tail disintegrated, but the dragon was too massive—and too quickly regenerating—for that to prove more than a momentary inconvenience. Enough of the tail survived to send the God of Destruction flying, snapping him backward with enough force to kill a mortal. Khored caught himself, using magic to slow his flight. He came to rest thirty feet from the lava, annoyed.

I suspected my odds of convincing Khored that I wasn't on the opposing side were growing narrower with each passing second. This was a problem for multiple reasons, not least of which was, again, I didn't want Khored to die here. Or at all. In fact, I really needed Khored to *not* die here, given my plans for later. I just had to hope that since he'd always been a master tactician, not to mention one of the most skilled soldiers I'd ever known, the man would be capable of holding his own against a crazed dragon for at least a few minutes.

No, the bigger problem was Ompher, who was merely "very talented" when it came to combat rather than qualifying as "one of the best that had ever lived." Unfortunately, he was facing off against an opponent who had lifetimes in which to practice playing different versions of this conflict in endless repetition. Xaltorath knew all Ompher's strengths and weaknesses—as well, if not better, than the god himself. Understandably, Ompher was having a rough time of things. I wasn't sure how much longer he could last. If Ompher was going to survive, he would need an unexpected variable. Something like me.

I launched myself at the demon queen. Again, the demon simply teleported away rather than allow me to move close enough to touch her. That bought Ompher time; he was bleeding from a dozen wounds that he hadn't managed to heal, and he was visibly weakening. Rarely had it been quite as obvious that the seemingly infinite power of the Guardians did in fact have limits.

Even as I drove off Xaltorath, a wave of lava rose from the ground and attempted to crash over me.

I glanced back at Ompher. *"Would you stop that?"* I muttered after dodging to the side. It was an empty request, obviously. Ompher wouldn't.

So I couldn't do much else except try to avoid Ompher as best I could and concentrate on Xaltorath, moving to siphon tenyé off the demon the same way another demon might. I managed to freeze one of her hands, but she immediately whirled around and summoned up Khored's red glass sword to fire off a beam of pure entropy in my direction. Simultaneously, three of her other arms also threw spells in my direction—with powers originally owned by several of the other Guardians. That blast almost knocked me back into the magical wall of force that Tya had set up around the Blight. Heat carried over from the firestorm inside kept the rock closest to the wall molten and cherry red.

Khored looked torn on who he should be attacking first, since either way he'd be helping an enemy. Ompher had no such reservations: he focused on Xaltorath.

We had little warning that yet another enemy had joined our midst other than a sudden gust of wind and drop in temperature. My gut clenched. *I* knew who that was.

The sky had grown brighter as Rol'amar's vast flight of dead birds dwindled and fell from the sky, but now it darkened again—this time with clouds. The storm had only incompletely covered the sky when the clouds parted again like the lightest and most delicate of silk curtains to reveal the gargantuan serpentine shape of Aeyan'arric the Ice Dragon, Lady of Storms.

Also, my daughter. Not in Kihrin's "sort of, in a past life, if you look at it sideways" fashion. No, since I was now running around in S'arric's body, that meant Aeyan'arric was my biological daughter. It was . . . I was trying not to think about it.

Unfortunately, I was out of luck in that regard, mostly because of my unexpected visceral reaction to seeing her—pure, violent fury. It caught me off guard. The anger of her betrayal hurt so much more than the others. I had to remind myself that I didn't know—had never known—what her motives had been. There was every chance that her uncle Rev'arric had lied to her about what the ritual was designed to do.

How I hoped so.

Aeyan'arric attacked Khored, extending her jaw to breathe out a long stream of razor-sharp ice shards. The ice blast was strong enough and fast enough to send lava spraying, creating a giant wall of blinding steam.

That didn't bother me. What bothered me much more was why Aeyan'arric was there at all. She shouldn't have been. Her preferred territory was thousands of miles to the north, in the icy wastes of Yor. I could understand why Rol'amar had wandered over. In theory, Rol'amar would have been somewhere near the Blight and thus in a fantastic position to respond to this catastrophe. But Aeyan'arric? She wouldn't have flown down without a very good reason.

What were the odds *all* the dragons had felt me die?

And what were the odds that *all* the dragons were now on their way?

I checked through that link that always hovered in the back of my mind, that many-threaded connection to nine other identities. Two of those minds were closed to me, but that wasn't unexpected. Relos Var had always been careful to erect a barrier to keep out Vol Karoth's thoughts, and now that Drehemia was sane again, the same was true of her. But for the dragon minds that remained, all snarling, yowling seven of them, well.

They'd all responded. Great.

The temperature of the air plummeted lower, until any creatures who needed to breathe or hadn't cast some kind of spell rendering it unnecessary found themselves exhaling little, white clouds with every breath. Cracking sounds filled the air as the ground under their feet turned to obsidian and basalt.

I studied the ground. I couldn't cool the lava because that wasn't how my power worked. I'd destroy it in the attempt. But an ice dragon was a different story.

*"Aeyanie!"* I shouted. ***"Leave him alone! Don't bother with the storm. Freeze the ground! I want you to freeze the lava!"***

Relos Var might be able to sense if I telepathically gave the dragons orders, but the link didn't allow the wizard to eavesdrop on what I was physically saying. I knew that for a fact and would have known it even if we hadn't asked the Name of All Things for confirmation.[2] Thus, I was perfectly capable of giving audible orders.

I just didn't know if any of the dragons would *listen* to audible orders.

But Aeyan'arric broke off breathing at Khored and turned her head to the side to gaze at me. It was a much less angry look than I'd seen the last time we'd met. The last time had been the hateful stare of a tiger about to leap at its prey. This time, it was hard to shake the impression that she'd perked up like a dog that had just received a new command from her master.

She circled around in the air and switched her target to the ground. Aeyan'arric didn't breathe again, but the land under her flight path began to freeze in large swaths, billowing more vapor into the air while simultaneously hardening the lava. Even if she'd stopped actively summoning up a blizzard (and she probably had), she was still sending enough water into the air to make the arrival of a storm imminent.

"S'arric?" Khored said.

I turned back. Xaltorath and Ompher were back to fighting, and that wasn't a situation Ompher was going to survive for long. But I couldn't go do anything about that as long as I had to fight Khored too.

But the look on Khored's face made me pause. His expression was marked with wistful bemusement, laced with equal parts suspicion and hope. It was the look of a man who desperately wished the world would give him some happy news, even though he knew in his heart that it wouldn't.

***"We have to get Ompher out of here or Xaltorath will kill him!"*** I knew Khored hadn't meant the question that way, but I answered it as though he'd asked me what we were going to do next.

Because I could remember a thousand times when Khored *had* meant it that way, when he'd followed every order I gave him.

I swear Khored started to follow my orders this time too.

But a scream rang out. It wasn't a physical scream. Rather it was a scream that reached out from the tenyé itself, vibrating painfully through all of existence.

I remember hearing once that when Tya had given birth to Janel, her cries had deafened every mage for three days.

---

[2] But please note that we did check, anyway, before we left the Lighthouse for what turned out to be the last time.—S

*"Tya,"* I said. If anything happened to her . . .

I had to pick a priority. Saving Tya—and keeping that wall intact around the Korthaen Blight—easily trumped any plans to save Ompher's life. Whatever spell, effect, or item Ompher had somehow used to keep me spiked to one location until he could drop a comet on my head was gone. I could only assume it had lost its grip on me during the many, many, way-too-many times I'd died and self-resurrected while trying to escape the enormous, churning firestorm.

So I left the others behind. I hoped that they'd do the sensible thing and gang up on Xaltorath instead of following me. Then I teleported to Tya's location.

If I hadn't already been in a war footing, I might have been caught unaware by the swarm of metal shards falling like rain on my position. I knew the attack hadn't been meant for me, nor that my attacker had any way to know where I'd be in advance. It was just coincidence because I'd shown up right next to Tya.

And two dragons—Morios and Sharanakal—were trying to kill her.

## 75. MOVING FORWARD

### Kihrin's story
### Khorvesh, just outside the Korthaen Blight
### Just after Tya screamed

A second after Morios stopped breathing destruction over the landscape, Sharanakal started, which had the lovely side effect of creating little molten puddles of metal—all varieties—dotting the area. I kept up the barrier I'd raised to fend off Morios's swords, knowing it would also need to protect against the Old Man's pyroclastic flows. I shielded Tya as well, who was gritting her teeth as she tried to keep the wall stable. She'd already taken several bad hits, including a metal shard through one of her calves.

She glanced over and saw me. For a split second, the terror was large and stark behind her red eyes, and then she blinked as she realized I was protecting her. I was starting to recognize that look of hope warring with cynical realism.

"I can't hold it," she whispered.

*"Let me help. Janel will never forgive me if I let you die,"* I told her.

She blinked. I watched as she jumped to the entirely correct conclusion. "Kihrin?" She at least didn't say it loudly.

*"Shh. Let that be our secret—"*

A wave of pain raced over me, settled into the cracks in my souls. I screamed as I felt Xaltorath attempt to rip my souls from my body using one of Thaena's powers. Never mind that Xaltorath hadn't eaten Thaena in this timeline. Clearly, at some point, she had.

But seriously, if it was that easy to kill Vol Karoth, Thaena would've done it a long time ago. Probably Xaltorath was just trying to get my attention.

\*\*\*NOW DON'T SPOIL MY FUN,\*\*\* Xaltorath said. \*\*\*WE WERE JUST GETTING TO THE GOOD PART.\*\*\* The demoness walked over from where she'd teleported in, giving barely a passing glance to the dragons, even though Morios had just started his next attack. She seemed in no rush.

There was a strange sort of energy balance to Vol Karoth. Too much and I couldn't hold it all. Not enough and I became so hungry I was a hazard to everyone around me. Put me in a position like this, where I was required to throw out massive quantities of energy to stop the attacks of two dragons while simultaneously absorbing the energy from those same attacks?

I could do this all day. Until it was too much or not enough and then I was back to being in trouble.

*"Attack Xaltorath, attack the demon!"* I screamed at the dragons, hoping that they too would prove suggestible to my commands. Morios immediately broke off from showering the area around Tya with knives and instead swiveled his head to focus on Xaltorath.

Xaltorath's mental voice was lyrical and sweet as she continued the onslaught. \*\*\*EARTHGOD ENRAGED, BY NATURE'S PLIGHT, PULLS THE SKY DOWN, TO DESTROY THE BLIGHT. DEVASTATE? NO, PERHAPS ANNIHILATE!\*\*\* She broke off in a snarl as I tried the other way of defending against her—getting in a good attack of my own.

Khored and Ompher teleported into the area at the same moment Tya lost control. The wall of energy surrounding the Korthaen Blight vanished.

Given the amount of debris, dust, and ash in the air, I didn't see any change. The magical barrier had stayed in position for long enough to contain the worst effects of the initial blast and heat wave, but that only meant the forces inside were still primed to leave. A giant wall of superheated matter began to collapse, rolling out like an avalanche while a black-and-red mushroom cloud lit from within by a thousand lightning storms soared up into the sky.

I had no idea how to fix this. This fell solidly into the "too much" camp.

Ompher soared forward on a moving band of molten rock. He paused for just long enough to stare at me. His eyes were haunted.

"If you really are S'arric," he said, "then make damn sure they find a good replacement for me. Xaltorath had the right idea. I *should* go join my wife."

*"No,"* I said. *"Whatever you're planning, stop."*

"Ompher, wait!" Khored yelled.

But Ompher was already moving, a rolling ground wave carrying him forward toward the inferno. Ahead of him, the billowing clouds retreated. Behind him, those same clouds drew in at his heels like hounds called to order. Matter fell toward him the way it might toward any planet. I lost him from view.

Inside the area, the giant fireball condensed, pulled in on itself. Ompher was fixing his mistake. I couldn't help but feel a sense of approval, of pride, but it was chased down by the realization that Ompher would kill himself doing it. *Which he'd known.* He was pulling all that energy into himself, and he wouldn't be able to channel it—

Wait. Where had Xaltorath gone?

I heard the flapping of giant wings. More wings. I began mentally reciting all the curses I'd ever learned from Tyentso as I turned to see Baelosh and Sharanakal fly in. Sharanakal landed with a momentous ground shudder while Baelosh continued to circle, unwilling to touch molten rock.

But Sharanakal? Sharanakal was right over—

The first Sharanakal gave me a look both simultaneously playful and hideously evil. He raised his head back to breathe, flickering as he did through every other dragon's shape. Not all at the same time either, so one moment he had Aeyan'arric's face, and the next moment Rol'amar's. So not Sharanakal, then. *Gorokai.*

*"No, don't you dare!"* I shouted, a spike of genuine dread racing through me. I didn't think Gorokai could hurt me—much—and I wasn't sure what he'd do to the other Guardians. That was the problem. There was no way to know. His breath would twist apart the landscape and mutate everyone nearby in a million unpredictable ways.

If any of the dragons were the literal embodiment of chaos, who couldn't be controlled, who would rebel against orders just for fun . . .

Gorokai's eyes twinkled, and I knew that yes, he was about to attack. Then a white blur of motion dove straight at Gorokai as Aeyan'arric slammed into the chaos dragon, sending both of them rolling into the shaking ground. Giant clouds of dirt and debris rose into the air as they crashed into the base of one of the mountains. Trees toppled in riotous chorus.

But all this was a distraction. I tore my eyes away from the sight. *Where was Xaltorath?*

Behind me, Tya was recovering and trying to restore the shield. It was only useful because the vast rising cloud was collapsing, falling back down to earth. Tya would have to restore the wall soon or it would spill out and wipe out most of Khorvesh and Marakor, even if Ompher's gravity did manage to gather it all back in again.

*"Don't attack anyone! That's an order!"* I shouted at the dragons, who seemed understandably mystified that I'd changed my mind on the whole "let's watch it all burn" plan that I'd pursued so vigorously for almost four thousand years. They were fighting my orders too, which boded especially well for how the rest of this battle was going to go. On a deeply fundamental level, the dragons *wanted* to destroy. Anyone telling them differently—even me—was suspect.

"There!" Khored shouted, pointing with the sword. "She's in the Blight!"

I blinked. *"In the Blight? Who's in the—"*

Xaltorath. *She was in the Blight.*

I didn't have time to feel sick or dizzy or shocked. No time to properly appreciate the horror of the situation. The last time I'd seen her, Xaltorath had been composing a bad rhyme to commemorate the event. Because she'd been writing what would no doubt be the first of many prophecies she would use to leave notes to herself when Xaltorath started the timeline all over again.

Which she was about to have enough power to do, thanks to Ompher's rash attempt to kill me. Even besides the power of the explosion itself, Ompher wouldn't have enough strength to resist her. Not after this.

I turned toward the Blight. The swirling clouds of fire and ash pulled back, collapsing into a ball growing smaller with each passing moment. I couldn't see either Ompher or Xaltorath—but I could feel their auras, and they were right on top of each other. And then, that quickly, there were no longer two auras. Just one.

Just Xaltorath.

She was ironically doing the same thing as Ompher—pulling in all the released energy of the explosion, but whereas he'd been doing it to save lives,

Xaltorath was doing it to provide the extraordinary energy she needed to twist back time itself.

I was unsure which of us had a larger capacity to absorb energy. That probably seems strange, since that's my speciality, right? But I had a physical body and Xaltorath didn't. I'd been mutated into something that was *like* a demon in my ability to absorb energy, while Xaltorath theoretically had no limits at all. A less powerful demon would have been overwhelmed, but after absorbing Galava and who knows how many other demons, I had zero doubt that she was capable of swallowing all the energy Ompher's tightly contained fireball could provide. Could I? Yes, but I'd damn well better have something to do with that energy afterward or all I'd do was delay the explosion.

But it didn't matter: I had to stop her, or this was over. For everyone.

I knew her location, and I knew where she'd have to stay in order to finish absorbing the explosion. Once she did that, Xaltorath would have enough power to perform whatever ritual or spell she used to loop time and begin again.

I didn't know what would happen next. Would it seem like nothing because from my own perceptions she would have shunted herself into a parallel dimension? Would we all cease to exist as reality turned back two thousand years while Xaltorath once more chased down her chance to take it all?

I didn't know, and I didn't want to find out.

That meant that, despite my best intentions, we had to proceed with the next stage *now*. The plan either moved forward or stalled forever.

I reached out to a group of minds I knew well. *"There's a problem,"* I told them. ***"Stage two starts now. Swords away when you arrive; nothing here will attack you."***

I felt confident making that claim. The dragons were too busy fighting each other, and Xaltorath was preoccupied. Still, each word felt like the tick of a clock, reminding me that I had no way to know how much time we had left.

First, I burned Senera's air glyph into everyone's clothing and then followed that up with a different glyph that protected against fire.

Then I teleported the entire group to my location and threw a chunk of my energy into keeping myself from killing anyone who wandered too close.

"Everyone" was not, in fact, *everyone*. But it was Xivan, Talea, Senera, and Thurvishar. Xivan because the plan hinged on her. Talea both because we needed the luck but also because she'd surely find a way to kill me if I left her behind. Senera and Thurvishar because they could guide Xivan through the spell and because, of all the others, they were the ones most likely to be able to survive this level of fighting.[1]

---

[1] I'm not sure he would have said this if he saw how easily Anlyr dealt with you back in the Capital.—S

Yes, it is truly strange beyond measure that I, a twenty-five-year-old man, might possibly have any difficulty in a one-on-one melee against a fourteen-thousand-plus-year-old mimic. Astonishing.—T

What about in your last life, when you were Emperor Simillion?—S

Ah yes. That would be the time I was murdered when I was twenty.—T

The four looked shocked when they arrived, but given the dragons present and the hellscape that greeted their arrival, I could hardly blame them. At that precise moment, Aeyan'arric was still wrestling with Gorokai, and Sharanakal and Baelosh had started snapping at each other because they'd always been like that, even before they were dragons. Rol'amar hadn't yet rejoined us, but I didn't give it very long.

I pointed toward the Blight. *"Xaltorath's going to drain the energy from that explosion to power her time travel ritual. She's going to restart the whole thing."*

"What are you talking about?" Khored snapped. *"Time travel?"*

Thurvishar eyed the still-raging mass of clouds, now shifting in odd ways through a combination of Tya's wall and Xaltorath's feeding.

"We can't go in there until they've pulled out the energy from the entire explosion, but if we wait that long, we also won't stop her from leaving for a private location where she can finish her ritual in peace." Thurvishar frowned. "We need to distract her so she doesn't want to leave."

"That's easy," Xivan said. "Her weakness has always been the same as Suless's. She wouldn't steer a boat across a river to save a drowning child, but she'd swim through rabid crocodiles to hold that same kid's head underwater."

"Kihrin," Senera said. "Why isn't Janel here?" she said in a way that made it clear she already knew the answer—sympathetic but also a little chiding.

I gave her a wry smile, aware that I was still a silhouette of darkness and she couldn't see my expression. There was no defending the decision, so I wasn't going to try. I hadn't brought Janel or Teraeth because I hadn't wanted to risk either of them.

*"She's about to be."*

Unfortunately, it'd just become necessary. Because Senera was right. Janel needed to be there. Xaltorath would always hold a special place in her vile core for her adopted daughter. If she thought she had a chance to rub salt in Janel's wounds, she'd grab it with both hands.

*"You're up next. We need to keep Xaltorath busy. I suggest challenging her to a fight."* With that, I gave Janel and Teraeth the same protections I'd given the others and brought the two of them over as well.

I couldn't leave Teraeth out of it for the same reason I hadn't left Talea behind.

By this point, the collapsing cloud of death had turned into an enormous fire whirl. The edges of it began to hit Tya's rewoven barrier as it sank down into a squat shape, all the while continuing to circle the center of the Blight. The volume was lowering fast, falling back to the earth inert and cold as Xaltorath tried to consume every single morsel of energy from the massive act of destruction.

"Janel?" The first person to speak was Tya.

Janel crossed to her mother's side.

"Yes, it's me," Janel said. "Please help us. Help him. I promise you that this isn't what it seems."

"Unless you think that we're the misunderstood good guys," Teraeth said, "in which case, carry on. But we need to leave."

"Teraeth," Khored said, and it wasn't clear if that word was meant to scold, cheer, or simply greet.

"We need to leave *now*," Teraeth said.

**I SEE YOU!** Janel shouted. **I SEE YOU, XALTORATH! DON'T YOU WANT TO COME OUT AND SAY HELLO? IT'LL BE LIKE A FAMILY REUNION–JUST YOU, ME, AND MY *REAL MOTHER*.**

"If this doesn't work, maybe Jarith?" Senera tapped her lower lip thoughtfully. "Or Sheloran?"

"If this doesn't work, I don't think we'll have the chance to try again," Thurvishar said in response. He was clearly keeping his eyes on the dragons, following their motions even as he spoke to Senera.

The tornado had become a gyre, now a dull dirty gray and black as cooled debris began to slow. The spreading wave of falling rock and dust spread from the center outward as Xaltorath made one final push, or rather, pull.

Tya dropped the wall. There was no need for it anymore.

And in the center of the Korthaen Blight, glowing from the strength of the stored energy inside her, waited the Queen of Demons, Xaltorath.

# 76. An Unceasing Appetite for Pain

*Janel's story*
*Just outside the Korthaen Blight*
*Immediately following Xaltorath's reappearance*

The moment Kihrin contacted her mind, Janel knew three things: one, that the situation was dire, two, that she was going to kick Kihrin's ass if and when they got out of all of this, because three, he was backsliding: putting her into a "reserve" category that he clearly hadn't intended to ever call upon.

The *if* part of that caveat presented itself in all Xaltorath's splendor. That would need to be dealt with before Janel could so much as pat Kihrin's butt gently, much less kick it. And Xaltorath was a problem under the most ideal of circumstances.

This was not the most ideal of circumstances.

**NO GREETINGS TO YOUR OWN CHILD?** Janel "shouted" at Xaltorath. **NOT SO EAGER TO CALL ME YOUR DAUGHTER NOW THAT I KNOW WHAT YOU REALLY ARE, ARE YOU? AND NOW THAT JARITH'S NOT UNDER YOUR CONTROL EITHER? WOULD YOU LIKE TO KNOW HOW I FREED HIM? TOO BAD! I'LL NEVER TELL YOU!**

Most entities would have pivoted, turned, swiveled, or in some other way rotated to face her at this point. Xaltorath merely made a face appear on her body facing Janel, because why even pretend to obey the laws of biology when you're a demon prince? ***THIS IS PATHETIC,*** Xaltorath replied. ***YOU'RE A CHILD. A CHILD BEGGING TO BE SPANKED.***

**I AM SIMPLY TREATING YOU WITH THE RESPECT YOU DESERVE, SULESS. WHICH IS NONE,** Janel corrected. **AND YOU HAVEN'T MANAGED TO KILL ME YET.**

***I HAVEN'T TRIED.*** Xaltorath raised her arms, which tripled in length and grew clawed fingers protruding in every direction. ***THANKS FOR REMINDING ME THAT I NEED TO DO THAT BEFORE I LEAVE THIS FAILED TIMELINE. DEPARTING WITHOUT COLLECTING YOUR MEMORIES WOULD BE INEXCUSABLY SLOPPY OF ME.***

Damn. Xaltorath had never eaten her soul—not in any of Janel's incarnations, not in any of C'indrol's, not on any previous "loop." So the demon didn't know all that Janel knew. Janel contemplated the possibility that this could go very badly.

Now Xaltorath *was* thinking about it, which meant that if this plan of theirs didn't work, things would be exponentially harder on them next time around.

Janel slammed her sword against her shield and gave the demon prince a feral grin. \*\*YOU'LL TRY, ANYWAY. SO DO YOU NEED TO PONTIFICATE SOME MORE? I KNOW HOW YOU LOVE TO HEAR YOURSELF TALK . . . PERHAPS I MIGHT CONJURE MYSELF A CHAIR AND A BEVERAGE IF YOU'RE GOING TO BE AT THIS A WHILE?\*\*

\*\*\*IS THIS YOUR IDEA OF RILING ME UP? EVEN YOUR INSULTS ARE INSIPID, DIRECTIONLESS, AND WITHOUT STING. ASSUMING I HAVE USE FOR YOU NEXT TIME, I'LL TRY TO TEACH YOU TO AT LEAST MOCK YOUR FOES INTELLIGENTLY.\*\*\* The demon queen appeared at Janel's side instantaneously, raking at her with those many-clawed arms.

Janel was already moving, raising her shield to her left while dodging right. The claws skittered across the shanathá shield, and Janel's sword flashed down in an arc. Several of those extra fingers fell, vanished into smoke on their way down, and were immediately reabsorbed. Janel stabbed cross-body at Xaltorath's head, but the head elongated, stretched, and flowed around the blade before re-forming so that Janel's arm was inside the monster's mouth.

Xaltorath clenched her jaws, but a burst of rainbow energy shone around Janel's arm. The demon's teeth couldn't penetrate it.

Janel yanked her arm free, losing her sword in the process. She glanced over her shoulder to see her mother, Tya, watching the fight with obvious concern. Sweat dripped from the Goddess of Magic's brow; containing the devastation had taken a toll on her, but she was still in the fight. Tya gave Xaltorath an ironic bow of her head. "Can you beat us both, Suless?" she asked, locking eyes with the demon.

\*\*\*EASILY,\*\*\* Xaltorath sneered. More eyes appeared all around her body.

Meanwhile, Khored attempted to sneak around back to flank. Xivan and Senera were focused on Kihrin, who appeared dazed or distracted.

Xaltorath paid attention to the people she perceived as threats: Janel, Tya, and Khored. She lashed out at Khored with hands glowing with tenyé. He rolled under the attack, coming to his feet and slashing with his blade, but the glass sword passed through Xaltorath's thigh and reappeared on the other side.

At the same time, several black tentacles with scorpion-like stingers on the ends burst forth from Xaltorath's chest, whipping toward Tya. The Guardian managed to avoid most of them with a sudden conjuration of energy, but one tentacle slipped past and wrapped around Tya's left arm. The stinger jabbed down, a mouth opening at the tip as it did, and it bit deeply into Tya's shoulder.

Janel could actually *see* energy being drained from Tya and flowing into Xaltorath through that connection. \*\*\*YES!\*\*\* the demon queen exulted. \*\*\*GIVE ME YOUR POWER!\*\*\*

Janel dove forward and slammed the edge of her shield against the tentacle, severing it and breaking the connection. Tya staggered back, while Xaltorath smashed the other tentacles against Janel's shield, crashing her into the newly-formed rock near Senera and Xivan.

Janel was close enough, in fact, to see Xivan produce a small star-tear diamond from inside her misha and hand it to Senera.

"Never thought I'd be glad to see this," Senera said, somewhat bemused as she examined the gem.

Janel rose to her feet, picked up a chunk of stone the size of a large man's rib cage, and began circling to the right.

Janel threw the rock when she was about thirty or so feet from the demon and yelled, **SULESS! TELL ME, WHAT KIND OF FOOL MUST YOU BE, TO PLAY THROUGH THE SAME GAME SO MANY TIMES WITHOUT EVER ONCE WINNING? HOW MANY TIMES HAVE YOU DONE THIS AND *ALWAYS LOST*?**

The rock did little except knock askew one of Xaltorath's arms (of which she had around eight at the moment) and cause her to miss an overhead slam against Khored. It did, however, buy her the demon queen's attention once more.

Janel needed to distract the demon and play defense for a while.

That star tear that Xivan had given Senera belonged to Suless. The Suless from *this* timeline. No matter how many times Xaltorath reset the timeline, she could never change her own origin. The core of Xaltorath's gestalt demonic entity would always be the angry, spiteful soul of Suless, God-Queen of Witches.

Senera was the master of sympathetic magic; changing the whole by affecting a part. She'd used that sort of magic in Jorat, in Yor, probably in many other places. She just needed time.

Time Janel was determined to buy her.

Easier said than done. The childish insults were having some effect: Xaltorath chafed under the accusation of foolishness and incompetence. The demonic face twisted in malicious rage as Xaltorath once more teleported into Janel's personal space.

The shield held . . . barely. While that defense saved Janel's arm and half of her torso, the shield was all but destroyed, forcing Janel to discard it quickly. She suspected her arm was broken.

***DON'T MAKE THIS TOO EASY,*** Xaltorath sneered. ***I'M GOING TO ENJOY TEARING YOUR SOUL INTO TINY PARTS BEFORE I EAT IT.***

**OH, THAT THREAT'S SO ORIGINAL,** Janel replied, sprinting for cover behind a rock. **DO ALL DEMONS STUDY FOR THE STAGE? WAS THERE A BOOK OR SOMETHING THAT I MISSED? SOMETHING TITLED *HOW TO TALK LIKE A SELF-IMPORTANT PIECE OF SHIT*?**

The boulder Janel wanted to hide behind exploded into shrapnel and dust as four of Xaltorath's arms crashed into it. Janel flung herself back and rolled, feeling the wind from the other two arms rush by, one of them scoring her from hip to shoulder along her left side. She staggered back with her hands raised.

"Janel!" a voice yelled. That was her mother; her real mother, Tya. Xaltorath extended her arms to grasp and crush Janel, but another rainbow energy field interposed itself.

Janel looked past the demon to see Tya, on one knee and holding one hand pressed hard against a bleeding wound on her neck, the other hand raised. Khored sprinted past her, his sword aimed at Xaltorath.

***HONESTLY, YOU PEOPLE NEED TO LEARN WHEN YOU'VE BEEN DEFEATED!*** Xaltorath bellowed.

"Funny," Senera said, "I was about to say the same thing to you."

Xaltorath manifested another head to look at her, Xivan, and Talea. On the ground in front of them, a series of rune-infused circles glowed with faint light as tenyé lit up the dust drifting in the air. In the center of the circle, a small, perfect star-tear diamond glittered.

Janel was impressed the demon even saw the thing, but Xaltorath must have felt some instinctive connection, some link to a soul that might have once been hers. The demon queen tried to teleport to the center, to pick it up, but nothing happened.

Khored's red blade glowed as it descended, severing one of the demon's arms. He created another sword out of nothing and tossed it to Janel, who caught it in her off hand and raised it in an awkward defense.

Xaltorath batted Khored aside almost casually and frowned.

"Can't teleport, can you?" Senera said. "You're pinned."

***IT IS NO CONSEQUENCE,*** Xaltorath snarled. ***I DON'T NEED TO TELEPORT TO KILL ALL OF YOU, AND YOU CAN'T DEFEAT ME IN THE TIME YOU HAVE LEFT ALIVE . . . ***

That's when Kihrin appeared.

Or rather, in this case, Vol Karoth. His hands, silhouettes of deepest black, grasped either side of the demon queen's head. *"They cannot."* His voice sounded hollow and distant but at the same time resonant and commanding. *"But now I'm ready for the feast of suffering."*[1]

Xaltorath screamed on both the psychic and physical planes. The scream was one of absolute agony, of feeling her soul being torn to shreds and consumed in exactly the way she'd done to so many others before.

Tya forced herself to her feet, one hand raised to intervene. While Xaltorath was bad, Vol Karoth must have seemed much worse, and the Guardian's loyalties were conflicted. Janel stepped forward to block her mother's path. "Mother, wait. It's okay," she said. *"Trust me."*

Out of the corner of her eye, Teraeth was having a similar conversation with Khored.

Tya's hand dropped. "But," she said. "Kihrin. How?"

"I promise all will be explained," Janel said. "Just help us."

Behind her, Xaltorath continued to scream.

There was nothing about what was happening that was fair or noble, noth-

---

[1] That's a reference to what Xaltorath said upon assaulting Kihrin in the Capital City of Quur when he was fifteen.—T

ing that adhered to any Joratese sense of honor or chivalry. This was an ambush, pure and simple. It was also, unfortunately, the only way they could defeat Xaltorath. They all knew it.

Tya's magic soothed the pain in Janel's body. She glanced down to see her arm healing and setting back into place.

Xaltorath continued screaming, the sound having moved now from agony to terror.

Janel turned to see what was happening.

"Oh no," Senera said.

"What?" Janel and Xivan both asked the question at the same time.

"We didn't expect Xaltorath to be so powerful when this happened. So literally power-full. We've never established what Vol Karoth's limits are."

"Limits?" Janel said. "He's the Endless Hunger, the Prince of Annihilation. He doesn't have limits."

Senera stared at her. "Are we *sure about that?*"

Kihrin continued to feed, consuming Xaltorath's souls and energy. The empty silhouette that was his body began to vibrate. Another scream joined Xaltorath's: Kihrin's.

"No," Janel said, the dread growing inside her. "We're not."

Kihrin didn't stop. But he was in obvious, agonizing pain. Absorbing all of Xaltorath's energy was pushing him to his limits. Past them.

Janel felt a dull ringing sound, a vibration that carried through the rock beneath her feet. Suddenly, all the extraneous sounds ended, leaving only a faint susurrus of wind. What was left of Xaltorath flaked to ash and drifted away.

Kihrin staggered. Janel moved toward him, reaching out for him before she remembered that touching him was one of the more effective ways to commit suicide. She yanked her hand back, then raised it again to block Teraeth from making the same mistake.

Kihrin swayed, screamed again. The ground around him trembled and cracked. A pressure began to build in the air. Teraeth pushed Janel's hand aside, and he ran forward.

Fortunately, Kihrin had already vanished.

## 77. THE YELLOW SUN

*Kihrin's story*
*One of Ompher's moons*
*Right after biting off more than he could chew*

I was burning up. I knew in the back of my mind that I'd teleported back to the moon again—it seemed safer than staying planetside—but I had more immediate problems. Problems like what I could possibly do with all this energy without making the entire situation a thousand times worse.

Certainly, I couldn't just *keep* it. The delicate balancing act of existence that had become my new reality was tipped all the way over. This was more than just the energy that had killed me half a dozen times over before I'd fought it off. This was that tenyé, and all of Xaltorath's, and all of Galava's, and all of Ompher's, and all of every demon that Xaltorath had devoured . . .

The thing was, I wasn't even sure it would kill me. I didn't think it would, any more than Ompher's cataclysm had. But if I couldn't hold on to all this energy, it would go *somewhere,* and I had a terrible feeling that the explosion would be a thousand times worse than anything Ompher had accidentally done.

I really could break the world.

I found little humor in the idea that I might accidentally fulfill the worst of Xaltorath's mnemonic prophecies after I'd not only discovered they'd never been genuine in the first place but had also finally managed to destroy their author. One might consider that irony.

I had a different problem too. While it may not have compared with my most pressing issue—what to do with all that power—I also needed to figure out what to do with all those *souls.*

Although Suless formed the kernel of Xaltorath's identity, thousands of unique, individual souls were included in that mix. People I knew. People whom I had never known because they had lived their entire lives in a different version of history. I was forced to sort not only through lifetimes but through all the many instances that Xaltorath had simply started over again, twisting the ribbon of time in a loop again and again as the demon tried to find exactly the right set of circumstances. The path that she'd needed to take in order to have command over . . . everything.

I didn't really want to think about just how close she'd come to winning.

Xaltorath hadn't wanted to just overthrow the gods and rule everyone. Oh, her ambitions had been extraordinary, nothing less than merging both universes and using the energy therein to restart creation. With Xaltorath in charge. A demon turned into God. Ironically, several loops-worth of devoured Relos Vars had put their own distinctive spin on the plans, lending their own insight and knowledge, but hadn't appreciably changed the goals. He was fine with becoming God too.

Those other lifetimes of Relos Var proved an odd tightrope to walk. They were identical to each other and to the Relos Var I knew—right up until the point where Xaltorath began manipulating the timeline, and then they splintered. There were Relos Vars who had never known Senera and Relos Vars who had become emperor, Relos Vars who had never fathered Sandus and Relos Vars who hadn't made pacts with Grizzst. It meant that nothing I learned from these almost doubles was reliable, when the entire reason I had targeted Xaltorath was to finally learn some solid, consistent information about Relos Var's plans.

I had grabbed the psychic equivalent of a double fistful of writhing, venomous snakes. Now I was forced to sort through the varieties without being bitten, searching for just the right species. Voices screamed in my ears as Xaltorath tried to threaten me, to cajole, tease, tempt. Worse, I couldn't just disregard the demonic rat-king. Doing that allowed for the possibility that Xaltorath might find a way to regain her strength, to take over. Even if I stripped away every single extraneous soul and released them into the Afterlife (and I honestly didn't know what the potential consequences of that would be when some of these souls were temporal duplicates of ones that already existed), the kernel soul, Suless, would still be a demon, and would still be capable of climbing her way back out of any pit I threw her in. So I had to keep Xaltorath trapped, adding the monster to an unfortunately growing collection of demons I was keeping imprisoned using my own body. Not ideal, but for the moment, I had no alternatives.

Anyway, back to the real problem: all the damn tenyé.

Xaltorath had been hoarding tenyé like she was preparing for a long winter. All that power had been necessary—required—if she would have had any hope of punching a hole back through time to restart the loop. That was the reason why Xaltorath hadn't just started over when first Janel and then Jarith had escaped her control and mucked up her plans—she hadn't accumulated enough power. At the moment I'd finally defeated her, she'd been brimming over with accumulated tenyé, the equivalent of dozens of god-kings, two Guardians (Galava and Ompher), and the total energy output of that comet strike. I could (and did) let Galava and Ompher escape back into the universe, but that didn't do anything about the tenyé they'd carried.

I could feel that pulsing within me, demanding freedom. Explosive, destructive freedom.

I couldn't contain it. And using it to turn back time in the same manner Xaltaroth plan allowed for far too many variables to be worth considering. I was equally sure that whatever physical object I tried to use as an energy sink would explode so violently that the devastation might well be total. I couldn't predict how bad, but I assumed "beyond reckoning." I couldn't think of a single thing on the entire planet capable of holding this much energy. Possibly Skyfire? But I'd never reclaim the Cornerstone in time.

Nothing on this world . . . I looked up.

I had a fraction of a second to make a decision.

I did.

*Teraeth's story*
*Just outside the Korthaen Blight*
*Just after Kihrin's disappearance*

How Teraeth hated that he couldn't do anything to sway the outcome of the fight. Although he did convince Khored to stop attacking Kihrin, which wasn't anything to scoff at. Still, his job was making sure everyone else was in a position to do theirs.

Which meant Teraeth paid close attention when he saw Kihrin attacking Xaltorath. Kihrin had sworn up and down that he could do this, that it wouldn't be a problem, that everything would be fine. Maybe that was even true. Unfortunately, even if that hadn't been true, Kihrin would've made the same claim. So he watched for any sign of a problem.

The screaming was a big clue.

At first, he'd thought that it was just Xaltorath. Pulling the tenyé out of that demon had to be the spiritual equivalent of soaking in a midden. Teraeth would have screamed too.

But that wasn't it. There was a strange distortion in the air—strange even for Vol Karoth. The faint blue-violet halo that outlined Vol Karoth's utter blackness grew bright enough to easily see. Grew brighter still. That's when Teraeth realized what the problem was: it was just too much power. Too much power even for Vol Karoth.

"You have to get rid of it," Teraeth whispered. "Get it out of your body. Just . . . send it up into the sky or something."

Kihrin turned to look at him. Teraeth couldn't tell, of course. He couldn't see more than that outline. But it was easy to imagine that Kihrin had done exactly that, that he'd given Teraeth a reassuring "don't worry, I know what I'm doing" kind of nod just before he vanished.

Wishful thinking. Kihrin absolutely didn't know what he was doing. That wasn't even an insult: How could he? Who had ever done this before?

Laughter threatened to bubble up inside him. Xaltorath. He supposed Xaltorath might have done this before.

An odd silence fell in the wake of Xaltorath's destruction and Kihrin's retreat. Not true silence—the dragons remained on the scene, biting and sniping at each other. It gave the whole situation an unsettled feeling.

Teraeth crossed to Janel, still standing next to Tya. Janel seemed uninjured, but he remembered that she had been just a few moments before. "Are you all right? You're healed, right? It's not—"

Janel grabbed him around the waist and buried her head against his shoulder. He couldn't blame her. What had just happened . . .

"To Hell with this," Teraeth's grandfather Khored said. "We're damn well going to talk. And you're going to tell us—"

A streak of white split the sky, pointed straight to the sun. The brilliant line dissected the heavens, traveling from somewhere beyond the horizon across the sky until it hit the sun. Six dragons stopped fighting and looked up.

Everyone looked up.

"What the fuck is that?" Xivan said rather succinctly, while also managing to convey a strong sense of "what is it *this time*?"

"Kihrin," Janel whispered, still in Teraeth's arms. "It's Kihrin." She gave him a stare that hovered between relief and panic.

Teraeth felt a rush of relief. Kihrin was doing what Teraeth had suggested. He was throwing the excess energy out into space.

Except he wasn't, was he? He was throwing the excess energy *at the sun*. To what end? It didn't seem like enough to do anything to it, good or bad. Sure, yes, the tenyé was more than enough to overwhelm Kihrin and supercharge Xaltorath, but that still didn't seem . . .

Teraeth found himself wondering how much energy it had taken Vol Karoth to destabilize the sun in the first place. What the magical mechanics of the whole thing had been.

"We need to leave here," Tya said. "Now."

"Might I suggest the Manol?" Thurvishar offered. Teraeth could only envy his calm.

"What about the dragons?" Xivan looked north where the dragons were still arguing among themselves. At that very moment, Sharanakal reared back and started to breathe at Baelosh. Gorokai smacked Sharanakal's neck, so he veered off course and ended up pointed straight at them. A great dark cloud of superheated gas and rock began to speed in their direction.

"Great suggestion," Khored said. "Let's do that."

The entire group vanished and reappeared in the Manol throne room.

Teraeth exhaled. He was still holding Janel, and wasn't honestly sure he ever wanted to let go. They'd been in so much danger back there that it had almost ceased to have any meaning. There were more than a few times where he knew for a fact that he would have been dead if someone hadn't thrown a protective spell over him—usually Kihrin, but quite often Khored or Tya too. Even if he was grateful, he hated the helpless feeling.

Everyone started talking at once. The entire throne room drowned in panic, not least of which because no one was ever supposed to be able to just "appear in the Manol throne room."

Teraeth glanced around. Khored was half a second from coming over to demand those explanations, no doubt eager to prove that he too shared the family temper.[1] Tya looked not lost but numb. And various vané or Grizzst or one of the Quuros was trying to wrangle answers from Senera or Thurvishar. It was chaos.

---

[1] If Teraeth thinks he inherited his temper from his father's side of the family, I would invite him to take a closer look at his mother.—S

Teraeth sighed to himself. He hated this. It was everything he hadn't wanted. Everything he'd ever told himself he'd never, ever do in this lifetime. He'd have abdicated immediately if it hadn't happened in the middle of all this nonsense. But not now, for so many reasons. For Kihrin's sake, he stayed.

He'd do a lot of things for Kihrin. Even this.

Teraeth kissed Janel's forehead and stepped away.

She frowned but didn't try to stop him. He gave her one last look and a soft smile before he turned away from her. Teraeth climbed the dais up to the perfectly shaped chair of interwoven living branches that the Manol vané sovereigns had long considered their throne. Everyone was arguing or talking or having not-so-quiet fits when he turned around.

Teraeth sat down. "*Silence.*"

His command carried to every corner of the room, loudly, and cut through every competing voice. Teraeth couldn't claim his blinding charisma was responsible—this was due to the spells set upon the throne.

"This—" he gestured toward the gathered crowd, ignoring the surreal knowledge he was about to shout down *gods,* "—is unproductive. Tya—" Teraeth paused as he realized the Goddess of Magic wasn't paying attention to him. She had a faraway look in her eyes. Teraeth didn't think she was daydreaming or being rude.

"Tya!" Teraeth repeated.

The goddess startled. "The sun—"

He gestured to her. "Yes, that. What happened to the sun? Can you show us?"

A dozen people started to ask questions, but Tya proved two things: first, that she had, in fact, been paying attention; and second, that she didn't take objection to being given orders. She waved a hand through the air and conjured an illusion toward the ceiling, centered around a vision of the sun that hung like a glittering ornament.

"It looks normal," Therin D'Mon said.

It did look normal. But that didn't mean—

"Light doesn't travel instantly," Doc murmured in Teraeth's ear. "Give it a few minutes."

Teraeth didn't react to his father's voice, but he was happy to hear it.

Khored didn't seem inclined to wait until the sun did something. He whirled on Teraeth.

"What happened?" The God of Destruction's voice was not in any way suitable for public spaces. "Did you cure S'arric? Because that wasn't Vol Karoth back there! What is going on?"

"Oh, I don't think we have long enough for that conversation," Xivan said as she stepped forward. She was scowling, but weren't they all? "People are dying. We need to concentrate on saving lives, and afterward, we figure out motives and orders of events."

"This is not an unimportant—" But Khored paused in whatever he'd been about to say to Xivan and stared at her. His eyes widened. In a much less concussive voice, he said, "You found Thaena's Grail." It wasn't a question.

Xivan shrugged. "My friends did, but they gave it to me. That's not important right now."

"Not important!" Khored snapped.

"Not even slightly," Teraeth corrected and then leaned past the God of Destruction to speak to the larger crowd in the room. "So let's get this out of the way. Ompher's—" He glanced over at Xivan.

"—dead," she finished.

"Right. Ompher is dead. Xaltorath is dead. Vol Karoth—or at least the Vol Karoth we know as the insane God of Annihilation who wants to destroy the world—*is dead.*"

Khored scoffed. "Then who did Ompher throw a comet at? Because it looked to me like Vol Karoth survived that."

"*Vol Karoth is dead,*" Teraeth repeated. "So's S'arric, in a sense. Kihrin, on the other hand—"

"Look!" someone shouted and pointed up, at the illusion.

Because something *was* happening; the sun deformed, morphed, condensed. It was like someone had taken the red-orange forge of the sun and doubled the fuel—it began to glow hotter, a brilliant yellow-white color. Audible gasps were heard from all around the throne room. An unusually high percentage of the people at court were Founders, old enough to remember trivia that had passed out of common knowledge.

For example, Teraeth remembered being told by his . . . by Khaemezra that the sun used to be yellow.

"Is this bad?" Khaeriel murmured from nearby.

She was too young. Too young by far. She'd never seen the original sun.

Teraeth felt a strange pull at his face and realized he was grinning. Kihrin had done it. He'd fixed the sun . . .

"That idiot!" Senera cursed.

Teraeth gave her a flat look. "Excuse me?"

Senera crossed her arms over her chest. "He might as well have sent Relos Var a damn signed letter. This wasn't part of the plan!"

Teraeth raised an eyebrow. He honestly wondered if she had any idea what the plan was. He didn't, mostly because it certainly had seemed like the "plan" amounted to "let's first find out what Relos Var is trying to do." The plan had already shifted several times. "There's never been a plan in the history of the universe that survived its implementation intact," Teraeth spat and ignored the fond look Khored threw him. "He found a way to deal with the unexpected without destroying most of the continent. I'm not complaining."

"Senera's not wrong, though." Janel's smile fell into something less pleasant as she stared at the illusion. "Relos Var's going to know exactly what's happened to Vol Karoth the moment he bothers to look up."

# 78. THE RITUAL OF UNMAKING

### Relos Var's story
### The Raenena Mountains
### That afternoon

"Revas? Revas, you need to see this!"

Relos Var raised his head from where he was carefully inscribing glyphs into the granite rock face. He'd hollowed out the cavern by hand (or rather by magic), and precision was vital. He wasn't even close to being finished. An earthquake earlier had wrecked hours of work.[1]

He'd also left orders that he was not, under any circumstances, to be disturbed. If it were anyone else doing the disturbing, he'd have made an example of them, but this was Drehemia.

The woman who entered the cave was strange and beautiful. People were always fond of describing beautiful skin as "poreless," but it was more literally true for the dreth than any other race. This particular woman did indeed have "alabaster skin"—less soft than like something carved from rock and made animate. She had no hair anywhere on her body, which made for a very odd appearance to anyone who wasn't dreth.

He'd missed her.

Var sighed and straightened up. "What is it, Drehemia?"

"You need to see this," she repeated. "The sun just fixed itself."

"What?" He dropped his tools and dove back into the tunnel, heading toward the entrance. He exited at the base of one of the Dragonspires into a wide, shallow valley filled with trees and a broad, meandering river. Scenic. Beautiful. Irrelevant. A crowd of wizards had left their tents to gather in a clearing, eyes focused skyward.

He shaded his eyes as he followed the direction of their stares.

Relos Var started to laugh.

"I thought you said Vol Karoth permanently messed up the sun," Drehemia said, almost an accusation. There was a great deal she didn't remember about her time as an insane dragon. Relos Var sympathized. There was a great deal that he didn't remember from his time as an insane dragon either.

"How in heaven did someone manage that?" Relos Var said.

Then he blinked. There was only one explanation. "They cured S'arric. They must have cured S'arric."

---

1 I suppose that was one unexpected benefit to what Ompher did.—T

"What? But you said—"

Relos Var raised a hand for her to be silent. "They cured S'arric. Vol Karoth's the only person—the only entity—who could have fixed what he caused in the first place. But *Vol Karoth,* either before he was fractured or afterward, wouldn't have. He would never give back the energy he'd absorbed. That fool D'Mon boy must have sacrificed himself—I should have known what was going on when I saw the state of Kharas Gulgoth."

Drehemia frowned. "I haven't even had a chance to tell you about Karolaen."[2]

Relos Var stopped. He turned back to her. "What about Karolaen?"

The dreth woman rocked back on her heels, hands on hips, looking like she was about to convey an invitation to a surprise party. "It's been destroyed. Ompher's work, as far as I can tell. He chucked something at the basin. An asteroid or comet, probably.[3] I'm sure you felt the earthquake earlier. I don't know who he was fighting, but he wasn't playing around."

Relos Var could only stand there, staring. One didn't casually slam a stellar object into a planet, not just morally but logistically. Asteroids never appreciated spontaneity. That implied that Ompher had either gotten impossibly lucky or he'd been able to predict Vol Karoth's location. He probably wouldn't have just thrown a giant rock at the place for old times' sake. Was it possible that Ompher had managed to *destroy* Vol Karoth?

No, impossible. Relos Var had designed that to be impossible.

He allowed himself the barest, tiniest fraction of a second to check the link. It was a thread that he would've severed the moment he learned of its existence, but it stubbornly defied any such attempts. He had to guard the link constantly, not just to keep Vol Karoth out of his head but also the hysterics of eight dragons screaming into the void.

The link was still there. Vol Karoth was alive.

The moment he had that realization, he also knew something was wrong. It was too much energy. Fixing the sun would have taken all the energy Vol Karoth had, forcing him into a state that would have been—to Relos Var's senses, at least—almost indistinguishable from death until Vol Karoth recovered. That hadn't happened.

"Something's gone wrong," he murmured.

"Or gone right," Anlyr said. "We just need to figure out which one it is."

Relos Var didn't bother debating the difference. He pulled Worldhearth out of his robe and held it up. Immediately, a pulsing globe of cool blue energy exploded into the air in front of him. Many of those points were particularly bright, some almost blinding in their intensity. There were a number of

2 Karolaen was Kharas Gulgoth's original name.—T
3 Apparently "shooting star" is a misnomer, and depending on composition, such objects are more generally called either comets (ice) or asteroids (rock). I would've assumed Ompher would use rock by preference, but evidently not.—T

I asked, and was told that comets often move at faster speeds, and thus are capable of causing more devastation on impact, assuming they don't burn up before reaching the surface. Or, to put it a different way, Ompher was being a dick.—S

brilliant lights that hadn't been there the last time he checked, but then again, god-kings were always coming and going.[4] It wasn't enough information to determine location, but he'd practiced enough—long before he'd given the Cornerstone to Qown—to be able to determine identity.

"Ompher's dead," Relos Var said.

"I guess the comet didn't help," Drehemia said.

But that was just an interesting bit of trivia. One less obstacle in Relos Var's path. Whoever had killed Ompher had done him a favor. But also . . .

His pulse quickened. Khored, Tya, and yes, even Vol Karoth were still there, still adding their energy signatures (or stark lack of one, in Vol Karoth's case) to the accumulated heat of the planet. But Ompher's energy signature wasn't the only one missing.

*Where was Xaltorath?*

He'd checked once before, just after he'd taken back the Cornerstone. Xaltorath had been the brightest thing on the whole planet. And now? Gone.

Relos Var glanced up at the sky. Yes. That would do it.

The wizard chuckled. "Thank you, dear brother. You have made my job so much easier." Dealing with Xaltorath had always been an inconvenience that he dreaded. Now it didn't matter. And better still, his dear heroic, stupid little brother hadn't even kept that power for himself.

Relos Var was glad he'd fixed the sun. It meant he didn't have to worry about maintaining the Veil after he killed Tya.

"Xaltorath's dead too," Relos Var declared. "So I suppose it's time to finish what I started, isn't it?"

---

4 What do you want to bet that two of those bright lights he'd just dismissed were Xivan and Talea?—S

# 79. The Empty Cup

*Janel's story*
*The Manol*
*After their return from the Blight*

"*Half of humanity?*" Grizzst's voice seemed too large for the space they occupied, a volume that conveyed all the anger and fury of shouting without technically qualifying.

Janel wasn't sure what to call this meeting. It struck her as one of those portentous gatherings that historians in later eras would name something reverent. Something that would utterly fail to capture the rabid, scrambling desperation that had proceeded it and that still hung thick and suffocating in the Manol vané sitting room. Something that wouldn't even hint at the barking, snapping, arguing of people with almost unimaginable power grappling with the unwelcome sensation of being so terrified they were all but shitting themselves.

The only good thing to come out of the whole ordeal was that Tya had immediately volunteered to shield them against magically scrying. At which point a nervous Qown had stepped forward to volunteer that he'd magically scryed on Tya herself, and she didn't know how to protect against World-hearth. Which stole all the fuel out of any attempt the two remaining Immortals might have made to control that meeting while burning with righteous fury. A not-too-subtle reminder that they were all there because Guardians too were no more immune to making mistakes than anyone else.

Said meeting included two gods (Tya and Khored), three people in the process of becoming gods (Xivan, Talea, and Dorna), an immortal wizard now trapped in an articulated metal statue (Grizzst), two former vané queens (Valathea and Khaeriel), the current vané king (Teraeth), his heir (Therin), a mimic (Talon), four members of Quuros royalty, including the empress (Thurvishar, Galen, Sheloran, and Tyentso), a former Vishai priest (Qown), a mostly reformed terrorist (Senera), a former assassin (Kalindra), her brother, Jarith, and herself.

Doc was probably in the room too, but she couldn't see him.

"Half of humanity at minimum," Tya agreed, "but that's assuming that Kihrin is correct about Relos Var's intentions. We don't know for certain Var intends to do any of this." She was visibly upset, visibly tired, and Janel had to pinch her own hand to remind herself not to devolve into screaming at her own mother.

Seriously. Seriously, after all this time, after everything that he'd done. Tya was still going to make apologies for that bastard? Unbelievable.

But Janel couldn't completely hide her disapproval. "Whatever his intentions, you didn't think this fact about demon souls was worth mentioning?"

"Why would we have said anything?" Tya said in response. While she hadn't ignored Grizzst's outburst, the goddess did a commendable job of gracefully conveying the idea that he'd rudely interrupted a private conversation. "To what purpose? So people whose only sin was the origins of their souls could wallow in the anguish and guilt of never knowing if that mattered? If a dark or evil thought was truly theirs?" She waved a hand negligently at everyone in the room so that it would have been impossible to tell exactly who she indicated.

Khored's voice was soft but cut through all others. "Feel free to dissect our mistakes if we survive this. In the meantime, what happens moving forward–"

"I cannot fucking believe this," Grizzst interrupted. Before anyone could make any further comment, he added, "And you're wrong, Tya. We do know Relos Var's intentions. I know, because I fucking *helped develop the ritual to do it.* Which I only did because someone didn't think the rest of us needed to know that its qualifying criteria included half the damn population–"

"You developed the ritual," Janel said, heart rate picking up.

"Helped," he corrected. "Gotta give credit where it's due. Var did a fair chunk of the work."

"But you know it? You could re-create it?" Janel pressed. If they knew what Relos Var was doing in advance, then that changed things. *That changed everything.*

Grizzst paused, but then made a clanking noise as he shook his head. "You won't have time. It takes ages to set up a ritual like this."

She laughed. "Me? No. You misunderstand. Relos Var's already setting up the ritual for us. We're just modifying a few glyphs."

Senera sucked in a breath. "That . . . that could work. If we knew what those glyphs were in advance . . ." She met Thurvishar's gaze.

He in turn raised his hands. "It might be an option, but it seems riskier than stopping the ritual in the first place."

"That's the problem: you won't."

Kihrin appeared at the far side of the room.

Given that Kihrin (albeit Talon shape-changed as Kihrin) was already in the room, a certain amount of consternation was to be expected. Khaeriel was one of the first to start moving.

"Kihrin!"

Janel stepped in front of the woman and stopped her. "No, don't do that. I'm sure Kihrin would like to still have a mother when this is all finished."

"What are you–?" Khaeriel's mouth dropped open in outrage. "Get out of my way!"

"No, no, Janel's right," Kihrin said. "Everyone should keep their distance."

Khored had already pulled his sword by this point. Janel thought it was likely habit. And possibly also that part about being terrified. He pointed it at Kihrin. "Are you Kihrin D'Mon, or are you Vol Karoth? Show yourself!"

Kihrin stared at the blade and then at the Manol vané man holding it. "Do you really think that I'm the problem right now?"

"We saw what happened to Ompher." Khored's stance was battle-ready and his expression grim. "This could still be a trick."

"It's not a trick," Thurvishar said. Then he paused. "At least not the way you mean."

Teraeth sent a glare in the wizard's direction. "Stop helping."

"Yes, because obviously I mind controlled Ompher into *dropping a comet on the planet*. That seems like a strategically wise play." Kihrin's voice dripped sarcasm. "Stop panicking and start thinking, Mithros. If I were your enemy, I wouldn't have helped you in that fight back there. Also, I'd be appearing here in the flesh and we'd be fighting right now." He paused. "And I think we can all agree that I wouldn't have fixed the sun."

"I agree that the sun part does seem odd," Tya said, "but perhaps you might make an exception and appear in person, anyway. Call it a mark of trust."

Kihrin threw the Goddess of Magic a sour look. "I'm not staying away to protect *me*, Irisia."

Tya's face went blank for a second, and then she inhaled. "How bad is it?" Her voice was softer, more notably concerned.

"Could be worse," Kihrin said. "At least I managed to not blow up the planet."

"*Was that an option?*" Therin's voice sounded strangled. He hadn't attempted to approach his son.

Kihrin didn't answer. No one else volunteered to explain either. Janel already knew the answer was yes.

Kihrin glanced over at Janel and smiled. "You all right? I saw you take a hit out there."

"I'm fine," she said. Whether that was true or not would have to wait. If she wasn't dropping unconscious or forced to abandon her body, she was "fine" for the only definition she cared about.

"Let's get back to the part about how we can't stop the ritual," Teraeth said.

"And even more importantly," Senera said, "did it *work*?"

A corner of Kihrin's mouth flicked up. "Yes, it worked perfectly. A small snag on the power levels, but otherwise exactly as planned."

There was an almost audible release of tension around the room, at least from some of the people present, Janel included.

"Xaltorath is dead," Kihrin continued, "and I have access to all their memories. Which is why I know that you're not likely to stop the ritual. At least, we never have before, in all the times that Xaltorath has ever replayed history."

"Replayed history–?" Several people, mostly the oldest and most powerful in the room, all began babbling at once.

"Xaltorath had figured out how to move through time," Janel declared loudly, giving Teraeth a glance that she hoped he would interpret as *"please use your fancy throne to shout over people as necessary."* "It required incredible amounts of energy, which is why she kept attacking Immortals. She needed their power. Each cycle she repeated, she would leave herself notes on what had happened before—what everyone else calls the Devoran Prophecies. They don't predict the future. They never did. They chronicle the past."

"But this time they made a mistake," Kihrin said. "Xaltorath decided that their job would be easier if they only had to deal with one enemy rather than two—and apologies for any egos this may trample, but the only enemies they cared about were Vol Karoth and Relos Var. So this last time through, they set up a chain of events that resulted in Elana Milligreest fracturing Vol Karoth's soul, which as a side effect resulted in three souls being reborn that never had been before: Elana, Atrin, and S'arric." He gave Thurvishar a shrug, which the man returned, an unspoken apology for leaving him out. "Xaltorath didn't care about that, though. Their true goal was making sure that what remained of Vol Karoth would be too spiritually and cognitively damaged to prove any threat by the time we reached this point."

"Oops," Talon said.

"Right," Kihrin said, smiling with grim satisfaction. "Xaltorath's plan worked in a way. They did a fantastic job of eliminating one leg of that triad: themselves. But as soon as Relos Var realizes that Xaltorath is gone, he's going to move on to what would normally be his next step—the one he's likely been delaying because any time he's ever tried it previously while Xaltorath was still alive, the demon was able to twist the ritual against him."

"Wait, so Relos Var knows about the time loops?" Tya asked.

"He does." Senera paused as several of the other people in the room threw her questioning looks. "I was the one who figured what Xaltorath was doing using the Name of All Things. We were trying to find out why the demon prince was so interested in Janel. Relos Var didn't accept it was just the obvious: that she was Tya's daughter."

Janel found herself grateful that Senera and Relos Var still hadn't known quite the right questions to ask back when she'd been their prisoner. They'd known about her previous incarnation as Elana. They hadn't known about her first incarnation as S'arric's lover, C'indrol. It had been a pivotal blind spot.

"Very well," Janel said. "Let's assume we can't stop his demon ritual. I'm betting we can modify it. We know more about demons than he does. We can be more precise so that it only affects actual demons and, instead of ejecting them from this universe, sends them to the Font of Souls to be reborn."

Very smart people were in the room. She wasn't at all surprised when those very smart people immediately looked concerned.

"Janel—" Teraeth said.

"I know," she said. "I'm an actual demon. So is Jarith. Knowing that, it may be possible to modify the ritual so it won't affect us."

"And if it isn't?" Kalindra's voice went shrill at the end.

**Then we do it anyway,** Jarith said.

"No!" Kalindra said. Teraeth looked like he was about to start voicing a similar objection.

Janel met Kihrin's eyes. He understood. He wasn't happy about it, but he understood.

"There isn't a single person here who won't be risking their lives," Janel said. "Any one of us might not come back. I don't plan on committing suicide."

"Then we'll have to make sure we do a better job of redesigning the ritual than Relos Var did," Tya said. "We'll do it together."

Janel nodded at her mother, throat suddenly dry. She knew that Teraeth was still giving her a worried, upset look that spoke volumes about how they absolutely weren't done talking about it, but that was fine. It was possible that her concerns meant nothing, that there might be an easy way to make sure neither of them were affected.

But it would have been wrong of her not to bring up the possibility.

"Once he realizes Xaltorath is gone," Kihrin said, "his next step will be to strip the Eight Guardians of their powers so he can claim those concepts for himself." He inhaled. "So let's talk about that."

"He can't do it," Tya said. "If Relos Var could steal our powers, he also would have done it by now."

"The problem was never the ritual," Kihrin corrected. "He created the ritual. He knows how to undo it. No, the problem is that it's all or nothing. Once he starts, all Eight Guardians will know that someone is trying to cut their links with their powers and they'll know where that person is. If he didn't wait until you were too weak to stop him, it would never work."

"I don't know if you've taken a head count recently," Talon piped up, "but there's a lot fewer than eight of you these days."

"Yes, that's my point. Now originally, he likely thought that once Xaltorath was out of the picture, he could just perform the ritual to strip the Guardians, perform a second ritual to destroy demons, use Urthaenriel to take control of me and force me into the Nythrawl Wound, closing it behind me, and . . . I don't know. Take a nap? He's engineered enough chaos and mayhem in the rest of the empire to make sure Quur is in no position to interfere. And had I still been diminished, he'd be able to control all eight dragons just in case any unexpected complications turned up. It would be impossible to stop him."

"Except he knows you're *not* diminished," Teraeth said. "He'll know the moment he looks up and sees a yellow sun."

"That reminds me," Tya murmured. "I need to remove the Veil or the planet's going to freeze."

"You might want to do that sooner rather than later," Kihrin suggested.

"You said we can't stop the ritual to destroy the demons," Valathea said. "Is there nothing that can be done about stripping the Guardians of their powers?"

"Of course, there is," Thurvishar said. "We beat him to it."

Silence.

It was a testament to how total the stunned surprise was in the room that no one said a word. Most of them just blinked at Thurvishar like he'd just told them that jumping into the Nythrawl Wound themselves was a perfectly rational solution to the whole problem. Most. Senera was nodding. Kihrin was showing no reaction at all.

Janel thought that was wise. Coming from him, the likelihood that someone would accuse this of being a trap seemed a certainty.

Grizzst broke the silence. "To what end? To make his job easier for him? If he has a way to claim those concepts, it doesn't matter who cuts the connection—"

"He's not the only one who has a way to claim the concepts," Xivan said. Her gaze was firmly fixed on Khored.

"Oh, I get it," Dorna said. "Can't empty a drained cup, can you? But couldn't he just . . . do the ritual again?"

"He has to know their names for the ritual to work," Kihrin said slowly. "Their true names. He's already denied Thaena, Taja, or Galava. He just doesn't know it yet. But once that first attempt fails, he'll start searching for answers. In previous runs, when that happened, he just asked the Name of All Things for the identities of the new hosts. This time, he doesn't have that option, because this time, Senera switched sides and used that Cornerstone to cure Drehemia."

"You would just have to strip . . . us," Tya said. "The only two left. The others are easy. We just hand out Greater Talismans."

"Greater what?" Grizzst asked.

Tyentso leaned over. "I have no idea either. Just shut up and listen."

"Hey, I'd like to know what's going on!" Grizzst snapped back.

"And I'd like Nemesan to not start a damn civil war. It's nice to want things." Tyentso stepped forward. "But just to cut through all the bullshit on this, am I understanding what you're proposing, Scamp? You want to do this ritual, making eight new Guardians . . . and then what? That doesn't fix the demons. That doesn't fix the Nythrawl Wound." She shrugged. "And while I realize this part's a bit more personal, it doesn't stop Nemesan from ripping the empire apart." She narrowed her eyes. "Why did you want to make sure that Relos Var has Urthaenriel, anyway?"

Kihrin grinned, big and wide and so like, well, *Kihrin* that Janel damned the fact she couldn't stop everything and kiss him right there. "Oh, because that way I can track his location."

"You can't track—" A half-dozen voices, all at once, saying some variation of Godslayer or Urthaenriel or in one case, the Ruin of Kings.

Kihrin met Janel's gaze and smirked.

"Not helping," Teraeth called out. "One at a time." He didn't quite roll his eyes, but Janel could tell he was fighting it.

"Kihrin can track Urthaenriel," Thurvishar said. "I've seen him do it. And that was before, when he was mortal."

Kihrin held up a hand. "Three steps. First, we make new Guardians. Two, we take Janel's suggestion and fix Relos Var's ritual for him. Three—" He hesitated. "Three's more complicated. I'd prefer not to use Relos Var's method of solving the Nythrawl Wound problem, but we'll have to see how it goes."

"Kihrin–" Teraeth leaned forward, a warning in his voice.

Janel commiserated. *"We'll have to see how it goes"* wasn't so difficult to translate into *"if I have to sacrifice my own life, I will."* But at least Kihrin wasn't making it the first option.

"You make that sound so easy," Tyentso said. "Like he's not going to have eight dragons and an entire army stewed on Warmonger fighting on his side."

"He won't," Kihrin said. "He thinks he controls the dragons. He doesn't. He thinks he can use Urthaenriel to force me into the Wound. He can't. And as for Warmonger–"

Tyentso addressed Jarith. "You tracked down Warmonger once. Can you do it again?"

**Yes. And teleport wards won't stop me.**

"You're still my favorite Milligreest," Tyentso told him, shaking a finger. "All right. That's almost starting to sound like a plan. We'll beat him to the finish line on the first ritual and then track him down and kick his ass before he can finish the second."

"You're all assuming we're going to agree to being de-powered." Khored was practically growling.

"You're damn right we are," Dorna said, whacking the God of Destruction on the arm as she did. "Sounds to me like you're losing that loaf of bread no matter how you cut it. What they're suggesting is giving you control over who comes next. Now come on, old man. Ain't you immortal and thousands of years old, anyway? So, you won't be a god. So what? Didn't seem to me that you enjoyed that half as much as fighting in the tournaments and wenching yourself sick after."

Khored gave Dorna an admonishing look to which the old woman seemed perfectly immune. "Damn it all, Dorna. Who told you to start making sense?"

"Must go with the job or something. We both know that it ain't natural behavior for me."

Sheloran snapped her fan closed with a hard metallic click. "So," she said. "I suppose the most obvious question is: Who do we choose as replacements?"

Khored frowned. "Does it matter? They won't have time to acclimate." He pointed to Talea and Xivan. "You two have come along faster than I would've expected, but there's little chance we'll have even that much time for our replacements. Which is fine, because until we can kill Relos Var, we'll have to keep all of you out of sight, or he'll just do the ritual again with the correct names."

"It damn well *does* matter," Senera snapped. "Because whoever is chosen will still have the job when this is all finished! Telling yourself that the compromises were fine because they'd only last until you accomplished your goals was how we ended up in this position in the first place!"

Khored's mouth twisted, but he didn't tell the wizard she was wrong. In fact, he didn't seem insulted by her rant. Janel wondered if she should blame too many years spent working alongside Khaemezra.

"There's one last thing," Kihrin said.

"Oh, for fuck's sake," Tyentso said.

"You have the option of resisting the ritual," Kihrin said to Tya and Khored. "But if you do, it will set up a fatal disharmony. It'll kill you. Relos Var probably doesn't mind that outcome. I do. So don't fight it. I know after all this time it will be instinctive to do so, so all three of us are going to have to make a point of allowing it."

Grizzst whipped back around. "Wait. It's going to affect you too?"

"I did say all or nothing, didn't I?" Kihrin said. "The ritual isn't piecemeal. He has to try to strip the powers from all eight of us, all at once. He won't *get* all of us, but as it stands right now, he will affect Tya, Khored, Ompher, Argas, and yes, me. It doesn't matter that Ompher and Argas are both dead. That just means they can't resist."

"No, that's bullshit," Grizzst interrupted. "Look, I get that it's possible, but he went through a lot of effort to make sure that you, in particular, had these powers. He's not just going to remove them."

Kihrin looked vaguely annoyed at the interruption, but he simply shook his head. "But he's not removing the powers he cares about. You forget I've been through this ritual *twice*. He'll strip S'arric's concepts away. Vol Karoth's will remain." He sighed. "Unfortunately."

Janel stepped forward. "We need to remove those powers and reassign them before Relos Var can. That's the point."

"We'll still have to find the right people," Tya said. "The Greater Talismans only respond to very specific resonances. Not just anyone can form the bond with them."

Valathea cast her gaze around the room. "Be that as it may, I see a roomful of people who likely qualify. With the additional bonuses that we both already know them and they're *here*. I see no reason we can't start this right now."

"Wait, you're not suggesting—" Galen started to say.

The mimic began laughing.

"I don't see what all the fuss is about," Talea said. "It's not like becoming a god hurts."

## 80. The Siege of Atrine

*Tyentso's story*
*The imperial army camp outside Atrine*
*After the Battle of the Blight*

Tyentso returned with her people (she decided not to examine exactly when a Black Brotherhood assassin and an actual demon had become "her people," but at least Fayrin legitimately took orders from her) while everyone back at the Manol made their plans.

Tyentso knew damn well that Relos Var wouldn't have cut a deal with Nemesan or Havar or Murad or whatever the hell he was going to call himself without it serving a purpose. Maybe it was as simple as denying his enemies that large a military force.

She suspected it was more than that. Tyentso had never known a time when Relos Var didn't work on multiple levels, usually all at once.

She didn't have to wait long.

When Havar's troops attacked, they did so in classic House D'Aramarin style: by opening gates into the middle of the camp and killing anyone who moved. The imperial army was well trained, but with Warmonger removed?

The soldiers were more of a detriment to their side than anything else. The Marakori troops might have overrun the camp in a matter of moments if they'd only been dealing with the imperials. But thank every star in the heavens they weren't.

They were also dealing with the Joratese.

There was no front line.

"I thought you said they were waiting for us to lay siege!" Tyentso shouted at Ninavis as she found the woman. She ignored the fact that Ninavis was in the middle of a fight. She seemed to be doing fine.

"Whoops?" the woman said. "What the fuck is wrong with your people, by the way? Did you forget to let them sleep? And where's Dorna?"

"Long story, they won't be much help. Dorna's busy. I have more reinforcements on the way." Tyentso fired a long beam of tightly vibrating sound waves that punched a neat whole through a Quuros war scorpion. Not one of hers. That fucker had brought his own and was trying to set them up so he could turn them on the local civilian population.

"Oh yeah, speaking of reinforcements, don't attack the shadow demon. He's with us."

Ninavis stared at her blankly. "What."

Tyentso rolled up her sleeves and prepared to start defending her empire in a slightly more personal manner than she'd been doing of late.

A few minutes later, however, everything fell quiet again. Tyentso searched around her only to realize the fighting had stopped.

"What the fuck? Where'd everyone go?" Ninavis searched around her, confused.

Tyentso blinked. Not everyone had vanished. The people they'd been immediately fighting had died like normal. They weren't replaced, however. No new enemy soldiers were showing up to reinforce the push.

"Oh," she said. "This was a feint. They were just testing our defenses."

"Stupid of them to let us know they can do that," Ninavis muttered.

"Stupid of you not to assume I could," Havar D'Aramarin said.

A whole lot of people started aiming spells and arrows and—

"Don't bother," Tyentso ordered. "He's not really here."

"No," Havar agreed. "I'm not."

Truthfully, Tyentso was assuming he was Havar because his voice sounded familiar. He didn't look like Havar D'Aramarin anymore. Presumably, he'd decided that there was no longer any need to pretend to be a normal human when he instead could be an incredibly handsome god-king with forge-red voras eyes. He still didn't look like the statues of Murad. He'd cast off that disguise too: this was Nemesan.

"What is it you want to say, traitor?" Tyentso asked him.

"Traitor?" Havar smiled. "That would imply that I ever owed Quur any allegiance at all. And I don't. I have always been at war with Quur. You simply didn't realize it. But there's no point in pretending anymore." He held up a silver-gray chunk of hematite, worn smooth and shiny. "Not when I have this."

Warmonger. Tyentso took a step forward before she could stop herself. "Really? You showed up here to gloat?"

"I showed up here to offer you one last chance," Nemesan said. "I'm a forgiving man. Surrender and have your people lay down their arms, and no one else has to die. Time is on my side, not yours. In a few hours, your people will be too sick to move, while mine will only become stronger. All your soldiers will die, and I won't be gentle to the civilian population. At which point, this offer will still be open—but only to your soldiers. Not to you."

Cute. Oh, that was cute. Pirate ships made the same offers while closing in on merchant prey. Turn against the captain and live or fight against foolish odds and go down with the ship.

"Damn, you're a cocky motherfucker," Tyentso said. "As if I didn't kick your ass out of the Capital, destroy your house, and send you whimpering back to Marakor. You aren't as invulnerable as you think you are."

"If you're trying to make me believe you still have Urthaenriel in your possession," Nemesan sneered, "I know better. You don't have Godslayer, while now I do have Warmonger. And I know what this Cornerstone can do. I'm not some pathetic high lord balancing accounts and selling spells for profit. I am the god-king Nemesan! It took a century for Quur to defeat me the last time I had this stone in my possession. You can't overwhelm me in a few hours."

Tyentso had spent a lifetime controlling her expressions, not letting her real feelings show in front of Gadrith or slavers or any number of enemies. She was confident her expression didn't change—or changed almost imperceptibly—when he first made his admission. Nemesan was making the big reveal, trying to impress her with the declaration of his real identity.

She snorted.

"Am I supposed to be shocked?" Tyentso told him. "I already know who you are. So we'll just see who can play this game of Zaibur better, won't we? In case it's not clear enough for you, my answer is no."

He smiled. "Good. I'd have been so disappointed if you'd said yes."

Nemesan vanished.

The duchess turned to Tyentso and slapped her arm. "What was that? A dick-measuring contest?"

"I fucking wish," Tyentso told her. "But heh, battles are won in the mind first, right? If he can convince us that it's impossible to win against him, then he's halfway there, isn't he? Anyway, he's nothing but a distraction, although it was awfully nice of him to confirm that he really is Relos Var's lackey." Nemesan shouldn't have known about Urthaenriel. Most people would have assumed that she'd never had the sword to begin with. No emperor had run around waving the damn thing in five hundred years. She chewed on the inside of her cheek. "Have everyone work on setting up defenses, demon-march protocols. Even if they say they aren't feeling well. I want everyone on their feet until they can't be anymore."

"And then what?" Ninavis was scowling. "We just wait for them to attack us again?"

"No," Tyentso said. "We're waiting for more information."

Fortunately, she knew just how to get it. Tyentso tilted her head toward Kalindra. "You and your wonderful husband can get that for me, can't you?"

Kalindra smiled. "It would be our pleasure."

# 81. THE NEW EIGHT

*Janel's story*
*The Mother of Trees, the Manol*
*After Kihrin's arrival*

Kihrin cleared his throat.

Everyone had done a commendable job of keeping their distance, although Janel knew that it must have been difficult for some. Possibly it became easier when people started to notice that in spite of Kihrin's best efforts, the side of the throne room where he stood was looking increasingly damaged.

No one wanted to look at him or anywhere else. Teraeth took Janel's hand and squeezed.

Kihrin gestured toward Khored and Tya. "We shouldn't wait. It's not like you weren't already starting to pick the next Guardians. I bet easily half the people you had in mind are already in this room." He pointed at Khored. "Teraeth or Janel?"

"Teraeth," Janel said before Khored could speak. She gave Teraeth an apologetic look. "Regardless of your answer, my dear, it *can't* be me. We don't know what it would do."

Janel didn't explain. She knew she wouldn't have to; Teraeth already knew she was pregnant. But she forgot one important detail.

That Dorna was the new Goddess of Life.

"You're pregnant? Bloody fields, stallion! What'd you go off and do that for?" Dorna looked like she hadn't quite decided if she wanted to be spitting mad about it or not, but she was leaning toward yes. The woman looked back and forth between Teraeth and Kihrin. "So which one of you did she tumble?" She didn't wait for them to answer, but crossed her arms over her chest and glared at Janel. "How are you supposed to raise a child without a herd! You know you can't just–" She turned to Tya and pointed back at Janel. "I didn't raise her to–"

"Dorna!" Janel said.

Tya shook her head. "Later, Dorna. We have bigger problems than who will raise my grandchild."

Khored stared at the women fondly as he summoned up a red glass sword, a smaller version of the one he typically used. "That does make my choice easier." He reversed his hold on the sword and handed it hilt first to Teraeth. "It's practically the family business."

Teraeth didn't look like he agreed. Indeed, Janel suspected he would rather bodily injure himself–shatter that sword and shove each shard through his tongue—than accept what his grandfather was offering. The Manol vané crown had been bad enough.

Senera also noticed his hesitation and rolled her eyes. "There are only so many synergies present, you know. Do you really want *Talon* to be the new God of Destruction?" Senera reminded him.

Teraeth grabbed the sword.

"I think I resent that," Talon muttered. "Although . . . fair."

"So what do I do with the damn thing?" Teraeth examined the sword with obvious disquiet.

"Nothing. Just hold on to it for now," Kihrin said. "Once we perform the ritual, you'll already have it, and then it will start to take effect."

"Lucky we know how to speed the process up," Talea said.

Tya, who had been one of the pair to invent the Greater Talismans, blinked at the new Goddess of Luck. "I'm sorry? What was that?"

"If a soul is injured," Janel explained, "it's easier for the talisman to attach. A bit like a wound making one more vulnerable to infection. In this case, the talisman heals the damage and, in doing so, bonds. What otherwise might take days or weeks happens instantly."

"An injured soul?" Tya cocked her head. "Are you referring to someone being gaeshed?"

"Yes," Janel said grimly.

"It seems to me," Valathea said as she walked over to the three remaining talismans, "that Thurvishar might work for any of these." She motioned to Tya's Veil, the Globe of Ompher, and the Book of Argas.

"If I were being extraordinarily petty, I would say it has to be the Book of Argas." Valathea had a dark, stern expression on her face.

Janel felt her gut twist. Yes, that would be extraordinarily petty. Appropriate, but rubbing Relos Var's face in the fact that he wasn't chosen for the role of Argas, would never be chosen for the role of Argas. That Valathea had chosen someone else.

Not just anyone else but Relos Var's grandson. His weakness was also family, if perhaps not quite in the same way as the people he targeted.

But Janel also thought that was something of the obvious choice, one Relos Var might well guess correctly once he figured out that the Eight had been replaced. Thurvishar was a good pick—but not for that position.

"Then it's a good thing I am not extraordinarily petty," Thurvishar said. He picked up the Globe of Ompher. "I know Wildheart is more associated with Galava than Ompher, but I suspect I'd still do well with this one."

Very well. Astonishingly well. The idea of Thurvishar controlling all the powers of Ompher was frankly terrifying.

Senera frowned at the wizard, visibly confused. "You're not picking Tya? I'd just assumed . . ."

"Oh no," Thurvishar said. "I wouldn't dream of taking that away from you."

Janel wouldn't have thought it possible for Senera to turn whiter, but it was difficult to dispute the evidence of her eyes.

"No," Senera said, shaking her head. "No, absolutely not. And I would be a terrible choice. The worst choice, honestly. You can't expect . . . Just *no*."

"I can't help but notice nobody's giving me the option of becoming a Guardian," Grizzst said petulantly.

"Yes, I wonder why that is." Kihrin answered. But his attention quickly snapped back to Senera. "I think you might be wrong about being a poor choice. What do you think, Irisia?"

The current Goddess of Magic looked thoughtful. "Not a poor choice at all, honestly." Then she nodded decisively. "Yes, I want you to have it."

Senera snapped at Janel, "Why did you have to get pregnant? You're her daughter! You'd be perfect."

Janel just smiled. Adorable. As if she hadn't spent her whole life running away from her mother's inheritance, even before she realized who her mother was. "I'm not the right one for that role at all, and you know it. Maybe in another lifetime."

"Oh, come on, Senera," Talea said. "We'd be the Three Sisters."

Next to her, Xivan just smiled, as if she'd known all along how this would go.

Senera closed her eyes, and Janel knew that Senera had given in. She snatched the veil off the table and glared at everyone as if daring them to say a single word to her about it.

When no one did, Senera snapped, "I can't be trusted with this kind of power! You shouldn't be letting me anywhere near this. This is ridiculous! What the fuck is wrong with you people?"

"Oh, now we ain't got time for that," Dorna said. "And I always did say you was on the wrong side."

"Yes, you're very smart!" Senera retreated to her chair, where she sat down with exactly the same expression on her face as a child who'd been sent to her room without dinner.

"One left," Valathea said. She tapped the cover of the book with a delicate violet finger while she scanned the room.

"I think this one's obvious, don't you?" Janel looked over at Kihrin, who nodded in reply. Sure, there were a couple of people in the room who wouldn't make a bad fit. Senera might have been an even better match with Argas than with Tya, given her thirst for knowledge. Thurvishar would also have been outstanding. But since they'd already chosen their jobs, that left one person who would do the job right.

"Is it?" Grizzst asked. "I mean, Valathea's not a bad choice . . ."

"I'm flattered," Valathea said, "but I'm quite satisfied with the part I have to play. I don't need a larger role."

Janel reached for the book, stopping just before touching it. "May I?" she asked Valathea.

"Of course." Valathea removed her hand.

Janel picked up the book. She didn't go thumbing through the pages, just in case the damn thing were to have some sort of odd reaction.

Then she handed it to Qown.

"Oh, now *that's* petty," Talon murmured.

"While I agree my pick is a glorious fuck you to Relos Var, that isn't the reason I'm suggesting him. That just happens to be the sweetest of desserts after the meal." She met Qown's eyes. "I'm nominating you because you deserve it, and you would do the job well."

Qown held the book to his chest, nodding slowly. His expression was one of shock.

"Apologies, Valathea," Kihrin said, "but that's not the last one. *Now* there's one more left."

Tya studied Kihrin. "That will require a new talisman focus."

It was almost comical how they'd forgotten this part. Just missed it completely. Yes, of course they were going to need a focus. Janel could tell by the look on Kihrin's face that he was unprepared. And what could he possibly have brought with him?

The answer came to her, and it was so obvious that she nearly laughed.

"I have it." Janel pulled the necklace of star tears from around her neck and tossed it to her mother. "This held Kihrin's gaesh for years. The star tears themselves are empty now."

Kihrin laughed, just once, then looked away. "Yes," he murmured. "You're right. That's perfect."

Janel's mother took the necklace and proceeded to stare at it with great solemnity for a good sixty seconds. She would occasionally glance up as if to study Kihrin, then stare up at the ceiling as if checking the sun outside. Which might have been exactly what she was doing. The necklace began to glow with a bright, golden light, which grew to blinding intensity before settling back down until the necklace looked perfectly normal. Or as perfectly normal as a necklace of priceless star tears ever looked.

"And who receives this?" Tya asked Kihrin. Janel suspected the rest of them weren't being invited to share their opinion.

Kihrin didn't hesitate. "Galen."

"What?" Galen said.

"You know, this is a bit like attending the world's most surreal will reading," Talon said. "Only instead of figuring out who gets the fifty-year-old wine in the cellar, we're handing out godhoods."

"Don't I get a say in this?" Galen asked. He seemed less upset than genuinely curious.

"Blue, don't even start." Sheloran elbowed her husband in the ribs and tapped the table in front of her. "Yes, he'll take it. Of course he will."

Tya didn't move. She stared at Galen. "I appreciate your wife's enthusiasm, but the answer is yes, you do get a say. If you don't want it, we'll find someone else."

"But seriously," Talon said, "*I* have so much sympathetic resonance with Kihrin and by extension S'arric. I would be a valid, logical choice for this position, which *nobody* wants, including me. So you'd better say yes."

"I was always going to," Galen said. "I just wanted to know." Tya folded the necklace into his hands. He stared at it for a long moment with an unreadable expression before fastening it around his neck.

"Now we're done," Kihrin said. "At least with that part. Next up–finishing the ritual before Relos Var does."

"And your mother and I need to talk to you alone," Therin said. The man had been silent the entire conversation. So had Khaeriel. They'd just watched from the back, so quiet it had been easy to forget they were in the room.

Janel fought back a flinch. It seemed unlikely that they hadn't pieced together exactly what was going on. And they looked as happy about it as one might expect.

Kihrin raised his chin. "Sure. I can do that too."

## 82. Questions of Identity

### Kihrin's story
### The Mother of Trees, the Manol Jungle
### Just before the De-Ascension Ritual

I met with my parents in one of the back parlors. Several were spread out through the private quarters of the palace, places where members of the royal family could find privacy, without the threat of courtiers or petitioners jockeying for a few moments of their time. The room also didn't have much in the way of furnishings compared to its neighbors, which was great because it meant that there was less for me to accidentally disintegrate.

I held a hand up when my mother began to walk up to me. "Stay back, please," I told her. "I've warned you that it's not safe for you to get close."

They both looked at each other, then at me.

"Are you Kihrin?" my mother asked cautiously.

"He can't be," Therin snapped. "I don't know why the others just seem willing to accept—"

"Are you Khaeriel?" I asked my mother.

She got the point immediately. Khaeriel, after all, wasn't in the body that she'd originally been born in. Thanks to the Stone of Shackles, she'd been switched into someone else's. But that didn't make her Miyathreall. Then she shook her head. "That seems a different circumstance. My souls were swapped because of the Stone of Shackles."

"The difference is that Miya wasn't a god," Therin snapped. "And Miya's souls didn't stick around after the transfer was done. We're supposed to believe that you're *not* Vol Karoth?"

"Dad, calm the fuck down," I told him.

He did not look even slightly calm. "How can you even say that—"

I sighed. I didn't need this. Fuck, I *so* didn't need this. "Were I actually Vol Karoth the Endless Hunger, Warchild, He Who Will Bring the End, and whatever stupid labels you feel like assigning, would I really be standing here letting my parents lecture me about—" I squinted. "What am I being lectured on? Saving the world, taking possession of my original body from my last life, the fact that I still haven't quite figured out how not to destroy anything I touch? I promise I'm working on that last one really hard. I'm up to an hour now."

"I don't care!" Therin said. "And yes! You're being lectured on all of that!

Damn it, Kihrin, I just got you back, and now I find out that you're already—"
He choked and turned away.

"I'm *not dead*," I repeated. "Yes, fine, your biological offspring *is* dead.
Which—okay, yes. That sounded better in my head. *I'm sorry*. It was unavoid-
able. I still consider you my father." Hardly difficult. S'arric barely remembered *his* father. He'd been a child when his family had left the man behind
in a whole different universe.

Therin didn't look mollified. He looked horrified.

"You must be aware that this ritual might well destroy you," Khaeriel said.
"We have no idea how it will affect you."

"Xaltorath's seen it done before, and it never has. I think we're safe on that
front." I shrugged. "No, the real problem is that this body is unstable, and if I
don't find a way to fix it, my options are—" I paused. Going back to that prison
wasn't possible. And the Guardians would be too immature in their power to
do anything on their own. So if this didn't work, I faced the real possibility of
having to walk myself through the Nythrawl Wound breach, because sooner
or later I would accumulate too much power and be in the same position I'd
been in after Xaltorath. "—not great."

Khaeriel put her arm around Therin's waist, turned her face in to his
shoulder.

"Please tell me that you intend on surviving all this," Therin said. "That
you aren't intending to defeat Relos Var at the cost of ending your own life."

"Janel and Teraeth have already given me this lecture," I said truthfully.
"I'm not planning on dying here. Just the opposite. In case you weren't paying
attention earlier, I have a child on the way. It would be nice to still be around
to see that child grow up." I paused. "Relos Var's expecting me to sacrifice
myself, you know. Now that he knows I'm back, he'll be expecting me to do
something selfless and heroic that he can exploit. He thinks he knows how
I'm going to behave." I grinned. "He thinks I'm S'arric. And if I have my way,
that mistake will cost him."

Therin's expression turned thoughtful then. "You really are Kihrin, aren't
you?"

I sighed. "Haven't I told you this?" I tucked my hands under my arms.
Honestly, I wanted to give them both hugs. It annoyed me that I couldn't. It
annoyed me a lot.

"They'll be starting soon," I said. "I'm going to go watch."

I vanished on them.

I wasn't in any mood for teary goodbyes.

## 83. OUT WITH THE OLD GODS

*Janel's story*
*The Korthaen Blight*
*Late afternoon*

Kihrin insisted that the best place to conduct the ritual was at ground level, on bedrock. Which eliminated the Mother of Trees or any of the other surrounding sky trees as ritual spots. Hell, it disqualified most of the Manol Jungle, large chunks of which were twenty feet or more underwater for most of the year. True, there were parts of the jungle that weren't flood zones, including places Janel had visited only recently, but very few that would serve their purposes. And a number of people, Janel included, refused to go anywhere near the Quarry.

So they ended up back inside the Korthaen Blight.

The fact that it made sense did nothing to lessen the sugar-sweet richness of the irony. Janel understood the logic, though; Kihrin wanted to lessen any variables that might possibly cause the ritual to veer in an unpredictable manner. Thus, similar surroundings to all the other times this ritual had been performed.

Or in this case, in the exact same place all the other rituals had been performed.

It seemed unlikely that it was *exactly* the same place, since the entire area was a mass of magically cooled volcanic rock that now covered the entire plain in a black stone blanket. It was difficult to say if they were in the center of the Korthaen Blight, impossible to say if they were standing on the same spot as the previous rituals. They were "somewhere within" the boundaries protected by Tya's wall, and later cooled to stone by a combination of Ompher and Xaltorath.

Close enough.

Kihrin had given instructions to Senera and Thurvishar, since both could interact with others far more readily and safely than he could. He still had a projection at the site, but a good hundred feet from anyone else, where a loss of control would give people enough time to respond.

Janel walked over to him.

"You should stay back," he told her.

"You should've thought of that before you decided Cursed God of Annihilation was a reasonable ambition," Janel said. Then she added, softly, "Can we do this?"

She wanted so badly to hold him. To hold him and touch him and make everything okay. She hated that there was no good sure solution to this, that ultimately their plan hinged on the frailty of human nature. And humans were always so surprising in when they were weak versus when they were strong. Often they were both at the same time.

"The plan's taken a few knocks, it's true . . ." Kihrin winked at her.

She allowed herself a sour chuckle in response and didn't even look up at the yellow sun and the shockingly blue sky. Janel knew he'd made his point, anyway.

Kihrin smiled in response. "But all plans do. We might still pull it off."

Janel took a deep breath. "We'd better, darling, because I'm afraid Teraeth will never forgive us if we make him go through waiting another five hundred years for the chance to romance us again." It was a poor attempt at humor. If they didn't make it through this, odds were excellent that they wouldn't end up in a position to be reborn. Relos Var would make it a special point to end matters for both of them. Teraeth and Janel would end up as tsali stones sitting on a shelf. Kihrin . . . Kihrin would have a far worse fate waiting for him. "If worse comes to worst—"

"Don't," Kihrin said. "Who told me 'don't plan to fail?'"

"—could you restart? Reloop the timeline the way Xaltorath did?"

He paused. At least Kihrin didn't dismiss the idea out of hand, but he shook his head. "No. I used up too much power fixing the sun. But would you really want that? You'd essentially be giving Xaltorath another chance."

Janel felt a shudder. He was right. That would be the result. But if there was nothing else . . .

"Don't fail," Janel whispered.

"Have you figured out a way to make sure the demon ritual doesn't affect you?"

Janel looked past Kihrin and made a vague motion in that direction. "I think they're almost finished."

They seemed to be. In this case, that meant lying six people down on beds that Tya had made especially for them.[1] She placed them into an enchanted sleep, because being gaeshed was horrible and grim whether one volunteered for it or not. Since at least one person in the group (Qown) had an active phobia about being gaeshed, it seemed only reasonable to spare him that discomfort.

"Janel," Kihrin said, in a tone that translated as "don't think I haven't noticed how you didn't answer my question."

"I know," she said. "Believe me, I know. But you don't get to say a word. We'll both do what we have to."

"I'm going to try talking to him."

It took her a second. Talk to him. Kihrin wanted to try to *talk* to Relos Var. Janel sighed. They'd been over this before, and it never made any more sense with repetition. "And do you really expect his answer's going to change? That

---

1 Xivan and Talea didn't need to be gaeshed because they'd already gone through this.—S

THE DISCORD OF GODS

this time you'll get through to him? How many bodies have to be piled up between you two?"

"Hey," he chided. "Play nice."

"Why? Relos Var's certainly not going to." Janel waved a hand. "Okay, fine. You want to bring him back to the light. I wish you luck."

"You don't think I can."

"I think it's not a contest," Janel said. "But more than that, I think you can't wake a man who's only pretending to be asleep. It's not that he can't change, Kihrin. It's that he doesn't *want to*. He thinks he's being reasonable. Logical. He knows he's right. We're the ones who're being obdurate."

His silhouette shifted, although she wasn't sure what meaning she should attribute there, if any at all. Unease? Anxiety? An itch?

Damn, she missed this man. It was killing her that he was right here and yet literally millions of miles away.

"I'll be careful," Kihrin reassured her.

"I know you will." She smiled at him and then went to join the others.

Janel contemplated what he'd just told her. She knew Kihrin wasn't naïve. He'd lived with Darzin; he'd known more than his share of bullies. She rather suspected that the problem was S'arric, and his memories of a brother he had trusted and loved for millennia.

Where was the cutoff for redemption? At what point were the sins too great for forgiveness? The number of people in her current company—even the number of people they were about to give godlike powers to—who could be accurately described as murderers and monsters implied that their side's requirements for atonement were generous. If Relos Var—if *Rev'arric*—came around and asked for her forgiveness, could she find it in herself to give it? Could she forgive all the people around her for their sins but *not* forgive Relos Var?

It didn't matter. Because if Janel had one simple qualifier for forgiveness, it was this: they had to want it. Not in a cute "I'm only sorry because I was caught" way but a genuine desire to do better. It was a simple stipulation, one which she knew Relos Var would never meet. He wasn't sorry for a thing he'd ever done. He might bemoan his failures, but he never regretted the motive that sparked those actions. He was, had always been, a blazing, shining star of self-acknowledged righteousness. Never in her existence had she known a better one-man definition of hubris.

It had drawn Janel to him once, in another lifetime. Confident, intelligent, deeply committed to the search for knowledge. He'd been appealing. It had taken C'indrol an embarrassingly long time to see beyond that, to realize that the man lived in a universe that revolved solely around himself. That he would do anything to make that universe reality.

Everyone was asleep when she reached the beds. Tya and Xivan both sat next to the others, tiny streams of light flowing from their hands to the bodies lying next to them. Her mother nodded at her. "Care to help?" She used her free hand to gesture toward a table where small talismans had been dumped in an undignified tangle.

Janel straightened. "I've never . . . uh . . ."

"It's sadly not that difficult," Tya said. "I'll walk you through it."

Janel hated every second of it. Not the lesson from her mother. That was fine. Pleasant, even. But just the knowledge that she could do this again—gaesh someone and so chain their soul—if the mood ever struck her. That she'd learned the specific requirements to accomplish it. It felt like dipping her hands in rancid oil. Slick and rotten.

Janel helped anyway.

When they finished, Tya took each of the gaesh control talismans and put them into a thick iron box, which she closed and handed to Khored. The box vanished the moment it touched his hands.

Janel frowned. "You didn't destroy that, did you?"

"No. Tucked it away somewhere safe," Khored said. "It would be a shame if it fell into the wrong hands at the wrong time."

After that, they woke the others. Everyone began to move quickly. Kihrin kept his distance while burning ritual circle markings into the ground, tracing down the necessary patterns.

Janel kept herself busy talking with Grizzst, who wasn't exactly her favorite person in the world, but at least remembered the second ritual they would need to do something about—the one that would wipe out half of humanity if it worked the way they suspected it might.

They were racing an invisible clock, not knowing when Var would start his own version of this ritual, or if he did, if it would take him the same length of time as it was taking them. Most of the people not involved were wandering the area, looking out of place. At one point, she heard Senera grumble that she should have asked Thurvishar to make chairs for everyone before they started.

"Once the Guardian positions are fully separated," Kihrin explained, "your Greater Talismans should vanish as your gaeshe are healed, and the integration process will begin. Any questions?"

People had a few, but they were all in a rush. Thurvishar conducted the actual decoupling ritual, and the rest of them stood back and kept watch.

In Mithros's case literally as he scanned the skies. At one point toward the end, he growled. "Oh, I hate this. I can feel it happening."

"Don't resist it," Kihrin warned. "Remember, it's extremely fatal if you fight it."

"How fatal is 'extremely fatal'?" Mithros asked. "On a scale from 'died as an angel of Thaena' to 'chucked body and souls into the Nythrawl Wound'?"

Xivan turned around and gave Mithros a long, slow blink.

"About an eight," Kihrin said. "Meaning it might be possible to bring you back, but neither Xaltorath, Relos Var, nor I have any idea *how*."

"So I'd best not do that, then," Mithros said.

"Best not," Kihrin agreed.

A grim look crossed Mithros's face. "He's started."

Janel leaned toward him. "What was that?"

"Relos Var—he's started his own version of the ritual. I can feel the pull."

Mithros didn't seem to be inclined to panic about it, so Janel didn't either. "Ours is going to finish first unless something changes."

Xivan appeared deep in thought. "I have an idea, but before I share, I'd like to confirm whether or not it's even possible." Xivan waved at the ritual site. "I'm not needed for this. I'm going to go back to the Land of Peace for a bit. I want to talk with the real Khaemezra."

Janel did a poor job of hiding her distaste, because Xivan immediately snapped, "I'm not her biggest fan either, but there's something I want to find out if we can do, and if so, how. She's the person to ask. I don't think Khae will know."

Janel nodded. "Then that's probably a good idea."

"Can I come along too?" Talea asked brightly.

Xivan smiled fondly at the other woman. "Of course you may." They both vanished.

"You didn't ask what she wants to do?" Kihrin's shadow seemed focused on her.

"It's Xivan," Janel said. "She'll tell me when she's ready. There's little point in trying to pry it out of her earlier than that. And she has Talea along to keep her out of too much trouble."

"True." Kihrin shook himself and then backed up. Backed way up. "Sorry about that. I didn't realize I'd drifted so close."

"You don't seem inclined to disintegrate anything, so I'm feeling magnanimous," Janel said. She tried not to show the pure longing seizing her. She wanted to hold him. And that was unwise for a dozen reasons. "How long have you gone this time?"

"A while," Kihrin said. "Let's just hope—" His words cut off as he shifted to one side, visibly clutching his side and bending over. Then Kihrin laughed harshly. "I see what you mean, Mithros. I'm feeling it too."

Janel felt a thread of something that might have been hope. "It's going to work?" The moment she said that, the hope dropped away, replaced by panic. What if his connection to the concept of "energy" was the only thing keeping him alive? What if stripping him of that link killed him? What if this was in fact the worst possible mistake? They were trusting Xaltorath, Xaltorath's memories. Xaltorath! If her memory was so perfect, she wouldn't have needed the damn prophecies!

Kihrin still had a hand to his chest, but he held out the other one as if to forestall her protests. "It's fine. I understand how this whole process works a lot better now. It won't kill me. I don't even think it will affect my powers, although wouldn't that be lovely?"

Janel swallowed down regret. It had indeed been too much to hope for, but yes, it would have been lovely.

Groans rang out from all around the chamber as the ritual came to a close. Tya, Khored, and . . . No. Irisia and Mithros were both bent over, suffering through it the best they could. Kihrin stood taut and straight, the rigidity communicating better than words that he was hurting too.

For just a moment, three glowing balls of light appeared in the center of the room, hovering in midair. They lasted for perhaps a second, probably less, before they brightened in color and then spread outward in an expanding ring of light, fading as they traveled outward until nothing remained.

"It's done," Thurvishar said.

Mithros had a rueful look on his face, and Janel's mother, Irisia, was only slightly better. But Janel's attention was almost entirely focused on the third person who was the focus of the ritual—Kihrin.

"Fuck," Kihrin said, with feeling. He'd bent over, holding himself as though injured.

"How are you feeling?" Janel couldn't keep the panic from her voice. "Is there a problem?"

"A little bit of one," Kihrin agreed. "Looks like Xaltorath misunderstood something. I guess that answers whether Relos Var would have included me in the ritual. He must have always intended this."

So, something had happened. Something bad.

"Spit it out, damn it," Teraeth snapped. "What's wrong?"

Kihrin raised his head, although he hadn't yet straightened up. "I can't feel the dragons."

"What?" Janel blinked at him. "What do you mean—"

"I mean, I can't feel any of the dragons. Something about breaking the link between S'arric's powers and Vol Karoth's also severed the link to the dragons. I can't feel them—and that means I can't control them." He laughed. "And just when it didn't matter if I did so openly or not anymore."

"That you don't control the dragons, that means *he* does," Janel said. "Relos Var."

Kihrin nodded. "Remember how I said he wasn't going to have those dragons on his side?"

"Fuck," Teraeth said. "He will."

"So that's a problem," Thurvishar agreed. "Good to know."

"Where's the sword?" Mithros asked his grandson.

"The sword? I just had—" Teraeth looked down at his belt, now devoid of any weapon larger than a dagger. "I had it a second ago."

"It's working," Tya said.

"Great," Kihrin (or rather his projection) said. "Now we move on to the next part."

"What is the next part?" Mithros asked.

"Oh, you know. The next part is where we keep Relos Var from wiping out half of humanity," Kihrin said. "But at least finding him should be easy. Because once he realizes that someone's beaten him to stripping the Guardians of their powers, he's going to know something's up. And being Relos Var, he'll seek out a nice primary source who might know something." Kihrin pointed at Irisia and Mithros.

"So in other words"—Janel looped an arm around Teraeth's waist and leaned in—"he's coming to us."

# 84. THE NAME OF ALL THINGS

### *Relos Var's story*
### *Raenora Valley in the Raenena Mountains*
### *Evening*

Relos Var suspected that rituals upturned the natural order in multiple ways. Unlike real life, where it was easier to destroy than create, with rituals, it was far easier to cause an effect than unmake one. It had taken him close to a thousand years to figure out how to reverse the ritual that had created the Guardians. Even then, it would only work because that first attempt had been the rough and unpolished precursor of what followed.

He could untie a group of humans from concepts that made them like gods, although not without risk—the harder someone struggled against the ritual, the more they'd hurt themselves. They'd shred themselves to pieces spread out over the universal firmament, not just dead but left desolate and scattered on a spiritual level. A fact that he no longer considered a flaw, given his plans. The most dangerous part of the spell had always been that the intended recipients of the same would immediately know his location. That would have meant a lot more back in the days when seven Guardians would have shown up. And now, with the steps he'd taken? Barely a concern.

Relos Var had never found a way to undo what had turned himself and his compatriots into dragons. That was a snarl of tenyé too tangled and dense to be freed.[1]

In any event, the ritual was a drawn-out remarkably lonely affair even if Drehemia and Anlyr were both patiently waiting for him to finish. Drehemia, at least, had been interested in the ritual itself; she'd taken considerable delight in discussing the details of his discovery, how he'd gone about testing it, what the possible ramifications might be.

She'd agreed that ritual would do what he thought.

Ultimately, however, there was only one way to know for sure.

What gave him pause when the ritual concluded was simple: no one had shown up to try to stop him.

No one had shown up at all. Not even S'arric.

Which meant that either S'arric, Tya, and Khored had died when he wasn't looking (technically possible but extremely improbable), they'd chosen to

---

[1] And given what we've learned from the Lash, this is almost certainly related to the existence of other dragons out there in the universe.–T

ignore the implications of the ritual and cooperate fully (equally improbable), or they hadn't thought the ritual would work.

This last idea seemed to have the most merit. He checked the prepared ritual circle. Nothing. It was empty. Even if he somehow hadn't felt the residual release of rebounding concepts, the energies *should* have gathered here. But the circle was empty and showed no signs of having ever been used. None of the Guardian elements of power had gathered within its confines, as he'd devised.

He scowled and walked back outside. Drehemia and Anlyr both trailed after him. Both knew better than to try to talk to him immediately.

He came outside to find it was night. When he looked up into the sky, he saw . . . stars. A beautiful, brilliant field of stars, luxurious and glittering in intensity. A sight to bring tears to one's eyes at the sublime beauty of it all. He was so visually arrested for that moment that he almost missed why it was so odd that he might see the stars this way.

Tya's Veil was gone.

He just didn't know if it was gone *before* he finished the ritual or *because* he finished the ritual. But no, he was certain that a Guardian's death or disimbuement wouldn't undo the magical effects of their actions. Perhaps the Veil would have faded when it eventually drained the tenyé needed to power its existence. But for it to fade now?

Tya had lowered the Veil.

"You there." Var pointed to one of the guards. "When did Tya's Veil vanish?"

The man looked up at the sky in shock, eyes widening. Var realized he had no idea; he'd only realized it was gone because Relos Var had pointed it out.

Anlyr slowly scanned the area before turning back to Var. "Early evening. About three hours ago."

"That's too early," Drehemia said. "That's much too early. The ritual hadn't even finished yet."

"Stripping the Guardians shouldn't have removed the Veil, anyway. I assume she did it because of how the sun's changed? We would've needed to lower the Veil, anyway, wouldn't we?" Anlyr was clearly looking to Relos Var for confirmation. Which was odd because Anlyr was nearly the same age as he was, give or take a few centuries.[2] There was no reason Anlyr couldn't understand the science just as well as Var himself.

"Yes, we would have. Lest we wanted a frozen world." Var looked toward Anlyr and confided, "I had quite enough of that in Yor, thank you." He ignored the brief, piercing ache as he thought of Senera. He put her out of his mind.

"But what does it mean?" Drehemia asked. "The ritual didn't work, did it?"

[2] This directly contradicts previous claims that there were no children born after the settlers arrived.—S

It's become evident that when they say "no" children, what they mean is "no children except for special exceptions." Also, it's possible the settlers brought babies with them.—T

"Indeed, it didn't. But why? No one should have been able to resist that. The only way it wouldn't have worked was if it didn't have a proper target—" Relos Var paused. "Didn't have a proper target," he repeated. "Because you can't loose an arrow at a target that doesn't exist."

He recognized the move and the style. C'indrol. Or Janel or whatever they wanted to call themselves. Janel, who loved big, bold plans and understood the importance of denying weapons to the enemy.

Relos Var began laughing. "They beat me to it. Ah, my students are too clever by half."

"Professor?" Drehemia looked understandably concerned.

"They conducted the ritual first," Relos Var said.

"How?" Drehemia said. "I thought you said that you were the only one who knew it. That even knew it was possible."

"That is what I thought, yes," Relos Var said, "but it's the only explanation that makes sense. Perhaps Grizzst left notes. They must have stripped the remaining Immortals of their positions before I could."

"So we progress to the next step," Drehemia said.

Anlyr gave her a scolding look. "You think they're going to give us time for that? Now why would they make our job easier if they didn't have a way of making sure we couldn't take advantage of it?"

"Do you have some sort of point? And if yes, could you please make it?" Drehemia squinted at Anlyr. "I have things to do."

"My point is that if we give them time, they will re-create the Guardians, and we won't have any idea *who* the next Guardians will be."

"The ritual to create the Guardians takes *days*," Drehemia said. "What we're doing doesn't. If we start now, we'll beat them to it. Easy."

"What does it hurt to take the time to confirm?" Anlyr said, "You don't know these people. They're not stupid."

"Excuse me? I don't know Mithros and Irisia? Who do you think—"

Anlyr shook his head. "I'm not talking about Mithros and Irisia. Whatever with them. I'm talking about *Senera*. We have to assume that Senera discovered how the ritual works and then told Thurvishar and his crew how to perform it. If they're smart—which they *are*—then she used the Name of All Things to re-create it before she restored *you*."

Relos Var began paying closer attention to the conversation.

"Yes, fine," Drehemia snapped, "I'm sorry that my sanity is proving such an inconvenience. Let's assume for the moment that they beat us to it and stripped themselves of their own godhood. How would they keep us from fastening a new source to those same concepts?"

"The same way you prevent someone from being gaeshed," Relos Var said. "They know how long the imbuement ritual takes. They must have taken steps."

Drehemia cocked her head. "From being *what*?"[3]

---

[3] She wouldn't have ever encountered the concept of a "gaesh"—T

Drehemia was already a dragon by the time Cherthog discovered he could use the Stone of Shackles to chain souls.—S

Anlyr waved a hand. "It doesn't matter. You think they've found a faster way to create Guardians."

"Exactly so."

"It really is a shame that we don't have the Name of All Things," Anlyr said.

Relos Var felt a curious sort of pain. Damn. Yes, it really was.

It had felt so nice to have Drehemia back too. So nice to have one of his old students back, someone loyal and smart, who trusted him. She'd understood him the same way Irisia had, but without the blasted insistence on "helping him be a better person." He'd been able to talk about the ritual sources with her—the dragons—when he hadn't dared mention them to anyone else. Most of all, it had been *Drehemia*. Despite her dreth ethnicity, she'd been like a daughter to him.

He was going to miss her.

Drehemia pressed her lips together, clearly unamused. "Yes, such a shame. If I could go back to being insane and give you the stone, I would." Sarcasm dripped from every word.

Relos Var said, "Good. I'm glad we're in agreement."

Drehemia startled and stared at her teacher. The surprise on her face melted away as she waited for him to deliver some punch line, let her know that he was joking. But no such punch line was forthcoming. A grim understanding replaced the fading shock, and Relos Var knew that she understood. She'd known him for too long to expect clemency because they were close.

Relos Var's lip curled. "Find solace in the knowledge that it's for the greater good. And I'll cure you once this is all over."

Drehemia stared at him like she held on to some faint belief that he didn't mean it, but any hope of that quickly drained from her eyes. "Revas," she whispered. "No."

"Run," Relos Var told her. "It would be a shame if our fight destroyed the camp, but you know it won't stop me."

Her eyes widened. She took one step back, then another, then turned to flee. Her body began to shift and flow, darkness wrapping around the draconic shape like veils as Drehemia took her shadow dragon form again.

She vanished.

It little mattered. Var had placed a spell on her that would allow him to continue tracking her. He gave Anlyr a single nod, then jumped into the air and let the transformation take him as he soared upward.

It would have been easy to say he hated being a dragon, and that was why he took the form so rarely. That would've been a lie.

He *loved* being a dragon, loved it with a singular focus and sense of purpose, which was terrifying when he returned to a human shape. Being a dragon felt every bit as elemental as he would have imagined, godlike in power, momentous in intensity. Every time he changed, he wondered if this would be the time he couldn't force himself to change back, not for lack of skill but for lack of desire. Every time he transitioned back into a human, he vowed to never turn back into a dragon except for the most extreme of needs.

Recovering the Name of All Things qualified.

He focused on the spell he'd cast, found the twisted coils of tenyé drifting through the air in Drehemia's wake, and followed her.

Relos Var hunted.

# 85. Trade Secrets

*Xivan's story*
*The Land of Peace*
*After the First Ritual of Unmaking*

"So we're looking for Khaemezra?" Talea pursed her lips as she gazed at the palatial halls of the Land of Peace.

Its appearance hadn't changed since the last time they'd visited—which had only been a day. Some indefinable quality about the place made it seem quieter. Like the dying hours of a party, when all the sensible people have already gone home and those who remain are either passed out or marshaling their strength for one more round.

"Yes," Xivan said. "The real one and not this shadow." She gave the old woman a dirty look, which was ignored. "I know we don't have much time, so let's hurry." The problem was that there was no way of knowing if Khaemezra had stayed in the main ballroom where Teraeth had found her or if she was elsewhere wandering through the palace.

She grabbed Talea's hand, then paused and let go of her.

"What is it?" Talea said.

"You lead," Xivan said. "Just go wherever your feet take you. I'll follow."

They found Khaemezra in the first place they looked. To be more accurate, they found Khaemezra on the way to the first place Talea had intended to look, in one of the gardens on their way to the main ballroom. She appeared in her dark-skinned voramer form, sitting by a fountain, one leg hanging over the lip of the pool. She seemed like she was about five seconds from going for a swim. The scene deserved a painting, something portraying a wistful young woman gazing off at nothing, contemplating her future.

Or lack of one.

Khaemezra turned her head. "Do you need something, or are you just—" She paused as she focused on Xivan for the first time. "You."

Xivan didn't know what had given her away. Possibly nothing. Likely all dead souls knew when they were in the presence of the Goddess of Death. Whatever the reason, Khaemezra had somehow known that she was staring at her successor.

"I need your help," Xivan said.

Khaemezra opened her mouth. Xivan quickly added, "And I'm willing to make you a deal for it."

The woman leaned away from Xivan, wariness sharp in her posture. "I'm listening."

"That thing that angels do. You know how you make it so they automatically come back to life after they die? How do you *do* that? Does it just happen automatically to anyone who becomes an angel, or do you have to do something special?"

Talea gave Xivan a sharp look, while Khaemezra's eyes closed to slits. It made her look less like someone who was suspicious or displeased than like a very satisfied cat, lounging after a meal.

Khaemezra splashed water in tiny little waves as she moved her toes through the water. "Ah, that. We developed it for exactly the same reason I assume you're asking about it, but it doesn't work. Even if it can heal or re-create the entire body"—she met Xivan's stare as she shook her head—"it won't be as good as what Galava herself might have done in person. It can't bring back a Guardian."

Xivan sighed. She would love to rip the woman to shreds over her presumption, but that would have to wait until she wasn't in a position to childishly hold back on vital information. "It's fine if it won't work on Guardians. I don't want to use it on Guardians, anyway."

"Oh." Khaemezra's brows drew together. She looked past Xivan to Talea. After a moment, she grunted and rose to her feet. "You've got to be Taja. I swear I don't know how that woman managed to find someone with the same smile, but she did it. Anyway, follow me. I'll show you. I assume you're in a rush."

Khaemezra led Xivan and Talea into a large room filled with tiers and tiers of waterfalls. Waterfalls set into the walls and pouring from impossible places along the ceiling or sometimes midair. Most of the waterfalls had dark bands set across them at regular lengths. Xivan leaned forward to study one and saw that someone had used magic to mark a name across the width. It flowed and smudged as the water moved past it, giving off the impression that it was a different kind of liquid, trapped.

There were a great many waterfalls, and a great many names on each.

"Argas built it," Khaemezra said. "With help from Galava and me, of course. Tya helped a little too. After it was built, well. It didn't work quite the way we wanted it to, but it had its uses. The others could give me the names of their most trusted servants, and I would write those names down here to form the link. And the next time that person died, they would be resurrected. It's not perfect, but it did the job. For anyone who isn't a Guardian."

"You mentioned," Xivan said.

Khaemezra scoffed. "It can't overcome the environmental hazards of the location where you died. If you were thrown into a forge so that your entire body burned to ash, you'd find yourself resurrected only to burn to ash a second time. If a non-voramer were chained to a weight at the bottom of the ocean, they'd simply drown again. Once a person dies, their name is washed away, and they have to be added again."

Xivan paused. "It can remake a body? Entirely?"

Khaemezra was less impressed, probably because she hadn't previously been in a place to benefit. "Yes, but does it? Consider that bodies are difficult to destroy that quickly. Anything that might manage such a feat will likely still be there when the person Returns. Ready to kill them again. It's no great favor under those circumstances."

The former goddess motioned toward the back walls. "All those waterfalls once held the names of angels, and with every death, the names empty one by one. They have no idea that their next deaths will be their last." She sounded genuinely heartbroken about that idea. "I can't add them anymore. Only you can."

Xivan might have been more sympathetic except for the part where, at least in the case of Thaena's angels, they were referring to assassins. She had no illusions about her own morality, but she suspected that killing people for money, no matter how she justified it, just might have been the point where Khaemezra started to diverge from her role as a sworn guardian of humanity.

"What are we doing here?" Talea whispered the question as if she were in a church.

The room did feel oddly church-like. "Just one more ditch for us to hide in, my love. And hopefully we won't need it." She glanced over at Khaemezra. "Relos Var has a way to strip the Eight Immortals of their powers." She held up a hand as Khaemezra started to protest. "He does. And since we don't have full access to our powers yet, it's exactly like you said: we're not in a good position to stop him if he tries. But if he kills us, or he steals our powers and kills us, or kills us and steals our powers—however that works—then your waterfalls will kick in. Which means we can Return to the Living World one more time."

"But not as Guardians," Khaemezra warned.

"But still *alive*," Xivan pressed.

Khaemezra looked thoughtful as she splashed water. "Yes, fine. I see no reason why that wouldn't work. You'll be able to Return the others." The corner of her mouth quirked.

Something in the way she said those words caught at Xivan, ripped a bright, sharp line across the back of her mind.

"I'll be able to return the others," Xivan repeated.

Khaemezra hadn't said that Xivan would be able to Return *herself.*

The voramer woman grinned in a manner more shark than human. "It's the nature of the connection. The first link has to be made to the world you're pushing the soul back into. That means every person you write down on this list has to be *in* the First World when you do it. If you try to add her name right now"—she pointed to Talea—"nothing will happen. You'll waste the effort."

"Which means I can't add myself," Xivan murmured. Oh, the black humor of it was just delightful. Death couldn't resurrect herself.

"I told you it won't work on the Immortals," Khaemezra snapped.

Xivan's eyes began to sting. She angrily blinked back any tears and lifted her head, glaring. "And I told you that I wasn't planning on using it on any. This was a worst-case contingency if Relos Var actually fucking wins—or at least succeeds in de-ascending the Eight."

"If he does that, he wins," Khaemezra countered.

"Don't be so sure," Xivan said.

Khaemezra scoffed. "Well, if you're not gods at the time, then it should work fine—for everyone but you," she said to Xivan.

"No, no, no," Talea said. "She can't add her own name? Not a problem. I'll add her name. She can add mine and everyone else's. We'll cover for each other."

Khaemezra laughed. "No. The Goddess of Death can add names. You cannot."

Talea's expression turned very still.

"It's fine, Talea," Xivan said and took the younger woman's arm.

Talea pushed her away. "Under *what definition*? How is that fine?"

"Because us dying is not part of the plan, right?" Xivan tried again, this time gently sliding her hands along the outside of the other woman's arms. "Relos Var won't even know the Eight can be replaced until he finishes that ritual of his and nothing happens. Then he'll have no easy way to find out who the new Eight are. It's unlikely that any of this will be necessary. I'm just providing a contingency. I'll feel better knowing that no matter what happens, at least I don't need to worry about losing you."

Xivan stared into Talia's eyes. Hers were the most beautiful deep pools, and Xivan didn't think she would ever grow tired of looking into them. She'd grown good at reading them, too, so she knew right away that she'd done a spectacularly poor job of persuading Talea that any of that was true.

Talea leaned up, kissed her way over to Xivan's ear, and then whispered, "Don't ever try to reassure me by giving me the odds." Before Xivan could answer, Talea kissed her, hard and deep. It was a kiss not only passionate, but apologetic and angry.

"I have to do this," Xivan whispered, "but I'm not planning to die out there. You know that."

Talea swallowed thickly. "I do know that. I hate everything about this, but I understand why you're doing it."

They kissed again. Slower this time and with something much more like goodbye in the taste of her lips.

When she finally pulled back, Talea said, "Don't stay out too long. We're fighting evil later." Then she teleported back to the First World.

Xivan hung her head. She really should have known better than to think she'd fooled Talea for a moment. She didn't know whether to laugh or—

Khaemezra cleared her throat.

Xivan thought she might have blushed. She hated herself for it, just a little. She didn't give a damn about Khaemezra's opinion, but they'd put on quite a show for the former Goddess of Death without the faintest shame.

Khaemezra didn't seem offended, though. Mostly amused.

"So, what do you want out of this?" Xivan asked quickly. "To be Returned?"

That was the price she'd come here expecting to pay. Teraeth would likely have a fit when he found out, but that was his problem.

Khaemezra looked genuinely surprised. Whatever snap answer she'd been about to give Xivan died in the woman's throat. Her expression turned contemplative.

"No," Khaemezra said. "No, I don't want payment for this. It was my job." Discomfort flickered over her features. "It should have been, anyway." She motioned to the waterfalls. "Let me walk you through what you need to do."

# 86. Asking the Right Questions

*Relos Var's story*
*The Raenena Mountains*
*After killing Drehemia*

When Relos Var returned to the camp, he carried the Name of All Things.

The very idea that the unification of a dragon and their Cornerstone might be reversible was a secret he'd kept hidden. It was a secret that he'd long suspected but never been able to definitively prove for all the obvious reasons, but mostly because he had no test subject besides himself.

And yes, he might have easily cured one of the dragons—Baelosh had always been approachable, with a real fondness for card games—and tested the concept on him as confirmation. But he hadn't because it seemed unlikely that such an act would pass unnoticed. If it worked, he didn't want his enemies discovering that this was a tactic that could also be used on Relos Var himself.

The other secret was that Relos Var could use the Cornerstones. *All* the Cornerstones, at the same time. He didn't know if he'd successfully kept that secret. Some of the opponents he'd faced along the way had been obnoxiously, inconveniently smart. It wasn't outside the realm of possibility that Thaena had guessed the truth and perhaps handed that suspicion over to the other Immortals during better, friendlier days.

But the time had come for all deceptions to end.

Drehemia would heal quickly from her murder. He'd guaranteed it, killing her so neatly that the worst damage to her body had been when he'd cut her heart from her chest. She'd be back to herself—the insane dragon form of herself—before the sun rose. Such was the price for knowledge.

He sat down with a stack of paper, a pot of ink, and a Capital-style quill pen. For this to work, he had to find out the identities of the new Guardians and strip them of their newly acquired concepts.

And then he would fix the world, starting with Vol Karoth.

Relos Var asked his first question.

# 87. Adaptation

### *Teraeth's story*
### *The Mother of Trees, the Manol*
### *After becoming an Immortal—kind of*

A curious ennui settled over Teraeth in the wake of becoming an Immortal. The early-evening hours had been tense and uncomfortable, particularly the part where he'd had to sit there and allow Tya to gaesh him.

*That* had created a dull, aching, hollow feeling inside him. Colors had dampened. Sounds had muted. The stars seemed to slip from the sky. He thought about Kihrin, having to live like this for *years*, and Janel, so inured to her gaesh that she hadn't been able to recognize the symptoms as anything but "normal." If this was even a portion of what their experiences were like . . .

At least the monster who'd gaeshed Janel was dead and would never again be a problem.[1] The one who gaeshed Kihrin, though . . . that had been Tyentso.[2]

Tyentso's part in this wasn't done yet. If Relos Var had been the one who'd convinced Havar D'Aramarin to break away from the empire, then Relos Var wanted Tyentso too busy to be a threat. Which implied she could be.

Whether or not Teraeth could be a threat was a different matter. He wasn't the God of Destruction *yet*. He had the title, but none of the perks or powers of the job. He was just a seed that had been planted in the ground and, with luck, would be left alone to become a Guardian. Oh, that wasn't even the right analogy. He was a seed stolen solely for the purpose of keeping it from growing in another man's garden. Whether or not he ever sprouted was inconsequential.

There was one advantage that he'd been able to identify from the start—tenyé. He now had access to what seemed like a never-ending supply of it. Teraeth logically knew that wasn't true, but it felt that way. He suspected Talea didn't previously use enough magic to have noticed, and he didn't think Xivan had used magic at all. So likely neither would have perceived that they

---

[1] That was Xaltorath.–S
[2] Actually, that was also Xaltorath. Tyentso was just the person who'd performed the summoning.–T

were pulling from an enormous storehouse of the stuff until they were further along in their control of their powers.

Janel shifted under the silk sheets next to him. After they'd finished the ritual, everyone had gone to bed. It seemed laughably prosaic, but what exactly would have been the point of staying up to greet the dawn? They knew they still had a long, tense road ahead of them. Relos Var would quickly figure out what they'd done, and then it was just a matter of predicting how he'd respond. Maybe Kihrin was right and the wizard would come after Irisia and Mithros. Maybe it would be Qown or Senera. Maybe it was always a danger to assume one understood what that bastard was planning.

Janel placed warm fingers against the small of his back, slowly skated her hands along his skin until she was fully resting against him, forehead on his shoulder blades. The sensation remained at once incredibly arousing and a stark reminder that he needed to do something about keeping the room cool. Sleeping with Janel was functionally equivalent to sleeping next to an oven. In the Manol, that wasn't the most comfortable of sleeping situations.

"I wonder if we'll be alive this time tomorrow," Janel whispered to his back. He tried to ignore the way his skin prickled in spite of her warmth.

"Janel . . ." Teraeth turned around and drew her back into his arms. "We're going to get through this." He paused. "You're not upset because it wasn't you, are you? I mean, I know how you've always felt about Khored . . ." It should have been Janel. She's the one who should have ended up as the new God of Destruction.

She shook her head against his chest. Her hands on his shoulders were the same shade as his own skin color, almost as if one color bled into the other. "No," she murmured. "No, I don't care about that. I just–" She inhaled sharply. "It feels unreal. After everything that's happened. There's a good chance that all of this–thousands of years of this–will be over *tomorrow*. I just . . . I don't know whether to laugh or cry."

Teraeth felt an odd tugging sensation, which quickly turned into an odd shooting pain. This didn't feel physical. It was spiritual. A horrible pulling, as if someone were trying to yank his souls from his body at a great distance and send them hurtling away, also at a great distance. Yet he knew where the feeling originated. Far to the north.

"No . . . not tomorrow. It's going to be today," Teraeth said. He normally would have cursed, but he was too numb. Oh, Relos Var had compensated much faster than they'd given him credit for.

"Teraeth?" Janel sat up next to him. She placed a black-socked hand on his arm. "*Today?* What do you mean?"

He rolled out of bed and walked over to the wardrobe, looking for a set of clothes that might be functional on a battlefield and not just in a court. What were the odds his predecessors hadn't kept exceptionally well-crafted armor?

"Teraeth," Janel repeated.

"It's not going to be over tomorrow," Teraeth told her. "It's going to be over *today*. Because—"

Someone started banging on the door to the suite. "Your Majesty? Your Majesty!"

Teraeth turned back to Janel. "Because someone in the Raenena Mountains just started the De-Ascension Ritual again, and this time, they're using my name."

## 88. The Problem with Cornerstones

### *Kihrin's story*
### *The Mother of Trees, the Manol*
### *Evening*

"It's all of us," Galen said. He gestured around the room at the eight men and women who'd volunteered to step into these roles only to find out that their terms were about to be cut very short indeed.

More than eight people were in the room. Besides the Eight, their predecessors, Irisia and Mithros, were present, as well as Talon, my parents, Khaeriel and Therin, Valathea, Sheloran, and Janel. Someone had brought out a banquet service for a midnight breakfast, so that was nice.

At least the apocalypse was proving well catered.[1]

"Can't we start the ritual again?" Talea said. "Take the positions away from us just like we did last time?"

Irisia sighed. "You can, but first, it's unlikely we'll finish before he does. We'd be starting late, not even considering you'd need to make a whole new set of Greater Talismans and none of you have enough power yet. And if you solve that problem, a new one takes its place, namely we're running short on candidates. If you give it up now? There's no one to take your place. Which means the concepts will just—"

"Be up for grabs," Mithros said. "And Relos Var is the one grabbing."

"I want to know how he found out so quickly," Xivan said, stabbing the table. "It didn't even take him half a day! And sure, it's easy to guess that Teraeth would be part of this, or Senera or Thurvishar, but me? Talea? He shouldn't have even thought of us. He should have assumed that Teraeth was going to be Death and Janel would be Destruction. He should have messed up at least *one* of our names."

"He must . . ." Senera bit the edge of her thumb. She wore an understandably sour expression. "It could have been a spy. It could have been some kind of trick . . ."

"Are we certain that Drehemia doesn't have any of the Name of All Things's powers?" Qown asked.

A sour taste filled my mouth. No, we weren't certain. And that wasn't the only option.

---

[1] I have to say that although the Manol Jungle was unpleasantly, unreasonably warm, the food was amazing.—S

"He might have killed her," I said. "Taken the stone back."

Janel glanced at me with wide eyes. "What?"

"What if the process can be reversed?" I asked. "If you can reunite a dragon with their Cornerstone, perhaps it's possible to separate them again too. If I still had my connection, I could tell you if Drehemia has gone back to being insane, but I'm betting if you killed Drehemia and ripped out her heart—"

"Veils. You'd have the Name of All Things back," Senera finished.

"In theory," I said. "I don't know how permanent death is when a dragon is killed after being united with their Cornerstone. I assumed that both dragon and Cornerstone would count as having been destroyed at the same time, but if not . . ."

"Oh, fuck me," Senera said. She slumped in her chair. "He found a way to get the Cornerstone back. That's why he was so quick to figure out the next Eight." She laughed viciously. "Relos Var has the Name of All Things."

"We don't know—" Irisia started to say, but then she seemed to visibly stop herself. "No, you're right. That's exactly what he's done."

"Fantastic," Janel murmured.

"Did you find a solution?" I asked Janel then. "Did you figure out how to exempt Jarith and yourself when you change the demon-banishing ritual?"

Janel blinked, exactly once. "I know what I need to do."

That wasn't a yes.

She stared at me as though daring me to call her on it. Daring me to point out that she would be going to her death when so many of us, myself included, faced the same risks. How would it change anything? At least if she was tossed into the Font of Souls along with the other demons, she'd be reborn. She'd have a next life. That was a better outcome than what would likely happen if Relos Var won.

Something ugly and frightened flickered over Teraeth's expression as he'd noticed too.

Neither of us said anything.

"So what next?" Sheloran asked. "I assume we're not going to just roll over and let him have this?"

"Oh, hell no," Teraeth growled. "Now it's war."

## 89. THE BEST VIEW OF THE END

### Kihrin's story
### Raenora Valley in the Raenena Mountains
### Nighttime

If the situation hadn't been so terrible, I might have taken the time to admire the panorama. This far north, the summer weather was crisp and cool compared to the nonstop rains of the Capital. The surrounding mountains were snowcapped and draped with evergreens. A small lake at the end of the valley glittered in the moonlight. We stood on a small bluff the next valley over, high enough up and far enough away that we could only see into the target valley because Senera had conjured up a distortion in the air that magnified the view.[1] It wasn't technically clairvoyance, so no one on the other end could sense it. Theoretically.

Anyway, if the large valley suddenly seemed small, it was only because it was filled with so many dragons.

I counted six of them. No Xaloma, no Drehemia, and no Relos Var, but everyone else was at the party.

"I know this valley," Grizzst muttered. "How do I know this valley?"

Thurvishar turned back to the man. "This isn't where you found Rev'arric when he was a dragon, is it? Where you cured him?"

Grizzst scratched the side of his helmet, all the more laughable for the idea that he might have developed an itch. "You know, I think it might be."

"That's odd," Senera said. "Why the attachment to *this* particular valley?"

"Perhaps instead of taking the midnight hiking tour," Mithros said, "we might concentrate on the dragons down there? Because Relos Var's brought all of them."

One of those dragons was Mithros's own brother. He was probably unexcited to be fighting Morios *without* his god powers.

"Not everyone," Janel said. "Let's split into two groups. Half of us stay here and deal with the dragons. The other half will go to Atrine."

A few people started to protest, but she cut them off. "Why does Relos Var need to distract the Quuros army? Why did he need to enlist Nemesan's help? I *only* see the dragons here. Not Nemesan's troops. Not any god-kings. Relos

[1] And it let some of us see in the dark. It's a handy spell.—T

Var's doing something at both locations, hoping to split our attention. This may be a diversion."

"A diversion which will succeed if you divide us up," Grizzst said.

"He can't fake where the De-Ascension Ritual is happening," Senera said. "But that doesn't mean he can't start a second one elsewhere. Or do something else. I think if we leave Tyentso and the Quuros army on their own, we'll regret it."

Several people turned to me.

I still wasn't technically there, but I'd grown comfortable enough with the projection business (and sufficiently well fed) that I was in no danger of melting my friends. But I hadn't expected anyone to want my opinion, mostly because they were trying to ignore my presence and what it meant.

"We need to split up," I agreed. "Talon, Khaeriel, Therin, and Grizzst can go to Atrine to reinforce Tyentso, Jarith, and Kalindra–"

"If you're just trying to–" my father started to say.

"Yes," I told him. "I'm just trying to stop you from fighting *multiple dragons*. I'm also sending you straight into the middle of a war, but I'll feel nominally better than I would if you were in the middle of what this mess is going to be."

"Fine," Therin grated, practically with clenched teeth to emphasize that it was not fine and he was not happy. He turned to Galen. "I can't guarantee we won't have to kill Havar."

Galen looked confused.

"He's your maternal grandfather," Therin reminded Galen.

Galen made a face. "Oh, that? Go right ahead. I don't give a damn about Havar D'Aramarin. He left my mother to rot, and he's never said a word more to me than was absolutely necessary at parties. No emotional attachments here."[2]

Sheloran squeezed her husband's hand. "I sent a message to my mother. Hopefully, she'll help too."

"Good." I turned to Janel. "Give Skyfire to Sheloran."

She frowned at me, probably because I knew she had it. Janel hadn't gone out of her way to advertise she'd been the one who'd picked up the diamond when Empress Tyentso had left it with us. A lot had been going on at the time.

Yeah, well, I may have been cut off from the dragons–at least for the time being–but I most certainly wasn't cut off from the Cornerstones. I could tell that she carried one.

Janel sighed and handed the diamond to Sheloran, who seemed more than a little stunned.

"What am I supposed to do with this?"

"Your job is to protect everyone from Morios while Qown takes him out," I said. "If Devors taught us anything, it's that you're perfectly willing to spellcast yourself to death in situations like this. But as long as you're carrying

---

[2] Given that Havar D'Aramarin is also the god-king Nemesan, I'm sure the feeling is entirely mutual.–S

Skyfire, you'll have all the tenyé you'll ever need." I spoke to Xivan. "How many dragons are in the valley? That's not a trick question: How many do *you* see?"

Thaena had proved hard to fool with invisibility spells and the like. I suspected Xivan was similar. Something about being able to see into both Twin Worlds at the same time made them hard to fool.

"Eight," she answered.

"Right," I said, "so *all* the dragons are there. We just can't see Drehemia or Xaloma. Xivan—"

"Xaloma's mine," Xivan said, sounding like she wasn't even slightly happy about it. Hard to blame her.

"Feel free to modify the plan as needed, but Thurvishar can use Wildheart to negate most of Baelosh's nastiness. Galen, I know you probably can't do much more than make a fire right now, but trust me when I say you can make it a large fire. And Aeyan'arric is vulnerable. Target her. Irisia and Dorna, you're going to need to find a way to distract Gorokai. Mithros, fill in where you see an opportunity. Senera—"

"I'll take Rol'amar," Senera said, giving Irisia a thoughtful look. "He's vulnerable to magic."

"Drehemia's a problem," I said.

"Oh, I'll handle Drehemia," Talea said with a grin and a wave. "Look, I even brought a bow and arrows!" She hooked a thumb under the quiver belt in emphasis.

I wasn't going to argue she couldn't do it. She was the first of the new Eight and seemed to be having the easiest time transitioning into her new role. Far be it from me to say she couldn't get in a lucky shot. Or that a lucky shot from Talea wouldn't be devastating, even to a dragon.

"Aw," Teraeth said, "you left my brother for me."

I winced. Yeah. I hadn't assigned anyone to take care of Sharanakal, the Old Man. And he was a problem too, if only because we were about to have this fight in one of the worst possible locations for a dragon capable of provoking volcanic eruptions.

"I'll help you," I told him.

"We both will," Janel said. "You two played with him last time without me. You're not leaving me behind again."

"What about Valathea?" Khaeriel asked.

"She's staying with me," I said, wondering if my mother was about to forget the whole "let's not mention Doc" discussion. A lot had happened since then.

My mother simply nodded at Valathea. "Good luck."

I thought she might say something to Sheloran and Galen, but fortunately, she seemed to recognize that this wasn't the time.

"One more thing," I said. "Once we start, I'll have to show up in person. When that happens, stay away from the big shadow cut out of the universe, would you? I won't be safe."

Nods and agreements all around, although some of those doing so looked uncomfortable.

Irisia opened a gate to Atrine for the second group. "Very well. We have our orders. Let's begin."

I nodded, mostly to myself.

Before I left the moon, I picked up a rock.

### Thurvishar's story
### Several miles from Raenora Valley
### Just after splitting up

Thurvishar felt the uncomfortable tugging pulling him into Raenora Valley, but he'd found no sign of the ritual itself. Just six dragons (plus two he couldn't see) who were uprooting trees and making a giant mess. The moment anyone showed up in the valley, that would transform into six dragons (plus two he couldn't see) trying their damnedest to kill them all.

It explained the lack of wards, the dearth of protection magics.

Who needed them with *eight dragons*?

"Just remember," Janel said, "that the goal isn't to kill dragons. Or even to fight dragons. The goal is to stop Relos Var from completing that ritual."

"Where *is* Relos Var?" Teraeth said. "I don't see him anywhere and I don't like it."

"Look for Rol'amar," Irisia said. "What's Rol'amar doing?"[3]

Galen squinted at the enhanced view. "Digging into the mountainside."

"Then that's where you'll find his father," Irisia said.

"Ready?" Thurvishar asked the other wizards.

"Multiple gates," Senera said. "We don't want to bunch up and be easy targets for flybys."

Galen let out a fast exhale that might have been either laughter or a sob cut off too quickly.

His wife took his hand. "You can do this."

"I've cast every protection spell on you I know," Senera said. "It's not invulnerability, but there are plenty of god-kings less prepared to fight a dragon."

"Sure," Galen said, nodding. "But I did assume that I wouldn't have to figure out what the hell I'm doing on the actual battlefield."

"That was silly of you," Talea said. "Haven't you met us?"

Galen covered his mouth to stop his laughter.

Thurvishar nodded to himself. He sympathized. And he worried. Qown was fantastic at healing magics, yes, but he also loathed combat. Mithros had been the God of Destruction for millennia, but how much magic did the man know without that link? Dorna was an old woman who, as far as Thurvishar recalled, knew a single witchgift. Teraeth ws an extraordinary knife fighter, but these were *dragons*.

Talea and Xivan would be fine. He wasn't worried about them.

Janel looked over at her mother. "Want to help us take down—"

---

[3] On several occasions previous, it's been noticed that dragons seem to be drawn to their non-draconic family members. It's an observation we've never had a chance to properly investigate.—T

"I'll help Senera with Rol'amar," Irisia said. "As you said, he's vulnerable to magic."

Thurvishar regarded the two women with concern. Rol'amar was Irisia's son by Relos Var. No one had expected that she would want to be one of the people fighting him. Rol'amar was also, he supposed, Janel's half brother. And Thurvishar's uncle. Thurvishar wrinkled his nose and looked away.

There was a lot of that going around this fight. Hell, Teraeth had a brother *and* a sister down there.

"Are we ready?" Senera asked in a tone that all but screamed *"you'd damn well better be."*

Nods and affirmatives from all around.

Multiple gates opened around them. People teleported out.

Kihrin vanished.

And in Raenora Valley, the final battle began.

# 90. THE BATTLE OF EIGHT DRAGONS

### *Sheloran's story*
### *Raenora Valley*
### *Fighting Morios*

Sheloran was glad that both Galen and Qown had been tapped to be on the Guardian list. A part of her would've liked to have been there too. She couldn't deny that she'd thought about raising a hand when suggestions were being tossed around. But if Galen was going to become immortal, at least Qown would be too.

Anyway, if one of the three of them would end up eventually becoming a god-king, it would be her. She considered this motivation.[1]

If holding Skyfire was what it felt like to be a god, she could see the appeal. Using Skyfire was like waking up in the morning to watch the sunrise on a day so full of potential that anything might happen. She floated in a warm sea of tenyé—as much as she wanted, hers for the asking.

Which was good, because about five seconds into the battle, she decided that she hated Morios's stupid metal guts.

The war dragon loved sending literal tons of shrapnel screaming through the air to impale her friends. Even for someone of her skill set—so good at metal-warping that she likely would have already been House D'Talus's chief Red Man if women had previously been allowed to hold that position, wielding an artifact that gave her unlimited energy—stopping all that metal was difficult.

And he wasn't the only dragon trying to kill them.

She found it curious that the dragons proved selective in their hatred. If there was a choice between pursuing Sheloran or chasing Qown—who wasn't attacking anyone—they'd pick Qown every time. Or any of the Immortals. Janel, Sheloran, Mithros, and Irisia had an easier time, simply because they were ignored as primary targets. This was even true in cases where the dragons had a personal connection.

Where had Valathea gone?

Sheloran didn't have time to search. She was concentrating as hard as she could on taking care of one dragon while simultaneously dodging the collateral damage caused by the others.

---

[1] Given that Sheloran comes from two generations of god-kings and has no fewer than four god-kings in her immediate family (unprecedented as far as I know) I would agree with her assessment. One does not "inherit" immortality, but there is such a thing as the privilege of access.–S

Just as she was having that thought, an enormous crack opened in the ground next to her. She jumped to one side to avoid the fountaining lava spilling up from it.

When the lava hit air, it turned hard and glossy like black onyx. Then the lava continued to grow, branching up in delicate crystal spires larger than the Rose Palace until they wrapped around Baelosh's tail. He yowled as the stone spikes snapped shut around his lower body, halting his fight.

That was Thurvishar's work. He might've been new to being Ompher, but he'd always been good with earth magic. This was just the deadly gilding on a skill he already possessed.[2]

She stepped around where Baelosh writhed and continued to focus on Morios.

### Teraeth's story
### Raenora Valley
### Fighting Sharanakal

Teraeth threw a dagger. It tumbled end over end and hit a huge, round, red eye smack in the center, blade first. It didn't even give Sharanakal a mild itch, but it caught his attention.

"Hey, big brother!" Teraeth yelled. "Remember how you wanted to keep Kihrin on the island, but then you accidentally killed him? Only you didn't kill him, he just escaped right from under your nose? Yeah, that was all me, you big dumb—whoa!"

The vané assassin threw himself to the side to avoid a burst of lava from the Old Man. Evidently, the dragon didn't consider him a real threat; he was saving his more impressive attacks for someone worthier.

Teraeth felt insulted by that.

"Hey, magma brain, I'm talking to you!" he yelled, following it up with a blast of pure annihilation, tenyé tinted with the entropic forces of Khored. It singed off one of Sharanakal's nostril horns, and the dragon bellowed in rage and pain. "There we go," Teraeth said. "That got your attention."

Which it had, so Teraeth ran.

He threw up a wall of energy to stop the flow of superheated gas and ash headed his way. He hadn't blocked all of it, but the grit that flowed around him was no worse than the sand in a Khorveshan breeze.

He glanced to the side and saw Janel beside him, hands outstretched as she fed on the heat that bled through his shield. "Thanks for having my back," he said.

"Your turn," she said in response.

Teraeth noticed the dragon's attention had been diverted; the Old Man must have assumed that his pyroclastic flow would kill Teraeth and had proceeded to focus on opening fissures at Sheloran.

"You should *really* stop ignoring me," Teraeth said, drawing in as much

---

[2] I know. That's why I picked it.—T

tenyé as he could hold and then unleashing it in a twin strike. With his left hand, he gathered a stream of Morios's flying needles and redirected it at Sharanakal's wings, while with his right he unleashed another blast of destructive chaos at his brother's head, hoping to injure it in the same place again.

There were advantages to having the memories of one of the most powerful emperors in Quur's history—namely, the ability to cope with suddenly having massive amounts of power.

The chaos blast scored another strike, just above the first. Half of a nostril crisped and shattered like so much pumice hit with a sledgehammer. The daggers did better than he'd expected; he'd meant them as a feint for the other attack, but a handful of them must have caused some damage when they pierced the Old Man's right wing. It was moving slightly slower than his left. The dragon took a deep breath. The red-hot cracks in Sharanakal's skin glowed brighter and hotter. The rest of Morios's metal fléchettes melted.

Janel picked Teraeth up without the slightest warning and started running, narrowly avoiding them both being crushed by a giant slab of ice. Why was there a giant slab of ice in the mountains? Oh yes, Aeyan'arric. Unfortunately, it seemed that Sharanakal's and Aeyan'arric's powers didn't necessarily cancel each other out. Because the magma didn't cool and turn to glossy black stone as it hit the ice.

Instead, it exploded.

A wall of earth stopped the magma bombs from smacking them.

"Thanks," Teraeth said as Janel set him down. "This seems like a good tactic: I'll play hand-slapping games with my big brother, you watch the rest of the battle and make sure we don't get squished by whatever the hell that is." He pointed at a giant whale with dragonfly wings the size of a mountain. Gorokai, he assumed.

"Gladly," Janel said as they both raced around the big block of obsidian to keep Sharanakal in their sight.

"I just hope he doesn't . . . Oh damn. He has," Teraeth said. For Sharanakal stood on his haunches, his torso thrust upward into the air. With both forelegs (arms?), he made slow lifting motions, and the ground trembled beneath their feet.

"He has what?" Janel asked.

"He remembered that he can trigger volcanic eruptions. Fighting him on a mountain is less than ideal, honestly," Teraeth said. He launched another bolt of chaos, but his brother was ready for it this time and whipped his head aside. "Fuck."

Just then, a voice started singing. Loudly, but not straining. Magic was clearly involved in projecting the melody over the roaring of the battle and the howling of winds at this point.

The tune was oddly familiar.

*Let me tell you a tale of*
*Four brothers strong,*
*Red, yellow, violet, and indigo.*

*To whom all the land and*
*Sea once did belong,*
*Red, yellow, violet, and indigo . . .*

Teraeth started laughing. He didn't recognize the voice; how could he? He'd never hard *S'arric* sing before. But both he and Sharanakal recognized Kihrin in the song choice all the same.

The dragon paused in his efforts to build up magma pressure and make the mountain explode. He turned his head toward the black silhouette hanging in the sky, man-shaped and from whence the music issued.

"What is happening?" Janel asked. "Why is . . . Oh right. Well, go on, while he's distracted . . ."

Kihrin launched into the second verse, Sharanakal distracted by a new target. Teraeth rolled onto the balls of his feet and sneaked forward. He reached within twenty feet or so of the dragon, practically under his head. Teraeth gathered more tenyé; more than that previous assault, more than he thought he could handle. He kept drawing it in, from every fight, every squabble, every argument currently happening in the world. Teraeth drew it from the lightning-cracked dead trees in forests succumbing to rot, from the brush fires in eastern Doltar and every chunk of rock eroded by wind or water on the Yoran coast. He drew it from this very conflict, and in that moment, he truly understood why Morios could never be defeated by violence. He drew in and in and in until he was positively bursting at the seams; his every nerve screamed in agony, his heart labored to beat within his chest, his ears rang with the untapped potential of it all. He molded it, willed it to flow and form the shape of his desire, and then with a release that was very nearly orgasmic in its intensity, he directed it all into Sharanakal's head from below.[3]

A sinuous serpent of roiling entropy flew up from where Teraeth stood and crashed into the Old Man's lower jaw. The stonelike armor powdered and flaked into dust. Magma blood cooled, congealed, and turned to ash. The serpent continued to issue forth from Teraeth, coiling ever up and up, disintegrating the upper palate, filling the sinus cavity, smashing through the upper jaw, and finally reaching the head. Disintegrating lava flowed from the Old Man's eyes, nose, and the gaping hole where his mouth used to be. The body twitched for a second, then solidified, turning to stone as the heart ceased to pump and the blood cooled to volcanic stone.

Sharanakal was, for the moment, dead.

[3] This is an excellent example of the power of literally not knowing your limits. I doubt Mithros would have ever tried something so foolhardy.—T

## 91. GOING TO WAR

### *Kalindra's story*
### *The imperial army camp outside of Atrine, Jorat*
### *Evening*

"I saw Anlyr," Kalindra said the moment Tyentso walked into the medical tent.

Tyentso cut off whatever she'd been about to say. "Where? What was he doing?"

Kalindra was wrapping a bandage around her thigh so the physickers would stop pestering her about it. She'd be fine, she'd had far worse injuries, they needed to keep their magic ready for more serious wounds. On the other hand, Jarith would keep nudging medics in her direction until she bandaged the damn thing, so . . .

"They're setting up some kind of ritual down there," Kalindra said. "Which isn't saying much because there's ritual magic painted on every wall in that camp, but this one has Anlyr setting it up. I'm assuming it's something Relos Var wants."

"Then that's something we—"

A portal opened in the center of the tent.

"Stop!" Tyentso yelled before anyone could respond with violence. It wasn't a D'Aramarin portal. This one looked . . . well. It looked like something Tya would have made.

Grizzst, Therin, Khaeriel, and Talon (still looking like Kihrin) stepped through.

"Hi. We heard you might want help?" the big walking suit of armor said.

But Kalindra wasn't interested in Grizzst. She was *very* interested in Talon.

"Hey," Kalindra said to Talon. "Want to help me kill a mimic?"

Talon grinned at her. "Aw, it's like you're reading *my* mind."

"A mimic? Where?" Khaeriel asked, although it didn't seem like she needed to know the answer as much as she was trying to distract herself.

"His name's Anlyr," Kalindra said with a distasteful grimace. "He's adorable. And he works for Relos Var."

"Oh, I see," Khaeriel said primly.

Tyentso waved her fingers at Talon. "Off with you, then. Make me proud."

"Where's Fayrin?" Kalindra asked.

Tyentso waved a hand. "He's doing a thing for me. But what's important right now is that I fucked up."

"Oh?" Kalindra perked up, because while she was distantly—maybe—starting to warm up to Tyentso, she'd still swallow a living seagull whole if it meant pulling the wind from the empress's sails. "Please tell me more."

Tyentso casually gave her a rude gesture. "You were here when Nemesan showed up earlier today to stick his tongue out at me and gloat. I thought he was testing our defenses, but that wasn't it at all. He did it so we'd turtle up."

"You stay in your camp, Nemesan stays in his, and nobody's trying to stop this Anlyr kid?" the walking suit of armor suggested.

"Pretty sure that Anlyr kid is *your* age," Tyentso told Grizzst. "But yes, basically. So that means this is no longer about defense. We need to attack."

# 92. The Battle of Eight Dragons II

### *Talea's story*
### *Raenora Valley*
### *Fighting Drehemia*

Drehemia wasn't used to fighting someone who could see her. It made her skittish and prone to skulking around the edge of the valley, attempting to see who she might be able to sneak up on and pick off in a moment of vulnerability.

Galen might have been able to perceive Drehemia. Talea wasn't entirely certain if his ability to see in darkness also translated into being able to spot Drehemia when she was invisible.

Talea certainly couldn't see where Drehemia was.

She was just taking lucky shots.

### *Senera's story*
### *Raenora Valley*
### *Fighting Rol'amar*

Irisia's portal closed behind those going to Atrine. Senera looked at the erstwhile Goddess of Magic and said, "You ready for this? I know it's been a while since you . . . Excuse me? Where are you going?"

Irisia was already flying toward Rol'amar, weaving rainbows of energy and launching them in oddly beautiful streamers of destruction. One detonated a large stone nearby, another drifted on the breeze and lashed Baelosh, who hissed in pain, but the majority found their way to their intended target.

The dragon of bound souls made a hissing sound that probably would have been a scream in a creature with a fully-intact throat. Ribbons of coruscating energy burned the rotting flesh from more of his bones.

Sadly, that didn't slow him down. He leaped aloft and began circling, snapping at Irisia, who was forced to dive under him, perilously close to the ground.

"Oh, for fuck's sake," Senera muttered. "I see where Janel gets it from. You're not a Guardian anymore! Conserve your tenyé!" She took off into the air, directing the wind to buffet and pelt Rol'amar from different directions, making it harder for him to fly. Hard, sharp gusts laden with pebbles and snow tore at his wings and slammed him sideways, down, back, and down again.

Rol'amar landed hard; a leg bone snapped. And then he was aloft again, shooting up and out of the wild winds faster than Senera would have expected. Some two or three hundred feet in the air, he let out a warbling keen, evidently having healed his vocal cords.

"What was that?" Senera asked rhetorically.

Veils, but she missed the Name of All Things.[1]

A plume of steam rose from the ground, obscuring her vision. Senera flew to the side only to see that Rol'amar had used the brief distraction to track her and was heading her way with his mouth wide open.

"Don't let him breathe on you!" Irisia cried out.

*No, really?* Senera thought. She focused her energy on teleporting above and behind the dragon. She followed that up with a spell to break bones. She'd turned a particularly annoying Yoran into jelly with that one once.

It cracked all the bones in Rol'amar's right foreleg, which hung limp. But even as she watched, the leg began to repair itself.

"Hey, you said he was vulnerable to magic!" Senera yelled at Irisia. "What exactly does that mean?"

But the former Tya wasn't paying attention to her; she was staring across the battlefield and casting spells to help someone else. Senera turned her focus back to the battle at hand.

And was hit by a flock of undead crows.

*Oh,* she thought, *that's what that was.* Rol'amar had called for reinforcements.

The crows buffeted Senera. She cried out in pain as beaks pierced her flesh. She made a gesture and dumped more tenyé into it than was strictly necessary; the flock exploded. Some of the crows shredded, others merely pushed aside.

Senera searched for Qown, saw he was busy with Morios, and decided she didn't need him all that badly just yet, after all.

Besides, Rol'amar was heading her way again, trying to breathe on her once more.

Senera teleported. It was amazingly easy with the power of the Guardians at her disposal. *I might never walk again,* she thought. This time, she arrived on top of Rol'amar's back. "Very well," she said, "broken bones and burned flesh don't bother you . . . Let's try something else."

Senera considered herself a competent healer, although Qown was superior in skill. She knew enough; Senera set a hand on the dragon's putrid flesh and began to heal him.

Rol'amar screamed.[2] And then he did something Senera hadn't expected: he rolled upside down and fell, attempting to crush her with his body.

His actions made sense in retrospect; most creatures wouldn't pull a stunt like that because it would hurt them too. But Rol'amar was, perhaps, the one creature in all of creation that preferred to be broken and torn.

---

[1] A little known property of the Cornerstone allowed its bearer to understand languages.—S

   Did you just footnote your own thought-comment?—T

   As if you're one to talk.—S

[2] I suppose this lends credence to Kihrin's belief that the dragon would be vulnerable to healing.—T

If she hadn't been the new Tya, that might have been the end for Senera. Opening portals took time she didn't have. Luckily, with all the power at her disposal, avoiding her potential fate as a piece of Doltar-flavored sag was simplicity itself: she wished herself elsewhere.

And was nearly squashed by a falling ice mountain. Aeyan'arric flew somewhere up above, dropping glaciers on the battlefield.

Rol'amar righted himself. The fall had undone the small amount of healing Senera had managed to pump into him, and he was back to his full, gross glory. He threw back his head and warbled again.

"Oh, just stop that!" Senera said. "Irisia, we need to . . . Irisia?"

"I'm here," the former goddess said from behind a wall of thorns incongruously growing out of the snowy mountainside. She stepped out, Mithros with her. He looked like hell; covered in blood and bruises.

"Okay," said Senera. "We need to . . . duck!" She threw herself flat as another flight of half- and fully-skeletal birds flew past. Irisia did the same, but Mithros was made of sterner (or more overconfident) stuff than that; he stood his ground and surrounded himself with a barrier of shimmering energy. Each bird exploded into dust and bits of feather on impact.

"As I was saying, we need to heal Rol'amar," Senera said.

"Because that'll interfere with his undead nature." Irisia nodded as if that were obvious all along. Senera resisted the urge to throw something at her.

Progress!

"Let's grab that Vishai priest while we're at it," Mithros said. "He'll be useful. I left him right over by Morios."

It was all somewhat anticlimactic after that. With three healers and Mithros to distract the dragon, they made short work of Rol'amar.

Then Talea started screaming.

# 93. A Previous Engagement

### *Talon's story*
### *The Marakori war camp*
### *Starting the search for Anlyr*

There's nothing quite like a military camp in the middle of an attack. The enemy soldiers might be using portals for their main strikes against Atrine, but the actual locations of said camps weren't so far from each other in terms of distance. The enemy's main group was situated right at the bottom of Demon Falls. Presumably, they had magic in place to keep everyone in Jorat from dropping rocks on their heads, because otherwise . . . whew.

Otherwise, she had to assume that Nemesan was an *idiot*.

Anyway, it wasn't difficult for Talon to find a soldier whose bladder didn't care about battlegrounds but very much did care about the anxiety of being near one. After that, she could come and go through the rank and file as she wished. Talon made it look like she had somewhere to be, a soldier with a mission. She occasionally called out a name and at least twice had to declare it was the wrong person when it turned out that someone with that name answered.

It took her longer than she would have liked–valuable minutes–but she eventually found her target. An efficient, hyper-competent officer who was holding things together and radiated neither the endless fury of the average soldier nor the normal fears of someone expecting an attack from the Quuros Empire. In short, someone who wasn't scared, and was good at his job.

Anyway, his aura was the giveaway.

He'd come up with a decent strategy. Anlyr had gone out of his way to develop a reputation as that weirdest of things: a mimic who didn't shape-change. And then he'd made sure to let himself be seen, so if anyone keeping the camp under watch recognized Anlyr, later on, they would search for . . . Anlyr.

Which meant there was never a better time in the entirety of Anlyr's existence for the man to bite down on a piece of leather, deal with the pain, and look like someone else. Talon had bet on someone else who was still capable, still competent, still effective, still pretty.

Every mimic had their tells.

She watched him check in with the group performing the ritual. The man leading the ceremony was no one Talon recognized: a middle-aged man dressed in the style of a Quuros Academy professor.

The professor wasn't her target. Talon followed the soldier as he walked between two tents, then struck. She jumped up silently, and as she came down, she turned her arm into a long, sharp spike. This she tried to slam down into his skull, intent on skewering his brain, but the "soldier" moved unexpectedly at the last moment. Her attack caught him in the shoulder and then pierced downward, all the way through his lungs and liver.

But even as she started to rip the spike from his body, the flesh of her victim flowed backward, away from the spike, and then coagulated into the soldier again.

"Anlyr!" Talon said. "Ducky, it's so nice to meet you!"

He tsked over the bloodstains, dropping the edge of a white shirt sodden with blood. "Now what if I'd just been a normal person?"

Talon shrugged like she was a little girl who'd just been caught picking flowers. "Oops?" She wasn't about to feel guilty. If he hadn't been Anlyr, he still would have been a competent officer working for the other side.

Otherwise known as fair game.

Anlyr checked his knives and the sword by his side as they circled each other, an interesting reminder that the items were genuine rather than extensions of his body. "I've been looking forward to meeting you. I remember Talon from the old days. Pretentious brat. Most of us were. Thought we had to take names like Talon or Chameleon or, my personal favorite, Fang."

She wrinkled her nose. "Fang? Seriously?"

"Yeah, those were simpler days." Anlyr drew his sword. "You know, Talon was all the crazy. Nice to see you're doing your best to keep up the standards."

"Now you're just being mean," Talon said. And she hadn't even done anything crazy lately. Or not massively crazy. Comparatively. She was trying! "Besides, it was a stupid question, ducky. If you'd been a normal person, I wouldn't have attacked you. Now where's the *real* ritual taking place, because we both know it isn't anywhere near that extravagant bull's-eye you've created over there." She used a lock of her "hair" to point back toward the ritual site Anlyr was all but begging people to attack.

He seemed surprised. They continued to circle each other, searching for openings. "You honestly think I'll tell you?"

Talon thought about that for a moment. "Okay, not really, no. Mostly, I just want to kick your ass for what you did to Galen." She paused. "He's my baby."

Anlyr didn't bother to respond to that. The two mimics stared at each other while standing between blood-splattered tents.

And then, upon some indeterminate signal that they both recognized, they attacked.

Talon was stunned by Anlyr's speed. They exchanged a dozen blows in a second as the two mimics tried to kill each other. The only difference between the two was that Talon was using her own body, and Anlyr was using blades.

Anlyr pulled a dagger from his belt and slammed it into one of Talon's tentacles. She felt a burst of tenyé. An unpleasant burning spread out from the entry point of the wound. Talon lashed out at Anlyr, hard. She felt something connect, something give, heard a grunt of pain. She pulled back the spiked tentacle, knowing if she didn't, Anlyr would repeat whatever he'd already done.

And whatever he'd already done to one of her tentacles hurt *so much*.

Talon tried to change the appendage back into an arm, to heal over the wound—and couldn't.

"What the fuck?" she muttered.

Anlyr snickered. She looked up to see him healing the hole she'd punched through his stomach. The dagger he'd used to stab her was gone.

"Funny thing about being a mimic," Anlyr said, "is that I've had thousands of years to figure out how to kill one. Stings, doesn't it?"

She tried to change the shape of a different tentacle—and couldn't do that either.

"What have you done?" Fear shot through her. Nothing in any of Talon's memories had even hinted that such a thing was possible. Teraeth had figured out a way to paralyze her, but that wasn't the same as this.

"Mimics don't carry talismans," Anlyr reminded her. "That makes us highly vulnerable to certain kinds of magic. All I did was remind your cells that you shouldn't be able to change their shape at all. Consider it a temporary vacation for your poor, tired body."

Talon didn't bother with denials or further questions. She knew from the uncomfortable fire rushing to fill every corner of her body that he was telling the truth.

"Fucking . . . bastard . . ." She cast her gaze around the alley, but there was nothing she could use as a weapon, which meant she'd have to use herself. Closing to striking distance of the other mimic with her physical body just became a much more worrying prospect than it had been previously.

Anlyr drew his sword.

"Let's get this over with. I have eight gods to kill."

Talon grinned her very best "*fuck you*." "You can try, anyway."

Talon ran.

## 94: TACTICAL MANEUVERS

*Kihrin's story*
*Raenora Valley*
*During the fighting*

I wasn't as much help as I would've liked.

The problem was that my assistance was all or nothing. Yes, I could disintegrate anything—even dragons. I had, in fact, killed Rol'amar at one point by using that very method. But I couldn't guarantee that if I let loose I wouldn't accidentally affect friends—a thing I wanted to avoid at all costs. So mostly, I was on the sidelines, taking advantage of opportunities.

Sharanakal was missing a wing from one such an opening. Grounding the dragon had helped, if only to predict where the overactive dragon volcano would attack next.

Then I heard Relos Var's voice in my mind.

*[This is a pointless battle. You and I aren't on different sides. We can find a way to work this out.]*

It was so out of character for the man that I wondered if I might have hallucinated that. But I knew I hadn't.

***"Unless you're going to stop trying to kill my friends, I really don't think that's true."*** I felt no small amount of skepticism. Relos Var had an angle. Perhaps as simple as what Janel had done with Xaltorath—create a delay for long enough for the special attacks to line up in position.

*[Whether or not they die is entirely their choice. They could always cooperate. But please. After I destroy the demons, there will be little reason for us to fight—]*

I felt a frisson of dread ripple over my body. That meant he'd already started. We'd been assuming—very stupidly—that he'd do the de-powering ritual first. ***"Destroy the demons? You mean with a ritual?"***

*[I'm almost finished.]*

***"Relos, listen to me. You can't—"***

The link between us slammed back down like a prison gate falling. I settled back onto the ground, mostly to keep away from any draconic aerial acrobatics. Dodging that was starting to interfere with my concentration. The approaching dawn turned the small river into a meandering band of bright silver, while evergreens swayed in the brisk breezes.

It was a trap. I knew it was a trap, but I also knew that Relos Var didn't have to be bluffing. After all, said ritual to free the world of demons would most certainly be on his to-do list. Nothing said that he couldn't mark off more than one bird with that same stone. I assumed both the trap and the threat were real.

So I was going.

As soon as I figured out where to go. But that wasn't as difficult a problem for me as it would have been for anyone else. I simply followed the faintest sounds of heavenly music.

Urthaenriel was close. And I knew in my heart that at this last stage, only one person would be wielding Urthaenriel, despite his stubborn refusal to touch the sword for so many years: Relos Var.

*[It's time,]* I told Valathea and Janel.

I left to find my brother.

# 95. THE BATTLE OF EIGHT DRAGONS III

### *Sheloran's story*
### *Raenora Valley*
### *Fighting Morios*

"Thanks!" Sheloran yelled in Thurvishar's direction. She looked around, taking stock of the fight.

Teraeth and Janel were fighting the big black-and-red volcano dragon . . . Sharanakal, she thought his name was.

Talea stood on a promontory with a good view of the battlefield, bow in hand, firing arrows blindly into a pool of inky darkness that Sheloran recognized as the handiwork of Drehemia. The fact that the shadow dragon was once again insane and on the bad guy's side irritated her on a personal level, as if all their pain and sacrifices on Devors had amounted to little more than a temporary holiday.

She'd have liked to see more of the battle, but Morios was still breathing those damnable metal slivers of his. "Does he ever run out?" she asked Qown.

"No, I don't think so," the former Vishai priest said. "Can you keep doing this?" He indicated the point twenty feet in front of him where the cylinder of fléchettes divided and passed to either side of them.

Sheloran laughed, holding up Skyfire. "With this little trinket? I can do this all day."

"Look out!" Qown yelled, pointing behind her.

She didn't look. She couldn't look. She might have been able to deflect Morios's hail of daggers, but that required sight. She couldn't look away. Instead, she threw herself flat and hoped that it was enough.

It was. A small flock of skeletal crows flew through the spot where she'd been standing. "Sorry," Senera's voice called from somewhere to her left.

Sheloran didn't reply, but instead stood and dusted dirt off her skirt. "We need to take this fight to him," she told Qown as she continued diverting the metal darts. "You weren't kidding; he really isn't going to run out of those things. The financial implications of something that can generate unlimited metal on command . . ." She shook her head.

"Plot the economic collapse of the Quuros Empire later," Qown suggested. "I think he's decided to change tactics."

Indeed, the district-size behemoth had stopped breathing razors at them and was now charging at them far faster and more gracefully than she would've imagined possible.

"I don't suppose you can . . ." Qown made a swatting motion as he back-pedaled quickly.

Sheloran laughed. The idea was absurd. And yet, with Skyfire's power . . . Why not? She tried to shove Morios aside. And it . . . sort of worked? The dragon stumbled. A moment later, he staggered as a huge chunk of obsidian slammed into him from the side. More of Thurvishar's doing.

But a several-ton block of volcanic stone smashing into the dragon didn't do more than idly inconvenience him. Morios resumed his advance.

Sheloran was reminded of a cat stalking a mouse. She hated being the mouse.

"You're not Panag Khael," Morios said, his voice like a thousand swords scraping against a thousand whetstones. "Why do you wear his aura?" The monster was clearly talking to Qown, so Sheloran took the opportunity to draw more power from Skyfire and weave the tenyé into a subtle pattern.

"No, I'm not Khael," Qown agreed. "But I am the new Argas. Just like your brother isn't Khored anymore." He pointed across the battlefield to where Mithros was helping the old Joratese woman Dorna fight Gorokai.

The distraction worked. Morios turned his head to look. "Brother?" he said, then snarled. "I'll kill him later. For now, you're right here and—what in Hell is happening?" The dragon craned his head to look behind him.

Sheloran had released the shaping she'd done. Morios's metal body stretched and thinned, starting at the tail, wrapping around itself into a massive coil of metal wire. Half of his tail was already elongated and wrapped around itself in this way.

The dragon's head whipped back, and Sheloran realized she'd made a mistake. Once again, she underestimated the dragon's speed. She was unable to stop the burst of razor-sharp daggers this time as dozens of them impaled Qown and herself. The last thing she saw was Morios bellowing in triumph, already turning to stalk after Mithros.

She stared down at herself, disbelieving. A large, nasty-looking stain of blood bloomed over her chest. It hurt, but just for a moment. Then it didn't hurt at all. Nothing did.

Everything turned black.

And then the world came into focus again. Sheloran turned her head and coughed blood. "Oh *fuck,* that hurts," she said, slowly rolling onto her side. The cold ice felt good on her still-stinging injuries. She fought down a sense of hysterical panic.

Sheloran knew what had just happened. She'd grown annoyingly familiar with the sensation of dying.

She just hadn't stayed that way for long this time.

"Are you okay?" Qown asked Sheloran. Qown had been impaled too, but with a Guardian's resources, had been able to heal himself faster than he could die.

"I'll live," Sheloran decided, then laughed darkly. "Again."

"It's better than the alternative," Qown agreed. "Come on, we still have a dragon to figure out how to kill."

The two of them helped each other to their feet.

"I think you were on the right track," Qown said. "But we need to do something to stop him from retaliating before you can finish."

"Yes," Sheloran said. "That was my one free death. So unless Xivan is . . ." She looked around. "Nope, still busy with Xaloma. We're on our own. What do you suggest?"

"Can you pull tenyé from Skyfire while at the same time using it to melt everything?"

"No idea," Sheloran said. "Let's find out." She found two of the metal shards that had killed her and levitated them into the air. She stretched one into fine wire and wove an intricate net with it, pulling on Skyfire's power to make it a trivially easy task. At the same time, she willed the Cornerstone to melt the second dart into slag.

The second dart glowed, softened, melted.

"Yes," she said, "but it's not easy."

"Oh!" Qown's eyes lit up. "Can you maintain concentration on one of your metal sculpture things without being able to see it?"

"Yes." Sheloran didn't need to experiment with that. She'd done it dozens of times. "Why?"

"I have an idea," said Qown. "First, we're going to need a bunch of those daggers he's been breathing at everyone. And we need to work quickly. I think he's about to kill Mithros."

"Okay," Sheloran said and gathered every fragment of unattended metal she could on the battlefield. "What am I doing with this?"

When Qown told her, she began to laugh.

Not long after, Qown landed in front of the dragon, between Morios and his brother. "As I said, I'm the new Argas. Knowledge. And the first thing I did was learn the secrets of life and death. You can't defeat me."

Morios cocked his head as though he'd just been presented with a riddle. On the ground, Mithros took the opportunity to heal himself, although the man was on his last legs in terms of tenyé. Sheloran imagined that having unlimited energy for millennia would cause quite the culture shock when you suddenly had only what your own body could generate by itself.

The dragon peered at Qown. "I doubt that. Life is Galava's realm and Death is Thaena's. What trickery is this?"

Qown spread his arms. "There's only one way to find out."

Morios slammed a giant hand down, crushing the man like so much paper. As he lifted his hand again, however, Qown stood up, unharmed. "Told you," said Qown's voice.

Mithros staggered away from the conversation. Sheloran could have kissed the old campaigner, for although he'd almost certainly figured out what was going on, he didn't give it away.

Morios shook his head. "Impossible," he said. "I know not what trickery this is, but you'll not survive it!" The dragon inhaled and opened his mouth wide to rain metal-barbed death on Qown.

But the moment that mouth opened wide enough, Qown moved forward.

Not at a walk or even a run. Instead, he simply flew through the air without otherwise shifting his position. He flew straight down Morios's throat.

From behind one of Aeyan'arric's half-melted glaciers, Sheloran muttered, "Here's a little trick I learned from Janel."

At which point, the metal simulacrum of Qown began to heat up. She'd crafted the basic form, and Qown had used his new powers to make it look like himself, sound like himself. The metallic mass softened inside Morios's throat, melted. The metal boiled as Sheloran poured the power of Skyfire into something ultimately forged from Morios.

Morios shook his head violently. He exhaled, which was his undoing. The metal darts hit the molten mass and were added to the mix as Sheloran poured more and more of the sun's energy into the growing ball inside Morios's throat. Each of his own fléchettes added to the superheated metal in his throat, and he'd taken a deep breath indeed. The dragon croaked something that might have been an angry curse.

And then his head fell off.[1]

Qown and Sheloran looked at each other and nodded in satisfaction. Then they stood up to see who else needed help.

---

[1] Morios is exceedingly difficult to kill, but he's not immune to environmental damage nor to his own power. Thus using Morios's own metal against him worked. –T

## 96. CAVALRY

### Tyentso's story
### The Marakori war camp
### Just before attacking

"You know these wards really remind me of Nemesan," Grizzst said as he examined the protections set up around the enemy camp.

Tyentso sighed at him.

"What? They do!"

"Yes, that's because they were created by *Nemesan,*" she snapped. "Can you take them down or not?"

"What kind of college dropout who never went to proper wizard school do you take me for?" Grizzst growled. "Of course, I can."

He was just a damn suit of armor. There was no way he was smiling.

It felt like he was smiling. Asshole.

"All right, then let's get ready to move," Tyentso said.

The suit of armor tracked her movements. She could tell because the helmet moved. "No offense or anything, but you and what army? Half your people are starting to stumble into their tents for nap time."

It was her turn to grin. "I'll show you what army. In fact, I'll show you three of them."

The Marakori soldiers (they probably had a different name, but Tyentso sure as fuck hadn't been paying attention to whatever idiotic label Nemesan had decided to grant his wet dream of imperial secession) had prepared for a siege. Nemesan had no doubt sworn up and down that it was impossible to open portals into their territory. And why wouldn't he make that guarantee? He thought it was true. Maybe he'd been promised that no Immortals would interfere. Nemesan had blocked any incoming gates, including ones made by the Empress of Quur.

But he still hadn't properly warded several miles up.

To be fair, it was impossible. He would've needed to have something to hook the wards onto, and what was he going to do that with, clouds? He'd warded against certain hazards. No chucking boulders from the top of Demon Falls, for example. See also scorpion casks.

But crops needed rain, so he hadn't blocked *water*.

That meant he hadn't blocked ice.

Giant balls of ice are shockingly destructive when falling on the enemy position from that far up.[1] And aimed at the right spots, fantastic at wrecking the wards that kept people from opening magical portals into your territory.

Which is when Tyentso attacked. Not with imperial troops, of course. Those had largely been taken out of the game thanks to Warmonger withdrawal.

But the Yorans had been pleasantly responsive to the idea of self-rule and the magical restoration of their cave systems. Likewise, the morgage could cover shocking amounts of ground under the magical guidance of their sorceress leaders.

And then there were the Joratese and those Marakori whom Ninavis and her people had been smuggling out of the Dominion for years now, the ones who wanted nothing to do with Royal House ideas about slavery. The firebloods were especially vicious on the battlefield.

If anything worried her, it was that this seemed too easy.

[1] This is in essence what Ompher did in the Korthaen Blight too. It's just that his ball of ice was much larger and dropped from much farther up.—T

## 97. The Battle of Eight Dragons IV

### *Galen's story*
### *Raenora Valley*
### *Fighting Aeyan'arric*

"Hi," Galen yelled at the giant white dragon. "We've never been properly introduced. I'm your . . . cousin? I guess? Your father's nephew. But also sort of your uncle, because I don't care what anyone says, Kihrin's always going to be my brother."

She breathed a stream of freezing wind laced with ice shards at him.

"Right. Don't mention your dad. Got it," Galen said from the other side of the steam cloud formed by all that ice hitting his hastily erected wall of fire.

"Look, I'd appreciate it if you'd stop doing that," he said a second later after she tried the trick again. "If you keep it up, I'll have to kill you, and really, I've lost too many family members this year. Granted, some of them weren't as lost as I'd initially thought . . ." He paused to deflect another ice blast. "And sure, my grandfather's sleeping with the woman who killed most of those family members, and I'm still sorting out how I feel about that . . ." He dove to the side and rolled through the snow as the dragon tried to swat him with a claw. "But all the same, I'm feeling pretty good about me and your—oops, I promised I wasn't going to mention him again. Sorry."

Aeyan'arric took off into the air, flew a tight circle, and tried to breathe on him from behind. That attack also turned to steam, which refroze in the cold air and fell like fresh powder.

"Not a talker, huh? I respect that," Galen said. "But seriously, stop trying to kill me—" He leaped aside as she crashed into the spot where he'd been. Then he had to keep rolling since she did too. She slapped out with a wing, which would have crushed him if he wasn't the new sun god. Instead, she singed her own wing and retracted it with a yelp.

Galen stood, cradling his ribs. "That does it. I'm going to hurt you now." With one hand, he blasted her with blisteringly hot jets of flame.

Aeyan'arric screamed as the fire hit her, and she launched herself into the air once more. She favored her left foreleg on takeoff, however. "Seriously, you could leave!" Galen yelled up at her. "I won't tell anyone. Just go away so I don't have to kill you."

Much to Galen's surprise, she flew up and up, spiraling ever higher until she was lost in the clouds. "Wait, really?" he said to no one in particular.

Then the giant ice boulders began to fall.[1] One crashed near where Kihrin's lovers were tussling with that fire dragon, another almost crushed Thurvishar, one hit the dragon who looked like he was a skeleton (it didn't seem to bother him at all, which Galen felt was fundamentally unfair). And, of course, one came right at Galen himself.

He wasn't sure he could melt something that big in time, and he hadn't mastered the trick of teleporting just yet. "F–"

A scintillating rainbow of energy surrounded him. Suddenly, he stood several dozen yards away as the ice boulder smashed harmlessly to the ground where he'd been.

"–uck," he finished, staggered and disoriented.

He made a mental note to find out later if that was Senera or Irisia who'd saved him.[2]

"Fine," Galen said. "I need to fly. I know it can be done because gods do it all the time.[3] It can't be that hard, right?" Galen visualized himself lifting off the ground and then poured tenyé into that idea.

Galen crashed into the ground, two ice boulders, and a frozen wave of obsidian before he figured the trick of aiming himself. At last, he lifted into the clouds in search of his technically-not-actually-related-to-him cousin.

He was disappointed to discover that clouds didn't count as darkness. Nor did being the new sun god allow him to see through them. *Think,* he told himself. *What would Qown do? Qown would use Worldhearth to look for the coldest thing up here. My power's fire or fire-ish. I can do that. Sure. Why not?*

He concentrated on using his connection to the concept of "energy" to "see" various degrees of heat. And very nearly plummeted to his death before figuring out how to keep himself aloft and do that at the same time.

There. Something even darker and colder than the icy clouds around him. That had to be Aeyan'arric. He flew toward that dark spot and almost smashed right into a falling ice boulder.

"Not her," he gasped, dodging the boulder and ascending once more. This time when he spotted what he thought might be the dragon, he launched a line of fire at it. A draconic cry of pain greeted his efforts.

"Found you," he said and began rising to meet her.

He imagined that the battle would be epic, a deadly aerial duet of finesse and cunning, feint and counter-feint, thrust and riposte . . .

. . . if only either of them could see what the hell was going on. Instead, he launched blast after blast of heat at a dark blob he dimly perceived through the clouds, and Aeyan'arric launched spray after spray of ice, to be melted at the last second.

In all his time training under his father, in all the fights he'd had since,

[1] This was a popular tactic, apparently.–T
[2] Must have been Irisia. I was up to my eyeballs in animated dead.–S
[3] They don't? Gods, either of the Immortal or god-king variety, very much do not do this all the time.–S

  Yes, luckily, nobody told him.–T

Galen had never imagined that a life-and-death battle between a fledgling godling and a dragon would be . . . tedious.

And yet, there they were.

Aeyan'arric must have felt the same way, because after about five or so minutes of this nonsense, she twisted and dove toward the ground, out of the cloud layer. Galen chased after her, too late to stop her from breathing a line of ice and freezing death toward . . . someone. He couldn't tell who from that distance.

The dragon banked. He threw more fire at her wing. Unfortunately for the brilliance of his plan, a flock of dead birds chose that exact moment to fly between them. They made spectacular flying bonfires as they fell, but also covered for Aeyan'arric turning around to rush at Galen at high speed.

"Whoops!" he said. Galen let himself fall backward, then caught himself a couple dozen feet above the rocks. As Aeyan'arric flew over him, he fired straight up at her underside.

The dragon opened from gullet to craw, her insides curling up into a black charred mass. She crashed to the ground, landing on top of a suspiciously life-like stone statue of a dragon. The force of the landing broke off the statue's head. It took Galen a moment to realize that the stone dragon was Sharanakal, now shattered into a dozen pieces.

Galen landed beside Qown and his wife. "And exactly where did you learn to do that?" Sheloran asked.

"Be amazing, you mean?" Galen grinned. "Natural talent."

### *Xivan's story*
### *Raenora Valley*
### *Fighting Xaloma*

They hadn't fought Xaloma that long ago, really. Less than a day.

And she'd kicked their asses.

That had been in the middle of a deathless sea, though. Now they were on land, in the Living World, where Xaloma would never be at her strongest. Xivan hoped that might give her an edge over the dragon.

Unfortunately, after a few ineffectual rounds, Xivan realized that she'd misjudged the situation. Their powers were too alike. They were immune to too many of the same things.

They couldn't hurt each other.

Xivan ducked under cover to avoid a Morios flyover and made her way to Dorna's side.

The old woman was facing off against a truly disgusting, shifting mass of flesh and bone. It animated, only to fall apart again, tendons and muscles failing to attach to bone.

For a second, Xivan thought Dorna was fighting Rol'amar. But no.

This was Gorokai. And every time he took a new shape, Dorna *dismantled* it.

"Hey, Dorna," Xivan said. "Want to help me kill a death dragon? I think you're the woman for the job, not me."

Dorna glanced over at her from where she was concentrating on the writhing bundle of flesh. "A bit busy here, dear."

"Sure," Xivan said. "But my dear old ghost dragon counterpart isn't really something I can kill, as it turns out. If I send her to the Afterlife, she just comes bouncing back. But this is *your* world. I could send her back, and then you could keep her from returning."

Dorna eyed Gorokai's monstrous pulsing flesh and pursed her lips. "I can try? Ain't no guarantee it'll work, though."

"Better than nothing."

Xivan wasted no time. She attacked Xaloma, this time trying to do so as the Goddess of Death, rather than just a girl from Khorvesh who happened to be exceptionally good with a sword.

She felt the dragon's souls rip free of their moorings (to which they'd always been poorly attached) and banished them to the other side of the Veil. Xivan had already done that a few times—it hadn't mattered when Xaloma could just dash back and inhabit her body again, often only a few seconds later.

"Now, Dorna!"

That was the moment it all went wrong.

It wasn't Dorna's fault. It's just that while Xivan had been concentrating on banishing Xaloma to the Afterlife, Drehemia had been sneaking up on both of them.

That moment of distraction was when the shadow dragon attacked. Drehemia tore a claw through Dorna's chest, scraping downward in a terrible spray of blood and gore.

Dorna went down and stayed there.

"Shit," Xivan cursed.

Drehemia didn't savage her kill. Instead, the dragon screamed as an arrow embedded itself in the soft tissues of her mouth, and she whirled toward the source of that attack. Xivan allowed herself a second of concern for Talea, but it was brief and quickly overwhelmed by a more pressing problem.

Gorokai had broken free.

The dragon expanded to full size—although even then, he didn't look like whatever Gorokai's natural form was. Instead, he was turning into an iridescent white dragon that Xivan knew only too well: Relos Var.

Relos Var's dragon form was a damn problem. Even worse, Gorokai clearly intended to vent his frustration in the general direction of the woman who'd been keeping him in literal pieces. Who would need a recoverable body if she was to have any hope of resurrection.

The whole battlefield spread itself out in front of Xivan for a moment. That awareness of who was doing what, who was nearby, who was available to help.

No one.

If she didn't do something fast—take Gorokai down so quickly that he had no chance to breathe—the dragon would destroy Dorna's body and Xivan wouldn't have anything to stuff the cranky old woman's souls back into.[4]

She slammed both hands on the dragon's writhing tail, concentrating with all her might on one singular act: death.

Xivan hadn't forgotten how fast Gorokai could move. It just didn't matter.

Black rot spread out from her fingertips, racing up over the rainbow-white scales, the cell death spreading viruslike through the dragon's body.

A wing spread up, curled around, transformed into a dragon head, staring straight at Xivan.

Gorokai breathed.

[4] The "angel contingency" would only activate if Relos Var's ritual succeeded in stripping away everyone's Immortal status.—S

## 98. HOW TO KILL A MIMIC

*Talon's story*
*The Marakori war camp*
*After the fight with Anlyr*

Talon ran. She ran like death was chasing her and hoped that Anlyr was too busy doing whatever a good lackey of Relos Var's did to chase.

Sadly, he had nothing better to do.

She heard his steps behind her, heard him laugh. She didn't dare look back. All around her, Nemesan's soldiers looked confused by the sight of one of their own in such a panic. At least, they were confused until they saw the tentacles, the ones she couldn't just dismiss at will because of whatever the fuck it was Anlyr had done. A spell, clearly. Maybe a spell wrapped around a poison. But how to heal the damage was less obvious, and she was out of time.

So, the shouting started right away.

No point but to lean into it, she decided. Maybe Warmonger had strong enough hooks into this crew by this point to make appealing to their paranoia a valid tactic.

Talon screamed as she pointed back toward Anlyr. "He cursed me! Look what he did to my arm! He's a spy!"

All that attention reoriented itself to the man behind her.

Anlyr laughed under his breath. "Oh, you little . . ."

She lost what he said after that. Talon grabbed some poor idiot's winter cloak and wrapped it around her tentacles like she was carrying a load of laundry. Talon needed to get out of there fast. Everything was starting to hurt, and several spots on her arms and side had begun to bleed. She wasn't wearing real clothing this time—she'd known she'd have to counterfeit uniforms—but now she was rubbing open wounds on herself every time she moved. She was forced to tear off her "cape" (and do so without screaming too, which surely earned her an extra helping of dessert and a kiss on the cheek), before dressing herself in the cloak she'd stolen. The cloak would help hide both the tentacles and the bleeding, she hoped. She picked up a sword, although all she could do was hold the thing in her hand since she couldn't create a scabbard for it

Talon searched for the source of the explosions, hoping she might find some kind of aid. But as she moved that way, she did a double take as she passed by the extra-obvious ritual site.

She was wrong about not knowing the man performing the ritual, for one thing. With a better look, Talon recognized Professor Tillinghast from the Alavel Academy. She recognized several attendants as the highest-ranked members of the wizards' school too, the sort who never *left* the Academy. Certainly not to hop over to Marakor and perform magical rituals for god-kings. Yet here they were.

Equally disturbing, the ritual apparently required an extra push of tenyé—a row of men had been lined up for the purpose. She would've thought they were slaves, but the uniforms belied that idea. They weren't gagged either but patiently kneeling. Talon sensed a little worry and concern, but not the out-of-control fear and panic she would expect from people condemned to death. Some were even excited to die for the glory and triumph of their new king.

The levels of tenyé made Talon pause. It was too much. Too much for a diversion. People here were going to die, and while yes, Relos Var was willing to do that, if the ritual was genuine and they were powering it with this much energy . . .

Then this *wasn't* a decoy.

"Shit," she said. The others were looking through the camp for a ritual that either didn't exist or would be a trap. The real ritual was happening right out in the open. Somebody had to warn them, and Talon didn't know how far along the ritual was. She could try—

In her condition? Please.

She started to leave when she felt the burning, white-hot pain of a sword slicing into her back, bursting out through her stomach. She screamed, shock and surprise warring with a childlike indignation. It had never hurt *that* badly to be stabbed before. Rude.

Anlyr pulled his sword from the wound and then stabbed her again, this time through the neck, through the *spine*. Talon had a fleeting moment of wondering why he hadn't aimed for her heart, then realized he'd expected her to move it.

Which, to be fair, she had.

Everything moved slowly after that. She heard the slow sound of footsteps, low and sharp and loud as thunder, as Anlyr walked away. His spell slipped off her with a prickly sweet tingle, control released now that it had done its job.

The world tilted sideways and drained away.

Then the world turned white, like being dragged backward from a cave into sunlight, dazzling in intensity.

Talon opened her eyes.

She was on the ground. She would have laughed if she had the lung capacity for it. But even as she had the thought, she realized her heart wasn't beating. She pulled no air into her lungs. But somehow . . .

Anlyr's spell had faded. She concentrated on healing her wounds, drawing the flesh together without making it obvious.

The other mimic hadn't gone far. He stood to the side, scanning the crowd as the Academy wizards continued the ritual. She kept her eyes closed while she opened other eyes in less conspicuous places so she might continue observing him. And this time, study him.

He *was* wearing talismans. She wouldn't have expected it, but he hadn't shape-changed except to heal the wound from her initial attack, had he? He wasn't wearing his natural form, true, but he could've done that earlier. Just fun morphing to shift his appearance, and then wear his talismans. Anlyr had returned to the same methods he always used—a wizard duelist using his powers to augment his speed and dexterity. The fact that he covered himself in enough talismans to hinder easy shape-changing just meant he would only polymorph under the direst of emergencies—to fix being cut in half, for example.

The problem with being a mimic (one of many, many problems—so many problems—people had *no idea*) was that any shape that couldn't survive on its own had to be supported with magic. Moving one's heart or even one's brain around wasn't a problem, except that one had to continue to spend tenyé to maintain the new location or put it somewhere that it would function successfully on its own. And weird fact: it turned out that it was really, really hard for the human brain to function when relocated to any other part of the human body besides the skull. Craniums were just fantastic brain homes, whereas most other places in the body kind of sucked at it. Go figure.

All of which was to say that there was an excellent chance that Anlyr's brain was in his skull at that very moment. If Anlyr suddenly lost his head, he might really die. And unlike Talon, he didn't have a friendly Death Goddess that had given him a one-use-only invitation to Return from the dead.

Talon would have one shot, and she couldn't afford to fuck it up. She'd have prayed to Taja/Talea, but that would only be a distraction for Talea, assuming the woman could hear her at all. Talon—Lyrilyn—began chanting a different kind of prayer to herself.

She channeled the knowledge she carried from two of the many different personalities lodged inside her: Surdyeh and Kihrin. Surdyeh had been a paid member of the House D'Jorax Revelers. He knew some shit when it came to drawing a crowd's attention.

Across the way, people turned as a sudden explosion of triumphant fanfare and sparkling confetti filled the air.

Everyone looked toward the unexpected sound except Anlyr, who turned to face the other direction. But even if he had been looking in the right direction, he still wouldn't have seen Talon, who'd turned invisible.[1] She feinted with two attacks, knowing he would have no choice but to dodge to the side. She let Kihrin's skills direct the strike.

Screams and shouts rang out around her as she landed, still invisible. Anlyr's body slid off her blade arm with a wet, disgusting sound. Soldiers began looking for the assassin, but Talon only had eyes for the wizard finishing the ritual.

Wait. *No.*

---

[1] I feel like I've missed out by not learning Kihrin's invisibility spell.—T
   You have. It's one of the best versions of that spell I've ever encountered.—S

Silver flashed in the professor's hand. Before Talon could move, he'd ripped open the throat of the first soldier in line. She still should've had enough time to stop the others, to close with the man or cast a spell or *do something.* The wizard must have bound the men sympathetically, because as he slit one throat, he slit them all, simultaneously.

The ritual wasn't playing around. The men dissolved into ash, flaking away like the bark of a heavy log in the fire. All their physical matter destroyed and converted to tenyé in an instant. The light around the circle intensified. That same glowing light shot up from the edges of the ritual circle, then spread out in eight glowing petals. Each flare spread out in the morning sky before all eight lines came together and streaked toward a singular destination.

Talon inhaled sharply.

The light show was beautiful, sure, except for what it meant. The new Eight, a group that included both *Galen and Talea,* were about to be stripped of their conceptual connections.

They were about to either be dead or powerless.

She prayed, prayed, prayed to any damn power that would listen that they'd just give in, not resist, not fight it. If they cooperated, they'd live. *Galen. Talea.* She wasn't ready to lose them. She didn't want to add them to her collection. She didn't want to do that anymore!

Maybe they wouldn't fight it. They wouldn't resist. Either way, they'd lose their powers, but at least they wouldn't die.

But she suspected some of them would be too stubborn.

"It's not fair," she muttered. "It's not fair! *I was doing the right thing this time!*" Talon eyed the soldiers around her with murderous rage.

She smiled as her hands turned into claws.

## 99. How to Kill an Immortal

*Talea's story*
*Raenora Valley*
*Just before Gorokai's death*

Talea had been firing haphazard but effective shots at Drehemia. She knew she was weakening the dragon. It was just a matter of time. Unfortunately, she couldn't *see* Drehemia, and that meant she couldn't track her.

She didn't notice that Drehemia had switched targets until it was too late.

Even then, she could only watch in horror as one event triggered another and then another. A horrible sequence of events, toppling down a hill. She tried to pull the odds, but she knew from the moment that Xivan rushed forward that Talea had failed to tilt the probabilities enough to matter.

"No!" Talea screamed.

Even the dragons paused for a moment, as if expecting another of their kind to show up or some further event to happen.

Gorokai's form turned black and skeletal, the flesh decomposing right in front of Talea's eyes, but she could see . . . she *couldn't* see . . .

Gorokai had breathed right on top of Xivan, and in the wake of that attack, Xivan was gone. Just gone. No, she must have escaped . . .

A twisted mass of dead roses lay on the ground that hadn't existed just seconds before. A mass that suspiciously resembled a human form. It was already breaking apart, disintegrating, dried petals blowing away in the wind.

Talea's voice choked off as she felt the tug.

She knew exactly what it was. Talea had felt it before. The ugly, stomach-clenching pull of the ritual designed to strip her powers.

But from a different location. From Marakor. And the one that had been ongoing in Raenena *stopped*.

"What just happened?" Teraeth screamed.

What just happened was that they'd lost.

Part of her didn't care. She really didn't. Whatever happened to her wasn't going to happen to Xivan.

Xivan wasn't coming back. She was the only one of them who *couldn't* come back. She was dead for good.

"What's wrong?" Janel shouted.

Talea opened her eyes and started yelling, because wasn't it perfectly obvious what was wrong? Then she realized Janel wasn't talking to her. The woman was speaking to Senera, who'd begun laughing hysterically.

"That bastard! That fucking bastard!" Senera shouted. "He copied my idea!"

"What?" Janel screamed back.

Senera was close to tears. "What I did to Shadrag Gor and Kharas Gulgoth! He linked two locations so they're sympathetically the same place. The ritual isn't happening here anymore. He's moved it!"[1]

Teraeth cursed. "We need a gate—" The request sputtered and died.

Numbly, Talea recalled that portals into Marakor were blocked. Even assuming they escaped these dragons, they'd have to fight their way through miles of enemy territory and who knew how many god-kings to get to where the new ritual was happening.

She calculated the odds.

"We're not going to make it," Talea murmured.

Fury rose over her in a wave. Without thinking, Talea pulled an arrow from her quiver and fired a shot randomly into the air. A moment later, she heard a draconic scream.

It didn't make anything better. Nothing could.

Xivan had always known this might be the price. She hadn't flinched. And knowing that didn't help either. Xivan had died while still Thaena. She'd died without leaving behind a viable body. That meant that either Galava brought her back to life or nothing could.

And Galava—Dorna—was dead. She'd stay that way until she wasn't Galava anymore. All of which turned a million probabilities and possibilities into one single inarguable result.

She'd lost Xivan.

---

[1] Looking back, Relos Var probably didn't steal the idea from me, but part of me will always wonder.—S

You could always ask.—T

Yes, I could. I don't think I will.—S

## 100. Three Rituals

*[I know where he is,]* I told Valathea, reaching across the distance between us and touching her mind directly. *[It's time.]*

*[Leave a marker,]* she said. *[Janel, Terindel, and I will follow you.]*

*Bless that woman,* I thought. At least someone was keeping her eye on the goal. The same certainly couldn't be said of me. I'd have to take a great many things on faith in the next few minutes, but most important of all would be that even though I couldn't see them, those three were doing their jobs. In Janel's case, to modify the demon-banishing ritual. In Valathea's case, to use illusions to hide Janel so Relos Var wouldn't stop her.

In Doc's case, to wait.

I turned invisible and followed Urthaenriel's voice, letting it grow louder in my ears until I traced the thread of her song to its source.

Then I teleported.[1]

I appeared inside the mountain, in a tunnel that I only knew from Relos Var's memories by way of Xaltorath. The room was well lit with mage-lights that highlighted glyphs—dragons carved in bas-relief on the walls and the sigils that had inspired Relos Var to create the Guardians in the first place. The Guardians, and later the dragons. I didn't have a chance to more than glance at them, but it was enough to make me wonder.

Drehemia, dreth daughter that she was, had originally found this cave. She'd shown it to her teacher, trusting Rev'arric to do the right thing.[2] With my new understanding and access to Xaltorath's knowledge, I identified it as a ritual chamber, created by a race long absent for a purpose that Relos Var had fooled himself into thinking he understood.

My brother waited for me.

He wielded Urthaenriel, which looked like a black silhouette in his grip. And he didn't, in fact, look like Relos Var. He'd returned to his original (if no longer native) form, Rev'arric.

---

[1] This isn't as dangerous as it may seem. Most teleport spells won't allow the recipient to appear in an occupied space, although they might do themselves harm for a host of other reasons.–T

[2] He didn't.–S

He didn't glance in my direction as I entered but instead continued concentrating on the ritual circles in the room. I knew enough advanced magical theory by that point to understand that rituals were capable of incredible feats but not without taxing both body and soul. Most people would be lucky to be able to perform a single ritual and, depending on their personal tenyé reserves, might not survive it,[3] but Relos Var didn't seem hampered by that limitation.

He was controlling three different rituals simultaneously.

None of them was the ritual to strip the Eight of their powers. The first one in progress was the one designed to banish demons back to their original universe. To my horror, that one was indeed ongoing, although I couldn't tell how far along. The second circle was filled with a tall column of energy, which appeared empty. The third was an incomplete portal circle, with an unclear destination. Relos Var stood between them, alone.

I left the marker for Valathea to follow toward the back of the room, where the shadows gathered, away from Relos Var's line of vision. I expected he had wards and other defensive alarms set up to cover every inch of this cave, however.

I was going to be disappointed in him if he didn't.

Relos Var glanced up from his work, recognized some change in lighting that gave away the game, and grinned. "Ah, I'm so glad you accepted my invitation."

It was funny how with just a single glance I knew that Relos Var thought he held all the cards in our little game. Rev'arric used to get that same damn look on his face when he'd just figured out a brilliant way to worm out of doing his chores. That smug, barely concealed look of satisfaction when he thought he was pulling one over on someone but this time layered around a core of poisonous hatred.

*"You can't complete this ritual,"* I told him. *"You don't know what it'll do."*

Relos Var shrugged. "I know exactly what it will do. But I wouldn't expect you to understand the nuances."

His tone suggested I was doing everything he wanted, that he was in control. Demon-borne doubt was quick to plague my thoughts, nagging that he was right. That I was still ten steps behind and would never catch my brother unaware.

I ignored those voices. Mostly.

He pointed Urthaenriel at me. "Step toward that portal circle. Now."

I felt the tug. The pull that just a brief time earlier would absolutely have forced Vol Karoth to do whatever Urthaenriel's wielder wanted. It was validating to know that I'd been right about why Relos Var had wanted Urthaenriel, that he'd known possessing the sword would mean having a way to control the tool he'd gone through so much trouble to make.

---

[3] For example, the Ritual of Night, which required such intense tenyé reserves that it traditionally killed its caster and everyone assisting.—T

I glanced at the smaller circle, the one I hadn't been able to identify. Ah. I had wondered how Relos Var planned to transport me to the Nythrawl Wound to plug up that leak, as it were. That solution was more elegant than what Thurvishar and I had devised. Still, I took some reassurance that the fundamental theories behind our ideas were sound.

*"No,"* I told him. *"I don't feel like it."*

He blinked at me. His flicker of confusion gratified me as his gaze lowered to the sword. Perhaps he wondered how he'd been fooled. If somehow he wasn't holding Godslayer when his every sense told him that he was.

But there were ways to fool the senses. He knew that too. He hadn't been able to recover Chainbreaker, after all.

Relos Var's jaw tightened.

*"I don't want to fight you,"* I told him. *"If we work together, there's nothing that we couldn't accomplish. If you finish that ritual to banish the demons, do you understand how many people will die?"*

I knew, the moment I spoke the words, that I'd said the wrong thing. I'd implied he'd made a mistake, that he was too stupid to piece together the truth. Unacceptable.

"Far better than you," Relos Var said, unclenching his jaw for long enough to speak. "But out of curiosity, what do you think it's going to do?"

*"Wipe out half of all humanity. What you're doing isn't just going to affect the demons but all the people who* used *to be demons in past lives. That's a lot of people who don't deserve to die."*

"Pfft." Relos Var gestured dismissively. "Don't be ridiculous."

*"It really will—"*

"Who told you it would *only* be half? It's going to be everyone who wasn't part of the original settlement, S'arric. Easily ninety-nine percent."

I stared. Turned out that asshole could still surprise me. Relos Var's placid, unconcerned expression left me with no doubt that he wasn't joking.

Fuck.

*"Ninety-nine percent. You . . . you know that, and you're going through with it, anyway."* My voice was perfectly flat and emotionless.

But of course he'd go through with it. Janel had told me that he wouldn't care. I felt a moment of sympathy with Qown. The realization that someone I cared about was *that* thoroughly horrible, wasn't misunderstood, had no interest in changing. That in the end, the only thing I could do was accept that they were a lost cause. Let them go.

The part of S'arric that wasn't on permanent sabbatical because of anger issues had known, cared for, and loved his brother for close to ten thousand years. Knowing that Rev'arric had viewed our relationship so differently was gutting. He'd never understood why I'd done the things I had. Just as I clearly had never understood Rev'arric at all. He hadn't been my brother—not in the sense that mattered—for a long time.

Relos Var had always known what the death toll would be. And he'd nodded, having decided those terms were acceptable.

"I'm sorry, did you expect me to allow the demons to wipe *all* humanity out when I can save one percent? That's still enough souls to repopulate. Without demonic souls in the Font, it *will* produce new ones, these untainted. We will recover."

*"And if you're* **wrong?"** The pure arrogance of Relos Var thinking that he could willfully destroy most of humanity without serious repercussions was dizzying in its hubris.

"I'm not."

*"For fuck's sake, Revas, there has to be another way!"*

"There isn't." His face might as well have been carved from stone.

*"No,"* I said. *"You stopped looking when you decided that the cost was acceptable. That's not the same thing."* I stepped forward. *"Please, I am begging you. Stop this now. You and I can come up with something else. We can come up with something better!"* I gestured to the room at large, to the ritual circles.

"You expect me to put aside a plan that I know will work for the faint, dim hope that my dear 'heroic' brother will come through and save the day? So you can be the hero? So you can turn this into your triumph?" Relos Var scoffed. "I'm not a fool, S'arric. And this is too important to pin on your idiotic optimism or your hilarious efforts to trick me."

*"Don't pretend everything's going according to plan,"* I snapped. *"We both know better."*

"Do we really?" Relos Var smiled.

He moved to attack then. But not to attack me.

Relos Var vanished before reappearing on the other side of the cavern. I'd have assumed that he'd teleported except for the fact that he was still carrying Urthaenriel. Which meant that either there was someone else was in the room creating phantasms (hilarious if true) or he'd created a series of spells and illusions that could be triggered remotely. Or the worst possibility of all, that even while carrying Godslayer, Relos Var could still use magic.

I suspected it was that last one.

A grid of light appeared, swirling around me as it marked my location. Swirling too around something that looked like empty space. Relos Var moved so fast it was just a blur of quick, dark motion as he stabbed forward against an invisible enemy.

A scream rang out. The light in the room flickered.

Valathea turned visible, clutching the spreading red bloom at her breast. She fell to her knees, Chainbreaker glittering green around her neck.

*"Valathea!"* I stepped in her direction, only remembering at the last minute that my proximity would be less than helpful.

"There you are," Relos Var said.

Valathea ground her teeth against the pain. I moved to attack Relos Var.

"Stop," he called out to me and put the edge of Urthaenriel to her neck.

I stopped.

"As I said, your hilarious tricks aren't going to work on me. Did you honestly think I had forgotten about Chainbreaker?" Relos Var's lip lifted in a cold sneer.

*"Let her go,"* I said.

"Or what?" Relos Var said. "You weren't already going to kill me?"

*"I don't have to make it a kind death,"* I growled and stepped toward him.

He pressed the edge of the sword against her skin, parting a thin red line of blood. She hissed in pain, but I was glad he couldn't see her expression. Couldn't see the way her eyes glinted hard and sharp.

I eyed the sword. It really was annoying to fight someone holding that damn thing. I could understand why Gadrith had been so upset.

But Urthaenriel didn't make its wearer immune to everything. There *were* some magical effects that the sword supposedly immune to all magic couldn't block.

For example, the Cornerstones.

So too, the world was full of non-magical ways to die, which was why a poison-tipped arrowhead or well-aimed dagger was what so often brought down a Quuros emperor.

Swords were a valid option. So I made one.

Relos Var's mouth quirked to the side at he glanced the weapon now in my hand. "Is this the part where I'm supposed to throw aside my leverage and have a duel with you? Honorable combat to decide the fate of the world? I'll pass."

*"I didn't expect you to accept. You know I'm better than you with a sword."*

He rolled his eyes that time. "If you think that I'm going to feel ashamed of an honest assessment of my skills, think again." Relos pressed the sword harder against Valathea's throat, so more blood spilled down. He hadn't yet pressed so hard that he slit a vein, but he'd get there.

I shook my head. *"Then I think we're at an impasse, don't you? Because you can't kill me any other way. Not while you're holding Godslayer."* And I won't move against you while you have a sword to Valathea's throat. I didn't say that last part out loud, but he understood.

Then the column of light brightened. Eight swirling streaks of energy settled into the magical container, circling each other. Which would have just been mysterious and vaguely menacing if I hadn't known what it meant.

Wherever the real dis-imbuement ritual had been performed, no one had stopped it. The powers of the Eight Guardians were once again up for grabs to the first person who could claim them.

And given that those links shouldn't have ended up swirling in a ritual circle underneath a mountain, Relos Var already had.

Relos Var also regarded the streaks. "Yes, I think everything is very much going to plan." He turned back to me. "My condolences on losing Teraeth. I know how close you were. And my condolences on Valathea as well."

*"No!"* I screamed.

But it was too late. I might as well have been shouting at the sun myself. He'd already pulled the razor-sharp edge of Urthaenriel across Valathea's throat and pushed her away from him. Her blood splashed garish and red against the stone floor, while she twitched once and then lay still.

He stepped to the side and raised his arm, and even before I could close with him, he blocked what would have been a lethal blow—from Janel. I'm not sure how he did it. How he'd even realized Janel was there. Possibly more of those wards. Possibly millennia's worth of experience dodging ambushes. Her sword came down across Urthaenriel and rebounded, although not without notching the edge.

"You're here too, C'indrol?" Relos Var laughed. "Very well. I suppose that's appropriate. You weren't there to see the beginning, but at least you'll see the end."[4]

Janel took a step back, circling to stay between Var and myself. "You son of a bitch," she spat. "I won't let you kill him."

"Oh, my dear," Relos Var said. "I have no plans to kill him. I never did."

She moved to strike him, and he parried again. He fought defensively, seeming in no rush to make a strong attack of his own.

I took the opportunity to begin closing with him from his other side, although the fight had just become more complicated. Now I had to stay away from Janel, which he knew.

*"You realize that you'll have to put down the sword in order to claim the power of the Guardians, right?"* I gestured toward the eight swirling lights.

Relos Var glanced back at me. "You're making the fallacious assumption that I ever intended to keep that power for myself. I have a much better use for it." He gestured meaningfully.

The wall of energy came smashing down. Eight streaks of power swirled out like spinning blades, before wrapping and slamming into the intended recipient of eight separate godheads. Except that recipient wasn't Relos Var.

All that power flew straight into me.

[4] Relos Var deliberately kept C'indrol away when he performed the ritual that turned S'arric into Vol Karoth and created the dragons. C'indrol died in the explosion after.—T

# 101. THE DEATH OF VOL KAROTH

***Kihrin's story***
***The ritual cave under Raenora Valley***
***After being given the power of the Eight***

I hadn't been prepared. I'd assumed—because it had been true in *every other version of the timeline* Xaltorath had tracked—that Relos Var intended to keep all the powers of the Eight for himself. That he was going to combine all that power and use it to ascend into something greater than the Eight. There'd been no reason to think Relos Var would deviate from that plan.

But he had.

If I'd thought the tenyé from Xaltorath was too much, it had *nothing* on this. I screamed as eight competing and in no way complementary conceptual frameworks tried to find a way to exist inside me simultaneously. Every fiber of my body was trying to fly apart, all at the same time. I had so much energy that I stopped pulling in new tenyé, new matter. I stopped disintegrating objects near me. I don't think I could've disintegrated anything if I'd wanted to.

I dropped the sword.

I also started *glowing*.

I had the power of eight god-like beings, and it meant nothing—less than nothing—because I was spending every single crumb of that power to keep myself from exploding like a dying star. Only not metaphorically.

This hadn't been part of the plan. Or rather, it hadn't been part of *ours*.

I heard noises. Clashing metal. Janel, attacking Relos Var.

"One ritual down," Relos Var said. "Now for the second. Really, C'indrol. I would think you'd like to watch this one, after everything the demons have done to you."

As much as I couldn't bear to watch, I also couldn't bear to look away. I knew what was about to happen. I couldn't stop it.

Tenyé vibrated through the floor as Relos Var activated the second ritual, the one that he would use to rid the world of demons forever, along with the vast majority of its human population. Janel stepped back, lowered her weapon, and stared at Relos Var with contempt in her eyes.

For a single instant of eternity, nothing happened.

It was only then that Relos Var glanced down at the ritual array itself. The smug look on his face vanished as he spotted the new configurations, the patterns shifted by a line here, a tiny addition there.

"What . . . what have you done?" he asked Janel.

"What you would have," she told him, "if only you'd been smarter."

Janel's eyes rolled up in her head, and she slumped to the ground. Her corpse looked small. Petite and fragile in a way she never had while alive.

Janel had always taken up so much room.

A small, ugly sob escaped me. Foreknowledge had been no defense against the piercing grief. Somewhere in Marakor, a shadow demon named Jarith had just vanished. Demons all over the Twin Worlds were vanishing, a wave of ritual force spreading out over the planet as all that energy and power accumulated, not into the array that Relos Var had prepared but instead flowing to the Font of Souls. The ritual wouldn't kill 99 percent of the population or half of the population or even 1 percent of the population.

It would kill none. Exactly none of the human population.

But it killed every demon. Including Jarith and Janel.

"What have you done?" Relos Var's voice was barely higher than a whisper, but I heard him. When I looked up, I saw that he'd bent down to check Janel's pulse. He rose, shaking his head.

"You stupid little fool." He sounded angry. Relos Var looked back at me over his shoulder. "Where did she send the souls?"

I scoffed as best I could while literally holding the cells of my body together through pure force of will. ***"Not to the other side of the Nythrawl Wound, that's for sure."*** Which hardly made this easier. At least Janel would be reborn someday. I'd take comfort in that. ***"Oh no. That's not what you were planning, is it? You were going to send all that power into me too."***

Relos Var squatted next to me, which is how I realized that I'd somehow ended up lying down on the floor.

"Yes," Relos Var said gently. "If I had to. If it had proved necessary. But let me explain how this will work. I know you're in a lot of pain right now, but it's important that you focus through that. Because if you release any of that energy, it will be devastating. I suspect such an explosion will be stellar in scale. At best, you'll take a sizable chunk of this planet with you. More likely, you'll destroy the entire world."

***"You'll die too,"*** I said through gritted teeth.

"No, I don't think I will," Relos Var mused. "But for the purposes of this discussion, all you need to know is that if you stay here, you'll destroy everyone you love. You still have family, friends. Or . . ." Relos Var smiled. "You can be the hero. The ritual circle is right next you. All you need to do is take a step. I'll finish connecting those two lines, activate it, and you'll be transported to the other side of the Nythrawl Wound. Where you can explode to your heart's content and harm no one but yourself. The Wound will be sealed, you'll have saved everyone's lives, and everyone you care about will live happily ever after. You can make the same sacrifice that Janel just did: your life for everyone's. You know it's a fair trade."

I let out a laugh and tried to grab the man's ankle, but Relos Var easily sidestepped. I found it hilarious that when I was theoretically at my absolute strongest—strong enough that I could destroy *everyone*—I was also at my weakest.

Perhaps *hilarious* was the wrong word.

I had to admire Relos Var's brilliant gamble. Yes, he was in theory giving all the toys to his enemy, but it was too much. I would hardly have enough time to learn to *use* those toys. More so, the moment I went through the Wound between our universes, those conceptual umbilicals would sever. At which point, Relos Var would be free to gather them all up for himself once more. I was pretty sure he didn't have my "problem" with power. He'd be able to handle all Eight.

He'd planned it that way.

I forced myself to rise to my feet. ***"That sounds like a great plan. Too bad for you. I'm not going to explode."***

I summoned my sword back into my grip and swung at him.

## 102. Demon Falls

***Fayrin's story***
***The Marakori war camp***
***Sometime during the attack***

Fayrin Jhelora sauntered through the opening of the tent like it was the front doors of a velvet house, a bottle of sassibim brandy in his hand and a rascal grin on his face.

Caerowan looked up from his book, widened his eyes, and shot to his feet. He reached behind himself for something. Presumably a trap or a gas or maybe just a dagger.

Fayrin cleared his throat. "*In a Green Land turned to war, the eight will become none, and the clash of armies will roar over the silence of battles won.*" He squinted. "Is that book five or eight? I don't remember. Quatrain one hundred twenty-four, though."

Caerowan paused. Fayrin carried no obvious weapons. He looked like he'd already taken a few generous pulls from that bottle.

"I didn't realize you were a fan of the Devoran Prophecies," Caerowan finally said.

"Are you kidding? I've read them forward and backward." Fayrin flopped down in a chair by the door, setting his feet on a trunk. "But you." He pointed a wavering finger. "Seriously? All this going down around our ears and you're reading? Shouldn't you be celebrating?" Fayrin leaned forward and stage-whispered, "We're about to win."

Caerowan closed his book and set it aside. "We? You work for Tyentso. For the empire."

Fayrin grinned. "Sweetheart, you have met me, haven't you? I work for whoever's paying me enough metal."

Caerowan rubbed his chin. "Tyentso didn't take you with her." Unspoken were the implications: that Fayrin wasn't under the effect of Warmonger, that his loyalty to Quur and its empress was certain. That, perhaps, Fayrin was telling the truth.

Fayrin hadn't spent the last decade carefully cultivating a reputation as a greedy wastrel who was always for sale to the highest bidder for *nothing*.

"No, the bitch," Fayrin muttered, "didn't trust me for some reason." He leaned forward a second time and slapped his hand on the desk. "But that's why we're having a drink!"

"I don't drink," Caerowan said. He sounded rather smug about the fact.

"Bah. You do today." Fayrin pointed a finger at Caerowan and took a healthy swig of brandy. "*In victory did the god-king boast his promises to make his followers rich. Many bottles were raised in toasts to the defeat of the blackhearted witch.* Book three, quatrain sixteen."[1] He held out the bottle to Caerowan. "Come on. You know that's got to be Tyentso. The prophecies say we have to drink."

Suddenly, Caerowan looked visibly torn.

The small man's lips pressed together in a thin line. "I always thought that referred to Jaakar's defeat of Olin during the Zaibur era, but maybe . . ."

"Better safe than sorry," Fayrin said with the somber seriousness of a very drunk man.

Caerowan started to reach for the bottle, but then stopped.

"No," he said. "I don't trust you."

"What? Why?" Fayrin schooled his expression into wide-eyed innocence, so overplayed that there was no chance of it being genuine, as he took another drink. Then he slapped a hand on the desk. "It can't be *tea,* Caerowan. Do you have any alcohol here? Hmm?"

"Of course not, I–" Caerowan paused. "The man who was here before left a bottle of something." He pulled a small tin cup from a drawer along with a bottle of amber-gold liquid. Not rice wine or sassibim brandy. Ara.

"Just one drink," Caerowan said sternly.

"To the defeat of the blackhearted witch!" Fayrin toasted.

### Kalindra's story
### The Marakori war camp
### During the attack

They'd been traveling through the back lines when it happened. Kalindra had taken it upon herself to prepare for a war that might continue beyond this single attack. Poisoning food reserves and sabotaging scorpion war machines in storage might not win them any battles immediately, but it would come in handy as the fighting continued in the weeks and months ahead. While she did that, Kalindra and Jarith both searched for the ritual.

At least, they searched until they heard shouting. Kalindra looked up to see eight colored streaks of light fly up into the sky and vanish.

"Shit," she muttered. That meant that not only had they not found the right ritual but they certainly hadn't stopped it.

She retreated to a section of auxiliary stables that had been repurposed as storerooms.

**Kalindra!**

She spun around, ready to defend herself. She'd assumed that Jarith had shouted her name as a warning.

But she was wrong.

Her husband had materialized a few feet from her. Right away, she knew

---

[1] Both the quatrains he quoted are real. And almost guaranteed to have nothing to do with the actual events here.–T

something was happening. It was like some force was trying to pull Jarith away but he was fighting it. Smoke trying to resist a hurricane.

"No," she whispered. The second ritual. The demon-banishing ritual that Janel had changed so it wouldn't wipe out most of humanity.

"No," Kalindra repeated. "She was supposed to find a way. She was supposed to figure out a way not to affect you!"

**I knew she hadn't.** Jarith's voice whispered in her mind. **But it didn't matter. Better me than my List.**

She choked. His list. How many people on it would have been affected by Relos Var's version of the ritual? Probably all of them. "Jarith, please–!" She had no idea what she was pleading for exactly. What she thought he might be able to do. Nothing. Nothing at all.

Every demon in the world simply vanished. No one but a few would ever understand what had happened to them, where they had gone, or who had died so everyone else might live.

*It wasn't fair.*

**I love you.**

And he was gone.

## 103. A Chorus of Dragons

*Talea's story*
*Raenora Valley*
*Just after the second dis-imbuement ritual*

When the ritual finished, Talea resisted.

Talea had never died before. At least, not that she remembered. She supposed it might have been possible that she'd died and been reincarnated and had lived countless lives before. She'd never asked. She didn't want to know.

So maybe she'd died before.

But in this life, it was her first time. The horror wasn't the idea of what was going to happen to her but knowing that it wouldn't fucking *take*. That she was going to Return, like it or not, because Xivan had set it up that way. She'd Return without Xivan.

Talea hadn't wanted to come back.

Her lungs had different ideas. She opened her eyes as she gasped and began breathing. No matter how hard she cried, she *kept* breathing too.

Talea cried, silently, head pressed to the ground as if she could somehow pray Xivan's body back into existence. If she'd come under attack, she would've died a second time. She had no interest in defending herself.

"Oh, child," she heard Dorna say, stricken. Talea didn't know who the woman was talking to. Then she felt the old woman's hand on her shoulder and knew that Dorna had been talking to her. The fact that Dorna *could* talk to her just underlined what had happened, that Dorna had been Returned and Xivan had not.

"I thought—" Qown's voice sounded so young. "I thought Xivan said we'd all come back."

As Teraeth gently began explaining how no, that's not how that would've worked, Talea began crying louder. She'd known better.

Then she grabbed Dorna's hand and squeezed hard, unintentionally making the old woman yelp before letting go. She stood.

"We're *not done*," Talea reminded them. "All of this is for nothing if Kihrin doesn't succeed. All of this will have been pointless!"

They hadn't traveled far. Just a small pass on one of the mountains overlooking the valley, enough out of the way that they could see what was happening and far enough away to be overlooked by the dragons. They were close enough to go back.

"It's out of our hands," Teraeth said. He looked like someone had taken a hatchet to his soul. His eyes were haunted, and Talea knew, just looking, that he'd already realized he was losing both his loves too. "He'll be wherever Relos Var is."

That was when each dragon lifted their head up into the sky and began to sing.

Talea had no idea if what they were singing was meant to have structure or if it was the equivalent of wolves howling into the sky, but it echoed through the mountains, vibrating high and low, at once discordant and harmonious.

Talea heard a rumbling that had nothing to do with singing.

"Avalanches," Thurvishar said. "This location isn't safe either."

Talea nodded. She was too numb to feel any fear about the idea that their position might be buried under a thousand tons of ice. Instead, she stared at the valley. The dragons were busy singing, which meant they weren't paying attention to the valley itself.

"This is the best chance we'll ever have," Teraeth told everyone. "Kihrin told Valathea that he'd leave a marker for her. Is that enough to follow?"

Irisia started to cast. "Let's find out."

The former goddess opened a portal.

## 104. Sleight of Hand

*Kihrin's story*
*The ritual cave under Raenora Valley*
*After being given the power of the Eight*

I swung at Relos Var with my sword.

Not a single one of Doc's lessons had ever prepared me for this kind of sword fight. Filled to bursting with tenyé, unable to use any of it, fighting an enemy who was immune to any spell I might use that magic to cast. Knowing that if I lost control, the consequences would be apocalyptic.

Relos Var looked annoyed, but he met me blow for blow.

*"Nice. You've been practicing,"* I told him. I kept my voice light. I had to. I couldn't just fight him. I had to pretend it was *easy*.

"Oh, fuck off," Relos Var snarled.

I put one hand behind my back, let my posture do the work of communicating an insouciant disregard. It wasn't the arrogant posture it seemed to be. I moved my fingers in a "gimme" motion while I slowly circled, waiting until the moment I felt someone slip the cool crystal facets of a rough Cornerstone into my hand. I tucked a finger under one of the chains.

I was running out of time. I could feel the pressure inside me pushing at the edges, seeking a violent escape. It took all my self-control to keep that energy inside despite the agony. My control was slipping.

But Relos Var knew that too; he was starting to look concerned. If I called his bluff and refused to enter the portal, there was an excellent chance that my death would take everyone with me.

Neither of us wanted me to destroy the world.

"Is this grief?" he said. "I can bring Janel back, you realize. Teraeth too. But not if you lose control."

*"Who said I was going to lose control?"* I sounded amused and just a touch arrogant. I gestured toward my chest. This was the point where I'd find out if matters had truly gone wrong or not. I'd had to take it on faith, for all this time, that Doc waited out there somewhere in the darkness. But now I knew for sure: he was the one who'd just handed me a Cornerstone, after all.

We'd known from the beginning that the only way this would work was if Relos Var was under Chainbreaker's influence. But we'd also known that Relos Var would be expecting that—that he knew I'd bring Valathea with me so she could use the Cornerstone on him the same way that she had on Thaena.

For this to work, he had to *know,* with absolute certainty, that he'd already taken care of that threat. That Valathea had been removed from the equation.

Which she was. If only she'd ever been the one wearing Chainbreaker.

And Doc? Well, Doc was dead. Everyone knew that. Even once he'd confirmed that his enemies had somehow imbued eight new Guardians, Relos Var had no reason to think that Xivan had been the Goddess of Death for long enough to make a difference.

On cue, the darkness dropped away from me, an "illusion" at last discarded to reveal my "true form." It also revealed the brilliant yellow diamond that lay glittering on my breast.

Skyfire.

I grinned. I didn't know what the illusion covering me showed, exactly, but I trusted Doc had made my smirk as annoying as possible. The man was good at this. ***"You were right to be upset when Gorokai stole what you were hiding at the Temple of Light. Turns out this bauble has an amazing capacity to store power. More than enough to hold all the bullshit you're throwing at me. But hey, thanks for giving me the powers of* all eight Guardians."** I cocked my head. *"Maybe not the way I'd have gone with that one."*

I twirled the fingers of one hand, and the shadow sword I'd been using vanished, replaced by a blade of red glass. Khored's sword. A visible reminder that he'd just given me the power of eight gods.

Relos Var's eyes widened. His expression was something a person less familiar with the man might've been inclined to call fear. Because if he'd been paying attention—and I assumed he had—then he might have noticed Sheloran using Skyfire earlier. He knew the Cornerstone was here. Doubt would creep into his mind. Had Sheloran using Skyfire been nothing but a ruse, so he wouldn't think to look for it elsewhere? Did I indeed possess Aeyan'arric's (and by extension, S'arric's) Cornerstone? Chainbreaker could've pulled off that illusion earlier, but not now, not when its wielder Valathea was dead.

Which meant I wasn't bluffing. Without the accumulated tenyé of practically the entire human race dumped into me in addition to all eight Guardians, perhaps I didn't have an overwhelming amount of tenyé, after all. Maybe I wouldn't explode. If so, I wouldn't have any reason to make a signature S'arric heroic sacrifice. Which meant the only thing preventing me from killing him outright was Urthaenriel. But even that artifact only granted him a reprieve. We both knew I was the better swordsman.

My brother panicked.

Time stopped.

I experienced a moment of perfect awareness. I might have chalked it up to Taja's powers—watching the dice fall one by one and knowing exactly how the numbers would land. But this was a bit like rolling those dice and knowing with absolute certainty that they'd keep spinning on their points.

A ludicrous, impossible, improbable gamble.

There was no small irony in how much easier Relos Var's own gambit had made this. Easier and harder. I could barely stand, and I had to grit my teeth and tense every muscle to keep the energy inside from cataclysmically exploding outward.

Relos Var hadn't miscalculated, even if he'd convinced himself otherwise. I didn't have much time before I'd have to dive into that portal circle and hope someone sent me to the other side of the Nythrawl Wound. Doc was using Chainbreaker to conceal my rapidly escalating condition—to keep any hint of the truth from sneaking out—but I knew how close I skirted the edge of catastrophe. I was an eyelash away from truly ending the world.

Especially since I wasn't carrying Skyfire.

That stone still rested in Sheloran's grip, being used to fight off raging dragons. Doc had slipped an entirely different Cornerstone into my possession, at the last possible minute, to minimize any chance I might accidentally damage the stupid thing before it could do its job.

I saw my brother think through all the angles, the solutions, all the ways he might possibly manage to salvage this calamity. I saw Relos Var glance down at Urthaenriel, which he'd previously only required in order to command Vol Karoth. Now it must have seemed like salvation.

I watched Relos Var come to the same conclusion that I myself had once discovered when faced with a similar situation against an opponent I couldn't kill: that Relos Var didn't have to kill me when he could destroy the Cornerstone instead. If he shattered Skyfire, I'd be right back where he wanted me. And if Relos Var injured me, that was perfectly acceptable as long as I ended up in that circle. Like the Cornerstone, I *would* recover, and by the time I did, I'd be locked away in another universe. Cost, risk, potential reward, all weighed, juggled, and assessed in an instant. I doubt it was a hard decision.

Especially for someone who was an utter bastard.

On the other side of the room, Janel inhaled. I glanced in her direction.

Relos Var took advantage of that moment of distraction. He stabbed me, piercing Urthaenriel through the Cornerstone hanging from my neck.

Making sure an attacker missed you was far easier than making sure they hit—but exactly where you wanted. I wasn't standing where Relos Var thought, so Urthaenriel didn't shatter the Cornerstone. Urthaenriel also didn't stop before she entered my chest. I ended up having to throw myself forward to make sure everything lined up correctly, but it was close enough.

Urthaenriel pierced my heart.

The death stroke was as precisely placed as if Doc had wielded the blade. Just one of several reasons that it had to be Doc using Chainbreaker and not Valathea. I loved the woman. She was much better at crafting illusions that fooled the senses. There was no one better than Doc, though, for crafting illusions that might trick you into killing your friends.

Or killing your brother, in this case. Relos Var had struck true. A perfect, fatal, final blow. Or final for eight seconds, anyway.

Eight seconds was enough.

Relos Var withdrew the sword. His brows drew together as he tried to comprehend what had just happened.

*"I couldn't kill my own brother,"* I told him. *"But I can't stop you from doing it to yourself."*

Doc always had a fine sense of drama, so every illusion in the cave fell at the same moment. My glowing silhouette returned, still unstable and gorged with power. I was revealed to be standing a foot in front of my previous position. But aside from those changes, I likely looked the same as I had before, except for two vital differences.

The clearest was the lack of Skyfire. As I'd said earlier, I wasn't wearing it. I wish I had been. It would have made dealing with all that tenyé so much easier.

But thanks to Doc, I *was* carrying a Cornerstone.

I'd been practicing relentlessly, for days, to make sure I could without destroying it. That it would still be there at the vital, pivotal moment.

I opened my hand and let Relos Var see what I'd been holding when he struck the killing blow.

*The Stone of Shackles.*

It fell from my fingers and hit the cavern floor with a grave and final sound.

# 105. The Switch

**Kihrin's story**
**Inside the Stone of Shackles**
**The instant of Vol Karoth's death**

I felt a cold, fierce pressure when Urthaenriel pierced my heart.

The world turned indigo blue.

The Stone of Shackles ripped my souls free from their usual housing, granting me a new, temporary residence while the old one finished dying. It wasn't a pleasurable sensation. All around me were strange angles of light and dark, looming shapes that I felt certain were both my old body and that of my unwilling killer. The dark line of Urthaenriel sang a discordant melody near me. Tendrils of cobalt energy arced through the space, wrapping around me as they pulled me forward from one dark container to the other. A blue tendril had wrapped around Urthaenriel as well, and I watched as the sword shivered and then jerked, once. A small ball of light from that direction flew at me.

Urthaenriel stopped singing.[1]

All was silence except for the slowing of a double tap of percussion: my heart, beating its last.

It would start up again in eight seconds.

My brother traveled in the opposite direction, wrapped in the same blue chains. We drew closer, much the same except for one major difference. He was struggling; I was not.

*[What have you done?]* he screamed at me without sound.

*[You did this to yourself,]* I told him. *[All of this has happened by your design.]*

His face contorted. *[Arrogant, egotistical maniac! You're no better than me!]*

I didn't reply. Some projections simply weren't worth commenting on.

We orbited each other half a turn before the tide began to recede, withdrawing us both to new sides. He to his new body and I to mine. The sound of a second heartbeat began to grow louder: my brother's body.

Normally . . . normally, the Stone of Shackles would force the souls of the murderer (in this case, Relos Var) to enter a corpse. But the Stone of Shackles wasn't Grimward. The murderer's souls weren't bound, so those souls (having

---

[1] While it's impossible to say if Urthaenriel lost its power at this moment, it seems likely that it lost that portion of S'arric's soul that had been lodged within it and might have (under other circumstances) allowed Relos Var to use the sword to control Vol Karoth. —T

little choice in the matter) then passed on to the Afterlife. Not this time, though. I didn't think the transfer was taking eight seconds, even if it felt like eternity plus a day. Relos Var would enter my body (S'arric's body, Vol Karoth's body), and then that body would self-resurrect, as I had so many times in the Korthaen Blight. Except this time Relos Var would find himself in a body he didn't understand and didn't know how to control.

Unless we timed this perfectly, what followed would be a very large explosion.

*[I want to understand,]* I said, arm outstretched toward him. *[Why? Why do all of this?]*

*[You'll never know. You always thought it was about you. You were unimportant. You were nothing more than the needle and thread I was using to darn a ripped seam. And now you've ruined it. You've killed everyone!]*

A thin, bitter stream of laughter welled up in me, too tired to break free into something more genuine. Veils, I was so tired. This didn't feel like victory.

*[Ruined it? Vol Karoth is going into the Nythrawl Wound. Just exactly as you had planned. You wanted to save the world, brother. I'm letting you.]*

Eight seconds. Probably half that. That was how long Doc and Janel would have to make sure he was on the other side of the Nythrawl Wound before he revived again. Before he woke, lost control, and exploded.

My velocity increased. Time began to speed up once more. Revas's healthy, whole heart beat faster in my ears.

*[Goodbye, brother,]* I said. If souls were capable of crying, I would have wept.

*[Go to hell,]* he replied.

Those were the last words Relos Var ever spoke—at least, in this universe.

# 106. THE HEALING OF THE WOUND

### *Janel's story*
### *The ritual cave under Raenora Valley*
### *After Relos Var slew Vol Karoth*

Janel knew Xivan had placed her name on the angel rosters in the After-life, but Janel hadn't been certain it would work. It wouldn't have changed anything if she'd known it wouldn't Return her. What had to happen had to happen.

Doc had been prepared to take this to the final stages by himself. It turned out to be unnecessary; Janel had one advantage compared to so many others (save perhaps Teraeth and the few other members of the Black Brotherhood with similar training).[1]

She was an expert at coming back from the dead.

Janel rolled to her feet even as Urthaenriel fell from Relos Var's fingers, a split second after the Stone of Shackles dropped from Vol Karoth's. Relos Var's expression was one of horror.

Across from him, Vol Karoth was dying.

"Do it now," Doc yelled. The man turned visible. He stood next to the last ritual array, the portal designed to send anything inside its circumference to the other side of the Nythrawl Wound.

There to explode and heal the Wound forever.

Or if she wasn't fast enough, to explode first.

Janel picked up Urthaenriel and threw it at Vol Karoth like a spear. Janel had no illusions that it would cause any permanent injury. Or even temporary injury. But she threw the sword with all her strength, and even without magic, Janel's strength was no small thing. Vol Karoth hadn't even started falling to the ground when the force of her throw sent both his body and the sword flying backward.

Relos Var, now in Vol Karoth's body, crossed the threshold of the portal array.

Doc connected the last two points. The circle activated.

Vol Karoth—Vol Karoth's body, anyway—vanished.

Urthaenriel vanished too. It seemed fitting that they'd go together.

A quiet beat of eternity filled the cave. Janel stood there, breathing. Doc kneeled next to the circle, looking like he wasn't entirely certain what would happen next, if anything.

---

[1] Oh, I think Janel's familiarity puts the Black Brotherhood to shame.—S

Across the room, Valathea inhaled, then started to cough. Doc was by her side in an instant, helping her up, pulling her to him. Janel couldn't blame him. It wasn't an easy thing to watch someone you love leap into harm's way. Knowing that you could not, should not, stop it.

They'd all known that Relos Var would kill Valathea if given the chance.[2]

Then the man still on the floor—the man who looked like Relos Var but absolutely was *not* Relos Var—began to moan.

Janel ran to him.

[2] We'd originally meant to fake her death using Chainbreaker, but when Xivan revealed that she could make angels, Valathea decided against using an illusion for that purpose. The risk was too great.—T

## 107. THE COST OF LIVING

*Kihrin's story*
*The ritual cave under Raenora Valley*
*Just after switching bodies with Relos Var*

It hurt so much worse than anything I'd ever experienced, which included being turned into Vol Karoth in the first place.

It hadn't been so bad when I was in the Stone of Shackles. Perhaps not a soothing, pleasant sensation, but I wouldn't have described it as pain.

That changed the moment I was in a physical body again. This was the pain of having one's souls torn from their body. Then having them stabbed into a different body like a splintering barbed knife, the whole wrapped tight with chains. Stabbed into a body to which I had no previous connection, no sympathy, no harmony. It was chaos and pain and the ugly sensation of being crammed into a vessel that was too small and the wrong shape besides. As much as it had hurt to be in Vol Karoth's cursed, perpetually hungry form, at least that had been S'arric's body. My body.

But this? This was something else. My very soul *rebelled*.

Not that it mattered. This was happening.

Dying hadn't hurt like this. Being gaeshed hadn't hurt like this. The pain turned red, then black, pulsing with each heartbeat as I writhed on the ground. Then the world lightened. Sound returned in odd, disjointed splashes of noise, until I recognized speech.

"Shh. It's okay. Everything's going to be fine. Just remember to breathe. You need to breathe again. Slow, even breaths," Janel's voice whispered. "I know it hurts. It won't hurt forever. I promise. It won't hurt forever, right?"

I remembered the screaming. I think I'd been the one doing it. My sore throat confirmed that idea. I opened my eyes (not *my* eyes) to see Janel hovering over me. And behind her, Doc and Valathea, his arm wrapped tightly around her, heedless of the blood spilled down the front of her dress from a slit throat now healed.

I'd known Janel was on the angel list, but I hadn't known that the demon-banishing ritual's completion would qualify as death. Although I suppose if any definition counted, it would be the forcible removal of one's souls before they were tossed into the Font of Souls. That did sound a lot like "death."

"No, it won't," Doc said. "Not forever."

"Revas?" I whispered.

"Gone," Valathea said.

"Dead," Doc corrected. "Janel tossed him into the Wound after you passed out, kid." My teacher grinned. "You know this whole thing almost didn't work. If we hadn't changed the demon-banishing ritual . . ."

I laughed weakly. If we hadn't changed the banishing ritual, I would've been overwhelmed. There'd have been no chance that I'd have been able to hold on for long enough to trick Relos Var. My brother's plan would have succeeded. Maybe later, in a decade or two, I'd be able to laugh about how close it had been.

"Is it–" I looked over to the side, toward the portal circle. It looked perfectly normal. Also, inactive.

Earlier, Janel had relayed to me what Khaeriel had explained–that using the Stone of Shackles had been the worst agony she'd ever experienced. I hadn't thought my mother exaggerating exactly, but I'd assumed that since I'd been through terrible things and knew more than my fair share about dying in painful, nasty ways that it wouldn't be a big deal.[1]

Dying while wearing the Stone of Shackles was a big deal. I don't recommend it.

I tried again. "Is the Wound sealed?" I whispered.

"We can assume so," Janel said, "because if it weren't, I believe we'd have blown up by now."

I coughed up a laugh. "Anticlimactic."

She smiled at me. "You know you've won when you're still around to listen to the silence."

"Kihrin!"

I'd never been happier to hear Teraeth's voice, with Galen and several others calling my name at the same time, just a sliver out of sync. I heard a lot of footsteps and a lot of noise, but I was really only paying attention to Teraeth's voice. Teraeth and Janel were the ropes I'd tied to myself to keep from drowning.

Teraeth came into view, but he didn't look happy. Just the opposite. But of course. They wouldn't have known if it had worked. He was staring at room that contained no one but Janel, Doc, Valathea, and Relos Var.

I had to let him know I only *looked* like Relos Var.

"Cold clam broth," I whispered to Teraeth.

He responded with a strangled sob of laughter, while Janel gathered me into her arms. "Everything's going to be fine," Teraeth whispered. "Rest now."

I closed my eyes and did exactly that.

---

[1] I suppose this does answer a question of mine–namely, why extremely jaded vané nobles never used the Stone of Shackles to switch out bodies like they were fashion accessories.–S

# PART III

## AFTER THE GAME
## IS FINISHED

## 108. HAPPY ENDINGS . . . OF A SORT

*Tyentso's story*
*Caerowan's tent*
*During the attack on the Marakori camp*

"Fayrin?" Tyentso pulled aside the curtain of the tent, prepared to start throwing spells.

What she found instead was an unconscious traitor of a Devoran priest, asleep on a cot and drooling on his own hand, and the youngest member of the High Council. Who was not unconscious but instead sitting cattywampus behind a desk, feet kicked up on a stack of books. He slowly sipped from a tin cup held in his right hand, and in his left, he was spinning a flat misshapen disk of hematite silver.

"Get your feet off of those." Tyentso smacked his boots. "Those are books, not a footrest." Then she noticed that the books in question were copies of the Devoran Prophecies. "Never mind. Forget I said anything."

Fayrin grinned at her. "Said what, Your Majesty? Thank you for coming so quickly. Anyway, I have a present for you." He slammed his hand down on top of Warmonger to stop it spinning, then pushed the Cornerstone in Tyentso's direction.

She gave him an incredulous look as she picked up the Cornerstone. "How on earth did you manage to steal this from Nemesan, Fayrin?"

"I didn't." He waved a hand at Caerowan. "I figured that if Caerowan worked for Relos Var, there's no chance that he was going to hand over Warmonger to Nemesan. I was right. He still had it. He gave it to me. I asked really nicely, though. Also the man has the worst alcohol tolerance of anyone I've ever met in my entire life."

"Well. Isn't that just great." Tyentso glanced down at the stone. She hated the damn thing, but for the moment, she couldn't be rid of it. Not just yet. "Three days," she said.

"Three days?" He pulled his feet back down and started to stand.

"One day to throw so much force at Nemesan that he can't see straight. One day to retreat with the Quuros army and leave the auxiliaries here to man the gates. One day to start preparations for weaning everyone off this fucking thing. Three days, then this goes to the bottom of the deepest, darkest hole I can find. If I tell you that I need more time than that, slap me." She quirked her lips, fully aware of just how little he'd be able to do about it if she changed her mind. But he'd proved himself resourceful many times over. He'd come up with something.

"Let's get this thing out of here." Tyentso started to open a gate.

"What about Nemesan?" Fayrin said.

"What about him? He ran. I'll hunt his ass down after I finish doing much more important things, like keeping my people from starving." She didn't hide her annoyance, but in hindsight, she shouldn't have been surprised that Nemesan hadn't stayed to fight to the last. He never had before.

"Okay, what about *him*?" Fayrin pointed to Caerowan.

Tyentso glanced at the unconscious man and sighed. Caerowan was something worse than malicious or evil. He'd been too wrapped up in ideas of shepherding prophecies and protecting the empire to realize that he'd somehow ended up on the side trying to destroy it. In other words, a fool.

"Bring him," she ordered. "He'll stand trial for his crimes."

Tyentso knew perfectly well that if it hadn't been Caerowan, it would have been someone else. But it was Caerowan, and because of Warmonger, there had been rioting in the streets, and who knows how many people had died. A lot, she would wager. Too many for bad poetry written by a dead demon to be any kind of excuse.

She opened a gate back to the Joratese camp.

### Kalindra's story
### The Joratese camp
### Several hours later

It wasn't a rout, not exactly, but the Joratese, Yoran, and morgage armies had been able to rush in and undermine or weaken key defensive points. The defending soldiers had been expecting a very different enemy; they hadn't been prepared.

The only reason Kalindra hadn't fought her way through the enemy until they either killed her or she was able to slit Nemesan from voice to viscera was because someone had reminded her that her son Nikali needed her.

Which was true, so she stopped behaving recklessly and retreated when the call came.

But it didn't mean she wasn't dying inside.

Losing Jarith once had been a nightmare. Losing him twice?

How she was supposed to survive losing him twice. What was she supposed to do. How she was supposed to live. All those questions existed in a place so far removed from answers they were nothing but dull, dark numbness. It felt the same as it had that first day, when her father-in-law had brought home the news that Jarith hadn't survived the Hellmarch.

Unreal. It just couldn't be real. But this time, she hadn't even been allowed the false comfort of disbelief; it had happened right in front of her.

Kalindra ended up back at the Joratese camp. She had no idea how. She thought a fireblood group had hauled her out of there. Conversations were happening all around her. Discussions of fighting and strategy and which god-kings were where, who had already surrendered, who would need to be dug out.

She was distantly aware that while they hadn't won yet, they had already inflicted losses that Nemesan's forces might not be able to recover from. Someone had found Warmonger and returned it to Tyentso. It wasn't an ideal solution by any means, but it would allow them to turn the full force of the Quuros army on the enemy. With the addition of the auxiliary armies Tyentso had raised, it was just a matter of time.

Kalindra didn't care. She sat in a tent and stared at nothing. Had they won the important battle? It seemed to her that either side winning would feel the same to everyone else in the world. Only catastrophe would be noticed.

That clearly hadn't happened. They were still alive.

Or at least some people were still alive.

Tears fell down her cheeks as she raised a hand to her face. She couldn't stand—

"Kalindra?"

She stood up and whipped around, eyes wide. Kalindra was hallucinating. She had to be. Because that was Jarith's voice—*his real voice*—which she hadn't heard since he'd left her in the Capital, forced to stop pretending . . .

Jarith stood in the tent entrance.

He was dressed oddly, in mismatched clothing that looked like he'd stolen them out of someone's laundry. Was that a horse blanket? And this was, without question, the best job he'd done of impersonating a genuine living, breathing human since Kihrin had helped him make that one copy on Devors. Maybe better, because the expression on his face was so confused, so astonished.

Maybe she was going insane. It didn't matter. She'd take it. She'd take it gladly.

Kalindra threw herself into his arms. "Jarith!"

"I'm so sorry," he whispered. "I didn't mean to leave. I didn't want to." He kissed her hair, her forehead, her cheeks.

Kalindra backed away from him, blinking, fingers digging into the cotton fabric of the Quuros soldier's shirt he wore. His clothing still smelled of soap and the nose-sharp scent of lye, except for his misha, which had a long streak of dirt down the front. The horse blanket he'd pulled around him like a cloak smelled, predictably, of horses. He was wearing sandals, and Jarith *hated* sandals. One of them wasn't even tied correctly. And yet he was perfectly clean, his face looking like he'd never once in his life shaved or needed to.

But all of this didn't add up to a counterfeit, an impostor. Just the opposite. This felt more authentic than any contact she'd had with Jarith since she'd first learned that he was something far better and far worse than dead—that he'd become a demon.

Her hands tightened. She stared in wonder at the feeling of his flesh indenting under the pressure of her fingers. This was real. This body was real.

Jarith had a body. *His* body.

"How . . . ?" she whispered.

"I don't know what happened," he told her. "The only thing I can think of is that Xivan must have put me on that list of hers. And that worked? I didn't realize that would work, but I woke up back in the Marakor camp, and I–" He laughed. "I think the only reason I got out was because both sides were too bewildered by the confused, naked man running through the fighting to stop me."

"You have a body. It brought you back and gave you a body." Kalindra smoothed her hands over his arms. "You're here. You're alive." A different sense of disbelief bubbled up inside her, but whereas before it had been cold and numb and bleak, this was a sharp, beautiful stab of hope.

She started crying. If anyone had made fun of her for it in that moment, she'd have absolutely, definitely stabbed them–while still crying.

"I am," he said. "I'm here." He smoothed her hair and ran a thumb under one eye, wiping away tears, before drawing her into his arms. She pressed her forehead against his shoulder and kissed his tears as they ran down his neck.

Kalindra wasn't sure how long they stayed like that. Long enough for both of them to cry themselves out.

Kalindra gazed up at him. "Let's go home. Your family misses you."

He smiled. "That sounds like a great idea."

### Kihrin's story
### The Mother of Trees, the Manol
### Several days later

I woke several times after that, but never for long enough to do more than take stock of my surroundings (the Mother of Trees, I was certain) and realize that either Teraeth or Janel was always somewhere nearby. Then I would float off to sleep again.

I woke, some indeterminate time later, to arguing.

"What do you mean you can't switch him back?" Teraeth tended to whisper when he was *really* angry, which was how I knew this was serious.

My mother's voice then. I almost opened my eyes, but decided to play dead a little longer.

"What I am attempting to explain is that by the end, my son was a cursed Immortal soul-swapped with a *dragon*. Even should we use Talon to craft a copy of Kihrin's birth form—which I must stress is not guaranteed to succeed— that body is no longer compatible. I have been informed that in previous attempts of this nature, the bodies would *explode*. In fact, it seems that Kihrin soul-swapped with one of the only entities in the entire universe with whom it would have been safe to do so."

"Yes, that was the plan," I interrupted, cracking open my eyes. "I mean . . . it was a plan I was hoping wouldn't be required, but it was a plan."

Everyone stopped talking and rushed over to my bedside. I noticed Janel was there too, standing next to Teraeth and looking thoroughly annoyed.

Janel placed a warm hand against my forehead, stroked my cheek. "How are you feeling?"

"Like my souls have been cut into a thousand pieces by a thousand knives and then stitched back together again before being pounded into a small jar that someone threw over a cliff." I squinted at my mother. "I now understand why your brother was able to catch you so easily after the soul-switch."

"Yes," Khaeriel answered with a wry smile. "I was too busy screaming to run. My respect for Terindel rose by no small proportion when I realized that he had somehow managed to both escape and *hide* after he switched bodies with his assassin. Rather extraordinary." She gave me a warm look. "Shall I leave you three alone for a bit?"

I nodded. "Thank you. We'll talk later."

Khaeriel nodded. "Of course. I shall send over something for you to eat as well." She swept out of the room with her typical elegance, leaving the three of us to stare at each other.

"That bad, huh?" I said when she was gone.

Janel sat down on the edge of the bed. "You're alive. That's all that matters."

I raised my eyebrows at her. "Is it really?"

She blushed. "At least you don't look like Father Zajhera."

"Or Relos Var, for that matter." Teraeth gave me a critical once-over. "I'll learn to live with it."

Janel started to say something and then stopped herself. I could guess what she was thinking. If my new face didn't remind Teraeth of Relos Var, it most certainly would remind Janel of *Rev'arric*. Maybe not the sexiest association, all things considered.

I was going to need to figure out how to change my appearance as soon as possible, but in the meantime, it wouldn't be that hard to remind her that I wasn't Relos Var. All I had to do was smile and not glare at everything.

"Nice of him," Teraeth continued, "to shape-change into someone cute at the end. I'd send him a gift, but—"

I quirked a smile. "This is what he really looked like."

Teraeth seemed genuinely bewildered. "Then why the fuck was he jealous of *you*? Did the bastard not own a damn mirror?"

I picked up his hand. "There's nothing logical about jealousy." I sighed and made a face. "Why was Darzin jealous of me? That didn't make any sense either."

"You're officially not allowed to have any more brothers," Teraeth said.

I nodded sagely. "I'll let my mother know right away that she is requested to only give birth to daughters from here on out." But that teasing reminded me of something less funny, and my gaze shifted over to Janel. "I never asked, but—"

She put her hand on her stomach and gave me a wry look. "Yes, still pregnant. Somehow. It's a tough little bean. Approximately the size of a grain of rice at the moment, but still holding on. And Dorna has reminded me about four times since breakfast that it's quite inappropriate for me to be planning to have a child when I haven't even chosen a herd to help raise it, let alone officially taken any partners."

My mouth suddenly felt dry. "And what did you say?"

"I reminded her that Relos Var and I are already married."[1]

I just stared at her for a second, mouth open. Because that was *technically* true, if it was completely untrue in all the ways that had mattered. Then I started laughing, because the irony of it was just too damn good. I caught Teraeth's eyes, and that was enough to get him going, and then we were both cackling while Janel watched us both with a smug, fond smile.

I cleared my throat. "You know . . . I'm pretty sure that sort of thing isn't legal until it's consummated."

"Is that so?" Janel said. "That is a problem, because it was certainly never consummated previously. However shall we fix that?"

"However indeed." I squeezed Teraeth's hand, put my other hand on the small of Janel's back. "We could make this official, the three of us . . . ?" I looked at Teraeth. "That is legal here, right?"

"Yes," Teraeth said, "and as an added bonus, I'm told three-way marriages hugely complicate succession, which I consider a significant point in favor of the idea." He added as an afterthought, "Oh, and King Terindel is back on the throne, so I am *not*. Which we should celebrate."

"That explains why we're not in the royal suite," I said. My gaze swept to the side and then stopped cold as I noticed several rocks had been meticulously placed in a line on a nearby table. The Stone of Shackles was easy enough to recognize, but I also saw Grimward, Worldhearth, Skyfire, and the Name of All Things. Warmonger was missing, as were Wildheart and Chainbreaker. I assumed the last two were still with their owners and Warmonger was . . . well. I didn't know. We'd need to find out.[2]

I looked back at my loves with what I suspect was a highly bemused expression.

"We rounded up all the Cornerstones we could," Janel explained.

"And you dropped the Stone of Shackles," Teraeth clarified, "before Janel pushed your old body into the Wound."

"Lucky us." Janel sounded like she'd have been glad if the stone had been lost. I smiled at she tucked a strand of hair back from my face.

Curly. Something very much like cloudcurl although not so fine in texture. Rev'arric had hated his hair, probably because it's difficult for students to take the stern professor seriously when he's graced with *adorable ringlets*.

---

[1] This is technically true, but since I am also "technically" married to Relos Var, I will vigorously argue that it doesn't count. They're just going to have to do this for real.–S

[2] Back with Tyentso, thanks to Fayrin Jhelora. She kept it with the Quuros army until they could be pulled back to the Capital, at which point, she began the rather unpleasant task of attempting to wean both the army and an entire city of its effects. We have since hidden the stone in an unpopulated area. No, I will not say where.–T

Teraeth wasted no time tousling said curls. "I cannot believe your entire plan hinged around 'get the bad guy to stab you.'"

I wrinkled my nose. "The best cons are the ones that exploit what the other person was going to do, anyway."

"Which is another way of saying, 'It worked, so shut up'?"

"Basically."

Janel just shook her head. "You may need to dig that explanation out of your pocket a lot. There's an entire herd of people out there waiting for you to wake up so they can shake you by the shoulders and demand to know what the hell you were thinking."

"An entire—" My eyes widened. "Who?"

Teraeth started laughing again. I think he was feeling a bit drunk on . . . everything. Living. Surviving what we had all assumed was unsurvivable.

"Everyone?" Teraeth said. "Galen, Thurvishar, Qown, Talea—" A flicker of something crossed his face, but he didn't explain.[3] "But we can tell them to fuck off until tomorrow."

I tugged him closer. "Tomorrow? I'm going to need more than one day."

Janel slipped away from my grasp as she stood. "More than one day for recovery?"

"Sure, you can call it 'recovery' if you like." I grinned at each of them in turn. "I promised myself that if I survived this—" I paused. "*When* we survived this, I was going to demand at least two days alone with both of you where we only left our bed when absolutely necessary."

"Three days," Teraeth countered. "We need *at least* three days."

Janel headed for the door. "I'll tell them to come back in a week."

*Thurvishar's story*
*The Mother of Trees*
*One week later*

Thurvishar found Kihrin in the private library of the royal palace at the Mother of Trees. He was sitting on one of the balconies with a book in his lap. If it wasn't for the rather extraordinary Manol vané clothing, Thurvishar would have thought he was doing a fantastic impersonation of a recovering invalid.

Which he was, by certain definitions.

Thurvishar knocked on the doorframe. "Are you open for receiving guests?"

Kihrin smiled and set his book aside. "I'm guessing you heard the news."

It felt odd to see this stranger and know it was Kihrin, but Thurvishar supposed he could at least be grateful that said strange man didn't look like Relos Var. Or at least the man Thurvishar remembered as Relos Var. The first was just odd; the second would have been a level of awkward that made him shudder to contemplate.

---

[3] We let Kihrin know about Xivan's death later.—S

"Do the Well of Spirals attendants think it didn't work because we wanted to use Talon for the template?" Thurvishar felt more than a little guilty over the whole thing. Ever since Talon had made the suggestion, Thurvishar had been operating under the assumption that once this was all over, the vané would be able to make Kihrin a new body and just move his souls into it. And Relos Var's body could finally and forever be laid to rest.

Apparently, it wasn't that simple.

"No, a more basic incompatibility."

"At least you should be able to shape-change," Thurvishar pointed out. "You can look like yourself again."

"Sure," Kihrin agreed, "once I figure out how to do that. If all else fails, I suppose I can go to Caless, but at the moment, I can't perform any magic at all. Tried turning invisible earlier this morning. Nothing." He wrinkled his nose. "Doc says it'll take me a little while to figure out how to spellcast with the new body." He paused. "That's not the worst part, though."

Thurvishar paused. "Would that be the dragon part?"

Kihrin groaned and slid down his chair. "I don't know how to do that either. I know he was a dragon, so in theory I too must be a dragon, right? But I have no idea how any of that works. And you know what else? I have all his *memories*. I hate it."

The comment confused Thurvishar immensely. "I thought you already did. Because of Xaltorath?"

"No," Kihrin said. "I mean yes, but that was like having a crystal ball I could pull out of a bag and look at whenever I had a question. It wasn't intrinsic. I could compartmentalize Xaltorath's memories the same way I did with the demons." Kihrin tapped the side of his head. "This is . . . everything. His whole life. I mean, I don't see it all at once because memories don't work like that, but I keep hearing things or smelling things, and it'll all come back to me, like *I* was there. Like they were my decisions, my actions." Kihrin scoffed. "At the very end, I asked him why he'd done it all, and he told me that I'd never know."

"But you do know."

"Oh yes," Kihrin said. "I know exactly why."

Thurvishar waited while Kihrin stared off into the distance. After a moment, Kihrin glanced at Thurvishar out of the corner of his eye, and his lip curled up in a smile.

Thurvishar flicked his shoulder.

The smile fled, and Kihrin scowled. "I know why, but it doesn't make explaining it easy. Turns out we were competing our whole lives, and no one told me." He paused and then rolled his eyes. "All right, I guess I knew. I just didn't think it was important. That's how brothers are, right? I never realized how much the little irritations built up, layer over layer, until finally, the foundations couldn't support all that weight, and it just . . . cracked." He shrugged. "He was insecure. And his way of dealing with that insecurity was to swing in the other direction as hard as he could. Quiet the voices by telling himself that he was always the smartest man in the room, and always right."

Thurvishar pondered those words. "I don't think I would enjoy having that in my head for any great length of time."

"No, I don't recommend it. Doc tells me that the memories fade eventually. It's like moving into a house the previous occupant hadn't moved out of. Sure, I showed up with all my belongings, but all the old stuff's still there. Eventually, I'll replace the old furniture with my own, but in the meantime, I keep tripping over the rugs."

"You've put a lot of thought into that metaphor."

"I've been thinking about it all morning for some reason."

"But wait." Thurvishar cocked his head. "You didn't say that was the worst part. What is the worst part?"

"Relos Var was tone-deaf," Kihrin said.

Thurvishar blinked at him.

"Tone-deaf!" Kihrin repeated with feeling. "I can't sing! I'm going to have to retrain . . . everything." He made a face. "The man was fourteen thousand years old and could change his shape. The least he could do was give himself perfect pitch."

"I question your priorities," Thurvishar said.

Kihrin studied him thoughtfully. "Have you by chance inherited a similar tone-deafness from me, your paternal grandfather?"

Thurvishar *froze*. "Oh . . . Veils." From a purely biological level, Kihrin wasn't wrong; he was now inhabiting the body of Thurvishar's grandfather. Or least living in the house his grandfather had built.

Kihrin started laughing. "The look on your face." He paused. "Although it probably wasn't nearly as good as the look on mine when Janel reminded me that, technically speaking, we're already married in the dominion of Yor. But then I reminded her that was never consummated, and so we had to drop everything and . . ."

"Stop. Just stop." Thurvishar slowly sat down in the chair next to Kihrin's. "I don't need to know the details."

Kihrin grinned.

### Tyentso's story
### The Mother of Trees
### Also several days later

The vané wouldn't tell her where Grizzst had gone, only that he would come back soon. So she stalked the hall outside his chambers—why did Grizzst have permanent rooms at the vané capital city?—and pretended her presence wasn't a walking diplomatic incident. For the moment, her hosts seemed willing to overlook little fiddly details like how she was the Quuros emperor. Perhaps because she was on a first-name basis with the new king. And with the king before that.

Or perhaps they were simply aware of how little the title *emperor* meant these days.

Their assault on the Marakori capital had been entirely successful. Nemesan hadn't had enough chance to fully acclimate his troops to Warmonger, after all. He'd probably meant to give it a lot more time before pushing for a fight, but what had Relos Var cared about Nemesan's plans? So he hadn't been ready, and then Tyentso had surprised him by bringing in three whole armies who'd never been under Warmonger's thrall.

It was mostly a mopping-up exercise at this point, but they hadn't managed to locate Nemesan himself.

She'd reached the point of wondering if it would just be best to go back to Quur and let the cards fall where they may, when a pair of vané escorted a tired-looking man with curly black hair down the hall in her direction. He looked like he might have been Grizzst. She'd never seen Grizzst in person before, so she was operating off descriptions. Thurvishar's had been particularly colorful.

As they approached, the man narrowed his eyes and looked at her in confusion. "I'm pretty sure we left Quur, didn't we?"

"You did," one of the vané reassured him.

"You're Grizzst, right?" Tyentso asked. Last she'd seen, he'd been running around as a suit of enchanted armor; either some princess somewhere had broken the curse or he'd just been wearing the armor, because he looked human enough. "I need to talk to you."

"Look, if you're here to give me shit about the Crown protecting you from Warmonger, you need to understand that I had no way to know—"

"I want you to come back to Quur with me," Tyentso said.

He hesitated for a split second. "Fuck off. I'm on vacation."

Tyentso narrowed her eyes. She didn't have time for this shit. She had a thousand things to do, never mind that Galen and Sheloran were showing up on the hour with more helpful suggestions for reorganizing the empire. Suggestions that were especially annoying because they were actually helpful.

Oh yeah, and she'd apparently adopted a son. Fuck if she was going to let Tyrin grow up in a country that was coming apart at the seams.[4]

"Fine." Tyentso pulled the Crown from her head and thrust both it and the Scepter in Grizzst's direction. "I quit. Take them back."

He stared at her.

The two vané looked at each other. "Shall we just give the two of you a moment, then? Excellent. Remember, no drinking, no heavy exercise, and no straining yourself for at least two days." With that admonishment given, the two vané retreated with impressive haste.

Grizzst looked not at all thrilled to find himself without his two helpers. He slowly walked to the door and pushed his way inside.

Tyentso followed him.

---

[4] Yes, she adopted Tyrin. All of us, but I suspected most especially Jira Milligreest, were shocked.—T

Translation: she's given the boy her family name, and very likely the Milligreests will do most of the actual "raising."—S

I imagine so, yes. But on the other hand, that's already a thousand percent better parenting than anything Gadrith did.—T

"Why the fuck," Grizzst said as he immediately poured himself a glass of wine, "would you be trying to hand the Crown and Scepter of Quur to *me*?"

Tyentso was about to point out that vané wine almost certainly counted under the "no drinking" rule, when he grimaced and lowered his glass. "Damn," he said. "It's fucking fruit juice."

She decided not to comment on it.

Grizzst shrugged. "Anyway, can't, won't. You're stuck with it until you die. Might as well make the most of it."

"Look, you made the damn things," she said. "And you built the fucking empire. So if you're not willing to help me fix what you broke–"

"I didn't break–"

"You broke it when you built it!" Tyentso said. "The empire was flawed from the start. It was built on slavery and the poor and the Royal Houses making damn sure that they were the only ones using magic. *You* didn't give a damn as long as you could use it to power the Crown and Scepter and set up a few altars." She twirled the Crown of Quur on a finger. "We need to re-create a gate system to replace what Havar D'Aramarin broke. For some reason, I don't think *Nemesan's* going to volunteer. So guess what? It's your job."

"I'm better at gates than that asshole–"

"Prove it," Tyentso said flatly.

Grizzst scowled at her. "And that's it? You just want me to rebuild the gate system?"

Tyentso huffed. "Fuck no. Have you been paying no damn attention at all? I just granted Yor their independence, but any peace is conditional on helping clean out their caves, which we poisoned. Marakor isn't completely retaken yet, and Nemesan's still out there somewhere. Most of my wizards at the Academy were either fucking useless or actively working for Relos Var. I gave the Kulma Swamp to the gods-damned *morgage*. The only reason Jorat didn't secede is because they're too fucking loyal to the 'Blood of Joras' to kick us when we're down. And likewise, the only reason the people in the Capital aren't going to starve is because the vané king's an old friend and cut me a sweetheart deal on grain imports. The empire is all but destroyed. I'm going to need your help with a hell of a lot more than a couple of fixed magical gates." She jabbed a finger at his chest. "You helped break it. You have to help fix it."

"I don't have to do shit," Grizzst said. "What do I get out of it? Do not fucking say something like 'a sense of satisfaction' or 'knowing that you've helped people.' I've helped enough people for lifetimes. I'm good on that."

Tyentso didn't press her luck with the finger pushing. She also didn't get upset. She'd spoken with Thurvishar about this. He'd told her what to say.

"No, none of that." She leaned toward him and said, "You. Won't. Be. Bored."

Grizzst stared at her, his face free of all expression. Then he cursed. "Godsdamn it. Hit me in the fucking balls, would you?"

"Every time," she said mildly. "But only if you say *please*."

Grizzst paused and considered her for a moment. "I might be in love with you," he admitted.

Tyentso rolled her eyes. So it was going to be that sort of relationship. Fine. She didn't care how he flirted with her as long as he *helped*. "That's nice," she said. "Too bad for you I like younger men. Speaking of, I believe you've already met Fayrin. He'll be getting you up to speed."

He snorted. "So when did you want to leave—"

Tyentso grabbed his wrist and teleported back to the Capital City.

# 109. And in Conclusion

## *Epilogue*

And so we come to the end of this chronicle.

It does not and cannot neatly wrap up every possible stray thread or frayed edge. Happily ever after is a thing that only happens out of context with history in the province of god-king tales and bardic stories. The end of these events left a world still on fire. Even that was a victory, given that the alternative was a world that wouldn't have existed enough to burn at all.

No longer can the dead be Returned by those privileged enough to have the right connections or wealth. The obvious assurance on the good behavior of the god-kings—Urthaenriel—is gone, but so too is the reason that humanity had little choice but to put up with god-king tyranny in the first place: the demons. The sun is yellow, and the sky is blue. A broken, singed Quuros Empire still exists, as do eight insane dragons. Nythrawl will gradually thaw, opening up a third continent. It may even be that knowledge thought lost to the ages will once again come to light when the ice retreats. The voras had needed neither gods nor kings, which is hardly so ill a model to follow.

The future remains uncertain, as futures always are.

Senera and I still have questions, of course. Questions about the true nature of dragons, about the Daughters of Laaka, about what kind of nation might be sewn from Quur's tattered cloth.

But those are different chapters in our history. This one, at least, is finished.

Or almost finished.

I leave you with a small addendum that Janel placed in my hands, which she insists is true. And this too leaves me with many questions. A reminder, perhaps, that it is always worthy to question our assumptions.

And why, for all I can say that the Eight are gone, I find I must add a troubling qualifier:

*For now.*

# 110. THE PALE LADY WALKS

### Xivan's story
### The Afterlife
### An unknown time later

Every soul in the Afterlife looked up to the sky when the sun rose that day.

Mostly because the sun had never risen before, at least not that any souls there had ever seen. The sun hadn't risen since the demons first arrived, when they'd punched through the boundaries between universes and broken something intrinsic to this place. Since no human souls had been there to witness it, no humans had ever known that it had stopped.

The Daughters of Laaka might have told them, but none had ever been asked.

The sun itself was black, surrounded by a halo of white filaments, eternally in eclipse. The sky was the color of blood.

What else had anyone expected of the Afterlife, honestly?

Souls wandered in a state of numbed shock. There was laughter and celebrations and people racing to the Chasm only to discover there no longer was a Chasm. At which point, they'd laugh and run to where the other side would have been, intent on joining the party at the palace or just jumping headfirst into the Font of Souls now that it lay open and unguarded. It turned out that a great many souls had held off reincarnation out of duty, determined to keep demons from making any further gains into the Afterlife.

As far as Xivan was concerned, every last one of them was a hero to beggar the bravest Quuros soldier. It was one thing to fight and know that you might well be Returned if you died—quite another thing to fight knowing the consequence of losing was to be absorbed into a demon that would continue killing your brethren.

Someone up ahead was playing a stringed instrument. As she drew closer, she saw that it was a young man sitting on a rock, playing a double-strung harp. No one gathered around him, but people shouted encouragements and praise as they passed.

It was easy to embrace the beauty of the moment. The rising sun, the wisps of fog swirling off forest floors, the haunting melody flowing around them. It wasn't just the people enjoying his concert either. The animals stopped to listen, the birds lined all the treetops nearby, the plants leaned toward him like he was a small sun playing light and warmth just for them.

Xivan stopped by the man's side.

He glanced up at her and smiled. The musician was a handsome man who'd no doubt learned early that music served as safe passage through many harbors. In this place, that was probably truer than anywhere else, although Xivan would've been surprised indeed if he'd avoided the fighting. He had a spear on the ground by his side; he'd likely served at the Chasm.

The harpist possessed both deep black hair that he'd gathered up at the nape of his neck, and an immaculately curled and groomed beard. His fingers were long and supple. His eyes were a green too bright to be anything but House D'Aramarin, although his manner seemed too casual for royalty. Perhaps an Ogenra.

"What's your name?" Xivan asked.

The fingers faltered, the music stopped. A frown crowded out the smile. He was silent for a long time, and then said, "I don't remember."

She nodded. Not unusual. Most people didn't. She hadn't at first either, but memories had filtered down like sunlight through the trees. She touched his shoulder. "Are you sure?"

He blinked and shook his head, like trying to get the water out of an ear. "I don't . . ." He leaned back, letting the harp balance between his legs. He blinked several times at nothing.

"My name is Surdyeh," he said. It was almost a question, asked with no small amount of wonder.

"Well met, Surdyeh. So I was thinking—the palace is beautiful and great for throwing parties, as we can all see—but don't you think we need a little more?"

"The Afterlife has grown a bit crowded of late," Surdyeh agreed ruefully.

"Right. Now, hopefully, everything will settle down, but in the meantime, we have a great many people who don't want to go but don't have a place to stay."

The musician gave her an odd look. "Agreed, but . . . wouldn't that be Thaena's job?"

Xivan's mouth twisted. "Probably. If someone finds her, they should let her know." She smiled at some private joke. "But for now"—she gestured toward the wide slice of earth where the Chasm had once stood—"want to help me build a city?"

His mouth opened at the offer. Perhaps he thought she was joking. When it occurred to him that she wasn't, he closed his mouth again. "Promise me we won't have an Upper and Lower Circle—that we won't push everyone into rich or poor."

"What would define *rich* and *poor* in a place like this?" Xivan questioned, but even as she said the words, she could think of ways. Some people would have more tenyé, or would figure out how to cast spells here, or just be more creative and stronger-willed than their fellows. There would always be two kinds of power: that which one wielded intrinsically through spells or sword or godhood, and the kind that one wielded because everyone else agreed that it should be so. It was shockingly easy to engineer the latter.

So Xivan smiled and said, "I can promise we'll try to make sure it doesn't happen. We'll have to be vigilant, though—old habits never fade without a fight."

*Jenn Lyons*

She reached out a hand, palm down. In response, a small riot of black leaves and thorned vines broke free from the ground. The bush grew so quickly that by the time it reached her hand, the only portion of the plant that brushed her fingers were the velvety bloodred petals of newly bloomed roses. She smiled fondly. Being dead hadn't changed how this world felt about her.

If anything, it had strengthened their connection.

Surdyeh stared at Xivan with wide eyes. "What did you say your name was again?"

"I didn't," she said, smiling.

He shook his head, still startled but now also a tiny bit scared. "I don't think you need to either." He slung his harp over his shoulder for just long enough to scramble up to his feet.

Together, they walked toward the land that had once been the Chasm.

In Xivan's wake, roses bloomed.

**THE END**

# GLOSSARY

**A**

Aeyan'arric (EYE-ann-AR-ik)—a dragon associated with ice, cold, and storms. Daughter of S'arric and C'indrol.

Afterlife, the—a dark mirror of the Living World, souls go to the Afterlife after death, hopefully to move on to the Land of Peace, where the Font of Souls is located.

agolé (a-GOAL-lay)—a piece of cloth worn draped around the shoulders and hips by both men and women in western Quur.

Alavel (a-la-VEL)—home city of the wizard's school known as the Academy.

Arasgon (AIR-as-gon)—a fireblood, Talaras's brother.

Arena, the—a park in the center of the Capital City that serves as battleground for the choosing of the emperor.

Argas (AR-gas)—one of the Eight Immortals. Considered the god of invention and innovation.

Atrine (at-rin-EE)—capital of the dominion of Jorat, originally built by Emperor Atrin Kandor.

**B**

Baelosh (BAY-losh)—a dragon, best known for the size of his hoard of treasure.

barrier roses—a magical ward preventing teleportation or gate-creation magics anywhere inside the Manol. Ten individuals are known to be able to ignore the barrier roses: the Immortals, Relos Var, and Grizzst, who created them.

Bertok (BER-tok)—god-king of war.

Blood of Joras (JOR-as)—a Joratese term for any wizard not of Joratese, Marakori, or Yoran extraction.

**C**

Caless (kal-LESS)—goddess of physical love and lust. Popular among velvet girls and boys of the Capital. See: D'Talus, Lessoral.

Chainbreaker—a Cornerstone, associated with the Manol vané. Has powers dealing with illusions.

Cherthog (cher-THOG)—a god of winter and ice, primarily worshipped in Yor.

Cimillion (seh-MIL-e-on)—Emperor Sandus's son, believed killed as an infant by Gadrith the Twisted, but in fact renamed as Thurvishar D'Lorus.

City, the—a.k.a. the Capital City. Just called "the City." Originally a city-state under the control of the god-king Qhuaras, its original name (Quur) now applies to the whole empire.

cloudcurl hair—originally a vané trait, now common in areas like Kirpis and Khorvesh, of hair so curly that it is cloudlike. While both vané groups can have cloudcurl hair, the Kirpis vané were especially famous for it. It's not an uncommon feature in people from Kirpis or Kazivar, suggesting that significant interbreeding has occurred—even after the vané were supposedly pushed out of the Kirpis forest.

Cornerstones, the—eight magical artifacts: Chainbreaker, Grimward, the Name of All Things, Skyfire, the Stone of Shackles, Warmonger, Wildheart, and Worldhearth.

Court of Gems, the—slang for the royal families of the Upper Circle represented by twelve different kinds of gemstones.

Crown and the Scepter, the—famous artifacts that may only be wielded by the Emperor of Quur. Created by Grizzst.

Culling Fields, the—a tavern and inn situated just outside the imperial Arena. Previously owned by Doc and now run by his adopted daughter, Taunna.

## D

Daakis (DAY-kis)—god of sports, swordplay, and games.

Dana (dan-AY)—god-queen of Eamithon, still worshipped as the goddess of wisdom and virtue.

D'Aramarin (day-ar-a-MAR-in)—the first ranked Royal House. House D'Aramarin controlled the Gatekeepers, the guild of wizards primarily responsible for running and maintaining the gate system. They were thus responsible for and control almost all interdominion trade. Their leader, Havar, had attempted to form his own nation by splitting off Marakor.

  Havar (hav-AR)—High Lord of House D'Aramarin. Secretly a god-king. See: Murad, Nemesan.

Daughter of Laaka (LAKE-ay)—a.k.a. kraken, an enormous immortal sea creature.

Delon (DEL-on)—first mate aboard the slave ship the *Misery*. He was killed by slaves in the galley as the ship was attempting to navigate the Maw.

Demon Falls—the artificial dam constructed by Atrin Kandor to form Lake Jorat, called such because the spillways are shaped like demon mouths.

demons—an alien race from another dimension that can, through effort, gain access to the material world. Famous for their cruelty and power. See: Hellmarch.

D'Erinwa (day-er-in-WAY)—a Royal House, primarily associated with slavery.

  Phaellan (FAY-lan)—a nobleman of House D'Erinwa, murdered by Gadrith D'Lorus. His ghost possessed Raverí D'Lorus (see: Tyentso) and was responsible for much of her early education.

Devoran Prophecies, the—a many-book series of prophecies that are believed to foretell the end of the world. Less well known is that they have nothing to do with actual prognostication and are instead a method used by the demon Xaltorath to remind themselves of important events in previous timelines.

Devors (de-VORS)—island chain south of the Capital City, most famous as the home of the Devoran priests and their prophecies.

dhole (dol)—a form of wild dog, domesticated in Jorat and also found throughout Marakor.

D'Kard (day-KARD)—a Royal House, primarily associated with crafting.

D'Lorus (du-LOR-us)—a Royal House, primarily associated with paper, books, schools, and education.

   Cedric (KED-rik)—High Lord of House D'Lorus. Father of Gadrith. Executed for treason by his granddaughter, Empress Tyentso.

   Gadrith (GAD-rith)—Lord Heir of House D'Lorus, an infamous necromancer and wizard, widely believed to be dead; also known as Gadrith the Twisted.

   Raverí (rav-ear-EE)—wife of Gadrith D'Lorus. Officially listed as mother of Thurvishar D'Lorus, executed after his birth for the charges of witchcraft and treason. In truth, she was Gadrith's Ogenra daughter, who entered into a platonic marriage with her own father in order to put herself in a position to enact her vengeance against the man. Later revealed to still be alive and using the name Tyentso, she has since become the Empress of Quur.

   Thurvishar (thur-vish-AR)—legally the son of Gadrith and Raverí D'Lorus, but in fact the son of Emperor Sandus and Dyana. Technically now High Lord of House D'Lorus, depending on whether or not House D'Lorus still exists.

D'Mon (day-MON)—a Royal House, primarily associated with the healing arts.

   Alshena (al-shen-AY)—wife of Darzin D'Mon and daughter of Havar D'Aramarin, murdered by being sacrificed to the demon Xaltorath a number of years ago. Mother of three children: Galen, Saerá, and Tishenya (note: this is not the same as Therin's daughter Tishenya, although they share the same name).

   Darzin (DAR-zin)—former Lord Heir of House D'Mon, slain by his "son" Kihrin.

   Galen (GAL-len)—Lord Heir Darzin D'Mon's only son, now theoretically High Lord of House D'Mon (depending on whether or not House D'Mon still exists).

   Gerisea (ger-IS-see-ah)—youngest daughter of Therin D'Mon, married to the Duke of Khorvesh's second-oldest son. Killed during the Glittering Feast.

   Kihrin (KEAR-rin)—youngest child of High Lord Therin D'Mon and only child of Queen Khaeriel of the vané. Also, the reincarnation of S'arric, one of the Eight Immortals.

   Saerá (SAY-ra)—eldest daughter of Darzin D'Mon.

   Therin (THER-rin)—former High Lord of House D'Mon, now living in the Manol.

Tishenya (tish-EN-ya)—oldest child of Therin D'Mon, murdered by her sister, Gerisea.

Doc—see: Terindel.

Doltar (dol-TAR)—a distant country whose people have pale skin and light-colored hair and eyes.

Dorna (DOR-na)—an elderly Joratese woman who served as Janel Theranon's nanny in childhood. An angel of Tya, Dorna now works with Duke Ninavis.

Dragonspires, the—a mountain range running north-south through Quur, dividing the dominions of Kirpis, Kazivar, Eamithon, and Khorvesh from Raenena, Jorat, Marakor, and Yor.

Drehemia (DRAY-hem-EE-ah)—a dragon, particularly associated with darkness and secrets.

dreth (dreth)—see: vordreth.

drussian (drus-E-an)—a rare metal, superior to iron, which can only be created through superhot magical fires.

Dry Mothers, the—the elders of the morgage, who rule the various tribal groups.

D'Talus (day-TAL-us)—the Royal House in charge of the smelter and smith's guild, known as the Red Men.

    Lessoral (les-SOR-al)—High Lady of House D'Talus. Secretly, also the god-queen Caless, Goddess of Love (or Lust) who has been worshipped in the Capital City since its founding.

    Varik (VAHR-ik)—High Lord of House D'Talus. Secretly, also the god-king Bezar, God of Forges and Smiths.

Dyana (DEE-an-ah)—a vordreth woman, married to Emperor Sandus, murdered by Gadrith the Twisted. Thurvishar D'Lorus's biological mother.

# E

Eamithon (AY-mith-ON)—a dominion just north of the Capital City, the oldest of the Quuros dominions and considered the most tranquil.

Eight Immortals, the—eight beings of godlike power created by a ritual performed by Relos Var.

Empire of Quur (koor)—see: Quur.

Eshimavari (esh-EE-mah-VAR-ee)—the real name of the Goddess of Luck. See: Taja.

# F

Festival of the Turning Leaves—a yearly celebration to the goddess Galava. Here petitioners may, after one year of service to the goddess, petition the goddess to change their biological sex.

firebloods—a race originally related to horses but modified by the god-king Khorsal to possess extraordinary size, power, resilience, loyalty, and intelligence. Firebloods are omnivorous, and although they don't possess fingers, some are capable of manipulating tenyé. They have an average life expectancy of eighty years or more.

Founders—in vané society, Founders are members of the race who founded the vané nation, meaning any Founder is at least fourteen thousand years old. Founders have specific legislative powers. Outside of vané society, it has also become slang for the original settlers who came to this world from another dimension and whose souls can be used to create a star tear tsali.

Four Races, the—the entirely mistaken belief that four immortal races once existed. In fact, there were only three: the voras, voramer, and vordreth. The vané were in fact an offshoot race whose immortality was not inherent, but the result of their retention of magical skill.

# G

gaesh (gaysh), pl. gaeshe (gaysh-ay)—an enchantment that forces the victim to follow all commands given by the person who physically possesses their totem focus, up to and including commands of suicide. Being unable or unwilling to perform a command results in death.

Galava (gal-a-VAY)—one of the Eight Immortals. Goddess of life and nature.

Galla Sea (GAL-la)—sea between the Devors island cluster and the Desolation.

gate—a.k.a. portal, the magical connection of two different geographic locations, allowing for quick travel across great distances. Only powerful wizards can typically create Gatestone-independent portals.

Gatekeepers—the guild who controls and maintains gate travel. Ruled by House D'Aramarin.

Gatestone—a specially inscribed section of stone that somehow makes gate travel much less magically onerous. Exactly how this is accomplished is a proprietary, heavily protected House D'Aramarin secret.

gelding—a Joratese term for any person, male or female, who does not fall into stallion or mare stereotypes. Note that this does not indicate the person is sexually neuter, nor is it indicative of sexual preferences. See: gender, Joratese.

Gendal (GEN-dal)—former Emperor of Quur, murdered by Gadrith D'Lorus.

gender, Joratese—Joratese customs define gender separately from sex or sexual orientation, falling into three categories: stallion, mare, and gelding. Stallions can roughly be considered "men" and mares "women." Geldings are those who refuse to define themselves within this otherwise binary system (which has all the flaws one might expect of a polarized gender system). Thus, it is possible to have a "mare" who is biologically male or a "stallion" who is biologically female, and "gelding" has nothing to do with whether or not one is capable of sexual reproduction. See: sexuality, Joratese.

Godslayer—see: Urthaenriel.

god-touched—a gift or curse (depending on whom one asks) handed down by the Eight Immortals to the eight Royal Houses of Quur. Besides giving each house a distinctive eye color, the Royal Houses are forbidden from making laws.

Gorokai (GORE-o-kai)—a dragon with the ability to change his shape, both to animal forms as well as mimicking other dragons. Responsible for the destruction of the Temple of Light in Eamithon.

Grimward—one of the Cornerstones, with the ability to bring the dead back to a semblance of life. Has been used to do so on Gadrith the Twisted, Xivan Kaen, and the Lash.

Grizzst (grizt)—falsely attributed to being one of the Eight Immortals; famous wizard, sometimes considered a god of magic, particularly demonology. Believed to be responsible for binding demons as well as making the Crown and Scepter of Quur.

Gryphon Men, the—a secret organization ultimately working for the emperors of Quur, since both Sandus and his predecessor Gendal seem to have had connections to this group. Their goals are unclear, but they seem to be working toward fulfilling the Devoran Prophecies, although that seems counterproductive considering how many of those prophecies predict the destruction of Quur.

Guarem (GOW-rem)—the primary language of Quur.

# H

Hamarratus (ham-ar-RA-tus)—a fireblood, previously a slave owned by Darzin D'Mon, also called Scandal.

Hell—distinct from the Land of Peace; it's an actual location—namely, the area surrounding the Nythrawl Wound, so named because it's on the continent of Nythrawl.

Hellmarch—the result of a powerful demon gaining access to the physical world, freely summoning demons and possessing corpses. This usually results in a runaway path of death and devastation. The ultimate cause of a Hellmarch used to be a demon escaping a summoner's control. Before the breaking of the Stone of Shackles, demons could only be summoned to the Living World by corporeal entities (such as humans or vané). But demons quickly discovered they could exploit a loophole by possessing a living body and forcing that body to summon more of their kind. Demons can also possess corpses in the Joratese/Marakori area but cannot summon more demons in this manner. Famous Hellmarches include the Lonezh Hellmarch and the Capital City Hellmarch.

Hellwarrior—a prophesied villain who will rise up to destroy the Empire of Quur and possibly the world. Also a prophesied hero who will rise up to save the world. Also a group of heroes who will do either of the previous two.

# I

idorrá (id-DOR-ray)—a Joratese concept of authority, dominance, and control. Roughly analogous to responsibility, duty, and authority, idorrá can be lost if the holder fails to protect or defend it.

Ir'amar (IR-ah-mar)—formal contracted name of Irisia'amar. See: Tya.

Ivory District, the—the temple district of the Upper Circle, in the Capital.

# J

Jazars (JAZ-arz)—god of parties, food, and drink.

Jhelora, Fayrin (zah-LOR-ah, FAY-rin)—imperial liaison of the High Council and Ogenra of House D'Jorax. Notoriously corrupt libertine.

Jorat (jor-AT)—a dominion in the middle of Quur of varying climates and wide reaches of grassy plains; known for its horses.

# K

Kaen (kane)—the Yoran ducal line.

Azhen (AHJ-en)—Duke, or Hon, of Yor, grandson of the Joratese Quuros general who conquered the region and slew the god-king rulers of the region, Cherthog and Suless. Eventually slain by Suless, who had not in fact been killed but enslaved and forced to serve the Kaen family.

Exidhar (EX-eh-DAR)—Azhen and Xivan Kaen's only son. Killed by Suless.

Veixizhau (vex-e-SHAU)—Exidhar Kaen's wife, formally Azhen's wife, but was divorced from her original husband after it was discovered she'd been having an affair with, and was pregnant by, Exidhar.

Xivan (JI-van)—Azhen Kaen's first wife; her Khorveshan ancestry made her unpopular with the Yoran people, and she was eventually killed in an assassination attempt meant for her husband. She was brought back by Relos Var as an undead being at the cost of Azhen Kaen's service. Briefly a wielder of Urthaenriel and more recently the new Goddess of Death.

Kandor (KAN-dor)

Atrin (AT-rin)—an Emperor of Quur who significantly expanded the borders of the empire; most famous for deciding to invade the Manol, which resulted in the destruction of virtually the entire Quuros army and the loss of Urthaenriel. This left Quur defenseless against the subsequent morgage invasion. Reincarnated as Teraeth.

Elana (e-LAN-ay)—a musician from Khorvesh who married Atrin Kandor. After his death, she returned to using her maiden name and journeyed into the Korthaen Blight to negotiate a peace settlement with the invading morgage people; responsible for freeing S'arric. Reincarnated as Janel Theranon.

Karolaen (KAR-o-lane)—former name of Kharas Gulgoth.

Kazivar (KAZ-eh-var)—one of the dominions of Quur, north of Eamithon.

kef (kef)—a style of trouser common in western Quur.

Kelanis (KEL-a-nis)—son of Khaevatz and Kelindel, younger brother of Khaeriel; former king of the vané, slain by Suless.

Kelindel (KEL-in-del)—the Kirpis vané king who married the Manol vané queen Khaevatz and united the vané people.

Key—a specialist burglar working for the Shadowdancers trained at unlocking magical wards and enchantments. Technically a witch. See: witch.

Khaemezra (kay-MEZ-rah)—a.k.a. Mother, the High Priestess of Thaena, and leader of the Black Brotherhood; Teraeth's mother; the true name of the first Thaena. See: Thaena.

Khaeriel (kay-RE-el)—queen of the vané, assassinated by her brother, Kelanis. Because Khaeriel was wearing the Stone of Shackles, she ended up in the body of her assassin and was later gaeshed and sold into slavery to Therin D'Mon by her grandmother Khaemezra. After her gaesh was broken, she slew most of the D'Mon family and kidnapped her former owner, Therin. Kihrin D'Mon's mother.

Khaevatz (KAY-vatz)—deceased Manol vané queen, famous for resisting Atrin
    Kandor's invasion. She later married Kirpis vané king Kelindel. Khaemezra's
    daughter and Teraeth's half sister, she and her husband both died fighting
    a god-king in the Doltari Free States.
Kharas Gulgoth (KAR-as GUL-goth)—a ruin in the middle of the Korthaen
    Blight; believed sacred (and cursed) by the morgage; prison of the cor-
    rupted god Vol Karoth.
Khored (KOR-ed)—one of the Eight Immortals, God of Destruction. See: Mi-
    thros.
Khorsal (KOR-sal)—god-king who ruled Jorat. He was particularly obsessed
    with horses and modified a great many of the people and animals under
    his power. Responsible for the creation of the fireblood horse lines and
    centaurs.
Khorvesh (kor-VESH)—a dominion to the south of the Capital City, just north
    of the Manol Jungle.
Kirpis, the (KIR-pis)—a dominion to the north of Kazivar, primarily forest. Most
    famous for being the original home of one of the vané races, as well as the
    Academy. Also, home to a number of famous vineyards. Despite the fact that
    the vané are supposed to be extinct in the Kirpis, vané traits like unusually
    colored cloudcurl hair continue to show up in natives of the region.
knight, Joratese, unlike knights elsewhere, Joratese knights are more akin to
    sports athletes, who fight as proxies to establish idorrá/thudajé relation-
    ships. This affects every aspect of Joratese life, from business deals to trials.
Korthaen Blight, the (kor-THANE)—also called *the Wastelands,* a cursed and
    unlivable land that is (somehow) home to the morgage.
Kulma Swamp (KUL-mah)—a lowland swamp area in southern Marakor.

# L

laevos (LAY-vos)—a Joratese hairstyle consisting of a strip of hair down the
    center of the head and shaved sides, echoing a horse's mane. Some Joratese
    grow their hair this way by default; it's considered a sign of nobility.
Lake Jorat—a large lake formed by the Demon Falls dam.
Land of Peace, the—Heaven, the place of reward souls go to after they die and
    are judged worthy by Thaena.
Lower Circle, the—area of the Capital City that exists outside of the safety of
    the tabletop mesa of the Upper Circle, thus making it vulnerable to flooding.
Lyrilyn (LIR-il-in)—a slave girl owned by Pedron D'Mon, later transformed
    by the Stone of Shackles into the mimic Talon. She was Khaeriel's hand-
    maiden and tasked with smuggling Khaeriel's newborn son Kihrin back to
    the Manol, a task she failed to carry out.

# M

Maevanos (MAY-van-os)—1. an erotic dance; 2. a holy rite of the Black Gate,
    the church of Thaena.
Malkoessian, Palomarn (mal-KOZ-ee-an, PAL-o-marn)—Aroth Malkoessian's
    firstborn son, now using the name Star.

Manol, the (MAN-ol)—an area of dense jungle in the equatorial region of the known world; home to the Manol vané.

Marakor (MARE-a-kor)—the Quuros dominion to the southeast of the empire. Politically important because Marakor is the only (relatively) easy entry point to the Manol Jungle. Consolidating the various rival city-state clans, which originally made up the region, has proved difficult.

mare—a Joratese person who identifies as a woman (note: different from being sexually female; see: gender, Joratese) and who expresses interest in mare attributes such as housekeeping, child-rearing, farming, crafting, art, cooking—and embraces teamwork, family, and subordinate values.

Maw, the—an area of ocean maelstrom to the south of the Desolation, near Zherias.

Milligreest (mill-eh-GREEST)

　　Jarith (JAR-ith)—only son of Qoran; like most Milligreests, served in the military; killed by Xaltorath during the Capital Hellmarch.

　　Kalindra (KAL-ind-rah)—the widowed wife of Jarith Milligreest, who died during the Capital Hellmarch. Secretly, a member of the Black Brotherhood, of Khorveshan and Zheriasian descent.

　　Nikali (ni-KAL-i)—cousin of Qoran Milligreest, famous for his skill with a sword. See: Terindel.

　　Qoran (KOR-an)—high general of the Quuran army, considered one of the most powerful people in the empire.

mimics—although commonly believed to be an entire race, mimics are actually a small number (either twelve or sixteen) survivors of a vané experiment in spell imprinting, which gave them all the ability for extremely fast shape-changing, telepathy, and memory absorption (through consumption of brain matter). They all promptly went insane. It's unknown how many of them now work as assassins or spies. See: Talon.

Mir, Hanik (MEER, HAN-ik)—see: Ompher.

*Misery,* the—a slave ship.

misha (MEESH-ah)—a long-sleeved shirt worn by men in Quur.

Mithrail (MEETH-rail)—Khored's son and Sovereign Kaevatz's consort, Mithrail was killed while attacking King Terindel (who was wearing the Stone of Shackles), who afterward found himself in Mithrail's body.

Mithros (MEETH-ros)—leader of the Red Spears, a mercenary company selling their services to the highest bidder for tournaments in Jorat; a Manol vané. The real name of Khored, God of Destruction.

Miya (MY-ah)—see: Miyathreall.

Miyane (MY-an-ee)—queen of the vané, wife of King Kelanis and previously wife of Queen Khaeriel. Note that Miyane is Miyathreall's biological sister.

Miyathreall (MY-ah-threel)—a.k.a. Miya; a handmaiden to Queen Khaeriel, secretly a member of the Black Brotherhood. Miya was slain while assassinating Queen Khaeriel (who wore the Stone of Shackles) and Khaeriel, trapped in Miya's body, was gaeshed and sold to Therin D'Mon.

Morea (MOR-e-ah)—Talea's twin sister, who was murdered by Talon.

morgage (mor-gah-GEE)—a wild and savage race that lives in the Korthaen

Blight and makes constant war on its neighbors. These are mainly Quuros living in the dominion of Khorvesh, but they hold a special hatred for the vané.

Morios (MORE-ee-os)—a dragon, also Mithros's brother.

# N

Name of All Things, the—a Cornerstone that will truthfully answer any question the owner asks while holding it. It cannot predict the future, answer
questions earlier than its own creation, or interpret opinions. The Name
of All Things was lost when it was used to cure the insanity of its paired
dragon, Drehemia.

Nameless Lord, the—the Joratese name of the eighth of the Eight Immortals.
See: S'arric.

Nathera, Ola (na-THER-ah, O-la)—a.k.a. Raven. A former slave and owner
of the Shattered Veil Club in Velvet Town, Ola was killed accidentally by
Thurvishar D'Lorus during Kihrin's attempt to run away. She was later
consumed and impersonated by Talon.

Nemesan (NEM-es-an)—a deceased god-king famous for his tactical ability,
intellect, and evil nature.

Nerikan (NAIR-eh-kahn)—a Quuros emperor.

# O

Octagon, the—the main slave auction house of the Capital City.

Ogenra (O-jon-RAY)—an unrecognized bastard of one of the Royal Houses.
Far from being unwanted, Ogenra are considered an important part of the
political process because of their ability to circumvent the god-touched curse.

Old Man, the—see: Sharanakal.

Ompher (OM-fur)—one of the Eight Immortals, god of the world.

# Q

Qhuaras (kwar-AHS)—a deceased god-king.

Qown (kown)—a former priest of the Vishai Mysteries who briefly worked
for Relos Var and has since become a companion of Galen and Sheloran
D'Mon.

Quarry, the—a prison used by the vané.

Quur, the Great and Holy Empire of (koor)—a large empire originally expanded from a single city-state (also named Quur) that now serves as the
empire's capital.

Quuros High Council—the ultimate ruling body of Quur, composed of repre-
sentatives nominated from the Royal Houses. Theoretically, the emperor
has authority over them, but no emperor has attempted to enforce that
authority since Emperor Kandor. It's widely believed that emperors are
gaeshed when receiving the Crown and Scepter, hamstringing their powers.

# R

Raenena (RAY-nen-ah)—a dominion of Quur, nestled in the Dragonspire
Mountains to the north.

Rainbow Lake—a small lake in Eamithon famous for being the home of Grizzst's Tower, which is widely considered to be mythological.

raisigi (RAY-sig-eye)—a tight-fitting bodice worn by women.

Rava (ra-VAY)—Raverí's mother. Executed for witchcraft.

Raven—see: Nathera, Ola.

razarras (RAY-zar-as)—a highly poisonous ore.

Red Spears—a mercenary company of Jorat, commanded by Mithros.

Return—to be resurrected from the Afterlife, always with the permission of the Goddess of Death, Thaena.

Rev'arric (rev-AR-ik)—see: Var, Relos.

Ritual of Night, the—a voras ritual designed to drain the immortality from an immortal race and use that power to recharge the eighth warding crystal keeping Vol Karoth imprisoned. The ritual kills its participants.

Rol'amar (ROL-a-mar)—a dragon.

Rook—see: D'Mon, Kihrin.

## S

S'arric (sar-RIC)—one of the Eight Immortals, mostly unknown (and deceased); god of sun, stars, and sky; murdered by his older brother, Rev'arric. Past life of Kihrin D'Mon.

sallí (sal-LEE)—a hooded, cloak-like garment designed to protect the wearer from the intense heat of the Capital City.

Sandus (SAND-us)—a farmer from Marakor, later Emperor of Quur.

Selanol (SELL-an-al)—the solar deity worshipped as part of the Vishai Mysteries.

Senera (SEN-er-AY)—a former slave of House D'Jorax who was freed, recruited, and trained by Relos Var. Being of Doltari descent, Senera is pale-skinned with pale hair, a rarity in the empire.

sexuality, Joratese—Joratese society defines sexual identity around partner preference. So, for example, anyone who prefers biologically female sexual partners "runs with mares" regardless of their own biological sex. People who "run with stallions" prefer male sexual partners, and people who "run with the herd" would be considered bisexual. Asexuals simply "don't run." All of these options are accepted without discrimination in Joratese society.

shanathá (shan-NA-tha)—a light, hard metal used to make some kinds of armor and weapons.

Sharanakal (SHA-ran-a-KAL)—a.k.a. "The Old Man." A dragon tied to volcanoes, capable of breathing out a pyroclastic flow and making volcanoes erupt.

Simillion (SIM-i-le-on)—first Emperor of Quur.

Soaring Halls, the—the imperial palace in the Capital City of Quur. Emperors have rarely used the palace as actual living space, although it has happened.

Spurned, the—an all-female warrior company under the command of Xivan Kaen.

stallion—a Joratese person who identifies as a man (note: different from being sexually male; see: gender, Joratese) and expresses stallion attributes such as leadership, assertiveness, guardianship, entertaining, contests, and combativeness.

Star—a Joratese horse trainer enslaved for stealing horses. See: Malkoessian, Palomarn.

star tears—a kind of rare blue diamond; also, the tsali of any soul not originally from this universe.

Stone of Shackles, the—one of the eight Cornerstones, ancient artifacts of unknown origin. The Stone of Shackles has power over souls, including the ability to exchange its wearer's soul with that of their murderer. The Stone of Shackles was destroyed, at least temporarily, by Kihrin D'Mon using Urthaenriel, which freed all gaeshe made using it (namely, almost all of them).

Suless (SEW-less)—god-queen of Yor, associated with witchcraft, deception, treachery, and betrayal; also associated with hyenas. Suless was the very first god-king, who was gaeshed by and forced to marry Cherthog. She was freed from her gaesh when the Stone of Shackles was destroyed.

Surdyeh (SUR-de-yeh)—a wizard and minstrel secretly working for the Gryphon Men who raised Kihrin D'Mon. Surdyeh was murdered and consumed by Talon.

# T

Taja (TAJ-ah)—one of the Eight Immortals. Goddess of Luck.

Talea (tal-E-ah)—Morea's sister. A slave girl formerly owned by Baron Mataris, who became second-in-command of the Spurned. Now the new Goddess of Luck.

talisman—an otherwise normal object whose tenyé has been modified to vibrate in sympathy with the owner, thus reinforcing the owner's tenyé against enemies who might use magic to change it into a different form. This also means it's extremely dangerous to allow one's talismans to fall into enemy hands. Since talismans interfere with magical power, every talisman worn weakens the effectiveness of the wearer's spellcasting.

Talon—a mimic assassin who was "taken over" by Lyrilyn because of the Stone of Shackles. She promptly went insane (as is tradition) but has since continued pursuing a garbled set of sometimes contradictory goals as her multiple personalities clash with each other. See: Lyrilyn.

tamarane (tam-a-RAN-ee)—a system of Joratese cooking with eight specific styles of heating.

tenyé (ten-AY)—the true essence of an object, vital to all magic.

Teraeth (ter-RATHE)—hunter of Thaena; a Manol vané assassin and member of the Black Brotherhood; son of Khaemezra.

Terindel (TER-in-del)—an infamous Kirpis vané who tried to assassinate Queen Khaevatz and usurp his brother's throne.

Thaena (thane-AY)—one of the Eight Immortals. Goddess of Death.

Theranon (ther-a-NON)—a noble family from Jorat.

    Janel (jan-EL)—a demon-tainted warrior who goes to the Afterlife when she sleeps.

    Ninavis (NIN-a-vis)—an outlaw who gathered together a group of like-minded bandits and now exists on the outskirts of Barsine Banner, mostly

sticking to the forest. Adopted by Janel Theranon; became Count of Tolamer after Janel's abdication and has since become the Duke of Jorat.

thorra (THOR-ah)—Joratese term for a person who abuses idorrá privileges;
bully or tyrant, lit. "a stallion who is not safe to leave with other horses."

Three Sisters, the—either Taja, Tya, and Thaena, or Galava, Tya, and Thaena;
also, the three moons in the night sky.

thudajé (thu-DAJ-ay)—Joratese term of respect, humility, and submission;
thudajé is considered an essential and positive Joratese trait. No matter
how high in idorrá someone is, the Joratese believe there will always be
someone to whom they owe thudajé.

Tillinghast, Professor (TIL-in-gast)—a professor who teaches at the Academy
in Kirpis. Infamous for giving very boring lectures.

tsali stone (zal-e)—a crystal created from the condescended soul of a person.

Twin Worlds, the—name for the combination of the Living World and Afterlife, when referring to both realms as part of a larger whole.

Tya (TIE-ah)—a.k.a. Irisia (IR-is-EE-ah). One of the Eight Immortals. Goddess
of Magic.

Tya's Veil—an aurora borealis effect visible in the night sky.

Tyentso (tie-EN-so)—formerly Raverí D'Lorus, now the Emperor of Quur; the
first woman to ever be emperor.

# U

uisigi (YOU-sig-eye)—undergarments, specifically underpants or loincloths.

Upper Circle—the mesa plateau in the center of the Capital City that is home
to the Royal Houses, temples, government, and the Arena.

Urthaenriel (UR-thane-re-EL)—a.k.a. Godslayer, the Ruin of Kings, the Emperor's Sword. A powerful artifact that is believed to make its wielder completely immune to magic and thus is capable of killing gods.

# V

Valathea (val-a-THEE-a)—a harp passed through the Milligreest family. Also,
a deceased queen of the Kirpis vané, Terindel's wife, who was sentenced to
the Traitor's Walk after her husband's death.

Valrashar (val-ra-SHAR)—vané princess, daughter of Kirpis vané king Terindel and Queen Valathea.

vané (van-EH)—a.k.a. vorfelané. An immortal, magically gifted race known
for their exceptional beauty. Vané appearance is mutable and can be
changed as the vané desires (although not quickly). Vané tend to keep the
skin colors they were born with unless they are making a big statement (as
happened when the Manol vané split from the Kirpis and the entire population of the new nation deliberately darkened their skin).

vané, Kirpis—a fair-skinned, immortal race who once lived in the Kirpis forest. They were driven south to eventually relocate in the Manol Jungle.

vané, Manol—the vané who settled in the Manol Jungle, in part as protest
against Kirpis vané isolationism and unwillingness to pay attention to both
the Blight and the threat of humanity.

Var, Relos (var, REL-os)—a powerful wizard, believed responsible for the ritual that created the Eight Immortals, and also the ritual that created both the dragons and Vol Karoth.

Veil, the—1. the aurora borealis effect sometimes seen in the nighttime sky; 2. the state of perception separating seeing the "normal" world from seeing the true essence or tenyé of the world, necessary for magic.

Velvet Town—the red-light district of the Lower Circle. Those who engage in the sex trade are commonly described as *velvet* (i.e., velvet boys or velvet girls).

Vishai Mysteries, the (vish-AY)—a religion popular in parts of Eamithon, Jorat, and Marakor; little is known about their inner workings, but their religion seems to principally center around a solar deity named Selanol; usually pacifistic; members of the faith will often obtain licenses from House D'Mon to legally practice healing.

Vol Karoth (vol ka-ROTH)—a.k.a. War Child or Warchild. A demon offspring crafted by demons to counter the Eight Immortals; alternately a corrupted remnant of the sacrificed god of the sun, S'arric.

voramer (vor-a-MEER)—a.k.a. vormer. An extinct water-dwelling race believed to be the progenitors of the morgage and the ithlané; of the two, only the ithlané still live in water. Many Zheriasians have ithlané ancestors, which is part of the reason they have a reputation for being "undrownable."

voras (vor-AS)—a.k.a. vorarras. Extinct race believed to have been the progenitors of humanity, who lost their immortality when Karolaen was destroyed.

vordreth (vor-DRETH)—a.k.a. vordredd, dreth, dredd, dwarves. An underground-dwelling race known for their strength and intelligence. Despite their nickname, not short. Believed to have been wiped out when Atrin Kandor conquered Raenena, but in fact, the largest dreth population lives under the Doltar region, which has more than its share of dreth-blooded inhabitants.

# W

Warmonger—a Cornerstone whose power seems to involve manipulating loyalty and anger over large populations.

Well of Spirals, the—a location sacred to vané, where they imprint their children and perform a number of miraculous biological magics. The mimics were created there.

Wildheart—a Cornerstone that allows its owner to control plant and animal life, as well as manipulate earth and rocks.

witch—anyone using magic who hasn't received formal, official training and licensing; although technically gender-neutral, usually only applied to women; in Jorat, anyone using magic who isn't Blood of Joras is considered a witch.

Worldhearth—a Cornerstone with the power to allow its user clairvoyance through heat sources.

# X

Xaloma (ZAL-o-may)—a dragon, associated with souls.

Xaltorath (zal-tor-OTH)—a demon prince who can only be summoned through the sacrifice of a family member. Self-associated with lust and war. Gender-neutral but identifies as female when dealing with her adopted daughter, Janel.

# Y

Ynis (YIN-is)—a god-king who once ruled the area now known as Khorvesh. Associated with death and snakes.

Ynisthana (yin-IS-than-AY)—an island in the Desolation chain, used as a training grounds by the Black Brotherhood. Destroyed by a volcanic eruption caused by Sharanakal.

Yor (yor)—one of Quur's dominions, the most recently added and the least acclimated to imperial rule.

# Z

Zaibur (ZAI-bur)—1. the major river running from Demon Falls and Lake Jorat all the way to the ocean, dividing Jorat from Marakor; 2. a strategy game.

Zajhera, Father (zah-JER-ah)—leader of the Vishai Faith / Vishai Mysteries. Personally exorcised the demon Xaltorath, who possessed Janel Theranon when she was a child. An alias used by Relos Var.

Zherias (ZER-e-as)—a large island to the southwest of Quur. Independent from Quur and anxious to stay that way. Famous for their skill at piracy and trade. Contains a high proportion of voramer ancestry, so that it's not uncommon for Zheriasians to go to sea when they're older.

# ACKNOWLEDGMENTS

Here we are. It's difficult to believe that I'm writing these words. That this saga, which has been a part of my life for so long, is finally coming to an end. I first began working on the characters that would eventually make their way into this story when I was fifteen (in case you're curious, the first character I created was the one who would eventually become Khaemezra, and the second one, Kihrin). I'm now fifty. Never in my wildest dreams did I think that I would have the opportunity to share them with you.

As always, but with no less enthusiasm than on previous occasions, let me thank my agent, Sam Morgan, my editors, Devi Pillai and Bella Pagan, and all the often unsung staff at Tor without whom these books would have been impossible. I'd also like to thank Lars Grant-West, whose cover art has been so utterly perfect throughout the entire series.

Eternal thanks to my husband, Mike, whose input and willingness to be the rubber duck I throw ideas against has so often carried me through in a pinch. I am forever thankful for his suggestions and for his patience—and especially for his understanding when I have ignored his advice. Thanks too to the members of the Author's Sack, active or otherwise, who have supported, cheered, and prodded me into getting my butt in the chair and my fingers on the keyboard. And last but certainly not least, thank you to my family and friends who have spent the last three years being told, "Sorry, I can't. I'm on deadline."

By the time I'm typing this I will have written over one million words for this series. I'm less certain how large the total would be if I counted the words that ended up in the trash bin, but I'll assume at least half again as large. The vast majority of that was written in the last three years.

I regret nothing.

# The Eight Guardians and the Nine Dragons
## Family Trees

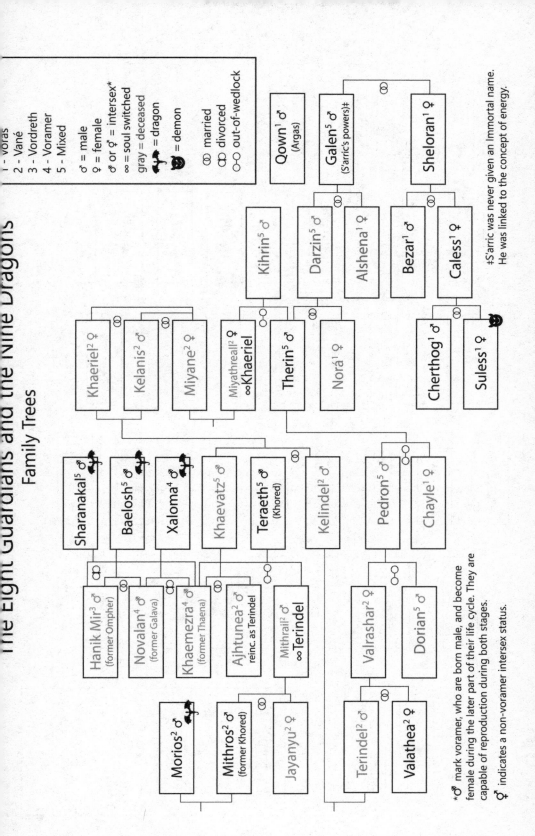

1 - Voras
2 - Vané
3 - Vordreth
4 - Voramer
5 - Mixed

♂ = male
♀ = female
♂ or ♀ = intersex*
∞ = soul switched
gray = deceased
🐉 = dragon
😈 = demon

⊂⊃ married
⊂⊃ divorced
○─○ out-of-wedlock

‡S'arric was never given an Immortal name. He was linked to the concept of energy.

*♂ mark voramer, who are born male, and become female during the later part of their life cycle. They are capable of reproduction during both stages.

♂ indicates a non-voramer intersex status.

---

Qown¹ ♂ (Argas)

Galen⁵ ♂ (S'arric's powers)‡

Sheloran¹ ♀

Kihrin⁵ ♂

Darzin⁵ ♂

Alshena¹ ♀

Bezar¹ ♂

Caless¹ ♀

Khaeriel!² ♀

Kelanis² ♂

Miyane² ♀

Miyathreall² ♀ ∞Khaeriel

Therin⁵ ♂

Norá¹ ♀

Cherthog¹ ♂

Suless¹ ♀

Sharanakal⁵ ♂

Baelosh⁵ ♂

Xaloma⁴ ♂

Khaevatz⁵ ♂

Teraeth⁵ ♂ (Khored)

Kelindel² ♂

Pedron⁵ ♂

Chayle¹ ♀

Hanik Mir³ ♂ (former Ompher)

Novalan⁴ ♂ (former Galava)

Khaemezra⁴ ♂ (former Thaena)

Ajhtunea² ♂ reinc. as Terindel

Mithrail² ♂ ∞Terindel

Valrashar² ♀

Dorian⁵ ♂

Morios² ♂

Mithros² ♂ (former Khored)

Jayanyu² ♀

Terindel² ♂

Valathea² ♀

# The Eight Guardians and the Nine Dragons

## Family Trees

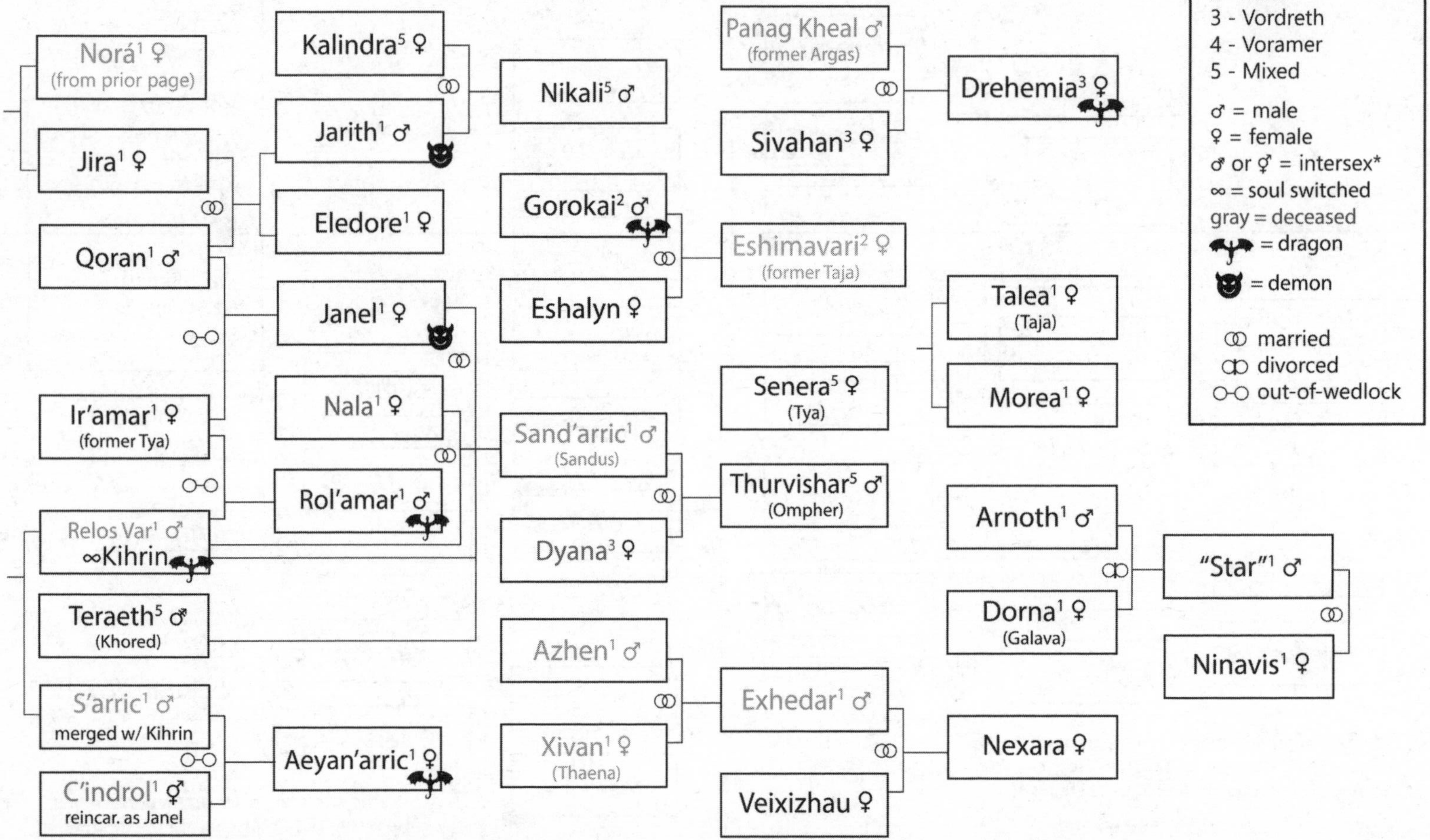